I0702779

LIBERATION

BOOK 1
of the
KEEPERS OF MIDGATE

Copyright © 2023 by R. M. Krogman

Cover art by Celebril Art | celebrilart.com
Typography by Miblart | miblart.com
Interior illustrations by Monon Saad with Etheric Tales | behance.net/monon-saad

All artwork commissioned by the author.

Edited by Dylan Garity | garityediting.com

All rights reserved. No part of this novel may be reproduced, stored, or transmitted in any form or by any means, electronic, mechanical, photocopying, recording, scanning, or otherwise without written permission from the publisher, except as permitted by U.S. copyright law.

This novel is entirely a work of fiction. The names, characters, and incidents portrayed in it are the work of the author's imagination. Any resemblances to actual persons, living or dead, events, or localities is entirely coincidental.

R. M. Krogman asserts the moral right to be identified as the author of this work.

For Mrs. Willis.

Thank you for looking at my words and seeing my world.
Thank you for seeing me.
(Sorry about the cursing.)

PREFACE

This novel exists because my husband told me to give up.

It's what I needed to hear.

I have talked about writing this book for over twenty years. The world of Midgate blossomed into existence in early high school, a vast world with its own history, cultures, and peoples. I sketched maps and animals and plants; I jotted notes on color symbolism and languages. I identified industries, located master training halls, and established an apprenticeship structure. I described religions and traditions and superstitions. I modeled wind and ocean currents, then determined climate patterns and resultant major biomes.

I did everything but write.

The story smoldered in my mind. At first, I thought it was about a man wrongfully kept from his crown, who overcame his circumstances and became the savior in a battle of good and evil. Then a girl appeared, and the story transformed. Then another man and woman appeared, shouting that they needed their fair share of attention, and my story exploded to an epic of people overcoming their past and freeing themselves from rigid destiny. Told through multiple points of view, this book is about freedom—freedom from the bonds of societal expectations, suffocating control, and physical binds. The next is about choice, allowing the pain and madness of the world to mold you and drive you, or not. The last is about love, about who we are when we choose others over ourselves or vice versa.

And after hearing about it day after day, year after year, for over a decade straight and still having no book in his hand, my dearly beloved said, "Either start writing, or admit that you're not going to do it and *give up*."

That had exactly the effect it was meant to, and I buckled down to put my thoughts into tangible form. I spent a month documenting the plot and establishing point-of-view characters, then about a year drafting this book and months upon months garnering feedback and revising.

So here we are.

I present to you *Liberation*, the first in series of an epic story about freedom, choice, and love, embedded in a magic-filled world of violence, madness, and loss. I hope you come to love the world of Midgate as much as I do, that your heart breaks and mends with the characters, and that you forget where you are for at least a little while.

ACKNOWLEDGMENTS

I thank my family and friends for their encouragement and enthusiasm providing feedback at the earliest stages, when I most needed someone to have faith in me. That momentum has kept me going for three years straight.

I thank the patient and tenacious readers who provided critical review at various stages of this book's development, especially C. Anderson, J. DeBoer, K. Krogman, B. Martin, E. McDermott, and T. Plyler. I deeply appreciate the time dedicated by L. Svane, D. Joiner, A. McFadden, H. Stewart, J. Krogman, and C. Krogman in reviewing drafts, C. Krogman in tweaking and finalizing files, and my many advance readers and launch team for helping to spread the word.

I also thank my editor D. Garity for his meticulous work—and C. D. McKenna for her outstanding recommendation of him—and my incredible cover illustrator E. Džamková and interior illustrator M. Saad. Your work helped turn this book into a beautiful thing.

A NOTE TO READERS

Liberation is a darker epic fantasy set in a brutal, medieval-inspired world of escalating war and disease, which includes elements of war violence, hand-to-hand combat, death and injury, sexual violence, trauma, emotional and physical abuse, miscarriage and trouble trying to conceive, racism, classism, sexism, mental sickness, coarse language, alcohol consumption, and consensual adult romantic relationships. Readers who may be sensitive to these elements, please take note and prepare to enter the expansive world of Midgate . . .

CONTENTS

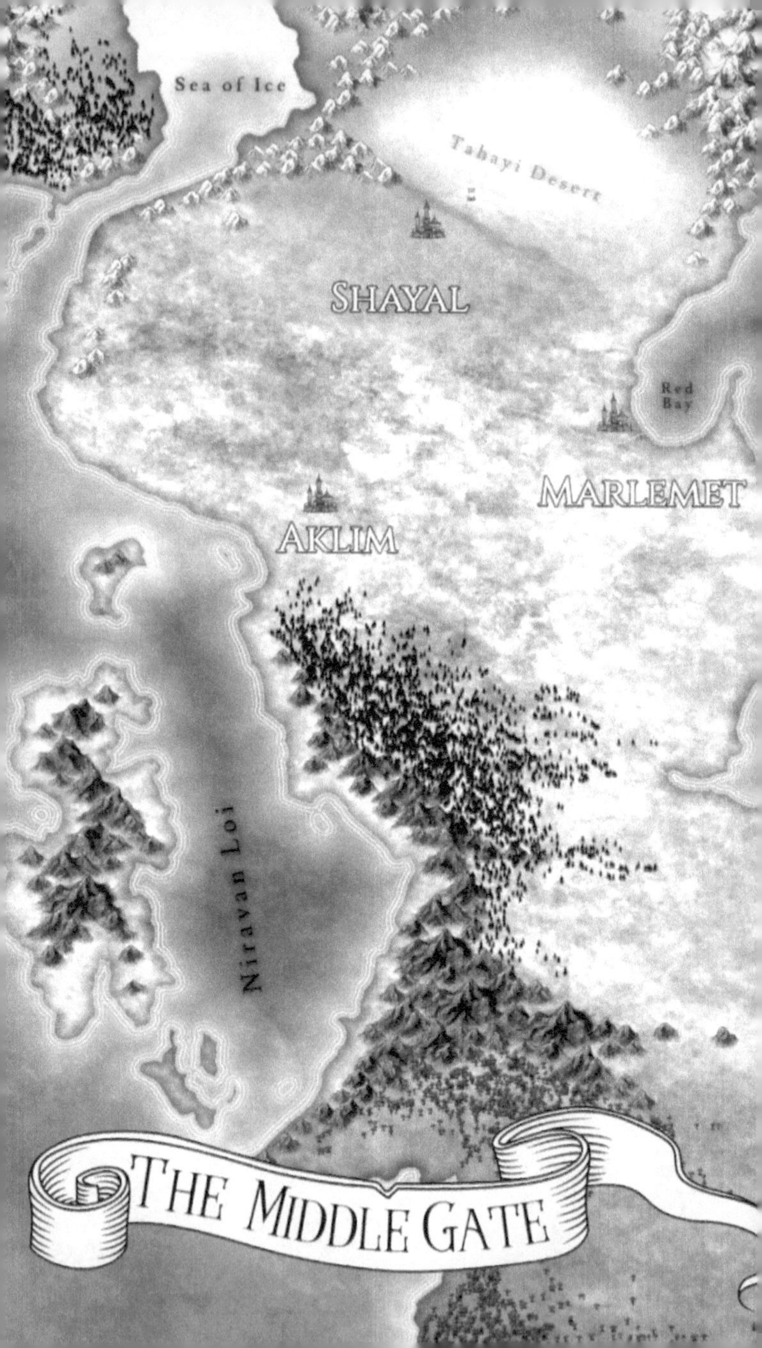

Sea of Ice
Tahayi Desert
SHAYAL
Red Bay
MARLEMET
AKLIM
Niravan Loi
THE MIDDLE GATE

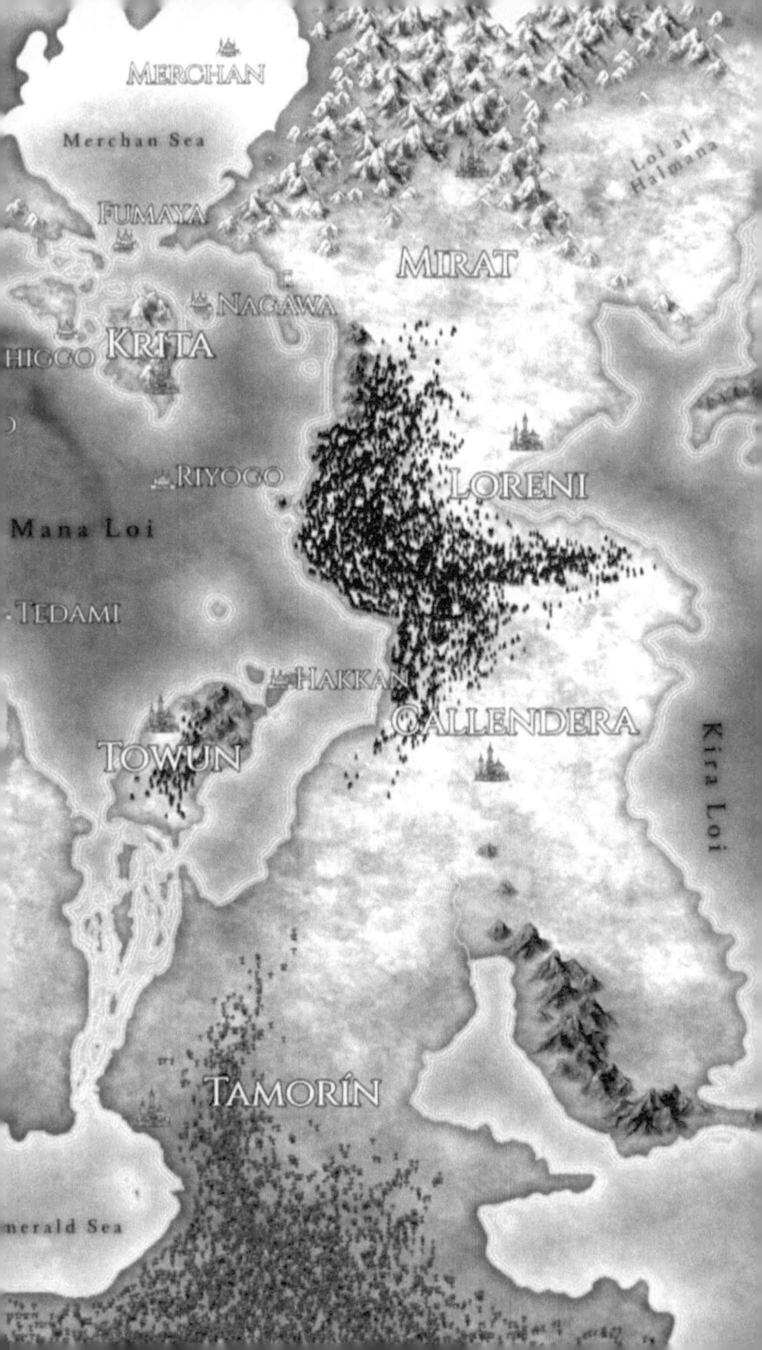

MERCHAN
Merchan Sea
FUMAYA
NAGAWA
KRITA
HIGGO
MIRAT
Loi al'
Halmana
RIYOGO
LORENI
Mana Loi
TEDAMI
HAKKAN
CALLENDERA
Kira Loi
TOWUN
TAMORÍN
merald Sea

PROLOGUE

THE SHARP, FAMILIAR METALLIC flavor of blood filled Konan's nose, an almost welcome reprieve from the stench of the sulfur mines.

If only it weren't coming from Isellan.

The older man gasped in erratic spurts, his stout chest heaving with effort, but Konan could hear the gurgle of blood in the lungs. Like everyone in Tahayi Mines eventually did, Isellan was dying, his life wasting into the sand in a bright red pool.

Konan knelt beside him, silent, every part of him feeling numb.

Isellan's eyes rolled up toward the cold sky as he wrenched another breath in; his sun-worn skin stretched into a grimace on his gaunt cheeks. His crow's feet, etched on by years of kind smiles despite the misery of the mine, creased with pain. A tremor took over his lower lip as he tried to speak.

"Son." The word bubbled out, and Isellan hacked a bloody cough.

The spray hit Konan's face, but he didn't flinch, just stared down with a furrowed brow. Could the Five-Faced God be this cruel? He made several quick hand motions, although Isellan's eyes were already losing their focus.

"Don't leave me," he signed. *Please don't leave me.* His vision blurred for a moment, but he blinked it away for fear of losing awareness of his surroundings. He glanced up to be sure the other prisoners had gone, then placed a protective hand on his mentor's laboring chest.

They were alone. The men who'd attacked Isellan had taken the rations and disappeared into the endless rows of wooden shanties.

Konan returned his gaze to Isellan, who was trying to speak again.

"Endure it," he managed. "Overcome—"

The complex words took too much effort. Frothy red spittle leaked from the corner of his mouth, and he shuddered once more under Konan's broad palm. The stiffness pulling at his face softened. The tension of a decade protecting Konan in Tahayi Mines eased from his brow, and the tremble in his lip stopped.

The constant gurgling died away, and Isellan's head lolled to one side, his bright eyes vacant of their typical hard glint. Konan had always likened them to diamonds, clear and impossibly hard. Isellan was exactly like that, a man forged of iron will and strength, a leader and a mentor.

A savior.

Isellan was the only reason Konan had survived the mines as a boy.

In truth, the man was the only reason he lived now. What purpose had life to offer Konan, bereft of the only person who cared for him? What was the point of waking, working, breaking one's back and growing weak with thirst, all for the glory of Tahayi Mines and its masters, the merchants of Shayal?

Something in him transformed, condensing any boyish, nonsensical hope of escape into a tight ball, then crushing it into a blackened, toxic pit. The pit burrowed his heart, digging deep into the layers of guarded emotion, and seeded itself.

Konan brushed a bloody hand over Isellan's face, pushing the eyelids shut. The tradition left sandy fingerprints everywhere, and Konan heaved a resigned sigh, taking the cold, dry air in through his nose and out through his mouth. It burned his nostrils.

His other hand still lay on Isellan's chest. Beneath his palm, the man's heart no longer beat, his lungs no longer labored. Behind the third rib on the right side, several small puncture wounds leaked the last of his congealing fluids, feeding the desert sands their rich life. Konan could taste the metal hanging in the air, and it reminded him to wipe the blood spray from his lips and cheek with a tattered sleeve.

He glanced around again, hovering protectively over the corpse, narrowing his eyes in suspicion. A few other prisoners watched, their impassive gazes no more or less than he'd expect. Death was no surprise in the mines, merely an eventuality. Sometimes, it was accompanied by the opportunity for new boots.

Other than the man with the dagger, no one would challenge Konan today. They had seen him fight, they had seen him rage against three or even four men with practiced jabs and hard knuckles and bodily tosses. Despite his less than twenty years, his natural height and brawn gave most prisoners pause. Combined with the massacre of pockmarked skin covering the left half of his body, his hulking presence was usually avoided, as he preferred.

Every fight avoided was a battle won in the name of survival. Isellan had taught him that.

But if you had to fight, show no mercy. Weakness, hesitation, and uncertainty could kill. Isellan had taught him that too.

That unfamiliar sensation of blurred vision returned, and Konan winced, willing it away with tightly squeezed eyes and a hardened resolve. He could feel the movement stretch the taut skin of his left eyebrow. His cheek ticced, an erratic and constant twitch that revealed his inner turmoil, and then he realized how sore his jaw felt.

He was clamping his teeth together so hard, an ache was emerging in his temple as well.

With another slow, deep breath of the winter air—that bitter chill that sucked warmth from the body and teased with skies as bright and clear as ice—Konan began to remove Isellan's boots and clothes.

The Tahayi Desert was miserable in winter, when the straight-line winds screeched down from the northern wastes and tore across the sands until they broke against the Bleeding Wall. Beyond that massive cliff of blood-streaked malagate and shale and slate, the raised steppe of Shayal's dry kingdom truly began. The edge of civilization.

Tahayi Mines had no guard wall, no sealed stone buildings, no hearth fires. Only an endless sea of leaking shanties with dilapidated roofs and empty sacks and rotting barrels—and the mines. The small fortress guarding the mines featured towers facing the prison camp, spaced regularly to ensure each section of the camp was monitored just enough to ensure consistent operation.

Konan had been inside the fortress once, according to Isellan: when he arrived as a boy, unconscious and horribly maimed. And since, he had been here in the camp, surviving from day to day on rations exchanged for mined sulfur and salt and occasional gemstones.

He fastened Isellan's boots onto his feet; they were tight. He'd have to cut the toes out. The pants and shirt would be used as cloth to augment his existing clothing, though neither would fit.

Konan stood, looking at the dead man one last time. Isellan was gone. His intelligent, glinting eyes and good soul were gone, passed through the Gates to the next life. This was merely an empty, naked husk. Konan slung it over his shoulder, his own expression frozen with neutrality, and headed to the waste pits.

He was alone.

PART ONE

1

THREE YEARS LATER

THE TUNNELS OF THE sulfur mine meandered in all directions, tracing the paths of yellow seams deeper and deeper into the sand and rock. Konan had memorized the network years ago, and now its familiarity felt reassuring. The cooler air, stagnant and musty with sulfur as it was, was also heavier somehow than that of the breezy desert above, comforting like a heavy fur blanketing one's bed. The sun, which blazed down without mercy during summer, couldn't reach more than twenty paces beyond the entrance, forcing miners to carry candles in the deeper recesses.

Konan stepped carefully through the gloom of others' candles, allowing his feet to wend their way through his memory of this section. It was safer to carry only one's quarry if possible, allowing a free hand for the undersized pick allocated by the sentries. Konan spun it with a flick of his wrist, its balance and motion perfected even in the dark.

Today was a good day.

He had pried a near-luminescent stone from the earth, one that glittered with flecks of rainbow color in the dim candlelight. He had nearly broken through it, but upon seeing a corner chip off and twinkle at him, had dedicated time to working a large, single piece out. It was worth weeks of rations.

Tucking it closer into the crook of his left elbow, somewhat hiding it under his piecemeal cloak, Konan hurried toward the entrance.

A dark figure emerged from the shadows, blocking the tunnel.

"What y'got there?" came a voice.

Konan paused. He had passed no one, he was certain. This man was alone.

The stranger angled his own pick at Konan like a weapon. "Give it to me, whatever it is. Must be a good'n, the way you was rushin' outta here before dusk."

Don't be a fool, Konan thought, steeling himself as the other man stepped forward.

He closed the distance enough that they could see each other's faces, then paused. A glimmer of hesitation and recognition crossed his haggard features, but just as quickly, he planted his feet. "Can't go no further till y'give it up. I'm starving."

Then use that pick to mine, Konan thought, narrowing his eyes.

The man swung wildly, and Konan sidestepped him. The tunnel was tight and low, making it awkward to move around. He swung again, swiping his pick at Konan's abdomen, and Konan lurched backward. They circled each other, wary. There was no going back now; this man wanted his prize. Unless . . .

Konan had circled the man, his gemstone clutched tightly to one side and his pick white-knuckled in the other. He was the one nearer to the entrance now. He spun and ran.

The man cursed and scrambled after him, and then Konan felt a yank on his flailing cloak as the assailant managed to catch it with his pick. The fabric tore.

Enough.

Konan turned back.

The man clearly hadn't expected that, as he stumbled forward with his own momentum, one arm outstretched to the edge of Konan's cloak. His face filled with fear as Konan swung the gemstone like a left hook; the rock hit with a sickening crunch.

The man tried to swing his pick once more as Konan fell on top of him. Konan caught the weak attempt and smashed at the clutching fingers until they were bloody and broken. The pick dropped to the ground. Then he struck the man's face once again for good measure. Blood poured from a crooked, ruined nose and jagged cuts on the man's cheek and brow.

He snuffled something about mercy through the blood and sinus fluid, and Konan straightened his shoulders.

"I don't care whether you live or die," he signed, his face neutral and cold. He adjusted his slipping veil and hood.

The man didn't understand him; no one could.

As Konan stood, careful not to bash his own skull against the sharp rock of the uneven ceiling, the man clutched his broken hand to his chest and sobbed. "Can't dig nothin', can't do nothin'." He snorted and spat a bloody mess onto the ground. "Can't get no rations. I'm gonna die here." He continued moaning to himself, and Konan ignored him.

After retrieving both picks to ensure the man didn't come after him again, he resumed his departure, his gemstone sequestered by his side. Konan wound his way up the tunnel, occasionally passing a small candle set on a jutting rock, adhered by its own wax and burning to its eventual death. He focused on regaining control of his fluttering heartbeat, inhaling the blessedly cool air in a calm, even rhythm.

Other miners glanced at him with vacant, hopeless eyes as he passed, then returned to their own labors. The closer he got to the entrance, the more there were, tapping mindlessly away at the deposits, trying to earn enough to get by. Most of them would receive only a portion of the rations gained, as they were obligated to give tribute to whichever gang leader they followed.

Konan stopped at the entrance and handed both picks to a sentry. The other sentry, an older man with sunburnt skin and a weary expression, scanned him for hidden weapons. His eyes widened as they caught on the bloodied stone, and his face twisted into a sour grimace.

"By the fucking Light, boy," he snarled. "Not again."

Konan stared down at him, the image of calm, his eyes dead. It was strange how the old-timers still called him boy.

The first sentry raised both picks in question. "We gotta go get a body, sir?" He glanced at the older sentry for confirmation, who looked at Konan.

Konan shook his head, and the older man's scowl softened slightly.

"Good. Lotta fuckin' work that'd be. Fucking molehill in there, stinks to the Nethergate. You do me a favor, boy?"

Konan didn't acknowledge, only listened, and the younger sentry leaned over and asked his superior if Konan was dumb. The man ignored him and continued.

"You kill someone deep in, at least carry them out so someone finds 'em. Damned rotten down there already."

With a slow nod, Konan turned away. Why had he defended himself? In the heat of any altercation—and there were many—his instinct was to fight, to operate with sheer white rage that filled his vision and warmed his core. To battle against whatever foe until that foe diminished or died. But why?

Had he allowed that man to take his life and his gemstone, perhaps Konan would be at peace. Perhaps he would find something better on the other side of the Gates, wherever it was Isellan had gone. Regret filled him as he recalled the bloody pulp of the man's cheek and nose. He should have allowed the assailant to end it, this miserable, pointless life.

He trudged along the fortress wall and watched the sun sink behind the distant horizon. Dusk had arrived. With the wall on one side and the sea of shanties on the other, Konan could now walk safely to the well and food window. It was the best-watched place in the camp, guarded by two nearby towers. Soldiers could pour from the adjacent iron-spiked gate if necessary, although that was infrequent enough. They seemed to better enjoy picking the rare troublemakers off with arrows from up high. Konan knew they kept score amongst themselves, small numbers that carried much weight in the monotony of guarding the mines.

After rinsing his bloodied, dusty hands, he cupped tepid fresh water into his mouth from the well. The stone pool built against the wall was fed by a small fountain, circulating enough to rinse away blood, urine, or whatever else soaked one's body and clothes. It was the only water available in Tahayi Mines, a sure way to control the prisoners. Drawn from deep underground into a well inside the fort, the water was pumped through aqueducts onto the salt flats—the other half of Tahayi Mines' operations—and to here, the drinking well. With a surreptitious glance around, Konan shuffled his empty water skein from under his cloak.

Skeins were rarities, and he had fashioned this one from the limited leather he had encountered over the years. He had sewn it with a needle, another rarity obtained only because the middle-aged woman at the food window, a Shay-alese named Tass, had known him when he was young.

She leaned out the food window now and grinned at him with yellow teeth. "What you got today, boy?"

Konan secured his full water skein to his belt and hid it with his cloak, then carried the stone to the exchange window. He was surprised to see a younger woman peering around her, first with a semblance of curiosity, though it was quickly replaced by fear and disgust. He stood back slightly, allowing them to appraise his offering.

Tass gestured at the younger woman. "Come now, he ain't one to be afraid of. I know he looks it, but he's fine. Look at this stone now, and light that lamp."

The younger one grimaced with distaste at Konan and at the blood-grimed stone, then leaned forward to help.

Tass gave her a prim look of approval. "This here's Dawna, new girl y'know. She don't know you yet, but she'll have to get used to you and the rest."

Konan didn't respond, but he was aware of other miners making their way from the far east end. He wished the woman would hurry so he could leave. Things got more dangerous in the dark, and he preferred to be back in his shanty, alone.

"See here, Dawna, he's brought us an entire sunstone," the older woman continued, pulling out a tiny pick and inspecting different sides of the rock. She seemed unaware of the blood, entranced by the rainbow sparkle showing beneath the gray stone in each place she tapped. "This here's worth weeks of rations."

Two maximum, he guessed, but she pushed three weeks' worth through the window with a wink. "Good work, boy."

Dawna mumbled something and flinched as Konan reached for the sack of food. She threw a dubious look at the older woman. Her reaction was normal—all the servants who worked the food window were frightened of the prisoners, as they should have been.

With a wary look around, Konan saw the other miners approaching and hurried away, his rations held close.

As he trudged off, he heard the other miners' lewd comments and laughter. They were teasing Dawna. He clenched his jaw at the rough words, which seemed to be getting rougher as he made distance.

Then he heard a yelp, and he looked back.

Dawna was halfway out the window, her reed-thin body too easy to manipulate. One of the men was covering her mouth, and they both yanked at her while Tass yanked back with a shrill curse. Her shouts were probably loud in her own ears, but they didn't carry out the food window very effectively, and a glance at the guard towers told Konan no one was really paying much attention.

In moments, Konan had shoved one of the men into the wall as hard as he could and begun punching him, first a hook to the face and then a strike to the gut. The man doubled over with a pain-filled squawk, but then the second man pushed Konan from behind.

He threw an elbow back, hard.

It connected with the second man's face, and he flew toward the well.

Konan returned to the first. His knuckles would bruise, again, so he grabbed a stone from the food window and used it instead, smashing it into the man's face over and over and over. The man slumped after a while and sank all the way to the ground, and still Konan beat him until his face was a mass of blood and shattered bone and burst eyeball.

When his rage subsided, Konan stood and looked around, nostrils flaring as he regained control.

Dawna sat in the sand, wide-eyed. Then she scrambled back through the window and disappeared with a terrified sob.

Konan placed the stone back on the windowsill without making a sound. The older woman took it with a grim nod.

"Thank you, boy. Hopefully she'll learn quick. Not all of 'em are like you."

Tass leaned out and examined the mess. Konan followed her gaze, which stopped first on the pulpy face of the man who was leaned up against the wall, then moved to the one still lying in the well.

"Move him, would you? Don't want the water sickened. The guards'll get 'em moved all the way out in the morning, when it's light." She slid the iron shutter down to bar the window, then closed the inner wooden doors as well, leaving Konan with only the remnant of orange light from the sunset.

Konan did as she asked, wondering at himself again. Why did he keep living, when it was so easy to die? But this time, he had an answer. Dawna. He wouldn't have interacted with those men at all had she not been grabbed and pulled through. He shook his head and heard a distant laugh.

Looking up into the failing light at the nearest tower, he saw one of the soldiers hold up a hand to him, with two fingers showing. The others had arrows nocked, but their bows were lowered.

Two.

The soldiers burst out laughing again.

Konan had a wall score now.

2

THE HEADY SCENT OF cactus flowers permeated the capital square of Shayal City, where a raised platform had been constructed out of shale blocks and mortar. The platform had five corners, as was proper in honor of I'ya. Surrounded by curated palms and smooth-skinned palmate cacti, the central plaza of Shayal attracted the wealthiest clientele and the greatest amount of patronage for the wayfarers' stalls.

Lyra stepped onto the platform to the raucous sounds of applause and ear-piercing whistles. She blushed but raised her chin with an open smile, as her mother had taught her to do. The crowd was harmless, and hopefully generous.

To one side, a secondary stage featured narrow stone columns, which held an airy white awning, stretched tight against the beating sun. The musicians, including her mother Elaisa, drew their bows and plucked their strings in blessed shade. Mam strummed at a sitar, and the first few notes twanging out to the crowd caused passersby to pause. Her skillful fingers danced into a teasing melody, and Lyra twirled into the center of the stage, her layered skirt flailing with ruffles.

Shining silver coins flickered in the bright desert light, accompanied by the shaking of the copper bells that edged her skirting. To the crowd, it was the "Dance of Maridi the Virgin," the ecstatic and teasing whirlwind of motions danced by Maridi, Maiden of the Mountains, after she escaped a man of dark intentions. The man pursued her across the Holy Mountains, trampling holy ground with blind anger and evil in his heart. And so I'ya and the gods of the Earth had damned him to chase his futile desires for eternity; they had given Maridi's dance to all of the wayfarer caravans.

Mam called it the Mocking Dance.

Every wayfaring maiden was taught to dance, to twirl, to tease, and to conceal the Maiden Maridi securely in their midst. Lyra danced, her lithe body moving in a whirl of brilliantly dyed silks. The copper bells tinkled furiously as she moved across the platform, bouncing and swinging her hips in time to her tambourine. For a while, she was lost in it, alight with the ecstasy of moving in time with the thrum of the sitar and the shivering whine of the strings. The air danced around her as much as she danced through it, her silent, twirling partner.

She finished with a flourish that flared her skirts outward in a mesmerizing display, leaving her lightly panting with the exertion. Controlling her breath beneath her tightly bound corset, as well as her demeanor, Lyra maintained an effortless and flirtatious smile on her lips.

There was a theater to this, but also pure pleasure as her body synchronized with the rhythm vibrating from each instrument. The music shivered through her entire being.

The crowd, mostly men, drowned her with applause, and she caught her breath while watching her little brother Elden slip through the throng, relieving several well-heeled men of their coin.

Lyra hid any hint of grimace. She didn't support the theft, but many of her watchers emptied their pockets on the stage regardless—it made no matter. With a final curtsy, her lips split apart into a real, joyful smile. Lyra left the stage, allowing a storytelling orator to step forward. He launched into elaborate gesticulations with a commanding voice that quieted the crowd.

Mam took her hand and squeezed it. "Your best performance yet, *beneshel*," she gushed, brushing Lyra's wild hair back and kissing her forehead.

Lyra blushed again, still grinning. Mam always called her that, a word from the Old Language. It meant "gift" or "blessing," although Lyra would have reserved that name for Elden, her unexpected little brother who had arrived in an undue season and barely survived infancy.

Mam led the way to the wayfarers' market stalls, which were more temporary. Constructed of thin fabric and wooden poles, the tentlike stalls could be constructed swiftly in any market in which the caravan settled, and deconstructed just as fast.

Several men nearly tripped on Lyra's skirts, they were following so closely. She could hear their hopeful commentary, wondering whether the Maiden Maridi had perhaps dropped something, or might need a cool drink or a handkerchief, or more brazenly, whether she needed a cozier place to stay for the night than her family's airy caravan wagon.

Mam glared most of them away, unless their cloaks were rich with dye and fastened with golden brooches, and Lyra ignored them all. Despite some suave words and a few somewhat handsome faces, most of these men were unworthy. Her maidenhood was a closely guarded commodity, after all. Mam said it was valuable enough that its sale could purchase Lyra a sedentary life, one with a bed that didn't jostle in wagon ruts or radiate dust when you adjusted the furs.

That was what Mam thought, in any case.

Lyra wasn't so sure, given her wayfarer blood, but she knew she wasn't willing to give up such a precious part of herself to just anyone. She may have been born a wayfarer, or *maunderer* as most people called her, but if she was chaste, she might be pretty enough to serve as wife to a young baron or knight. To have land, to have servants even.

She could hardly imagine what such a life was like. To have a place to come home to made of timber and stone, with a woven rug and even a wall hanging. To have a pretty window made of glass that looked out on a garden during summer, that sparkled with frost as it guarded the house from winter's chill. To have a fireplace with a chimney that emitted a curl of white smoke, heralding visitors welcome.

And her husband, a kind and simple landed man. Perhaps he would be a knight, born or elevated to nobility, but perhaps not. She didn't care either way, only that he might be gentle, giving her a peaceful life. That he might open his doors to her family's caravan when they passed through, and not look at her like she was lesser. *Maunderer.*

It was a secret desire shared between Lyra and Mam, the bright spark of hope that she, unlike her mother, might rise above the scorn given to their kind.

The silver-tongued followers, recognizing defeat before they made complete fools of themselves, dissipated into the market crowd. Lyra released a small sigh of relief. Although she did dream of marrying well and lighting Mam's eyes up with joy and relief, she didn't think any of those men were the one. Usually, the ones who hounded her immediately were rude, overflowing with brazen words they said were brought on by her irresistible dress and dance.

Pathetic excuses to get a closer look at her cleavage, according to Mam. That same physique, however, would eventually draw the eye of someone more worthy. Someone like *them* had to somehow garner that attention in the first place, before having the vaguest hope for marriage negotiations. The suitor would find so much more beyond that, though, if only he would look long enough.

Elden met them at the leatherwork stall, an enclosed tent where Mam sold their tanned hides, worked belts and straps, and fine sheaths and purses. Elden broke into a mischievous, gap-filled grin; only one adult tooth pushed its way out of his gums. He reached for one of his hidden pockets, but Mam stopped him with a subtle flick of her hand.

The tent flap was parted by two men, each vying for first entry.

"Bright day," said one, nodding to Mam and Lyra. He wore a long, light cloak with tattered edges where it swept across the ground.

Lyra gave a slight curtsy. Apparently not all of the crowd's men had given up.

"It's a pleasure to host such a talented wayfarer caravan here in Shayal," the man began. "Miss . . . ?"

"Lyra of the Maskalan Caravan, my daughter." Mam's tone was utterly polite, smooth as the silk of Lyra's skirts and sonorous with the notes of a contralto singer. Yet it was also edged, imperious. Her eyes dropped down to the man's ratty cloak edge as she took his measure, and her lips tightened.

"Miss Lyra, what a lovely name," said the man, avoiding Mam's direct gaze by fawning at Lyra. "And you have just arrived in the city?"

"We have." Mam spoke for Lyra, who stared at the floor with her jaw set and her cheeks burning. "The caravan brings goods to trade, for those with a spare penny, Sir . . ." She gestured at the display tables with her eyebrows raised just enough to look doubtful.

The man minced over the wares, then subtly patted his pocket and subsided, a half-controlled look of dismay painting his face. He bowed again. "I hope to see you again tomorrow, Miss Lyra." He backed out of the tent and disappeared into the throng of the plaza.

The second man watched him go with disdain, then stepped forward and took Lyra's hand. He gave it a soft kiss, as a noble or high-ranking guildsman would do, then bowed deeply. "Poor men have no place speaking to a young lady like you," he said, his derision obvious.

"Thank you, sir," said Lyra. Her politeness was more genuine than Mam's, although less practiced. Mam was doubtful of every man who pursued her, but this one looked like a reasonable option.

His cloak was a finespun fabric, not quite silk but smooth in texture and tightly woven, and dyed a unique shade of blue. His open-toed sandals indicated not only that he could afford leather as fine as that produced by the Maskalan Caravan, but also that his labor did not require boots. His face was clean-shaven, and although he was a bit older than Lyra would have preferred, he had no silver streaks in his dark hair.

He addressed Mam with a bow far more respectful than was due to a wayfarer. "May I beg your name, madam?"

"Elaisa ol'Maskalan, sir," replied Mam with a pleased expression.

The man launched into pleasantries with them, extolling their leatherwork and fine products with what seemed to be a genuine knowledge. He welcomed them to Shayal and bragged about his horses, who could use new straps and bridles.

"Have you many horses?" asked Mam innocuously. "We have saddles as well, several quite fitting for a nobleman, Sir . . . ?" Again, her deeper voice lilted high, inquiring after the man's name and rank.

A partial smirk crossed the man's face, which he covered by turning toward the table. For a moment, Lyra saw a disturbing level of arrogance. He said his name, but she didn't hear it as her internal thoughts raged against each other in a sea of doubt.

Which was better? A rich nobleman with an absolute assurance in his own excellence, or a poorer man who was more earnest but less prideful?

"I do, madam," the man went on.

Mam pulled a saddle from beneath the table; it was embedded with the ornate gems mined in Shayal, a fine example of the Maskalan blending of northern commodities and southern design.

The man marveled over it, explaining that his steward was in need of a new saddle.

Lyra's mouth almost dropped open. A gem-studded saddle for a steward? She controlled herself as Mam caught her eye.

Mam had Elden pull several other saddles out that had been tucked away for security, her attitude growing friendlier and friendlier as the man extolled their individual virtues. Clearly, he met at least some of her requirements.

Lyra's stomach churned as she answered the man's intermittent questions. Something about him grated, and it wasn't only his age. That wasn't all too important, in the end. It was something in the way he spoke, as though he were talking to a child—never asking difficult or interesting questions, only grazing superficial and empty topics and then disregarding her answers. Polite and meaningless. Was that the life she had to look forward to?

"I'll send my servants to retrieve it all tomorrow then," said the nobleman, handing Mam a clinking purse.

"Shall you accompany them, sir?" Mam inquired. "We'd be pleased to see you again."

The man straightened his shoulders and raised his chin, preening over himself. "I had hoped I might return this evening, if it pleases Miss Lyra."

Lyra berated herself as she put on a show of agreement and excitement. Arrogant or not, this man couldn't possibly be that bad. He was giving them business, and he was polite. If he was high-ranked, he must have a reason to be proud of his nobility. And besides, he couldn't broach more interesting topics while also bartering with Mam. Perhaps, this evening, he would take Lyra on a walk through one of the green oases tucked inside the noble houses' high walls, and they could speak of their dreams and goals, their fears, and their families.

"As my lord pleases," said Mam.

Lyra echoed her words, feeling the man's lips brush her fingers once more. Then he was gone.

Mam placed her palm on Lyra's cheek. Her pale green eyes sparkled with excitement. "What a suitor, Maiden Maridi," she gushed in a low voice. "You carried yourself well. He's a man of highborn blood, being a baron. Your uncle Terrasa will accompany you." She moved to the drawn tent flaps and loosed the strings, closing them off from the rest of the world.

"Mam, do you think he's kind?"

Her mother paused, then wrapped her arms around Lyra. "He's landed, beneshel, and seemed kind enough. However, you will have to evaluate that yourself when he courts you this evening. Terrasa will report his impressions as well."

Lyra leaned into the hug. Mam was thicker than she, but with the same long ringlets of pinkish-blonde, although her mother's was a shade redder.

Mam stroked the wild fray down and pressed Lyra's cheek into her shoulder. "We won't make an agreement without ensuring you'll be well cared-for, beneshel," she murmured. "You're worth far more than that."

I'm just a maunderer.

Mam must have felt her slight stiffening, for she pushed Lyra back and looked her in the eye. "You deserve better than this life. You must believe that. Everything we strive for is to give you that dream."

Lyra nodded obediently, and her mother released her.

Then Mam placed her hands on her hips and scowled at Elden, who capered from foot to foot, nearly bursting. "And you, little rascal? I think you might be the reason people believe wayfarers are nothing but thieves."

Elden produced coin purses from multiple pockets with a giggle, and their mother quickly stowed the gold away. She patted him on the head and bid him go.

"No more today, young bird," she called after him as he scampered into the crowd. A doleful smile stretched across her face as she turned to Lyra. "Full of mischief, that boy is. Praise the Light you were never so intent on making trouble." She refastened the tent flaps open as wide as they would go, allowing the fresh desert air and sunshine in.

They both stepped behind the main display table and worked the market, calling passersby to their tent not only for leather, but also for spells.

Laughable things, spells. The minor workings of people blessed with far more magika than the customers of Shayal could comprehend. Spells of love, spells of hate, potions that could turn a man's bowels into jelly and powders that could harden the heart for battle. These tiny scrips and mixtures were sometimes more profitable than the leather, despite the material's tangibility.

This was especially the case in the more superstitious corners of the world, including Shayal. The northern regions had always been more superstitious than the south, perhaps because of the influence of the wild and magical peoples that resided beyond the edges of civilization. Past Shayal City lay the Tahayi Desert, a temperate desert filled with nomadic tribes who had never been under the Empire's chokehold. Some were even said to have Fire-filled blood, although she suspected that was a rumor without truth. On the eastern continent, it was known that the fyrpeople populated the grasslands at the edge of Mirat, as well as the icy northern Merchan Coast.

Of course, these spells were low magika, independent of one's blood or natural gifting. Almost anyone could practice some form of low magika, although there were certain differences in talent and resulting efficacy.

The Maskalan were quite gifted, as many wayfaring caravans were. Like the fyrpeople, they'd lived outside the structure of Empirical rule a thousand years ago, thereby escaping not only its politics but its genocide of gifted commoners. Most of their wares were green magika, the careful mixtures of herbs and flowers in various forms. Perhaps a bit of black—the metallurgic properties added substantial power to spells of strength and fear. The Maskalan didn't touch red magika. It was too dangerous, with too many nefarious uses.

Lyra winked playfully at a tight-lipped man as he bartered over a curse with her mother. His gaunt cheeks and bitter look implied that he was certainly going to close a deal, if only he would meet Mam's minimum, but then Mam hesitated. Her eyes, ever so briefly, moved beyond the miserable creature to a tall, barrel-chested man in royal attire who stood in the entrance. He was accompanied by eight knights with yellow capes edged in orange. Mam closed the deal quickly and took the tight-lipped man's coin to pocket before dropping into a ground-level curtsy.

Lyra curtsied as well, her eyes fixed on the lord's shoes. He wore fine riding boots, thicker-soled for riding with stirrups but otherwise incredibly thin and supple. Although Lyra took them in, her focus remained on her peripheral, on Mam's composed expression.

"Your Highness," her mother murmured. "You honor us with your presence. Do our wares please the king's eyes?" She kept her face trained to the ground, as did Lyra.

King Hemil, ruler of the kingdom of Shayal, stepped carefully into the large tent and perused the display tables. "You may rise, lady," he said, removing his glove to touch each jeweled leather belt in turn.

Mam eased Lyra up and back, moving all the way behind the table to give the king and his men space.

"I require a belt for my nephew," King Hemil stated, his voice deep and gravelly. "He shall earn his first sword soon. Have you any gems hidden beneath the cloth? The Maskalan usually do."

Her mother let out a light chuckle. "M'lord knows a wayfarer well." She summoned a belt wrapped in red silk and laid it upon the table with reverence. As she unfolded the silk, a ruby glimmered in the afternoon light. The belt itself was tanned and colored with a deep black burnish; winking, embedded rubies outlined the shapes of soaring birds. Each bird hung on the breath of diamond wings, minute gemstones that sparkled in every direction. It shone like no belt Lyra had ever seen, a stunning gift worthy of a prince.

King Hemil picked the belt up with gentle hands, a look of approval flashing across his face. Lyra finally gathered the confidence to glance at his expression in that moment and was surprised by his handsomeness. His face was broad and brown like most people's in this part of the world, with a coarse but closely trimmed goatee and mustache. His loose-curled hair was a deep, dark brown reminiscent of the burnished belt, with silver streaks at each temple. Above all, his eyes were a shocking blue, stark against his sun-tanned cheeks.

A handsome man, a lordly and authoritative man.

The king was looking back at her, still holding the bejeweled belt.

Aghast, Lyra returned her gaze to the ground, her cheeks burning with a furious, self-deprecating fire.

"This is certainly an unexpected gem you had hidden away, wayfarer," King Hemil said, tracing the outline of each bird with a finger. "A gem worthy of a young lord."

Mam huffed a small sigh of relief. "It pleases m'lord, then?"

"Yes. I always find such rare value in the humble tents of the Maskalan; I'm grateful to the Eye you returned to my fair city."

Mam's smile creased the corners of her eyes, and Lyra could tell it was genuine. "Please, let this be a gift then, from the Maskalan Caravan. M'lord has always used us well, though it has been many long years since our wagons entered Shayal's capital."

King Hemil shook his head. "Nay, lady. I cannot rightfully gift another's gift. I shall pay."

"Very well." Mam closed the agreement with little bartering, giving the king a fair deal before curtsying deeply once again. "You honor the Maskalan, Your Highness. May the Light of I'ya shine upon you always."

Lyra mimicked her motion and words, still shocked at the king's presence and friendliness.

King Hemil thanked them both with a gracious nod, then marched out with his escort. Mam watched the contingent of yellow-garbed knights, now mounted on gorgeous black stallions, disappear among the throng. Her expression was carefully sculpted in detached interest, her red lips pursed and her cheeks flushed a light pink.

"Mam?" Lyra inquired after a brief silence. "Was that really the king of Shayal? In our tent?"

"Yes, beneshel, the King Hemil, Alis al'Shayal."

Lyra giggled, all of her nerves frayed. "He's handsome."

Mam shushed her. "You mustn't disrespect one of such high blood. We are only wayfarers, after all. Remember your place." She beamed at Lyra even as she said it though, wrinkling her rounded nose. "Tread carefully—at least until you're secure in a noble house, a lady yourself, and bound to be mother to noble-blooded children."

Mam sent her to the wakeway as the reddening sun sent hazy golden rays across the baked steppe south of Shayal. The wayfarers' wagons were stationed on the southern edge of the city, not far from the lazy river that snaked through the city proper. The wakeway wound around a large cove, forming a crescent shape of docks and fish hawkers and trade stalls.

At the middle, the wakeway intersected the Black Road, Shayal's main crossroad, which went straight to the center of the city, including the plaza in which Lyra had danced earlier. The Black Road spanned all the way from Shayal's southern cove to its northern edge, paved with perfectly squared malagate stones and partitioned with stone murals detailing Shayal's somber history.

Shayal had a long and dark history, caught between the Tahayi Desert clans, the aggression of the Empire, and a thousand other infringements. Each event was etched into the hard malagate face, brought to life by a rainbow of paints and cheap gemstones: the War of the Triad, the Siege of Ramar when the High Temple burned, the invasion of the Haralal thousands of years ago.

Lyra needed only to pick up enough fish for Mam's evening stew, and then she would be free to join the nobleman for a short evening of social pleasantries. How glorious if she could see one of the Shayalese gardens, congested with outstretching fronds and overarching palms, occasional thorntrees with complex leaves and spice-smelling bean pods, and delicate flowers that could never thrive without extra water and care.

She didn't waste any time, closing a deal with one of the rivermen for the basketful swinging in the crook of her arm now. The wares at the wakeway had been minimal but adequate for a warm supper. The Maskalan came from the southern edge of the larger trade sea, the Mana Loi. The fish there carried spars on their bodies and shone like blue jewels in the ocean. Their flesh was thick, meaty, and satisfying.

The lazy Shayalese river yielded somewhat less, its fish sparse and quite different. The small-bodied cichlid Lyra had purchased would be mild in flavor, a strange food but good texture for the stew.

She meandered toward the Black Road and its pretty murals, taking in the sharp, fishy scent and industrial sounds of men unloading their catch from the countless wooden skiffs anchored on each dock. She stopped to admire one particular carving.

It was the Tale of Five Kings. Lyra knew the tale as everyone did, but she had never seen such a beautiful portrayal before. The images were engraved with the detail of a painting, with lighter etching giving the appearance of texture and shading on each figure. Gattlin the Grim's hardset features glared stonily at the demon Mek'asal; the Grim wielded an emerald-inlaid battle-axe high above his head. The black demon cowered, its smoky form shying from the fearsome power in Gattlin's gauntleted fist. It had no color, save in the eyes, which burned with hateful crimson acid. The Grim's armor shone with lesser green gemstones, forming the ancient signet of Callendera. His chainmail was flecked in obsidian, and his eyes gleamed a deep, calm jade.

In stark contrast to the Grim's serenity as he delivered death, Shastid the Boy King grinned wide as he swung a massive battle-hammer upon the demon Mek'harar. The Boy King's mouth was half-open with utter delight, and bloodlust shone in his wild eyes. His brawny figure was far from diminutive, towering over the other warrior kings, and his alisite armor was painted in silver.

Lyra pondered the mural from an appropriate distance that wouldn't draw the guards' ire. She relived the great battle to which she sometimes danced. The Five Kings Dance was far less joyful and light than what she had displayed that afternoon—it required an entire team, which marched against each other in a rhythmic war drumbeat. The violent clashing of their prop weapons was accompanied by shakes of the tambourine and the pounding of boots on the stage.

A shadow fell over Lyra, and a pair of yellow-gloved hands grabbed her and yanked her into an alley. Shoved against a wall, she peered into a guard's face.

"Pretty little thing, ain't she?" he snickered.

Lyra spat in his eyes and pulled away, but his grip on her arm was sure. He slapped her, and a second guard grabbed her other arm with an indifferent expression.

"Aye, she'd do in a pinch, heh."

"Let me go!" Lyra cried, dropping her basket of fish and wrenching one arm free.

Please, she thought. *If only that nobleman would appear with his knights. All I was doing was looking; I didn't touch the mural.*

"Stop struggling, maunderer," said the first one.

She didn't stop. She strained toward the Black Road with her entire body. Several passersby stole glances toward her, and one even paused, but they all rushed on when they recognized the guards' uniforms.

The second guard backhanded her cheek hard enough to knock her off balance, and she would have stumbled if not for the other's grasp. They dragged her farther into the alley and shoved her down.

She landed with a huff as the breath was knocked out of her. Dust alighted, then resettled on her fine silk skirts. Lyra would have to change outfits before meeting the nobleman.

Then she noticed expensive sandals in front of her, peeking out with the sparkle of diamonds from underneath a roughspun cloak. Then a voice.

"Look at me, maunderer."

That word.

Lyra's hair was gripped and yanked back. She stared into a delicate, well-bred face, most certainly a noblewoman.

The woman's eyes were like fire. Her gaze leapt from Lyra's eyes to her hair, to her clothes, back to her eyes again, jumping almost as if irritated. It made Lyra think of sweat bees, the ones that seemed to touch every part of your arm before deciding which spot to bite. The woman beckoned Lyra to stand, and Lyra obeyed with trembling knees. She could feel the noblewoman's examination crawl over every part of her.

She crossed her arms and looked down, but the woman grabbed her chin and wrenched it up to look her in the eye once more.

The noblewoman inspected Lyra with a silent fury and . . . was it disgust? "Get rid of her."

"But I didn't do—"

Another slap, this time from the noblewoman. Her jewel-encrusted rings drew blood on Lyra's cheek, a fact that clearly irritated the woman even further. She sneered at Lyra with untempered hatred before turning away. The glittering shoes were gone.

"As y'please, m'lady," one guard snickered and struck Lyra's skull from behind.

They bagged her head and hauled her out of the alleyway without ceremony, dragging her, hacking and gasping in the filthy bag, through the black stone streets of Shayal. Any time she tried to scream or protest, they would strike her again.

Lyra kicked her feet out several times before being struck in the stomach and reprimanded, and then someone grabbed her legs and carried her.

They removed the bag, revealing her surroundings—a dungeon—where they beat her until she collapsed on the damp stones. She shuddered, barely able to breathe with the sudden pain in her ribs and eye. Had they removed the bag merely so they could hit her in the face? Then they began to tear her clothes away, first pulling at the dyed leather corset which she clutched to her body, then at her copper-belled skirt.

Her screams were unrestrained now but fruitless. No one would hear her in a dungeon. Panic bubbled up as she realized they might do more than hit her.

"Begone," came a wizened voice, "or I'll send you through the nethergates myself."

Both soldiers paused, and their greedy looks fell into sullen disappointment.

"I'll send your fuckin' balls separately if you take any longer. Out of my dungeon, now." The old man, the dungeon keykeeper, pushed them out of the cell with a snarl, but not before one of them tossed Lyra against the wall.

Her skull slammed into the rock with a crack that echoed through her mind, and she lay where they left her, a ruin of copper-belled silk and blood-spackled blond curls.

3

Lyra's head lolled to the side as she stumbled a fine line between nightmarish dreams and an unpleasant, painful consciousness.

Her left eye throbbed, and she tried to open it to peer at her jostling surroundings. It was swollen nearly shut, and she winced. She imagined it was purple and green, like the time she had been kicked by a horse; Elden had thought that was hilarious. Ada had been a little more empathetic, groaning and saying "sorry" over and over and over. As one of the stable keepers, he blamed himself, but it certainly hadn't been his fault.

Memory flooded back, and the pounding in her head made sense.

Her last memory was of the guard's gloved hand lancing into the hair by her ear, of his cruel expression as he shoved her to one side. Then, a crack that echoed from one ear to the other.

Wincing, Lyra tried to assess her situation. She wasn't in the dungeon any longer. She was in an enclosed wooden wagon lined with metal sheeting; the only opening was a tiny grate of a window at the back. She tried to sit as the wagon clunked along, every jolt wracking her bruised body and nerves. Her wrists chafed against rusty shackles that held her hands high; her fingers and hands stung as her heart struggled to push enough blood into them.

Her corset was looser than it should have been, with several of the tightening strings ripped out. Her breasts were a sickly yellow hue, and the ache in her ribs told her they were the same if not worse. The delicate light skin on her arms was marred with more bruises, and the tightness of her cheeks was uncomfortable.

Thankfully, her teeth were intact, as was her nose, although it had bled profusely and stained her white under-tunic.

What did I do? she reflected as she was jostled left and right in the prison wagon.

The caravan would have to leave without her, and quickly, if they wanted no part in whatever this mess was. She whispered into the wind for her family to depart Shayal, to pack up the wagons and leave immediately. She whispered her capture, wrongful imprisonment, and the possibility of danger to them. Lyra was afraid for herself, but she was even more afraid that whatever had happened to her might happen to them.

This was how wayfarers were treated.

Whatever offense she had committed or been accused of, she would be punished without trial or hesitation. It didn't matter whether the offense was real.

To Elaisa, she said to the Whisper before it squeezed through the window grating and flew off. A faint sense of relief entered Lyra.

Perhaps the Whisper would be quick enough. This was not the first time one of them had been marked by a noble and taken. Isellan was the cautionary tale told to all Maskalan children.

Isellan had led the wayfaring caravan when she was a babe. He had bounced her on his knee and let her play with his grizzled red beard as he sat on the second wagon in the train, his deep, guttural voice grounding out commands as his whip snapped by the ears of both beasts and men. Some time later, he had offended the lord of a prominent castle, supposedly robbing him in the market square. Twenty knights had sworn to the event's truth—they'd heard the scuffle and rushed into the maunderer tent where their lord had gone, saving their beloved master and overcoming the murderous, road-roughened vagrant.

That was the story, and it sounded as fictitious as the others told by orators late at night.

Lyra heard it muttered among the uncles that Isellan had indeed offered the lord a beautiful charm, blessed with a powerful green magika, but for a price. No wayfarer would give up such wares for free; her mother's offering to King Hemil had been a rare and generous moment in a lifetime of hard bargaining and pursuit of coin. Isellan had apparently been arrested, his crimes and punishment announced that afternoon, and his previous wagon replaced by a much different one as he was shipped off to Tahayi Mines. No one knew what ever happened to the charm.

That was the way it was for wayfarers. That was why Mam wanted Lyra to escape this life, to settle with land and a stationary husband. Even with leaders as strong as Isellan, cousins as caring as Ada, and the protection of family, the caravan was less than Lyra deserved, according to Mam.

Isellan had been Lyra's father, or so the uncles said. You never knew with wayfarers, and you never needed to. The Maskalan Caravan had been one family, and family took care of their own. Lyra had been cared for by ten more fathers and twenty more mothers during the years after Isellan was taken, and she had nearly forgotten about him until now.

Would he have snapped his whip at the ears of the Shayalese noblewoman? Or the guards? Lyra thought so. Despite her aching bruises, she managed a half smile in the darkness. Then she faltered.

Isellan had been sent to Tahayi Mines. That had to be her own destination now too.

By the Light, she had sung enough ballads and danced enough stories of treachery and just punishment to know the suffering that awaited her in Tahayi. The mines were for the most demonic of evils, the most shameful of deeds, the most treacherous of lies.

Surely, this was her death. Tahayi Mines held no prisoners forever. She heard they died in the sweltering heat, burned and naked beneath the Eye, their sins bared to the open. In Tahayi Mines, their repentances were offered in vain, and the desperation to survive rivaled the desperation to die. As expected, Isellan had never returned, nor had a single Whisper reached their ears of his fate.

Again, Lyra whispered a warning into the wind. *Leave Shayal. Elden, Adrian, Mam, uncles and aunties, get out. Get away.* She sighed as the second Whisper disappeared into the darkness.

Hopefully, they had already gone.

Long hours passed, and the tingle in Lyra's hands faded to a dull numbness. Her slender fingers were pale but not broken.

In the dry, creaking darkness, she was alone. If she was bound for Tahayi Mines, no one was coming with her. A strong, westerly wind nudged at the wagon as it trundled northward. The air tasted of salt and sucked the moisture from her tongue, like eating unripe fruit. Even in the cloistered twilight of the enclosed wagon, Lyra was aware of the Air around her, its flavor and character. Its power.

As it buffeted the side of the wagon, she thought of how great its source must be, far beyond *hamanool* comprehension. Even she had little understanding of the Air, and she was more gifted than anyone she knew.

She scowled, then winced as it pulled at her cheek's tender skin.

Why hadn't the Air burst from her when she was attacked? It usually did, when she was truly afraid or startled. When Elden scared her, leaping from the shadows of wagons with a scream, she would sometimes fling the Air like a tumultuous breeze and knock him over. When she was upset, she would accidentally manifest a tempestuous wind much like the one harassing this prison wagon, one which irritated the horses but cooled the sweat on their skin.

Because they were soldiers, legitimate men-at-arms in the service of King Hemil, their shoulders carrying the weight of golden-edged yellow capes.

That was why it hadn't occurred to her to fight back immediately.

She resolved not to forget the next time. Whatever Tahayi Mines held, she was certain it was going to be frightening.

The wagon lurched to a halt, and she heard the driver whistle.

"Hai, y'useless cunt. Hai!"

One of the haulbeasts groaned, and Lyra heard the whip lashing out with a hard snap.

"Piss off, boy," came another distant voice.

The driver laughed. "That Pensik I hear up there? They let you run the gate? Let me in—I'm hungry for a hot meal."

The gatekeeper grumbled curses, but Lyra nonetheless heard the creak of rusty hinges as the gates swung open. The wagon moved once again, bouncing onto a smoother, rhythmic surface—chiseled stone blocks. She listened to the familiar sound of it as the wagon rolled along, then stopped.

No one came for her.

The driver hopped down and gave curt instructions to a stablekeeper, then yelled insulting greetings to several others. One passed by the small window, carrying two tankards.

"Just in time for a meal, as always," the stranger said.

"Been doing this a while," replied the driver with a chuckle.

Lyra heard a knock on the side of the wagon.

"Whatcha got this time? Just the supplies, or a batch of criminals?"

She shook her shackles against the side in response. "I'm not a criminal! Let me out, please. Let me go home."

Lyra heard the driver snort liquid, then cough with laughter, but the stranger clambered up the back of the wagon and peered in at her. He raised his eyebrows.

"Please, I'm not a criminal," she repeated.

He sneered. "Convince the warden of Tahayi, and then maybe you can go home." He leapt down, leaving Lyra staring after him.

Warden? Like a dungeonkeeper?

The dungeonkeeper in Shayal had been fair enough, at least forcing the guards to leave her alone. Perhaps the warden would be a fair man too. A faint hope lit inside her tight chest, and she sat immured in her thoughts until the driver returned an hour later, as dusk settled with orange light beyond her window.

They dropped off the pavement of whatever fortress they had been in, then began a steep descent, the driver cursing the entire way. Orange light faded into twilight.

At first, Lyra took his oaths as artifacts of his obvious foul mouth and irritability. He had certainly not slept since departing Shayal, unless he'd dozed in the driving seat.

But then, the wagon jolted to one side, and his exclamation was fearful rather than irritated. With the wagon still lopsided, he leapt from the high driving platform and jostled around the wagon, cinching ropes in place.

Lyra could see one of the ropes lashed around the window grating. Then she heard him urging the haulbeasts forward, and the wagon moaned, its sluggish weight shifting from the rear left to the fore right. Lyra was jolted again as the stray wheel finally met ground.

The driver wordlessly removed the ropes, peering in at her with a lantern in hand before resuming his place on the driving bench. His eyes were wide.

They kept moving downward, slowly, erratically, and Lyra remained alert to every bump. The driver had been afraid. She could see it in his nervous expression and muted curses. The wagon negotiated a tight turn, and another. Sometimes she saw a dark rock face, and sometimes she saw only the starlit sky.

Her heart fluttered with realization. They were descending a cliff, sidling back and forth on a narrow, perilous trail in a cumbersome wagon. She shuddered.

The Bleeding Wall. The legendary break in the Tahayi Desert that separated the civilized kingdom of Shayal from the vast northern waste. The high malagate cliff that bled with intricate crimson veins.

Lyra realized that the first event had seen her precariously balanced between imprisonment and death, one wheel dangling off the edge and near to tumbling sideways. By the Light, no wonder the driver had been afraid.

She mumbled a prayer to I'ya, the Five-Faced God, for protection, but her heart was brimming with doubts and too much fear. Every time they turned, Lyra gaped out at the shadows.

The next day dawned, and still they descended, slow and careful, the driver ever meticulous as he chose his precise path down. Lyra gaped at the bleeding rock face every time it swung across her vision, disbelieving the terrible height of the cliff and understanding now how Shayal resisted incursions from the desert tribes.

Finally, as the sun began to plunge to the other side of the horizon, the road flattened out, and the driver let out a whoop.

"Hai, y'cunts," he shouted. "Haaiiii, ssshhhh." The wagon jerked to a stop, and he appeared at her window, clinking a key around until the entire door swung open. He examined her shackles before putting a sloshing skein to her chapped lips.

Lyra gulped greedily, but he pulled the water away too soon.

She pleaded for more. "Or food? Please, sir?"

The driver stared at her dispassionately, then grabbed the front of his trousers with a lewd motion. "You can suck my cock, maunderer, if you're that hungry." He slammed the door, and she heard the lock click into place. Then he called back, "All I have to do is get you there alive; that's all they pays me to do. And I sure as nethers ain't sharin' my rations with you."

Alone again, Lyra heaved a sigh that made her ribs ache. All she could see out the tiny window was the black malagate wall. Hearing the driver settle down, Lyra fell into an uneasy sleep plagued by nightmares of falling over the edge and being impaled on a bloody spire. Every time she awoke, the wind gusting against her wagon as if nudging her out of the fearful dream, she realized they were at the bottom. She was alive. But each dream felt as real as waking, and she found little comfort in her reality.

Again, she tried to pray, but her entreaties to the Eye that burned above were suffocated. Dry dust settled on her eyelashes and stung her eyes, accumulating in her throat as phlegm.

The prison wagon moved again, and the bouncing of rocky ground changed to a sinking, laborious drag. The black wall, at first filling Lyra's view, slowly lost its detail and at last broke against sky far in the distance. They had entered a new terrain.

The sands.

Lyra lost track of the time, but it was somewhere in the afternoon when the wagon creaked and groaned to a halt. Shaking herself out of a stupor of soreness and worry, she looked around. She hadn't been asleep, but neither had she been awake.

The last sounds had been the clop of hooves on cobblestone; they were in a courtyard somewhere. Was it the mine?

Lyra felt the jostle of the driver leaping from the bench, then heard him unfastening the haulbeasts. They clopped over to somewhere nearby, where the thirsty creatures slopped at water. The splashing sound would have made Lyra salivate, but her mouth was parched.

She whimpered relief when the driver appeared at her window, clanked at the rusty door, and reached toward her with the skein. Then a hand appeared on his shoulder, and he was shoved aside, revealing a Shayalese soldier. The man's gaze traveled from Lyra's face to her cleavage, then down to her waist and ripped skirt. He glared at the driver.

"She looks a little rough, boy."

"I didn't do nothing," the driver whined as the soldier smacked the back of his head.

"Get her out of those shackles and clean 'er up in the trough."

To Lyra's disappointment, the driver set the skein down with a frustrated huff, but then he pulled the keys from his belt and unclasped her shackles. "I ain't fuckin' paid to wash 'em," he muttered, shoving her toward the soldier.

Lyra's limbs had no strength, and she flailed, nearly falling from the wagon.

The soldier caught her and waited as she recovered. His grip was iron, and she looked up at him with desperation.

"Sir, is this Tahayi Mines? I don't belong here; it was a mistake. I didn't even have a trial." Her voice cracked in the dry air.

His smile was strange as he set her on her wavering feet. "You want to see the warden?"

"Yes please, sir." The kindling of hope flared into a small flame, and she offered a quick prayer of thanks to the sky. She had to have faith that I'ya would protect her, and her family.

"Driveboy, clean 'er up. You brought her in this condition; the warden won't be pleased."

The driver groaned—he had already moved away to care for the haulbeasts. They were idraka, the strong, durable creatures of the desert. Their round humps, slender legs, and large, padded feet were odd to Lyra, but they belonged here in the sands. Their necks were even spindlier than their legs; their heads were all eyes and tongue with flexible flaring nostrils. Their bodies were colored like sand pebbled with darker stones. The driver patted one of them before gesturing Lyra over to the trough.

She cringed at the long basin. The froth of idraka saliva clung to the edges, and the orangeish-brown grit of sand danced across the bottom.

As the driver shoved her forward, she cracked her knee on the cobblestone and her hands splashed in the water. A few soldiers snickered along with the driver, and one of the idraka groaned at her as it slurped more water.

Lyra glared at the driver, but he merely shrugged.

"You can clean yourself up, right? Do it, then. Not my fuckin' job."

Her limbs shook violently as she worked blood back into each one; her fingers tingled. The odd numbness in her fingertips hindered her washing, but she nevertheless tried to splash the dust from her face and the dried blood from under her nose. She had no reflection save the trough water, but with luck, she looked presentable.

Respectable, not a criminal.

Perhaps the warden would believe her.

She scooped the sand from the bottom of the trough and used it to scrub her arms and chest. The red chafing on her wrists and the bruises on her arms wouldn't wash off, though, and she imagined her face had bruising as well. She could see a hint of it in the murky water.

Lyra looked up, realizing the courtyard's industry, the banging of barrels getting moved off the wagon, the chatter of bored soldiers, had ceased.

Many of them were watching her. Her cheeks flared with an uncomfortable heat.

Just get to the warden.

Under the weight of the lewd stares, she adjusted her undertunic and retightened her corset, knotting broken strings back together. Her silky skirt was ruined, but it still covered her legs with its many layers. Lyra tried to rinse its tattered edges clean in the trough, but silk was delicate. The skirt would never be platform-worthy again.

Finished, she stood tall and looked at the lead soldier. "I'm ready to see the warden, sir."

The soldier snorted, looking at her as though she were still filthy. *Maunderer.* Nonetheless, he extended an arm to escort her.

She took it, still a little unsteady. With a deep, grounding breath, she thanked the burnished orange Eye as it sank toward the horizon. The mote of hope stirred and danced inside of her, a leaf dancing in the wind. With her honesty and obvious innocence, she might be able to convince an authority like the warden of the truth. And maybe, just maybe, she'd be able to go home to her caravan.

Lyra practiced polite and eloquent words as they entered the fortress keep and ascended a set of stone stairs. Her strappy leather sandals made no sound on each step, but the soldier's heavier boots pounded in the echoing stairwell.

Or was that her heartbeat?

They pushed into a larger room, an office with a small table and several chairs, a larger desk at one end, and a fireplace. A middle-aged man with jowls wrinkled from constant scowling sat at the desk, turning when they entered.

"My lord warden, the latest shipment from Shayal City has arrived," said the soldier with a bow. "The woman requested an audience." He pushed Lyra forward.

The warden dismissed him, and the heavy office door shut behind Lyra with an ominous groan and a click. The man sidled closer, his deeply lined face twisting into a semblance of a smile. "I don't grant many audiences, but then, most criminals aren't interesting."

Lyra examined the floor. "I'm not a criminal, my lord warden. It's a mistake for me to be here. Please let me go home."

The warden laughed, a cruel, mocking sound that bounced from the hollow office walls. "So say many who come to me, their excuses thick and their lies obvious. Why should I believe you?"

Lyra looked up, her vision blurred by the sudden onslaught of tears. She struggled to find words, despite the whirlwind of practiced phrases she had considered in the wagon and stairwell. Her breath hitched as she fought back a desperate sob. "Sir, you must. You must help me. Aren't you a man of justice?"

The force with which he struck her swept her from her feet, and she banged into the table and chair on her way down. All the air was forced from her lungs as she landed, and she looked up at the warden with surprise and terror. The small candle of hope inside her flickered out.

He was in her face, his hot breath on her cheek and his dark eyes glittering. His nasty snarl of a grin incised even deeper lines into his face as he spoke.

"I *must* do nothing. I am lord warden, and nearly everyone who comes here is innocent in some way. It doesn't matter. They're mine now."

4

Konan stared across the open walkway and peered through the fortress's iron gate by the light of both moons. The quick moon, which grew full and then emptied over the course of a few weeks, waxed near full in the sky, casting a bright light. The slow moon was lower on the horizon; it never rose very high, instead traveling in a subdued arc to the south. Its half crescent reflected a soft light, having started to wane weeks ago. Together, they cast mismatched angles of light across the camp.

He leaned in the shadows of a dilapidated shanty that had been vacant for a year, but he knew others were doing the same, driven by a morbid curiosity to see what pathetic soul was destined to join them.

The supply wagon that had arrived several hours earlier was unloaded and pulled around, leaving the courtyard open and empty. With any luck, they would be generous with bread for a week or two, but he doubted it. More intriguing was the delay in prisoner release.

Konan would have expected them to shove the bedraggled man—whomever he might be—through the iron gate before the sun went down, so they wouldn't have to risk opening the gates in the dark. As with the incident with Dawna, they preferred not to come out in force at night. There were too many violent prisoners, and they were too organized into coordinated factions led by vicious men: Thordrin in the west camp, Selen in the central camp, and Scrap in the east camp.

His sharp eye caught movement, and he heard the shuffling of feet and clinking of spear butts on cobblestone. He stayed still, a black shape in the shadows, but he saw movement around him as other miners perked up.

The gate swung open, and a squadron of soldiers emerged. They moved in concert across the walkway and just past the first row of shanties, their steps hurried. One in the center had a slender body slung over his shoulder, which he dumped on the ground.

The soldiers turned outward, glaring furiously at the prisoners, who seemed to emerge from every doorway and shadow. The squadron backed away, spears pointed out and swaying with unspoken threat, and then they were back through the gate. It screamed with the metallic clank of locking mechanisms, the sound harsh in the night.

If any of the gangs hadn't been paying attention, they would be by now.

Curious, Konan edged closer, emerging from his hiding place on the edge of the central camp. With a few steps, he was into Selen's territory. He could hear others doing the same. The rustle of half-shoed feet and ragged, rough-spun cotton swept across the camp in a muted whisper.

All eyes turned to the body. It was a girl.

Dropped unceremoniously to the sandy ground, she lay at first like a rag doll, although he could tell her sparkling eyes were open as she stared at the starry sky.

Konan sucked in a breath, then clenched his jaw. The tic on his cheek quivered. There were so few women in Tahayi Mines, and none so soft-looking as her.

The leader of the central camp appeared. Selen. He swaggered toward the girl as if he were the one responsible for her appearance. "What have we here, boys?" he called out in a jaunty tone. "Finally, something fuckable." His men jeered and began circling.

Konan counted eleven of them. They were like scavenger birds circling a corpse.

The girl seemed to struggle to sit up; her scrawny arms trembled visibly. Her chest heaved as she examined her surroundings, and Konan could see the subtle signs of growing panic—the slight widening of her darting eyes, the depth and speed of her gasping breaths, the stiffening of her posture.

Her cheeks looked swollen and off-color, likely tender from a beating by the guards, and her forehead bled just on the edge of her hairline. Had she resisted arrest?

She sobbed once, then nothing. Her eyes, at first glittering like the stars above, seemed to glaze over, and she went still, almost as if she were in shock.

Surely, this soft creature hadn't resisted arrest. She had already given up.

A stubborn, angry voice inside of him railed at her. Why didn't she scream or lash out? Did she really have so little fight? Weak, tender hearts didn't last in the mines. Konan knew.

The circle of Selen's men tightened around her. One of them grabbed her wrist; she turned her hazy eyes upon him and brought her other hand up in a defensive motion.

A churning wind tore into the group, seemingly from her. It twisted, picking up gritty sand in a wild, pulsing whirlwind the size of two men, then engulfed the man who grabbed her. The air shrieked and hissed, overwhelming his scream.

He stumbled backward, his hand clutched to his throat, but the others advanced with a shout.

The girl's hands flung toward each man, seeming to direct the windstorm, which crashed around her in a chaotic pattern. Four more men fell, consumed and asphyxiated by the flurry of sand.

Two men ran. Konan watched as they sank namelessly into the crowd of prisoners.

Selen, the burly gang leader who commanded the central camp, grabbed hold of her hair from behind and dragged her against his chest. He pinned her arms against himself with a nasty grin, and she yelped with more pain than Konan would have expected.

Then he noticed the black bruising showing through a rip in her undertunic. Her ribs were broken, no doubt.

Nevertheless, the girl kicked out, frantic, resisting Selen's grasp. Her colorful skirts, now marred with muck and blood, flailed about her legs.

Then a wall of air slammed into them with a roar. Konan stumbled, but so did everyone else. Two of Selen's men howled as grit ripped at their skin and pummeled their eyes. Even Selen hacked at the dust, tightening his grip around the girl's neck and using the other arm to cover his face.

Konan tightened his face wrapping as he recovered his own balance.

The prison was chaos.

"She's a mage!" someone cried.

"Course she's a fuckin' mage," Selen growled, squeezing more tightly until the girl choked. The gale died down. He growled into her ear, loud enough for all to hear, his voice guttural with phlegm and sand. "One more summons and I'll break your neck, witch."

She lashed a leg out at one of Selen's men with one more bodily effort. Red with fury, the man groaned, then punched her in the abdomen.

The girl screamed and doubled over, but she seemed to be fading fast in Selen's grip. He pulled at her corset strings with his free hand, and she pushed ineffectually at his fingers. The corset fell off, revealing the shape of her breasts, hanging loose under the filthy undertunic.

Selen's men jeered. "Start her slow, boss!" "No, hard and fast, so I can have a turn."

Konan snarled with disgust.

The girl was barely conscious, but he could see the tears streaming down her pale face. When she'd summoned her magika, the bright glitter of her eyes had glazed to a terrifying cloudiness, a violent storm about to break upon them all, but now they were different. Dull. Blood foamed from the corner of her mouth, and she managed to utter a few quiet words.

"Don't . . . please . . ."

Her desperation was met with raucous laughter from Selen's remaining men, and one of them kicked her. They grabbed her and spread her out on the ground, then began ripping at her tattered skirts.

With a deep sigh, Konan stepped out of the shadows and grunted a warning to the four men. He hadn't made a sound in so long, it seemed like an animal's growl, but it was the best he could do.

They ignored him.

He strode forward, revealing his tall stature and hooded cloak in the moonlight.

One of the men glanced up, and a look of fearful recognition flashed across his face. Then he nudged Selen.

The leader snorted with derision. "Little far from your camp, aren't you, boy?" He sneered, jutting a chin at his men and the surrounding crowd, his implication clear. *These are my men.*

"Stop," Konan signed, unblinking. He was painfully aware of how far he was from his shack, but he couldn't retreat now. He wouldn't. His glare encompassed not only Selen, but the entire circle of miserable prisoners. Few would join the man's ravaging, but even fewer would do a damned thing to stop it. Konan breathed the situation in slowly through his nose, shaking his shoulders loose. White rage and disgust flashed through his body like an incendiary flame. He was ready.

Selen eyed his hand motions for a moment, then scoffed and turned back to the girl. He gestured to one of his men to keep an eye on Konan as he unfastened his own belt and crawled over the girl.

"I think he said stop." That cocky voice. Konan guessed who it might be, but the origin of the voice was hidden. Thordrin, gang leader of the west camp. Thordrin continued, "I don't fuckin' know, but I agree. I'd rather see you fuck a pig. At least it'd be small enough to feel your prick."

This time, Selen's head snapped to attention, and his arrogant sneer twitched with doubt. He and his men turned toward the voice as one and began to stand.

A white-handled knife flashed through the air and embedded in the eye of a man holding the girl's shoulder. He keeled backward and plopped into the sand.

Thordrin hooted as if it were the funniest thing he'd seen in months, and he and Konan rushed in together.

Konan leapt over the fallen man and tackled another, rolling him off the girl and landing on top of him, his fists already flying. He broke the man's nose, then his jaw. He ignored the pain in his scarred knuckles. It was temporary. This man's pain was not.

Feeling someone grab at his hood, he shot to his feet before the attacker could hit him. A knee clipped his chin, but Konan deftly flipped the man over his shoulder, grabbed his jaw, and broke the man's neck with a loud crack. Another swiped at him with a chipped rock blade, and he hissed as it sliced his arm open. He twisted the blade out of his attacker's hand and dislocated the man's shoulder, then broke his neck as well. The crack seemed to echo, and the chaos paused for a moment as Selen's men reevaluated him.

He glanced around.

Thordrin had yanked his knife from the dead man's eye and was swiping at Selen's men in an acrobatic dance. His movements were so graceful, his grin so wide, he seemed like a court jester. Thordrin howled with mad elation as he lunged into a man and opened his throat, then danced away.

More of Selen's men rejoined the fray, seeming almost frantic to support their master in a time of need, but they died in moments.

Konan jabbed another prisoner in the cheek, then smashed the heel of his palm into the man's nose. It snapped inward and upward, and the man dropped. Konan broke another's arm and tossed him aside. One of Selen's men stopped short, his chest heaving with terror as he looked up at Konan; then he spun and ran.

The only one left was Selen himself, and Thordrin seemed to be toying with him.

Konan steadied himself, willing the rage down to a controlled simmer. He knelt beside the still body of the girl and placed a protective palm over her, then looked up at the crowd with a territorial glare of suspicion. Satisfied that no more would attack, he turned his attention to her.

The delicate skin of her neck was marred with red fingermarks, and she was unresponsive when he touched her chin. He turned her head one way, then the other. Her nose wasn't broken, but both cheeks were marred by fresh bruises, and her eyes were shadowed with blackened rings. One was swollen shut. The whites he could see were a vermiculated pinkish-red, and her gaze was nearly lifeless—but not quite.

Relief washed over him.

Thordrin spun with a joyful grin of rage and unrestrained hatred, finishing his dance with a flip of his knife into Selen's calf. The other man fell to one knee with a yelp, his leg spurting onto the sand. Thordrin kicked him in the chest, knocking Selen into the pool of his own blood. The west leader cackled as the man flung bloody sand aside.

Cursing continually, Selen dragged himself backward, leaving a bright blood trail that shone crimson in the moonlight.

Thordrin prowled after him, sidestepping the mess so it didn't get on his boots, then pounced. He grabbed Selen's collar and leaned in close. "You move, Selen, and I'll pull your innards out one by one." His disarming smile didn't match his cold, hard gaze. Then he winked. "Didn't know you liked girls. All this time, I was watching for a pig to come through the gates and give you and your boys a good time. I know you've been lonely."

"We can make a deal, Thordrin," Selen stammered. "You can have her first. You can have for all night, all week even. I'll take her when you're done."

Thordrin seemed to consider this, glancing briefly at Konan and the girl, then smiled even wider. "No."

Selen paused, but then turned his expression into a sneer. "You may have the west end, but you ain't in the west end, Thordrin." His voice grew louder. "All these men watching, they're my men. You can't touch me here."

"Yeah, you must be right," Thordrin replied equably. With a mad smile, he trailed his blade across Selen's throat. A thin red line appeared wherever the sharp dagger kissed.

Selen's sneer froze, and any confidence he had fronted melted away. "I'll make a deal, Thordrin. C'mon, I ain't never touched the west end."

Thordrin's hearty laugh echoed through the night, a sound at odds with the tension in the prison. He leaned in closer. "Call your men. Call for help. Go on."

Selen's eyes shot desperately through the crowd, landing briefly on Konan and the girl, growing bigger as they did.

Thordrin continued to encourage him. "Ask for help, Selen. I think you need it. I'd hate to see you go down without a good fight."

Selen took a deep breath. "Men, take him! Take him now!" he cried, his voice cracking.

Nobody moved, although Konan's muscles had tensed in preparation for another fight. He hovered over the girl, his heart quickening. He dared not pick her up until he knew the fighting was done.

Thordrin took a casual look around, then leaned even closer to Selen's ear. "I think you're out of luck." The whisper barely reached Konan.

"Then kill me," replied Selen, his voice ragged with despair.

Thordrin chuckled. Again, his mirth didn't really meet his glittering green eyes. "So easily?"

Selen shuddered and wet himself.

The other man looked up and shouted to the watching prisoners, "The girl is mine."

Konan grunted to get his attention, then signed. "And mine."

Thordrin shot him a measuring glance, then a disarming smile. "You like her too? That's fine. We can share."

Konan scowled and pointed at Selen. "And him?" he signed.

Thordrin's grin widened; he seemed to understand Konan's meaning. "He's mine." He choked Selen with one knee, leaning heavily upon him so the central camp leader couldn't move. Sliding his knife down the man's chest, he popped the man's damp pants open with the blade and tickled the skin all the way down, leaving a meandering trail of blood from neck to groin. Selen groaned, a pathetic sound, and begged for mercy, but Thordrin's merry expression didn't change, his green eyes remaining locked with Selen's.

The knife sliced cleanly through, leaving a stump. Blood spurted all over the sand. Selen screamed.

5

KONAN LEANED AGAINST THE door to Thordrin's shack, crossing his arms and squinting at his new surroundings. He had resided in west camp before, but nowhere near Thordrin's gang. Their shacks centered on the man's preferred location, a sturdier-than-average wooden shanty with a solidly hung door, located an adequate distance from the guard towers in each direction, enough not to draw attention.

Thordrin sat on a barrel like it was a throne, propped up by sand-filled food sacks, with another barrel serving as an armrest. He slouched with one knee resting on a sack and picked at the dirt under his fingernails with his white-handled knife. Not a care in the world.

His gang languished in doorways and against shanty walls, and his watchmen stood on the roofs that could bear the weight. One of the men goggled at Konan, and Konan scowled back at him. He looked away.

"So who the fuck are you?" Thordrin said, not even glancing in his direction.

Konan allowed his grimace to shift from the watchman and settle on Thordrin. He uncrossed his arms. "Doesn't matter," he signed to himself.

As expected, Thordrin sneered at him and waved his knife at Konan's hand motions. "That mean somethin'?"

"Maybe he ain't right in the head, Cap," suggested one of his men, a shrimpish man with oversized eyes and a receding hairline. His rags were those of a mariner, the blue faded to a filthy gray.

"You may be right, Moon." Thordrin chortled and pointed at Konan again. "You right in the head, or did your mam try to drown you when she saw how fucked your face was?"

Moon and the other men laughed, but it was a nervous sound, and Konan noticed how sharply Thordrin watched him for a reaction.

Crossing his arms again, he ignored the insult. It didn't matter. Very little mattered.

Thordrin goaded him once more, feigning a glance at Moon. "I'd say it's the latter, wouldn't you, Moony? A mother's love only goes so far."

"Looks like a fruit been left too long on deck," Moon replied with a broken grin.

"Looks like a horse's ass," Thordrin shot back.

"Wrinkled like a woman's—"

Thordrin cut him off with a derisive laugh. "You been alone too long, Moon. You can't compare that face to a lovely whore's flower; it's an insult to all the women waiting for me back home."

The men chuckled as Moony's face turned bright red. His gap-filled grin faded. "Cap? The girl . . ."

"She's mine, Moony," Thordrin answered, straightening on his throne. He pointed his knife first at Moony, then at the other men watching. "And I ain't one for sharing, unless I have to." He nodded at Konan with exaggerated tragedy. His eyes glittered with cruelty, which he then turned back on his men. "Come to think of it, my girl might be awake by now. Moon, bring the fresh rations. If she ain't ready, at least I can eat *something*."

Moon nodded and returned after just a few seconds with a bowl of tepid broth, which Thordrin took with a wink.

Konan listened to the gang's hooting laughter as he and Thordrin entered the shack he had been guarding.

The door swung shut, and they paused as their eyes adjusted to the dark room. Konan gave the smaller man a long, measuring look.

Thordrin pushed the bowl at him and raised an eyebrow. "You ain't stupid. That's obvious. Why the fuck don't you talk?"

Konan shook his head.

"You got a name?"

Konan didn't respond. What did it matter? He knelt over the young woman, who lay on a lumpy bed made of sacksful of sand. As he got closer, peering through the shadows, she cringed and turned her cheek an inch, then whimpered.

It was a muted response, but likely all she could muster. His examination of her injuries revealed far more than he expected: multiple broken ribs, severe bruising on her arms, legs, and torso, and terrible marks on her neck and face from the abuse. At least her lungs hadn't been punctured. He didn't know how he knew, but he was certain they were clear. He blinked away a brief flash of Isellan's wheezing, the froth on his lips, the gurgled hacking, then shoved the memory away. This was different. The girl could live.

He pushed the bowl to her lips, but she made no effort to incline her head. A violent shaking overtook her body, and her less swollen eye sparkled with fresh tears. Still, she wouldn't look at him. She flinched again as he touched the back of her head and pulled her up enough to drink.

Konan fed her slowly. Every other gulp seemed to trickle down the wrong way, for she kept breaking into a weak cough accompanied by moans of pain and spasming in her chest. By the time she finished the bowl, she looked exhausted, and she lay back with a gasp.

Her eye, a bright glint in the shadowy room, finally sought him out, lingered on his masked face, then shifted distrustfully to Thordrin, who stood over them both with one hand on the hilt of his dagger.

"Finally awake, girl? Still hungry?" He produced a sack of dry rations and handed it to Konan.

The girl flinched at the sudden movements and let out a sob.

Thordrin crouched to get closer. "You scared?" he scoffed, jutting his square jaw outward, conveying pure disgust. "We saved you, mage—show some fucking appreciation."

Her lower lip trembled as she looked from Konan to Thordrin, then back. She began to cry.

The lines of Thordrin's scowl deepened, and his narrowed green eyes creased even further. He stood. "By the nethers, I should have let 'em rape you, if you're gonna be this annoying. Did you hear me? You're *safe* with us. We saved you."

"You were too late," she sobbed in faltering, over-shallow breaths. She tightened her arm, which had been laid across her stomach, against her rib cage, wincing each time her chest heaved.

Thordrin's jaw moved from side to side with a grinding sound. He spun and left without another word, slamming the door behind him. Dust motes flew into the air as the entire shanty shook. Outside, the man made a lewd, light-hearted comment about Konan having a moment with the girl, followed by raucous laughter.

Konan's own cheek ticced with irritation. And yet, his shoulders and neck eased with relief. Thordrin wouldn't hurt the girl either, regardless of the crass boasting in front of his men. He turned his attention back to her.

She was still clutching at her rib cage, clearly struggling not to cry but failing. He caught her wandering gaze and started. Bright with tears and icy in color, it shone like a diamond in the darkness. The blinding rays of sunlight that peeked through the cracks in the walls seemed to make her iris glitter, and he was reminded of its terrifying shine the night they met. There was such power behind those eyes, such wildness and passion. Were all mages imbued with such unsettling characteristics?

Konan realized he was leaning over her, peering at her face, and that she was trying to turn away with the little strength she had. He rocked back on his heels, resting his hands on his knees.

The girl stared at him, her brow knitting and unknitting with bewilderment. As he went to stand, she gasped a breath in and whispered, "Please don't leave me."

Konan resettled himself and swallowed, his throat suddenly dry. The girl's fingers flickered as if reaching, and though hesitant, he reached out in response. He paused, clenching his hand in and out of a fist, but then her fingertips touched his. A shiver ran through him, and again he wondered at how her power shimmered out of her like a mirage. Konan wrapped her fine fingers into his, and she clutched his hand tightly.

In that moment, she seemed to break. Whatever frail, silken webbings had held her together dissolved in a deluge of tears that trickled to the sand beneath her head. She winced repeatedly, her broken ribs no doubt screaming in anguish every time her body convulsed with fresh tears.

The girl's weeping was echoed by a sudden buffeting of wind outside the shack. A sandstorm was on its way.

Konan watched her for a while, returning her grasp and sitting quietly. Too late, she had said. How could that be, unless— That white-hot anger broiled up in him again, searing through his veins with furious energy. The time between her wagon's arrival and her deposition in the camp had been far too long. Someone, perhaps multiple someones, had hurt her long before Selen had a glimpse of her fine curls and lithe body.

There was no one like her in Tahayi Mines.

There were women. Not many, but some. They were coarse and rough-hewn like the men, women of blood-covered steel and rusty iron. Some were harsh enough to match the demands of men like Thordrin and integrated with the gangs, and some were feral enough not to be of interest.

He had never seen a creature like this one, though. Soft. Delicate. Entirely out of place in Tahayi Mines, like a blue-petaled flower amongst craggy rocks.

Had this been what Isellan saw, the day Konan was dumped in the mines as a boy? Something that didn't belong, that shouldn't have been. This girl didn't deserve the misery of this place, no matter what she had done.

Another whimper from her caught his attention. She batted her eyelashes at their hands, unable to do much more, and he realized he was clutching hers so tightly that her fingers were turning white. He dropped the grip and retreated into the shadows, overwhelmed with dismay. He had hurt her.

"Don't leave me alone," she repeated, so softly he almost didn't hear it. "Please."

Her entreaty forced his feet forward in a shuffle, despite his renewed sense of reluctance. Irresistibly, he returned and knelt by her side.

"Who are you?" she asked, her voice tentative in the deep silence.

Instead of acknowledging the question, Konan checked her wounds and adjusting her bandages. First, the cut on her forehead, a gash along the reddish-blonde hairline. It had scabbed over. One of her eyes was nearly shut with swelling, puffy and purple, the iris behind it streaked with visible blood veins. It was unlikely she could see from that one. The other was merely blackened, surely painful but not hindering her vision. Her high cheekbones were both marred with a ghastly rainbow of hues ranging from sickly yellow to black.

He had checked her teeth when she was unconscious. By some miracle, none had been loosened or knocked out, but it appeared she had bit her tongue at some point.

Shuddering at the thought, Konan moved on. The red marks on her neck would heal. The abrasions on her wrists and the cut on her arm would too, although right now they were covered by silk wrappings from her skirt. He felt her cringe, and when he glanced up, he found her face full of fear once again.

It would be necessary to check her stomach, to see if the blackish color had spread. If she was bleeding internally, she might not survive. His scarred cheek and eyelid quivered. He couldn't pull the thin cloth covering down without frightening her.

"Forgive me," he signed. He emptied the food sack Thordrin had tossed at him, dumping the contents onto a barrel. Stale bread, mild yellow cheese—standard rations. The girl would have trouble eating them until she could sit up further, but at least she had her teeth. Returning, he placed the sack across her chest, then gave her a meaningful look. She seemed to acknowledge him, so he pulled the covers down enough to see her ribs and stomach.

Severe bruising again. In several places, the skin was obviously swollen and tender to his probing touch. The black spot on her stomach hadn't changed, and Konan was satisfied she wasn't bleeding further inside. Her taut stomach shuddered with her tears, and he pulled the cover back up, torn between shame and necessity.

"Forgive me," he repeated, signing, but that only earned a strange look.

"Thank you," she whispered, sounding unsure. Nevertheless, she strained to raise her arm, a movement which showed only as the quivering of her weak fingers.

Konan took them and placed her hand back on her abdomen, and the slight tightening of her hold told him to remain there. The wind continued to howl outside, and it didn't die down until she drifted off to sleep.

6

Despite the misty sunrise, the day of the Grand Festival of Remembrance was bright by noon, blessed with the white light and tentative warmth of spring sunshine.

"Praise the Light, I thought it might be unpleasant after that morning chill," murmured Priscilla. She shivered as they looked out from their main balcony.

Reylin adjusted the shawl over his first wife's shoulders, nudging the edges up to her lace collar. "I thought you were hot all the time, my lady."

She pulled a face without screwing her features up too much. "It comes and goes, my lord."

"Perhaps you should go inside until it warms a little more," suggested Syrana, Reylin's second and Chosen wife, from his other side. "Such chills could lead to a fever."

Priscilla blushed and rubbed her protruding belly. "Yes, that may be wise." She began to move away, but Reylin caught her hand.

"Would you like an escort, my lady?"

She shook her head and leaned up to kiss his cheek. "I'll be all right, my lord. Perhaps I'll soak in the heat of the large fire in the south parlor; I may take some tea before the feast." She had to stand on her toes to reach him, and he turned his head to brush against her soft lips. Then he watched her go. Although she lumbered a bit less gracefully than she used to, her growing physique was a source of pride for him. With any luck, and by the grace of the Five-Faced God and numerous prayers sent by the Temple mages, the form growing inside her was his first son, prince and heir to the Kingdom of Mirat.

"Such a sickly woman—she really ought to be more careful," said Syrana in his ear. "Today shines bright, and it's not overly cold. Shall we go for a walk before our civic duties?" She shimmied under his shoulder, and the temperature of her pale skin implied she was being strong.

Reylin adjusted her gauzy green shawl as well and held her to him.

She had dressed to match him. Her decorative, plaited corset was bleached and dyed a light spring green, reminiscent of the growth spurting from the ramparts and walkways of the castle. Its underbust style, cinched tightly with silk ribbons, emphasized her glorious shape, which spilled out from the white blouse. She had demanded silk from Tamorín for that, and its quality showed in the weave. Its edges shimmered with rose thread, and the corset dangled with strings of rosy pearls and diamonds, her favorite gemstones after the orange Gems of I'ya that declared royalty. Similar strings draped from her black hair trusses, affixed by diamond-studded hairpins.

Over her breasts, a brilliant orange gemstone drew the eye and hung on another string of pink pearls, a clear indicator of her status as a princess of Mirat. Intricately interwoven threads of gold formed her circlet crown, smaller than a queen's for two reasons: she was not the first wife, and Reylin had not yet Ascended to his kingship.

Reylin frowned.

"We don't have to go for a walk, my love," Syrana rushed to say. "Whatever pleases you, pleases me."

Reylin caught himself, realizing she had misinterpreted his expression, and rubbed her arms. "No, my Chosen, I—"

He grimaced. "I was merely contemplating how, even when I place a larger crown upon your head, it would fail to out-shine you."

Her worry shifted to pleasure, and she trailed her painted nails up his chest. Reylin was wearing newly tailored festival garb, commissioned at the behest of the Elder Council: a dark green tunic the color of frostmoss and accented by the same fresh verdigris as Syrana's outfit. The colors not only sang of the season, but also proclaimed his love for his parents, lost all those years ago in the terrible fire. His white cloak fluttered nearly to the backs of his knees, trimmed in rose and gold. The diamonds embedding the out-facing side sparkled in the sunlight as he moved.

But Syrana didn't seem to notice any of these details as she focused on his face. She played with his closely trimmed goatee. "My lord is pleased?" She bit her rouged bottom lip just a little.

Reylin stirred and broke into a smile. Although he had not been allowed to marry his Chosen *first*, at least he had been allowed to marry her.

The Council had insisted he first bind the Miratian throne to one of the petty kingdoms to the south as a form of alliance and friendship, and in truth, Priscilla was lovely. In the past year, she had proven herself a considerate and kind person, and she shared his bed willingly. She seemed to love him.

Yet Syrana was his chosen wife, selected and courted for passionate love alone. By the Light, she was perfect in every way.

Reylin looked down at her now, feeling the hunger in him growing. "I'm quite pleased, my beautiful lady." He consumed her with his eyes, outlining every part of her and lingering on the dark shadow of her cleavage.

She tossed her hair with a coquettish smile. The loose curls hanging from her pearl-and-diamond fixtures moved like silk, framing her face and emphasizing her dark eyes. Then she dragged her finger down his chin, along his clean-shaven neck, to the rose pearl buttons at the top of his tunic. She lingered on the whisper of scars on his collarbone. "We don't have to go for a walk," she repeated.

The soft words carried just enough hint of salaciousness to let him know what she wanted, and he pulled her into the sanctuary of their bedroom. He had managed to remove her shawl and unlace the corset when a knock impeded their pleasure.

"Your Royal Highness?" came the gravelly voice of his High Guard commander, Sir Gillead, from the other side of the gilded doors.

Reylin grimaced as Syrana continued to pull at his belt with a look as desirous as it was mischievous.

Gillead continued through the wood. "Your Highness, forgive me for the interruption, but the Council has requested your presence for the festival opening speech."

"Now?"

"Yes, Your Royal Highness."

Reylin groaned his frustration but called back to Gillead nonetheless. "Tell Galltry we'll be down as soon as we can, and please inform Her Highness Priscilla to meet us. You should find her in the south parlor."

"Yes, Your Royal Highness."

Reylin could hear the big man marching away, then turned his attention back to Syrana. "You'd think I could decide for myself what time the festivities should start," he muttered. "Am I not the crown prince?"

Syrana continued tugging at his belt, unhooking it and whipping it off. "So you are, my love."

He took her hands and hesitated. "We must ready ourselves, my Chosen, and you are doing precisely the opposite."

She pulled her hands free and tugged at his rosy pink leggings. "You are ready." Then she pulled him toward the bed. "We should give Priscilla a little time. She moves quite slowly due to her poor condition. Love me, my prince. Love me now."

Reylin adjusted his belt once more and examined Syrana with renewed appreciation. She was as splendorous as before their short diversion, her hair perfect and her corset tightly relaced. She was his, and only his, and by the Light he was thankful for it. What had he done to deserve her? Priscilla was lovely, but Syrana was his passion, his Chosen, and he had done nothing to deserve her love. She made him forget his ire, release the tightness in his shoulders, and relinquish the worries that plagued him—was he good enough to be king? Was he strong enough, clever enough? Did he belong on that coveted throne?

She crept her hand into the crook of his arm and fawned at him. It bolstered his confidence. If the Council wanted to see a proper crown prince, they would see it. Reylin straightened his shoulders, emphasizing his height and build. Above all, he enjoyed the fact that he had surpassed Lord Galltry in height this past year. The man could no longer look down at him, as though Reylin were naught but a snot-nosed child.

Priscilla joined them at the door to the main dining hall, and Reylin was obligated to switch Syrana to his left arm. He smiled sheepishly at her, hoping she wasn't too miffed, but Priscilla *was* first. (What man in his right mind wanted two wives? Especially if they weren't friendly with each other, like Priscilla and Syrana were.)

They entered together to the sound of a herald and accompanying music.

The massive hall echoed with the shuffle of hundreds of feet and whispering nudges as the people of Mirat and neighboring kingdoms watched them walk to the head table, a long, crescent-shaped affair with spaces not only for him and his wives, but also for the highest-ranked lords and ladies. Galltry gave him a welcoming smile; his friendliness was echoed by his wife's. Lady Shildra beckoned him up to his position in the center. Lord Lío, the scornfully all-knowing duke of the western coast, acknowledged him stiffly. His first wife, Lady Falicia, was friendlier, waving at Priscilla with a warm, maternal smile. Two more royal couples sat closest to Reylin's central position: the generously proportioned King Brigg of Loreni and his consort Queen Wenfa, and the pinch-faced and dour King Rigaran and his equally somber wife Queen Déllani of Krita.

Despite Reylin's frustration, he had to acknowledge the respect garnered by Lord Galltry, the duke of Mirat's east range and valley. Sporting a snow-white beard and streaked hair, the man was as wise and venerable as he looked, and therefore the head of Mirat's Elder Council. Shildra, his bashful and kindly wife, was nearly as respected despite her sex. Although several other lords had been displaced by the visiting royalty, Galltry and his wife remained at the head table, being by far the most influential of their rank.

As Reylin began to take a breath to welcome the crowd, Galltry stood, and the rustle of the room quieted. He indicated Reylin with a broad gesture. "And now, our crown prince would like to speak a few words of welcome to the Grand Festival of Remembrance, our annual celebration and memorial to the beloved King Rolis and beautiful Queen Leyalin." He lowered his voice and spoke more softly to Reylin. "Go ahead, son." He sat.

Realization struck Reylin, and his shoulders sagged a little. The Council had already initiated the feast, likely with fine and eloquent words from Galltry, before Reylin had even made his entrance. His own speech was secondary, its richness lost on the crowd like a tertiary dessert.

Both Syrana and Priscilla squeezed his arms, and Syrana looked up at him with utter adoration. He tried to straighten again, but his height held no authority. He said a few words, but he choked on his own frustrated fury. Then, pasting a smile on, he guided first Priscilla, then Syrana to their chairs. When he was seated, the elderly High Holy Mage Ma'thell spoke a blessing over the room and meal, again making him feel sandwiched betwixt two more important things.

The mob cheered as Father Ma'thell creaked to his seat at the benches (a place for commoners, but mages refused to acknowledge their station in situations like this one). Unlike the first few years after the fire, a period of melancholy, the festival was now a celebration of Rolis and Leyalin's lives and memory. They and others had been consumed in the terrible fire that swept through Ironhold Castle, and Reylin had been the only survivor of the central keep. He subconsciously touched the light scar on his brow, the only remnant of his terrible near-death experience. Its shadow reappeared on his collarbone and arm, but only if you really looked for it. The Temple's healing mages were quite talented, led by High Holy Mage Ma'thell, a master of healing arts.

Many had come for this spring gathering as the news of Princess Priscilla's pregnancy and Syrana's newfound sovereignty had spread over the winter months. Residents were eager to see their new lady and to bless the prince and his get, whereas strangers were keen to collect gossip they could natter about back home. Reylin spied the orange of Mirat, but also the greens and blues of Callendera and Krita interspersed throughout the crowd.

Reylin seethed as servants piled from the kitchen bearing steaming trays, rolling carts, and covered platters. He sat at the center of this affair, and yet he felt invisible.

The head table was laid with a massive oval platter. The entire room gasped as the chef removed the lid, revealing a fearsome giant bird from the barbarian grasslands, its long, muscular neck wrapped around the front of its body and baked flawlessly. Although the rest of its body was plucked, the bird's wildly plumed head had been taken off beforehand and was now set perfectly in line with the neck, its brilliant green crown of feathers splayed out like a fan. Its marble-black eyes gazed out at the cavernous hall, indicating how freshly killed it really was. It had to have been flown in by a dragonkeeper, perhaps even taken by a vicious dragon, for who else would dare venture into the dangerous Loi al'Halmana? The giant birds were herded like cattle by the barbarians, even ridden, and using one as the centerpiece was one more reminder to the crowd of Mirat's superiority over the wild north.

Arranged around the bird's basted body were sweet fruits from the equatorial regions, and on one side were three round eggs, poked through the top of the shell and crammed with a dozen spices and minced vegetables before baking. The display was faultless, a credit to the Miratian head chef.

Other savory platters emerged from the kitchens, borne by hulking slaves from the Sea of Ice north of Merchan: lath of aromatic thindelwood bearing the smoked backstrap from a wild haulbeast, laden with springtime vegetables in a dark gravy; a tiered cake that was brought out in four sections and assembled on the table, its vividly pink frosting indicating that it was flavored with delectably sweet magasberries from the mountainside; a bowl of tubers mashed and spiced and mixed with cream and grains—a dish so spicy it burnt the tongue without milk to wash it down. Meats dripping with juices and marinade, breads fluffy and fresh, and a myriad of desserts ranging from pies to cobblers to sweet creams and fruits littered the tables throughout the cavernous hall.

Ale was poured by maidens in silk, their outfits naught but strips of thin veneer. Marlemetian wines were poured at the upper tables, to the delight of the eastern lords who received shipments from the western kingdom of Marlemet less frequently than they desired. The ale was a local favorite, brewed in one of the lesser valleys of Mirat with a winter grain. It was strong and dark, a perfect bride for the thirsty men of the Miratian mines. The children scattered through-out the tables received pitlan cider, as did some of the mages. High Holy Mage Ma'thell restrained himself from the consumption of alcohol, as he did most amusements, activities he referred to as the "diversions of the young." By his lead, many of the older holy men refrained from drunkenness, although they encouraged it in the younger mages. "One cannot understand the human soul without experiencing its desires," they said wisely. "Drink up, my son."

My son. Reylin enjoyed little of the meal, distracted as he was by Galltry's constant treatment of him as a boy. He hadn't been a boy for years. He had not one wife but two, and was soon to be a father with an heir for the kingdom. What more could he do to prove his manhood? He ground his teeth.

Priscilla gagged and covered her mouth at her plateful of steaming spiced tubers. "Oh Light's end," she murmured through her hand.

Reylin leaned over her immediately. "My lady? Are you well?"

She shook her head, paling, and he waved Sir Gillead and Sir Patreagh over.

Priscilla swallowed hard and tried to recover her composure, but it was clear she had no more interest in the meal. "Your son is kicking like a horse today, my lord, and he did not like this dish." She heaved a breath, then drank some wine.

"Does he want something lighter?" Perhaps the heavily spiced meats were too strong, but the head chef had also brought out a spongy light white cake, sticky with baked egg white, and a variety of fresh fruits from the south. Reylin scooped clotted cream and sugar on top and offered it to her.

"Would you like to rest?" he asked when she winced.

Gillead and Patreagh stood behind her, ready to escort her, but she shook her head again.

"I just need a moment, my lord. I'm so sorry."

"Don't be," he whispered.

Priscilla regained some of her poise, nodding her apology to Queen Déllani, who sat beside her; the Kritali queen merely raised an eyebrow before resuming very polite conversation.

Reylin almost wished she had capitulated to the desire to leave. He would have escorted her, with a more than adequate excuse to avoid the humiliation he felt. Instead, he and his wives now endured the long meal, the capers and songs of wayfarers, the jestering of Halmani slaves, and the eventual degeneration to drink.

He left the feast as soon as was socially acceptable, having enjoyed nothing and desiring only to get away. He felt a fool. Called like a dog, and then kicked like one.

"Damn the Council," Reylin snarled when he finally reached his chambers. He flounced onto his canopied bed and rubbed his temples.

Both of his wives were silent, but he felt the bed move as they sat beside him.

"When will they recognize that I can do more than give some silly, meaningless speech?" he lamented, too furious to withhold his feelings in front of them.

"Of course you can," Syrana agreed enthusiastically. "Initiating any part of the festivities without you was incredibly rude, and Galltry had to realize that."

"He likely doesn't," said Priscilla, keeping her voice soft. She looked apologetic once more as she added, "He's been head of the Council for so long, he's used to being the one in charge."

Reylin ground his teeth again and turned away from Priscilla, but she caught his knee.

"My lord, you are right to feel the way you do, but it's already happened. What matters is how you react now. You are worthy of their respect." She rubbed her round belly.

"You're a man grown, sire of a child and husband to me, husband to Syrana, a man trained by knights and learned in history, survivor of a terrible fire that nearly destroyed your lineage. You are *Reylin*. Show them who you are."

His sense of pride warred with his sense of impotence, but the latter won out, and he scowled. "I deserve respect regardless of who I am, and I'm tired of begging for it." He pushed her hand off his knee. Turning away, he heard her labor to her feet and shuffle out.

Syrana's cool touch flickered across his hand, then up his arm, shivering through him like ice. "My love?" There was just enough query in her voice to encourage him.

Reylin scrubbed his face and looked at her. By the Light, she was gorgeous. She looked at him with dark concern shining in her gaze, further emphasized by her long, black lashes. She adjusted herself in his lap and leaned close to his ear.

"We didn't fully satisfy ourselves earlier, did we?" she whispered, a touch of danger in her voice. "And you *are*, after all, a man grown." She nibbled his ear, and her breath was hot against his skin.

He shuddered and caressed her shape beneath her dress. "Tell me you love me, my Chosen."

"There's nothing I want more."

Reylin felt some of the tension in his neck and shoulders release as she brushed them with her lips, and then he pulled her to himself and kissed her with all the urgency he felt. It may have been too rough, but then again, so were his hands as he felt the delicate fabric of her dress tear under his probing fingers.

He stuttered an apology as she undid her fittings.

"The Master Tailor can fix it," she murmured, tossing the dress through the door with an imperious command to Sir Gillead, who stood beyond with the other High Guard. She turned back and posed for him in all her naked glory. Porcelain skin, black trusses cascading past her breasts, black hair below.

He licked his lips as she climbed back onto his lap and hungrily undid his own fastenings.

"Show me what kind of king you are," she demanded with all of the authority of a queen, and all of the lust of a courtesan.

Reylin obeyed.

7

"You presented yourself with such grace at the festival, my young prince." Galltry's familiar, conciliatory voice controlled the room with a gentle but utterly unyielding strength. "It reflected well upon you to focus on your parents' memory with modest words."

Reylin clenched his jaw and slid his gaze across the other faces in the council room. The other lords were nodding enthusiastically. Of course they agreed with Galltry. Didn't they always?

Your role is not to speak, Prince.

"I would have liked to say more, Lord Galltry, but I didn't relish a redundant speech about the tragedy of Ironhold." His words were somewhat clipped, and Lord Galltry's smile twitched with the slightest bit of chagrin.

"It's been a wise move to shift the focus of the festival to your miraculous survival, rather than the tragedy itself," said Galltry.

Lord Lío grunted an affirmation, which was echoed by several others sitting around the table.

Reylin took a deep breath through his nose. Galltry always made him feel like an errant boy, while simultaneously implying that the state of things was a result of Reylin's influence. He annually recalled how Reylin had pushed to make the festival a celebration of life, rather than a somber burning of candles and donning of black garments. If Reylin thought back, he only recalled being a lonely boy who whined about how depressing the former event was. It exacerbated everything he already felt. The event had changed after that, but not by his adolescent hand.

"I'd like to discuss my Ascension," he managed, straightening his shoulders. "By next spring's Grand Festival of Remembrance, I'd like to be the one giving the opening speech, with my wives and children by my side. I am ready."

"Children?" Galltry raised a gray brow at the plural reference, and Lord Ennedrew grinned openly, light dancing in his eyes. "Are you expecting another already?"

How subtle, thought Reylin, to cast doubt while also changing the subject. He cleared his throat. "I would think the Princess Syrana will also bear a child by then, but my Ascension need not await yet another indicator of my readiness to rule. I have waited patiently for years, my lords regent. I have studied all you've given me, I've trained with Lord Commander Gillead, and I've begun to build a family. I am ready now."

Galltry's smile tightened, and he gestured apologetically. "We appreciate how much you've grown and matured in the last few years, Your Royal Highness, but you must understand we wish only what's best for the kingdom and for you."

Reylin's cheeks and forehead felt hot, and he was thankful for the cool spring air wafting through the chamber's windows. "Yes, I have grown and matured. I *am* ready. It is you who are not." He hated that he had repeated himself three times.

Galltry's reasonable tone dominated the room. "My prince, the Council debates your Ascension at least once a new moon. We wish only to ensure that the future of Mirat is in steady hands."

Reylin clenched his jaw and praised the Light that Syrana wasn't in the private room. This was humiliating. His voice began to shake as he tried to speak with care. "Lord Galltry, you have provided steady leadership, and you, Lord Lío—" He nodded at the dour man on his other side before continuing. "And I am thankful for the Council's stewardship over the years since my parents' deaths. Because of your stewardship, your attention to my education and training, I have been groomed to be a good king. But training cannot last forever. I am ready now. It is not a debate any longer."

"As you say, Prince," said Galltry with a respectful but meaningless nod, "but the Council must be unanimous in this consent."

Reylin's temper flared. "And who denies me?" He glared down the table as the councilmembers dissembled. Only Galltry and Holy Mage Kaiadin, a junior mage of the Temple of I'ya, met his eye. Lío scowled at the wooden tabletop, his lips curled up in a poor-tempered snarl, and Porin looked helplessly at the others. Lords Yarris and Shiften stared straight ahead with blank expressions, and the bright-eyed Lord Ennedrew smiled awkwardly at High Holy Mage Ma'thell. Reylin couldn't tell if Ma'thell's vague and wrinkled smile was directed back at Ennedrew, as the old man's cloudy cataracts neared blindness.

Reylin tried to rein his anger in and continue in a reasonable tone, that same steadiness that Galltry always seemed to carry. "This situation has no precedent, and thus no rules. The Council has done well enough in my parents' stead, but Mirat is ready for her king. We did not emerge from the ashes of the Empire to fight over Ironhold's seat. My bloodline has ruled since those dark days, providing the steady hand of which you always speak."

Holy Mage Kaiadin nodded briefly in agreement, but he looked down when Lío redirected his frown.

"A unanimous decision is necessary," muttered Lío, "not only to ensure that your training is complete, but to ensure stability in the transition."

The thought of disaffected lords rejecting him filled Reylin with a burning fury from deep within. His tenuous hold of his temper failed. "And stability there will be, with the Council still intact as an advisory group. But you must—" Reylin pounded the table with his fist. "You *must* relinquish rule to me, the rightful king!"

Galltry looked doleful and fatherly, placing his hand on Reylin's to quell his anger. It was infuriating, and Reylin shook him off with a glare.

Lío affected an expression of offense, as if Reylin's demand for autonomy implied his own incompetence. "We have done all for the glory of Mirat. *We* rebuilt the castle. *We* added the new iron mines!" he stated, raising his loose chin high.

"The mines at Southface Pine are now nearly spent, Lord Lío," Reylin interrupted.

"*We* expanded North Mara's port to handle the stone coming through, and strengthened the route to Krita," Lío continued as if the younger man hadn't spoken. He had an irritating habit of doing that, like Reylin's words didn't matter.

"The road from the Camdry Quarry needs repaved and widening," Reylin insisted, "and the kingdom road from here to Loreni."

"Before the road to Tallgrass?" muttered Porin, sounding unhappy. He still looked everywhere but up, his arms crossed, hunched inward. "Our farms need better accessibility."

"That stone isn't getting a fair price either," continued Reylin, feeling more and more passionate. "Krita needs it locally for that construction project of Rigaran's, not to mention the numerous forwards from there to the western shore. He needs our export more than we do; an internal road project would provide even greater leverage against his sour, thieving trademasters."

"We already bartered for a good trade deal," Lío grumbled.

"I had lheard Marlemet was building some sort of seawall to guard the Red Bay," muttered Yarris.

Reylin nodded emphatically. "And Fumaya and Shiggo are expanding their royal castles. You know they don't produce a lot of their own stone, especially high-grade for facings."

"You want to trade with the *myr*?" Lío's voice was derisive.

"We already do, and you know it." Reylin refused to lower his gaze from the glowering duke, who controlled Mirat's best seaports.

"A minor route, to be sure," said Galltry, sparing a stern look at Lío, "but *those* people are not ones with whom we wish to foster a relationship. They're not . . . trustworthy."

"Barely even people," snorted Lío with disgust.

"Leave these worries with us, my young prince," said Galltry. "Lord Lío is most familiar with the complexities of the Krita relationship."

The lord snorted again. "Nothing passes through my ports without my approval."

"But imagine if we could gain a hundred mark more per ton?" Reylin pushed.

"Krita would never accept," Lío replied.

Galltry broke in, speaking to Reylin like a youngling, utterly calm. "Imagine is all we can do, young prince. Krita loves her profits and punishes through harsh tariffs. Our stone prices have been set amicably for several years now, thanks to Lord Lío. Worry not, son."

Reylin prickled at the last word. Galltry always used that tone when he had stopped listening. He drew a long breath in, steadying himself. It was not this day either, was it? They would hear no more of his trade ideas or his construction projects than they would of his Ascension. He acquiesced, feeling the anger inside churn like acid. "I've imposed on the Council's consultation time long enough then. I realize your private session awaits, so I'll take my leave. Please consider my comments regarding a road project, and northward prospecting in alliance with the miners' guild."

Galltry bowed respectfully, while Porin looked visibly relieved. The junior mage Kaiadin also rose, leaving the lords and his own superior Ma'thell to further discussion and decision-making.

It galled Reylin that they frequently made final decisions without him present. Could he not even listen to their full discourse? What did they hide from him? But this was how it had been since the fateful fire. This was the process, and its conduct had held the kingdom together for over a decade. He heaved a sigh as the council room door shut, unaware that Kaiadin stood next to him.

"My good prince, it is no fault of yours," murmured the mage in a smooth bass. "The fault is theirs, in failing to see your readiness to Ascend."

Reylin gave him a sharp look. The tall man was draped with purple robes, an indigo band painted across his brown eyes. His spectacles looked strange over top the elegant holy decoration. The priest bowed, a quick and awkward motion.

"I'm sorry. I do not mean to interfere, Your Royal Highness."

"You are one of the Council."

"Yes, and I can promise you they have your best interests at heart, but they still see a boy. The Eye of I'ya has cycled twelve times since you became their charge, but time does not seem that long to those who have seen sixty cycles." Kaiadin smiled in a friendly, if clumsy, manner.

"Or seventy." Reylin pictured Galltry's gray hair and beard and snorted. "Stuck in their ways?"

"Indeed, Your Highness." Kaiadin gave another bow, deep this time, barely catching his glasses as they tumbled off his nose. "I counsel patience, if you would be so gracious as to accept my counsel. Patience will see you king before long." The junior mage turned and glided sedately down the hall.

Reylin stared after him, hoping he was right. Ma'thell, would speak well for Reylin, and Ennedrew seemed supportive. Galltry was difficult to read, sometimes seeming to want to believe Reylin was ready in a paternal sort of way, yet failing to stand up for that with his verbal representation of the Council as a whole. If the Council required unanimity, it would take only one voice of dissonance to prevent Reylin's timely Ascension.

Perhaps he should focus on proving himself to that one. But who was it? Lío? Porin? Or was it in fact Lord Galltry, the gatekeeper of the entire Council, a man capable of intertwining fatherly encouragement and insidious doubt? They did all seem to follow his lead.

At least he knew it wasn't Father Kaiadin, and he suspected it wasn't Father Ma'thell. Both mages were men of faith, and their benevolence seemed to extend not only to doing good in the world, but to *believing* in good in the world.

Reylin shook his arms out, hoping to dispel the shiver of energy gained from arguing with the Elder Council. He stalked back to his quarters, trailed as usual by his High Guard.

When he was in a mood like this one, Sir Gillead wouldn't initiate any conversation, acting as demure and invisible as a Halmani slave. His fellow High Guard followed suit. Sir Patreagh withheld his careful commentary, and Sir Ronidann clamped his mouth over any smart jokes about the councilmembers. Sir Jonathan merely grimaced.

Reylin found Syrana in the adjoining parlor as he had hoped.

She looked up from her embroidery and smiled, but her expression shifted to concern as she examined him. She tossed her project at her handmaiden and rushed to him.

"What did they say?" she asked, nearly breathless.

When he didn't reply, she slid her jeweled fingers around him and caressed his back, then leaned her head against his chest. Her heavily perfumed hair flooded his senses with the delicate floral of roses and kiltberries, and he leaned into her intoxicating presence.

"Tell me, my love," she whispered.

And he did.

He told her of his assertion and subsequent denial, followed by their disregard for all of his concerns for their economy. This was yet another rejection in a string of requests, which had lately come to chafe uncomfortably as Reylin came of age.

"Galltry wouldn't even admit he made an error, not allowing me to speak first at the festival," he complained. "He wouldn't even allow for the promise of my Ascension before next spring."

Syrana balked. "They don't know your potential, my love. They are fools."

He went to grimace but found his features had already been molded into a permanent frown. He made an effort to mask his expression, suddenly embarrassed that he had revealed such insecurities to the woman he wanted most to impress.

"You're handsome, even when you scowl," Syrana said, her voice turning sultry. Her fingers began to explore further, sending prickles of delight up his spine.

Dipping his head, Reylin gave her a long kiss. How could he focus on anything with her near? He trapped her wandering hands and looked at her appreciatively.

Her soft lips curved into a superior smile, the expression a queen *should* wear, and she tilted her chin high. "So what are you going to do, my love? How can you show them what kind of king you can be?"

He half shrugged. "I need to think through the options. Nothing I say seems to be welcome in the Council meetings, but perhaps if I presented a complete plan, they would consider it more seriously."

Reylin led her to the outer balcony, and they settled on a cushioned chaise that overlooked the endless valley south of Ironhold.

Mirat was truly beautiful. Her craggy shoulders embraced the royal castle and city, reaching out on either side with distant fingers, the last vestiges of the Sikrat, before giving way to a rich high plain soil. The valley was broad and flat, with a river meandering through the middle. Beyond his immediate sight, where the foothills ended, the valley opened into an expanse of shortgrass and mountain forbs, interspersed with boggy wetlands and crisscrossed with glacial brooks. Now, in the springtime, delicate blossoms appeared in hues of violet, sunny yellow, and rose pink across the plains, and periwinkle shrubs washed the hillsides. The wild herds would migrate northward from their winter homes in Callendera, marching their way through the pastures and into the Sikrat. Crops would be sown, and exports would move in caravans to the sea.

He was no king of this land still. The Council's denial stung more each time.

Reylin had understood the Council's reticence when he was younger. He had only seen ten years when he first asked to pursue an education in the Temple; he displayed no blessing of magika, but it had seemed like a fun calling. Seeing the brawn of the mining guildmaster, Daiunek, he had asked at twelve to apprentice as a miner, but the dangers of the mines were too high, and the Elder Council had said no. Instead, he should invest his energy into learning history, diplomacy, and courtly manners.

And he had done so.

"Something that demonstrates my capability in war and diplomacy," he murmured, snapping his fingers at Syrana's handmaiden to bring them a fur.

She murmured agreement. "Why not both? Mirat has been weak with Krita, all thanks to that Lord Lío and his policies in trade. It's hurting Mirat's profit, despite how much we export."

"We can't go to war with Krita," Reylin said without pause. The Council would laugh him out of the room for such a suggestion.

"No, my love, of course not."

"But we could demand more in trade, if we had better resources to trade and in more limited amounts."

That, he mulled over. He needed to make some difficult decisions that the Council had been tabling for months. Their trade routes were threatened by the growing sea trade, and he believed a strategic alliance with other kingdoms of the eastern continent would be wise to defray the power of Krita Port. He also worried for the concerns Master Miner Daiunek shared in private: the primary iron mine was nearly spent, and some of the gem lodes were waning. Greater resources were to be found where he and Wethers had been prospecting, at East Face Mine and beyond, but pushing the boundary carried greater risk. The Council wanted nothing to do with border arguments, especially in that direction, although they found obvious pleasure in reallocating land within the kingdom as suited their needs.

"You know, Master Oyerton came to me seeking help."

Syrana raised a delicately drawn eyebrow.

"He said Southface Pine's lodes are nearly exhausted, and that we should be prepared for a flagging in our iron trade."

Syrana gasped. "Our entire economy would destabilize."

He knew she understood the gravity of Oyerton's report. She came from a mining district, Camdry, over which her father served as baron.

Reylin nodded. "The Elder Council wouldn't listen when I passed it along. They seem to believe we'll be magically gifted with more, but they haven't done the planning to find a new source as rich as that one. And that's just the iron. Oyerton suggested that his master, Daiunek, had prospected to the north and east and found more promising metals and gemstones. Gallite, rubies, sapphires, perhaps even orange gems."

"I'm sure the Council didn't want to hear that either." Syrana pursed her lips just slightly, but not enough to twist her face in an unpleasant way. If anything, the expression made him want to bite those protruding lips, to caress them with his own and remind himself what they tasted like.

He tried to focus. This thought had potential. "If we could push northeast just a little farther, toward the Loi al'Halmana, staying high on the east face, the savages would present little threat, and we could derive more valuable items for trade. We could develop a new diplomatic agreement with the Miners Guild, and we could use our improved position to renegotiate with not only Krita, but with Loreni and Callendera."

"Rigaran is a snake," Syrana warned.

"I know. All the more reason it may impress upon the Council that I can seal a beneficial agreement with another kingdom. Success would prove to them that I'm capable and mature." One more step forward, one more weight upon the balance to demonstrate his readiness.

Syrana played with his goatee, then touched the subtle scar that traced his forehead on the left side. He turned his head, ashamed of the mark.

"You are more than capable. A hard man to deny..." Syrana bit her lip again.

She denied him nothing, and he likewise.

Reylin's last fleeting thought was that he hoped the renovated royal bedroom didn't look the same as it had before the Great Fire. They had rebuilt the collapsed walls and scrubbed the ash marks from the stone, then hung massive tapestries and tall curtains, laid plush rugs on the floor, and canopied the bed. Reylin had moved into the massive suite formerly belonging to King Rolis and Queen Leyalin, and now shared its vast rooms with his wives. Renovated or not, he rather hoped the pattern he nuzzled his cheek into each night was his own, making the rooms unique to him and not a copy of something else.

Reylin tapped his fingers impatiently on the fine-grained tabletop. Then he shifted his legs, placing one ankle as casually as possible on the other knee. His foot invariably began tapping as well.

Lord Galltry finally looked up from reading the proposal and removed his reading glasses. He smiled. "Son, you've done a fine job with this. The Council will have ample detail to consider its merit," he said. He shuffled the papers back into tidy order and handed the proposal back to Reylin.

"Thank you," Reylin replied, straightening his posture. "I hope to present to the Council this week, with your support."

Galltry agreed, but with some reservation. "The potential increase in gemstone exports to Krita Port is likely unsustainable." He shook his head. "No, you may have to dispense with that portion of the proposal."

"Not if we push north and east, as the Miners Guild wishes to continue doing." Reylin's enthusiasm came through, and he tried to reign it in again, realizing Galltry would not appreciate the youthful impulse.

"It is risky, son, to push the northeast border with people like the Halmani. The positive effects on our trade capacity are substantial, justifying some renegotiation in export prices and quantities, but we must consider the requisite military component."

"Yes, I've considered that," said Reylin, launching into a description of their standing knights and ground troops in a somewhat more measured tone. Still, he found himself rambling in his excitement. Galltry would see this as a sign of immaturity, so Reylin forced himself to stop talking.

"My own troops are best positioned to assist the guild, although I wish no loss of life should we encounter a border conflict," suggested Galltry. "Yes, with that adjustment, I would be confident in the viability of the plan." Some royal funds would go into Galltry's coffers to pay his knights, thought Reylin. Then he berated himself for thinking so poorly of the man. He wasn't Lord Lío or Porin, after all. The senior duke continued, "Note, my young prince, that Lío will not appreciate exclusion from the negotiations with Krita. You may have to convince him—and include him."

Reylin offered an eager nod. "We can give him a good basis of quality soldiers to assure the East Face Mine's safety, and he can reciprocate with shipments of iron and gallite. Let us strengthen our solidarity with the Mining Guild." Those were words Galltry liked to hear: reciprocate, solidarity.

The lord stroked his beard thoughtfully. Cut close on the cheeks to leave only a goatee and mustache, but allowed to remain along the jaw line, it reminded Reylin of Sir Gillead's but far whiter. "Perhaps," Galltry murmured, "perhaps you are right." Another few strokes, and he shook his head. "We must not aggravate the Halmani though, young prince. We mustn't start a war. No, you must rein that portion of your proposal back. Be conservative with how far east and northward you propose we push, or this will surely be rejected by the rest of the Council."

Reylin stiffly thanked the man for his input and dismissed him. Lord Galltry departed, murmuring pleasantries to Syrana on his way by, to which she responded equably. Reylin stood up to greet her. She looked as eager as he had felt not long before.

"Did he approve, my love?" she asked.

Reylin tried to smile, but the proposal had only partially won Galltry over. Syrana's hopeful smile faded, and she took his hands.

"They would be fools to ignore a good idea."

Reylin snorted a little. "Sometimes I think they ignore good ideas because they didn't think of them, especially when they come from me."

Syrana ran her fingers up his arms. "Then they are fools," she said stoutly.

He gave her a passionate kiss. "Thank you." She kissed him back, making him shudder, and he lifted her onto the meeting table, sweeping the proposal papers off. They would have to be rewritten anyway.

8

SYRANA SPUN IN FRONT of the full-length mirror, exulting in the lift and flow of the sheer layers on her hips. Her new dress was not overly heavy, constructed as it was from innumerable gauzy lengths with a vivacious slit up one side. The gown was perfectly suited to the summer solstice celebration for which it had been designed.

She took one more flouncing turn, cranking her head to see how the gown lay upon her buttocks. Yes, she was quite satisfied with this one. The tailormaster had done well, emphasizing her ideal proportions with every cut. The summer always arrived quickly after the Festival of Remembrance, as the fire had occurred in late spring, and the solstice celebration would be notably more mellow. Nonetheless, she wished to look spectacular.

She beckoned her handmaiden, a demure Halmani girl, to undress her.

"Have a care," she snapped as she felt an overt tug at the lacing. "You'll ruin it before it's even been worn."

The handmaiden apologized.

Syrana had to maintain this charade of elegance, if only to please Reylin. He had grown more and more embittered since the last festival, no matter how hard she tried, and she suspected some of it revolved around her and her empty womb.

What kind of man could he be, when he couldn't even plant a seed in his own wife?

She knew he worried, but she also didn't have the heart to tell him that it wasn't likely his fault. He did all the right things (she shivered at that thought), but her body seemed combative and hostile.

Syrana couldn't tell him that either, for fear of losing his favor.

She controlled a grimace as her handmaiden redressed her for the day. Twisting her features in such a way would not serve her well, and she forced a prim smile. She pooched her lips out for the application of rouge, and then held perfectly still for the addition of kohl and color on her eyebrows and cheeks.

Shortly after, Syrana swept into the High Temple at a reasonably early time for her morning prayers. The space was quiet but joyful, a natural aura deriving from the light-filled design of the building. True to the tenets of I'ya, the temple was five-sided, with a private room in the center. The purest of glass prisms served as windows, angled to cast rainbows across the open gallery throughout the day and seasons. Mirrors covered the outer walls of the private chapel, reflecting light back outward while providing privacy to those within.

Syrana ducked into the room's small arched door, leaving her handmaiden outside. High Holy Mage Ma'thell welcomed her with a wizened smile and open arms.

"Is that Lady Syrana, my dear young princess?" he said. Despite his dimming eyesight, he knew well she had arrived, as was her daily routine. "A bright morning to you, child of I'ya."

She responded in kind and settled on her knees in front of an altar. Sparkling light spattered the walls and floor from the faceted crystal chandelier above, bathing her and the mage in flecks of color. She prayed silently for a while, then looked up. Father Ma'thell stood quietly on the other side of the altar.

"Do you have any sins you wish to confess, child of I'ya?" he asked, offering both open palms over the altar.

Syrana nodded, then stood and placed her hands palm-down over his.

"Confess them to the Eye, and let your heart be light."

Responding to his entreaty, she overcame her misgivings and acquiesced. She confessed her bitterness over Priscilla's pregnancy and her own lack of conception, and her fear of losing Reylin's love should she fail to provide him with children. She confessed her daily terror that she was broken inside, and her desperation to be able to fulfill that one duty as his wife.

Syrana didn't confess her darker thoughts, the truly sinful ones. How she had delighted in Priscilla's social stumble at the feast, and how disappointed she had been when Reylin comforted the first wife instead of chastising her for her indignity. How she had prayed for the curves on Priscilla to progress to unsightly weight, for the bump on her abdomen to manifest as a girl. How she, Syrana, second wife of Reylin of House Harkin, might grasp the chance to bear him a son and be the Heir-Mother.

Ma'thell listened, and when she had done, he ruminated for minutes, allowing her to process her own confession.

Had she been foolish to say so much? Did I'ya even care for such earthly troubles? What could a god care for such minutia? Syrana already regretted her stumbling words.

The father's gray eyes seemed to pierce right through her, as though he could see the darker thoughts in her mind clarified as writing on the wall.

"You came from a small house, did you not?" Ma'thell finally asked.

"Yes, High Holy Father."

Ma'thell indicated that she may remove her hands from the altar, and he stepped around to shorten the distance between them. He placed a shaky hand on her arm; his fingers were knobby and arthritic, his skin thin as paper. "I'ya sees your fear and forgives you. Love does not depend on an heir; it is pure. Like a wine, it is young and can sometimes be sharp, but it can last the ages if you let it, growing only better with time."

Syrana fought the tears welling up.

It was true that Reylin had pursued her fanatically from the day he met her, a naive maiden at court only recently come from that lesser house of Camdry, the place she had formerly called home. She'd hardly stepped from her carriage before he had taken her hand and kissed her sigil ring. But was that love? She had likewise pursued him, enamored with the way his dark eyes flashed with those iron and gold flecks that matched his crown, his heady masculine scent that consumed her, his proud stature that proclaimed his kingship. But was that love?

"I can see it between you," said Ma'thell, as if he knew her thoughts, "like a string of light between two souls. Trust that bond, and give your fear to I'ya this morning." He squeezed her arm one more time before escorting her to the door. "Let your heart be light, child."

Syrana thanked the high holy mage and stepped out of the central chapel, nearly falling into Father Kaiadin's arms. The gawky man stammered as he dropped an armful of writings.

"My dear princess, I didn't realize you were there. Please forgive me."

He stooped to collect the scattered papers, as did she and her scrawny handmaid. They were spells, minor magika mostly, but one caught her eye.

Motherhood.

The sheet was mixed in with others on birthing and pregnancy health, which she shuffled into a messy pile. Syrana made sure to be discreet as she slipped that one under her skirt and stood with a disarrayed pile in her arms. She handed the pile to Kaiadin, who beamed at them gratefully. He nudged his spectacles up his long, slightly bent nose and nodded.

"Thank you, my lady. Again, I apologize for my carelessness." He stuttered something more, then bit his tongue. Bowing, he clutched the papers to his chest.

Syrana gave him an innocuous smile, pawing at the papers to ensure he didn't lose hold of the loosely fluttering edges. "Are you preparing for something specific? Such spells, I hope it's nothing too concerning."

Kaiadin graced her with a kind smile. "Oh, nothing to fear, my dear lady consort," he assured her. "The Temple is merely preparing for the first lady's babe, to ensure its health and that of the mother. An important event for the future of Mirat."

Syrana agreed wholeheartedly, and the junior mage rushed away on his errands.

Her stomach turned over as her fears returned in full force. Priscilla's baby was important. Providing an heir was important. How could Reylin love her if she, Syrana, could not provide that for him as well? She scanned the temple gallery for anyone who might notice her, but the other worshipers were engaged in their own praises and supplications, and Kaiadin had gone. She bent to retrieve the spell sheet from under her skirts, folding it several times and tucking it in her dress. Perhaps it could give her some advantage, make her body more amenable to accepting Reylin's seed. They had tried enough times—something should have happened by now.

She left the temple in a stately glide, but her heart was racing as she returned to her quarters and spread the sheet out, pushing the creases flat so she could read it.

Motherhood: A collection of green and red magika for the development of male or female children, and the alteration of said development.

Syrana caught her breath. Alteration?

She scanned the sheet. There was nothing on enhancing fertility. Instead, the sheet contained several potions, including the use of *cha* to encourage the development of a female child. The scroll warned of blood thinning with that method, but it also recommended it as the simplest solution. Syrana had already known that one, but there was more, all documented in a factual, scholarly script.

To encourage a male, use of dried frostmoss using the same tonic method.

And then the red magika . . .

Red magic was frowned upon, although she knew it was still used quietly in the backrooms of shops on every corner. She read the instructions. *To produce a female babe: Burn the feathers of one dove with the hair of the mother, producing an ash. Combine the ash with water and pulverized rabbit bone to make a paste, and speak the following words . . .*

What followed was Old Language, words she didn't understand but could at least read phonetically. Application of the paste would be difficult as well, but it was natural for her to care for the first wife in her late stage. She, Syrana, was a kind and caring fellow wife, a trustworthy friend and companion. Her lips curved into a smile. It could be done, with enough care and cleverness.

What *exactly* could be done? Her mother's voice echoed in her head, doubtful as ever.

Syrana paused. Was she really willing to go this far? She didn't even know if her words had power with red magic. Witchcraft wasn't an inborn talent for everyone, and she knew very little beyond the cha seed trick.

Furthermore, Father Ma'thell had counseled peace and trust in her love with Reylin.

She dismissed that. Ma'thell didn't understand. He had never married, and priests didn't raise children even if they fathered them. It was possible Reylin would still love her in her barrenness, although she doubted it, and this step simply provided . . . insurance. Besides, she could hardly return to Camdry without a seed planted in her womb; she'd be unable to face Baroness Ana. Syrana resolved herself to her decision and turned to her handmaiden, who waited expectantly.

"Retrieve the first wife's hairbrush, quietly," she said. What she was about to do wasn't wrong. It was for love, and love justified all sorts of actions.

Syrana's next days of prayer were more lighthearted, and Father Ma'thell praised the light in the sky.

"Trust in I'ya, daughter," he wheezed. "How much joy it brings me to see the youthful hope in you once again."

With a respectful bow to the mage, she departed the private chapel.

Her Halmani handmaiden slunk up to her.

"Did you find anything?" Syrana snatched the slip of paper the girl held. Surprisingly, the savage girl could read a little, and she had been far more useful than Syrana would have imagined. Her mission to peruse the library during Syrana's prayers, looking for more spells, had proven fruitful. Slaves like her were rarely questioned and for the most part ignored.

Syrana sucked in a sharp breath. The slip of paper had another bit of red magika, this one for making a baby die in the womb. A dangerous one, one she couldn't be seen with. She scanned the ingredients, then hid it in her bodice.

"Your Highness, bright morning," came a deep, stuttering voice. Father Kaiadin.

She barely pulled her hand from her hidden pocket in time, turning to greet him casually.

He bobbed into a bow. "Are you quite well, my lady? You seem a bit troubled of late."

Perhaps he could read her better than the "wise" Father Ma'thell could. Then again, Ma'thell was blind as a cave bat. Syrana tried to smile. "Father Kaiadin, may the Eye smile upon you. I'm well, I assure you."

"Good, good. That is well. I have been praying for you both, you and the Lady Priscilla, for your health." His encouraging expression should have been warming, but a coldness entered her at the mention of Reylin's other wife. Kaiadin placed a large, gentle hand on her arm. He was quite intimidating by his stature alone, and he would have been elegant in his indigo robes if not for his awkward bearing. "The Light has revealed to me that you worry for your health, Princess, but you must trust me when I say that all will turn out as it should."

She agreed with him automatically, although she doubted his words very much.

"That said," he continued, "we do not only wait with idle hands for a blessing to come from the sky. We do intervene sometimes."

She kept her face frozen in a politely inquiring expression, as if she didn't know what he meant. There was no way he could know of her cha seeds or her feather-laden paste.

"That's why we assist with Lady Priscilla," he finished. "She's been quite dizzy of late, which I'm sure you already know being so close to her. The Temple is happy to support her with fortifying potions and spells for the child's well-being."

"Father Ma'thell instructed me to trust in I'ya," Syrana said. Catching the bitterness in her own tone, she smiled to offset it.

Kaiadin squeezed her arm as if he understood. "And so you should, certainly, but also keep yourself active in pursuing your own good health. You are important to Mirat, important to Prince Reylin. You matter, my dear lady. And do not fear asking for assistance. Would that Mirat were favored with *both* its ladies bearing strong sons for House Harkin." With that formal blessing laid upon her, he walked away on whatever task he had been given.

Syrana wondered at him as he disappeared. He seemed far more in tune than High Holy Mage Ma'thell, for which she was grateful. Although she didn't think she could be entirely honest with him about her malevolent witchcraft, at least she might ask for help for herself. Kaiadin had been recently assigned as the dedicated mage for Ironhold Castle, which meant she would see him more frequently. She could feel him out more before revealing her deep-seated fear of barrenness—perhaps there was more he could do than offer empty blessings and humbling words.

9

"Take good care of Priscilla and my son," Reylin said, nibbling Syrana's ear and inhaling her perfume one last time.

"I will," she murmured with a sweet smile. "Worry not, my love."

Reylin bade Priscilla goodbye last, as was appropriate. She lumbered up from the chaise that had been placed for her at the top of the keep stairs, and he gave her an affectionate kiss on one cheek, then the other, and finally on the lips. Her mouth was hot, as was her skin. He'd noticed how feverish she felt for months now, like a baker's oven. He smiled as he ran his hands possessively over her belly.

"Bright day, my son," he whispered, lingering on the sense of life under his fingers.

Priscilla beamed. "Go on now, he's not coming out to see you yet. You have plenty of time to do what you need to do."

"You sure?" Reylin grinned, somewhat foolishly. He couldn't help it.

Priscilla pushed him gently toward his waiting carriage. "Yes, my lord. Now show them what you can do."

He schooled his expression in case Galltry or Shildra were watching from a window. The Elder Council had deliberated on his plan for too long, and finally approved it with numerous caveats and warnings of all the things that could go wrong. Lío's reaction had been far from friendly, and Shiften had muttered about some factor that seemed entirely unrelated to Reylin's proposal. Galltry, however, had stood firmly in Reylin's corner, encouraging the Council to collaborate more closely with the Miners Guild. Porin had whined that any military supplementation would likely come from him, drawing his troops away from the southeastern coast, but he had quieted once Galltry pointed out they would be paid. The final decision, of course, had been made behind closed doors.

Despite the approval to move forward, Reylin knew the Council doubted his ability to follow through, and they awaited his missteps almost eagerly.

He rejected the carriage departure, instead beckoning for his warhorse, a sleek stallion with an ebony brown coat. Patting the horse's muscular neck, he leaned in. "Let's ride out properly, shall we, Farrion?"

The stallion whipped his head, impatient to depart as usual, and Reylin leapt onto his back and wheeled to the front of the party. The empty carriage would follow behind in case he desired it later, but he sighed at leaving both his wives behind.

Regardless of his wants, he wouldn't be wise to bring them on this particular expedition, exploratory as it was. And wasn't that the point—to demonstrate his wisdom and forethought?

Sirs Gillead and Patreagh took their place immediately behind him, and they set out from Ironhold's inner courtyard followed by a contingent of mounted soldiers. Sirs Ronidann and Jonathan held the rear. Father Kaiadin moved up to Reylin's right, just a step behind, serving as the retinue's spiritual guide.

They headed northward over several days, first along main roads that were well-kept, but then onto lesser secondary roads, and eventually toward subtle paths tread only by shepherds until recently. There, they would meet with a guide from the advance prospectors who could lead them to the site of the intended mines.

They rode in silence at the front, although Reylin occasionally caught laughter from the rear, where Sir Ronidann was undoubtedly entertaining his comrades. Reylin was too far into his thoughts, stewing over his own self-doubts, to joke, and Sir Gillead was too stoic to laugh in any case.

"My young king worries?" Holy Mage Kaiadin's deep voice broke through his mulling. The middle-aged man rode comfortably on a long-legged white gelding with silver tack; his indigo robes looked all the more glorious draped over the animal. Reylin welcomed the mage's company, and Kaiadin spurred his gelding forward a few steps.

"Do not be troubled, Your Royal Highness," the mage added with a warm smile, his eyebrows twitching awkwardly over his glasses. "I'ya smiles brightly upon your mission, and your family will be safe at Ironhold. Priscilla is far from ready to deliver your son, and even if he decided to enter this world early, High Holy Mage Ma'thell and I can keep contact through his Whispers. You would know her status within hours of any change."

Reylin thanked him, noticing that Kaiadin called him "king" without a hint of reservation.

They rode without further words for a while, but Kaiadin kept clearing his throat and adjusting his spectacles.

"Is there something else, Father?" Reylin finally asked.

Kaiadin blanched as though he had erred, then straightened. Although lankier than Reylin, he was tall. He answered, half stuttering, "I am grateful to attend you this journey, my king, for these are dangerous times. A mage can provide additional protection and blessing to your expedition." He spat to one side for luck.

Reylin raised an eyebrow, wondering if the man was worried about pushing the northeastern border. "I've considered every contingency, Father, and Mirat is prepared to answer any threat."

"True, true . . . for a typical threat," the man muttered. "But I must share something with you which I have been constrained to tell. The Temple receives some tidings from farther off."

"How far?" asked Reylin, intrigued now rather than angry.

"I hate to worry you." Kaiadin hung his head, focusing on his saddle pommel. "Perhaps it's nothing the Temple can't handle, as Father Ma'thell insists."

"A king well informed is a king well prepared," said Reylin, quoting Gillead's words from past lessons. "Please do tell. The fact that you brought it up concerns me."

Kaiadin gulped and nodded. "As you wish, Your Highness. The Temple received Whispers of a madness in Krita, men losing their minds and becoming like wild animals." He spoke low so as not to be overheard, and Reylin leaned in closer. Kaiadin continued, "One man killed his wife and child, and a woman threw herself off a cliff. They even say"—his voice grew quieter—"a man was found in an alley in the Kritali capital, eating another man's innards."

"That's absurd," Reylin scoffed, straightening on his horse. He glanced back at Sir Gillead, who watched them with sharp attention as usual.

"Temple Whispers don't lie, my young king," said Kaiadin sincerely. "These are reports of holy mages, who were deployed to each site to investigate the madness. They've kept the reports quiet as Ma'thell ordered, but King Rigaran and Queen Déllani know the extent of the issue. It's only right that you know as well, with Krita being so close and exchanging so many goods with North Mara Port."

"Does Lord Lío know?" The idea irked Reylin.

"No, Your Highness. I don't think so. Father Ma'thell discouraged this word beyond the Temple until they had a better handle on it, but I believe it is time you knew. You are king, or will be soon. I am beholden to inform you of something this important."

Reylin acknowledged that with appreciation, his temper cooling. "What would cause such a madness? Disease?" Although he wanted to doubt the mage's words simply because they were frightening, he knew the mages of I'ya kept close contact among all the temples, and they would know such a thing before anyone else.

"Yes, a disease of the mind," said Kaiadin. "The Temple received word recently that the madness had even spread to Marlemet through the main port in the Red Bay."

"What happened?"

Kaiadin shook his head, looking sad. "Violence, senseless violence. So far, the madness has only touched the common folk. It may be that nobility are immune to such a mental decay. Regardless, the Temple has been attempting to intercede on behalf of the commoners' souls."

"And?"

Kaiadin pursed his thin lips and adjusted his glasses. "And they have not been very successful yet. The madness follows the sick to their death, then spreads."

Reylin considered that troubling piece of news for many miles, until they encountered a mounted mining apprentice at the foot of a goat path. The young man, adorned in an earthy russet and forest green, tugged his hood up to cover his hair, indicative of his inferior station. He bowed as best he could from the horse, then led them up the subtle, single-track road. They left the carriage behind with two men and continued on, deeper and deeper into the Sikrat's eastern range.

"Nearly there, Your Royal Highness," he said over his shoulder. His voice cracked with adolescence, and Reylin felt a vague sense of jealousy slipping through him.

He really had wanted to apprentice with the Miners Guild.

Guildmaster Daiunek was an admirable man of considerable brawn, with the shoulders and muscle of a warrior and the loyalty of his comrades that any king could envy. Reylin had wanted to follow him based on his charisma alone.

But that was one of a hundred illusions that had burned their way through Reylin's imagination, each one immediately doused and smothered by one or more members of the Elder Council. Mining was too dangerous. Temple service was for those with magika. Painting and drawing weren't useful enough, whereas smithing was too common.

Reylin had been allowed to pursue training with the orators, managing to draw a Master from Krita Port, until Galltry had realized his interests lay in music rather than elocution. Upon that discovery, Reylin's formal orator lessons ended, and he was redirected to focus on speech writing and reading to broaden his vocabulary.

"Here we are, Your Highness," called the apprentice. "Watch that bough."

Reylin ducked under the low pine branch and found himself in an eastward-facing glade, milling with industry. A host of burly men and women scurried about, some of them still erecting a rough cabin and some entering a hole in the rock face.

A frostbear of a man approached with a glad smile and a handshake that made Reylin realize what a sturdy grip really felt like. "Prince," the man began. His guttural voice, rough from years of shouting commands and breathing dust, boomed in the peaceful afternoon of the glade. "I welcome you and thank you for Mirat's protection detail. Come now, slake that road thirst." He nearly pulled Reylin from the saddle in his enthusiasm. "The iron from this mine will be enough to supply our weapon forges for years," he continued proudly, gesturing at the east-facing opening in the rock face.

Reylin couldn't help but grin at the guildmaster. Unlike the others, the man's head was entirely exposed, a sign of his high rank in the Miners Guild. Even Oyerton had to cover the lengths of his dark hair with a brown bandana twisted over top. Daiunek, however, was the master over all miners, based out of the guild Masterhall in Ironhold and subservient to no one, not even Reylin. Nonetheless, Reylin couldn't help but like him. "I knew the old gallite mine was strained," he said. "I'm proud to be part of the search for a new one; Mirat believes it is important." He watched as industrious miners entered and exited bearing tools, lanterns, and lumber.

"Aye, she was a blessing of a find," Master Oyerton, Daiunek's next-in-charge, added. He poured Reylin and his master a glass of steaming cider. "And fit to burst! We haven't found a lode like this—"

"The rock hears you," a surly man interrupted, raising his own mug, which emitted a telling odor much harsher than cider. Reylin wondered at the man, but his superiors said nothing as he drained the mug with a sway.

The guildmaster clacked his mug against Reylin's. "The Earth listens and gives as she will, and takes as she will. To the mine!"

"To the mine," they chorused. Oyerton and the drunk journeyman reentered the dark entrance and disappeared.

Daiunek leaned forward, almost furtive in his body movements, but when he spoke, it was in a loud, gruff voice. Perhaps he wasn't capable of whispering. "As you know, this mine is the first in this valley, the farthest east we've dared go, but its riches are barely tapped. We figured we'd find gallite this high, but Wethers believes there is much more farther east. I concur with his sentiment."

Reylin instinctively looked eastward, down the mountain toward the open plains of the Loi al'Halmana. "Downslope?"

"Yes, Prince. There are rubies eastward, and perhaps even . . . something more rare. I can smell it." Daiunek sniffed loudly and heaved a sigh. "I can *nearly* taste it, and Wethers says he actually can."

"The journeyman?"

"Don't underestimate him, Prince Reylin. The only thing he has a stronger nose for than liquor is metal." Daiunek chuckled and refilled both their mugs. "Now, this one is for you, for your generous allocation of soldiers to our expedition." He raised his mug.

Reylin swelled. He had brought the soldiers himself, despite the resistance from the Elder Council for him not to be overly risky. Reylin didn't see the risk. They were high on the mountainside, far from the savage plains. If anything, the risk was to the Council, revealing the over-conservatism of their border policies.

Now Reylin could claim direct responsibility for helping the guild push eastward into new territory, into lands they had been begging to prospect for years. Mirat was not obligated to help, as the guild could have chosen to prospect without military support, but Reylin believed they should, given the guild's long history of collaboration with the kingdom. Mining was by far Mirat's most important industry, and if the only hindrance was a few wildlings from the Loi al'Halmana, what did that matter?

He raised his own mug. "And this one's to you, Guildmaster. To your courage to push to the ends of civilization in the name of progress, a courage that has been sorely lacking in my own circle."

Daiunek unceremoniously slapped him on the back and chugged. "I'll drink to that. To the ends of the earth!"

Reylin straightened, torn between scolding the older man for his familiarity and accepting the friendly words. Few people could treat Reylin that way, but Guildmaster Daiunek owed him neither allegiance nor fealty. In the guild, his rank was considered equivalent to Reylin's high nobility.

The prince swallowed his pride with another gulp of cider and smiled.

They spoke for a while, watching the erection of the cabin and mulling over the terms of their agreement in a casual, cider-fed manner. As a good host, Daiunek offered cider to the High Guard and to Father Kaiadin as well, but they all denied the offer politely. The knights were on high alert in the new territory, and Gillead paced through the glade without pause, staring hard at the valley below.

Kaiadin suggested he'd had quite enough imbibing as a magus-in-training. "Can't stomach it anymore," he said nervously, almost apologetic for resisting the host's generosity. "I only brought the one set of robes."

Daiunek guffawed and poured another for Reylin, then excused himself for a few minutes as he entered the mine and returned. He sat without ceremony. "Forgive us for not allowing you further into the mine, Prince. It's not fully fortified yet, and Lady Shildra would kill me if I let anything happen to you down there."

Reylin controlled his grimace. "Not just Lady Shildra."

"Aye, you're right. Galltry would have my balls after Shildra cut them off—pardon the bluntness."

Reylin snorted out some of his cider. The sugar burned his nostrils. "I would like to see the mine when it's safer, if that's acceptable."

Daiunek shrugged, noncommittal. "Should be fine, once we brace the walls and assess the weak seams. Perhaps next time you visit." He leaned in, the smile within his nearly black beard turning to a serious frown. "Prince Reylin, I have another request, if you're willing."

Reylin nodded.

"Wethers and I do wish to prospect down the mountainside, as you know. But his nose is telling him to push even farther eastward than I initially suggested, to the foothill range on the south side. It's dangerously close to the fyr. We will gladly pay Mirat with a portion of the gains, whatever we find, in exchange for more soldiers."

Unease twinged through Reylin as he glanced at the men he had brought. The cavalrymen lounged in the glade, making their horses comfortable and setting up tents. He had thought he'd brought enough, but Daiunek was already implying he'd miscalculated. "The Council was reticent to give me more men than this," Reylin stuttered, feeling unsure of himself now. His heart pounded in his ears.

Daiunek nodded as though he understood. "And a platoon was a reasonable start, but not if we push that far downslope. I worry. Remember, my people are not fighters."

"And you believe it's necessary?"

"Wethers smells alisite. So do I."

Reylin's eyes widened. Alisite, the ore of kings, harder than any other metal. Blended by a master swordmaker with the right ores, alisite made unbreakable, holy weapons that swung true and cut through bone like butter. Mirat would make a fortune. "It's in the valley?"

"In the rock, but at a lower elevation." Daiunek's guttural whisper carried more excitement than Reylin had ever heard before. "We're already bordering the tribe lands, even up here, and we dare not go much further without stronger accompaniment."

Reylin considered it. For years, he had pushed the Elder Council to expand their territory northward and eastward, to take the rich Loi al'Halmana from the savage fyr, a primitive people who were said to be half monster. Reylin knew it to true, for a portion of any fyr slaves they procured would transform trying to escape, and they would have to be put to death. The slaves retained in the castle were demure, small people with light frames, most fit for entertainment and household duties. In large numbers, however, he imagined their savagery would be more obvious. Here, on the edge of the plains, he wondered how many there were, and how near they might be. He strained his eyes over the darkening valley, seeing no sign of human habitation.

"They live in dispersed houses of woven straw and mud, with few villages, and rarely use fire," said Daiunek. "Trust me, they're there. Make no mistake."

"You seem to know a lot about them."

"I've pushed the boundaries my entire career," Daiunek intoned, almost to himself. "I've established new mines in every face of the Sikrat but this one, Prince. I've mined the low southlands, consulted at Shayal's western range, and established gold sources in Aklim's Sukrat. The edge is where civilization meets the earth and stops to bow in admiration, and every once in a while, as your nose touches the ground, the earth gifts you with a boon to let you know she welcomes your steps."

Reylin considered the zealous guildmaster and decided. The Elder Council wouldn't like it, but if he made the agreement, they could hardly say no, especially if the guildsmen were at risk in Mirat's borders. "I'll send another platoon upon my return to Ironhold, Guildmaster Daiunek." He offered his hand, and they shook. Daiunek's massive paw enveloped the prince's more refined hand, and the deal was struck.

10

LYRA SLEPT FOR THE greater part of a day at least, maybe longer. She woke at least once to drink more of the tasteless broth, though she needed the masked man's assistance to do even that. Grease swam on the liquid's surface, a slightly nauseating texture that smeared her lips and slithered down her throat. Or perhaps it was that black spot on her stomach that made her insides churn.

She couldn't remember how many boots had smashed into her abdomen, how many times a new, searing pain had flashed through her consciousness. All she knew was that her ribs felt shattered, but her heart even more so.

The warden had ruined her. He had hurt her. Before she even had a chance to speak, he had beaten her, undressed her, and torn everything precious from her. The tears in her clothing and cracks in her bones were nothing in comparison. Her soul felt as though it lay in slivers on the ground, and she wasn't sure if she even wanted to gather the pieces.

By the time she had been dumped in the camp, she had already been bruised and broken beyond redemption.

Mam would be heartbroken too. Their hopes for Lyra to have a better life were gone, a vain and wishful thought as fleeting as a Whisper. This was how maunderers were treated, after all, and that was all Lyra was. All she could be.

She sniffled, but she couldn't hold the torrent of emotions back. Every part of her body hurt, and her head spun in a continuous whirlwind of haziness and fear and horror. The wind outside echoed her hazy confusion, churning up in erratic bursts and whistling across the cracks in the walls. She could hear shouts when its buffeting switched direction, along with curses at the irritating dust.

She gasped when a movement in the shadows resolved into a silhouette—tall, broad, far stronger than she. The masked man's approach was slow, and he held his palms up as if to indicate he meant her no harm. Though his clothing hid it well, he was young. He wore a blood-soaked strip of pink cloth tied around his left arm, and she realized it was silk from her skirt. She glanced down in dismay, realizing her skirt had been removed, but her legs were still covered by the tattered cloth. She almost sighed in relief. The man also sported a large bruise on his distorted left eye. She squinted in the dark shack as she tried to see its color. His other eye seemed nearly black, but occasionally it caught the light beams with a golden flicker. His skin was darkly tanned but smooth and firm, at least on his forearms, and his muscles were well defined.

Lyra hesitated when he offered her his hand. A part of her was desperate for comfort, but another part of her shrieked for death, for an end to her physical and spiritual torment. Its voice was bitter and harsh, and above all, angry. That part of her wanted to shove his hand away and scream at him, and weep. And die.

Then she saw his expression. He wasn't looking at her. Instead, he looked into the shadowy corners of the shack, blinking with a forlorn look she couldn't place. He didn't seem to fully close his eyes, as though he were dreaming while awake, his mind fluttering through dark memories without ceasing and without mercy. His brow knotted into a scowl, and he bowed his head as if defeated.

His hand hung limp by her fingers, and Lyra stretched out enough to meet his skin. He jolted, as though her touch burned him, then shook himself and took her hand, squeezing it in light comfort. Nonetheless, he soon fell back into whatever rumination had taken hold of him, and they stayed in awkward silence for a long while.

The other stranger—the unkind one—did not appear until dusk, when the beams of light had dimmed to a bearable reddish-orange. He strode in without warning, trailed by laughter from the men outside. Stopping short, he tossed a bread crust at the hooded man, who deftly caught it.

Lyra was forced to sit up a bit, a movement that screamed pain in her rib cage and abdomen, but she was starving. Her mouth watered at the mere thought of bread, and soon she was chewing small pieces of it, trying to ignore the ache on her jawbone. As she finished, weakness enveloped her like a heavy blanket, demanding that she rest, and she lay back on the makeshift bed, panting with the exertion.

"You got a name, girl?" The green-eyed man crouched next to her other side, balanced comfortably on his toes, playing absentmindedly with his dagger. When she didn't immediately answer, he sneered and put a hand on his chest. "Thordrin. And you are . . ." His sarcasm couldn't be missed, and she flushed with nervous energy.

"Lyra," she managed.

"You're a mage," he stated, not inquisitively but as a matter of fact. "Not of the Temple, though."

Lyra gulped.

He continued, balancing his knife on a finger. "Mages of the Temple don't end up in Tahayi Mines, now do they? And they don't get treated like you did. They're all so damned holy, it's unthinkable. You, though." He smirked. "*Maunderer*, southern I'd guess. They can do whatever they want with you."

"How could you know that?" she whispered. Every word was an effort to begin with, but speaking to Thordrin was also frightening. He was like an ill-tempered bull, keen for signs of weakness and quick to anger.

As if hearing her comparison, Thordrin snorted his derision. "Your accent, your clothing, or at least what they left you with. Fuck's sake, love, you're not a difficult read."

So lighthearted, so careless. Lyra felt something welling up from her nauseous stomach at his attitude. "My name is Lyra."

Thordrin snorted again and gave her a merciless grin. "Well, love, no one here will notice your name, just your pussy. You better get used to it."

Lyra shivered. His words were so cold, so detached, as though he really didn't care what happened, and yet he had rescued her from the other prisoners. A hot blush burned down her body, and her frustration mounted to hot tears. How could this horrible man toss her innocence aside so casually, like it meant nothing?

Her vulnerability struck her. She was nearly naked except for the sheet, her body so broken that any defense would be a futile effort. "Give me my clothes." Her demand came out as a weak whine.

The flash of irritation on Thordrin's face reminded her that there was nothing she could demand from him. Then he chuckled. "There's not much left of your clothes. Boys tore 'em apart, and we fixed you up with what was left. Your skirt's wrapped around your ribs, and that one's arm." He jutted his chin at the other man, then went to retrieve a small bundle of cloth from the corner, which he tossed her way.

Lyra cringed as it landed on her bruised abdomen and unrolled partway. It was her undertunic, but it was ripped down the front. She plucked at it to cover herself, uncomfortably aware of Thordrin's cold glare. She pursed her lips angrily.

"Shadows save me, you're fuckin' needy," he said, shaking his head.

"Why help me then?" The words faded in and out, half of them barely audible.

He merely shrugged in response, then flipped his knife again. "I hate men like Selen. It was a good excuse to kill him, and it was fun." White teeth flashed in the dark shack.

She wondered if Selen was the prisoner who'd attacked her. A sickly feeling spread through her gut, and the vicious, bitter voice inside spoke. "Is he dead?"

A gloating and lop-sided smile curled across Thordrin's face, the mischievous kind of look she would have expected from Elden. It was as if he had just gotten away with the most terribly funny prank. It was the most genuine expression she had seen him wear. He barked a laugh. "A most unfortunate and *sudden* loss of blood killed that man."

Relief mixed with guilt flooded Lyra's body, and the bitter voice battled with the other inside, back and forth in shrill cries. Selen and the other prisoners had deserved to die, and yet it was evil to wish death upon others. She silently prayed to the Five-Faced God, who surely saw her elation in heart-breaking clarity; she prayed he might forgive her. Simultaneously, she hoped that Selen's soul had passed the Nethergate, the lowest of Gates, where he would be eternally tortured by monstrous demons along with his fellow wretches, rapists, and murderers. The two prayers left her mind together, twisted and intermingled such that she couldn't call only one back.

Such fantasies were sinful, she corrected herself, but praise the Light that at least Selen was dead.

Then another, more insidious thought struck her. Why praise the Light? I'ya hadn't saved her from the warden. The bitter woman inside her had won, filling her with a vile poison that flooded her being. Paired with wretched guilt over her own lack of faith, the sense of abandonment was overwhelming.

Thordrin was oblivious to her inner turmoil. He pulled another husk of bread from somewhere and munched on it, alternating with draws from a water skein. Lyra's mouth became suddenly parched as she watched him. Then she turned her gaze on the masked man, curious as to whether he would finally speak.

"He ain't got a name," Thordrin said amiably through a flurry of dry breadcrumbs. "Been here a while though, ain't that right, brother?" He nodded at the masked man, who acknowledged him with a solemn expression. "Thought I'd have to kill him when I got here, gotta let people know where you stand, but the boys warned me not to fuck with him. In exchange, he wouldn't fuck with me, and it's held true."

Lyra looked to the masked man with new appreciation. Knowing he wasn't Thordrin's man made him that much more trustworthy, and she began to believe he really did mean well with his ministrations. He didn't look back at her, instead taking the edges of her newfound undertunic and spreading it more evenly across her.

Thordrin continued. "Here, love, I'm a king, understand? No one messes with the west end. That fucking twat Selen, he was king of the central camp. This one, though—" He pointed the tip of his blade at the other man. "This one's his own man. Never seen anything like it."

Lyra raised her eyebrows at that, trying not to adjust her stiff neck.

Thordrin read the question in her eyes and chuckled easily. "Meaning he's on no one's side, love. But he's still alive. That shouldn't happen in a place like this, especially with someone who's obviously so useful." He winked and finally offered the water skein, but she was too exhausted to hold it. Instead, she allowed it to slump into the crook of her arm. Thordrin shrugged and rolled his eyes, then departed. She could hear him outside talking with others, their conversation punctuated by occasional laughter, terse commands, and scuffles.

The masked man lifted the skein and helped her drink till she could no longer bear it, and she lay back to rest.

"You'll protect me?" she whispered in the darkness.

He didn't answer, but she could sense the weight of his looming presence, the sharpness of his attention. His bulk was a dark shape in the shadows, blocking her from other, worse things. Despite his silence, she felt she knew the answer, and for a moment, she felt oddly reassured, even as the war within her raged between desire to live and desire to give up, to rest.

The following days blurred by as Lyra slept fitfully, with many lucid dreams and nightmares, waking only to sip water and rancid broth. Occasionally, Thordrin or the masked man brought her bread, but rations were sparse. Her body healed slowly, and it was over a week before she could even partially sit up by herself. Her ribs ached constantly, and every effort to rise from her bed resulted in fiery pains that shot through her torso. The welling of her black eyes was finally reduced to a mere irritant, and her vision on the one side cleared. The bruises on her arms and torso became first a deep purple—strangely reminiscent of the color worn by holy men—then a sickly yellow green, but at last they faded into her fair skin.

Twice, she gathered the energy to Whisper a warning to her mother Elaisa, but no Whispers returned to her. She wasn't surprised. She had never sent a Whisper farther than the other end of the caravan, and no one could Whisper as well as she. Not even Elden.

Pray for me, Mam, as I pray for you, she spoke to the Whisper, guilt gnawing at her as she recalled her very real doubts of any godly protection. *And forgive me for . . .* She trailed off. For being sullied. For losing her grasp of her most precious thing. For being weak.

The shrill voice inside berated her for apologizing, and she watched the Whisper siphon through a crack in the wall as a lone tear trickled its way down her cheek.

She was alone far more than she would have liked. Her nerves were frayed, and as she regained motion, she jumped at every unexpected sound. Thordrin would often leave and not return for several days at a time, although Lyra frequently heard his confident bass through the thin plank walls. Despite herself, she leaned on his deep voice as an anchor, realizing that none of his men would dare enter his shack without express permission, and for better or worse, he had vocally declared her to be his property.

The masked man would only disappear for a few hours, reappearing as quietly as he left and often bringing rations. He tended to hide a skein under his fluttering cloak, and it was always full. Whenever he returned, he would sit with her.

Sometimes, that was all. Other times, she would tremble violently and whip her head from side to side, desperately trying to shake the nightmare of the day they met. It plagued her, clawed at her, laughed at her. Sometimes she would cry, and other times her furious emotions would manifest in a tumultuous windstorm that tore through the mining camp in a frenzy of anger and sadness. When this happened, Lyra would rarely form a single tear; she would merely stare at the dark ceiling with haunted eyes and an obsessively working jaw. She mumbled words from the holy writings, Old Language words of healing, but none of it made her feel better.

The masked man would sit, seemingly detached but always there. When she reached for his callused hand, he would take it and stroke the top of her knuckles with his thumb. He never smiled, and he frequently fell into a dark expression, his eyes blinking in that half-formed way. He had his own nightmares, she realized, and they were as vivid to him awake as were her own.

She wondered what he had done to be in Tahayi Mines.

One day, after several weeks had passed, he entered as usual at the sun's highest peak.

Lyra scooted herself up with an effort, managing to rise halfway, her body still covered by the sheets. "How long have you been here?" she asked. Her mind had finally stopped reeling, clearing somewhat with her clouded vision, and she needed to know.

He made a hand gesture and looked away with a morose frown, rummaging in a barrel for a hunk of cheese for her. "A long time."

Lyra sucked in a breath. It was sign, like the caravan used to talk to Adrian. She had thought she recognized his gestures before, but she had been so immersed in her own blur of miserable emotions and memories that she hadn't been certain.

The masked man never responded to anything verbally, although he seemed to listen and seemed intelligent. She knew so little about him, although he was the one closest to her in this hellish place. "How long?" she repeated.

He didn't answer, slamming the barrel shut in what seemed like frustration. He handed her the food and signed repeatedly to himself. His body was turned partially away, and she could hardly see what he was doing. She reached for his cloak and pulled him down till he sank to his knees.

"Please, how long?" Lyra asked again, hearing a hint of exasperation in her own insistent tone. "Will you at least tell me your name?"

His surprise at being pulled toward her hardened into a closed expression, and his signs shifted. "Konan." He repeated it multiple times, like Adrian would often do.

"Konan?"

His face whipped up, and he stared at her with wide eyes. She realized they really were two different colors, the left carrying pale splotches on the iris. The right was an inky brown with coppery flecks that shone like her skirt bells. The discolored eye was smaller, restricted by tightly drawn scar tissue that came from beneath his hood and ran through his eyebrow, up his forehead. She couldn't see the rest of his face.

He signed rapidly, leaning forward. "You understand?"

She nodded. *Konan* was an ancient word taken from the Old Language, a vocabulary from years long faded in common man's memory but still maintained by wayfarers and mages.

He was breathing hard. His entire bulk moved in the shadowy shack, and she strained to see him better. Lyra took his hand and pulled him closer. A single tear leaked out of his good eye as he regarded her.

"Where are you from?"

He shook his head, just barely.

"Why don't you speak?"

Konan gave her such a mournful expression that she regretted asking. She apologized. How long had it been since someone had been able to speak with him? She couldn't imagine the loneliness, being so disconnected from others, and in a place that was lonely to begin with. She spoke with Mam and Elden and Adrian every day; her entire caravan was a social unit. They sang and told stories and chattered on the long roads from Shayal to Marlemet to Litis. "Where did you learn to sign?"

He took a deep, shaky breath and pulled his hand away to sign. "A man who was here . . ." He trailed off, lost in thought, and Lyra saw that troubled darkness overshadow him again.

"What happened to him?" She urged him to continue, hoping to pull him back.

"The desert took him."

She hadn't thought it was possible, but his eyes became even sadder, and she felt guilty for unearthing this deeply embedded hurt that was obviously still fresh in Konan's heart. He began signing to himself again, partial gestures that were difficult to follow. "He was the reason the desert did not take me. He was the only reason."

Lyra caught his frantic hands and squeezed them in heartfelt solace, as he had done for her so many times in the previous weeks. She surprised herself, but his pain was so obvious, so genuine. It made her think of her own losses. Lyra pictured her father, the man they had sent to Tahayi Mines, as he cracked his driver's whip through the air and snapped at the ears of boys from passing caravans. The boys would smirk and hand her sisters a flower from the roadside even as their ears and rear ends paid the price. Her own longing memories of a simple childhood with family, her own *missing*, was a pale echo of this man's sadness.

They shared that deep, never-ending melancholy that accompanies loss, although her feelings were much duller and more distant. For her, thinking of her father was like seeing something familiar through a crude looking-glass. For him . . .

Lyra realized he was staring at her, hard, taking in her hair and face until her skin began to crawl with discomfort. "He looked like you," Konan signed. "His name was Isellan."

Her mouth dropped open and became suddenly dry. She had no words. What fate had brought her to this moment, to this man? A few slow, large tears welled up and meandered down her cheeks for the father she had never really known.

Konan took a pink silk from his cloak—the one that had been around his arm the week before—and dabbed her cheeks dry. He looked like he might need it himself, but then he seemed to shake it off.

"When did he die?" Lyra managed, her voice tremulous.

"A few winters ago. He was a good man."

"I know." Lyra watched him tuck her pink silk away like a normal kerchief. "Konan, did he tell you what your name means?"

Konan shook his head.

"It means *son*."

Konan's cheek ticced wildly. He bowed his head, seeming sadder than ever, and she wondered if maybe she shouldn't have told him that. Isellan had clearly been important to him, perhaps more important than to her, blood connections be damned. His head jerked with a violent twitch, his expression hardening again as he raised his hands. "My family is gone. Yours is still out there. You need to return to them."

They sat in silence for a long while, both lost in their memories. When Konan finally left, Lyra fell into a fitful, nightmarish sleep, hounded by Isellan's tragic death and the warden's grasping hands.

11

KONAN STRODE BETWEEN THE rows of leaning shanties with the sack of rations tucked close. The less attention drawn, the better, for Dawna had given him an extra loaf of the dense, flour-heavy bread that sustained the prisoners much of the time. She hadn't said anything, merely pushed it through the food window. The older woman, Tass, raised an eyebrow at her and gave Konan a knowing look.

A wind had raged for two days, a tumultuous beast of a storm. It lacked direction.

He wondered if the guards noticed its unusual characteristics, the way it escalated at particular times of day and then shifted southward as though seeking something, the way it abated for several hours at a time.

It had to be her.

He approached the gang's epicenter, stalking through several men with a rough shoulder. They cursed at him but moved aside.

"Done proving your mettle in the mines for the day?" Thordrin jeered from his throne of barrels and sacks. He laughed. "Who do you think you're proving anything to? They ain't watchin'." He jutted his square jaw toward the guard tower, then flinched as a gust of wind blew sand into his face. "Would you tell that bitch to cut it out? She's really ruining the ambience."

Konan nodded, but several of Thordrin's men glanced at each other.

"What d'ya mean, Cap? Cut what out?" said Moony, the goggle-eyed ex-pirate.

Thordrin waved his hand in front of his face as if dusting the air away. "That's *her*, you shit-headed muckworm."

Moony's eyes widened further than normal. "Oh."

Konan began to push on the door, but Thordrin grabbed his cloak and yanked him close.

"Tonight, brother. My spies said it would be tonight." His deep voice was a gravelly whisper, and then he coughed and spat sand. "Fuck me, go take care of this before I kill her."

Konan nodded again and entered the shack.

Lyra lay halfway off her makeshift bed, tossing and turning with one cheek doused in sand. Her faltering moans paired with full-body twitches. Whatever she was dreaming, it looked unpleasant.

Konan knew what those were like. Was it better to let her sleep through it? Nightmares, as tangible as they sometimes seemed, were amorphous and fleeting demons that tended to skulk away if not acknowledged. If he woke her, the demon's shape would sear into her memory, freshly burned and tender to touch. He hesitated.

The wind battered the shack, followed by Thordrin's impatient pounding on the wall. "Wake her the fuck up," he shouted.

Lyra's eyelids fluttered, and she gasped a little, then fell into a hacking fit as she struggled to get the sand out of her nose. She clutched her ribs and rolled back onto the bed, chest still heaving. Her cough gave way to a low groan as she caught her breath.

Konan looked away. They had fashioned a binding for her from pieces of her undertunic, but none of it was adequate. None of it was civilized. None of it was right.

When she seemed settled again, he approached and offered the bread.

She barely moved her head, her features twisted in pain and grief. "I'm not hungry," she whispered.

"You have to eat, Lyra."

"Why?"

The single word seemed to hang in the air, which had stilled. The sandstorm outside had paused, matched by the lifeless, dull color in her gaze. She met his eyes and bit her lip, waiting for an answer.

He didn't have one, not immediately. He had asked himself the same question countless times. The number of times he wondered *why* seemed greater than the grains of sand in Tahayi. He set the bread aside.

"You must eat in order to heal," he signed methodically.

"You think I can simply heal? Like nothing happened? All I see, whether I'm asleep or awake, is him." Her high voice cracked on the last word, and her eyes glistened with resentment.

Konan looked away, feeling heat on his cheeks. If they had allowed her to sleep through it, perhaps she wouldn't have remembered the most recent nightmare. Too late now. "I think that something difficult is not impossible for someone like you," he signed at last.

Her indignation shifted to tragedy once again. "I couldn't even defend myself, Konan."

His hands cut through the air like a knife. "*No one* can defend themselves against a dozen men. You must realize that. You hurt at least as many as Thordrin and I killed individually."

He thought that would make her feel better, but instead guilt flashed across Lyra's face, and she shuddered. "I've never hurt anyone with my magika before," she whispered. "It feels . . . even worse. Like I've scorned a gift. And you still haven't answered my question. Why? Why should I want to be part of this world when it hurts as much as it does?" Her eyelashes fluttered, and she looked away, the corners of her mouth twitching as she battled tears.

Konan felt his own cheek convulse. Always the left one, and always out of his control. He understood, and yet he couldn't accept that her fate should be as dire as his own, that her future was as bereft of hope. He couldn't let her give up.

"You have something to live for, Lyra." He saw her watching his signs from the corner of her eye. "Your family. Your life." By the Light, it was a relief to be able to communicate with someone.

She seemed to ponder that for a while. "I miss them. I don't understand why this happened, why any of it happened. I had a good life, a good family. I didn't do anything to deserve this."

"Lyra, the world is cruel. It leaves scars." He paused, making sure he had her full attention. She stared back at him. "I know what it's like to lose everything you had and end up here. It feels like being abandoned." He glanced upward, as if the Eye could hear him, but a part of him doubted it. The Eye was blind to his torment, his trials. Perhaps Lyra's prayers would travel farther. "Isellan would say, overcome it. Endure."

The memory of the man cut through him, and he took a faltering breath of his own.

"It's not that simple," Lyra murmured, seeking his hand with a sigh. "But I do want to see my family again. I suppose I would do almost anything to be with them again."

Her pink lips curled into a brief but brilliant smile, though her gaze was far away.

Konan bowed his head to her, hoping she had found a small trace of solace in the warmth of his hand and her own memories. The sandstorm had died down, her inner turmoil calming from a boil to a simmer, and he marveled again at the power that ebbed from this slight young woman. She was a tempest: passionately sad, intensely frightened, and just as intensely joyful at the thought of her family.

If she was dedicated to returning to them, then he was equally devoted to helping her to do so. For what other reason had he been spared a bloody and senseless death? For what other reason would the Five-Faced God force him to endure, to continue drawing breath when all he wanted to do was slip away?

Lyra wrinkled her face and groaned, then clutched her mouth.

"Stomach bruises?" he signed.

She shrugged, then spoke, muffling her own voice with her fingers. "I can't tell if I'm hungry or if I never want to eat again."

Konan encouraged her to eat the bread, although she seemed dubious, then helped her recline. "Rest."

"Konan, why did you save me? I know why Thordrin did it. It's like a game for him." Her tone was bitter, almost resentful, but he didn't think it was directed at him. When he examined her, she stared right back at him, her delicate eyebrows knotted, eyes glittering with the need to know.

"What happened to you was wrong," he said. "I've seen so much of the darkness of man, so much depravity and cruelty. I couldn't tolerate it. When I saw you, it was like seeing a candle in a dark room, lighting up the walls and revealing the shadows for what they were, and Selen trying to snuff it. I knew in my heart that I must try, even if I died doing so."

Her eyes widened at that. "You could have died that night." She chewed on the words, as if she had only realized it in that moment.

He shrugged. It meant nothing to him.

"How can you not care? You don't want to live?"

Konan shrugged again. "My life hasn't been my own for a long time."

Her knotted brow shifted into something he could almost call a scowl. "You're a hypocrite. How can you expect me to overcome all of this, when you won't?"

"You deserve better."

"So do you."

He took a deep, slow breath. His heart hammered a dull drumbeat; he was certain she might be able to see it flickering under his skin. Surely she could see his cheek fluttering, his eyelid twitching along with it. She knew nothing of the things he had endured, nor the things he had done. "Rest," he instructed once more, then jumped to his feet and left.

Konan could feel her eyes burning into him as he closed the door behind himself and leaned against the frame. By the Light, she made him uncomfortable.

He watched them coming, furtive shapes slipping from shadow to shadow. They seemed quite confident of their stealthiness, for Thordrin's gang raised no alarm. The watchmen sat, hunched over and half-asleep, their legs swinging over the roof edges. Thordrin had wandered off with his favorite gang members, as he often did, intent on intimidating a different section of the west camp to keep them in line, and his remaining men slumped at their posts.

The night hours had slipped by, and the second moon had finally risen in the vast desert sky. It skirted the southern horizon in a low arc.

The shapes of eight men formed and faded between the tightly packed buildings, nearly silent. Their steps were covered by the restless stirring of the breeze. They converged on Thordrin's shack, and as they were forced into the light of the moon, they glanced around warily. Edging along the walls, they remained out of sight of the watch on the roof. One, wielding a dagger, nodded at the others and pushed the door open. The low creak was hidden by the sounds of the wind shifting through the camp, an expanse of rickety, creaking buildings. The man smirked and stepped into the shack, filling the doorway.

Thordrin, disguised as a sleeping watchman, sent his knife sailing from four shacks away. It embedded into the man's back with a thump. That was the sign.

Konan leapt out from his hiding place and kicked a man down, then grabbed another, who swung a fist past him. He yanked the man off balance and smashed an elbow into his face. The man crumpled, but the first had recovered and now stood with a small chipped stone blade in his hand. He swiped toward Konan, who stepped back. They danced around each other, and the man sliced at him twice more before overreaching. Konan feinted and closed with him, snapping the blade from the man's hand with a twist. The wrist cracked audibly, and the man cried out, but Konan didn't release him. Instead, he kept twisting, rolling the man over his shoulder just as another attacker brought his blade down upon them. The man with the broken wrist cried again and slumped to the ground, hacking blood.

Konan eyed the third man, who stumbled, at first seeming disconcerted by stabbing his own comrade. Then he lunged. Konan dodged and grabbed the man's hair, using his momentum to bring a knee up. The man staggered back, dropping his blade as he clutched at his disfigured nose; blood sprayed down his front. Konan took the opportunity to advance, connecting once more with a jab to the broken features. The man retreated, holding up a bloodied hand in defense, but Thordrin's gang descended. Konan left him encircled by four others with eager grins.

He swiped the two chipped stone daggers from the ground and headed into the shack.

The leader lay facedown in the sand by the entry, and Thordrin stood inside with a casual smile as he wiped his knife on the dead man's clothes.

"Well, that was easy," he said.

Konan peered over at Lyra, where she lay on her makeshift bed. She had managed to rise to her elbows on her own. Her arms quivered with the effort, and her eyes were wide, catching the moonlight that poured in through the door.

Thordrin tucked the knife into his belt and patted it. "You good, mage?" He lifted the corpse by its shaggy, greasy hair and grinned proudly. "I got you some new clothes."

Lyra blanched. "Who . . ." Her voice cracked, and her mouth moved without making sound. She tried again. "Who were they?"

"Central camp scum," Thordrin replied easily. "Figured they would have come a week ago."

Lyra stared at them both, paling as she processed Thordrin's words. "You knew they would come?"

"Course I knew." Thordrin gestured at Konan to remove the dead man's clothes.

"And you left me alone?" Her accusatory tone made Konan look up. She had paled, and the terror in her expression made his stomach churn.

Did she not understand why they had to do it? The central camp had buzzed for weeks about retrieving her. Better to let them come at a time Thordrin and Konan could predict. He bent to undressing the man, setting the rags and belt to the side for Lyra.

Thordrin scoffed. "You're welcome for the new wardrobe, y'little cunt. Let me guess, they're not tailored correctly. Fuck me." He grabbed the dead man by the ankle and dragged the corpse out.

Konan focused on folding the rags into a pile. Thordrin dropped another pile of clothing and boots next to him from the corpses outside and shut the door.

He could feel Lyra watching him. Resentment, perhaps rage—its intensity burned into him.

When he finally looked up, he realized his error.

It was betrayal.

Taking a knee beside her, he set the pile of clothing down. Lyra remained as she was, propped up on wobbling elbows, panting with the pain and exertion and fear.

The silence between them grew, and the sour smell of urine wafted into his nose. She had no doubt been frightened beyond her ability to cope, and he regretted more and more not warning her of their plan. The central camp gang was routed of leadership now, though; no one else would come for her.

"I thought I was safe with you," she murmured. Her soft words forced him to look, and he began to understand.

"You are safe. We knew they would come, and we were ready." He paused and thought harder. Then, "I should have warned you."

That seemed to break something in her, and she groaned as she lay back down.

Konan helped with a gentle hand on her shoulder, easing her into a comfortable position, and as he drew away, she clutched for his hand.

"It's only . . . I was starting to *feel* safe," she said, biting her lip again. "And now that feeling is gone." A shiver ran through her, and she hiccupped. "I thought the man in the doorway was Thordrin, and when I realized it wasn't, every part of me screamed. But I could do nothing."

She grimaced as if disgusted with herself, then began to cry.

Konan watched the tears carve moonlit streaks down her cheeks, along her small nose and into the curve of her mouth, down to her narrow chin. He squeezed her fingers to regain her attention and pulled the small, chipped knives from his pocket.

"We can teach you to fight."

She blinked at the weapons, then at him, then toward the door. "Out there?" Her voice shook.

"Selen and his gang are dead." Konan punctuated his words with a shake of her limp hand. "Now you must overcome your fear. You must survive and escape, and return to your family."

Lyra pulled away, fresh tears streaming out. "I don't even have clothes that cover me, just patches and pieces. And I . . . I made a mess of my clothes. I can't go out there." She flushed in shame.

Konan nodded his understanding, then gestured at the pile of rags. There were rope cords for belts, worn tunics and pants. He pulled the precious needle from his pouch and placed it in her palm, then closed her fingers around it.

"People will hurt you, Lyra, and they will leave scars on you that never go away, but they can't kill you. Only you can do that." He nodded toward the door. "Do whatever you have to do to go back out there, and I'll be with you."

She clutched the needle in a tight fist, her eyes wide. As he moved to stand, she reached for him once more. "Thank you."

Konan inclined his head in respect, and for the briefest moment, a stunning smile crossed her face, pulling at the corners of her lips and alighting her crystalline eyes. Then it was gone.

12

THE OCEAN REEKED OF the scent of battle. It both excited and unsettled her deep within, but she raised her chin and ignored it. Hachi shifted beneath her, sensing her slight agitation, but she patted his blubbery neck. He calmed.

"A nice little fight," remarked Vice Commodore Reihotto beside her.

They observed the destruction ahead with little emotion or concern, for their troops had easily decimated the small group of myr bearing the black and white stripes of Jijito.

Upon the word of her scouts, Taiuki had sent the troops into the headcurrent, undetected by Jijito's trackers, sharks attuned to the foreign scents of forged steel and tanned leather. Her own trackers had swayed their heads from side to side, baring their jagged maws as they worked. Her army crept behind, advancing through the murky water of the Mana Loi until they spied the small group of Jijiton-jin.

The invaders had attacked a small underwater village, one set in an open swath of kelpland, a somewhat open landscape with occasional towering kelp plants and numerous bands of wild waterdogs. More orderly rows of kelp lined the fields beyond, and the idyllic village boasted an elaborate garden behind every home.

Most of Taiuki's fleet didn't even unsheathe their jianswords or loose bolts from crossbows; they held back in reserve, almost bored.

"I suspect this was a first advance party," she finally answered Reihotto. "Scoping the area for Jijito's next move."

"Yes, my Second." Reihotto acknowledged her with a respectful nod. "Does it strike you odd that they would send such a small school? A single platoon's worth of soldiers is hardly enough to travel into enemy territory."

"Agreed, much like the village to the north."

Reihotto shook her head. "Strange behavior. Shall I prepare a report for the arch commodore?"

"Thank you, Vice Commodore, but I'll take care of it." Taiuki dismissed the woman, who turned her whale mount Tsuya away from the battle and toward the area in which their army made camp.

Reihotto was the closest thing she had to a friend, if Taiuki dared call their impeccable working relationship such a thing. As the vice commodore, Reihotto served as second-in-command of all of Shiggo's armies, the highest military rank carried by one without royal blood.

When Taiuki's uncle Sashiro retired, Taiuki herself would fill his position as arch commodore. Until then, she was the Second, the second child in line for the throne. Such was the way of the myr, as it always had been.

She took a deep breath and winced, recalling the strength of wafting blood and humors from the dead upcurrent. *No blood in the water, Taiuki.* Underwater, the scents were also a flavor, an intermingling of senses confounded by the gills on her neck. She knew Hachi could smell it too, for he groaned a light complaint to her.

Unlike Reihotto's Tsuya, Hachi was a blackheaded whale, a naturally pacifist species. Although highly trainable and eager to please, they weren't lusty for blood like saw-toothed whales and blues. He had been with her nearly ten years, and she loved him for all his foibles. She patted his neck again and guided him toward the growing war camp.

Taiuki squinted.

Another whale-mounted figure careened toward them, waving wildly. Before long, she noticed the distant clicking of the underwater myr language tapping through the water in a cadence the entire army could likely hear.

"Yuki! Yuki! I'm here! Sash let me come!"

The adolescent boy launched from his whale's saddle and bowled her off of Hachi in a gleeful, tumbling hug. He squeezed her tight, tails intertwined. By the current, he was stronger than he used to be with those thickening arms.

"Tan-sho, decorum," she managed as the breath was pushed out of her, resisting a grin to match his.

Her little brother Tan released her with a look of dismay. "Oh, right." He looked so crestfallen that she broke into a smile and grabbed him by the shoulders, scruffing his hair. He hated that.

"What in the darkest depths are you doing here?" she said when he broke away.

Tan's grin threatened to split his face in half, and he straightened while slicking his short black hair in place. He placed both palms to his forehead in exaggerated deference. "Tan, Third of Shiggo, reporting for duty at the front. Old Sash thought I could use the experience with you and Rei-hotto."

She looked at him sternly, and he cowed, letting his salute fall.

"*Arch Commodore Sashiro* thought I could use the experience," he mumbled, but the glint of mischief remained in the yellow flecks of his eyes.

Taiuki raised an eyebrow. "I see." She glared at him a few moments longer, then eased, slinging her arm around him once again. "You know I'm not sending you into battle, right? You're here to observe, from a distance."

He rolled his eyes. "I'll be fine, Yuki-sho."

"Precisely. I'll make sure of it."

She clicked for Hachi to follow, and they swam slowly toward the camp. Tan's mount, another blackheaded whale named Nimoka, followed at his command, happily wavering alongside Hachi. One wouldn't expect either of these whales to be vicious fighters, but their demeanor would shift the moment they knew they were working.

Tan brightened. "I could have fought in this battle. It looked easy."

A torrent of feelings rushed through Taiuki at the idea, but she steeled herself, revealing nothing. She merely squeezed his shoulder. "You will obey my orders, if you are to stay here at the front. If I say to stay back, you will do so. Do you understand, Third?"

"I shall conform, Second," he replied formally, but the mischievous curl to his lips gnawed at her darkest fears.

"I'm not joking, Tan-sho," she clicked quietly, making sure the traveling language reached as few listening ears as possible. "War is not a lighthearted jest."

"I thought it was just a border dispute." He looked genuinely glum as he realized how serious she was, but she wouldn't relent. Tan huffed, flaring his gills out.

There was something off about the last few battles, something strange about the Jijiton-jin behavior that flew in the face of myr ways, the Way of the Current. She couldn't put her finger on it yet, nor could Reihotto, but they were both uneasy.

With one last squeeze of encouragement, she released Tan. "You can train with the other soldiers, maintain your gear, and attend Nimoka as a member of the unit, but when we get to the next village, you must stay back with the bannerman and observe. Learn, think about the strategy, and tell me what I did wrong after."

He snorted at that. "Like I could give *you* any advice."

She and Tan entered the camp side-by-side, no longer casually touching. Taiuki threw her shoulders back and swam slightly ahead, inspecting the quick work of the soldiers in making camp. Most were already settled in circles of several dozen apiece, their sleeping arrangements in the center and their mounts on the outside in a barrier of protection.

They maintained separation by mount species, for the sawtooths disregarded their kindred blackheaded whales as mere prey. They were never aggressive to their humans, however, and Taiuki smiled softly to herself as she reminisced on those rare moments when the wild ones migrated by the castle every year. She would often talk to them, as much as they *could* communicate in a base language of emotions and intuitions, as they passed by.

The ferocious blue sharks moved to the outer ring of the entire war camp, according to their aloof and independent nature. They were highly intelligent, schooling with their conspecifics and naturally providing border protection both in the field and back home, where they edged the outer villages of Shiggo City. Arch Commodore Sashiro would call his blue shark Benn a partner, rather than a vassal.

Soldiers saluted as she passed, covering both eyes with their palms and touching their foreheads, heads bowed in submission. The soft chatter of myr clicking hushed, interrupted only by respectful greetings of "Second" from timid and admiring voices. Taiuki would have nodded back, but few met her eye after saluting, instead keeping their gaze averted in deference to her position.

Tan smiled at them and waved at a few, recognizing them from training at Shiggo City. Most of Taiuki's companies had only recently deployed, drawn from the capitol in response to troubling reports of violence on the Jijiton-jin border.

As Tan implied, border incursions were common. Myr territories ebbed and flowed like the ocean around them, pulsing with great power and shrinking with weakness and cowardice. Intimidation, confidence, and aggression were adequate weapons by which to claim a border township, ameliorating any need for bloodshed.

They settled in the center of the camp, with Tan gaining a tent of his own beside Taiuki's and Reihotto's. The canvas reduced the rush of the current past their ears, although it provided little in terms of insulation. Myr didn't tend to get cold in any case.

They had barely slept a few hours when Reihotto woke Taiuki from her rest.

"My Second, the scouts have returned from the next village to the southwest."

Taiuki was up almost before she finished speaking. She prayed the village had fared better than some they had seen, but she allowed the hope to wash away. It served no utility, filling her busy mind with blank, bright space that could be better applied to planning the next attack.

She spared a glance at Tan's tent. Her brother slept soundly, although Nimoka peered curiously at her from the dark water beyond. Tan would be better rested if she heard this without him; he could help deploy the next round of scouts in the morning.

The report was grim, and she dreamt of dealing death for the remainder of the night.

"By the current, every spring they push the border," Vice Commodore Reihotto said, watching from her position on Taiuki's right. Tsuya snorted under her tight rein, spraying water from his blowhole as they sat just above the ocean surface.

Taiuki agreed with a stony smile. "And every spring we push them back." Her response was automatic and rich with fervor, despite the unspoken tension.

This wasn't like every other spring, and they both knew it.

They peered through the ocean to the atoll in the murky distance, a hill that rose up from the bottom and pushed above the surface just enough to form a crater edge of sand and coral. Their fleet waited for Reihotto's hand signal, and Reihotto waited for Taiuki's command.

"Give them a volley, top line only."

Hachi nickered, and she patted his neck. He didn't like waiting, holding back as the vanguard took first blood. Although he didn't go wild with blood like the blues sometimes did, he liked the excitement of battle. Taiuki wondered if whales were smart enough to understand leadership, the concept of leading the school into the fray at the point of the echelon, versus rear command.

She intended a balance between the two.

Reihotto signaled a command, which traveled forward in hushed clicks and rapid hand motions, and the frontmost upper line of Shiggon-jin soldiers, who were barely submerged, popped from the water. Their bolts arced through the air in a shadow of gray and landed on the exposed atoll. Jijito's soldiers, tiny figures from this distance, screamed. Crossbows reloaded, the top line sank once again below the threshold of return fire. The upper platoons of soldiers clicked with raucous celebration of their archery skills.

Reihotto dipped down and reprimanded them harshly. Discipline, above all, would bring them victory.

The atoll ahead looked innocuous enough on the outside, but behind its coral walls lay an inner crater of open water. It had been a village, but Taiuki doubted they would find much intact given the bodies that had been posted on the lip. The corpses had lost their eyes to the gulls already, but their whipping cloaks were relatively whole. A week they had been hanging, perhaps?

Tan looked rather pale on her left side as he stared at the distant corpses.

"Advance," Taiuki commanded. "Six platoons at depth, moving up the atoll wall to plug holes. Six subsurface to sweep over the edge, preceded by another bolt volley from the top line."

"My Second, we still don't know how many are inside the atoll structure," Reihotto warned.

"It can't be more than six platoons, Vice Commodore," Taiuki replied. "I've been there before, and it's not that deep."

Reihotto saluted, obediently placing both palms to her own face and touching her forehead with her fingertips. "It shall be done, Second." She melted beneath the water.

Taiuki watched, restraining Hachi as he pranced back and forth under her hold. She chastised him in a gentle tone, and he calmed. Tan remained motionless on Nimoka, his hands clenched on her reins so tightly they were turning white at the knuckles.

Her commands were carried out flawlessly. The top lines—surface-level archers—held only a few paces below the ocean's surface, emerging just before the subsurface vanguard smashed into the atoll. Bolts flew in perfect coordination. The vanguard cavalry leapt off their mounts, shifting midair and landing on the atoll for hand-to-hand combat as Jijiton-jin soldiers poured from the atoll's center. Swords clashed and daggers flashed in the sunlight, and men and women screamed in a musical cacophony of violence.

Taiuki urged Hachi below the surface so she could see the deep attack. Led by soldiers riding vicious, blood-wild blues, the deep platoons circled round the lower part of the atoll walls, catching Jijiton-jin who escaped through small holes and tunnels pocking the coral-formed island. She watched as a blue shark ripped open the whale mount of a Jijiton-jin soldier. The myrman swam off, signaling his own surrender and begging for mercy. The Shiggon-jin soldier called the blue off, then dismounted for hand-to-hand underwater combat. His blue shark circled the two in a tight loop, whipping its head in frustration.

Taiuki approved. It was a more honorable kill, rather than letting the blue have its way.

Ascending once again, she could see the surface battle. More Jijiton-jin troops had fit inside the atoll than she had expected, although she was confident her soldiers were enough. Nevertheless . . .

Hachi clicked at her impatiently.

"Yes, let's go," she answered. "Tan, stay here until the fighting is done."

He didn't answer right away, and she gave him a sharp look. "Tan-sho."

That earned a quick nod and a gulp.

"Watch above and below. Observe the formation used to take the base of the island. I'll be back."

She and Reihotto advanced with the reserve, spreading in a pincer shape and enveloping the atoll, then rushing up its walls like a tightening noose. Many with whales leapt over the wall and joined the fight inside, while those with blues patrolled the edge to eliminate escapees. Others abandoned their mounts and shifted to human form, emerging on the sand with bare feet and bloodlust.

Taiuki was one of them. The moment her feet touched the sand of the atoll, she was running, spinning and jabbing with a short jiansword in one hand and a dagger in the other. Her leather and mail skirt flailed as she spun in a deadly dance. She felt her blade enter a man and exit the other side, breaking through the scale mail with a pop. Another required a more personal touch as he tried to rush her; she rolled his momentum into a controlled tumble. They landed together with her knife stuck in his throat. Blood spattered on her cheek and the stray wisps of black hair that escaped from her helmet.

"Ol Shiggo'lo!" She heard the stirring battle cry echoing across the atoll, bouncing across the open water to assail the ears of their foes.

Yanking her knife free, Taiuki turned to her next fight. This soldier was formidable, reasonably talented. She was forced to parry, dodge, feinting once and sliding across the soldier's side with minimal damage. He scored her unprotected leg below the skirt, and she cursed. As the soldier closed with her, she surprised him with a nearly vertical kick, jabbing his nose so hard with her heel that he flew backward into the sand. She plunged her knife into his chest and moved on.

This battle was a demonstration for Jijito, a harsh reminder of why they should keep to their territory. Only a few lives would be spared to tell their superiors what had happened; the rest would be given to the current.

Gritting her teeth, Taiuki took in the bloodshed around her and was grateful to be on land, where the scent did not spread as easily. Men and women bled out at her feet, giving most of their Water to the wet sand. She took a series of deep, slow breaths, controlling the tremble of bloodlust that surged through her body.

The Jijiton-jin deserved as much. They had violently expanded their kingdom during the last few months, setting up stronger outposts like this one along the relatively shallow flats west of the Lai'akala Trench. This atoll, like so many others, was Shiggon-jin land and water. *Her* land and water. And its population had been wiped out, exterminated by merciless soldiers from the more westerly myrkingdom. The small villages from weeks previous were nothing like this.

Unlike most border disputes, this had become a war. The Way of the Current demanded blood for blood, and she, Taiuki ol'Kada ol'Tatami, Second of the royal house of Shiggo, would dispense it. This was her purpose, to protect her people as military commander and diplomat.

She signaled for the top liners to vault the atoll wall and clean up. Their speed with bolt reloading was admirably efficient, and safer for dispatching mounts not amenable to retraining. With one more deep breath, she cleaned her blades on the leather skirt of a dead woman's breechbelt. The woman had been an officer, if Taiuki read the rankstones correctly. In charge of several platoons, most likely.

Not anymore, Taiuki thought as she dropped the bloodied leather material and sheathed her jiansword.

Reihotto, nostrils flaring and equally covered in blood, saluted her once again and bowed respectfully. "Second, it is done."

"Injury report?"

"Minimal. Four dead, thirteen injured, but most travel-worthy. One should not be moved. You're bleeding, Second."

"I'll heal," she said dismissively. "The Jijiton-jin?"

"Five survivors." Vice Commodore Reihotto eyed Taiuki's bleeding leg without touching it and wrinkled her nose. "Normally I would suggest the herbsman, but you always heal so quickly."

Taiuki ignored Reihotto's concern. "Five? Make it four. Wait, I'll do it."

She hesitated for a moment as she examined the five remaining Jijiton-jin soldiers. They knelt in a line with their hands bound. Border disputes never ended in this much death or mercilessness, and she didn't like having to do it, but Jijito had gone too far.

Jijito had murdered the myrfolk living around this atoll. The remains of their village were smashed and dismantled, and their farms had been left to decay. Even their animals, domesticated waterdogs and whales, had been butchered and left on spits both above and below the surface as a warning to Shiggo.

She drew her jiansword once again and stalked in front of the line. "I have a message for your king," she said coldly, holding on to the rancor those thoughts had given her. She pointed at each soldier with the tip of her blade.

One of the Jijiton-jin spat on the sand. "We know who you are."

"You should."

"You're the *Second*," the soldier continued with a sneer. "We've heard all kinds of rumors about you, but I doubt any of them are true."

Taiuki controlled her expression, but her stomach twisted uncomfortably. She forced a smile. "You're a talker. Will you deliver my message?"

The soldier spat again. "I don't deliver messages from anim—"

Before he could finish, she jabbed him in the throat, and he slumped over with a weak, gurgling cough.

Taiuki slid her gaze to the other four. "I have a message for your king," she repeated calmly, despite the internal distress she felt from the dead soldier's words. The Jijiton-jin were the ones acting like animals. "A small school might get home safely to deliver it, despite the blood in the water."

"Coward," sobbed one of the remaining soldiers. "He was bound. It's not honorable."

Taiuki nodded at Vice Commodore Reihotto, who raised her eyebrows but obeyed, cutting the soldier's bonds and giving him the dagger from her belt. If he wanted to fight one of them to the death, fair was fair.

As expected, the Jijiton-jin whirled on Reihotto, attempting to stab her in the leg between the flaps of chainmail skirting, but she rocked back on one foot and popped forward again with a second knife in her hand. She drove it into the soft muscle between the man's neck and shoulder, then calmly retrieved her other knife from his hand as he fell. She stooped to wipe the blood on the dead man's sleeve, then sheathed both weapons.

The trio of remaining Jijiton-jin trembled.

"If you three have enough honor to deliver my message, then we will release you," said Taiuki in a reasonable tone. "But make no mistake, I will kill all three of you if I have to, and your king will have to wonder what happened."

They exchanged timorous looks and quickly agreed, and she gave them a simple warning.

"Listen well, King of Jijito: Shiggo will not tolerate another incursion such as this one. We will reclaim every village, every life in full measure, blood for blood, according to the Way of the Current." She paused for effect. "I, Taiuki, Second of Shiggo, *will* take blood for blood."

She sent them off without any mounts. "A school of three is enough," she said in a harsh voice when Reihotto asked.

"They'll be able to make it to the next Jijiton-jin village. Let's move to the next atoll."

Taiuki turned away from their hasty retreat, confident she had made an impression, and found Tan, pale and still, standing a few rows behind the other soldiers on the atoll sand, his jaw slightly slackened. Her stomach dropped—until she realized his hair was only water-slicked, his uniform pristine, his armor unscratched. Then she grew angry.

"But Second—" Reihotto lowered her voice, begging with her eyes to be forgiven for speaking out as Taiuki's expression darkened. "One of our soldiers can't be moved. The school must stay together."

Taiuki clenched her jaw. There were other villages along this border that had been attacked, destroyed. "We can leave a squadron with him." She needed to reprimand Tan.

"You are an exceptional leader; your fleet *wants* to follow you. Don't leave them behind, my Second." Reihotto was pleading now. Despite her seniority in terms of experience, she ultimately had to adhere to the Second's decisions as arch commodore-in-training. The only one who might supersede Taiuki was Arch Commodore Sashiro himself, and he wasn't here.

Taiuki realized that leaving the injured man behind was not the myr way, but she couldn't justify waiting for him to heal enough to move. The next village to the south had also been attacked, as had the next, and the next for who knew what distance along the Lai'akala Trench. Shiggon-jin people were dead. Were they not also part of the school? Were not all Shiggon-jin under her care?

"We shouldn't give up this ground now that it's been gained," she mused, contemplating an alternative that would allow her to take troops south. "Send to Sashiro for another company," she decided. "He's not far; they should arrive in less than three days and can turn this place into a fortress. We'll leave two squadrons for defense of the atoll and one of the herbsmen for the injured, and move south tomorrow. Now, I must speak with my brother."

Vice Commodore Reihotto's discontent was obvious in her crinkled forehead and her dark, begging eyes, but she obeyed.

13

DESPITE REIHOTTO'S RESERVATIONS, THEIR fleet—a battalion composed of three companies—swept southward early the next day. In Taiuki's eyes, the injured man was stable, and she had left him with a protective unit and one of the better herbsmen. She didn't understand what more could possibly be needed, given Sashiro's imminent arrival.

"It's still a division of the school," Tan suggested quietly from her left. He looked away, concentrating exceptionally hard on handling Nimoka and maintaining perfect alignment with Reihotto.

Taiuki, who led at the point of the first echelon formation, ignored him. How could he have disregarded her orders to stay far back? What if he had gotten hurt?

The horror of it threatened to overwhelm her.

Tan claimed that he had waited until the battle was over, his sword hand itching to participate but clamped on the hilt with obedience, and that he had accompanied the bannerman forward after.

That wasn't the point. She said she would come back for him. What if his judgment had been wrong? What if some hidden Jijiton-jin force had burst from the atoll's lower caverns, a hidden passage, and overcome him as they fled?

"A platoon is large enough," she muttered stiffly, her clicking a staccato in her ears. "And a school is not defined by size so much as conformity." She forced him to meet her eye, and he reddened with shame. "Give me a battle report. How would you describe the last confrontation, and what did you learn?"

He stumbled through a description, falling into more of a rhythm as he defended her use of the reserve as a second wave, her multitiered attack formations, but then stuttered as he described the paltry line of survivors. He paled as he re-called her merciless execution of the first soldier, the mouthy one.

"Should I have allowed him to live?" she asked, curious of his answer. She doubted nothing in her actions, but Tan had rarely seen executions so close. In fact, now that she thought about it, that was his first full view of death, the necessary brutality of war. It made her empathize a little more, but she held her composure.

Tan blanched. "I'm not saying that, Yuki—I mean 'Second'—I guess I meant that I wasn't expecting it. Five is so few to send back to Jijito."

"Four is the minimum viable unit," Taiuki replied easily, "if sending a message was necessary. Otherwise, we should have killed them all."

"Blood for Blood," Vice Commodore Reihotto agreed from her right.

"It is the Way, I know," said Tan, but he was still wan with unease. "I just . . ."

"You hadn't seen it so close before." Taiuki finally relent-ed and eased Hachi over. She touched his smooth cheek.

He still hadn't formed a single facial hair. Maybe he wouldn't. Father hadn't had much to speak of either, al-though their uncle Sashiro had a thin mustache and a long, braided triangle of mostly black hair jutting from his chin. Tan still had his baby fat, making his cheeks rounder and his expressions softer. His voice had dropped, revealing a pleasant alto reminiscent of their father, and his lean body had formed into that of a young man, all lanky elbows and knees strung together with corded muscle.

He gave her an abashed look and covered her touch with his own hand. "It scared me, Yuki-sho," he clicked so quietly she almost didn't catch it. His eyes had gone pink, the only underwater tell that one might be weeping.

She gave his chin one last affectionate squeeze and pulled back into formation. "Death is a reasonable thing to fear, Tan-sho. Or at least, to respect. A healthy appreciation for its permanence makes you a better leader in the field, where every one of your choices is a parlay with the current for the lives of your men and women."

He attempted a halfhearted smile. "I don't want to parlay with death. I'm not even an officer."

"But you could be. That's why Arch Commodore Sashiro sent you here, to learn. You may be Third, Tan, but that doesn't mean you can't attain a high rank. I *expect* you to be one of my commodores someday."

Over the next few days, Taiuki pushed from village to village and found each manned by a small contingent of Jijiton-jin. The forces of Shiggo destroyed them.

After the first atoll, she left no one alive. The slaughter was another message for the king of Jijito, a message of a different kind. No more messengers would be deployed to the foot of his throne, blubbering about the massacre of their companions or the threat of Shiggo's retribution.

She prayed to the rushing current that he would take it seriously. She didn't enjoy killing, but she would do whatever was required to guard her kingdom.

Tan was mortified, but he knew it was right. At least he hung back after the first reprimand.

They would rebuild in the wake of this war. They would repopulate the villages under the watchful guard of strong border fortresses. They would replant the kelp farms and bring livestock back into the pastures. They would strengthen Shiggo's border towns until Jijito would not even consider such an offensive incursion ever again.

As Taiuki rested after the fourth village in a row, a messenger unit sped into the camp.

"From the arch commodore, Second," the leader said, handing her a letter.

Tan rested his chin on her shoulder as she read it silently.

> *Taiuki ol'Kada ol'Tatami, Second of Shiggo, I commend you on your successful reclamation of the atoll and subsequent villages. However, beware division of the school; the injured are equal members, not liabilities. Have a care for the Way of the Current, niece. I also relay a command from the queen: Return immediately with the Third to Shiggo City for further orders, leaving command with Vice Commodore Reihotto. She will ensure the completion of the current mission.*
> Arch Commodore Sashiro ol'Kada ol'Tatami

"What does that mean?" Tan furrowed his brow. "I've barely been at the front. They're sending me home?"

Taiuki squinted at the brownish-black letters inked onto the thin vellum scrap. Rarely did Sashiro recognize their familial relationship; he was usually so proper.

Her disregard for the school dynamic must have troubled him greatly, although she still thought it silly. She had repeated her tactic at each reclaimed village, leaving the wounded with a team and advancing. Her speed in moving southward had maintained the element of surprise, giving them a distinct upper hand in every battle with the Jijiton-jin. If they had slowed, or stopped altogether, that element could have been lost. Her aggressiveness was part of their successful strategy.

But she did notice the soldiers whispering, clicking in quiet taps and sounds that blended with the trickle of the water, and sometimes they seemed to peer through their fingers with something that was not entirely respect. Was it intimidation? Fear? Of being left behind? All she knew was that they saluted faster, almost as if fearful of backlash, and that they mumbled awkwardly instead of making conversation. They covered their eyes and avoided direct gazes.

Or perhaps she imagined their odd glances, for few of them ranked high enough *not* to look away.

"Are they sending me home?" Tan repeated.

"They're sending us both home," she said softly, chewing on the meaning behind the words.

She and Tan swam through the camp toward the saw-toothed whale pasture. Reihotto was there, rubbing salve on Tsuya where his halter chafed. She had removed her helmet and pauldrons, but still wore the tight-fitting scale mail and skirt armor; she was at ease. Taiuki waved the letter at her, then handed it over.

Reihotto scanned it quickly and handed it back with a grave acknowledgment. "I shall try to lead well in your stead, Second. Do you have any final orders for me before you go?"

"No, I entrust the fleet to you, including the next move. I know our strategies differ, but there's no one I trust more."

A brief expression of appreciation touched Reihotto's lips, then disappeared. "Which squadron will accompany you home?"

Taiuki shook her head. "No, I shouldn't take any of them with me. It will weaken the force you have."

Reihotto frowned, pausing her treatment of Tsuya, who nickered at them and pushed into her still hand. "You shouldn't travel without a school, Second. You *can't*, forgive my bluntness."

"I can and I will, if it means leaving a squadron here for you."

"I cannot allow it, my Second." They stared each other down, but Reihotto finally bowed her head and looked away. "I beg you to find another way. You and Tan, with your mounts, are hardly a school."

Taiuki halted, reconsidering. She had forgotten about her brother. That changed everything. She sighed and placed a friendly grip on Reihotto's shoulder. The vice commodore was one of the best women she knew, and worth trusting, but Taiuki couldn't bear the thought of reducing their force on the front for her own sake. For Tan, though, she would. "I'll take those who won't rejoin you in combat for convalescence in Shiggo City, and one fully functional blue team for escort. I leave the rest in your capable hands, Vice Commodore."

Reihotto's shoulder slumped with her relieved sigh, and she brightened. "I shall conform, my Second. May I'ya smile upon your journey, Second. Third."

Tan smiled back at her.

Taiuki nodded but didn't reply. I'ya's oversight hadn't helped the dead villagers of the past weeks, and she doubted it would help on the road back home either. The only protection they had was their own wit and speed, their own discipline and vigilance. I'ya's shining light faded quickly beneath the waves of the Mana Loi.

Mother's mouth was moving, enunciating each syllable and sound with prim exactitude and authority.

Taiuki heard the wretched words formed by Mother's hateful tongue, and yet, she didn't comprehend them after the first few words. *You are no longer the arch commodore-in-training.* She stood at attention, feet slightly apart and perfectly balanced, head high and back straight, and yet the world spun around her.

Very little emotion escaped from Queen Regent Furuhaki's facial expression, her brow smooth without a hint of dismay or doubt that her words would not be followed to the letter. Steward Wehan scribbled furiously behind her, documenting the court announcement in full detail upon his vellum scroll. Taiuki should have known something of import would happen, as he sat at his scribing pedestal rather than standing behind the throne to the right side. Her elder sister Keiki stood to the left of the throne, wringing her hands.

Mother's eyes flashed.

So there was emotion: irritation, ripening into fury.

Thank the current Tan wasn't here to see this humiliation. Taiuki waited for Mother's mouth to stop moving, waited for the sounds of Shiggo Castle to return to her prickling ears. Her eardrums seemed overwhelmed by a dull roar, somewhat like being in the midst of battle, instead of the familiar crackles and rushing whisper of the cavernous, air-filled halls of the myr royal castle. Where the water was held back—a trick of the Waterpriests—the thrumming and gurgling noises of the ocean beyond were louder, an arrhythmic melody to which the entire underwater portion of Shiggo City danced.

Mother glowered and stood, and then her strident demand cut through Taiuki's shock. "Conform, Princess," she hissed.

Taiuki attempted to stand her ground, but a nauseating feeling crept into her toes and feet where they were stationed on the stage, facing the throne. "And who shall replace me, Queen Regent?" she managed, tightly controlling her voice so as not to convey sarcasm or sadness. Neither was acceptable to Mother.

"One who deserves it," she declared, narrowing her eyes. "And you shall support him. Now conform."

The ache climbed up her legs and into her belly, gripping her gut and making her want to curl into a ball. Instead, she raised both palms to her temple, fingertips touching, and dipped her head in acquiescence. "I shall conform, Queen Regent," she intoned. She remained that way, awaiting release.

"Am I not deserving of a bow?"

Taiuki bent at the waist, fighting the torrent of feelings rushing through her. Humiliation, demotion, and for what? Because Mother loved Tan more? Why wasn't Kei saying *anything*?

"Get on your knees," Mother shrieked.

Taiuki dropped to her knees and leaned down as far as she could, her nose mere inches from the stone flooring. The imperfections of the coral- and crustacean-infused limestone were crystal clear at this distance, filled and smoothed to a polish with some sort of magical chemical.

She heard Mother flutter her skirts as she re-situated herself upon the throne. The regent had developed a poor habit of wearing heavy, over-long skirts like the landwalkers did, absurd clothing for a species meant to shift and swim underwater.

"You may rise, Princess. You are dismissed. I have more important things to attend to."

Taiuki rose slowly, harnessing all of her strength to keep from boiling over.

Kei stood behind the throne, pale, speechless, and trembling.

Mother flicked her ring-bedecked hand toward the door to the castle interior. "Do pull yourself together before the next few days. We'll have a distinguished guest."

Taiuki snarled wordlessly at the soldiers who moved to escort her out. None of them touched her. In fact, most looked sorry to be there. Regardless, they funneled her toward the door and out.

The heavy door boomed to a close with a sense of dreadful finality, leaving Taiuki alone and trembling with rage as she finally perceived Mother's words.

You are no longer arch commodore-in-training. You will be wife to the heir of Krita, Crown Prince Godrig of House Crayer.

Godrig? A Kritali pig, and not myr. In fact, the people of Krita didn't seem to have much connection to the higher realm in general. No magika, no alternate forms as the body shifted with its element. And no intuition. How could one rule over an island without a connection to the sea? An island was merely a mountaintop. Godrig had no Water in his blood, and no right to be with someone who did.

Father would never have locked her out of all discussion, ignored her for days on end, or allowed Mother and Kei to bully her into a landwalker marriage. Father would have—

She paused her mental tirade. Father wouldn't have stopped it either. Sad as his sudden death—a failure of his heart—had been, it hadn't changed Taiuki's life all that much. Mother was in charge now, with Kei as her pretty puppet, but she had been giving the commands for a long time from her place behind the throne.

Taiuki looked down at her dress uniform and clenched her fists so tightly, she could feel her nails breaking into her palms.

She had changed formally for this audience. The cuisse skirt hung loose, covered in front by a jeweled, decorative fauld breechbelt indicative of her rank as arch commodore-in-training, the second in line. The carved abalone was elaborate, but she was missing the bright orange gem in the center and the obsidian rankstones to mark her as supreme commander of the Shiggon-jin fleet. Such an honor would await her uncle's retirement. Above the cuisses, a simple sealskin tunic was overlaid with silver-gallite scaled mail that flexed with her form. She had affixed an ornate gorget to her neck, and pauldrons beaten into scallop shells decorated both shoulders. Her arms were likewise covered with scale mail and ended with gauntlets matching the gorget. Finally, a servant had drawn back her long black trusses and placed upon her head a pointed helm with a scaled hem. She looked the part.

And now, she was a jester. The court fool, dressed in a pretty costume wildly beyond her station.

The guards posted on either side of the throne room doors stared ahead, not daring to acknowledge her. They seemed to examine the fine striations on the hallway walls, no doubt just as complex and beautiful as the throne room's flooring. The layered limestone encapsulated thousands of tiny whorled shells and colorful pigments, thousands upon thousands of years of ocean life compressed into rock. Taiuki used to look at it for hours, seeking patterns and commonalities between the animals contained and the ones she saw still living in the ocean beyond.

She clenched her jaw several times, her focus extending through the closed door. Beyond, in the spacious and elegant, yet somehow empty throne room, Mother sat prim and straight in the place that should have been Kei's, beckoning to Wehan for the next item of business or for a glass of effervescent wine. The steward would be ready with quill and vellum parchment to document her decisions. Both would ignore the closed door to the castle interior, and certainly her standing behind it.

That dizzying sense of dread and resentment surged through her again, and she intensified her gaze, as though it could break through the door and force Mother to look her in the eye again. Wooden splinters seemed to flake off the door as she glared, lightly undulating to the floor like ocean detritus. The door shuddered and groaned on its hinges.

The sound woke her from her dark meditation, and she shook herself and spun, heading to the Garrison Gate. Enough of this. As she distanced herself, she thought she heard heavy sighs of relief from behind.

Taiuki rolled over and caught her breath, then pulled her nightshift back on to cover her chest. She scrubbed her face and huffed in frustration.

The man next to her was from Reihotto's company, one of the injured blue shark cavalrymen who had accompanied her back to Shiggo City. He wasn't very talkative, but she didn't have much to say. Her malcontent hadn't worked itself out during numerous rounds of sparring or meditation at the training hall, which he had noticed, as he sometimes did.

Taiuki didn't feel any better now, unfortunately.

She glanced over at him. He lay against her silk pillows, his bare chest showing above the covers, waiting. For what? Another round, or for orders?

Resigned, she sighed. "You may go."

"As you wish, Your Highness." He climbed out of the bed immediately, wincing as he put too much weight on his injured leg. (Hers had already healed, she realized.) He slipped his tunic back on, then adjusted his breechbelt. "Are you certain that's all you need from me, my Second?"

She gave him an appreciative look but waved him out, then sank back into her pillows and stared at the ceiling high above. A mural of battle scenes adorned it, reflecting moments from the lives of past kings and queens from House Tatami. Her walls were likewise covered in tapestries interspersed with tall glass mirrors. For some reason she didn't like looking in those. Something about her reflection instilled a seed of shame that churned in her belly like rotten food, something that was much easier to ignore if she avoided looking.

She turned her head, gazing out the portal window.

Beyond lay the sea. Her room, like the other royal sleeping quarters, lay a level below the surface of the Mana Loi in a part of the castle that could be flooded if need be, one more defense against attack from landwalkers. Her window was a shutter of glass, but that was for appearances more than anything, for the Waterpriests used their magika to hold the water beyond back. The castle was kept dry by their intervention, as were the Water Temple, the Lower Market, and the main access tunnels.

The door burst open, and Tan bounced in. "Him again?" he said, grinning as he raised a playfully dubious eyebrow. "Gross." She straightened her tunic and the covers before he jumped on top and looked at her. "I'm bored. Are you going back to the front soon?"

She shook her head slowly and folded her arms across her chest. "Tan-sho, I'm not even dressed. Give me a minute, and we can talk."

Tan rolled his eyes, but got up and went to her liquor cabinet. "You weren't at supper. You want that bitter stuff from Merchan?"

"By the current, yes."

"Gross."

"Someday you'll probably like it," she teased as she pulled another layer over her tunic and affixed a light skirt over top. She thanked him as he handed her a glass and plopped back onto the bed. "Someday you'll like girls, too."

Tan wrinkled his nose and shrugged. "They're okay. Some of them are pretty. Hey, don't change the subject. Why weren't you at supper?"

"Kei didn't tell you?" She took a long sip from her glass; it burned like fire in her throat. The only thing better was the numbness that followed. She explained.

Tan's face couldn't have scrunched any further with his confusion. "But who will be Second?"

"Tan-sho . . ."

"I don't want to do that," he mumbled, then slumped onto her shoulder with an exaggerated sigh. "I just want to ride Nimoka all day and go hunting, and watch *you* fight battles, and eat street food at the Lower Market."

"I know."

"I don't want all that pressure on me, to fulfill a duty where I can't screw up." His tone became serious, and instead of confusion, Taiuki could see lines of fear contorting his face. "A duty where people depend on me, and could die if I make the wrong call. I couldn't even stomach watching you do it up close."

She put her arm around his shoulder and squeezed. "Neither of us was born for that duty, Tan," she said quietly, thinking of their brother Taifun as she spoke.

But he turned his face toward her, the lines of fear dissipating and revealing a round, smooth young face once again. He smiled. "You were. Maybe tradition doesn't say so, but you're a good Second, and you'll be a great Arch Commodore when old Uncle Sash retires."

"I'm afraid that's not going to happen, if Kei and Mother have their way."

Tan snorted. "You're not afraid of anything." She shook her empty glass, and he bounced up to get her another. He kept chattering as he did so. "And anyway, how can they send to you to Krita when you're already courting someone here?"

Taiuki couldn't help but laugh. "I'm not *courting* anyone."

"Yeah, but don't they care about that in the land kingdoms?" Tan waved toward the door, gesturing after the soldier who had just left.

Taiuki shrugged. "That's Krita's problem, not ours. They can't hold me to some landwalker standard." She gladly took the refilled glass and drained it. She was no lady by their strange ways, but she was everything proper by myr standards. Well, mostly. She wore respectable clothing and decorative breechbelts for formal occasions, did her silky hair like the queens of old, and served in the military like all the other men and women. She enjoyed the beautiful, unique blooms of underwater plants and the gorgeous colors of wildlife beyond her window, things she got to inspect more closely when she was in the field with her soldiers. She wasn't much for embroidery, but that was less than important in Shiggo. She was damned good at the fighting arts and knew the Way of the Current due to Sashiro's mentorship.

And she liked men, although even her current interest maintained an aloofness from her that she couldn't quite put her finger on. Although he came to her bed occasionally, even he seemed unsure of her, maybe even intimidated. Did he come to her out of duty and allegiance, or eager desire . . . or fear? She thought back to the averted gazes of her soldiers, the way they clicked softly amongst each other and saluted her so formally.

Taiuki didn't know the answer, but she was glad when the numbing feeling of the liquor extended beyond her throat and crept through her veins.

14

Nausea swelled over her in waves.

It was like drowning, this sense of helplessness. This feeling of being at the mercy of those around her.

"By the nethers, she's fucking whiny," she heard Thordrin say through the walls. "Don't fuckin' gesture at me, you tongue-tied asshole."

Lyra scowled into the darkness. It was early morning, pre-dawn by a few bells. Glowing white beams cut across the room from the double moons; both were shining brightly beyond the enclosing walls that were supposed to separate her from the threats outside.

Her heart pattered in her chest and ears; she could see it flickering on her wrists and feel it on her temple. Lyra stretched her hands up, forcing her hair back from her face, and sat there for minutes. Fear coursed through her veins, an insidious poison that infiltrated her chest and stomach and legs. The torpor made her want to give up, to hide. Even with these two men, was she ever safe? How many more in the central camp wanted vengeance for Selen's death? How many in the west end were trustworthy? She could hear the mutter of strange voices beyond her walls, day in and day out. To whom did the voices belong, and what if they decided Thordrin wasn't strong enough to lead them? What if Konan, loner that he was, went to the wrong place alone?

We knew they would come, and we were ready.

Konan's signs traced lines of light in her memory, and she subsided somewhat. Neither he nor Thordrin were fools. She pondered his words as she assessed the pile of clothing. Threadbare shirts, ill-fitting pants, belts, patches, and other pieces she could certainly use.

She opened her fist, revealing the needle. Where Konan had gotten one, she could never guess. He surprised her constantly, first with his quiet intelligence and then with his ability to push her onward, to reinvigorate her when all she wanted to do was surrender to the ache inside.

In that sense, he was a paradox. It was obvious he himself had given up. His expressions were dull and sad, his own goals seemingly nonexistent. Yet he insisted on saving her.

The only time she had seen him light up was when he realized she could understand him. In that moment, his brows had lifted, and the golden flecks in his right eye had shimmered against their tawny brown backdrop. The whites had seemed to shine in the dim light, and for the briefest moment, Lyra had seen hope.

She worked to remove her soiled skirt and exchange it for pants, groaning again as pain and nausea swept over her, and she lay back. She couldn't sew much in the dark, so she resigned herself to rest.

Dawn arrived, and with it, Konan.

Lyra entered a new rhythm, in which she assessed what she needed and he helped her. He washed the soiled clothing somewhere, returning with the colorful fabric sopping wet and clean. It dried almost immediately in the parched desert heat, and she incorporated it into her plan. The torn pants could be mended with cloth from a tunic; the legs of another pair could be used as sleeves for the tattered shirt she already wore. The other tunic and skirt could be fashioned into a loose cloak, and additional pieces could be used as undergarments.

She cursed her body as she recalled her need for bindings. Why had Mam praised her precociousness in that area? Lyra hated herself for ever being proud of the admiration she'd garnered dancing. All those suitors, all those slobbering men tossing copper into the air, what had they wanted? She knew now.

"Are you all right?" Konan caught her eye, his brows knotted with concern.

Lyra shook herself from the memories.

She had loved dancing, but now the recall was tainted by an undercurrent of sickening fear.

Pursing her lips, Lyra bent to sewing.

She could feel Konan's gaze weighing on her. It wasn't predatory or malignant, nor did it burrow under her skin or clothing like that of other men, but it was earnest. He had a tendency to only flicker his eyelids, as if closing them entirely might cause him to miss something. He was seemingly aware of everything, of peripheral movement and slight sounds, and he was always tense. She wasn't sure which of his eyes was more observant, for the milky iris quivered across his surroundings just as avidly as the other.

"I've never been so afraid or aware of my appearance," she finally admitted, feeling heat creep up her chest and neck.

Konan nodded and adjusted the fabric as she stitched. It was a slow process, limited primarily by Lyra's own physical state. She couldn't easily sit up or try the clothing on for size. Any attempt at mobility was accompanied by searing pain and nausea, mostly from her rib cage and gut. Konan forced her to rest intermittently, taking over the simpler sewing with an experienced-enough hand.

Several days passed as she regained the strength to get up and dress herself.

Lyra felt the first cautious vestiges of hope in weeks. Despite the lingering pain in her chest, her body was ready to become strong again. Ready to walk, to feel the sun shine upon her face. Ready to use the waste pits on her own.

She felt heat on her cheeks as she looked up at Konan and leaned heavily on his arm, an extra pressure he didn't seem to notice as he led her toward the door. By the Light, the last weeks, month—however long it had been—were certainly the most embarrassing and frustrating she had ever experienced.

They paused at the threshold.

The sun was bright, casting a yellowish-white pallor across everything, including Lyra's sandaled toes. She could feel its warmth already, and she curled her toes with muted pleasure.

Beyond, there were voices. Deep, gravelly voices; harsh voices making caustic commentary; needling, nasally voices.

Konan's forearm flexed beneath her fingers, drawing her attention to his signs. "Overcome it, Lyra. I'm with you."

With a shaky breath, she stepped out. When the sun hit her face, she squeezed her eyes shut against the brightness, then blinked rapidly as she tried to adjust.

They were in a cluster of wooden shanties, walls rife with cracks and splinters, roofs in various states of disrepair. The sandy ground was well-packed from constant traffic, but a fine layer of dust lay over everything, lending a subtle shimmer like a mirage. To the left, an open walkway extended toward the fortress wall in the distance. To the right, the walkway was blocked by another shanty wall, creating a three-sided yard.

Thordrin's gang lounged on the walls and a few roofs: scabby, rough-hewn brutes and vicious-looking, hefty women, all wearing the same vaguely amused leers as they looked Lyra up and down.

Her stomach twisted, and she backed into Konan, startling herself as she felt his body heat envelop her. His cloak fluttered into her face, and she realized she had summoned a gusty breeze.

Thordrin cursed. He was sitting on a barrel along the wall of her shack, one knee propped up on a bag of sand and one stretched out in the sand. He waved a hand. "Damn it, girl. There's enough sand in this fuckin' place, I don't need more."

She reined herself in, and the powdery shine of dust drifted down.

Thordrin dropped his hand and looked her up and down. "Pretty sure the boys preferred your clothes before, maunderer." He snorted laughter at her chagrin, a sound that was echoed by his gang.

"Don't call me that word," she managed. "And don't look at me that way." Her voice was so soft, she doubted he even heard her over the gang's crass laughter.

A dangerous look crossed Thordrin's face. "Love, I'll do whatever I want. Lucky for you, I don't want a fuck from a maundering peasant girl. What I'd do for a good experienced whore, though . . ." His eyes glittered like emeralds, and she looked away.

Her nails dug into Konan's forearm, leaving blood-red crescents indented on his marred skin. She looked up at him with surprise and mouthed an apology, but he didn't reply. Instead he pulled her forward to a shanty with holes in the wall but a sturdy-looking roof. He pried her fingers off carefully.

"We're safe in the west end, Lyra. Stay close, and I'll show you."

He clambered up the pockmarked wall and disappeared over the edge of the roof, then reached down for her.

All her nerves were tingling, prickling across her skin and alerting her brain to danger. Every step away from the shack terrified her; every new face frightened her to her core. She could feel the quivering as palpable in the air as inside, matching her pulse.

Lyra reached for him, and he clasped her forearm firmly and pulled.

One moment, she stood in the yard, and the next she was high above them, raised effortlessly to the roof and settled back on her feet. She turned slowly, peering around Konan to see an endless expanse of desert beyond the edge of the camp, then the west end shanties, a sea of rectangles in poorly planned lines. The fortress wall and its towers.

Lyra spied a man on the edge of her vision as she continued to turn, and then she realized she could smell a peculiar musk of rancid sweat and rotten gums. She started, flinging a defensive hand up with a frightened squeak.

The wind that burst outward from her disoriented Konan, but he didn't loosen his grip.

The other man, however, grunted and flew backward, over the edge, and landed below with a crash. Lyra rushed to look. The watchman sprawled awkwardly across a broken barrel; blood poured from a cut on his skull. He groaned.

Thordrin hooted with merriment, doubled over and clutching his own stomach. Several of his gang members looked up at her, their leers turning to doubt. No one helped the watchman, who whined as his palm came away from his head covered in scarlet.

Lyra stepped back from the edge and glanced back at Konan.

He seemed neither shocked nor amused by the watchman's mishap, more so disinterested. Instead, he began to point things out.

"That line, from that tower to that burnt shack, is the border of the west end. That's the gate you came through, and there's the water well and food window. You have to bring what you mine to trade for rations."

"Is that where you go when you leave?"

Konan nodded and pointed across the camp to where a large, rocky outcropping pushed its way through the sand. "That's the sulfur mine. And those—" His finger swung toward the north, a series of sparkling white flats with people laboring in many of them. "Those are the salt mines. They pump the water into the flats and let it dry, then harvest the crystals."

Lyra took it all in and berated herself for any misplaced hope she might have had in escape. Beyond the camp lay nothing but desert. The sulfur mine was the only rocky outcropping she saw; the rest, to the east, north, and west, was sand. Heat emanated off the salt flats in waves, and the horizon held only mirages of mountains or trees, tempting shapes of the imagination that flickered into nothing when one looked too close.

To the south was the fortress, a high wall studded with watchtowers. She could see at least one man standing in the shade of each roofed turret.

"They watch for runaways, and to make sure workers can reach the mines. Notice how most of the camp is a space away from the fortress wall? They keep it open as a pathway, even with men like Selen or Thordrin guarding their kingdoms." Konan snorted, as if he found that connotation amusing somehow. "Their only job is to ensure we are producing in the mines. Our only job is to work, until we die."

Lyra felt her legs waver, whether with exhaustion or simply from being overwhelmed, she wasn't sure. Konan helped her lower to a sitting position, and they pondered the view silently for a while.

"How can I see my family again, if I can't escape?" she asked, her voice soft.

"There must be a way, with your power," Konan replied. He patted his chest. "You choose when you die, Lyra, in here." Then he gestured northward at the expanse. "Something has to be out there. I'm certain. And southward is the Bleeding Wall, impassable."

"I see nothing but sand, Konan." She reached for his comforting hold and bit her lip, recalling the terrifying malagate cliff. Southward was fruitless, but northward was eternally empty.

His large, callused hands enveloped hers, and he fell into the usual habit of caressing the skin on top with his thumb. At first, Lyra found the touch too confusing, for it stirred a strange feeling inside her of both fear and something else, but she found it oddly soothing. In particular, she knew Konan was doing it absentmindedly, for his focus was on something in the distance, and his eyelids fluttered in that erratic blink of his. He scowled at nothing, and his left side twitched with emotions as he relived some memory.

Finally, in the light of day, she could see him—or at least that which he didn't cover. He wore a short-sleeved tunic beneath a long cloak with a cowl. His face was covered, showing only his eyes, and most of his body was hidden as well. He wore better boots than most, although the toes had given out. Nevertheless, she could see the skin of his forearms, smooth and well-muscled with soft, dark hair. Medium-light skin, but not sporadically freckled like her own. He was young, although he didn't act like it. Younger than Thordrin, she was certain, but battle-scarred and jaded. She shook his hand.

"I'll try, Konan. I'll try to escape, if you'll come with me."

He bowed his head in acknowledgment and returned to his reminiscing, then grimaced at the scene below them.

The watchman had finally stood, and he glared up at them with a nasty look before turning to Thordrin. "Boss, you really ain't gonna do anything about this? I'm bleeding. You should punish that fucking cu—"

Thordrin's white-handled knife sailed into the watchman's gut with a wet thump, and he grunted.

"Don't tell me how to run west camp, you bloody shit stain." Thordrin eased up in his throne. How he had thrown his knife so accurately from a lounging position, Lyra didn't know, but now he gave his full attention to the watchman. In fact, he got up and marched over to the man, grabbed his knife handle, and yanked the blade out.

The watchman clutched at the hole in his abdomen, his mouth turning downward as his breath grew more ragged.

Thordrin wiped the blade on the man's shoulders and tucked it into a sheath at his belt.

"Why, boss?" the watchman managed. His lower lip trembled, and Lyra thought for a brief moment of Elden when he was pouting.

Thordrin grabbed the watchman's collar and began dragging him toward the shack that formed the third side of the yard. The man coughed and retched as his own clothing strangled him. Thordrin propped him against the wall, then made a show of adjusting his collar and straightening his tunic. He brushed sand off the watchman's arms and legs, then stepped back.

"How could central camp know when I planned to patrol the rest of west end?"

Thordrin's challenge hung in the air for moments, and several of his gang snickered. The watchman groaned again.

"Selen may have been a fairly stupid pigfucker, but he did have more than two eyes, didn't he? Not a wise choice of loyalties on your part." Thordrin tapped his dagger hilt in a thoughtful rhythm.

The watchman sobbed, but he made no move to get up. "C'mon, boss, it wasn't me."

"They set a plan of attack not a day after I told you about the patrol. You fucked yourself." Thordrin smiled, still tapping his dagger, then looked up to Lyra. "Love, get down here. Come meet the man who betrayed you to central camp."

Lyra began to shake her head, then saw the warning in Thordrin's gaze and obeyed. Konan lowered her down, her ribs screaming the entire way; then he followed.

"C'mon, love, I don't got all day for you." Thordrin waved her over, his impatience clear. "You got your knives?"

Lyra fumbled, finally pulling a total of five chipped stone blades out of a pocket. Konan had chipped them further down to match each other, making them a set.

"Good. Now throw them." Thordrin gestured toward the pitiful watchman, who merely moaned.

Horror filled Lyra, followed by indignation. She still carried guilt for the previous deaths, even the injuries. Although they were bad men, that wasn't the point. The point was what was in her heart, and I'ya didn't condone cold-blooded murder. She shook her head.

Thordrin narrowed his eyes, then leaned in, his voice dangerously low. "Kill him, girl."

"No." Her mouth formed the word, but hardly any sound came out. She found herself backing up a step and soon ran into Konan.

Thordrin's scrutiny flickered up to Konan, then back to her. With a broad gesture, he spoke up, light humor playing through his deep voice. "I suppose I haven't taught you proper yet, have I? No worries, love. Now's a perfect time for lessons."

He swept the blades from her hand and spun, tossing one into the watchman's stomach, dead center on the belly button. Another flew into his chest, just below the sternum, and a third buried itself in the neck, perfectly centered between the collar bones. The watchman rasped in his damaged throat, hands flailing, unsure which knife to grasp first. He goggled at all three, and then both eye sockets received their own blades with a pop.

Thordrin hooted and raised a fist. "Did you see that, Moony?"

"I saw it, Cap!"

Thordrin strode to the watchman's corpse, which had finally slumped over. He sliced the blade in the man's belly button upward, opening his gut further, then dipped a rag in the blood and painted a large circle on the wall above.

Standing back, he pondered it, then added another concentric circle before he seemed satisfied.

He turned with a wide grin.

"Now we can practice. You'll have to get your knives out, though. I tossed 'em a little deep."

Lyra stared. The target, first a bright red, was already darkening in the dry desert air. It dripped in a few spots, congealed blood making new paths along the splintered wood. Traveling down, down, down toward their origin. The watchman lay with his guts half out, her throwing knives puncturing him like a cursing doll. The scent of stomach acid and waste hit her nostrils.

Sour bile bubbled up from inside, and she convulsed, spewing it onto the sand. Konan grasped her shoulders and eased her down as she spasmed again, all of her body rejecting the violence and blood. Lyra could hear Thordrin and his gang chuckling, but she couldn't do anything but puke till her stomach held nothing but acidic froth and sickly belches. She panted, her ribs screaming anew from the convulsions.

A glance around reminded her of what a wretched place she was in. Thordrin's men watched her with slitted eyes, obviously interested but restraining themselves from any rash action that would result in the watchman's fate. One of them licked his parched lips as he leered. More watchmen stood on the roofs beyond, keeping an eye toward central camp. They would probably come for her again, or maybe Thordrin's own men would, seeing how easy it would be if they could only get her alone.

Konan appeared in her hazy vision, signing. "May I?"

She tried to nod.

Then his grasp tightened, and he swung her into his arms and carried her inside, laying her back on her familiar bed and covering her with a threadbare sheet.

Lyra cried until her ribs couldn't take it anymore. "Why did he do that, Konan?"

"The watchman had to be punished."

At first, she was shocked at his cold response.

"He tests his people constantly, and that watchman was the only one who could have warned the central camp of his absence. It was he who revealed you were alone that night. Does that kind of betrayal not demand punishment?"

"But death? A horrible death, Konan. Killing is a sin; it separates you from the Five-Faced God and disallows you from the higher Gate." Her words sounded empty even to her own ears, full of doctrine but lacking in the conviction they once had.

Konan squinted. "I am already separate. Lyra, justice is not the same as senseless killing. Self-defense is not the same either. You have to embrace these necessities to survive."

Lyra huffed, trying to overcome her emotions and expel the acidic flavor of her own breath. "I can't. You saw."

"You'll learn."

"The men were watching. They'll hurt me the first chance they get."

Konan launched into a series of emphatic motions. "They *have* been watching. They watched the first night, and they have felt your power every day since. They are afraid of what you can do. I've never seen power like yours before."

"It wasn't enough to stop the warden," she whispered, and a turbulent wind screamed outside. She heard surprised shouts, as well as Thordrin's cursing. He pounded on the wall, which did nothing to calm her, and she soon lost control of her breathing.

It heaved in and out, and her world seemed to pulse with it: first outward, then zooming inward, then out again. Everything was blurry and dark. The shack crumbled around her, then exploded.

She was no longer aware of the sounds, only of the sense of the structure around her collapsing—until she felt herself embraced, not too tight, but firm and warm. Lyra tensed at first, but she knew that smell, that musk and heat, and she buried herself in it.

She didn't know how long she wept; time didn't seem to exist. There was a past, certainly, but it was distant and colorful as a dream, and she doubted now whether it was real. Nor did it feel like there was a future. There was only now. And in this now, she was bereft of her joy, her innocence, and her family.

Konan held her, one hand cushioning her springy hair and the other resting on her arm. His shoulders enveloped hers, and she found herself leaning into his broad chest, attuned to the rhythm of his heartbeat. It was steady as a drum.

The shack stopped spinning as she regained her breath, looking up at him in the new stillness.

"Overcome it," he signed. "You must overcome what you feel."

"Why?"

"It's the way of the world, to cut you and feed on your blood, to leave scars that never heal."

Her look in return shifted from doubt to contempt. "Like you? Did you overcome your own pain? Your own scars?" she asked bitterly. Pushing away from his embrace, she scooted back. He was a hypocrite. "You cover your face, but it's obvious you have scars too. Did you magically overcome whatever did that, or magically overcome Isellan's death?"

Lyra subsided, seeing the hurt and anger in his eyes. Discolored or not, they were expressive, and now they returned her gaze like molten metal. The right one leaked a tear, which he blinked away.

Shame flooded over her. "I'm sorry. I shouldn't have said that." She pulled herself into a huddled position, but this time, he didn't reach for an embrace, and she cried alone, knowing she had hurt him with her careless words.

When she stopped, he was still sitting there, watching her. His expression was a little colder, a little stiffer, and she apologized again.

"This isn't about me," he signed, cutting the air with his hands. "And I am not ashamed of my scars. They're a part of me. They shaped me, and they guide me."

After his hands went silent, they stared at each other for a while.

"Then why do you wear a mask?" Lyra whispered.

His hard look softened, and then he looked away. "I didn't want you to be afraid."

She stared, but he would no longer meet her eye, and she finally loosened her grip on her knees and reached out to touch him. First his hand, then lightly tracing the edge of the purpling bruise on his arm. That was her fault. The rough texture and white discoloration of scars wasn't, though, and it disappeared beneath his tunic sleeve. She moved up to the fragmented shamble of cloak and hood, made of frayed brown cloth patched from pieces with the very needle she had used the week before.

Lyra tugged his hood down. Dark hair fell in thick locks on his right side, but the left side on the temple was patchy and pitiable, giving him an uneven hairline. A scar crept up the side of his face and temple, leaving one partial, mal-formed ear, and onto his forehead and the top of his skull; his hair grew haphazardly through the damaged tissue. His left eyebrow was broken as well.

Trembling, she pulled his face covering down, letting it hang loosely from the other side.

His face was terrible. A massive, ridged scar ran up his neck, along his left jawline and up, encompassing the discol-ored eye and a somewhat misshapen nostril. The cheek was rough and pitted, as was his forehead. His wretchedness was nearly unrecognizable, for when he wore a mask and hood, the only thing she had noticed were his brooding eyes. They met her blue eyes now, and she was ashamed at her horror.

"I'm not afraid, Konan, not of you." She could hear the tremor in her words, but they were the truth. "I—I'm not afraid of you." She forced herself to look at him. "Even though I don't understand who you are, where you're from, or why you're here. I don't know anything about you." She traced the pitted line below his eye like a tear, whispering down to the jawline. Then she realized that the scars con-tinued down his neck, connecting with what she had seen on his arm. A gasp of horror escaped her at the extent of his injuries.

A tic spasmed on his damaged left cheek as he regard-ed her sadly. "Whoever did this took away my voice too." His signs were ponderous and deliberate, as though he were moving through water instead of air. A groan escaped his lips. "I would speak to you if I could, Lyra. I would tell you to be strong, to endure, to be patient for the time to come when you can avenge yourself and claim your strength. Claim your scars."

15

THORDRIN BURST IN AS he usually did, throwing a sarcastic comment over his shoulder and smirking at the laughter it induced. He glanced with vague expectation at Konan, then rolled his eyes.

"Your sense of humor is as refined as your face," he muttered, standing over Konan as he carefully stitched a new skein from the leather of Lyra's corset.

"Do you ever have anything nice to say?" Lyra scowled at the man. The expression didn't fit her well. Her features were too open and soft—her chin too round, her lips too full. Hers was a face meant to smile. Instead, she pouted at Thordrin, who returned a mischievous leer.

"Sure, love. What I meant was, your face matches your personality very well." He knelt beside Konan, balancing on his toes. "Seriously, brother, what the fuck happened to you?"

"His name is Konan."

"Whatever." Thordrin waved a careless hand in her direction and peered more closely at Konan's face. "Tell me. *Who* are you? Sir Konan? Master Konan? Yeoman?"

Konan sighed and set the partially made skein aside. "Who are you?"

Thordrin smacked his fingers away. "I don't understand your fucking hand motions, damn it. Why don't you talk?"

Konan gulped back his anger, but his cheek ticced nonetheless.

"He can't, Thordrin," Lyra interjected. She reached for both of them. Her palm on Konan's knee was cool in the stagnant heat of the shack, and she looked from one to the other with a face full of worry.

Thordrin raised an eyebrow and nudged her hand off with a finger. "Well, that's annoying. I take it you can understand him?"

Lyra gave an emphatic nod. "It's the Empire's sign, the same as we use with my cousin Ada, and for communicating from a distance."

"So what did he say?"

"He asked who *you* were."

Thordrin raised his chin and thrust his thick, blond beard toward Konan. "I am Thordrin—*Sir* Thordrin in fact, of the Phantom Guild and sworn to House Crayer."

"Sir?" Lyra's shock echoed Konan's, although she showed it more.

"Damn straight, love. Best of the Kritali High Guard."

"Sworn to House Crayer of Krita?"

"But they're not sworn to me, apparently."

"Why are you here?" Konan asked. Lyra translated like an echo.

Thordrin's expression turned to a snarl, but his tone remained light. "Because no one is truly your friend, girl. No one is trustworthy, and the world is shit. Now, your turn." He looked pointedly at Konan.

"I'm Konan."

"Just Konan? Or are you really an exceptional peasant, blessed with the *exceptional* good grace not to die and cursed with *exceptional* scars?"

"It doesn't matter." That heavy weight of regret washed over him, an unwelcome reminder of the many things he had done and seen since being dumped in Tahayi. Gone was the innocent boy, naive to terror and malevolence, in love with the simple joys of horseback riding and stealing pie from the kitchens and reading with his mother.

What remained was a scarecrow, a man-shaped husk filled with straw and dust, but no more a man than that.

Thordrin narrowed his eyes. "Nethers, you're as dramatic as her. Well, Konan-whoever-you-are, you're more intriguing than the other cunts out there combined. You'll have to tell me eventually. We got a lot of time to kill."

"Not if we escape." Lyra's quiet interjection made both men turn to her. She clamped her mouth shut and pulled her knees up, as if embarrassed by her own audacity.

Konan caught her eye. There it was: that same light he had seen the first night. That fierce tenacity in the diamond blue of her gaze, a color so unique and bright that he still wondered if it was the magika inside her shining through.

The corners of her mouth twitched up as she returned his gaze. Then she looked away, abashed. "I'm ready to try, at least. For my family."

Thordrin scoffed. "Look, love, you're in the safest place in the camp, but no one leaves. There's nowhere to go. Konan's been here . . . I'ya knows how fucking long. Tell her, brother."

"I will help you, Lyra," Konan signed. Something about her, the light in her eyes, was like a match burning in the darkness, a match which lit a candle of hope in his heart. Perhaps he could seek a better life, one where those he loved weren't ripped away in violence and fire, their desiccated remains swept away like grains of sand. Even if *she* didn't need him afterward, at least he would be free. "I will do anything."

"The fuck did he say?" interrupted Thordrin.

This time, Lyra didn't look away, and her lips finally curved into a real smile. By the Light, it was beautiful—and sad. "Konan will help," she said.

"How? And where would we go after that? There's nothing but sand out there." Thordrin was cynical, gesturing out the door and reminding them both of the hopelessness of any plan.

Konan shook his head. Deep down, he knew Thordrin was wrong. "To the north, there is life. I'm certain. The wastes cannot go on forever."

"They can, and they do." Thordrin snorted. "The tribes don't even cross them to harass the mine."

Lyra lit up. "If there are tribes, then there must be something. Water, food, life—like Konan says."

"But we'd have to reach it," Thordrin replied without pause. "And we'd have to escape in the first place. You've seen what they do to escapees. They chase them down on armored idraka, shoot their legs out with an arrow. String 'em up on the gate and let 'em rot in the sun."

"I could try to hide us," Lyra suggested.

Both men considered that for a while. Konan believed she was capable of it, with practice. Her summonings thus far had been chaotic, but rich with power that shivered through the air.

Thordrin looked dubious, scratching his beard. "Dust storms that kill a few men are one thing. To be honest, I've never seen anyone do that before, but . . . can you really do something big enough to hide us? A sandstorm?"

Lyra hesitated. "I've never actually tried."

"I think you can," Konan signed. "I know you can."

Again, that brilliant glimpse of a smile before she faltered. "It will be a while before I'm strong enough."

Thordrin slapped his knees and stood. "That's all right. We need some time to prepare. Yes, I'm coming. I owe some favors in Krita Port. If you help me, I'll help you. Oh wait, you owe me anyway." He flashed a grin at Lyra.

"What do we need to do?" Lyra asked.

"Save up some rations, some water, teach you to throw knives . . . Plenty to do."

"We should acquire more rations," Konan signed. Lyra translated.

"I ain't fuckin' mining," Thordrin replied. "I didn't claw my way up the chain to do drudge work."

"We need enough for a journey. Your men only bring enough for subsistence."

Thordrin and Konan locked stares, and Thordrin cocked an eyebrow. "Well, I ain't fuckin' mining," he repeated. "But, you can take my man Moony. We will need more if the wastes are as endless as they look." He cleared his throat and jutted his chin at the half-made skein. "That was a good idea, brother. Bet you didn't like giving up your corset, did you, girl? Trust me, that water will be more important when the time comes." He smirked once more and left.

Lyra stared balefully at the work in progress that Konan had retrieved. He stitched carefully and tightly, creating a doubled-over seam as watertight as it could be. He knew she would have wanted it back, but leather was a rare commodity.

"Forgive me," he signed.

She wrinkled her nose. "I understand, Konan. I can't imagine something like that cinched on my ribcage now; everything already feels tight." With a long sigh, she lay down stiffly and watched him work.

"Will you tell me who you really are?" she whispered.

His hands were busy. At least, that was the reason he told himself for why he didn't immediately answer.

She rolled over, closer, and leaned her cheek on his knee like a pillow, searching him for answers.

"I am the son of Isellan."

Lyra smiled again, closed her eyes, and slept.

She had nightmares that night, as she often did. They seemed worse than usual, escalating halfway through the night until the camp shrieked with a shrill wind that buffeted the shack wall and poured sand through the cracks.

Konan had no doubt she could summon a sandstorm, if only she learned to control it.

He slept nearby, sitting up with his back against a barrel, between her and the door.

Thordrin, as usual, was elsewhere, possibly with one of his female compatriots, although Konan didn't think so. The man frequently disappeared, wandering through other parts of the camp to stir up trouble or harass prisoners into working for him in the mines. Recruitment, he called it.

Lyra tossed on her makeshift bed, and a desperate, frightened sound emitted between her gasping breaths.

He squinted through the dusty shadows, his eyes stinging.

She rolled again, huffing harder. Her eyelashes flickered over wildly rolling eyes.

Again, he hesitated. Waking one in the midst of such a dream was surely worse. Kneeling next to her, he searched for her hand in the dark and found it. It was clammy with sweat.

Her grip tightened around three of his fingers, and she emitted a shuddering sob and pulled herself into his lap, clinging to the one hand and nestling her cheek on his leg as she had earlier that day. Konan could feel her tears making his pants damp in one spot, but her crying slowed to a whimper as she fell back asleep.

Afraid to move, he remained where he was. He willed his heart to stop pounding and his chest to stop heaving.

The wind outside stopped battering the shack, but she still slept fitfully, moaning occasionally and wincing at some unknown assailant. No, not unknown. Konan had a guess as to who she had seared into her memories.

Hesitantly, he reached out with his free hand, hovering over her head for what seemed an eternity, then stroked the damp hair back from her sweating temple. He tried to make a comforting, shushing sound, but it came out as a low hiss.

Lyra seemed to calm, falling into a deeper sleep, and he breathed a sigh of relief as he ran his fingers over her crimpy hair. It was undoubtedly knotted so he couldn't do more than that without hurting or waking her, but it seemed to help. So he continued, and eventually Lyra stilled along with the winds outside.

He bowed his head, conscious only of the frizzy texture beneath his hand, of the increasingly rhythmic pattern of her breathing as the shack returned to normal, and of the muttered curses of the watchman outside. All was well.

"If I knew I'd get head, I would have stayed." Thordrin's cocky bass shattered Konan's restful sleep like a hammer striking ice. The man leaned over them, his face in Lyra's and his blade tipped to her chin as she slept.

She woke, and a look of fright crossed her face.

"Surprise," said Thordrin.

The timid squeak of surprise that came from her mouth contrasted with the powerful gust of wind that blasted outward.

Thordrin flew backward and hit the wall with a smack, then landed on his hands and knees. Enraged, he clambered to his feet and raised a hand, then realized his knife had embedded in the wall. Laughing, he yanked it out and approached. His voice was ingratiating, fake as nearly every other expression he put on, as one might speak to a wild horse. "What I meant was, *brightest* of mornings, lovely mage. Eaaaasy does it."

Lyra panted, her one hand still extended outward and shaking. Then she lay back down with a frustrated huff and nestled against Konan's leg. "You scared me."

"That's not hard to do. Time to get up." Thordrin's gentleness was replaced with impatience. "If you're serious about learning to defend yourself, you gotta get up and toss some knives." He threw the five chipped blades at her feet, glossy and clean, then spun and left, muttering about how long it had been since a woman was in his lap.

Konan looked down at Lyra. She blushed, seeming to realize she had crawled to him half-asleep.

"Thank you for staying with me," she said, looking anywhere but him. "I couldn't seem to escape last night. It was like running through a dark tunnel, with lights flashing, and I kept tripping on my skirt. Then I was on a stage, but the floor was covered in blood and straw, and the walls were grungy stone instead of open to the air . . ." Lyra cringed.

He brushed her wild hair back from her face, then nodded toward the door.

They emerged to a bright morning, every surface sparkling with a fresh layer of fine sand.

Thordrin waved them over to the far shack, where his target remained painted. The watchman's body was gone. "Hurry up. I don't want to do this later, when the sun bakes our fucking skin off. You thrown a knife before, girl?" He exaggerated his dismay at her silence. "I thought you maunderers were well-rounded. Take out a knife."

Konan gave Lyra's shoulder an encouraging squeeze and stepped back, leaning against the wall to watch.

Lyra fumbled with the chipped stone blades, pulling one out and gripping it tightly.

Thordrin shook his head again, then approached to loosen her hold and adjust her finger position. Konan noticed how he was careful not to startle her, and how the gang members present all scrutinized the scene with more nervous glances than he had ever seen from them before. Thordrin mimicked the motion of a throw, demonstrating how Lyra should do it, and then his knife appeared in his own hand as if from nowhere. He sent it flying at the target, where it pounded into the wood and shivered, its point at the small, blood-marked center.

Lyra swallowed visibly, heaved back with a slight wince, and threw her own blade.

It flew into the ground at her feet, any force (had there been any) muffled by the sand. She sighed, and a pinkish hue crawled up her neck.

Nonetheless, Thordrin indicated she should try again. "Let go sooner, love. Let go right when you're pointing your hand at the target."

Lyra readied a second blade, and Thordrin again adjusted her grasp, then flipped the knife around in her hand. She threw again.

The knife went sailing, clattering against the shack high and to the left before falling to the ground.

Konan could see the pinkish hue darkening into scarlet, up her neck and across her chest and onto her pale cheeks. Her nostrils flared.

Thordrin nodded. "Again. Flick your wrist more, not your arm."

Konan could see Lyra trembling as she fumbled for the third blade. Nevertheless, she adjusted her hold, an attentive student. She really was trying. Thordrin made some minor adjustments before demonstrating the throw once more. She let loose, and this time the knife flew high to the right, and stuck. It was no closer to the target than her second attempt, but Lyra seemed relieved. The tension in her mouth and forehead eased slightly.

Thordrin clapped her on the back, and she shrank from him with a piqued scowl. He seemed immune to her discomfiture, but Konan was certain he knew what he was doing. He continued on as if oblivious to her censure. "Good. Try to think about how hard you threw it, how quickly you moved your arm and turned your wrist. Do it again."

Lyra flushed all over again. "I don't know what I did."

Thordrin hardened. "Again. Don't make me repeat myself, love."

Lyra obeyed, staring doubtfully at the last chipped knife and then at the target. It wasn't far, but that distance could feel like an eternal chasm without experience to bridge it. In reality, Konan couldn't throw knives either. He had grown up fighting with his fists, elbows, knees, and whatever resources were at hand. With good knives being fairly rare in Tahayi, he had about the same level of experience as Lyra when it came to throwing.

A vision of leveling a sword at someone flashed across his memory. Staring down the wooden blade, eyeing his brawny opponent, who wore light armor and an orange cape. Konan blinked. He had some sword-fighting experience, but by the Light, it had been a lifetime ago.

Lyra threw the last knife. It flipped wildly through the air and clattered off the wall.

"By the nethergates, you really are useless," muttered Thordrin.

Lyra bolted toward the shack, crying, chased by mocking laughter from Thordrin's gang, then pivoted toward Konan. She buried her head against his crossed arms. He stood stiff as a board, unsure how to respond.

He glared over her at Thordrin, the Phantom assassin of Krita. Thordrin sneered right back and plopped on his barrel throne, then waved a hand at the target.

"She ain't gonna learn if she's gonna bitch about missing. Everybody misses sometimes. Except me."

"I can't do it," Lyra muttered into Konan's chest.

"Not if you don't practice, love. I've never trained a novice before; I see now how my masters felt." Thordrin's cruel laughter was echoed by his men, but Konan knew he was right.

Lyra pounded her forehead against him. All he could see was her halo of pinkish-blond curls. He uncrossed his arms and pushed her back to see her face. Her eyes were red, and she chewed her lip, giving him a mirthless smile.

"You're going to tell me to try again, aren't you?"

Konan nodded.

Lyra searched his face, and her expression tightened with resolve. "Okay."

She trudged over to the target wall and retrieved each blade, taking her time. Then she returned to the line in the sand Thordrin had drawn and gave him an expectant look.

His smirk looked genuine for once, and he hopped up. "Good. I thought for a minute I'd be bored today." He launched into a lesson, repetitive and interspersed with various insults to Lyra's skillset, but she no longer wavered. At least not at first.

Despite constant intervention from Thordrin, she continuously failed to make anything stick to the wall with regularity, let alone hit the mark. Her frustration manifested as an erratic gust that worked its way outward from their yard, pushing the watchmen off balance enough that they took to sitting. The breeze defrayed the heat of the summer sun as it rose in the sky and intensified, bearing down upon them without mercy.

A part of Konan doubted whether it was truly the Eye of I'ya, for how could it see everything it did and not intervene? On the other hand, it did send its burning rays downward without mercy, a contemptuous treatment of the suffering souls of Tahayi Mines. Perhaps it *was* I'ya, the Five-Faced God.

In the end, Lyra quit in a sweaty fluster. Although she didn't run for the shack, she did sit down in a huff next to Konan, who had been leaning casually against the wall. He slid down to sit next to her.

"Well done."

"I missed almost every time."

"Before today, you had never thrown a knife. Now you have."

She let out a bitter laugh, her tone flooded with self-effacement. "Konan, before today, I've never held a weapon."

He raised his eyebrows, feeling the tautness on the left side, and gave her a look. Lyra returned it, seeming to realize what she had said, and then accepted his compliment.

16

"The myr are the children of I'ya, and the blood cannot be watered down. Our blood *is* Water." Kei smirked at her own reflection in the vanity mirror and primped her black curls.

"A blending weakens the blood, Kei, and you know it!" Furious and disgusted, Taiuki paced behind, occasionally glancing up to verify that Kei was still ignoring her.

"Don't speak to me in that tone, sister." Kei's voice was cold. She spun around in her chair and stood, allowing her to look down at Taiuki by a few fingers. Arching her slim shoulders back, she pushed out her chest for greater effect. "I am queen."

Taiuki snorted. "Crown princess."

Kei glared, but her stature slumped a bit, and her expression tightened. "Well, Mother agrees. It's what's best for us, and your duty."

"My duty is to command the army. My duty is to serve the kingdom. I should return to the front. My duty is *not* Godrig!" Godrig, of all people? The haughty, overbearing crown prince of Krita, the one person she hated more than almost anyone else. Had Kei forgotten everything?

"It's already been arranged."

"No!"

Kei backhanded her without hesitation, and Taiuki staggered back rubbing her cheek. Kei winced and examined her palm, irritated, and adjusted the rings she wore. "You will. You *will* be queen for Krita. You'll live with the landwalkers." Kei smirked. The idea seemed to please her.

Taiuki battled the sting on her cheek and the sudden blur that accompanied it. Tears, in front of Kei? *Fight them.* She shook her head, dispelling the unwanted emotions. "How could you just stand there and do nothing to prevent this?"

Kei turned back to her mirror and continued lacing strings of pearls into the arrangement of curls. She snapped her fingers for help, and Taiuki obliged, waiting for an answer.

"An arrangement with Godrig will assure desirable terms for trade with Krita. They've been getting stingier, you know, and much as I hate to admit it, we need those routes. It's far easier than going across the ol'Loi plains to Marlemet, where we have to worry about Jijito's northern border." Mother's words and reasons and excuses spilled from Kei's mouth as if she were a mockingbird. That coldhearted, seemingly logical explanation that remained at odds with everything a true myr would do.

"And yet *you* cannot have him?" she pointed out.

Kei wrinkled her nose. "Certainly not. The royal bloodline would be polluted."

"And *Tan* will take command of the fleet, of all the armies of Shiggo?" But Taiuki already knew the answer.

"Yes."

"He's still a boy, Kei."

She scoffed and raised her chin, in exactly the haughty manner their mother would have. "Tan is perfectly capable of becoming arch commodore. And you're barely trained anyway. You're not even arch commodore yet; Sashiro is."

"He's a child, and he's afraid of blood."

"So are you, if I recall." Kei laughed and shooed her away from her hair. "You're just making it worse, Yuki." She re-pinned the last few strings until she was satisfied. "Now let me do yours."

Kei pushed her into the plush, cushioned chair. Like everything in Kei's room, it was upholstered in a delicate lavender color and trimmed with brassy ingots.

Taiuki averted her gaze from her reflection as her sister brushed out her hair.

"Kei, you know Tan is no arch commodore. He's been training, but . . ."

Were she or Kei to die or become incapacitated, Tan would step into their rank, as was tradition. But *she* was Second, not Tan. She was destined for it.

Taiuki felt the burn of shame on her face. No. Kei was destined to be arch commodore, and Taifun—she gulped back sour bile—*Taifun* had been destined to be king. He had been brave and strong. And handsome. A tall boy, he would have been a tall man. Their father, Rentai, had been a tall man too, regal and commanding: characteristics Taiuki did not have. In fact, she was a bit small for her age, neither well-endowed like Kei nor broad-shouldered like Taifun. The only things she seemed to have in common with them were her straight black hair and dark, yellow-flecked eyes, but those were characteristics common to all Shiggon-jin. She certainly didn't feel regal.

Still, the soldiers obeyed her in battle, followed her drills, and rarely met her eye. She was fast and strategic. Under Master Sashiro's tutelage, Taiuki studied tactics, geography, history, everything that affected Shiggo's diplomatic and battle approach, with the intent that she would one day replace him. When she wasn't deployed on the border, she trained almost daily with the other soldiers, myrmen and women, in weaponry, hand-to-hand combat, and riding, as well as battle theory and strategy.

Tan attended some of Sashiro's trainings, but they weren't all requisite yet. Although talented, he preferred sword fighting with dulled wooden sticks to the sharp points and metal edges of the sparring ring. It made the process more of a game to him. He'd been instructed to put some of that energy into the pastures and stables where the whale mounts were kept, to muck out slimy corners, a task which he never resisted. Tan enjoyed working with the animals and had a natural way about them, calming even the wildest, newly broken steeds. He had never feared them, even as a baby, as he had never feared the feral beasts that roamed beyond the water gates. Always, he embraced the wild and untamed.

"All I want to do is hunt and ride Nimoka all day," he had lamented.

Taiuki heard the breakage of hair as Kei yanked a knot out.

Her sister scowled. "It's out of my hands, and he'll be fine."

"You like to call yourself queen, but you can't stop Mother? Or you're not willing to try?"

Kei threw the brush down with a clatter, and patches of red colored her flat cheeks. "I'm trying to be nice, but you can't talk to me that way. I *am* going to be queen." She clenched her fists at her side.

"Apparently, so am I."

Kei tried to stare her down, using her standing posture to emphasize her superior position. Her elegant gown certainly matched the part of crown princess and First, cascading behind her in an asymmetrical flare of more lavender. The bodice curved across her form in the myr fashion and glittered with gold thread and tiny clear gemstones that refracted the low light of the underwater caverns. The cloth covering her upper arms and chest was a soft beige, and each elbow fluttered with a serrate flounce of purple silk. Her finely embellished breechbelt was gold, embedded with a nacreous center design like Taiuki's to indicate her royalty, and further supported by an orange gem ringed in diamonds.

Taiuki stared back, neither bothering to stand and face Kei nor retracting her challenge.

She could see Kei's hand twitch with the desire to hit her again.

Then a supercilious smile curved across Kei's lips. "Do you even *know* why we're getting dressed up for supper?" she asked mockingly, knowing full well that Taiuki didn't.

"Mother said a guest was coming. Why it matters, I don't know. We just entered a war, and I have more important things to do than host some Shiggon-jin noble for idle pleasantries."

Her sister snickered. "It's not some noble family. It's Lady Anella. Godrig's sister, from Krita? You look like a dying fish with your mouth open like that."

With a deep, slow breath, Taiuki shut her eyes. "*Why* is Lady Anella going to be here for supper?" Shiggo never hosted landwalkers. Never.

"For fostering," Kei answered flippantly. "She'll stay for at least a year or two."

Taiuki's stomach twisted at this new development. Why in the darkest depths of the Mana Loi would they send Anella here, now? "Who accompanies her?"

Kei continued with a cruel laugh. "Honestly, I don't know how you get by knowing so little. It's quite normal for members of a royal family to foster with another, especially if there's a marriage contract or a trade agreement involved. We have both now. And she's coming alone, although Mother suggested Godrig may come soon."

So Kei and Mother had drawn her from the front, away from the battle she desired with Jijito, placed her in a marriage contract with the crown prince of Krita, and accepted a foster to show good faith. For what? For better trade with a bunch of landwalkers? Taiuki sneered at the thought. No myrkingdom had ever lowered themselves to such a thing, not even Jijito. Blending weakened the blood of the myr.

"It's really not up to you," Kei muttered with scornful disdain.

It's not up to you either. She sighed. Mother would likely get what she wanted. She always did, and Kei didn't help.

Taiuki stood and faced her sister.

Although she was shorter, she was far more fit than the softened First of Shiggo. Kei bore minimal muscle, even in her legs, and her hands lacked the calluses derived from a sword grip or a crossbow. Her smooth copper skin was unmarred by a single scar, for she had dropped her military training the moment Taifun was gone.

Kei quailed the tiniest bit, then gave her a nasty look. "I'm *not* going to finish helping you with your hair. Go get a servant. You should have curled it first anyway."

"You should be ashamed of what you're allowing Shiggo to become," Taiuki said, keeping her voice calm, knowing her comment would result in another slap. It did, and she resisted wincing as she felt the heat flare on her cheek. One of Kei's rings had certainly cut her this time. Without another word, she stepped around her sister. Perhaps Lady Hannaka would help her get ready.

Lady Anella, Princess of Krita, arrived later that afternoon.

Taiuki avoided the fanfare at the port, indicating that late notice had delayed her in getting ready to receive such a guest. In truth, she had gone for a short ride with Hachi, working the jitter out of her limbs and taking the pure, early-summer water into her gills. This season always tasted uniquely floral with the underwater tanko blooms and flowering undercanopy of the kelp forests. Before too long, those flowers, so different from their land counterparts, would morph into solid tanko apples and savenberries.

She rushed back, knowing lateness to the meal would be punished, and changed into ceremonial clothing in the vein of the Tatami line. Far more traditional than Kei's dress, her azure skirting hugged her hips and hung just to her knees in front, with its primary decoration being the beading and gemstone chains of her breechbelt. The back of the skirt ruched tight to her rear, then flared out behind, hanging only to her ankles. Her tight bodice glittered with drapes of gemstone chains, and her sleeves were long and equally close-fitting, down to the ruching at her forearm. She chose turquoise for her necklaces and bracelets. Combined with the azure, they declared the beauty and perfection of the Way of the Current, of the myr lifestyle.

"Stunning," murmured the middle-aged woman who was primping her hair. "No time to curl, but you'll look incredible nonetheless."

"Myr do not bear curls when they come from the womb," Taiuki replied. "I don't see why I need them now. Traditional style, Nurse Hannaka. I want it no other way."

"Very well, Yuki-sho." The woman tittered as she pulled Taiuki's lengths up and pinned them. "It's just, I thought it would look so nice if you and Kei-sho matched."

Taiuki resisted shaking her head at the motherly woman. Hannaka had cared for her as long as she could remember, back to the murky years she intentionally avoided in her mind. The time *before Hannaka* was foggy like a summer upwelling, half-rotten with the carcasses of the dead and drenching everything in the slime of decay.

Hannaka was the only other person besides Tan who used the epithet "sho" to imply her affection. It sounded strange on the woman's lips after so many years of receiving military deference.

"Turquoise and diamond comb."

"Cape?"

"The azure silk."

Lady Hannaka affixed an elegant traditional length of blue gauze to a rondel at the center of Taiuki's back, allowing the train to drape down like a flaring fin. A riotous mix of blue shades, the silk cape could easily be removed should she decide to shift to swimming.

True to the situation of meeting a potential adversary, her outfit allowed for no hidden weaponry, unlike Kei's looser gown. It was a diplomatic, highly traditional choice from that perspective.

Tan knocked and entered without waiting.

"You about ready?" He grinned as he settled on her bed, mussing the covers. He was likewise well-dressed in a two-toned, layered skirt that reached his knees. His tunic was similar to hers but without ruching on the sleeves, and he wore a scaled vest over top in iridescent blues. A cape hung over his shoulders as well.

"You don't have to do your hair," she answered, moving to get up.

"Even so, I was dressed two bells past, and met her at the castle gate." His mischief faltered at her glower. "She seems nice, Yuki. You should give her a chance."

"She doesn't belong here," she retorted. "Let's go."

They moved on to other subjects soon enough, and they burst into the Great Hall laughing.

A stiff assemblage awaited them at the tables, and Taiuki swallowed back her mirth.

Queen Regent Furuhaki glared them into their seats, then nodded at Wehan to announce them. Afterward, she said in a falsely sweet voice, "I apologize for that interruption, my dear. You were saying?"

A girl younger than Tan nodded politely from her seat next to Kei. Her posture was excellent. "Grace be to them and you, Your Royal Highness. I was only saying that my father and mother offer their greetings and I'ya's blessings, and that they are very pleased to convey their desire for greater connections between Krita and Shiggo."

"We are so happy to have you here in our court," the queen regent replied graciously. "You are *most* welcome."

The girl looked around, first at Kei, who smiled sweetly, then at Taiuki, whose expression must have made her uncomfortable, because the girl quickly shifted her glance to Tan. Tan gave her a spritely grin.

"You know, you are the first foster we have had in a long time," the queen regent continued in a motherly voice. "The children will be ecstatic to get to know you."

The first foster ever, thought Taiuki with untempered disapproval.

"And I them," the girl assured Mother. "I have always wanted to visit a myrkingdom." She smiled awkwardly, seeming unsure whether she had stumbled socially with the brazen statement.

Taiuki certainly took offense to her careless words. As if they were animals in a bestiary, displayed for entertainment and gleeful commentary.

Kei masked her reaction with an even broader smile, and Mother changed the subject to Anella's travel companions, who would remain with her. A few servants were all, and their names glossed over Taiuki's mind without sticking. King Rigaran and Queen Déllani had sent their daughter to Shiggo with a minimal delegation, and apparently expected their carriage and driver to be returned to the ship. However, Anella had come with chests of clothing and books, and a landwalker mount that she seemed very fond of.

They ate supper with a few more guests to whom Anella was introduced: Master Mariner Apakun—the commodore of ships—and Marshal Kinota, master of the stables above and below the ocean surface. Anella's eyes widened at Kinota's introduction, but she regained her composure in a blink, straightening in her chair and clearing her throat. She used her forks out of order, Taiuki noted, and she seemed not to know when certain items were meant to be eaten by hand.

Tan was still learning some of those minutiae as well, although she noticed he offered to help the girl immediately. Taiuki shook her head again.

"Would you like a tour?" Tan offered enthusiastically when supper was over.

Anella dipped in a polite curtsy. "Yes, please, Your Highness." Then she faltered. "Actually, the trip was very long. Beg pardon, but perhaps we can look at my apartment?"

Tan laughed. "It's just Tan. You can call me Tan." He offered an arm, but Kei beat him to it.

She curled her arm around Anella's and gushed at her. "We can go anywhere you'd like, Princess. It is our castle after all."

Despite Anella's youth, she nearly matched Kei's height, but the fawning look she gave the First immediately illuminated their age difference. Her smile turned bright. "Forgive me for saying so without knowing you better, but you are *so* beautiful, Your Highness." She looked at Taiuki. "As are *you*, Your Highness. I've never seen eyes like yours before."

She seemed to bite her tongue at Taiuki's stiff expression, but Kei didn't notice. Instead, Taiuki's sister preened a little, tossing her chin back and primping stray hairs that didn't exist.

Tan snorted a little, and when Kei turned a glare on him, he merely shrugged and made a gesture. *You're not the ugliest.*

"Ignore my baby brother," Kei said, returning her attention to the younger girl. "Thank you for your kind words. I love your dress. Is that the new fashion in Krita?" She prattled on, forcing Taiuki and Tan to follow behind.

They wandered from the Great Hall through the adjacent galleries, which featured stately windows overlooking the sea and adjacent beach gardens. Anella marveled politely at it all, but then she paused at the opening to one of the massive stairwells that led to the lower levels.

"Do you want to go down? The Lower Market is still open," Tan suggested.

Anella's breath seemed to catch in her throat, easily observable given the wildly revealing cut of her dress. The girl was barely a woman, and yet the Kritali would have her display herself as crassly as a worn-out camp whore.

Anella shook her head. "No, thank you. Perhaps some other time. I'd like to get my bearings a little better first. Which way did you say my room was?"

A subtle flash of resentment crossed Kei's face as she slid her gaze from Anella to Taiuki, who looked away in shame. Anella, sister of Godrig, had to know all about the past encounters between House Crayer and House ol'Kada ol'Tatami.

"That's all right," Tan declared with an encouraging grin. "We have all the time in the world to show you. I know land-wa—er, people from the land kingdoms aren't used to being below surface level." His cheeks turned bright red from his stumble, and he pushed ahead of the group. "I know where your quarters are. I had Steward Wehan bring your things up already."

Anella nearly tripped on her skirts to follow him, obviously relieved. "Do you know where my horse is stabled?"

"Absolutely, I can show you after this. Did you ride her most of the way?" As usual, he was interested in the new animal more than anything else.

"Of course she didn't," Kei snapped. "She took a ship from Krita."

Tan's blush returned. "I meant from the docks."

"The crossing was pleasant, less than a week to the port on a galleon." Anella remained gracious, smiling at Tan. "Then I took the carriage to the castle, but I hope to ride my horse frequently now that I'm here, if that's okay. Riding is my favorite part of the day."

Kei pursed her lips. "See how stupid boys are, Anella?" She rolled her eyes at the girl, whose mouth dropped open in shock.

They reached her apartment, a room designed for land-walker guests. Situated in the outer bank wall's southeast-ward-facing tower, it gained warm sun for most of the day through massive windows. Each panel was carefully poured glass from Litis, a piece of artwork in itself with colored bits reminiscent of the city temple. The room decor was a purplish burgundy with elaborately woven carpets and duvet, gossamer purple curtains around the bed, and large paintings with gentle scenes of ladies sewing and chatting, or sitting under a tree with their adoring lover. It seemed like a landwalker room.

Anella's trunks of belongings sat in the corner, while Lady Hannaka industriously unpacked, arranging the princess's clothing in the wardrobe and dresser.

"This is matron-in-waiting Lady Hannaka," said Kei in introduction.

Hannaka paused her work and touched her forehead. "Welcome to Shiggo, dearie," she said warmly.

"She's Tan's wetnurse," added Kei.

"Not anymore," Tan protested. His face reddened—it seemed he realized how rude that may have sounded to the nurse. "I mean, she was."

Kei laughed, but Hannaka merely ruffled his hair and addressed the newcomer. "I'm their caretaker, dearie, and yours. Anything you need, I'm here."

Anella nodded and smiled, giving a small curtsy. "Pleased to make your acquaintance, Lady Hannaka."

"Dearie, you can call me Nurse. The other children do."

"Oh, I mustn't," said Anella, dipping into another nervous curtsy.

Hannaka's noble background and elder status did demand a formal title, but Taiuki never used it. She was just "Nurse."

Kei changed the subject, bidding the matron-in-waiting return to her work with a flick of her hand. "Tell us about Krita. How are your brothers?" She arranged herself comfortably on the long chaise by the window. The others, including Anella, sat in cushioned chairs.

"They are well, thank you for asking," Anella replied. "Godrig has been very busy working with Father, and Branig has been spending more time with the master mariner. He likes sailing."

"I remember Branig," Tan butted in, as if trying to resurrect his dignity. "He met Apakun last time he was here with the trade delegation. I'm surprised he didn't come with you."

Anella blushed. "He told me about Master Apakun, but . . ."

"What?" Kei asked.

"He's afraid of water, a little," she admitted. "Otherwise he would have loved to spend more time here."

Taiuki scoffed. Afraid of water? That was like being afraid of air, or the sun. Landwalkers were not only strange, but also foolish.

"Taiuki." Kei tried to stare her down with a scathing look, like one would give an errant child. Another thing she had learned from Mother.

Taiuki couldn't hold back. This girl didn't belong here, any more than Taiuki belonged in Krita. "Krita is an island country, borne of water. How could he be afraid? And how is he going to be a mariner?" How could one govern an island while fearing the sea? The entire concept was absurd.

Anella looked down at her neatly clasped hands and didn't answer.

Landwalkers. Taiuki couldn't hide her scorn, and she didn't try to. They were as silly as their horses. She didn't understand Kei's disapproval, but she guessed it had to do with making a positive impression. To a landwalker? Especially this one, the younger sister of Crown Prince Godrig?

Taiuki crossed her arms and leaned back in her chair, glaring evenly back at her sister.

Kei shook her head, just enough for Taiuki to see, then moved the conversation along with a light voice. "What else can you tell us from back home? Anything interesting?"

Anella searched for something to talk about, but she was clearly out of sorts. She swallowed a few times before stuttering, "There's some sort of sickness going around. Godrig called it a plague."

Tan and Kei perked up. Taiuki pretended not to be interested, but she listened closely.

"Some kind of *madness*," Anella continued, looking more confident as they gave their attention. She paused. "I'm not supposed to talk about it."

Kei leaned forward. "Madness?" she repeated, urging the princess into more gossip.

Anella pursed her lips and adjusted her clasped hands, now gripped even tighter.

"We won't tell anyone," said Kei, "but royals should share this kind of information. For the kingdoms' sake."

Bolstered, Anella leaned forward and spoke low enough that Hannaka couldn't hear. "It infects the common folks. Godrig says it's because they're weaker of mind."

"That would make sense." Kei nodded her encouragement.

Not to mention they're only human, Taiuki thought, *without the gift of Water in their blood.*

Anella spilled everything she knew. Three families murdered by their own household members in the outlying villages, eight suicides, and an uptick in violence in the capital. Rumors of cannibalism and desecrated bodies. The Temple was working to quell the issue, but so far without success. Anella's own Temple mage had been so busy, he had paused her daily ecclesiastic lessons.

"Is it contagious?" asked Tan, his eyes wide.

"Godrig says it isn't for us," said Anella, "but it seems to be spreading through the poorest neighborhoods. Of course, we could become victims if we lived among them."

The circle grew quiet as they pondered that possibility. Kei looked at the little girl with what appeared to be respect; she loved intrigue, and this one was especially good.

Taiuki measured the Kritali girl more dubiously. Anella couldn't have been a year or two off Tan's age. Although she was slightly shorter and plumper than Taiuki's brother, she was tall for her age. Her skin was much lighter, but her hair was still dark. Its rich brown hue reminded her of the expensive roasted nuts they received from Tamorín. Anella's face was round with the chubbiness of youth, and her body immature. The harder Kritali features revealed in Godrig and Branig's faces—square jaw and protruding cheekbones—didn't show on her yet. With any grace, they wouldn't. Anella had a soft, kind face.

That didn't change Taiuki's opinion of her, however. Anella was borne of the same union as Godrig. Fostering her here, in Shiggo, could only have one purpose: to smooth over the relationship between the two kingdoms until a marriage contract could be worked out and fulfilled. Myr *never* fostered landwalkers. In fact, they rarely fostered at all—it weakened family units. Although, there were occasional long visits from Fumaya and Nagawa. This had to be an innovation of Mother's, attempting to emulate the

Kritali ways to garner their friendship. It disgusted Taiuki far more than anything else her mother had done.

She stood and made an excuse about reading her histories. As she paced to the door, Anella called out, "It was lovely to meet you, Your Highness. I pray you sleep well."

Taiuki didn't look back or reply.

MONON H. SAND

17

TAIUKI WHEELED HER HORSE around to check on the progress of the others.

Marshal Kinota wanted her to ride her land mount more frequently, but she found it far less enjoyable than leaning into Hachi's hydrodynamic, powerful form, cutting the current and finding new joys in the Mana Loi. Horses were foolish, emotional creatures without an ounce of the intelligence shown by Hachi or Nimoka. Not to mention the awful jolt of riding on land. Master Sashiro insisted there was a fluidity in it if you had the proper form, but it certainly did not come naturally like it did underwater. Taiuki noticed, however, that the arch commodore frequently handed them off to Marshal Kinota, who was younger and far more comfortable on the land beasts, for horsemanship.

Taiuki smirked. As strongly as he encouraged cross-training, Master Sashiro had his own preferences, and he rode his blue Benn almost exclusively.

As if to exacerbate her annoyance at landwalker riding, Lady Anella accompanied them. Her white teeth gleamed from here as she laughed at Tan's jokes and enthusiastic gestures. At least Kei hadn't wanted to come, and they were shadowed only by a few distant riders: Anella's maidservants and a single Shiggon-jin escort assigned to her.

How Taiuki had wanted time alone with Tan-sho.

She huffed, and her horse pranced beneath her in an echo of her irritation. The two finally caught up.

"If we don't hold an adequate pace, we won't reach the shrine before the afternoon prayer," she said, turning a cold look upon Anella.

The princess blanched and apologized. "I'm so sorry, Your Highness. I didn't realize. We can canter if you please."

Taiuki looked the girl up and down. She wore a Kritali riding dress, an overlayered behemoth of skirts subtly split up the back to allow her to sit astride her saddle. Her feet barely showed in the stirrups, so tangled were they in shrouds of gauze and cloth. "*Can* you do so, Princess?"

Anella gave a quick nod, but her eyes flickered down to Taiuki's unencumbered legs, then away.

Tan must have noticed too. He was observant like that, which would serve him well in the field. He trotted up to her with a kind smile. "You're a fair rider, Anella. But if you want better riding clothes, we can easily provide them for you."

Anella's lips twitched, and she stuttered. "I appreciate that, but I'm not allowed to wear such revealing— I mean— Oh, I'm so sorry, Princess Taiuki, I don't mean to offend. I can't wear what you wear, though." She heaved a sigh and examined her saddle pommel.

Tan shrugged. "Why not?"

Anella's eyes widened. They were an interesting shade, reminiscent of the aquamarine of the southern coves and ringed with a darker cerulean. Did Godrig have those eyes? Taiuki didn't remember his being striking, not that she'd really looked.

The princess took a deep breath. "Please forgive me for saying, but I couldn't possibly reveal that much of my skin. It's . . . not allowed."

"Oh." Tan shrugged again. "Well, you're not in Krita, Nelly."

"Am I supposed to abandon what I've been taught, being here?" She seemed near to tears all of a sudden, but she kept looking to Taiuki instead of Tan for an answer.

The girl's confusion was incendiary, but Taiuki's anger wasn't directed at her, despite the snarl of disgust that overcame her expression. *Am I meant to abandon everything I've been taught for Krita?* She forced a slightly kinder look. "Perhaps we should trade outfits," she managed sarcastically.

Tan snorted, and a slight look of relief crossed Anella's face. She gave Taiuki an open smile. "Perhaps we should." She blushed hard. "I really *can* gallop if you need me to."

Taiuki restrained her with a light touch on the reins. Her own doubts and frustrations reeled through her mind, an amalgamation of hatred for Kritali expectations, resentment at being thrust into a foreign culture herself, and frustration at her lack of agency to stop it. She leaned toward Anella, her gaze intense. "Do what you are comfortable with, Princess. Adopt our ways if you choose, or don't. You are not Shiggon-jin and never will be, but at least learn and respect our ways, and respect yourself."

Anella nodded, touching Taiuki's hand. A thousand questions seemed to shimmer in those watery eyes, but she didn't ask any of them. Instead, she thanked Taiuki. "I really like it here. I'd like to learn more, if that's okay."

They cantered the rest of the way to the Shrine ol'Noriko, a smaller place of prayer built in the center of a vast water garden on the far end of the city. Anella marveled at the place, praising the lotus-covered pools and curving, asymmetrical edges. The area felt both wild and manicured, a unique combination reflective of myr architecture. Swaths of color filled every nook, bursting with freshly bloomed flowers and carefully clipped greenery. The air was fragrant with lilac and cherry blossoms.

"Feel free to explore," Taiuki instructed, "but do not enter the shrine out of respect for our Way."

Anella's face fell, but she agreed.

Tan gave her an encouraging smile and brought her hand to his forehead in a gesture of respect. "It's all right, my lady. We won't be long. You can go anywhere in the garden, just not the building."

Taiuki nearly dragged Tan into the shrine, where they knelt for prayers with several others. After the necessary rites, she pulled him deeper, to a private corner.

"Feeling devout today?" Tan said with a smirk.

Taiuki gave him a look. "I needed to talk to you, Tan-sho. Why did you invite her?"

"She's lonely, and she likes riding." He shrugged. "What's so bad about her?"

"She's different."

"So what?"

Taiuki grimaced and realized how pale her brother's light brown skin was beneath her grip. He said nothing as her nails dug into his bicep. She released him. "Tan, who am I without my rank?"

They sat on a bench in the dark corner, and Tan released a breath. "I've never seen you unsure of yourself before," he murmured. "You're still you."

"But if Mother follows through on this, and Kei doesn't stop it, I'll never fight again. I'll never lead Shiggo to victory against Jijito, and I won't be able to protect you."

He was quiet for a while, his face contorted with thought. "Mother said you should support me in my new role, right? Why not obey, by helping me? I need help, I think."

"Train you?"

The idea matured quickly into a plan. If she dedicated herself to mentoring Tan, he would not only benefit, but she could demonstrate her own ability, her own aptitude. She could continue showing the people of Shiggo that she was the right choice to become arch commodore upon Sashiro's retirement. Strange to even consider it a choice, of course—it was the traditional way, with no exceptions. But she could continue working with her men and women, developing rapport with the troops and solidifying her leadership.

She mussed Tan's hair, then hugged him. "You never did take it seriously enough, Tan-sho."

He slicked his hair back down with a mock scowl. "I have to now, I guess. But at least then you'll be with me."

"Until they finally ship me off." Taiuki frowned. The true issue wasn't anywhere near resolved. She could mentor Tan all she wanted, yet in the end, she still might prove nothing to Mother. *Conform, Princess.*

Being obedient to this assignment flew in the face of myr tradition.

No myr had ever contracted marriage to a landwalker nation, blending royal lines from different peoples. It simply wasn't done. And as far as she knew, no Second had ever been denied their station. These precepts formed the solid foundation upon which the myr had built a powerful society. They ruled the Mana Loi and every other ocean in Midgate.

Tan shook her shoulder. "Hey, they'll see, Yuki. They'll see you're the obvious choice. I don't want to be Second."

They emerged from the shrine together, and Tan got a panicky look on his face until they found Lady Anella wandering along a meandering path between pools in the far north corner.

She smiled brightly. "This shrine is one of the most beautiful places I've ever been. Did you say Noriko was a warrior queen? How can that be?"

Taiuki raised an eyebrow.

"Queens can't be warriors, right?" Anella seemed genuinely confused.

"Noriko Tatami was one of the greatest warriors of all time," said Taiuki sharply. "She was the second in line, so she was trained as a soldier before she married Kenji."

"But . . . women can't be soldiers," Anella protested.

"Of course they can," Taiuki snapped. Shiggo's military force would be half the size without women.

Anella looked embarrassed and confused. "Like that Reihotto and Marshal Kinota?"

"Vice Commodore Reihotto," Taiuki corrected her, "and yes."

Tan intervened. "Maybe it's different in Krita," he said. "Here it's more about birth order."

"So the second-born is a soldier?" Anella really was trying to understand, and Taiuki realized how cruel she was being to the girl. It was a hard habit to break, for everything about Anella reminded her of her engagement to Godrig.

Of course Kritali wouldn't understand their ways, and it wasn't Anella's fault she had been raised differently. Those landwalker traditions were the same ones that irked Taiuki now as they were foisted on her, traditions she would be forced to learn in order to marry the crown prince of Krita.

Taiuki sighed. "The first in line is trained for leadership of the castle and kingdom, as either king or queen," she explained, forcing herself to have more patience with the girl. "The second-in-line is trained for leadership in battle, as arch commodore."

"So shouldn't *you* be arch commodore?"

Taiuki and Tan locked gazes. Tan looked beyond apologetic, his cheeks flushed and his forehead wrinkled with worry.

Anella noticed. "Sorry," she whispered. "I'm third-born, you know, and a daughter. So I don't really matter either, not in Krita."

Dawn broke in Shiggo City much as it always did, with a dull gray luminescence seeping through the depths to reach the lowermost portal of the city. The Sanctuary Portal was ironically named, as no one came down this deep. No one sought its harsh pressure change, its bleak darkness and mystery, except Taiuki.

As the deepest in the city, the Sanctuary Portal sat at the distant end of the air-filled tunnel network of city ways, far beyond the Lower Market's bustle, away from the farms of the Whale Gate, and so secluded one might not realize the capital of Shiggo sprawled many levels above them.

Although the darkness intimidated some, it was the great pressure and cold that limited most from using the portal. Relatively few myr could tolerate the pain of shifting when passing through, going from a world of air to one of water, from feather light to deathly heavy. It collapsed the air from one's lungs, seared the eardrums, and churned the insides to nausea. When Taiuki entered that deep, it was like the weight of the entire world on her shoulders. She had practiced incrementally, moving from shallower portals to the deeper ones over the course of years, honing and refining her form shift and increasing her tolerance of the change.

It still hurt, but she embraced the pain. She owed the sea a penance in Taifun's name, and the splitting of her ears was the least she deserved. *Blood for Blood,* she whispered. *For you, Tai.*

She stood inside the Sanctuary Portal, silently watching the dark ocean beyond as it lightened to a deep slate gray. This was as much light as she would get. She might as well get going.

The sunken lands were fascinating, mysterious, and beautiful in their own way. Many considered the ocean bottom this deep to be a wasteland, a desert of death and detritus, but she didn't see it that way. Every rock was covered in tiny crustaceans and a crust of colorful growth; fish entirely unique to this depth zipped in and out of cracks and picked at her fin with curiosity. Farther on, bizarre-looking tubeworms grew in fields, and soft-bodied creatures floated, never ascending to the higher zones.

Taiuki had missed the land beyond the Sanctuary Portal during her deployment against Jijito, but now she was aggrieved to face it, for the only reason that she *could* explore was because she wasn't to be redeployed soon. Mother had ignored all of her requests for an audience, and Kei had laughed her out of the room with a cruel, mocking sound, refusing to listen to logic. Only Tan-sho listened and commiserated. If only Taifun were alive.

Whenever she couldn't get him off her mind, she came here, seeking whatever remained of him.

With a slow, calming breath, she stepped through the portal. The sea closed in around her body, pushing and straining to crush her fragile human bones, expressing all of the volume from her lungs in a spasm. She focused on the water, muttering as she summoned the powerful magika of the myr to shift. Slowly, her body equalized. Her bones hardened and compacted. By then, her fins had reformed, bursting from her skin in translucent waves. Her caudal fin was naturally dark with white and yellowish tips that matched the flecks in her eyes, a common color for Shiggon-jin myr. The scalelike texture of her tail shimmered up to her hips and faded out at her navel. She floated comfortably in the pale dawn light, breathing in the freshness of unpolluted, wild water.

She peered into her surroundings, the water speckled by fallout drifting downward like lazy snowflakes from the sky.

The ocean bottom was not far, she knew, but it descended rapidly toward the Lai'akala Trench. That was her destination.

Taifun, if you're there in the current, please tell me if what I'm doing is right.

The prayers at the Shrine ol'Noriko were empty of feeling or fervor, but this plea was earnest.

She cracked her wet lantern, and the fusion of ingredients glowed into a sudden ball of light, illuminating the path downward. Directly below the Sanctuary was an area rich in carboniferous spouts, which emitted steam and pale-cream molten rock. The spouts were laden with life, carpeted in clams and crustaceans, as well as an odd purple seaweed that grew in low, tangled mats. The seaweed beds harbored massive numbers of small fishes, particularly longworms and eels and blackeyes. The blackeyes were a deep fuchsia, with a black spot on their cheeks reminiscent of the black streaks at the base of the seaweed stalks.

Taiuki had only to keep watch for one creature, the eclipse jellyfish, a massive animal with a large, round body and bioluminescent tentacles. Although its tentacles were shorter than most jellyfish, its body was large enough to completely envelop a grown myrman, and its soft grasp was inescapable. Some said it was a star flung from the heavens by I'ya. The pulsing glow of its thin tentacles certainly reminded one of a star, but that legend was nonsense.

Light did not come down this deep, and Taiuki didn't particularly believe I'ya did either. Although the Way of the Current touted I'ya's true form being water, no one could deny his Eye traveling across the sky every day. I'ya was a god of the sky, if such a god existed, and the sky stopped far above. The sea was impenetrable, and the bottom was a kingdom of shadows, bursting with its own kind of life that thrived without sunlight. Taiuki admired the tenaciousness of the creatures that persisted here.

She held the wet lantern in front of her. The rocky desert lay before her now, a short stretch peppered by ghostly rock formations. She thought them almost cairn-like, as though someone had piled them perfectly and purposefully in celebration of the gods—or perhaps in mourning for the dead. A few considerably sized squids patrolled these rocks, jetting along the borders of their respective territories obsessively. They had attacked Taiuki the first time she had ventured here, but her knife and jiansword had defended her well enough. From that time on, she swam over the formations, and they ignored her.

At last, Taiuki reached the trench. It yawned before her, blacker than any night and countless fathoms deep. Taiuki paused. She held out the lantern, and her arm was shaking.

It's just the cold, she told herself. *It's just very cold.*

She drifted down to the sea floor, peering hesitantly over the edge. It was the furrow in the brow of Father Mana Loi, a crevice that stretched a distance beyond knowledge across the sea to the west and southeast. Taiuki had never come so far before, but she needed . . . something. To find a connection to the sea, to find that connection to Taifun that she had lost so long ago.

Tai, why did you have to leave me? If only you were here, I would be Third, and Tan would be able to continue being just a boy. He's hardly ready, and I'm terrified for Shiggo and for him.

Beginning a cautious descent, she kept to one side as much as possible so she could feel the reassuring brush of stone on her fingers. She passed by a bubbling funnel that was leaking white-hot lava; strange fish huddled around the stream, nipping at the small, nektonic crustaceans that danced in the heat. A spiny anglerfish eyed her querulously as she passed by in wonder. She gazed upward as the lava community faded away and the only light once again was from her lantern. Taiuki was shaking uncontrollably now, her arms spasming and her fingers twitching.

Why have I come here? she thought. *Why do I search the frozen depths while Kei bathes in the sunlight? I don't even know what I'm looking for.* Mother had said that she'd chosen this foolish, dangerous pastime of exploring the depths because she was a selfish deviant. Kei agreed.

You're looking for me. She was certain she was imagining Tai's voice (and smile), for he was long gone. The depths could do strange things to the mind, a combination of great pressure and darkness. Still, Tai's words were comforting. All that he had been was here, dispersed in the Mana Loi in a violent water burial. His regal look of pride, the breadth and bearing of his shoulders—Taifun, firstborn of King Rentai and Queen Furuhaki, had been a clone of Father.

Taiuki's stomach twisted with grief.

I need you, brother, she lamented. *I have never disobeyed an order, but I cannot accept these machinations of Mother's. They are not the Way.*

The ocean didn't answer, and she felt the sting of invisible tears. Perhaps this deep exploration was folly. There was no reason to go so far save for curiosity, and she wouldn't find Taifun down here any more than she would find him at the surface. He was gone with the current.

Tan thought it was fascinating, leaning on her for descriptions of what she found, of the phenomenal natural beauty of the underworld, and that was the only truly motivating factor that told her to stop. Her little brother (and her people) needed direction, not needless risk-taking. Tan needed a positive example.

And a mentor, she thought acerbically, shaking herself back to the present. *A mentor for his new appointment as Second. By the current, I'm not even a commissioned soldier anymore! What am I?*

She trembled from the cold that seeped into her bones, moment by moment turning blood into ice, then took one more long look at the never-ending depths below her. The Lai'akala Trench went on and on. Little could be seen, only rocks and motes of fallout sinking down from the pelagic zone. Taiuki's lamp barely reached beyond a few lengths. It was time to go back up. She could warm herself near the volcanic seepage, then return to the Sanctuary Portal.

Farewell, brother, Taiuki thought to herself. *May I see you again, when the current finally takes me.*

Farewell, Yuki-sho.

She swung her lantern around and hissed as a terrifying glow lit up in front of her, flashing its multiple layers. Her lantern pushed into cushiony flesh, and the circle yawned around her. Startled, she dropped the light and went for her knife.

The wet lantern sank away, disappearing into the trench. The only light came from the eclipse jelly's tentacles pulsing in a disorienting pattern. Taiuki stabbed all around her, even as the cushioned body surrounded her. The jelly flesh seemed to give without splitting, no matter how many times she thrust her knife into it. She grabbed at the tentacles, but they were slippery and sent searing twinges of electric shock through her. Panic unlike anything on the battlefield devoured her.

One remained in her grasp long enough for her to shear it from the jellyfish's body, but it continued burning in her hand. She grabbed another stinging tentacle and cut it as well. Her eyes hurt, and she was forced to close them. Taiuki could already feel her skin burning. The digestive juices were too strong now; she could feel her skin corroding. She fought furiously, nicking everywhere with her knife and occasionally slicing something. Though she dared not open her eyes, she could taste blood in the water. Her blood.

A new assault of fire burned onto her eyes, and she tried again to close her eyelids in the darkness. It felt strange, as if there was little to close. Her muscles spasmed, and the shaking in her limbs became exaggerated. In a stupor of pain, she continued to fling her knife, but all she could focus on was the flavor of her own flesh and blood in her mouth and gills.

"You're afraid of blood too," Kei laughed in her mind.

Blood for Blood. Blood in the water. Her mother was lecturing her again.

"No blood in the water," the queen regent had said severely, "or someone else will die."

"I can swim fast enough, Mother," she had answered.

Mother slapped her, then pointed at her sister and baby Tan. "You may be able to, but they can't."

"We were only playing, Mother," she replied with tears springing to her eyes.

Mother slapped her on the other cheek. "If you can't take care of your siblings, then play by yourself. *No* blood in the water."

The intensity of the memory was like a hallucination, and Taiuki brought her screaming hand up to protect her face from another slap, shaving the watery body with her knife again.

Suddenly, the gelatinous body opened back up.

Taiuki drifted out, her motions haphazard. In the dim light, she could see that the creature had drifted them up to the volcanic vent. It fanned out to its scavenging form, spasming and rippling its remaining tentacles in pain. It pulsed a few times, its bioluminescence a bright blue glow in contrast to the white light of the lava. Then it ascended.

The water slowly cleared of acid, but the taste of blood hovered all around her.

Taiuki shook uncontrollably. Unable to swim, she sank slowly into the trench. She was in too much pain to move, and she knew she was bleeding everywhere, even from her eyelids. Luckily, her eyes seemed to be all right, but something would smell her before long. No sharks came down this deep, but there were certainly squid and other sea monsters she had only read about.

No blood in the water, Taiuki repeated to herself as she sank into the pitch black, drifting through the still water like a mote of detritus. *No blood, or you play by yourself.*

It was peaceful, at least. Her body hurt, but her mind was calm. Maybe she would find Taifun on the other side of the Gates, if they were real. Maybe she had found a way back to him after all.

With that last, happy thought, she gave in to the overwhelming desire to die.

18

THE FYR CAME IN the night with a screech and the flutter of wings.

Reylin was sleeping in the newly built rustic cabin, thrown together with roughhewn logs and still fresh with pine pitch. His High Guard manned the entrance, one inside and three out, and the platoon he had brought were situated beyond. He startled awake at the clamor outside, sitting up and blinking. Father Kaiadin, who insisted on sleeping on a floor cot at his feet, sat up, rubbing his eyes and clambering blindly for his spectacles.

"Still, my prince," said Sir Gillead, raising a hand to his lips. "Draw your sword quietly, and be ready."

"Oh dear me," Kaiadin mumbled, pausing his search in fear.

Reylin nodded, shock running through him. The fyr were here? But they were far up the mountainside, nowhere near to the foothills, let alone the waving tallgrass. Why would a grassland people care so much about their little mine? Thank the Light he had come with a large contingent.

He heard Sir Patreagh shout outside, followed by a thump on the roof above.

"They're airborne," Patreagh cried, followed by a grunt and the whistle of swooping wings.

A shriek pierced the air, then the sound of something thumping to the ground.

Footsteps on the roof. Reylin glanced up, fearing the creature would bust through the barely serviceable roof.

Gillead thrust his sword up between the rafters, and another screech sounded. The creature tumbled off the roof, landing with a thud outside. They heard Patreagh curse.

"Fine thrust, sir," Sir Ronidann called merrily from the darkness. "If only you could do that in the sheets."

Gillead shook his head, ever stoic. As lord general, he was the leader of Reylin's High Guard and commander of the armies, and although his brows had become wilder in recent years, his temperament was as serious as ever.

Ronidann, on the other hand—

Reylin's thoughts were interrupted by another shriek, and a body slammed into the door, bursting it open. A fyr body tumbled onto the floor in front of them, and a burst of indigo light flashed around it. It rolled in an unconscious heap, and Gillead slammed his sword into its chest without waiting to see if it was still breathing. The savage, though small, appeared to be human—no signs of its monstrous nature remained.

Gillead stared hard at Father Kaiadin, whose hand was still extended outward from tossing the potion.

Kaiadin nestled his glasses on the bridge of his nose. "That was closer than I'd like," he stuttered.

Reylin squinted at the corpse, which still exuded a violet mist, then peeked through the door. Gillead growled at him. Only the slow moon was out and nearly full; the quick moon had waned to a mere sliver. By the slow moon's light, he could see shapes in the sky and in the trees, melting into the darkness and blocking the stars, but he couldn't get a good view. His Miratian soldiers battled at the sky, seeming like madmen as they swung at shadows. Their mounts were useless now. He had expected them to be running cavalry charges across the grassland, not tied up in the trees as a guerilla army of savages attacked from the heavens. Gillead shoved the door closed.

The sounds of battle died down, and a knock finally came.

"My prince, Lord Commander." Sir Patreagh's voice was muffled through the wood. "All clear."

"I'll keep the prince inside until dawn's light," Gillead replied.

"Very good, Lord Commander."

"My king, praise the Light you were here," said Father Kaiadin, making a holy gesture of blessing in Reylin's direction. "Had you not brought the soldiers you had, imagine the terrible consequences."

With a sigh, Reylin sheathed his sword and lay back down on the lumpy bed. Gillead disliked adventure. Even this mine visit had taken some measure of convincing; Reylin had barely managed to get here. It shouldn't have been dangerous, merely invigorating as Reylin saw a new area and ventured farther from Ironhold, overseeing the work of his own clever hands. Instead, Gillead would report the attack to Lord Galltry and the rest of the Council, and the noose around Reylin would grow even tighter. He sighed again and closed his eyes, willing sleep to come, but instead he mulled over the possibility of new restrictions until dawn came.

When he was finally allowed to emerge from the hut, he paused at the threshold. The clearing in front of the mine entrance was covered in blood and feathers. Most of the bodies had been cleared away, but not all. He inspected each one, hoping to see what the savages looked like in fyrform, but they appeared surprisingly human. Small, gangly humans, adorned in brightly colored headdresses and skirts, their upper bodies bare and painted in bright, gaudy colors.

Daiunek approached, grim-faced. "Praise I'ya it was no worse than it was. We're already too close to the fyr—they must know this land is rich and want it for their own."

"Did you lose any men?"

He shook his head. "Most were inside the mine sleeping. Your soldiers saved us, and I thank you for it. But we will need more, as discussed."

Reylin bobbed his chin down as he had seen Lord Galltry do—a statesman's concurrence, as if he already knew well what had been stated. Indeed, he understood thoroughly.

And yet his mind was still racing. He had been a fool to bring only a cavalry platoon. He should have brought at least one or two squadrons of skilled swordsmen, as his High Guard would not remain. Their personal swath of damage around the hut in which he had slept was clear as a timber cutting; the sword-wielding knights had cut down everything that had come at them from ground or air. Even if the fyr attacked from the sky, ground troops could effectively guard the mine entrances. And archers—a whole platoon would be wise, perhaps two. Archers had the range to keep the fyr away in the first place.

If Daiunek wanted to prospect farther down, then perhaps double that number was wiser.

"Thank you, Prince Reylin," Daiunek repeated. "If not for your timely arrival, we would have suffered casualties. Miners are not knights, brawny as we might be." He smiled sheepishly for a moment, but it faded as he looked eastward, toward the dawn. "We must advance, claim this territory for civil-minded folk. The miners are often first, along with the hunters, but I should expect more to follow if we can reach the fertile soil of the Loi al'Halmana. Glory not only for the guild, but for Mirat. Imagine the farms, the cities we could build on the flat expanse."

Reylin agreed. "I've always wanted to expand Mirat's borders in this direction. The Council is not bold enough, but I am."

"You're much like your father, Prince Reylin." Daiunek stuck his hand out once again in farewell. "Be careful on the road, and perhaps I'll see you at the Summer Solstice Festival. May I'ya light your way home."

Reylin gave the guildmaster one more solid handshake, as an equal, although the man's words made him queasy inside. Was he anything like King Rolis? Reylin would never know, as he had not known the man.

The Elder Council had raised him since the Great Fire, and the more timid Lord Galltry was the closest to a father figure he had. Galltry hardly deserved that honor either, as his rules and limitations kept Reylin from ascending to kingship, from achieving great deeds, from pursuing his dreams of glory and greatness. Too long, Reylin's shackles had chafed, and now he looked all the more a fool for underestimating the fyr savagery.

His frustration mounted as he surveyed the damage to the glade from horseback. He would return to Ironhold with only his High Guard, leaving the platoon of mounted soldiers to guard the mine, but he felt terrible leaving at all. Perhaps they ought to stay a few more nights to ensure the fyr would not attack again.

Patreagh had reported a near-total slaughter, though.

"They won't be back anytime soon," Gillead snorted, curling his lips back.

"Scattered like a flock of gulls, with about as much leadership," Ronidann agreed. "Our platoon is enough for now, my prince."

"And we'll dispatch more as soon as we return to Ironhold." Reylin sighed his acceptance. He knew Gillead wouldn't desire a prolonged stay in any case, as it placed Reylin in potential danger.

With one more respectful nod to Master Daiunek, Reylin turned toward the narrow path that led back to Ironhold. One successful but unexpected battle, one stumble as he misjudged the miners' need. He clenched his jaw. He could do better. He would do better. After all, he was the crown prince of Mirat, and he *would* push this border for the betterment of his people.

His conviction flagged under Galltry's stern scowl.

"I strongly suggested you not accompany the troops to that hole in the rock, not even a finished mine," Galltry reprimanded with all the tone of a parent. He scrubbed his face, then fell to tugging at his beard. "Son, do you not realize the harm that could have come to you?"

Lady Shildra echoed her husband's words, her arms crossed and her lips pursed tightly.

Reylin felt one more spurt of self-righteous anger burst out. "I didn't accompany them. I *led* them, and it was by I'ya's hand that I did, for the fyr would have attacked either way, and a lot of guildsmen and women would have died."

This time, Shildra came to him, beseeching him to be reasonable. "My dear young prince, do you not realize that the fyr may not have attacked had they not seen a fighting company arrive in numbers? They have not been aggressive with us for years."

Crestfallen, Reylin subsided. Perhaps she was right. If that was the case, Daiunek's miners would have been safer without his military presence.

He shifted uncomfortably on his chair. They were in the council room, but the other lords wouldn't meet for a number of weeks. Galltry and Shildra were there alone, being only a short distance away as they were. Galltry had seemed to know that Reylin's expedition had not turned out as hoped before Reylin's boots even touched the cobblestone of the inner courtyard.

Now what? he wanted to ask, but he wouldn't. He didn't want to show his uncertainty to Galltry. Shildra beat him to it.

"What is the wisest next step?" she asked, looking at him sternly. It was the same look she'd used when he was a boy and had shattered a vase, then hidden his mistake under a rug and lied about it.

Galltry gave him the other familiar look: *Tell us the right answer, or you're in trouble.*

By the Light, they both made him feel like a stupid little boy with their tones and expressions. He tried to ignore his rising temper and consider the best answer.

It was his project, his responsibility, his future.

"I suggest a timely withdrawal," said Galltry in his mild but omniscient way. "Back off from the Loi al'Halmana, and send the miners northward to search the deep Sikrat for the gallite seams. We know there's plenty there."

Reylin clamped his jaw to prevent a scathing response. *Stop speaking over me.* Be reasonable, be logical, he warned himself. He maintained more composure than he felt. "Lord Galltry, although I appreciate the advice, I've consulted with Mining Guildmaster Daiunek regarding the feasibility of northward expansion, and the logistics of moving both men and metal through those passes are unrealistic and dangerous, with a good chance of being deadly for a good portion of the year due to ice and rockfalls."

He found a little more confidence and straightened. "I believe the answer is to bolster the East Face Mine and send enough troops to not only deflect any Halmani attacks, but to halt them altogether."

"That would require a significant number of troops, a high level of aggression . . ." began Galltry.

Reylin slammed his fist on the table. "So be it. The Halmani savages *should* fear attacking us."

You're much like your father, Daiunek had said.

"Son—"

"Stop calling me that." He glared at Lady Shildra, then reined his temper in again. That unbridled impulse was never appreciated by Galltry, and even less so when directed at his wife. Reylin stood so he could tower over both of them, then forced himself to speak calmly. "I am the crown prince, sole heir of House Harkin and rightful leader of the Kingdom of Mirat, and I have already decided that Mirat will honor its agreement with the Miners Guild. I will dispatch enough swordsmen, archers, and mounted cavalry to assure not only the protection of East Face Mine, but also allow for safe prospecting farther east."

Galltry moved to speak, and Reylin leaned over him, using his broad chest and height to his advantage. Then he flicked a hand toward Gillead.

"Lord Commander, make it so."

Gillead bowed deeply. "As you please, Your Royal Highness." He left without a glance at Galltry, which gave Reylin a jolt of satisfaction. Gillead needed no authority but Reylin's, and he could dispatch whichever troops he so chose. As lord commander, he had authority not only over the troops of Ironhold's garrison, but over all the others scattered across Mirat.

Galltry's face fell, as if he had just realized the same. He dipped his head toward Reylin in a minimally respectful motion.

"I pray you're not erring in this choice, Your Highness. A lot of Miratians could be hurt in a war with the fyr."

19

Syrana preened under Reylin's attentions.

The trip to East Face Mine had rattled him, and he expressed his frustration almost violently. He must have thought Priscilla in too delicate of a state, for he had come to her immediately. She may or may not have suggested Priscilla's condition was precarious. Being so far along was certainly stressful, and the woman didn't need any kind of rough treatment. And so Syrana got Reylin all to herself, precisely as she desired.

"Do you recall our first meeting?" he murmured. His chest rumbled beneath her head, and she turned her chin up to see him.

They lay prone on the thick frostbear fur in front of the fire. Syrana draped herself over Reylin's stomach, playing with the fine hair that trailed from his navel to his chest. In return, he traced his fingers through her long trusses and along her arms, his touch feather light.

Syrana gave him a playful look. "You mean when you helped me from the carriage, newly arrived from Camdry? I nearly tripped on you. I wasn't expecting the lord of the castle to be acting as a coachman or a steward."

Reylin smirked. "Gordrew was busy, and I wanted to see who was arriving. But that's not what I meant. I suppose, do you recall our second meeting?"

She moaned at the warm memory and brushed her lips against him. "Dancing at the festival . . ."

"I wanted no other partner."

Syrana gloated internally at that, but her thoughts still warred against each other. She had met Reylin before Priscilla had, and yet she was still second. "Why did you make me wait so long?" she asked, keeping the whine from her voice, only displaying flirtatious entreaty.

"Oh, my lady, I didn't want to."

She felt him stir beneath her, and she favored him with a dramatically heartbroken look. "I doubted that you loved me."

"I doubt that you love me every day," he answered, pulling her up to his lips. "What kind of man am I, to garner the attention of such a gorgeous woman?"

She reveled in his desperate search for her own response, for his earnestness. When he was bothered, he often endured for longer, his mind torn between her and his angst as he worked his feelings out. She didn't mind that at all.

As expected, he left after a while, his angst getting the better of him. He would pace the hallways for hours, likely head to the barracks to reassess the available men-at-arms and chat with Gillead, then spar with Ronidann until he felt capable again.

She had time.

Syrana got up quickly, beckoning for her handmaid just outside the open door to the next room. The Halmani girl immediately prepared a tonic, as indicated by the stolen scripts from the Temple.

It was wretchedly bitter, sapping the liquid from her tongue and sticking to her teeth. She coughed after drinking it, but she managed to keep it down. "Light's end, which one was that?" she muttered, disgusted by the flavor.

Her handmaiden apologized. "Brownbed root, green magika, milady, for quickening the womb."

"Make me something to wash it down."

"Yes, milady."

Syrana winced and tried to lick her teeth, but her tongue felt like parchment. These spells and potions varied in complexity and efficacy, depending on their ingredients and the maker. She and her handmaiden had prepared numerous tonics and salves, philtres and teas, anything that looked like it may work, and only a handful had seemed to affect Syrana.

The bitter tonic was one, but they had found several others conducive to conception—and one to encourage development of a male. Syrana took each one depending on her sense for which was right; perhaps that was a sign of successful witchcraft. She didn't really know.

The other recipes were for Priscilla. Syrana had escalated her treatments drastically beyond the incorporation of cha seeds in the first wife's tea. The dove-feather-based paste was a standby. It felt powerful between Syrana's fingers, and after several successful applications on Priscilla, Syrana had realized she ought to wear gloves. Priscilla's health seemed fine, and the baby in her belly continued to grow, but if all went as it should, that babe would be female. Priscilla, trusting as she was, was none the wiser.

She nearly choked when a knock on the chamber door interrupted her thoughts.

"My young king?" Kaiadin's deep voice.

Syrana shot a warning glance at her handmaiden, who scuttled about, cleaning up the ingredients of her work while Syrana threw a long nightdress over her nakedness. This was an opportunity, she thought, still trying to suck the nasty taste from her mouth.

Kaiadin knocked again.

"I'm coming, Father," Syrana called.

She welcomed him in.

"Reylin's not here at the moment, Father, but I praise the Eye you've come."

Kaiadin bowed awkwardly, almost successful in disregarding her skimpy clothing. "I felt called, my lady. What troubles you, daughter of I'ya?" His voice was rich in tone, a surprising contrast with his sometimes ungainly nature.

She stammered as she tried to get her words out. "I need your help, Father."

"My help, or the help of I'ya?" asked Kaiadin.

"I'ya, I suppose."

Kaiadin gave her a knowing look, a slight amusement sparkling from the indigo band across his eyes. "I can help you, daughter. Tell me what's in your heart."

Syrana took a deep breath and glanced toward the door. Content no one would hear, she told Father Kaiadin her deepest worries and fears. She didn't mention any of her dabblings in magika, and certainly nothing of jealousy. Instead, she played the narrative she had practiced to High Holy Mage Ma'thell. She was barren, and heartbroken, and so desired to be a mother. The nearness of Priscilla's term made her heart burn hotter. How Syrana longed to hold a babe of her own!

Kaiadin listened, nodding occasional encouragement when she paused, and then ruminated for a while when she was done.

"Did you know there are spells to help one conceive, and to help one produce a boy?" he finally asked.

Syrana feigned some ignorance, as knowledge of the red magic was usually frowned upon. "I've heard such things existed, Father, but I didn't want to go through any unordained channels," she replied carefully.

Kaiadin nodded. "Likewise, there are spells to cause one to abort, or to produce a girl. Of course, one is less likely to be interested in those spells."

"Of course," Syrana agreed, feigning a horrified look.

Kaiadin continued, "There is magika in everything, my daughter, and *for* everything, if one only knows how to use it. There are several solutions we could attempt."

"And they are acceptable to I'ya?" Syrana asked. The last thing she needed was a public embarrassment to drive her apart from Reylin.

"These solutions are all derived from scholarly work at the Temple," Kaiadin assured her, "and we can start with the less invasive techniques, the green magics. Perhaps we will not need to elevate to other things." He encouraged her with a warm smile that crinkled the purple dye around his eyes.

Syrana hesitated. "Father, can you give me your silence with my husband as well? I cannot bear to have him know . . ." *That I am broken*, she thought caustically.

Kaiadin agreed, then added, "And Princess, I suggest you continue to work with me, and me alone, to resolve this problem. You have my word that I will do all I can to assist you, and that I will be subtle. I cannot promise the same of other mages, who may not remember the desire of family or the desperation of love."

"Thank you." She suspected he was speaking of the older ones like Ma'thell, and she agreed. Ma'thell would never understand; he had almost certainly forgotten what young love was like, if he had ever known it in the first place. Satisfied, she listened to all of his initial advice, producing a gentle herbal tea similar to one she had already tried.

Her handmaiden watched silently, observing each ingredient's measure and committing it to memory.

Kaiadin left them with the promise to find more solutions in the Temple records. "What a joyful mission," he declared. "To assist in the fertility of both royal wives, truly I am blessed." He bowed his way out and disappeared.

Syrana collapsed with a hefty sigh and glanced at her handmaiden.

"Hopefully he finds more than that," Syrana complained. "You already found better."

The girl nodded agreement.

Reylin stomped in a week later, slamming the outer door behind him in a rage.

"Those idiots," he snarled.

Syrana and Priscilla both looked up from their board game.

"What's wrong, my lord?" Priscilla began, moving to stand. She was too slow, and Syrana waved her back down to her cushions.

"Don't get up, Priscilla," she cautioned. She turned her attention to Reylin, who paced the room as he flung one item off at a time: his gloves, his cape, his crown. It smacked against the tapestry behind a long couch and bounced to the cushions. She rushed to him.

"The Council refused to allow my troops to depart for East Face Mine," he growled. "Galltry, that spineless son of a bitch, won't deploy the men I wanted from his barracks. But it's not up to him. They're my men, in the end." He scrubbed his face in frustration. "By the Light, his cowardice will ruin my plans."

She guided him to a bench and kneaded his shoulders, nodding to her handmaiden to draw a bath in the large tub. The girl disappeared into the next room.

"Of course they're your men," she said soothingly. "He cannot refuse you what is yours."

To Syrana's dismay, Priscilla did labor to her feet and come over, stationing herself on the bench beside Reylin. She patted his hand.

"My lord, this changes nothing. You laid out a reasonable plan, knowing you would provide military reinforcement to the guild as they pushed toward resources we need. The Elder Council did approve that plan, despite their temerity, and now you must carry that plan out. You're the only one of them with the courage to do so, and they know it."

Damn her to the Nethergate, Priscilla was well-spoken.

Syrana redoubled her efforts to soothe Reylin's tension.

He rotated his shoulders and groaned, then stretched his arm out and around Priscilla. His other hand found her belly, and he leaned against the first wife. "That's the truth of it, but I feel as though I'm commanding an army of four. The High Guard are loyal, but the rest churn in confusion whether they should obey me or their local duke's demands. This absurd situation would never have happened if not for the Council refusing to disband, to acquiesce to my kingship."

"Then make them acquiesce," Syrana whispered in his ear. "You are king."

That did it. His hand on Priscilla's womb paused, and he turned up to her with a hint of relief in his smile. He thanked her.

Syrana gave him a peck on the lips before he turned his head back, then continued rubbing his tight neck and back.

"Sir Gillead commands all of the soldiers, and you command Sir Gillead. They cannot deny you that, if you wish to deploy troops to East Face."

Reylin nodded—a slow, thoughtful motion. "They cannot deny me, especially if I am at the head of those troops."

Priscilla sat up a little straighter. "Pardon, my lord? Isn't that a bit dangerous, now that the Halmani have actually attacked?"

He stiffened. "Is that meant to stop me? I should be able to lead my troops. I'm not Lord Porin, hiding behind my status at the back of the army by the bannerman."

"You are none of those men, for those men are only dukes, whatever they think they may be," Syrana said agreeably. "None of them shall inherit the crown of Mirat."

At first, she thought he had ignored her, for he leaned down and kissed Priscilla's belly, but then he turned on the bench and pulled her to him and kissed her taut belly as well. He wrapped his arms around her hips and looked up at her, his beard catching on the delicate fabric of her dress.

"Any interest in accompanying me this time? We'll pass by Camdry on the way to East Face Mine, and you can visit your mother while I continue onward with the troops."

Syrana's eyes widened. She hadn't been home in a long time. She clutched him close and ran her fingers through his neatly cropped hair. "Of course, my love," she said. "I would enjoy that."

Priscilla smiled. "Hurry back this time, both of you." Reylin caught his breath, but Priscilla waved at him as if telling him to leave right away. "Now, don't worry. High Holy Mage Ma'thell is never more than a few minutes away, and he can Whisper to you if anything changes. Don't let me keep you from this. It's important for you to finish what you started, the way *you* want to do it."

Syrana's handmaiden interrupted them with a polite bow. "Your Highnesses, the bath is ready."

Reylin cracked his neck in both directions, obviously still tense, and gave Syrana an appreciative look. "Telling me to calm down?"

"Making you calm down," she asserted, guiding him away from Priscilla and into the heavily scented room, strewn with oils and soaps and dried flowers.

This was precisely what she wanted: Reylin, all to herself.

20

Reylin patted Farrion's neck and straightened, jutting his chin out in hopes of making an impression on anyone watching their departure.

Farrion had been draped in his battle armor, a fact that seemed to elate the stallion, although his exposure to real battle was truly limited. Just like Reylin. The chest guard was an elaborate fixture of steel chainmail and plates, ornately decorated in orange gems. Any leather was bleached a creamy white, and the saddlecloth declared House Harkin in a riot of burnished and bright oranges.

Reylin gave the retinue one more survey before trotting out, with Father Kaiadin one step behind.

Priscilla waved at him from the top of the steps; he blew her an affectionate kiss. She caught it, then hefted herself back onto the chaise set out for her.

He fretted for her gravid condition, that his son might enter the world without him, but he had to deliver the troops to East Face, and Priscilla couldn't comfortably ride at this point. Even the carriage cushions were inadequate, as the minor roads to Camdry Quarry and beyond were rutted and narrow. No, she had to be left behind.

Syrana too would be bored without much company other than his own. She rode in the carriage with only her hand-maiden, a Halmani girl they had captured and broken several years ago. The girl was useful, if barbarian, and seemed to provide some minimal level of conversation, but Reylin was sure it was not comparable to having another noblewoman available.

He spurred Farrion onward and out of the city. This trip would be expedient, if only for his wives' sakes.

They departed through Ironhold's west gate and entered the valley's extensive farm fields, an array of irregularly shaped pockets of grain interspersed with sheep and haulbeasts and homesteads. The main road here was paved and well-kept, wide enough for two wagons to pass, and Syrana's carriage settled into the track. Reylin reined Farrion back until he was even with the window.

"Are you comfortable, my Chosen?" he asked.

Syrana pulled the curtain back and simpered at him. "I am."

They chatted for a while, until Reylin no longer felt the harsh judgment of eyes from the castle behind them. He knew Galltry and Shildra would be watching from their guest suite high on the southeast tower. Galltry had been quite irritable when they parted ways.

With some measure of satisfaction at his own boldness, Reylin kissed Syrana's hand through the window. Bolstered, he moved back up next to Kaiadin for the long ride. Camdry Quarry was four days away with the marching ground troops, and longer with the carriage if he wanted Syrana's experience to be tolerable. Their second day would bring them through Lupine, a small town in the foothills where the men could rest.

They reached Lupine just before dusk on the second day. Reylin was grateful for the safe haven, for he didn't want to draw the carriage with his precious cargo at night, and the first moon was new. Despite his own optimism that he was being wise, a heaviness had entered the air, dragging at the feet and hearts of the soldiers. Reylin felt it, the shift in mood as they headed northward.

Kaiadin's news of madness had bothered him since the previous expedition, and Reylin was torn between appreciation for the mage's honesty and fear of the strange disease festering in Krita. Kaiadin had little more to tell about it, indicating that Ma'thell had neglected to share pertinent information even within the Temple's cloisters.

They entered the town of Lupine and rumbled past the inn, drawing a great deal of attention from locals who rushed to escort them along the road. The party stopped at the home of the knight Sir Cordan, an older man who had served under King Rolis years before.

Sir Cordan opened his double-doored home immediately, welcoming Reylin's officer and mage entourage in. He paused only momentarily as he beheld Reylin. "By I'ya, you look so much like your father," he said, almost breathless.

Reylin's reply caught in his throat. "You served under him."

"For many proud years. It is good to see that his blood is strong in you," answered Sir Cordan. His nostrils flared. He looked away as if embarrassed and nodded to himself, then called over his stablekeeper. He then joined Reylin in opening the carriage door and escorting Princess Syrana into the manor.

Sir Cordan's home was not extravagant, but it was adequate for hosting some guests. The fire had been stoked, and a large pot of stew simmered over it. Numerous rabbits and squab had already been cooked and were laid over the mantle to keep hot. A table had been set in the middle of the main room, with space for only eight, and so Reylin nodded to some of his officers to find a place outside.

"Oh no, my king," said Sir Cordan, intervening. "We've a second table set in the kitchen, and we can throw up another outside for those remaining. My own people will eat after. Please, rest and let your heart be light." He bowed low and then beckoned a servant with a washbowl for Reylin to rinse his face and hands of road dust.

Reylin thanked the man and settled in for a good meal. He noticed that Sir Cordan seated Syrana first, then Holy Mage Kaiadin, then his High Guard, leaving only one seat for himself to host. Cordan's own wife, introduced as Lady Amber, scuttled back and forth with the servants, bringing fresh bread, fruit, and beer, then doling out stew and rabbit meat. Sweet cakes with kiltberries were served last, along with a heavy, chocolatey stout. There was ample for all, even his men in the other room and the servants outside. The bulk of the soldiers made camp in Sir Cordan's pastures.

He complimented Sir Cordan for the fine meal, which yielded a humble and grateful nod from the man. Reylin couldn't help but appreciate the knight's stature and neatly trimmed, pure white beard, although age was making the old man a bit gaunt. He had served King Rolis? He seemed a trustworthy and faithful man.

After the meal, Sir Cordan showed them to their sleeping quarters. The knight had tidied his own room with extra furs and pillows, and added two cots along the walls to ensure Reylin's closest guards could sleep nearby. Furthermore, the man had prepared his children's adjacent room for Kaiadin, so the holy man could have his own space. True to the tenets of the Temple, however, the mage insisted he sleep somewhere of lesser status and returned the bed to Cordan and his wife. The dinner tables were moved, and more cots appeared throughout the house. Those who didn't fit were given room in the stable, for which Sir Cordan apologized profusely.

"Please, Sir Cordan, we appreciate the room and board on such short notice," assured Reylin, as Syrana echoed the same words to Lady Amber. The hosts worried over them for a while more, then acquiesced. The last of the beer was consumed, and they went to their beds.

Reylin shifted on the mattress. Sir Cordan was not especially wealthy, but he was a gracious host and decent man. Syrana spun uncomfortably as well, finally nestling her head on his chest and laying one leg over his. Reylin took a deep breath, stilling his muscles and thoughts. The second moon hadn't yet risen, and it was dark in the room save for the flicker of a candle by Gillead's cot, which was promptly blown out. Reylin shut his eyes and slept.

Reylin heard a light rasping and relinquished his dream, letting it fade into nebulous memory. The crescent of the second slow moon had risen, and pale moonlight streamed into the small window above his head. He blinked and yawned, then squinted. Sir Cordan stood in the doorway to the children's room. The man's silhouette was distorted; one shoulder hung low, and his head bobbed. His breathing was erratic, making muffled sounds in the back of his throat. The old knight took an uneven step into the room.

Reylin struggled against his tight muscles to sit up, feeling that something was off, when Sir Cordan turned suddenly to one of the High Guard knights sleeping on a cot. Jonathan, maybe? His glance was so predatory, Reylin froze.

Cordan fell onto the man and bit his exposed neck, emitting a horrifying slurping sound, then ripped an entire chunk out. His right hand flashed up and down on the knight's torso. The man screamed, waking the entire house, but Cordan had already turned to Reylin.

He advanced, ungainly but quick. While Gillead stumbled out of his cot with a cry, Sir Cordan clambered onto the bed, jabbing the knife into the thick furs around their legs. Syrana was shrieking in terror. Their host crawled spider-legged onto their laps and peered at them, wild-eyed. His white beard dripped with fresh blood, and his eyes were as black as the Nether-hour. He looked directly at Reylin and cocked his head as if considering, then slid his attention to his screaming wife. Sir Cordan raised his bloody knife with an elated, toothy smile and brought it down upon Syrana.

Reylin saw the world slow. *Not her.* He lunged over her to block the blade, and instinctively brought his hands up in self-defense. With all of his will, he denied the reality of what was about to happen. Not her. Not his Chosen.

Time stopped, and the room shuddered as something inside him broke. Power emanated outward like an explosion, an invisible wave that rattled the walls and shattered the glass windows.

The blade melted away in the moonlight, and Sir Cordan struck Reylin's palm with a closed fist. The knight growled like a feral beast, battering at them even as Gillead thrust a blade into his back. The madman slumped over with a raspy gurgle and fell to the floor, utterly still.

Reylin stared at the body and clutched Syrana close. Her terrified wailing was muffled in his chest, and he was certain his own heart was going to leap from his chest.

The house's chaos drifted to his ears like an avalanche from the mountains. A low rumble, then a concussive sound that slammed into his eardrums.

The house was in an uproar. Gillead was shouting commands; children were screaming. Reylin's guards scoured the house, collecting the servants and Sir Cordan's young ones. Patreagh emerged from the children's room and informed them that Lady Amber was dead in her bed, her throat slit wide. The children were shrieking and the dogs outside were barking. The entire town would be alerted.

"Move them away," Father Kaiadin commanded with surprising forcefulness. "They don't need to see this." The holy mage examined the scene, taking it all in through his blessed eyes. The indigo band painted over his vision would provide clarity, Reylin hoped. Kaiadin adjusted his spectacles and knelt over Sir Cordan to examine his face.

Sir Gillead stammered at the unusual source of authority. "But they're traitors." He looked at Reylin for guidance.

"No," said Kaiadin dismissively.

Reylin found himself looking to Kaiadin to explain. The holy mage had turned over Cordan's body. He pointed at his blackened eyes, then indicated the bladeless knife hilt clutched in his stiff hand. With the children gone, the room had gone silent.

"The madness," Kaiadin whispered. "The madness was here."

A knight by the bedroom door took a step back, but Kaiadin stopped him.

"Do not worry, it is gone," he said, with far more assuredness than Reylin felt. "However, I beseech you all to be wary on the rest of the journey. This is the first report of the madness so far into Mirat."

"What madness?" Gillead asked. He looked expectantly at Reylin. "I should have been informed."

Patreagh nodded his somber agreement.

Ronidann sobbed as he examined Jonathan, who was still in his cot. The knight had died quickly, but not without fear.

"And what was that pulse of power?" continued Gillead. "It came from you, Your Highness."

Reylin clutched at Syrana for grounding. The world he knew spun. Jonathan was dead. Sir Cordan was dead. Lady Amber was dead. He looked to Kaiadin. "Father?"

Cordan and Amber's servants were released as Kaiadin insisted that there was no treachery, and they scattered into the town. The children were retained for mutual protection, and all of Reylin's entourage were assigned to guard the house. Only Kaiadin and the three High Guard knights remained with Reylin and his trembling wife.

"My king, I thank I'ya you weren't hurt," Kaiadin said, shaking. He knelt by the bed and bowed formally to Reylin. "I saw I'ya intervene, through you: a miracle."

Syrana sobbed into him, oblivious to their conversation. Reylin shook her, and she looked up at him; he settled her on the bed.

Kaiadin, still staring hard at the floor, raised his hands up, revealing the knife hilt. "Do you understand what happened, my son?"

Reylin shook his head, and Gillead grumbled. "Get on with it already, Holy Father."

Kaiadin's voice trembled. "My dear king, you have power from I'ya. The power to destroy." He emphasized the knife hilt. "And the reciprocal power to create. *You* did this."

Reylin took the hilt from Kaiadin's hands and examined it. The entire blade was missing, as if it had never been. He nearly dropped it. "That's impossible," he said.

Kaiadin insisted, still refusing to look him in the eye. "Nay, my king, not impossible. The power of external transmutation is rare, but it exists in those of high enough blood, pure enough blood. You, son of Mirat, son of House Harkin, are the greatest gift of this generation from I'ya." The priest lowered himself even farther, touching his nose to the floor.

Reylin begged him to get up. Syrana was staring at her husband in awe, and he tried to ignore it. Would he ever just belong?

"No, my king," said Kaiadin, finally relinquishing his bow. "You were not born for such a mundane purpose as belonging. Your gift should be embraced and used, and I can teach you. I have a good deal of knowledge to share, and anything I don't know, I can help you find."

"That explosion was from him?" Gillead repeated, voice gruff with irritation and confusion.

Kaiadin glanced around the room, then at the closed door, and nodded verification without explanation. He placed a finger to his lips. Then he stood and excused himself to check the house again for any sign of madness. "Sleep well, my king. You are a miracle among miracles. It is safe now, for I'ya has seen you and your lovely wife through."

The High Guard remained, all awake and refusing to even sit, and Reylin tried his best to quiet his racing thoughts and rest.

They departed Lupine the next day. The streets were empty, and the few townspeople they saw were somber. Kaiadin had given them enough information the night before to quell any sedition and to ensure the villagers knew to inform them of any new disease. The local temple was small, and the mage couldn't whisper, but they had pigeons at least. Kaiadin sent a message to Ironhold with minimal detail, as Reylin didn't want the Council to demand his immediate return.

Father Kaiadin reassured him that the madness was gone, although Reylin didn't understand how. Sir Cordan's children were left in the hands of Lady Amber's family, who lived nearby. They buried the dead that morning, and Reylin watched the entire process with shame and grief. Somehow, he believed it was his fault, although he could never have known the madness would infect Sir Cordan, nor where it had come from.

Reylin quickened their pace, trotting the horses out of the town and trying to ignore the red eyes and grim expressions of those mourning. The lord and lady had been well-loved.

Clenching his jaw, Reylin rode onward. Camdry Quarry was several days away yet. He lamented yet another threat to his plans and person. This event, like the Halmani attack on East Face, was yet one more cause for the Council to declare his independence too dangerous. He'd barely had a chance to initiate his plan, and it was already endangered by the Council's meekness. He wouldn't return to Ironhold, not until he delivered his troops to Daiunek.

Father Kaiadin rode next to him, and Syrana's carriage trundled behind, bouncing on ruts and bumps in the poorly maintained road. Yet Reylin was acutely aware of the difference in the party.

Patreagh led at the front with a number of other knights. Gillead followed immediately behind Reylin. His horse's leading hooves seemed to clop in Reylin's ears and tread on the backs of Farrion's. Gillead's breath was on his neck. Ronidann carried the rear by himself. He was quiet. No winking or brash jokes, no lightening of everyone's mood as he mourned his fallen brother, Jonathan of the High Guard.

They would have to promote someone, but neither Reylin nor Gillead had the heart to do so just yet. There were plenty of quality men in their entourage, and Gillead would ensure another was chosen before they reached Camdry. Reylin didn't have much preference, trusting his man's selection.

Something else ate at him, though. Why had he been able to perform some miracle, and why had the windows shattered?

"I don't understand, Father," he murmured.

"Sometimes his will is mysterious, my king, but he has revealed something great and holy in you."

"But how? I was tested by the Temple when I was a boy. I had no magika back then."

Kaiadin's face contorted, and he looked everywhere but at Reylin. He adjusted his glasses once again, and the sweat on his indigo-painted brow made his fingers slightly purple. "My king . . ."

Reylin stared at him, expectant.

"My king, I—I cannot say." He looked as frustrated as Reylin felt.

"You must. Please, Father. How could the Temple not know that I had this gift, if it's so powerful?"

"The explosion . . ." Kaiadin began, busily rubbing the paint on his fingers off. "The outward pulse of power. It woke me and all the others—"

"What was it?" Reylin demanded.

"A break, son," Kaiadin finally answered, looking directly at him with a tragic expression. "Some sort of ward. Someone placed a magic ward on you, a powerful one. I wasn't aware of it, nor anyone else I know. Wards are invisible once placed."

Reylin's mouth went dry. Yet another way his autonomy was controlled? "Who could do such a thing?" he demanded, feeling the heat rise within.

Kaiadin shook his head, apparently just as shocked. "It would have to be someone with incredibly strong magika and extensive training." He paused, his mouth half-open and his brows raised. "Someone in the Temple. Someone trying to control you. My king, I don't know who, but it would have to be a High Mage. That was the most powerful ward I've ever seen."

Reylin burned with instantaneous rage, and all he could do was ride for a while, thinking in circles and clenching his teeth. Someone in the Temple, a High Mage. Someone knowledgeable, someone interested in keeping him in his place. The fury caught in his chest. Someone who knew his true place and didn't want to risk him even knowing his own power.

The ward had to have been in place since he was young, for he had never shown any magical aptitude until now. So it was someone who knew him as a child, a baby even.

"My king, I swear to you I do not know who would have had the audacity to rein your power in, but they were wrong to do so. All these years, all the lost opportunities." Kaiadin sounded just as upset as he was, just as livid; Reylin fully appreciated him in that moment.

Reylin didn't know his enemies, but they were surely in the Temple. Did they work with his parents? With the lords? Could Galltry and Shildra possibly have known all this time?

"So the ward finally broke?"

"*You* broke it, son, by the strength of your own will. Despite the shackles placed upon you, you broke free to save your wife." Kaiadin's admiration was obvious. "You did it, and in so doing achieved a kind of magika that is quite exceptional." The father's basic explanations of transmutative magic seemed limited by his own understanding, for he had not been elementally gifted himself. He specialized in spells and canonical knowledge. "We must learn more when we return to Ironhold," he suggested. "There are scrolls, practicums, and teaching mages—"

"I don't trust anyone, Father," Reylin interrupted. Who would teach him, if not the very people who had betrayed him? Whoever had placed the ward on him was in the Temple. It may even have been High Holy Mage Ma'thell.

Kaiadin nodded. "I will do my best to teach you. I do know a great deal, but there is much I do not, much that is not well-used simply because external transmutation is so uncommon. If only I had known *sooner* that you had such a gift . . ." He trailed off, and Reylin noticed that the man's forehead and cheeks around the indigo band were flushed. His hand clenched so tightly on the horse's reins that his knuckles had paled, and he ground his teeth audibly. He met Reylin's gaze and urgently leaned toward him. In a low voice, he whispered, "My king, I swear to you that I will do all I can to help you. You are a *beneshel*, a blessing given to this world by I'ya. I believe the breaking of the ward was a sign, that you have a greater purpose than any those in Ironhold could have imagined for you." He swallowed. "And it has something to do with the madness, I'm certain of it."

21

REYLIN CANTERED INTO THE district of Camdry with thinly disguised relief. After Lupine, the road had seemed very long. Despite Holy Mage Kaiadin's assurances, the madness seemed an imminent threat around every turn of the road, buried in each commoner's mind. How had it come to Mirat? How did it spread, and how could he stop it?

At least Syrana had her handmaiden for company. Despite the sullenness of most of the party, occasional laughter and light conversation emanated from the carriage. Reylin hadn't felt that light for long miles.

They turned into a stone-walled property on the edge of Camdry town proper and reined their horses in. The carriage rolled to a stop in front of the manor house, and the broad, iron-clad doors opened. Slaves streamed out, taking reins and baggage, while the primary servants staged on the steps for introduction. A dour, pinch-faced man and an elegant woman stepped out and greeted the travelers.

"This is our stewardess, Lady Hominy, and our chamberlain, Sir Bonnehad," said the man. Hominy, a plump woman, curtsied politely, and Bonnehad bowed. The head of the house continued formally, "Please use them as you need, and be welcome at the House of Camdry."

Reylin left his reins with a slight Halmani boy and stepped forward to grasp Baron Bonneser's arm. "I remember, father. It is good to see familiar faces, and to be welcomed into your beautiful home." He then kissed Baroness Ana's hand, but she pulled him in for a warm hug.

"It's wonderful to have you here, son," she murmured in a smooth voice, "and you wisely brought a precious cargo, I see?" She raised her delicately drawn eyebrows toward the carriage.

Reylin turned back to open the carriage door for Syrana and escorted her up the short steps to her parents, where she was grabbed by Baroness Ana in a fierce embrace.

The baroness was tearing up. "Oh my dearest, it's good to have you home. It's been so long!"

Reylin felt almost guilty, for he was the primary reason for Syrana's absence, first with her position as lady-in-waiting at his castle, then their winter wedding, and somehow they had been busy in the months since. He followed Baroness Ana and Syrana inside.

Sir Bonnehad, Bonneser's brother, settled them in the drawing room, where Reylin informed them of the purpose of his visit, the madness they had discovered in Lupine, and the subsequent tragic loss of Sir Cordan and his wife. Bonneser scowled gravely at the news of sickness so near, requiring numerous assurances from Father Kaiadin that the disease hadn't traveled with them. Nonetheless, Bonneser sent for the local mage, who resided at the temple in Camdry proper. The elder man joined them shortly to hear the news from the road. Reylin repeated some of the story with Kaiadin's assistance.

Bonnehad interrupted to inform them the evening meal was ready. The meal was pleasant, but their hosts realized the stress of the journey and sent them to their beds without excess delay.

Promising more socialization in the days to come, Reylin gratefully retreated to his room, the Frostmoss Chamber adorned in shades of green. Tucked under intricately embroidered evergreen blankets, Reylin mulled over his close encounter with the madness. He still hadn't processed Kaiadin's insistent declaration: he had *magika*.

He shifted in his bed, reaching for Syrana. Pulling her closer, he contemplated the nearness of death. It had been a moment on a knife's edge, teetering toward disaster. If he had lost her . . . He couldn't stand that thought, so he redirected his reflection to the moment itself. The blade had dissolved in front of him, dissipating into minute metallic droplets before hitting the duvet. If he could learn to control that power, could he not only destroy, but also create? Kaiadin seemed eager enough to provide him with the Temple's resources, as the mages kept extensive collections of knowledge. Although the magika Reylin apparently had was rare, there were histories and guidelines for helping one manifest.

He shifted again, caressing his wife's smooth skin, her tight stomach, the curve of her pelvis. Half-asleep, she mumbled and cuddled closer, pushing her lithe figure into him. Even if Reylin only learned to destroy, he could at least use such power to protect his wives from an incident like Lupine.

Father Kaiadin bobbed a gangly bow before Reylin left his morning prayers in the private chapel on the south side of the Baron's home. The tall man quivered like an aspen in the wind from his own excitement, and he attempted to maintain his composure by clasping his hands together beneath his long tunic sleeves.

"My king, I know you intend to allow the marching men to rest briefly before advancing up the mountain. At the risk of being poor guests, might we set aside some time to investigate your gift?"

Syrana squeezed Reylin's arm; she wore a slightly troubled look.

"My Chosen?"

"My mother will have prepared a sumptuous meal to break our fast, I'm certain," she stammered, "but we could suggest taking the noon meal on the road."

Crestfallen, Kaiadin bobbed again. "Of course, she and the Baron have been more than gracious hosts. I apologize. I shouldn't wish to offend."

"You've not offended, Father," Reylin assured him. "But we should take our breakfast with the lord and lady of the house first. Perhaps afterward?"

Father Kaiadin excused himself from the early meal, suggesting he might find something in the local temple, and reappeared at nearly the same time Reylin emerged from the dining room. He adjusted his spectacles and smiled awkwardly. "So little written in the records here," he muttered, "but even a small temple must be able to assess its local population."

Reylin broke into a relieved half smile, realizing that the tension in his belly had been riding with him since Lupine, and turned to Syrana. "My Chosen, I don't wish to keep you from your mother. She wanted to go riding with you this late morning, did she not?"

Syrana's delicate black brows twitched for only a moment, and then she smiled winningly. "She did, but I'll remain here when you go on. Are you certain I should not stay?"

"My dear lady, actually you are quite the distraction for His Highness," suggested Kaiadin. He ducked his head, seeming to realize what he had said, and seemed to redden beneath his indigo face paint. "I don't mean to offend, but . . ."

Reylin encouraged Syrana out, and Father Kaiadin led him to a parlor with bookshelves and a desk, at which Reylin sat.

Kaiadin removed a scroll from his robes and unrolled it carefully across the desk. The faded scrawl was Old Language, or the Language of I'ya as the Temple mages called it, an ancient tongue that had disappeared from common use. Reylin could read it phonetically, but he didn't understand the meaning behind the sounds. He peered over the title from his upside-down vantage point, but Father Kaiadin tapped it with an index finger and rolled it up.

"Yes, this is a fine start," the mage muttered. He raised his inspection to Reylin, then removed his glasses and wiped them on his robe. "You see, we don't know where your power comes from. I don't have a good sense for these things, as I'm not a sensitive."

Kaiadin traced his finger along the scroll, reading in silence. Then he looked up with greater confidence.

"When you destroyed Sir Cordan's knife, it dissolved, leaving bits of metal? That's a disassembling, if you will, but it required no transformation. Healing, however, requires changing, reassembling, and is easiest using the element you are linked to."

Reylin thought back to the moment and shuddered involuntarily. "I'm not sure it dissolved into bits of metal. I don't remember there being pieces left . . ."

Father Kaiadin continued interpreting the scroll, then looked up with the glint of an idea sparkling in his eye. "To determine the power gifted, present an element to the apprentice . . ."

"I should have gone through this years ago," Reylin lamented.

"You are right, son, and you are *in* the right to be angry," said Kaiadin, "but all we can do now is try to learn to use your gift, and to find out who it was that betrayed you. Now, cover your eyes please."

"Why?"

"Trust me, my son. You must use your other senses."

Reylin removed his crown and pulled a kerchief from his pocket, then cinched it tightly around his eyes. He heard Kaiadin rummaging around the room, then returning to the desk.

"Reach out your hand, son, palm down."

Reylin did so, reaching out blindly. *You are in the right to be angry.* Father Kaiadin seemed as infuriated as Reylin was for his ignorance to magic. The knowledge gave him a deep satisfaction that battled with the churning fear in his stomach. Syrana could have died, if not for this fluke of a moment and a breakage in his ward.

"Stay in that position, and try to search outward. Feel what is on the table, and tell me what you feel," Kaiadin ordered.

Reylin thought hard, considering his outstretched fingers and open palm. He imagined his hand hovering about six inches off the desk, held over . . . something. He tried to imagine what that thing might be, but nothing seemed apparent. He could only feel his hand, lightly shaking in the air, a reflection of his nerves.

"I feel nothing," he murmured sadly.

He heard a slight clink as Kaiadin moved items on the table. Then, the mage urged him to try again.

Reylin focused once more, starting at his tense shoulder, traveling down his bicep and forearm, then moving to his hand and fingers. But nothing was beyond those fingers. There was just blank space. His cheeks began to feel hot, and he was thankful for the kerchief covering his face.

"Anything, my young king?" asked Kaiadin. "It is well. Let's try another."

Again Reylin heard the muffled sound of shuffling items. He wondered if Kaiadin could discern his frustration and fear. Destroying Sir Cordan's knife in the heat and desperation of the moment was one thing, but manifesting some unknown power intentionally, thoughtfully? That was something else entirely. Reylin recalled only the despairing cry of his own soul as the blade flashed down. *Not my Chosen. Not her.*

"Excellent, my son." Kaiadin's voice brought him staggering back to the task.

Reylin refocused himself. Had he imagined that? He searched out with his fingers once again.

There it was: a refreshing pool of energy, still and concentrated. He touched it with his mind and imagined it rippling. Or did he imagine? He could swear he felt it moving.

Relieved, he pulled his kerchief off his eyes and found a bowl of water sitting in front of him. Its clear surface undulated with miniscule ripples that bounced back from the edges.

To either side was a small stack of coins and a flickering candle. Kaiadin smiled triumphantly from the other side of the table.

"Your gift is Water," said Kaiadin decisively.

"You're certain, Father?"

Kaiadin nodded somewhat sheepishly. "Well, we did not test Air, but I wasn't entirely sure how to present that, given it is present all around. However, you felt the Water, did you not? I saw you alter its surface without touching it. Miraculous."

"But how does that relate to destroying the dagger?"

Reylin watched the mage remove the other elements, placing the coins back into his purse and blowing out the candle. Kaiadin seemed to be pondering an adequate answer.

"Destruction and construction are reciprocal powers," he answered, pulling a chair up to the other side of the desk. "If you can destroy the knife, you can most likely build from your element as well. You can bind things together, healing them, and you can even create new things. In your case, you can best use Water to do so." He continued into a somewhat vague lecture on healing practices.

Reylin listened attentively, trying to understand how such instructions translated to practice. He stared at the bowl of water in front of him. He could feel its essence, but it was water, not flesh and blood.

Kaiadin seemed to sense his confusion; he stopped reading. "Perhaps another perspective could help us," he suggested. "Do you remember exactly what you did when you destroyed the knife?"

"I remember Sir Cordan attacking Syrana," said Reylin, "and wishing for it not to be. Not her." He looked down, embarrassed.

"Wishing it, or willing it?" asked Kaiadin. The junior mage did not seem to judge him for his passionate, desperate plea for his wife to be saved.

"I don't know."

"You willed it to be so, prince," the mage asserted. "Perhaps healing is the same. *Will* it to be."

"How?"

The unexpected speed of the mage startled Reylin as a dagger appeared and sliced across Reylin's forearm, nicking his skin. He goggled at the injury. Then anger welled up.

"You dare strike me?" he demanded, but Kaiadin stood. The mage was tall, and in this moment far more authoritative than Reylin would have expected.

"Will it to be, Prince Reylin," he commanded. His gangly arm swept out, pointing at the trace of blood. His presence filled Reylin's perception: strong, sure, unrelenting in its confidence.

Burying his initial fury, Reylin obeyed, turning all his attention to the injury. He could feel the blood seeping out, the break in the skin, the delicacy of the cut from a sharp blade. In his flesh, a great deal of water in the form of blood. He touched the cut on one end with his index finger. Tentative, he sought deeper into it. He could feel how the pieces needed to be joined, and how the water in his tissue could be bound back together. As he traced his finger slowly along the cut, it sealed partially shut, leaving a pale trace of the cut line. However, it burned as it went, searing like a fresh cut as it healed.

He stared at his arm in shock.

"I could put you to death for that," he spoke into the silent parlor. His voice sounded as empty as his threat, for he knew the mage was trying to help him.

"I know, my young king," said Kaiadin, "but I am willing to show you the path to your own strength, unlike your enemies." His commanding stature had diminished, and his beckoning was clearly an entreaty. "I am so proud of you, my son."

Reylin stared at the mage for a long time, then back down at his arm. It still seeped blood and clear fluid along the partially healed cut. With a deep, slow breath through his nose, he focused on it again.

The blood burst with substance, but the clear fluid was tasteless. Both were subtle, and little felt out of place. He ran his finger along the cut, absorbing the sensation of slivering skin as he attempted to complete the healing. The injury closed, and the white scar faded somewhat. It had the appearance of a weeks-old cut, one which had already shed its scabs to leave behind fresh, pale skin.

He heaved a sigh.

"Thank you, Father."

Kaiadin beamed. "Anything for my king, even unto betraying my Temple. We know now it is corrupted from within. Whoever warded you . . ." He shook his head, making his glasses slip down his hooked nose. "Someone did not want you to have this power of healing."

Reylin grimaced at the reminder.

Someone with great magical and political power.

"My son? There is another aspect to this which I do not believe is a coincidence."

Reylin raised an eyebrow.

"The disease, this 'madness' which the Temple has been monitoring in Krita and Marlemet. Perhaps it can be healed, but few have the ability accorded to you, and now your gift has been revealed. You may be part of a divine plan."

"And you believe Sir Cordan was part of that divine plan?"

"A light will always cast a shadow. Cordan was a revelation, a fearsome and terrifying one, but he is likely only the beginning if this madness cannot be stopped. You must be prepared to grow your skills, as you are one of few with the capacity to do anything about it. Even I cannot do what you've done. I rely on spells, incantations, lower magicks to defend myself."

Reylin wavered between overwhelming horror and immodest gratification. He relished the idea of having a rare gift that could shift the future dramatically. Lord Galltry would be obligated to admit that it set Reylin apart, that it implied purer, older blood and greater nobility. It legitimized his claim to the throne, being chosen by I'ya for such a cause and calling.

It also came with a heavy burden. He had to investigate this madness, especially now that it had entered Mirat and come so far inland, and see if he could somehow fix it as Father Kaiadin suggested. He had to develop his skills of destruction to fight enemies like Sir Cordan, drooling with vapid hatred and wild for blood. And above all, he had to protect his beloved wives and children.

If he had lost Syrana in Lupine, he wasn't sure he would have survived. It would have broken him to have to live without her, to face the future without a shadow of her remaining. They didn't even have a child together yet; she would have become nothing but a memory.

He shuddered again, trying to shake off the wretched thought, and looked at Father Kaiadin. "Teach me everything you can, Father. Let us continue until Syrana returns, and every day thereafter. You must remain by my side, for I can trust no others."

Kaiadin beamed and bowed as deeply as he could in his chair. "As you please, my son."

22

Even in the darkness, the Light shines.

The grating voice rumbled through her mind, stumbling through her confusion like a high double tide, sweeping over everything with its power.

A blue glow erupted around her, and she realized her eyes had been open. Despite blinking intentionally, nothing changed. The eclipse jellyfish had frayed her eyelids away, and what remained was so swollen she couldn't move them.

A thrum pulsed through the water, echoed by another slightly different vibration, followed by yet another. The water shimmered with sound, a cacophony of thrumming. More glowing eyes appeared, an entire school of something in the darkness.

Help me find the Gates, she thought morosely, imagining she was surrounded by monstrous predators. Taiuki had known something would find her. She was leaving a trail that screamed for attention, not only of blood but also of thin bodily fluids and dissolved skin. Its taste was all too familiar to her—the taste of death.

The Gates are not ready for you, child of I'ya, said the voice in an oddly practical tone.

Something nudged her in the dark. As she regretted her consciousness, knowing she would be eaten alive, she landed on a flat surface.

A bright, glowing spout appeared near her, as if the entire ledge had turned to blue fire. She could see a dark cave opening in the trench face, with the glowing patio ledge jutting out in front, and around her, monsters.

Taiuki gasped.

Burning blue eyes the size of her head stared back over a prominent muzzle with long, curved fangs. The creature's scales were nearly black, and they gave off an iridescent shine.

This was why she played by herself, why she deserved to be alone. As she drifted toward unconsciousness, her last thoughts were of Tan and Kei. Thank the Light they were safe.

Saltwater did wonders to a wound, if one managed not to bleed to death. Taiuki struggled out of a rigid torpor, but her body resisted any movement. Where had the monsters gone?

She was still perched on the ledge, and the blue light that had emanated from it was faded and dull. The ledge was empty and flat, as though some creature had scoured it smooth over time. The cave mouth yawned in front of her, the height of at least six men and twice as wide.

You are well, myrmaiden. That deep voice. It was more a statement than a query, so Taiuki didn't respond. She peered toward the cave, but she couldn't see beyond a few paces. *Would you prefer more light?*

"Yes," Taiuki clicked into the darkness, bewildered. That voice was inside, not clicking like a myr would underwater.

A fresh spout of blue light appeared, drenching the cave entrance in a puddle of renewed glow. A sea monster lounged before her, its head resting upon its forewings and its eyes fixed upon her. They must have been closed before, because now they shone like opals, like perfect pearls in the moonlight, and they whirled as if interested. The monster's head was long, ending in a fierce, predatory mouth with a sharp, hooked beak. A line of sensory organs stitched its way from behind the slit nostrils to its ear drums.

"What are you?" Taiuki asked, not daring to guess. Her mind was a muddle.

A guardian, came the reply.

"A . . . a dragon?" Taiuki was astonished. "A Water dragon?"

Yes, I believe that is what the hamanool called us, the creature replied. *It has been so long.*

Taiuki urged herself up despite the pain, willing her stiff body to move. Her skin was taut and sensitive, and her joints ached. In the dim light, she could see the pockmarks pitting her arms and tail, the searing lines slashing her hands where the tentacle stingers had touched. With a suppressed groan, she stretched her caudal fin and tried to swim erect, facing the Water dragon. "I'm alive," she said, half clicking and half thinking the answer as she drifted without control. Controlling her movement was too painful.

I am alive, child, stated the dragon, cocking its head sideways. *You are only half as alive as you should be.*

"Do you mean I'm dying?"

Every creation under the Eye of I'ya is dying, but that has nothing to do with being alive.

Taiuki was lost. Part of her wanted to be left alone, to slip into a stupor and not wake up, but the other part was fascinated with this sentient monster. "Why am I here?"

My child, you came to us.

"I'm not a child, actually—"

Myrmaiden, when you have seen the ages pass as I have, everyone is a child.

Taiuki detected a hint of humor in the dragon's comment.

The elder guardians believe you are here by the will of I'ya.

"I don't believe in I'ya," Taiuki responded softly. "I was severely injured and sank into the trench, unconscious."

One question has many answers, and often they are all true.

Why am I only half-alive? She thought the question, fully immersed in her mind. Everything the dragon said was confusing.

Your soul is restless, always searching, always seeking. Is that not why you are here?

Taiuki shivered and wrapped her arms across her bare chest. Her leather shirt had been eaten away by the eclipse jelly, leaving only rags over her metal breechbelt.

You are cold. Come inside, child. I am Uth'hal, Elder of the al'Laiakala.

The dragon pushed himself up and turned. He was so large, he had to duck his sinuous neck to enter the cave, and his wings were folded closely to his sides. His long-finned tail slid by like an eel's as it followed him in.

Taiuki didn't move. Everything spasmed, as if all of her nerves were firing at once. Even her gills burned from breathing the digestive acid of the creature that had attacked her. She desperately wanted to blink, even though she didn't really need to do so underwater. Nothing moved right; her muscles didn't respond. And she was so tired.

The dragon returned, and for a terrifying moment, she believed he had changed his mind. He scooped her up in his beak-like mouth, and she waited for him to clamp down. He didn't.

Instead, he glided into the dark cave, along a winding tunnel.

Water dragons were rare, ancient monsters. She had never seen one, but she heard rumors that there was at least one in Towun, the isle of fishermen. As far as she knew, it had never killed any fishermen. Perhaps this dragon was similarly passive.

The tunnel meandered, the walls and floor worn on the edges from travel of countless ages. The ancient creature whipped its elongated tail in a lazy back-and-forth, moving them forward with its wings tucked close to its body. Although membranous, they reminded her of the diving birds that migrated through Shiggo each year. The dragon's long, sinewy back was very eel-like, with a soft, black dorsal fin running its length. Razor-sharp spikes began on its forehead, elongating to fearsome spearpoints at the crest and shortening down the neck. Its head was otherwise bare, as the creature lacked ears, much like the other ocean creatures Taiuki had seen. Altogether, it was a bizarre combination of predatory seabird, eel, and scaled fish.

The water was getting warmer, and Taiuki realized that she had stopped shivering, although she kept twitching involuntarily from the pain of her raw skin. In fact, she could see the dim suggestion of orange light ahead.

They emerged into a massive cavern, its ceiling high above in shadows, its floor far below traced with bubbling lava creeping its way between cracks and overflowing in various places, cooling rapidly to form black levees that would divert the following lava flow elsewhere. The room glowed with orange and sputtering yellows, illuminating numerous other cave openings. One opening, halfway up on the opposite side, was dark and empty, but several others each contained a pair of glimmering opals, spinning with interest, surrounded by dark shapes shrouded in shadow. Dragons. They lounged in cave mouths and on ledges in the massive cavern, eyeing her with silent curiosity.

The dragon who had taken her through the cave passage floated out, gurgling a strange guttural to its conspecifics despite having her in his mouth. They replied with a variety of sounds she didn't understand, then emerged from their caves, drifting out and then sinking down to follow.

Taiuki gasped as the dragon dumped her on the cave bottom near a pedestal-shaped rock surrounded by bubbling steam vents. Dragons packed around them, huddling and uttering bubbling sounds and so many whispering thoughts that they overlapped nonsensically in Taiuki's head. All eyes were on the stone dais, and Taiuki struggled to focus through the distraction of pain.

She promptly forgot about everything, even Tan.

Taiuki had never seen anything so beautiful.

Not the sun drooping below the horizon after a ferocious squall, striking gallantly through the dissipating orange and red clouds like a fire. Not the Ice Castle of the Northern Merchan, its sharp, glistening towers delicately chiseled with the whispers of a thousand Waterpriests' spells.

This orblike miracle was more enchanting, more amazing in every way. She had been laid next to it days ago, and it almost seemed as if it pulsated encouragement as it hardened.

Encouragement to live, to not succumb to the pain she felt across her entire body or to the exhaustion that filled her. The egg was the only reason she had wanted to wake up at all the first time, and she had stumbled between that knowledge and wretched dreams of vicious sharks attacking Tan, lucid half-memories of an entire school of eclipse jellyfish crushing into her, and visions of Jijiton-jin soldiers massacring a village. Mothers screamed as their babies were slaughtered and their buildings washed away to become detritus in the current.

The pockmarks on her skin had filled in from the edges, and the angry red slashes from the jellyfish tentacles had mellowed to a pink that zigzagged across her hands and arms. The burn had lessened to a more tolerable tingle, and she had finally been able to close her eyes. What a relief it was, to be able to achieve such a simple, familiar movement. The acidic flavor in her gills had disappeared, and her skin was less taut than before. She doubted she would scar; she never did.

"You always heal so quickly," Reihotto echoed in her mind. The vice commodore's disbelief was obvious, and Taiuki remembered to glance at the older injury inflicted by the Jijiton-jin soldier. The cut on her leg would appear now on her fin. There was no sign of it.

The dragon egg glimmered with heat and light, emanating feral power. She turned to look at it.

At every heartbeat, the illumination revealed a shadowy shape inside. It was curled into a ball, wedged in the shell and squirming to be freed of its sharded prison. The occasional flicker came from the shape, matched by a knocking on the shell. Tap, tap, tap. Taiuki could feel its haste, its unruly impatience to be free in the world.

The tapping became more insistent, more demanding and furious. Then a deep thrumming began, a pulsating, powerful drumbeat that coursed and vibrated through the water. The dragons were humming in time to the egg's tapping. It filled Taiuki with joy and anticipation.

She knew no stories of dragon hatchings; no one in Shiggo had witnessed this ritual in hundreds of years, at least. In the Age of Blood, dragons had been closer to men. Dragonkeepers were frequently encountered and even welcomed into human society. They were looked to as leaders of godlike quality, demigods with a deeper connection to I'ya than any mere mortal could be capable of. Dragonkeepers led battle, kingdoms, and worship alike. They acted as generals, kings, and priests. No one disputed their rule or their righteousness in the Eye of I'ya.

Those legends were inspiring, fair words artfully placed in ancient tomes, but no more than stories in Taiuki's personal experience. Dragonkeepers were far too rare now to have that kind of influence. They were isolated, not only by society but often also by choice. They were hermits who placed themselves in remote locations and lived with their dragons, away from other men. Odd creatures—Taiuki's father Rentai had often warmed her that isolated people were dangerous, at odds with nature. Myrpeople swam in schools, typically numbering at least four if not more.

Taiuki's singular love for exploration made her deviant, and her independence was quite troubling to those who knew about her forays to the deep. Sashiro and Reihotto were terrified of her lack of reticence over leaving men behind, as well as her willingness to leave the front without an escort. Her mother was even more disturbed by her lack of fear or loneliness when away from others. How could she lead the kingdom if she had no schooling mentality?

Isolation created odd and dangerous creatures. The sharks that hunted alone were fearsome, unreasonable animals, and one simply could not communicate with them. Schooling sharks were more amenable to parlay, and even to friendship under the right circumstances, like Arch Commodore Sashiro's blue Benn. In exchange for a good head scratch and parasite removal, a hammerhead would patrol the kingdom's shallows and report shipwrecks. Blues would patrol the deep and forewarn of oncoming trade vessels or warships. But bluebacks, the vicious hunters of the open ocean, and lacers, the patterned predators of the kelp forest, could not be trusted. She assumed the same held true of dragonkeepers.

All that aside, the god the dragonkeepers served, I'ya, was a god for the weak, a holdover from a distant time of war and repression when gods were needed to explain the terrors of the world. His Eye might pass over the sky, but its light and warmth weren't necessary for the myr.

Taiuki shook herself. The thrum had intensified to a deep, droning beat. The egg in front of her shook, rolling from side to side as the shadow inside shifted. The circle of dragons thrummed loudly, vibrating the warm water with oscillating, throaty hums.

A crack rent the water, and a shard floated away. A hooked nose poked out, nudging small pieces of shell aside along the broken seam. It pulled back into the shell and pushed another large fragment off. As Taiuki watched in awe, the dragling clumsily emerged from the ruined shell, nosing about and whining. Taiuki remained motionless, fearing to end this sublime moment. A light push from behind startled her.

She is looking for you, child of I'ya. You are come at the will of He Who Sends the Light. It was the elder dragon Uth'hal.

Taiuki hesitated, then swam forward, taking her time. Her eyes met with the little dragon, and in that moment, everything she had thought important ceased to exist.

The little dragling flapped its translucent blue wings in awkward excitement, stepping off the stone and drifting toward her in a haphazard tumble. It squawked, which came through the water as a short, rough gurgle. Taiuki rushed forward to meet it, catching its lower jaw in her palm and stabilizing it in the water. They stared at each other, silently exchanging words.

I am It'tholl. Who are you?

"I am Taiuki."

We are One, yes?

"Yes. Oh, yes."

Taiuki's heart overflowed, its cracks and empty spaces surging full of warmth and happiness. Its thudding hammered into her ears and pounded out her limbs, racing to her fingertips until they tingled. A shimmer seemed to pass over her own scales, as though the dark gray of her tail had gained deeper hues of life and color. A wave of dizziness surged through her, foggy as an upwelling, and then her mind was utterly clear. Joy made her tremble, and she could sense It'tholl trembling as well. The smooth, finely scaled jaw quivered, but Taiuki could feel it in her heart too, a deeper knowledge of everything It'tholl felt and knew and thought. They were One. It'tholl loved her eternally and unequivocally, and Taiuki knew she would die for the dragling. She would be It'tholl's keeper until her last breath left her.

It'tholl stretched her thin wings out, her beautiful, sleek body shimmering azure like a sapphire. Her eyes spun like opalescent pools as she took in her surroundings, Taiuki, and her fellow dragons in the glowing light. She arched her back, chirping with joy, and her long tail fin flicked back and forth as she took control of her balance. Taiuki swam back, giving the little dragon room to stretch. Magika emanated from the little creature, power over Water shimmering outward like a wave. Taiuki could feel the strength coursing through her own blood, clearing her head, empowering her limbs and tail. She felt more powerful than she ever had in her life, more potent and more dangerous. It was both terrifying and fulfilling. She felt as though she could transform her entire body into a great fish and back again without hesitation, shift placid water into waves the height of cliffs, break the land apart and crack open the world.

With It'tholl by her side, anything was possible.

The pair drowned in their newfound glory, dancing around each other in a drunken spiral. It'tholl chortled, a strange sound underwater, and flapped awkwardly as she lost equilibrium and rolled. Taiuki righted her each time, guiding her about the hatching chamber as the elder dragons watched.

It'tholl is hungry. The dragling's plaintive cry was manifested in Taiuki's grumbling belly.

"Yes, I am too."

Taiuki glanced at the lead elder dragon Uth'hal questioningly. Could he hear their conversation?

You speak loudly, myrmaiden. Uth'hal sounded somewhat amused. *Please remain with It'tholl.* He turned and entered a nearby cave mouth, from which he retrieved a large carcass. The squid was freshly killed; its eyes hadn't even whitened yet. Uth'hal placed it next to the pair. *Please eat, young ones.*

"Thank you." Taiuki nodded at the great beast. These were surely not monsters. This great creature was intelligent and thoughtful. It'tholl was pure and good . . .

The dragling tore into the squid, ripping into the meat messily. A cloud of blue blood emanated outward, filling Taiuki's nostrils. It'tholl's hunger became more intense, and she wrenched the baby squid in half, bathing in its blood and keening loudly. The high-pitched sound reverberated through the chamber.

Taiuki backed away from the mess. *Blood in the water.* But her hunger drew her back in, tugging at the shredded remains of her shirt and pulling her forward. To eat. She was exhausted from the last days, and the intensity of her hunger coursed through her belly, overwhelming her. She found herself again side by side with It'tholl, who ate with a single-minded focus.

The squid was raw and fresh. Taiuki gagged a little but gulped it back. She needed to eat something, and there were no cookfires in this underwater realm. She focused on It'tholl, her serrated maw, hooked on the end like a diving bird. Her teeth were much like those of a cliff pike, that stony-eyed and vicious predator that patrolled the dropoffs for foolish sea creatures who wandered too far from the shallows. That was what she needed. Taiuki embraced the change without thinking, drawing power from the water around her and guiding it into her form. Her stomach churned as her digestive system changed slightly, and her mouth screamed as each tooth elongated to a fine point. Her tongue receded and hardened, leaving her with a toughened mouth full of chiseled razors, perfectly aligned for tearing. The squid looked somewhat appetizing now, and she grabbed a large chunk floating nearby.

As she bit into it, a primitive joy overtook her. She and It'tholl didn't notice the elder dragons as they queried each other about the unusual transformation and the miraculous myrchild who had come into their midst from the Land of Light.

23

THROWING KNIVES DIDN'T GET easier.

Lyra had no talent for it, and every dawn was a new challenge to rise from her lumpy bed, shuffle past the shack's threshold of safety and into the blinding open yard, and embarrass herself once again.

How many times the chipped stone blades clattered off the wall, she couldn't count.

Thordrin, for his part as teacher and mentor (if such a generous term could be used), alternated between moments of humorous tolerance of her performance and snarling impatience. Even as he molded her fingers into the proper form, he made rude comments that caused her heart to shiver with shame.

If Konan was nearby, he might encourage her, but often his gaze was hard as stone and his stance stiff. If she could have borrowed his stolid attitude, she would have, but it wasn't in her. If he wasn't nearby, it was because he had gone to mine for rations. Neither of these situations made her feel much better, although Konan's patience was the only reason she kept trying some days.

As soon as she began striking the congealed blood target, now blackened by the harsh sun, Thordrin would pull her another step backward, altering her method and throwing her off balance. She often wanted to cry at the severity of her own incompetence, and many times did.

Her last blade barely stuck in the distant wall, tapping the wood but then slumping toward the ground, the tip barely embedded.

"My grandmam could toss harder than that," muttered Thordrin, blanching comedically and shaking his head. "That would bounce off armor, Lyr."

That sick, frustrated feeling boiled in her stomach, and she scowled at him. "At least I hit the target."

"The target is a damn building." As if to emphasize his point, he flicked his own knife over his shoulder without looking; it planted in the center. The shivering impact made Lyra's blade dislodge, falling soundlessly to the sand.

She huffed her frustration and stood in the middle of yard, trembling as his gang chuckled at her expense. Anger fluctuated with fear, the slimy black kind that slipped out from deep inside her bones, a reminder that his gang could see all of her weaknesses on display every morning. Warmth crawled from between her breasts and out her bindings, up her neck, and settled on her cheeks, an extra burning layer on top of the desert heat.

Konan appeared at her elbow.

"We're done," he signed toward Thordrin, who merely waved a hand away.

"You two are no fun," he complained. "Get my knife."

They retrieved the blades. Lyra had learned that she couldn't avoid retrieval, regardless of where they landed; the precious chipped pieces were her responsibility and hers alone. She recalled the first day, realizing that Thordrin had removed them from the watchman's eye sockets for her in the dead of night. He had said nothing at the time, but the warning in his eyes was not to make him deal with it again.

Konan pulled her onto the roof of one of the shacks, and she settled next to him with a light groan.

"That almost feels good, stretching the muscles out," she said, flinging her arms toward the sky and opening her chest.

Konan's mouth twitched. "Most of the bruising has faded."

"Has it?" She looked down at her body, which was covered by her makeshift clothing, and wiggled back and forth. Her mobility was far better than it had been, although she was still stiff and exhausted, and specific movements lit up like lightning crackling in a summer sky. She twisted to see her back, where a nearly black mark had shifted to a pinkish-red. The mark on her stomach was now the same color, an uneven crimson with clay-brown and yellow edges. The various cuts on her arms and legs had closed, the former scabs mostly frayed off to leave pale white lines.

Konan caught her eye, then brought his hand up to her chin, gently turning it to look at her bad eye. That was still tender, aching whenever she rolled her eyeball to look in different directions. The swelling had reduced, her lid incrementally pulling back and finally folding properly. She blinked at him, and again his mouth twitched. He dropped his hand.

"I thought they had blinded you at first," he signed, his one cheek reddening. He looked down at the yard where Thordrin lounged. The man was flipping his knife and catching it, occasionally tossing it at the wall for Moony to retrieve. Konan signed again. "I have trouble believing he has a grandmam."

Was that a joke?

His facial expression gave nothing away. The man's mouth was locked into a permanent neutral position, and his left cheek was stiff with scar tissue. His brows were almost always furrowed together in an uneven scowl.

But there, that slight gleam in his eye, the tiniest bit of sparkle in the golden flecks, embedded in a sea of brown—he *was* joking.

Lyra couldn't suppress a giggle, and she quickly clamped her hand over her mouth. There was very little to laugh about. In fact, she was frightened most of the time, worried and intimidated. The very thought of laughter seemed offensive, and yet here she was, sitting on a half-rotten roof of an impoverished shack in a prison mine, staring out at a hopeless future, and laughing like a maniac.

The thought was sobering, and the moment soon passed. She peered down at Thordrin. "I don't think he could have been born. Someone molded him from steel and vinegar."

"You're not far wrong, if he's a Phantom as he said."

Lyra regarded Konan. Was he joking again? "I thought they were rumors."

No, this time he was serious. So there was a Phantom Guild, the unsanctioned guild of assassins. She had never been sure—for what reason would a wayfarer ever encounter such a person? Thordrin had said he was in high-level service to someone, that he had been knighted. She didn't believe him at first, given his lack of chivalry or manners, but perhaps he had been telling the truth. There was no way he was noble-born.

Lyra's stomach rumbled. Her appetite had finally returned, at least in intervals between bouts of nerves and nausea.

Konan must have heard it, for he produced his skein and a hunk of pale cheese.

"Mmm, watered red wine and a fresh milk cheese from Marlemet?" she mumbled, closing her eyes as she ate. "I miss food, or maybe . . . I miss the tradition of eating a meal with my family. Do you like watered wine?"

"I've never had it."

"Do you like Corroneili cheese, the stringy white kind?"

"I've never had it, that I recall."

She pondered him as she took another bite into the soft cheese. "Do you like fruit pies? The little hand-sized ones, dusted in sugar, that you buy on the street?"

Konan nodded slowly. "That I remember." Then his expression closed, and he seemed to grow sadder. Every time she mentioned the past, he went through the same cycle of tentative thought: vague recall of good, then obvious recall of bad. Her gut tightened with sympathy before rumbling again with hunger.

"I miss the peace that comes with a meal at the end of a weary travel day," she murmured, hoping he would open back up. "The caravan sometimes hustled to reach certain places before the weather turned. The horses would sweat, and the haulbeasts would chafe and strain over the ruts, and the wagons would bounce mercilessly. Not idraka like they use here, the plains beasts, tan steers with wide horns. Ada hated when we pushed the animals that hard." She smiled at the thought of her cousin. He was the stablekeeper of the entire caravan, although not in title since he couldn't speak. Her uncle Terrasa was the official stablekeeper, but in truth far less of a deft hand than Adrian.

She took a deep, slow breath and realized that his hand had enveloped hers. His fingers were brushing over her knuckles, and his intense stare cut right into her as he drank her words in. When Konan looked at her, he always met her eyes, never straying to the maturing figure she loathed so much, never lingering on the silhouette of her long legs. Maybe that was why she could tolerate his touch. He made no move to speak, so she continued.

"We would rush ahead of thunderstorms to avoid the boggy roads, and then make camp in a large circle of wagons with our fire in the center. You know how wild haulbeasts, the ones in big herds, sleep with their young in the center? It was like that, and we would cook and sing and dance and tell stories late into the night, then rest."

"Can you sing?" he asked, looking unsurprised when she acknowledged that she could. That sad look returned. "My mother sang."

That was the last word she could draw from him, so instead she talked about the caravan's route and how the food changed from one stop to the next. Heavily spiced mashed gingerroot in a mouthwatering red sauce, topped with fresh prawns and sticky sweet mango chunks, when they stayed near the Dark Passages south of Litis. Delicately sugared flowers on sweetcakes in the vast grassy plains, sometimes filled with chunks of a far-western montane fruit from the lone dragonkeepers who ventured close enough to trade. Rich and savory rice stews overflowing with hearty chunks of tart tomatoes and spiced sausage on the outskirts of Corronei.

She didn't mention Shayal. The thought of river whitefish led her mind elsewhere, down a path she didn't want to tread, and she distracted herself by telling him more about Marlemet's vineyards. When the caravan passed through the

Marlemetian countryside beyond the capital Corronei, Lyra would reel from the permeating sweet flavor of crushed, fermented grapes that emanated from the wineries. It nearly made her drunk with its immersive power.

When the sun rose higher, and the heat shimmered off the salt flats, they retreated from the roof and returned to the shack. Thordrin followed them, yanking Moony along with him, and shut the door.

"You eat too much, girl," he declared. "All this talk of food . . . Time to earn your keep." He pointed his knife at Moony. "Moon, my man, help these two in the mine. Get me three weeks' extra rations, and you can have one of my blades."

Moony's wary glance jumped to the tip of the knife and traveled along its length with covetous desire. His eyes bugged out even further, and he revealed a mouthful of rotten teeth and one of gold. "Yes, Cap!"

Thordrin leaned toward Moony and lowered his voice. The tip tickled Moony's throat, and he gulped visibly. "Moony, don't fuck around. I want those rations."

Moony barely nodded. His weak chin shook with the effort not to tremble against the knife tip.

"You keep her safe"—Thordrin nodded toward Lyra—"or I swear by the lowest Gate, the black abyss of the Nethergate, by the God of Darkness himself, and by all the nethergods who serve him, that I will gut you with this same knife and feed your innards to your crewmates. She's mine, and I'll not have her fucked with. Understand? And don't tell your mates about the rations."

Lyra couldn't have imagined Moony's eyes getting any bigger, but they did. He backed out of the shack with his jaw working, a tiny point of blood beading on his neck.

"Yes, Cap," he muttered as he disappeared.

Thordrin turned to them with triumph in his face. "There, now you can mine with an extra hand." He winked at Lyra.

Fear renewed its grip on her as realization struck. They needed food, more than they had, if they were to succeed in surviving the wastes. She was just as responsible as Konan or Thordrin for getting it, but that meant . . . going beyond the yard. Passing out of the west camp, edging by the central and east camps, and delving into the darkness of the rocky outcropping on the far end.

She staggered at the thought, and Konan lowered her down to her bed to rest.

"I'll be with you," he reminded her.

"Don't fret, Lyr," said Thordrin at the same time. "You'll have Konan and Moony. Moony's good in a fight too, used to be a mariner." He snorted. "Actually, he was a pirate, but what's the difference? One takes your money with tax, and one doesn't."

The following days were repetitive, until Lyra was unsure how many had passed: mining in the morning, knife throwing in the heat of the day with only a brief respite at the worst time, and more mining in the late afternoon. Every day, she overcame the fear restricting her footsteps, although it didn't seem to get easier. She focused on Konan's feet most of the time when they were on the move, then squarely placed herself between him and Moony in the mine. Thordrin took all of the rations they earned, squirreling them away to a hidden spot in the shack.

The mines reeked of sulfur, and the rot stuck to her hands like a fine, invisible powder. Most days were uneventful. Most of the residents of Tahayi worked for their rations—or someone else's—quietly. Only once had they found trouble, after she had filled a small bag with sharply angular chunks, identical to bags carried by Konan and Moony. On their way out, a haggard old man with a wheedling voice had begged her for it, and when she shied away in fear, he had tried to steal it.

Moony beat him with a piece of sulfur, bashing his face into a bloody mess and leaving him in a crumpled heap. After a short debate, Konan insisted on dragging the man closer to the entrance where he could be found, and they left him there, leaned at an odd angle. Moony took the old man's tattered shirt without hesitation.

The trio exchanged their quarries for two lean days' worth of bread, and slaked their thirst at the well. As always, Moony goggled at Konan's water skein. Lyra was beginning to understand how rare water skeins were in Tahayi, and was even more glad for the usefulness of her leather corset. In Tahayi, water was power. Konan ignored Moony entirely and proceeded back to the shack with Lyra in his tracks.

Thordrin ejected Moony after taking his rations, then spread the day's labor out with a satisfied look.

Lyra glanced at Konan with surprise. "The girl at the window gave you two extra pieces of bread compared to me."

Thordrin snorted and shook his head in disbelief. "He's been here a long time. Must've shown a scullery girl a good night. I've heard they'll climb through the food window for a good fuck." He eyed Konan. "What's her name? Dawna? Or do you go for the older one? She always seems to give you preference, and with age comes experience, if you know what I mean."

Konan didn't respond.

Thordrin packed the rations away, then left.

Lyra sighed as she curled up next to Konan. The day had been taxing; her body ached and her feet were sore after so many days of immobility and bedrest. Her delicate hands, acclimated to wearing gaudy bracelets, were tender with shallow cuts. But even more so, she was exhausted from the effort of going out to the mine. Her adrenaline had buzzed when the old man tried to rip her quarry out of her hands, and her mind had resisted each trudging step through the central camp. Still, the day had concluded with no other troubles, and now she could rest.

Late one afternoon, the wind rose of its own accord, whistling past the mine entrance and ruining the work on the salt flats. Lyra had procured a pick at the entrance, which she now swung in awkward arcs in the deep, cramped recesses of the mine.

Konan and Moony worked beside her as usual, using their hands and simpler chisels to break yellow chunks off the wall—the guards never gave a larger group multiple picks. They were deep into the lefthand tunnel, down a winding side chute that twisted hard left and down, effectively cutting off any stray sunlight and forcing them to work by candle.

The cave echoed with tapping and cracking, as well as shuffling footsteps, and Lyra constantly turned to look over her shoulder. Every time, their sphere of light dissipated into still darkness, the only movement being the motes of yellow dust that never seemed to settle. Or perhaps a glimmer of light would pass by farther down the tunnel or through another side chute; no other miners were close by.

Every time, her stomach would flutter, and she would tell herself she didn't need to turn around the next time. After all, she was the least observant of the three, and Konan and Moony knew what they were doing.

A muffled footstep close by betrayed her confidence.

A rock cracked into Moony's skull, and he staggered to a knee with a cry. At least three shapes infringed on their tiny sphere of light; the men had carried no candle.

"Run," Konan signed as he spun toward them and dodged the next stone. It smashed into the wall beside his ear.

Lyra whimpered and stumbled farther into the mine, into the dark. Behind, she heard a scuffle break out, and terror ripped through her body along with a surge of energy. She blindly slipped over rocks, clambered over steep inclines, and slid down loose rock in the dark. Then she tripped, falling forward and landing painfully on her arm. Her left hand burned; it was cut. The other hand clutched her pick, and she had scraped her knuckles hard upon landing.

She looked back. A bouncing candle followed her, held by one of the attackers, who was rushing toward her, scanning the corners and shadows methodically. He was alone.

Panting, Lyra got to her feet to face him in the dim light, still grasping the pick. She adjusted it in her hand.

Hearing her movement, the man looked directly toward her, peering beyond the candlelight in his hand. A victorious sneer came over his ruddy features. He advanced even faster.

Fear consumed Lyra, manifesting in a straight-line wind that blasted toward the man as she flung her pick. As she released it from her hand, she uttered a sound halfway between a groan and a sob. Then she turned and fled deeper into the mine, away from the candle that revealed her position, into the dark. She tripped again, falling into a rough wall with a startled whimper.

She collapsed into it, sinking to the ground and pulling her wobbling knees into her body. She trembled there for moments before realizing that someone was pursuing her yet again. The candlelight approached more slowly this time, seeking her.

Lyra pulled her knees closer, cringing into the shadow cast by the uneven wall and curling her toes in. Her arms gripped each other so tight, they felt as if they'd been cut off. Her fingernails dug into her palms.

The light got closer.

It was Konan.

His arm had fresh bruising and red marks, but he otherwise appeared to be fine. As usual, his garments covered most of his torso and face. He raised the candle toward her, gesturing for her to come.

Lyra let out a sob of relief, but she couldn't move at first.

"It's safe now," Konan signed, kneeling beside her and offering the candle. He preferred not to carry it, if they had one.

Lyra realized her nails had left bright red imprints in her palms, and she forced herself to release. The adrenaline made everything shake: her knees, her hands, her chest. She battled the surge of emotion that came with it, instead focusing on inspecting Konan's arm.

The ugly wreck of miniature cuts and abrasions were the aftermath of being struck with a rock, but in truth it was a minor wound. Nonetheless, she reached inside his cloak and pulled out the pink handkerchief he kept tucked away. Cinching the silk over his injury, she felt the molten heat of his gaze as clearly as she felt his hot breath. Her fingers fumbled with the knots.

When she was done, she got up, wincing with the soreness in her shoulder and buttocks, and reached for the candle.

Konan hissed when she revealed her hand, freshly sliced open and seeping. He set the candle aside to inspect it, and she saw him glance at the kerchief on his own arm.

"Don't take it off," she scolded, seeing the direction of his thoughts.

He clenched his jaw and examined the cut more closely, then turned her hand over and drew it to him. A shiver ran through Lyra as his lips brushed over the top of her hand, and her mind flashed back to that day in Shayal City, in the tent with Mam. The nobleman (a baron?) kissing her hand politely and inclining his head. The thought of the walled gardens, lush with thorntrees and a rainbow of delicate blossoms.

Konan placed the candle in her other hand and gestured for her to follow.

Around several bends, she nearly tripped on her attacker.

Konan crouched down. "Look," he said, rolling the man over and beckoning her closer.

Lyra stared.

She had buried the pick in the center of the man's chest.

Konan gripped the pick handle and yanked it out with some difficulty. A sickening scraping sound implied that he had pulled its tip from bone. The spine perhaps. Lyra shuddered as he handed the bloody tool to her, then stripped the body.

The man had nominal clothes, but he did have sandals—a valuable enough spoil—along with a rope belt, a pouch with a length of cord, and a small, chipped blade that matched Lyra's others. She tucked that away immediately.

Farther up the passage, they recovered clothing and minor items from the other two corpses, and lastly, Moony.

Lyra couldn't help but cry as Konan stripped the man in silence.

Moony, for his part, stared up at them in surprise, his vacant orbs wider than ever and his jaw slack open. His skull was bashed in, revealing a grayish-pink matter.

Lyra looked away but found only greater destruction. One corpse had a chisel shoved up beneath its ribs and its cheek smashed. Its arm hung popped out of socket. The other was a pulpy mass of white bones and soft tissue where a face should have been. It stared balefully from where it half-hung from a jutting rock, propped by an intact jawbone and tongue showing through the gaps in its teeth.

Lyra retched, but her stomach was nearly empty. She spat the yellowish slime out and tried to swallow back the rest.

Lastly, Konan hefted their sacks of mined rock, trading an armful of clothes for the pick that lay limp in Lyra's hands, and they departed the mine.

When Konan handed the bloody pick to the guards at the entrance, they started in surprise.

"How deep?" asked the older one, glancing first at Konan and then at Lyra with a sour look.

"Left tunnel, eighth chute on the right," she whispered. "Four bodies."

"Damn it, boy." The older sentry jutted his chin toward the mine, and the younger sentry grabbed a torch and disappeared into the mine with an expression of resignation.

Lyra apologized, but the sentry ignored her. He was already waving for more hands from the guards nearby.

She went through the next motions in a daze: trudging to the well, rinsing blood from her knees and hands and face, exchanging their quarry for food at the window, and finally ending up at the west end. Her heartbeat tapped in her ears, louder than the sarcastic commentary of Thordrin's gang as they entered the yard and providing a beat for her to march to. She entered the shack, laid the rations on a sack cloth, and curled up in the corner, trying to process what had happened.

Konan didn't follow her in immediately, for when they had entered the yard without Moony, he had taken interest with a glower.

"Where the fuck is my man?" Lyra could hear Thordrin's anger coming low and dangerous through the walls, and she pulled her knees closer. "Damn it all to the nethers, I'll go ask *her*." He burst through the door, making dust shimmer off the walls. The glare he gave Lyra was worse than she'd ever seen. "What happened to Moony?" he growled. His gaze was like a makran, the lithe feline predators of the Marlemetian grasslands. Cold, emotionless, intense, and full of death.

She shrank deeper into the corner. It was like being in the mine: pursued and seen.

Thordrin stepped forward, but Konan placed a restraining hand on his shoulder. The man whipped it off and drew his knife. His eyes burned like copper dust, an intense green that screamed death instead of life. He pointed the blade at Konan, then slowly turned it toward Lyra. Its edge gleamed in the low afternoon light from the door. "You've been a pain in my ass since I saved you. I'm only helping you to help myself, and now my man is dead. Tell me why."

Konan edged around him and knelt by Lyra, and she realized she hadn't been breathing. "Tell him what happened," he signed. "Tell him Moony is dead."

She searched him, first the dark eye, then the pale one, and repeated the words in a small voice.

"How?" Thordrin demanded.

"Tell him we were attacked, by east enders."

She did.

Thordrin snorted his derision and tucked his knife back into his belt. "Shame. Moony was a good man to have. Empty head, sharp eyes." His usual humor was reduced, but so was his livid anger. "Fucking east enders—never did get their taste. Was it Scrap or his lackeys?" His appraisal made Lyra want to shrink further, but Konan was with her, and she didn't. Thordrin returned her look with a grimace. "You know, I didn't have this kind of trouble before I had you to look out for. You need to be able to take care of yourself, maunderer. It's fucking exhausting worrying about keeping you alive."

"She killed one," signed Konan, scowling. "With a pick."

"What's he saying?"

Lyra interpreted in a voice so quiet she didn't think anyone would hear. She pursed her lips and examined her scraped knees.

"Threw it?" Thordrin's disbelief was obvious. "You finally hit something?" Moony was forgotten. His sarcasm had returned.

"With wind," Konan continued, signing at both of them to draw them together. "She can use that power to fight, if she can direct it like she did today."

Lyra repeated the words dumbly, translating without really registering the words. She was still processing everything she felt: terror, shock, and overwhelming guilt. She had killed a man. Not like Selen, who had died *because* of her but not by her own hand. Not like the warden, whom she had wished dead in a hidden, sinful, vengeful part of her heart, but who still lived in his well-appointed fortress on the other side of the iron gate.

She had killed the man in the mine. Buried a pickaxe in his chest and pierced through to his spine, like he was nothing.

Lyra shuddered.

Thordrin, meanwhile, snorted. "She should've been using that the entire time. Stupid maundering . . ." He drifted off into curses, but it was obvious he was pleased with the potential of the idea. With one hand on the hilt of his knife and one side of his mouth turned up in a thoughtful grin, he stalked out. After one last insult cursing her idiocy, he slammed the door shut.

Konan remained beside her. The shack whistled with the breeze, and Lyra could feel the air infiltrating the walls, pouring through the cracks to kiss her skin. Its power tickled the fine hairs on her arm and brushed her cheek like a mother would. Despite the horrors of the day, she felt comforted by that small blessing of her gift.

The Air spoke to her, sang to her, and bathed her in glorious comfort. Even in Tahayi, she was surrounded by it, a tool that no one could take away.

She waded through her feelings, torn between triumph at having won a fight and disabling, gut-wrenching remorse, and was grateful when Konan distracted her by wrapping her hand. The nausea rose and fell in waves, the jittery nerves and the horror, but when he finished with a neat knot and a delicate touch, she could almost forget. Almost.

24

LYRA PAUSED IN THE doorway, squinting in the brightness, her feet wavering instead of following.

Konan turned back. "You're not going to the mine."

Thordrin echoed his signs. "You're not mining anymore, Lyr," he called from his throne. "Too many hungry men in need of a soft girl. Too much work for me."

She heaved a sigh and seemed to shiver despite the sunshine. Her cheeks were wan and her slender fingers nearly white; the few freckles on her arms stood out against a pale canvas.

Konan pulled her through the threshold and guided her toward Thordrin. "Knives only. I'll mine alone."

She looked like she was about to protest, but he shook her hand. "I'll be fine."

Konan escorted her to her spot, a good distance from the dark brown ring that was flaking off in the constant sun and breeze, then stepped back.

"You're going now?" Her lip trembled as he turned away, making a guilty knot twist in Konan's gut. She had tossed about all night, no doubt reeling with new nightmares. He recalled the terror on her face when he found her after, having scrambled on bloody hands and knees deep into the mine without light. She had seen Moony fall, and she had thought Konan dead.

"He'll be fine, love," Thordrin called. "Been alone before, that one. And he doesn't have anything they want." He sat up with a grin and dusted sand off his new cloak, poached from one of the dead men the day before.

Konan traipsed down the yard and turned a corner, rounding one of the shacks and heading east. She needed to believe him to be gone, so they could see what she would do. The knot cinched itself tighter, a serpent eating its own tail. He slipped amongst the buildings and peeked at the scene from the shadows.

Thordrin stood between Lyra and the target, looking her up and down. She hugged herself and inspected the sand at her toes. Thordrin continued to leer until she finally looked up, a glint of fury shining in her eyes.

She was about to speak when Thordrin interrupted her. "So you hit your target yesterday?"

Clamping her mouth shut, she nodded. Konan barely shook his head. Thordrin had been known to kill for less boldness than that. Only Lyra . . .

"You remember what you did?"

The fire went out, and she shook her head in misery.

"Lyr, you did good. Fucking useful, for once."

She whipped her head in a vehement but wordless rejection, her curls bouncing, and the tears spilled out despite the way she squeezed her red-rimmed eyes shut. "I killed someone," she stammered.

"There are two kinds of people in this world, girl," Thordrin stated, his voice hard and nonnegotiable. "Those who kill, and those who serve."

She continued to cry. "Magika is a gift, meant to heal and help the *hamanool*," she managed, sniffling.

"Magika is a tool, to be used however you need it." Thordrin was getting impatient. "You want to be on the other end? You already have been. Soft, weak, useless. Is that really what you want to be? A fucking pawn for people to manipulate and hurt and use at their leisure? Kill by necessity if that makes you feel better about it, but you won't survive without killing. Now get your knives out, by the fucking Light!"

Lyra whimpered, but she pulled a chipped blade from the bracer sheath Konan had fashioned for her.

That seemed to please Thordrin, and he eased back. Despite his average stature, the Phantom was effective at intimidation, given his brawny shoulders, corded arms, and hard, square jaw—and most of all, his attitude. Konan had a good hand of height over the man, but it meant very little in terms of authority.

Lyra adjusted the blade between her fingers as Thordrin continued.

"What did you do exactly? You have to remember, so you can do it again."

Her words were soft, and Konan leaned forward to hear. "It was dark, and I ran. When I turned, all I could see was a dim light shining on his face. He was coming closer and closer. Everything around him was a blur . . ." She stuttered through an explanation, with Konan only catching half her words. Thordrin interrupted frequently, trying to make her elaborate.

"Konan said you used Air magika to direct your throw? You focused on the target, right?" Thordrin was checking items off his fingers methodically. "You adjusted for proper grip, aimed, and channeled Air during the throw?"

Lyra gave a noncommittal shrug and bit her lip, but Thordrin cracked a grin. "Konan said you buried it deep. The blast of wind nearly knocked *him* off his feet. So do it again." He checked her grip, verified her throwing form, and gestured toward the wall.

She tried, launching her first blade at the wall with some strength, but it clattered off the target. The next did the same. Her aim was erratic, and the breeze pushed around her, seeming to interfere with her stance. She let out a frustrated huff.

When the third knife clattered uselessly off the target, Thordrin struck her with the back of his hand.

Konan nearly broke from his hiding place, but caught himself. He knew what Thordrin was doing, and he knew she could defend herself, but that didn't keep the indignation from pouring out. He blinked back his rage, trying to focus on the scene without being overtaken by his instinctual anger.

Lyra staggered back and reached a hand up to her reddening cheek. Her mouth dropped open, and her eyebrows rose in shock and fear.

The yard was silent.

Thordrin advanced, his green eyes glittering ice, the coldest things in Tahayi Mines. He shoved her hard in the chest.

As she stumbled backward, something in her expression shifted. The fear was still there, but interlaced with it was fury. She retaliated, flinging a hand forward and summoning a powerful gust of wind.

Thordrin grunted with the force of it. His feet flew from beneath him, and he landed dangerously close to smashing his head against a wall. He sat up immediately and thrust a fist in the air. "That's it, love!" he declared, triumphant. "That's what you need to do. Channel your emotion. Direct it."

Lyra stared at him, then dropped her outstretched palm with a gasp. She rubbed her chest and glared at him. "Don't hit me again." She started to get up.

"If you understood the lesson, I won't have to," Thordrin sneered. He snuck a glance directly at Konan, who had remained in the shadow between buildings.

"Don't ever raise a hand to her again—" Konan signed, but Thordrin rolled his eyes and redirected his attention to Lyra, effectively cutting him off.

"What you just did, direct it onto the target when you throw," he said.

"I've never done it so intentionally," Lyra muttered, flipping a blade over in her hand, weighing it, testing it. "I guess, if it's anything like sending a Whisper . . ." She drifted off, her expression closing into thoughtful focus.

Konan could feel the air change. It seemed to lift around her, to swirl with her at the epicenter. The sand suspended itself around her feet. As she readied a throw, the wind joined her in a forward blast. Her knife flew.

The thud as it struck the wooden wall resounded in the yard, and Thordrin let out a whistle.

"Better," he exclaimed as he went to pull the blade from the wall. "Aim next time," he added with some acerbity, for she had missed the blood-painted target completely. Thordrin's grin gave him away, however, and then he grunted as he struggled to remove the deeply embedded weapon. "Damn, girl," he muttered when he finally pried it loose. He returned the four blades to her and gestured for her to continue.

Konan watched her throw her five once more before emerging. Three stuck to the wall, one of them inside the target, and she broke into a relieved half smile as she retrieved them.

"Well done," he signed as she trudged back to her line.

The way her expression lit up when she saw him made a strange feeling shiver through him. It weakened his knees and parched his throat and lips, and his heart leapt in his chest.

"Did you see that?" she asked, her tentative smile growing as she gestured back at the wall.

Konan reached up to inspect her pink cheek. Thordrin had left a mark.

"I saw everything," he admitted. "I'm sorry I didn't stop him."

She froze for a moment, then blanched. "If I had known you were still here, I wouldn't have been afraid, and I wouldn't have figured it out." She rubbed her sore cheek and winced, then glared back at Thordrin, who leaned back on his barrel with a leg propped up. "Not that it makes it okay," she added loudly.

"You about done, you two? We got practice to do—anytime this morning would be great," Thordrin answered.

Konan stepped back to his place by Thordrin and leaned against the shack wall.

"You're staying?" Lyra said hopefully.

He nodded, and she spent the rest of the morning practicing. As her enthusiasm grew, she chattered about the Air and how different it felt to direct it as she was doing, how difficult it was to manipulate the Air and aim the throw simultaneously. Each attempt varied wildly in accuracy, precision, and strength. Thordrin made numerous sarcastic comments about how much easier it might be if she shut her mouth and concentrated, interspersed with occasional sound advice.

"By the nethergates, imagine how good she'd be if she fucking focused," he muttered to Konan at one point. "She was a novice this morning. Now she's . . . still a novice, but a deadly one. She could kill something." He nodded in affirmation to himself as one of her blades pounded into the target with a smack that echoed across the yard.

Konan glanced at the few members of Thordrin's gang who remained: the ones who bullied enough they didn't need to mine, and the watchmen. They all observed Lyra's progress with interest. Whether that interest was friendly was doubtful, but at least they might see how dangerous her manifested power could be.

As the Eye ascended, Lyra tired, then started shifting from foot to foot as the sand beneath her became unbearably hot. Thordrin ended the lesson, and she and Konan ascended to their rooftop to eat.

She was strangely silent at first, swallowing down an entire chunk of bread before coughing. He offered her water, which she took. Then she sighed.

"I feel . . . so many things. I don't know how to process it all," she began, her voice so soft he had to lean toward her to hear. Her triumphant confidence from knife throwing was gone, her smile absent. "I learned how to control something today, an aspect of my gift that I've never before achieved, but I only learned it because I—" She stopped and clamped her mouth shut, battling tears as she leaned into his shoulder.

He awkwardly moved his arm and wrapped his cloak around her as she scooted closer.

"I killed someone, Konan." Again, her words wavered like a whisper, so faint that he could nearly believe he'd imagined them. They seemed almost ethereal, as though she hadn't really spoken aloud.

The sun beat down on them, and Konan noticed how much of her arms and face were exposed. He pushed her back and removed his cloak, then wrapped it around her. They needed to do a little more work with the clothing poached from the dead men from yesterday.

"Do you realize that wearing a dead man's clothing is ill luck?" Lyra said with a sniffle.

He nodded, but what did luck matter in Tahayi Mines?

Lyra's laugh was disingenuous, catching his attention. "Konan, I *killed* someone, using the help of my gift from I'ya, and now I'm considering wearing his clothes. All Five Faces will turn away from me now." She broke into a desperate, horrified sob and fell back into him, forcing him to simply hold her rather than speak.

Konan didn't know what to tell her. Death had been his companion for so long, he had somewhat discounted its presence. The Nethergate seemed to be continuously open, an ominous and eternal world that infected Tahayi Mines with despair, perhaps even with greater evil than it already held. All the prisoners could look forward to was the day they passed through.

When she eased slightly, he tried to encourage her. "Perhaps I'ya gave you your gift, knowing you would need it. Perhaps he has a greater purpose for you." He hardly believed his own words, but she held greater faith than he.

"To hurt people?"

"To defend people," he answered. "To do what needs to be done to safeguard the innocent."

"And you don't believe that's murder?"

"That's justice, Lyra, a function of I'ya."

She pondered that for a while, but he could sense the stiffness of her posture, the frustrated digging of her chin in his chest as she adjusted position.

"Is it wrong for me to wish the warden dead?"

"No."

"It feels wrong to me." She chewed on her lip.

He didn't believe his answer would have swayed her either way, so strong was her conviction, but so was his own. "Those with evil hearts deserve death," he insisted, his heart pounding in his ears. "The warden, those who sent you here, those who sent me . . ."

Lyra shook her head, tickling his chin with her curls. "I don't even know who sent me here. Do you?" She turned her chin up to look at him.

He willed his hammering heart to slow, for the fire burning through his veins to stop before it consumed him. She had peeled back an exceptionally painful layer, one he had ignored for over a decade.

He admitted he did not. "But I know what was taken from me."

She lit up with curiosity. "What is it? I live for my family, for the hope of being held close in Mam's arms, for touching Elden's scruffy mop of hair and seeing that grin of his. You know, by now he's probably lost at least one or two more teeth. Surely one; he likes to pull on them till they loosen." She wrinkled her nose in a somewhat comical look of disgust, then sobered. "What do you want to get back to? What did you lose?"

How much should he tell her? Did it even matter?

"I lost my mother and father," he admitted at last. "And I lost my home, to a fire."

As she had done only once before, she crept a tentative hand up to his neck, where the wicked lines emerged from his tunic. Ever since the day he had revealed himself, she had discouraged him from wearing a mask, insisting she could read more of his expressions without it. He still wore it occasionally to protect his face from the sun, but it was a relief not to hide himself in the stuffy interior of the shack.

Or now.

Her light fingers played across his collarbone, then up his neck to his chin. As he had inspected her cheek earlier, she inspected his with a look of utter anguish on her face. Her glossy eyes welled up again, and she shook her head as a few empathetic tears rolled out. "I'm so sorry for what happened to you," she murmured. Her fingertips traced across his brow, and he found himself staring directly at her, torn between terror at being laid bare and gratitude for her compassion. "Where was your home?" she asked, oblivious to his turmoil.

"Mirat."

Fresh tears fell. "That's so far away. What was it like?"

By the Light, it hurt.

Konan battled for control over the emotions that leapt up. He likened them to snarling wolves, dangerous and unruly and likely to get him killed. He glanced around, but most of Thordrin's gang had retreated to the shade.

"It was in the mountains," he signed. The small admission was the breaking of a floodgate. "In the summer, herds migrated through the valley to the south, heading to the high meadows, and we would hunt. In winter, snow from the peaks came down and covered the valley in a blanket of white. In spring . . ." He trailed off.

Lyra was giving him a strange look. "I knew you were a noble," she whispered, glancing down at her hands. He had fallen into the habit of stroking the top of one with his thumb, a thing as near to silk as he remembered.

He recalled pulling those slender fingers close, his chapped lips daring to brush against them, once. Was that how she thought she knew?

"People like me can't hunt the wild herdbeasts, Konan," she said, as if it were obvious. "Not without permission from a lord." She stared, daring him to deny it.

He didn't.

He did, however, feel like an animal straining against a trap, caught by the hand and bare to the revelations of daylight. No one had known who he was, save Isellan.

"Do you really have *nothing* to go back to?"

He began to deny it, then shrugged. In truth, he didn't know what remained.

"Could you not seek an answer, when we escape? Perhaps some of your extended family lives." The hope made her light up. "Perhaps you can reclaim your home and identity."

He gave her a sad look, but she kept pushing, leaning close.

"I felt so lost when I got here, Konan, so hopeless. Before all of this, I knew exactly who I was and where I belonged. I had dreams and wants. And all of it seemed stripped away from me, until *you* gave me hope." She almost glared at him. "So how can you believe I can escape this place and reclaim my life, if you can't believe it for yourself?"

Her challenging words suffused through him as violently as the moment before a fight; his pulse quickened and his cheek twitched. By the lowest Gate, she made him uncomfortable.

And she had to know it. She had sidled closer and turned toward him, her face only a hand's length from his as she stared directly at him. Her eyes were hard like Isellan's, and her lower lip pouted out with her frown. She had raised her jutting chin up, intractable as a queen on a golden throne.

"Well?" She raised her eyebrows in expectation of an answer, but he had none to give her.

He decided to change the subject. "What life did you dream of?"

Lyra narrowed her eyes, then broke into a self-deprecating smile as she looked out across the camp. "Silly dreams," she murmured. "Dreams of working the black soil of a backyard garden, growing speckled squashes and fresh lettuce and carrots. Of having a big enough table to seat my entire family, uncles and aunties and cousins, for a shared meal at Winter Solstice. Dreams of having a single window of Litisian glass that casts its colors across the floor, or even of having a paneled Litisian lamp, one of the spinning ones. I've only ever seen them in the finer shops of Corronei, but they're so beautiful, the way they throw pictures onto the walls and tell stories."

"None of those are silly dreams."

She sighed and played with the calluses on his palm. "Yes, they are, but they're mine. What are yours?"

"For you to have yours," he answered. His own dreams had frayed and faded into dust long ago.

Lyra rejected his answer with an emphatic shake. "That's not enough, Konan. Not nearly enough." She returned to picking at his calluses. It felt strangely good. "You need your own dream. Hmm . . . to open a tailor's shop. No? To find the edges of the world, by ship or horse, and break free so thoroughly you forget this place ever existed? Cross the Niravan Loi to the west and see what lies beyond the Forbidden Shores?"

He could have smiled at that and pulled his hand away to sign, wondering as he did whether the slight glint of mischief he spied was similar to her brother Elden's. "Your dream is better."

He offered no other clues, for he truly had no plans beyond helping Lyra escape. Her dreams were beautiful and flawless, and worthy of pursuit and realization.

Did he have anything worthy of pursuing, of pouring his entire will and heart into like she did? A thought flickered through his mind, emerging from the black and dingy recesses, and he blinked.

Vengeance, perhaps?

No.

Judgment. To make things right. To punish those who'd taken his tongue and seared the wound shut so he wouldn't choke to death on his own blood. To reclaim what was his. Perhaps such a mission was a worthy dream.

He still thought hers was better.

25

KONAN REDOUBLED HIS EFFORTS in the mine. The accumulation of supplies was slowed by Moony's death, but Konan could make up for the work with longer days and more careful prospecting. Another sunstone of good size would be enough, but those rainbow-flecked rocks were extremely rare in large sizes.

He knew Lyra worried about him mining alone, but it was hardly different than any other day before she arrived. He also noticed Thordrin had a handful of other men furtively mining and dropping extra provisions off. Konan suspected the assassin had promised each of them the bone-handled blade at his belt. Since each man worked to advance himself, none would mention their deal to the other, and Thordrin could successfully play off their mutual distrust and selfishness. Their deliveries didn't stand out much from the usual train of offerings that funneled to Thordrin's gang from the less powerful prisoners.

Konan trudged into the yard, finding it empty, and settled next to Thordrin as the sun set. It blazed orange in the cloudless sky. Tahayi was always dry, even in winter when the brittle winds howled from the north. Konan had contemplated this sunset for years now, at first with a pining desire to chase it over the horizon, to find the place where the sand shifted to pavement and then to rich earth. Where the desert ended with coastline, and the gem-laden foothills of Shayal's western range stretched down. Where there might be civilization with whom he could parlay, and broker a deal to get home.

After a few years, the sunset had become a flickering tease, and its burnished colors reflected and fed into his rage and frustration. He imagined returning to Mirat in full-fledged knight's armor, not to be home, but to wipe his enemies from the Middle Gate. Isellan had declared him an angry youth. But what did the man expect? Of course Konan was bitter at all he had lost.

With discipline and practice, Konan had tempered himself, allowing Tahayi to burn the weakness from him and channel the anger into productivity. And he had survived, working with Isellan at his side, until that fateful day Isellan was taken from him.

Then the anger returned in full measure, bright and hot like the Eye, and again he wondered if I'ya was a vengeful god. If the Eye watched the world, then it must be as furious as he, to burn eternally as it did. And if I'ya was indeed as harsh as he seemed, then Konan was his true disciple, a man of greater faith than he realized himself.

"We're close to freedom, brother," said Thordrin quietly from his throne. He leaned his head to one side to peer at the sunset through a space between shacks. "Ever closer." He held his hand out expectantly, and Konan passed him a heel of bread. He chewed it, looking thoughtful, the stale crumbs catching in his unruly blond beard. "Pretty soon, I won't have to dream pretty dreams about sticking a knife in someone's throat. By the darkest and lowest Nethergate, I need a good fuck too."

He spoke in a low voice, and Konan glanced up to the lone watchman on one of the roofs. The man was oblivious, his attention on the sunset for the moment.

"You been with a woman, Konan? Or have you been here too long?" Thordrin sniggered. "Or am I asking the wrong question?"

Konan ignored him, eating his own meager supper of bread. He could sense Thordrin's eyes sparkling dangerously from his peripheral vision. The man didn't like to be ignored.

Then Thordrin eased back in his throne. The bright sliver of sun had disappeared, leaving only a swath of color behind. "Yessir, a good experienced whore is what you need too. You got too much tension stored up, exacerbated by a certain curly-haired mage, I suspect. I bet you'd burst like a stretched skein, make an undignified mess all over her. Better have the whore first, so you don't embarrass yourself." He chuckled at Konan's discomfiture.

"I have no interest in whores," Konan signed, "nor in your choices."

"Whatever, brother." Thordrin waved away his gestures. "Look, when we get out of here, the first thing I'm gonna do is take a hot bath, then fuck a girl so dirty we'll need a second wash. Nethers, maybe I'll need two of 'em to adequately express myself." He leaned toward Konan with a merciless grin. "You need lessons? Shave that scruffy shit off your face, and then put it somewhere she won't have to look at you."

Konan clenched his jaw, although he could feel his tic.

Thordrin shifted, a disappointed look on his face. "By the Darkness and the Light, you're really no fun at all. How the fuck did I get stuck with you? Come on, we gotta talk more, and we need the girl."

Konan followed him inside and secured the door.

Lyra glanced up from her stitching with a brief smile of relief, the same look she gave him every day he returned from the mine late. Then she bent closer to her work, finishing a seam in the failing light.

"Pay attention, love, we gotta talk," said Thordrin.

"Almost done with this seam," she muttered, sticking her tongue out as she worked the needle back and forth. She finished and held it up, the beginnings of a cloak made of a dead man's clothes. Despite her misgivings, Lyra had accepted the necessity of fashioning more protective layers from the resources available, regardless of where they came from. She worked on it when Konan was mining and Thordrin declared it too hot for knife practice.

Konan gave her rations for the day and settled beside her, while Thordrin leaned against a sack and closed his eyes.

"Lyr, can you summon a wind to hide us?" Thordrin's question was direct, his tone no longer joking like it had been minutes ago.

"I think so." A sudden and unnatural breeze arose and whistled outside the shack.

They heard the watchman yelp and curse, and Thordrin sat up. "Ease it down. We don't want to alert the guards to anything unusual."

"How can I practice, or even know if I can do something that large—" Lyra began.

"You have to make it look more natural," Thordrin interrupted. "When we do decide to make a run for it, we'll want them to believe a sandstorm has arisen. Those are common enough, but they don't come out of nowhere. They rise up with a breeze from one direction, then escalate and intensify. You need fine enough control to make it look like that."

Lyra wrinkled her nose. "So, I should try to control the scale and direction of it, for longer periods of time? At lower power?"

"Exactly. But that's not the only reason I'm here. Translate." Thordrin leaned back against his sack and relaxed. "Escape is so close I can taste it. A few more days for Lyr to finish the cloaks, a few more days of rations from mining, and we'll have what we need to at least try. I don't know what's out there, but the only viable direction is north. The south is impassable, and the east and west are both known to be wastes to the coasts."

"I'm certain there is something out there," Konan signed, then waved toward the north. "I can feel it."

"Feelings are meaningless," Thordrin snapped. "But we have to go some direction, and at least we know there are tribes somewhere that way, which brings me to my next question. Once we get to civilization, Konan Whoever-You-Are, Noble-Hearted Son of Tahayi, do you have someone to kill?"

Konan regarded the assassin for what seemed like minutes. "Perhaps." He could feel Lyra's nervous judgment, for she still wasn't convinced that such reprisal was justifiable for the soul. Thordrin, however, broke into a wide grin.

"Good, then I'd like to make a knight's agreement, a handshake between gentlemen. Don't scoff at me, girl. I'm a man of my word. I propose that, after we return Lyra to her caravan, you and I mete out a little justice together."

"Upon whom?"

"I promise you they're bad people, Konan. Is that not enough? Traitors, backstabbers, liars. Come on, you've killed plenty of bad people. It's almost fun, isn't it?"

Konan hesitated. "I don't celebrate the blood I've drawn, Thordrin. Every death has been necessary."

Thordrin chuckled and peeked at him with one eye. "I can see by the scowl on your ugly mug that you disagree, even without Lyr translating, but I have found no greater satisfaction than watching the blood drain from a target. When you hit 'em just right, they don't even scream. They grunt, expelling their soul and slipping away like morning fog on the sea. And afterward the sun shines through, bathing you in glory from the gods who live beneath the waves."

Konan shuddered as Isellan's spittle-covered mouth flashed by; he could hear the hoarse breathing and gurgled words like it was happening in front of him. He grimaced.

Thordrin's face soured. "You know better than most, life can deal bad cards. My mysterious Noble-Heart, allow me to help you play the hand you were dealt. It's obvious you have scores to settle with someone, and it's obvious you don't belong here, just like Lyr. In return, help me play my hand. That's all I'm asking."

Konan ground his teeth.

"Maybe you should just tell us who you're after," Lyra suggested. "How can we make an honest oath without knowing what we're agreeing to?"

"I'm not asking you," Thordrin said with a sneer. "I'll get you to your family, a fair trade for you helping me get out of here, and you can go live your life. No, this knight's agreement is between the two of *us*, for what comes after."

Lyra subsided, her cheeks flushing.

"Anyway, they're bad men. You'll be dispensing justice. In exchange, I'll help you find whoever did that to you."

Konan wasn't sure he wanted to pursue that dream yet, but if he ever did, he would need help. Thordrin, for his part, was good help. He finally extended his hand, and the Phantom knight took it with a firm grip. They looked at each other solemnly for moments before Thordrin cracked another merciless grin.

"This will be fun too, though. Someone needs to teach you to have fun." He nodded to himself. "Honestly, Konan, you could have been a king here, as dangerous as you are. You don't see that, do you?"

Konan gave him a blank look. All his life, he had only tried to survive. That was all.

"By the nethers, you really don't." Thordrin shook his head. "As naive as the girl, and as worried about morality. I don't get it. This place is a hellscape, but it's better to be a king of hell than a slave of heaven."

"Tell me how exactly I can help you, Thordrin." Konan hoped to redirect his attention to something productive.

Lyra recovered herself and scoffed, then threw an obviously irked look at Thordrin, who smirked and scoffed back in imitation. "I'll tell you this: before I was the king of hell, I was a Phantom in service of a very powerful client. For years, I served him faithfully. I really am a man of my word, Konan, know that. And my allegiance was sworn to the guild and to him. He, for his part, betrayed me, as did one of my brothers. When we are free of this place, we will have to deal some bad cards. You'll get the steward, and I'll get the king." He laughed.

"Why is that funny?" asked Lyra. Konan wondered the same, thinking Thordrin was merely continuing his analogy of card-playing, in which the king and the steward were two of the high cards.

"Because he really is a king," Thordrin chortled. "You've already made a knight's agreement, Noble-Heart, so you will be a part of this, or I'll leave you here. We're going to kill a king."

"Krita?" Konan asked.

"Oh yes, Rigaran of House Crayer, high and mighty suck-my-cock-and-then-thank-me king of Krita." Thordrin continued to chuckle to himself. "I haven't looked forward to a job this much in years."

"You're not going to do that, are you?" Lyra asked, her voice low with horror.

"I've already given my word," Konan answered.

"And if you break it later, thinking you're a free man, I'll kill you," Thordrin added. "But I'd rather not." He groaned as he stretched against his sack, then rolled over with a yawn and ignored them.

Lyra stared at his back with her jaw slack, then shifted her gaze to Konan. She switched to signing, although her own signs were somewhat slower and more deliberate.

"What if the king is not evil?"

"I do believe Thordrin. He's a man of his word, as he said," Konan tried to reassure her.

"But he's a king."

By the Light, she was so trusting in the institutions around her, so naive in her belief that noble blood meant nobility. "A king is still a mortal and flawed man," he replied. *Very mortal. So very mortal.*

TIME DID NOT SEEM to pass in the Lai'akala Trench. The dragons were bathed in eternal night but for the slowly bubbling magma fissure, which provided relief from the cold and darkness. They could spit luminescent fire as well, but they tended to use it only for Taiuki's sake. They had adapted to this deep realm, living and hunting with occasional forays to the land of light far above.

Taiuki spent her days by It'tholl's side, teaching her to swim and move with grace whilst healing herself. The dragling was uncoordinated and flailed wildly whenever she lost orientation, once slicing Taiuki's arm with her pinion. Both of them screamed simultaneously at the pain.

Uth'hal, the elder dragon Taiuki had first met, and It'ma, a large female, oversaw most of their activities, bringing them food and guiding them when they strayed too far from the lit cavern. Taiuki thought perhaps It'ma was It'tholl's mother, but she wasn't sure whether it was appropriate to ask. The dragon order seemed to work as a fluid unit, hunting together and sleeping together, and familial relationships were unclear. They also seemed to have little hierarchy—no clan head or king. The creatures did not seem to argue with each other, but they also seemed somewhat dispassionate. She wasn't even sure Uth'hal and It'ma were mates, if dragons had mates.

Her life became a cycle of sleeping and waking, healing and stretching, feeding and swimming, and she began to wonder if she was missed at the surface. Had it been a week? Perhaps. Had it been two? Taiuki wasn't really sure, but she began to worry that she should return. She raised her concern with Uth'hal and It'ma.

How long would you be gone?

Taiuki hadn't really thought about it. "I—well, I live there. I need to return there."

It'tholl cannot live without you, and it is not safe for her yet. She is too young.

"But I really must return, to my brother and my people." She worried for Tan and Kei, and she worried for her soldiers. She worried for Reihotto and Sashiro, and the war. Did they worry for her?

Then we must go with you.

Taiuki was taken aback. "But this is your home."

Uth'hal rumbled. *Our home was never this dark place.* Other dragons echoed his grumble.

It'ma chimed in. *Our home was with the children of I'ya. With you.*

"But you can't." Panic filled Taiuki, forming a knot in her chest. "They wouldn't understand. They would fear you, and they would kill you." Her tears mixed with the ocean, detectable only to her. They didn't know what they were asking.

We have waited so long for a sign from I'ya, that we could return to the Land of Light. It'ma continued. *You were delivered to us.*

"It was an injury, a coincidence! It'ma, be reasonable." Taiuki could almost hear the derision in her mental voice. The jellyfish had been nothing but chance. They were fools to believe anything else.

A sign. We shall return with you.

"They will kill you, Uth'hal." Taiuki tore at her hair in frustration. "It's not safe, for the Order or for It'tholl."

It is decided. Both Uth'hal's and It'ma's voices merged with finality.

Word passed through the Order quickly, and a renewed energy filled the cavern. Taiuki couldn't help but feel some apprehension as the hunting pack returned and the dragons came together. This time, no food had been found, but none of them were disturbed, as they were about to ascend to a land of plenty, a land they had not frequented for centuries, a land into which they had made only brief forays when the food below was scarce.

They departed the cavern together, with Taiuki and It'tholl nested in the center. Several dragons on the perimeter held luminescent fire in their mouths to light the way and guide the others, and they ascended slowly, matching the pace of the baby dragling. It'tholl flapped her wings and waved her long tail, gliding erratically upward, but Taiuki could feel how exhausting it was for the baby. Taiuki moved over her and grasped her back ridges, helping guide the dragling in a straighter course. And so they moved gradually upward, leaving the caves in the dark below and entering the chasm of Lai'akala. They followed the wall on one side, which was only stone for a long time, then was spattered with crusty growths and minute worms. They passed a glowing spout of lava that bubbled from the surface, white hot on the edges but morphing into a cold black worm over which tiny crabs danced. Taiuki thought it seemed familiar, like a dream or a vision, and then it was gone, below them and out of sight.

They emerged from the trench, bursting onto the cairn fields in one large school and startling a giant squid who slipped away quickly, abandoning its coveted territory. At this point, Uth'hal asked Taiuki which direction they should travel, and she considered misguiding them. But home was that way, across the empty field of volcanic towers, up the slope to the red beds and blackeyes. It must have been daytime, because she could see across the fields in the dim gray light. She pointed, immediately regretting it.

Mother would never accept these creatures in her kingdom. She would exterminate them if she could.

Taiuki could see the Order in the dark ocean, an entire school of massive sea monsters, with predatory mouths and wings built for speed. Whether they spoke or not, they looked dangerous. They were dangerous.

It'tholl glanced up at her with concern, feeling her discomfiture.

"I'm okay," Taiuki assured her. "We *are* going home."

She guided them slightly west and north, not toward the city. The dimmest of light, like a gray, cloud-covered dawn after a stormy night, materialized above, and they could see the reed beds extending onward in the distance. The beds slowly gave way to long, green and purple kelp scattered in clumps. More fish appeared, of all sizes. Cliff pike serenely scanned the edges, and small, bottom-feeding sharks snuffled along below, sucking up the minute shrimps and worms hiding in the substrate. They swam through this dim world for a long time, skirting the myrkingdom capitol of Shiggo City on its southern edge. Hopefully they were still deep enough and far enough from the lower gates and its outer villages to evade any people.

They traveled for many hours in the twilight. Uth'hal and It'ma understood that she was not taking them to the myrkingdom, and the Order silently slipped through the water. The only disturbance was when they surprised a wild sawtoothed whale and her calf. It'ma and another dragon dispatched both quickly, and It'ma called for a brief stop to eat. They fed It'tholl first; the rest of the meal disappeared rapidly. Taiuki politely refused, somewhat sickened by the thought of eating whale despite her raw diet for the past days. Whales were a domestic animal, and an intelligent one. She was hungry, though, and instead gathered some orangebloom kelp. It was organic and crunchy. Realizing her shameful nakedness, she wove some of it into a rough shirt, the first covering over her breechbelt in weeks. The party moved on.

They traveled down a long valley and then up another mountain to the east of the city, steadily ascending to shallower waters. The landscape changed again; kelp abounded into a thick forest. Tree corals appeared sporadically, then shifted to colorful sections of reef groves as they moved toward the surface. Wild waterdogs scattered as they passed by, hiding in the shadows of the kelp beds and peeking out between stalks. Light danced through the foliage, and Taiuki could feel the joy swelling among the Order, especially from It'tholl.

It'tholl is happy, declared the dragling.

Taiuki smiled. "This is my world, It'tholl. Our world."

The Land of Light, said It'ma in wonder.

The Land of Light, echoed the Order.

It'tholl likes the Light. The dragling trilled, then slowed. *It'tholl is tired.*

"We're almost there, It'tholl." Taiuki hadn't actually been to this island, but it wasn't much farther. Another few hours?

We can rest, child of I'ya, suggested It'ma. *The dragling is not as strong as we.*

Taiuki nodded with relief. She was exhausted too, and hungry. She wasn't sure how much of that feeling was her own, and how much was It'tholl's.

The Order settled in a large open field of sweetgrass. It'ma rolled her massive body in it, exuberant; sweet scents filled the water around them. Several others did the same, crying with pleasure, and curled themselves into balls to rest. It'tholl was placed in the center, where she immediately fell into a deep sleep. Taiuki saw her settled, then foraged for fruits in the nearby forest. Her belly grumbled as she ignored the antennas waving from under each rock and swam over the clam beds. She was willing to wait for cooked meat. After she had slaked her hunger with fruit, she lay down next to It'tholl, nestling under a wing, and slept.

It'tholl is hungry!

The dragling's whine stirred Taiuki from a deep slumber. Groggy, she stretched and groaned. She had been in myrform for a long time, longer than she was used to, and her bones felt set. She needed to stretch toes and rotate tired ankles that weren't there, and to breathe fresh air and eat cooked meat, to feel the heat of a fire. The island she sought wasn't far. Refreshed, she recalled it should be only a half day more of swimming through this open plain and up the mountainside, through the forest and reefy glades.

Hungry!

"Sorry, It'tholl. I was distracted. It'ma, can you get something for her to eat please?"

The large dragon rumbled. *We already have.*

A goliath fish carcass was delivered promptly, and It'tholl attacked it voraciously. Taiuki watched with a combination of disgust and gratitude. Shreds of tissue and scales floated out from the carcass, making her uncomfortable, but she could feel It'tholl's hunger subside too.

When the dragling was done, the party moved on, continuing through the sweetgrass for a while, then reentering the kelp forest. The plants grew from the substrate to the surface far above, clustered thickly and creating a world of flickering shadow and light. The densest of stands had never been touched by a myrman's blade, and they created such a tangled thicket that the Order had to go around. The dragons glided through narrow lanes and glades where the sunlight danced on the bottom rocks and fed the emergent corals. Life abounded here. Striated kelpfish flickered between plants in flashes of violet, yellow, and orange; spiny urchins glided along the bottom; and bracken crabs foraged in each glade. Thousands of small fish fluttered around the coral outcroppings in an eternal game of chase, and colorful starfish worked their way through the clam beds.

The forest suddenly opened into a massive coral bed, with some corals towering upward to the surface. Among the towers soared greenback rays and, turning toward them, a massive lacer. The beast was half the length of the adult dragons, with powerfully built sides that rippled with each sweep of its tail. Taiuki's stomach dropped, and she felt suddenly cold. *It'tholl.* Her breath caught; she was immobilized. The creature directed itself immediately at It'tholl and launched at them, teeth bared. Lacers didn't circle, and they didn't think.

The shark burst into the middle of the Order, and its nose nearly touched It'tholl who screeched in fear, when it was yanked violently backward. Uth'hal had it gripped behind the dorsal fin, and he shattered its spine in a moment. The adult dragons crushed in upon the lacer, ripping chunks from it with tooth and claw. And it was no longer. The dragons didn't eat any of it, instead leaving the pieces to float outward in an explosion of parts, bone fragment, and skin.

The flavors of organ meat, brain tissue, and stomach acid hit Taiuki like a wave, and she retched uncontrollably. She sobbed and clung tightly to It'tholl. This taste of death was too familiar, the danger too imminent and real. The lacer's viciousness was too reminiscent of her nightmares for her to face.

It'tholl trembled and nestled into her despite the mess of vomit. The two exchanged emotions, consoling and frightening simultaneously, until the water around them cleared of detritus. Matter seemed to disintegrate around them, creating an orb of clear water around the pair, which grew outward. The sand began to whip at the bottom, and pincer shrimps and minute fish scattered away from the orb.

Stop!

Uth'hal's command broke into Taiuki's chaotic thoughts, and she finally took a full breath and opened her eyes. It'tholl's head was tucked entirely between Taiuki's body and her own wing. The orb of clear water weakened, then faded as it mixed into the surrounding water. Taiuki's heart slowed, and It'tholl peeked out.

It is all right, assured It'ma. *It is dead.*

They reassembled and moved on through the coral towers. Their new home was close.

Their passage through the coral towers was otherwise serene. Greenback rays and turtles glided by, barely flapping as they soared through the water. The coral grew in a rainbow of colors and shapes, piled one upon the other in a cluttered yet perfect ecosystem. The amount of food here was overwhelming, and Taiuki's stomach growled and churned. As they neared the surface, she picked a few fruits, only enough to carry in her arms. The purple tanko apples were ripe, and she ate a handful of kelpblooms as she swam.

They reached the island shoreline, and she bid them stay while she scouted the land. The dragons' excitement made the water itself hum, and Taiuki realized a heartbreaking reality. They had not seen the sun or breathed the air for decades. All the sunrises and sunsets missed; all the crisp ocean breezes that had whipped her hair and enriched her nostrils had been nonexistent in the dark below. This was a new day.

"I'll be quick, friends," she assured them, and went up to the surface, peeking her head out to scan the island. It was empty, as expected. The island itself was heavily vegetated further inland, a mixture of tall trees, broadly shading ferns, and tangled bushes beyond a clear sandy shoreline. The island was steep, rising up into rocky outcroppings and a twin-peaked mountain, which smoked continuously from both sides. The Mountains of Mourning. There was no sign of human life: no smoke from cookfires, no trees laid down for timber, and no boats on the water. Taiuki sighed in relief.

She called down to the Order, who immediately ascended, bursting in jubilation from the water. The dragons shifted to air-breathing, like she had, and their gills melted into their bodies. It'ma trumpeted loudly, a brass sound that echoed across the water and frightened hundreds of birds into the sky. Uth'hal did the same, followed by tens of others. The entire order rolled in the sunlight, spinning and leaping about.

It'tholl appeared by Taiuki's side in the shallows. She shifted, tenuous, peeking shyly from underwater. *Just like Tan-sho when he was little*, thought Taiuki. Babies could shift without thought. It'tholl's gills wavered shut, and she snorted saltwater out of her nose. Her eyes shifted as she blinked in the sunshine, until blur became clarity, and she pushed her head all the way out of the water.

It'tholl likes the Light!

Taiuki grinned at the dragling, even as she kept her righted and floating. The infant had no fear of this new world. Taiuki spoke aloud; her reformed vocal cords felt tight after such a long time without use. "Shall we go to shore?"

Yes, It'tholl likes the shore! Likes the sand! Likes the birds! It'tholl's joy was infectious, and the pair swam awkwardly together as Taiuki helped her navigate the tumbling waves.

Once It'tholl got her back flippers under her, she clambered her way onto the sand, splashing with delight.

The adults did the same. Taiuki held back her laughter as the dragons emerged from the water, bugling to each other and running ungainly about the beach. She noticed these dragons retained their eellike caudal fins and streamlined back flippers, designed for water rather than the land. Their wings, so fluidly coordinated in the water, were used as crutches as they stilted their way up the beach. Uth'hal rolled around in the sand, scratching a centuries-old itch, and fell into a deep sleep in the sun. The others followed shortly.

Taiuki knew they needed to find shelter soon, somewhere hidden where they could stay, but at least they were here, they were home, and the sun was warm. Her naked legs soaked in the light, and her heart was full. It'tholl slumbered, and shortly, so did she.

27

TAIUKI'S BRIEF NAP IN the sun was interrupted by the realization that they really did need to find shelter for It'tholl and the other dragons. Although the island she had chosen was isolated (haunted, some said), it was always possible some mariner or trader might stray too far from the roads and shipping passages.

It'tholl slumbered as Taiuki carefully detached herself and made her way down the shoreline to scout. It'ma appeared beside her, and they walked together for a while.

The forest pushed into the sandy beach, stretching out to an ocean it couldn't quite touch. The apita trees grew alone or in loose copses, their roots grasping into the sand and rocks, clinging even to the steep cliffside rising up to the smoking mountaintops. Where the trees receded, thick green grass and low flowering shrubs covered the steep rocks and outcroppings like a blanket. It'ma and Taiuki navigated the shoreline with caution.

They crested a steep outcropping that ended in cliff, dropping down several dragon lengths to a long, sickle-shaped shoreline. Waves tumbled gently into the hidden cove, which ended in a long beach and a dark crevasse in the cliffside. It'ma lurched down the cliff right away, stumbling once with her flippered hind legs. Taiuki picked her way inland through the forest, hoping to find a different route, and reached a portion that was half the height; she climbed down a step at a time, slipping once near the end and falling hard into the sand.

Come, child of I'ya! said It'ma, padding her way to the cave mouth.

Taiuki rubbed her bottom and caught her breath, then followed. The crevasse was tall enough to admit It'ma's grand stature and snaking head, and the dragon disappeared entirely inside the cave. As Taiuki's eyes adjusted to the darkness, she could see that the sunbright opening was dwarfed by the size of the cavern inside. It'ma's movements echoed in the vast space.

"This is perfect," whispered Taiuki, in awe. The cave continued into the mountain, splitting into two massive tunnels and pockmarked with holes and side caverns.

I'ya provides, It'ma responded in a knowing voice, the tone coming through clearly.

Taiuki shook her head and didn't answer. A freshwater stream trickled through the middle of the cave, collecting thousands of drippings from the cave ceiling and walls into one place. She tasted its water; it was rich with minerals and so refreshing that her head spun. It had been so long. It'ma lapped it up greedily as well. Taiuki could hardly imagine what the dragon was feeling. Years of darkness, solitude, and salt. An eternity of deprivation of some of the dearest experiences of life. It'ma had missed how many cool drinks from a stream, and how many brisk breezes in the evening? How many days had the Order lived without even the murkiest of light to tell them the sun had risen and set? Taiuki had missed home, and she had only been with them for a few weeks.

Home.

Now that they had found the cave, they needed to retrieve the Order and bring them to the safe haven. Then Taiuki had to make sure Kei and Tan were okay, and that her troops were well on the front. No time to waste.

It'tholl is lost! Lost! Lost!

It'tholl's faint cry came into Taiuki's mind. She was panicking.

"I'm here," Taiuki said aloud. Her voice bounced off the cavern walls.

Lost! Lost! The dragling couldn't hear her.

It'ma and Taiuki left the cave and, examining the cliff face they had ungainly dismounted, returned to the water to more easily move up the coast. As they swam, Taiuki could finally reach It'tholl and calmed her. She told the dragling they had found a home, and It'ma likewise told the Order to come to them. The dragons met midway, and It'ma and Taiuki guided them back to the hidden cove.

When they were settled, Taiuki explained to It'tholl that she was going to be gone for a little while. The upset dragling cried.

"I'll be back as soon as I can," reassured Taiuki, scratching the dragling's jaw. It'tholl's luminescent eyes sparkled with contentment in the moment. Her indigo scales were iridescent in the sunshine, but so itchy. Taiuki scratched more, getting It'tholl's shoulder and neck. "I really must go, It'tholl."

We will be here, child of I'ya, stated Uth'hal, sounding serene. *Go with the Light, and don't be gone too long. She needs you.*

Taiuki saluted and bowed low, thanking the elder dragons, and left.

"What were you thinking?" Mother's cold voice struck Taiuki harder than her palm. "We've had search parties looking for you for weeks, wasting their efforts instead of working the fields and cattle. Instead of training and fighting the Jijiton-jin. Do you realize the war you started?" Another strike, this time a backhand on Taiuki's right cheek. The queen regent had drawn blood with the multiple rings on her fingers. "You are selfish, and unworthy of your nobility."

Taiuki didn't respond. She didn't raise her hand to protect her cheek, nor press against the fresh, fine cuts. She couldn't tell Mother the entire truth, only that she had near-ly died when the eclipse jellyfish attacked her, that she had passed out and sunk to a ledge in the darkness.

"I couldn't move for a long time," she stammered, "and I was badly hurt. By the time I could swim back up without risk of attracting predators, I was lost too. It took me this long to find my way back, Mother. I'm sorry."

Kei and Tan watched the scene, looking uncomfortable. Kei was wearing her royal arraignments for judging; she had been working under Mother's watch in the throne room today. When Taiuki returned, attended by two pale guards who kept staring at her, they had ejected all callers from the room and closed the door. Now she stood in front of Mother, like a criminal receiving sentence, while Kei stood awkwardly to the side of the throne she had vacated when Mother took over. The queen regent stood tall over Taiu-ki, glaring down at her with distaste. Taiuki had never had her stature, and likely never would. She was still half-naked, wearing only her ragged kelp shirt and a breechbelt with bits of leather hanging from it, revealing in full her mus-cled legs and arms. Her hair was disheveled, and she looked half-starved even to her own eyes.

Mother gestured to a guard. "Get the steward."

Steward Wehan entered and bowed. "My queen regent." He bowed to Kei. "Your Highness."

"Get fresh robes or a skin, something, Wehan." Mother gestured with disgust at Taiuki's dirty figure.

"Immediately, my queen regent." Wehan left, then re-turned almost without pause, with Nurse Hannaka and a robe to cover Taiuki's nakedness. Hannaka removed the kelp rags from Taiuki's body and covered her with the robe, a humiliating process she endured in front of her siblings. Both of them looked away in shame. After sending Hannaka out, Wehan stayed by the door.

The queen regent stared down her nose, examining Taiu-ki's messy hair, her flushed cheeks, her slight stature.

Taiuki stared at the gilded hem of her mother's dress.

"Why did you go so far and so deep?"

Taiuki knew no answer would be right. "I don't know."

"What were you looking for? Him?" Mother's strident hostility grew. "You won't find him, and you'll meet the same end if you continue this foolishness. No more excursions, no more wandering and shirking your duties, Taiuki. You are needed here!"

"It was an accident, Mother." Did she even care that Taiuki could have died?

The queen regent leaned forward, eyes piercing through her. "The Kritali trade deal collapsed because you disappeared, because you could not accept your role, your duty to the kingdom. *You* are responsible, and you have failed your sister and your brother. You should be ashamed, Taiuki."

Taiuki forced her voice to remain level and strong. "You hardly need me here or in Krita," she said, defiant. "The soldiers need me at the front, where I can make a difference."

"Then you failed them too." This time, Mother's strike hit hard enough to knock Taiuki backward, and she landed with a muffled thud cushioned by the robes. Mother continued in a steady, cool voice as she rubbed her palm with the other hand. "Jijito redoubled their border guard and pushed an advance to the villages you left behind because of your reckless violence. Three villages have been lost again, their paltry garrisons destroyed, and any hope of diplomacy is lost."

The tears Taiuki had been withholding rolled freely down her cheeks now. She regretted ever coming home. She focused on the hem of Mother's dress, blinking to keep her eyes clear, but the tears made everything a blur.

The queen regent straightened suddenly. "Children, leave us," she said, calmly but firmly.

Kei hesitated, then took Tan by the hand and pulled him to the door. They took one last look over their shoulders at Taiuki, who was like a fallen statue facing the throne. Wehan closed the door behind them and stepped closer to the pair.

Mother stared at her for what seemed an eternity, both of them silent. Then, towering over her, she whispered, "I am ashamed to have borne you, Taiuki. If only it had been *you*, and not him."

Taiuki began to cry uncontrollably, bowing to the floor at Mother's feet. She was right. Why couldn't it have been her?

She dreaded meeting her mother's gaze, so she continued focusing on the skirt hem, the silver-and-gold needlework, the nacre beads, the even cut. Was it even? Or was there a divot right there? She couldn't rightly see in the blur.

"I'm sorry, Mother," she stammered between gasps of breath. "I didn't mean to—"

"You never mean to. You don't *think*, and you don't think of anyone but yourself. You stupid, selfish, awful curse of a child."

Now Taiuki felt rage well up. "It was an accident, Mother." It came out as a shout. "And I will *never* marry Godrig. I cannot!"

"You will, if it means we trade more freely through Krita Port."

"I won't! Please, Mother. Please reconsider this . . ." Taiuki trailed off, torn between a righteous anger and a sadness she couldn't define. It pervaded her, shook her to her bones. It was good she was already on the floor, because her legs felt weak and her heart pattered unevenly. She returned her attention to the skirt hem and stated in a dead voice. "I could have died, Mother. I *did* almost die, and all you care for is the trade deal." Her words would have as much effect on her mother as they had on the limestone wall, yet she still felt the need to say them.

Taiuki blinked. The tears had slowed enough that she could see how Mother's skirt had been eaten away at the hem. A few nacre beads and bits of gold and silver metal thread littered the floor. She directed all of her anguish at the tiny focal point, the only clear thing in her vision.

"Wehan!" Mother's voice was demanding, and a sudden shock blasted through Taiuki's body, knocking her over. Pain seared through her veins like lightning. Her muscles twitched and contracted, and her hands clenched into fists as she writhed on the floor. She would have screamed, but her jaw was shut; she tasted blood where she had bitten her tongue.

It didn't seem to end. She writhed in an endless cycle of pulsating agony. It blasted every tangible thought from her mind, every attempt to make sense of her torture. It wiped everything clean to a senselessly bright white stupor.

Mother backed away from Taiuki, scoffing. Then she gingerly stepped around her, scattering nacre beads as she strode from the room with her head high. Steward Wehan followed.

Taiuki lay there, curled in a fetal position, until Hannaka quietly entered and propped her up.

"Come along, Yuki-sho," she said, pulling Taiuki up. "Let's get you bathed and dressed. Your mother will expect you timely for supper."

Taiuki felt herself nodding dumbly. Her mind was scattered, broken apart by what had just happened, and she couldn't process it. Leaning on Lady Hannaka, she stumbled forward, leaving the great hall empty save for a servant who scuttled in and removed the evidence of her outburst from the floor, scrounging the valuable nacre beads in his pocket.

28

MATRON-IN-WAITING HANNAKA CARRIED HER charge by the shoulder to her royal quarters, where a hot bath was drawn. The young woman sagged against Hannaka, despondent. She had rarely seen her this quiet, at least not in many years.

Hannaka gently removed the temporary robe from Taiuki's shoulders, as well as the damaged breechbelt. Wisps of desiccated seaweed adhered to it, along with bits of her makeshift shirt. The girl was filthy, although not scarred. In fact, the princess's skin was flawless. No outward signs of a jellyfish attack remained—surprising, given the severity of wounds the princess claimed. Why, the princess had said her eyelids had been eaten away! Hannaka shook her head a little at the unmarred body before her. The girl was beautiful, if somewhat diminutive compared to her sister.

"Where have you been, Yuki-sho?" she murmured.

Taiuki didn't respond.

Hannaka lowered her into the wash basin, where she sat in an uncharacteristically sullen daze, then started with the girl's unkempt hair, a black mass of tangles. She attacked it with soap, something the long, wild mess hadn't seen in a while from the looks of it. As she scrubbed, she could feel the grit of sand embedded on Taiuki's scalp. Next, a rinse, and then she gently washed the girl's face, rubbing the smears of the last few weeks off her cheeks with a soft woven cloth. Her skin was olive underneath all that dirt.

She worked her way down Taiuki's slight shoulders and back. Small-statured as the young woman was, she was strong. Lean muscles, no spare cushion like Hannaka's own plush body, and rumored to have wickedly fast reactions. She had watched the girl become a woman, fierce and unrestrained in practically every way. Hannaka had seen Taiuki fight not only her youngest charge Tan-sho, but also older boys and young men in the training circle. And she knew the young woman had gained a reputation on the real battlefield, though Hannaka hadn't seen that herself.

A loving smile creased her face at the thought of Tan. Such a good and curious boy, excitable to a fault. Tan's attention was too short for serious battle training so far, but the enthusiasm was there. Whether the boy could formulate a plan or lead battalions was questionable, but again, he was just a boy. It would have to be so now, with him announced as Second and Yuki-sho being destined for Krita.

A shame, that.

Yuki-sho was a decent girl too, curious like Tan-sho but not excitable. She had always been eerily calm and measured for her age, rarely raising her voice except at her sister. Now she was older, she was a hard-faced and stolid anchor for the men and women who followed her in battle. Strong like the myr *should* be.

Hannaka had entered their lives shortly after a terrible accident, something the queen regent staunchly refused to talk about. Furuhaki had brought Hannaka in from her distant home far to the south, by the Dark Passages, and Hannaka really didn't know why. She was thankful for the employment, though. Tan-sho was her baby boy, and she loved him dearly. Taiuki, even at that young age, had always remained more distant. She had been old enough not to need a wet nurse, only some oversight. When Lady Hannaka first arrived, the child had gone weeks without leaving her quarters for more than meals and some mysterious "lessons" from the former Waterpriest Merridan. Merridan, of course, was a depraved rogue of a mage, and he had shortly been ejected from the castle under Queen Furuhaki's watchful eye. After that, Taiuki had sulked for months. Somewhat like now, but at least the girl had stayed out of trouble for years.

Thank goodness she's grown a bit, thought Hannaka. She didn't typically sulk anymore; she fought and trained. The only concern Hannaka had now was over Taiuki's love for exploring the deep or the distant on her own. Hannaka wasn't all that surprised by her brush with death; the young woman was always putting herself into dangerous situations. She shook her head again.

This girl.

It had been years since Taiuki had allowed Hannaka to bathe her, but this creature in the wash basin had reverted to obeisance, sitting and allowing her arms to be lifted, her palms and feet scrubbed with a pumice rock without a glimmer of acknowledgment. When the princess was younger, she had been ticklish, much like her little brother. Hannaka hid her frown. It had seemed cruel to undress her in front of her siblings.

When Taiuki was rinsed, Hannaka massaged oil into her long black hair, teasing out the roughness and assuaging the knots until the hair flowed like silk. She dressed the princess according to her station as lady of House Tatami for the evening meal: a soft fitted shift under a tougher seal-leather jerkin, which was overlaid with nacre and turquoise beads; a false cuisse skirt of dyed leather covered with delicate fish scales; a stunning silk cape; and a new breechbelt, this one wrought of strands of gold and silver, braided into a covering over her front. The larger abalone piece was framed by white gold and shone brightly. This breechbelt no longer had an apprentice's rankstone of andesite or colors of the commodore, only a rankstone indicating her royalty. Hannaka slipped sparkling bracelets on Taiuki's limp hands and a matching necklace around her neck. Finally, she pulled the now-dry hair back with pearl strings, revealing the princess's face.

Taiuki's eyes were dull.

The woman's reversal to Hannaka's early memories as wet-nurse was stunning. She took Taiuki by the shoulders and shook her to the present. "Yuki-sho," she said gently. "Come now, you're dressed."

Taiuki blinked but seemed to become more alert. "Yes, Nurse." Her response was childlike, reminiscent of when

Hannaka had been the highest authority in her daily life. She arose without expression and walked out the door.

Hannaka followed discreetly, about ten steps behind, to the Great Hall, a massive open cavern with skylights on the ocean surface above. The tables had been set for dining, and after Princess Taiuki had been announced, the young woman entered and sat at the raised dais between Keiki and Tan. Hannaka smiled as Tan-sho gave his sister a long, powerful hug from his seat. Such a sweet boy. Taiuki didn't hug him back.

Keiki leaned over without reducing her proper posture and said something into Taiuki's ear, then patted her on the knee. The Kritali princess, Lady Anella, gaped at the newly returned princess openly, then snapped her mouth shut and tried to politely eat as though nothing had changed. Tan-sho proceeded to chatter, asking Taiuki where she had been and what she had seen and how badly she had been hurt. He went on and on, even though she didn't seem to be answering. Kei extracted herself somewhat, glancing overtly at Queen Regent Furuhaki on her other side, and talked over them to Lady Anella.

The queen regent sat in her padded chair, overseeing the filling of the room with the last of the nobility and ranking servants. She spared no more attention for the children, and her expression held no emotion whatsoever. Princess Taiuki had been nearly last to arrive for the meal, and those present were trying hard not to gawk at her presence. Like Hannaka, most had believed the princess to be dead. Arch Commodore Sashiro, who was visiting from the front, and Master Mariner Apakun approached her directly and saluted before taking their seats beyond Steward Wehan. The room settled, and the meal began without fanfare.

Hannaka thought it somewhat strange that Queen Regent Furuhaki said nothing regarding Taiuki's renewed presence. But, she was only a matron-in-waiting from a small village and knew little of the ways in a castle as large as this one. They were far more formal here and had traditions she didn't understand. She bent forward to eat her stew. Crab today, with savory mint and a pinch of spice. What a fine meal.

29

TAIUKI DIDN'T RECALL MUCH about her supper, and eventually she ended up back in her quarters. Kei, Tan, and Anella followed, still unbelieving.

Tan kept hugging her unabashedly, and Kei kept touching her hand or shoulder as if to reassure herself Taiuki really was alive. Anella trod on their heels, speechless for once. She managed to work a few words out of her open mouth, asking permission to enter Taiuki's room. Kei waved her in.

"I'm so glad you're back," Tan was saying. "Old Sash was making me train daily. He's such a boring teacher."

"*Master* Sashiro," Kei corrected absently, pushing Taiuki into a chair.

"Decorum, Tan-sho," Taiuki whispered, her response automatic. She still felt as though she were wading through a fog, a suffocating cloud of festering memories and fresh pains. Her joints hurt, her skin prickled like it had been burned, and her mouth tasted metallic.

Kei looked around the room and grabbed a comb, then went about removing the pearl strings from Taiuki's trussed hair.

"Can I help?" Anella asked in a shy voice, then moved to her other side. "Princess Taiuki, I'm so glad you're okay. I was so worried the last few weeks."

Taiuki ignored the girl on one side, the woman on the other as they yanked her back and forth. She caught Tan's eye.

"The Merchan, Tan-sho," she said. She thanked him when he brought her a glass, but then caught his hand. "Master Sashiro is knowledgeable, and a fine commander. Be respectful of him."

Tan made a snoring sound and flopped onto her bed.

Kei sighed. "Tan, you do realize why Master Sashiro was training you, right? Why he returned from the front?"

Tan shrugged.

"Because, regardless of where Taiuki was, you are to be his replacement."

Tan scrunched his brow together. "But Yuki is back now. I didn't think Mother really meant that."

"She's bound for Krita." Kei turned back to Taiuki, yanking the knot she had been working out. "In all seriousness, sister, where were you? Did you run away?"

Anella's eyes widened at the query, and Tan sat up.

Taiuki struggled to answer. *I was looking for guidance. I was looking for him, although I know he isn't there.* "I was exploring the Sanctuary."

Kei pursed her lips. "That's stupid, especially alone."

"What's the Sanctuary?" Anella asked.

"The deepest portal of Shiggo City," Kei answered. "A miserable place, impossible to use and uninteresting in any case. There's hardly anything down there anyway."

"That's not true," Taiuki retorted.

Kei yanked the last pin from her hair and tossed the pearl string to the side table. She looked irritated.

"The Sanctuary Portal leads to the deepest waters of Shiggo, a place bursting with unique life," Taiuki explained, her focus on Anella, who seemed to appreciate the detail with a happy, awe-filled smile. "There are creatures there who survive an entirely different way, combining the energy of the cracks in Father Mana Loi's mantle and the detrital rain from above."

Kei sneered. "Tubeworms and crawling mollusks."

Taiuki ignored her, for both Anella and Tan looked fascinated. Then the Kritali princess's face fell.

"I wish I could see it, but that also sounds terrifying," Anella mumbled. "And you went out alone? Without even an escort?"

Taiuki scoffed. "Myr women don't need escorts."

"But they do need a school, Yuki." Kei had regained some of her composure. "*You* need a school. You can't just go wandering off, doing your own selfish things whenever you feel like it. You're needed here. You have a role to fulfill, as is your duty."

By the current, she sounded like Mother.

Nonetheless, Taiuki felt her stomach drop. "Mother admitted the trade deal fell apart. Thus I should head back to the front as soon as possible. If Master Sashiro is here for Tan's training, then the vice commodore is on her own, and I'm sure she would appreciate the help."

"The deal *did* fall apart, thanks to your disappearance, but we can resume negotiations now that you're back."

"I can't stomach the thought of marrying Godrig, and you know it." She bit her tongue, realizing that Anella was staring at her with a look of great injury.

The princess placed the strings of pearls on the table and stared at her shoes. "I didn't realize you disliked him so much," she said, her cheeks turning pink and her eyes glassy.

Taiuki felt the slightest bit guilty, then hardened. "Our people are not meant to mix, Lady Anella."

Anella scuffed the hard floor with a shoed toe, then nodded. "Please excuse me, everyone, but I'm feeling quite tired. Such an eventful day . . . I praise the Light you are well, Princess Taiuki. Um, bright night." She left quickly.

"That was mean," said Tan when she had gone. "She's not her brother."

"He's the firstborn of Krita. It would be a good placement," said Kei in a very practical tone. "You'd be a queen, like me."

"I don't want to be a queen, Kei. Why don't you understand that?"

"What *do* you want? Branig the Mariner? Would that be good enough for you?" Kei said the name with haughty disgust. "Or maybe that lowly soldier you like so much? Someone who brings no value whatsoever to our kingdom's standing? That *would* be a choice you'd make."

"I want to work with Sashiro. I *want* to lead our people, in battle and defense. It's what I've been doing, what I've trained and bled for. It's where I belong."

Exasperated, Kei turned Taiuki's shoulders and forced her to meet her gaze. It was now cold and calculating, like Mother's. "No, it's where I was meant to be." With that, she strode from the room, hot on Anella's heels.

Tan was quiet for a long while, but in the end the words burst from him uncontrollably. "She's talking about Taifun, isn't she?"

Taiuki found herself fighting the sting of tears again. She willed them away.

Tan got up the from the bed where he had been sitting and gave her another long hug. He clung to her as if he were afraid she would disappear again. He was growing tall so quickly—she could tell the difference from just a few weeks.

Squeezing him back, Taiuki ruffled his jet-black hair. "You're so much like him, Tan. I'm so glad you're okay."

Tan cocked an eyebrow. "Why wouldn't I be?"

She shook her head. "I don't know. I was worried."

"I'm fine, except for having to train constantly. It's you we were worried about. Kei really did think you ran away. She told everyone so."

Taiuki had considered it. But she couldn't protect Kei and Tan by running. She couldn't fight Jijito by running. Yes, It'tholl needed her too, but somehow she'd have to divide her time, slipping her precious moments with the dragling in between duties here. She would train hard at the garrison, so her mother and sister would see the necessity of keeping her intact as future arch commodore. She would guide Tan, mold him into a formidable warrior.

Marrying her off was a waste of an asset.

Renewed vigor filled her, and she finally was able to form a genuine smile.

Tan seemed confused by her expression, but he grinned back anyway. He half skipped to the door. "Glad you're not dead, sis," he called carelessly as he left.

Taiuki reeled back in her chair at his comment. Then she spent the next few hours thinking about Taifun.

Taiuki arrived at the training hall shortly after the gray light of dawn peeked through the Garrison Gate, adorned in her training mail. She practiced fighting forms in the courtyard as the barracks awoke, and she was shortly joined by Master Sashiro.

She bowed her head deeply to him, placing both palms in front of her face as a sign of deep respect. "Bright morning, Arch Commodore," she clicked.

He returned the salute and waited until she finally raised her head. His smile was gentle. "My heart is far lighter today than it was, Princess."

"How is the front, sir?"

"Reihotto has it in hand, and I shall rejoin her soon."

They shifted to dual fighting forms, running through the elaborate waltz of attack and defense that they had practiced for several years. Some of the barracks' young soldiers departed for a hunt, while others initiated their own knifeplay or shooting practice, but some gathered to watch the pair. With their fighting force deployed at the Jijiton-jin front, most of the remaining troops were in training, junior soldiers who had not experienced live battle.

After they had run through their forms, Master Sashiro handed Taiuki a short knife, and they battled hand-to-hand. It was as it had been for years, and the sense of familiarity brought Taiuki greater confidence that she was where she belonged. The duel was well-matched, as Sashiro was more experienced but Taiuki was faster. It was almost as if the water parted before her blade, easing its passage through. She nearly scored him once, barely overreaching as her knife hissed through the water, but he crashed down on her in rebuttal and smacked her skull with the butt of his blade. Taiuki staggered back, recomposing herself, but Master Sashiro had disengaged.

"I'm sorry, Your Highness," he clicked quietly, "but I must work with Tan. Please understand."

Taiuki looked around, scanning faces, and realized Tan was waiting on the edge of the ring. He wore a breechbelt nearly identical to hers, featuring an abalone shell and a royal rankstone, but his also featured a single rankstone of andesite, a stone hers no longer had. He met her gaze sheepishly as he rubbed the sleep from his eyes.

Master Sashiro exchanged his knife for one made of dull-edged ironwood, then gestured to Tan to take a position next to him so they could walk through forms. Tan did so, but with a beseeching glance at Taiuki to somehow extract him from the situation.

Taiuki awkwardly exited the courtyard, her cheeks burning, and joined the watching ranks. Sashiro had obviously returned to guide Tan in his new role as Second, and true to his dutiful nature, he would do so.

She was highly aware of the golden belt hanging over her front, shining with its lack of andesite and her desired but rejected rank. This was going to be more difficult than she had thought, if only because of the blow to her pride. She turned away, hoping to find something productive to do.

Soldiers parted before her as she entered the air-filled training hall, a large dome adjacent to the barracks that was maintained open by the Waterpriests, like most of the castle. The training hall was useful for exercises needed in a land battle; the weaponry and fighting strategy were so unique. She took a deep, quavering breath, allowing her anger to dissipate. She would go on practicing with the other soldiers. Later, she and Tan would train together as well, for his betterment.

Taiuki joined a battalion's morning session, which consisted of land spear forms and sparring. Taiuki enjoyed the spear, although she preferred the staff to some degree; it was more balanced. Nonetheless, she engaged fully and tried to ignore the small voice that reminded her of Tan's presence just outside. Sashiro would spend several hours with him, first with forms and slow-paced knife training, then a lecture on underwater strategy for unmounted troops. He often paired the weapon of focus with a battle strategy that was appropriate, or he would regale stories of a battle where that weapon was primarily used or became strategically important. Unlike Tan, Taiuki thought Master Sashiro's lessons were fascinating and well-planned.

When Master Sashiro lectured, many of the trainees would attend, so she would not be out of place, she thought as she struck a soldier successfully with the dulled spear. The soldier exhaled at the sharp prick, despite his thick hauberk, then increased his vigor. Taiuki defended herself well, backing up and circling, trying to keep herself away from the wall. The man would pin her down if he could. He had likely watched Sashiro do so many times before and was emulating the arch commodore's technique. They exchanged several blows, each attempting to find a solid mark with the sides or butt of their spears, but to little avail. The soldier playfully called for his platoon mates to join in, and three more attacked Taiuki from different directions. The fight quickened, and she spun and twisted in every direction, finding a foe at every face. She was forced to dive in escape, dropping her spear in a graceful but ill-conceived tumble. The first soldier was not far behind, and he made to jab at Taiuki in feigned victory.

Taiuki put her hand up in protest and winced, knowing the strike of the spear on her mail would bruise, serving as record of her defeat.

Instead, a blasting fire burst through her veins, alighting her arm and coursing across her chest. Everything—the soldier, the incoming spearhead, the domed ceiling above—became a hazy blur of pain and fear. Her heart felt like it would explode, and she cried out.

When she opened her eyes, the training hall had gone silent. The soldier stood over her, trembling with a bladeless spear in hand. He mouthed a few silent words before regaining his voice, which shook.

"My apologies, Princess." The soldier bowed and backed away, clutching the damaged spear. Another soldier did the same, mumbling, "I believe Master Sashiro is preparing to lecture soon. We don't want to keep you, Your Highness." The soldiers scattered abruptly, and Taiuki thought she saw a glimmer of castle silks in the hazy chaos.

She was alone yet again, and painfully so. Taking a deep breath, she stared at the ceiling from where she had fallen. Then she massaged her arm, which felt as though she had been punched. Her elbow creaked with renewed joint pain. Her heart physically ached; each beat pulsed blood into quivering arteries. Taiuki didn't understand what had happened, but a faint thought nagged at her. Her mind was scattered like beads across the floor; she couldn't think.

Taiuki blinked as Master Sashiro and his entourage, including Tan, entered the hall, chatting as they settled on benches. Sashiro launched into his lesson, extolling the virtues of the slim underwater blades made by the myr of eastward Nagawa. What made a quality blade? How were they tempered, of what metal were they? Master Sashiro's enthusiasm for weaponry was matched only by his keenness for fighting; he was an admirable man, worthy of leadership. He had been like a father to her for as long as Taiuki remembered. She allowed the strange electric feeling that pervaded her body to fade as she focused on the lesson.

She engaged in the remaining training that day, including a noonmeal with the soldiers. She sat next to Tan, who was still embarrassed at their apparent contention; only Master Sashiro joined them at their table. Tan kept them chatting about nothing, although Taiuki could feel the arch commodore's wordless inspection constantly washing over her.

Afterward, the afternoon was spent riding underwater, delayed for a moment when she and Tan vied for the secondary command position in the echelon formation. She had realized her error and acquiesced to the third position, to Sashiro's rear and left.

Before long, she and Tan were removing their saddles in the stables and rubbing salve on their mounts' shoulders. Hachi leaned into the rub, begging for scratches with an entreating nicker.

Tan was oddly quiet at first, but she suspected he wouldn't be able to hold his thoughts in for long. "Hachi missed you," he clicked.

Taiuki grinned a little as they put the salve away and moved into the air-filled training hall; they both shifted without thought, tails splitting and reforming into legs. "I missed him too. Was anyone giving him some exercise while I was gone?"

Tan nodded. "I did, and one of the other stableboys."

"Thanks."

"He bit him twice." Tan paused again. This corner of the hall was empty, and they sat in an alcove with a window to the barracks yard. He cleared his throat. "Are you coming back tomorrow?"

Taiuki nodded. She knew her normal place had been taken, but she refused to walk away now. "I'm not giving up on the troops—or you. I came back for that very reason."

Tan's stare was doubtful. "Mother's not going to like it."

"I know."

Again, he paused for a breath. "What happened with that soldier earlier? I heard the men talking about a spear . . ."

Taiuki furrowed her brow, thinking. What exactly had happened? It seemed blurry, like her mind was rejecting the event. She remembered searing pain in her arm, confusion, fear. The soldier backing away with a rushed bow. A dark, familiar face melting into the crowd. She felt fine now, and looked at Tan in puzzlement. "I don't know."

"I heard you broke it somehow." Tan shrugged. "Not sure why they were so worried about it. No one would talk in front of me."

"I just remember it hurt."

Tan shrugged again. Like her, he didn't know what had happened, but he had moved on already. "I'll be on time tomorrow. We can swim over together."

Taiuki smiled and agreed. "I'll make sure you wake up." She jostled him. "I'll send Nurse Hannaka in to get you out of bed!"

Tan rolled his eyes and batted her away with both hands. "I don't need a nurse anymore!"

"Then why is she still here?" Taiuki let out a laugh at Tan's discomfiture. Hannaka had stayed long after Tan needed a wet-nurse, but she fulfilled a useful role as their primary caregiver. She was a good woman, with a thick southern sea accent belying her origin from a smaller rural district, but she was noble nonetheless and of strong *myr* blood. Taiuki knew she had children whom she very occasionally traveled to see, but Tan was truly her baby. Taiuki ruffled Tan's hair to get him riled up again. "Tan-sho, dearie . . ." she crooned in Hannaka's voice.

Tan slapped her hand away in protest and got up, then straightened. Master Sashiro was standing in front of them. "Arch Commodore Sashiro." He bent at the waist while saluting.

Taiuki did the same, bowing deeply.

Master Sashiro bent his head back at the pair, then addressed Tan. "You will be timely tomorrow, I trust."

"Yes, sir."

"You are dismissed then."

Tan nodded and bowed again before departing.

Sashiro examined Taiuki for minutes. She stood at strict attention, not daring to anger him or make him question her discipline. He already questioned her understanding of the Way of the Current.

Finally, he gestured for her to be at ease, and they both sat in the alcove. Master Sashiro began, "I received orders several weeks ago, after you disappeared, to begin earnestly training Tan for leadership. He should do well enough, although he has much to learn. But you, Princess Taiuki, you are not expected on the front again."

Taiuki's lip trembled, but she stayed steady. "Sir, please allow me to continue as a soldier. I'll join a regular battalion if I must, but please let me remain with you."

Sashiro continued as if she hadn't spoken. "Your brother is enthusiastic in some things, but his attention wanes with battle strategy and forms. I saw him work harder today than ever before, truly a remarkable improvement."

"Please, sir—"

"Clearly, your presence made him work harder." The pause that followed his words was significant, and Taiuki clamped her mouth in apology. He continued, "He idolizes you, and he wants to impress you. I think the best route for him is to train with you and beside you, to learn from you, as you have learned from me. You'll need to be part of his training from now on, until you are assigned elsewhere. In fact, given my own duties at the Jijiton-jin front, alternating with Vice Commodore Reihotto's, I think it would be wise to engage you in training many of the young troops here, including Tan. The trainees respect you, and they can learn much from you in my own absence. When you deem them ready, you can send them to me in the west."

Taiuki wanted desperately to hug the man, but such impropriety would be rejected by the arch commodore. Instead she thanked him politely.

"Taiuki?"

"Sir?"

"All for Shiggo."

"Ol Shiggo'lo, sir," she affirmed.

"For the school, and for the kingdom."

He dismissed her, and she wandered back to the Garrison Gate, swimming slowly as she pondered. What had happened with the spear? What had happened with the lacer, when that empty orb of clarity had appeared around her and It'tholl? Her questions intermingled with pure elation at Master Sashiro's support.

She sought out her favorite corner in the Lower Market, an expansive, bustling cavern containing a sprawl of Shiggo City's businesses, all situated in stacked towers and tightly entwined walkways at the opening to the Mana Loi. The Market Gate. Beyond that, the city continued on in buildings of stone and water, rather than air.

From her spot at a seat recessed between a breechbelt maker and a jeweler who worked in tandem, Taiuki could see the long way toward the Market Gate. Townspeople and traders moved back and forth between the air-filled cavern and the sea, shifting seamlessly at the vertical wall of water. Soldiers posted to either side of the gate, leaning on their spears with bored stances. As far as she knew, the gallite portcullis had never been lowered in her lifetime.

She beckoned a drink vendor over, and he poured a generous glass of ale before saluting with both hands.

"Your Highness, I can acquire some Marlemetian red wine for you, if you give me but a short while."

"Please do," she answered, raising an eyebrow. That couldn't be easy to get ahold of, given the exceedingly weak trade lines connecting Marlemet's land kingdom to Shiggo. Their trade caravans were allowed to go to the myrkingdom in the Red Bay, but no trade was sanctioned to Marlemet, and the trickle of quality wine that came in passed through multiple hands under tables before reaching here.

She set her ale down and kicked her legs up onto a small barrel.

Ever since bonding with It'tholl, she had felt imbued with greater power than anyone had ever told her about. Everything around her seemed to pulse and shiver with Water, even the ale between her fingers. She raised the glass and inspected it.

What happened to the spear point?

The answer lay in some murky mass of confusion accompanied by searing pain, and she didn't know why. The point hadn't stabbed into her. It had seemingly snapped off and flown into some unseen corner, startling everyone. The soldiers had marveled, then feared. Even the blue shark cavalryman had avoided her after that.

What if it hadn't broken? The thought both intrigued and frightened her, leading to that familiar sick feeling that she would rather avoid.

She downed half the ale, and her stomach gurgled in protest.

Then she set the glass down and inspected it. Her composure would've looked casual to anyone watching, but her mind was intent upon the glass. During both the lacer and the spear incidents, she had been afraid, belting out emotion in waves. What if . . .

The glass beaded with condensation. Droplets slid down the side, wetting the table in a growing pool. Taiuki controlled a shuddering breath, and unexplainable terror froze her veins.

She twitched as the drink vendor reappeared with a small skein under his arm and a self-satisfied look.

At that moment, the ale glass cracked apart, sending fragments and liquid outward. It splashed upon Taiuki's skirting.

"Oh, Your Highness," the vendor cried in dismay. "Forgive me, I beg you. I didn't know that glass was damaged. Please allow me to give you a different one. It will be better not to pollute the wine in any case." He cut himself grabbing for the shards and tossing them into his apron.

"Peace, man. Leave the skein and a new glass."

He did so, bowing and averting his eyes as he backed away. "Call upon me whenever you wish for anything, Your

Highness," he mumbled, red with embarrassment. "I won't be far."

Taiuki swirled the red in her new glass, taking in its character and depth of rich, sweet flavor, then glanced at the mess on the table.

A small, confused look of satisfaction crossed her features. She didn't understand it, but it had to do with It'tholl. *My beloved It'tholl, I miss you.* With Sashiro's blessing, she had only to get her affairs in order, a defined and defensible schedule, and then she could return to her dragling.

30

REYLIN'S ARRIVAL AT EAST Face Mine was heralded with cheers, respectful salutes, and a hearty handshake from Guildmaster Daiunek despite the ominous clouds pushing from the north.

"A bright day to you, Prince, and a drink for all your men!" Daiunek declared. He wiped the blackish dust from his brow with a filthy sleeve, but the motion merely smeared the mine's gifts across his forehead. The big man hacked and spat, clearing his lungs, then directed his servants to pour mugs for all of Reylin's officers and High Guard.

Reylin thanked him and sipped, then caught his own wince at the thick stout chew of tar beer. Damn.

"Sit, Prince, and let us speak," suggested Daiunek, ushering him toward a set of long tables. The clearing before the mine opening had been expanded, trees cut and applied to the construction of a set of cabins. The original cabin in which Reylin had slept had gained numerous adjoining rooms, a stable overhanging, and a smithy work area. Daiunek gestured in that direction. "Aye, your sleeping quarters are better than they were; we've made excellent progress establishing East Face as a frontier mine."

"Can you even taste that beer through the grime?" Master Oyerton sat and handed Daiunek a wet rag.

The brawny man nodded gratefully and scrubbed his face, then continued speaking as though he hadn't been interrupted. "I'm telling you, Prince, this is a quality seam. Wethers and I are growing more excited with every bit of rock chipped out, every pace deeper we go . . ." He grumbled a sound like a man filled at banquet, then licked his lips. "The Earth gifts those brave enough to seek her."

"I'm pleased to hear it. And no attacks beyond the rare individual?"

Oyerton brought a finger to his lips, as though bringing up the possibility might curse them, but he dropped it just as quickly. He was in no position to reprimand Reylin.

Reylin steeled his jaw and redirected his attention to Daiunek, who had turned down the corners of his lips and was rubbing his jaw in thought.

"Aye, only a few, entirely uncoordinated. The creatures dive from the sky alone as a hawk would, hiding in the brightness of the Eye, but their mistake is believing us to be the mice. Your cavalrymen did well enough dispelling them, although I believe one or two of them were injured." He raised an eyebrow in query.

"Five," muttered Sir Gillead from Reylin's side. "We received that report while in Camdry, Guildmaster Daiunek."

Daiunek nodded slowly. "I see you brought archers—a wise move, Prince. The cavalry have so little range of motion up here on the mountainside, and although a portion of them have bows, they're obviously more effective with sweeping sword. That said, I can use them. I've half a mind to push downslope, now that you're here."

"Wethers is nearly drooling at the thought," said Oyerton, scoffing into his mug.

Reylin glanced around the open glade for the drunkard journeyman, doubting whether that was the reason Wethers might drool.

"He's deep in the mine," said the guildmaster as though he read Reylin's mind. He drained his mug. "We've been following a seam in, toward some flavor of gemstone. He's not quite sure what it is yet."

Reylin tried to convey a sound of respect and awe, rather than his true feeling of derision. What right did a man like Wethers have to carry such a gift of Earth? The man could hardly stand on two feet, and yet he fulfilled a highly valued role in the Miners Guild.

He focused on reporting the troops he had brought: one squadron of swordsmen, one squadron of pikes, and a platoon of archers. "They can handle their own supplies, but the cost shall be borne by the guild," he concluded as they watched the soldiers evaluate where best to set up camp.

"As agreed," said Daiunek pleasantly. "Their commanding officer?"

Gillead pointed, and Daiunek partially stood from the bench.

"I have some ideas to open this clearing up further." He smiled at Reylin. "I've half a mind to establish a town, Prince. In your name, a fortified Miratian settlement, around East Face. From here, we can cultivate multiple mines downslope with adequate military support."

Oyerton nodded silent agreement, sipping at his tar beer.

Reylin hesitated for only a moment. After all, a fortified town was hardly more aggressive than a mining encampment. Both were advances upon Halmani territory, both advances of proper civilization into the wilds. Both enhanced Miratian prestige and dominion, but one was strategically wiser if they were planning to stay long term.

"I support such a move, Guildmaster," he agreed.

Daiunek shook his hand again, then excused himself to speak with the commanding officer of the newly arrived troops. "Enjoy the evening and rest, Prince. Tomorrow, let us speak of supply management for colonization, an expanded agreement between guild and kingdom."

Reylin watched with satisfaction as a large camp sprang into place in the few hours before dusk. Trees were felled, and the glade emerged from the shade of hundreds of years of growth. The pines were straight as arrow shafts, and their trunks were dragged to a pile with the combined sweat of horses and men. Canvas tents popped up in creamy tan disarray, scattered amongst the spaces between tree stumps, and small cookfires appeared as evening drew on.

The mountainside around East Face Mine now appeared as a summer pasture, firebugs flashing over the grass in singular bursts. It was beautiful.

The grayness of clouds to the north darkened to black, churning through a low point between two heights and spilling toward them. Reylin inhaled the growing humidity, his awareness of its weight far enhanced by his realization of power. The Water was coming; the air was pregnant with it.

He savored the view from the largest lodge, in which Daiunek had gladly placed him and Kaiadin once again. Gillead and Patreagh sat on either side, doing the same. The clouds gathered behind them and to the north, and the valley far below them stretched out without sign of lamp or habitation.

"Gillead? You knew my father well, did you not?"

The man nodded solemnly. "Yes, Your Highness."

"What would he have done?" Reylin was unsure what answer he wanted. Daiunek's implication that he was much like his father had seemed complimentary, contrasting with the meekness of the Elder Council. On the other hand, Reylin wished to be seen for himself, not as the shadow of someone else's memory.

Gillead scowled, a natural expression for him, as he pondered an answer. He played with his peppered mustache. "He would have brought war to the fyr years ago, with or without a mine."

"Why didn't he?"

"He did several times, but never with the intent to colonize the Loi al'Halmana. Sir Patreagh and I both commanded men during those times."

Patreagh muttered an acknowledgment, then broke into a dark grin. "Bloody, glorious days."

"That they were," Gillead agreed. "Days that made a man proud to be Miratian. We battled for honor and security, settling the border lines, letting those Halmani savages know their limits. None dared to venture into Galltry's district back then."

"Why did we stop fighting?"

"King Rolis died."

Patreagh clenched his jaw and bowed his head in silent mourning, and Gillead leaned forward to look at him with a measure of sympathy.

"Patreagh knew your father better than I, Prince. He was drill master when your father entered knight's training."

Reylin seethed as he mulled over those words. The Elder Council, fearful and over-conservative to the last, had reined the military prowess of Mirat back after the Great Fire, undercutting the ambitions of men like Gillead and Patreagh. Men who had the spine to face the endless expanse of grass in the Loi al'Halmana and see potential rather than peril.

"I am not my father," he said quietly. "Nor am I Galltry. I will forge a new path, expand Mirat's borders, beginning with fortifying East Face and then taking the war to the Loi al'Halmana. I will leave my own legacy."

"I've always believed so, Your Highness," said Sir Gillead. He didn't crack a smile like Patreagh did, but Reylin thought he spied a twitch of pride in his lord commander's stiff, lined cheeks.

Reylin and his High Guard oversaw the settlement of East Face, staying another two days under the cover of a misty, somewhat miserable rain. The deployed men cleared the stumps, constructed lodges and work buildings, and began to lay out a fortification plan. The commanding officer, a knight captain by the name of Sir Theodar, was highly capable. Reylin had known him for years, for his tenure had lasted since Gillead was promoted to the High Guard.

Theodar, for his part, recommended a young knight named Dorian from his ranks to replace Sir Jonathan on the High Guard. The substitution was made quietly, with a formal blessing by Father Kaiadin and oath-taking by Reylin. Ronidann was nowhere to be seen during the ritual; he mourned his beloved fallen comrade in seclusion.

Kaiadin kept Reylin occupied with small experiments, pushing and sensing and touching the crystalline waters of a nearby stream that tumbled its way down the mountain. The stream had swelled with the rain, its power engorged and wild, and Reylin marveled at its pure and energetic character.

The rain cleared late in the day, the grayness of the sky brightening to a pale yellow. The expanse of the Loi al'Halmana at their feet now seemed an ocean, its edges immeasurable and unseen. Reylin imagined he could see the peaks of mountains, a different aspect of the mighty Sikrat, far away on the other side of the plains, but he knew it was imagination only. The grass extended beyond the horizon.

The fyr attacked with the dawn.

"You must remain inside, Your Highness," declared Sir Gillead, blocking the door as screeching battle cries sounded through the walls.

Reylin scrambled into his chainmail and beckoned for Patreagh to help him with the straps cinching his armor tight. "Gillead, I want to command my own men, not hide in this hovel like a coward."

"It's not cowardice, my prince. It's wisdom," Gillead countered with a grimace, but he didn't interfere with Patreagh's work. "Our sole duty is to ensure your safety, and we did not prepare you to fight."

"You've been training me since I was a child, Gillead." Reylin took his helmet from Patreagh and shoved it on, then held a hand out impatiently for his sword. "I know what kind of king I want to be, and I can't become him in this room."

Sir Gillead stood in front of the door and ground his teeth for a moment. As the one on primary guard duty, he wore his full armor already, whereas Patreagh was rushing to adorn himself.

"If you must go, then I bless your steps," said Father Kaiadin, tossing a cloud of powder over Reylin. The mist seemed to hang in the air and hiss, then dissipated to nothing.

Gillead scowled to himself and handed Reylin his sword with a bow. "Stay beside me, Your Highness, and Patreagh will cover your other side."

"Just as we do in sparring. It will be fine, Gillead." Reylin tried to sound confident, planting a stern look of authority on his own face. They had sparred thousands of times in the yard, but what good was sparring if it was not in preparation for real battle? Whether the Elder Council liked it or not, Reylin would and could bring war to the fyr, and he fully intended to be part of it, not an observer.

His adrenaline surged through his limbs, and he grinned hopefully as he heard Sirs Dorian and Ronidann outside. Gillead led the way.

Reylin found himself immersed in chaos, at least on the part of the fyr. The winged savages swooped low through the clearing, raking at soldiers with wicked, clawed greaves. The ones who landed rolled gracefully and shifted, bare-chested and painted in bright colors that matched their feathers; these would pull weapons from their back straps and attack with wild, acrobatic spins. Most double-wielded slender swords, while others swung hand axes.

"Loose!" cried Sir Theodar, and a wave of arrows flew.

Fyr tumbled from the sky.

"For Mirat and the mines," Reylin shouted, buzzing with excitement.

"For glory," Patreagh and Gillead replied in unison.

He leapt forward and swung at a fyr warrior that had landed. The smaller fyr barely managed to parry against Reylin's heavy broadsword, then rolled to one side. Reylin followed, meeting the creature's defensive bracing with a ringing clang. The fyr's strength was lesser, and he grunted as Reylin bore down upon him, then swept his blade smoothly to one side.

He opened a massive wound in the fyr's shoulder. Another sweep of his blade, and the fight was over.

The fyr slumped to the ground.

He looked like a man.

"Well done, Your Highness," cried Ronidann. The man was in his element, dancing among the dead with his own broadsword, back to Sir Dorian. It was the most joy Reylin had seen in him since the loss of Jonathan, and he seemed to direct his angst at the feathered creatures that poured from above.

"Loose!" cried Sir Theodar again, and another volley filled the sky.

The onslaught of fyr slowed, but many of the surviving monsters attempted to land.

Reylin stabbed into several before hearing Ronidann suggest that the fyr were no more than chickens on a skewer. His harsh laughter, interspersed with the heavy breaths of battle, was echoed by Dorian, who suggested that that might be why the savages didn't like fire. Both men hooted with merriment.

The one beneath Reylin's blade had fully shifted, leaving bare arms where colorful wings had been. The fyr wore no bracers or mail on their arms, for such garments would interfere with their ability to form wings, and in this state he could almost believe they truly were men.

The dead fyr, smaller and scrawnier in stature than himself, had five fingers on each hand, now-normal proportions of forearm and bicep, and a bare chest that looked like any other man's, although it was partially hairless. The creature's face, though ruddier than Reylin's, was a human one, streaked with paint. His nose was more hooked and his hair oddly grayish-white, but he shared the hazel eyes of many northerners.

Those eyes were vacant, dull with death, and Reylin shrugged his thoughts off.

He mustn't be distracted.

The fyr were monsters, attacking like cowards from the blinding morning light of the Eye. Attacking a harmless mine that, if not for Reylin, housed only miners and their servants. Reylin hated to think of the tragedy the guild's men and women could have endured had he not arrived in time.

He was breathless by the time the attack ended. Like the one before it, the assault seemed an uncoordinated flush of fyr from the sky. None of the corpses seemed to differ from another: no officer garb, no elite armor or especial weaponry, and certainly no indicator of higher intelligence.

"The creatures really thought they could take us down with these pigstickers?" Sir Ronidann sneered, retrieving and then tossing one of the slim blades away with a clatter. He was covered in blood. Colorful down stuck to the damp on his boots, a rainbow of remnants from the creatures thoroughly integrated with mud and blood.

"Praise the Light that's all they're capable of," Sir Dorian agreed, wiping his blade clean.

"Don't underestimate them," snarled Gillead, but he eased when he spied the wide grin splitting Reylin's face. "It was well fought, Your Highness. Your first battle." He knelt in the blood without consideration and dipped his head to Reylin for a long moment, exaggerated enough that the surrounding soldiers and other High Guard emulated him. "Congratulations, Prince. Your father would be proud."

Reylin acknowledged the compliment and felt a strange, almost hot sense of self-consciousness fill him. Would Rolis have been proud? Would he have loved his son for the glory of spilling fyr blood on the mountainside, for repelling the wildling attack and driving them away from the mine? Reylin indicated for Gillead to stand. "For Mirat, Sir Gillead."

"For glory," intoned the men in a rising swell of voices.

Reylin demanded they remain long enough to verify Sir Theodar was prepared for further incursions. The knight captain established a closer watch, establishing sentries on a number of prominent outcroppings and sending scouts out to find more vantage points. He compiled a list of supplies desired to construct a fortification more quickly, and Reylin promised he'd have it.

Reylin stayed busy as the profuse stacks of spindly bodies disappeared from the glade. They were piled and burned, sending a pyre of black, rotten smoke downslope and into the endless grasses. The evening breeze worked in the mine's favor, as Daiunek and Oyerton had suggested.

"Do you think they can see it?" he asked.

"I'm sure they're watching everything now," Gillead answered, crossing his bulky arms and glaring outward. "But the mine is secure under Theodar."

Reylin nodded, thinking back on how few of the fyr died in fyrform. Most transformed before passing the Gates, leaving behind a manlike shell. "It seems strange they can make themselves look so much like us," he muttered.

Gillead grumbled deep in his throat. "A farce, my prince."

"They're no more human than my horse," said Patreagh, his tone dripping with disdain. "Good for service with adequate training and discipline, but some can't be broken. Many, in fact."

Gillead inspected Reylin with a thoughtful look in the oncoming darkness of evening. "Patreagh and I spent many years on the Halmani front, Your Highness. We've seen the fyr atrocities, their uncivilized way of life, but I know you haven't. Trust us when we say you did well today, and you did right."

"I know that, Gillead," Reylin replied, somewhat testy. He tried to mask his transparent sense of dread over the fyr, over the memory of those five human fingers replacing a splayed-out wing, over the ghastly sight of bright awareness fading in each fyr face. It didn't matter, not in the face of necessary justice.

But Gillead pressed on. "I had fifteen years when I slew my first man, Your Highness. I was serving as a page, and my master was injured. I ran into the battle before thinking twice, and I ran his enemy through. The other man was young, only a few years older than I, and I saw the fear in his eyes as he died. I saw the specter of death in that moment, but I would never have traded it for failing my master. He is alive yet, because of my actions that day."

Feverish irritation burned through Reylin, touching his forehead and ears and settling like a furnace in his chest. Gillead saw through him so easily.

Patreagh added his own story, describing a border incident with a petty kingdom on the coast, one which had tied itself to a group of smugglers. Reylin only half listened.

"Being responsible for the death of another is a hefty weight," Gillead concluded, grasping his arm lightly. "I didn't look forward to this day, but if you are to be a king, then you will continue to carry that burden beyond today, for all of Mirat."

Reylin clenched his jaw, somewhat irked by Gillead's familiar touch. He glanced at it, and the man released him immediately. So both Gillead and Patreagh believed him to be suffering from the guilt of his first kill.

"Ensure that we are ready to depart in the morning," he commanded, forcing both men to leave. He leaned back on the bench, sensing the grounding wood of the wall behind him.

Father Kaiadin appeared and bowed, ungainly. "My young king, I have overseen the eradication of the fyr bodies, assuring their souls moved on to the proper nethergate. May I sit?"

Reylin waved him down. At least one person respected him adequately.

"I sense an unease in you," said Kaiadin. "Might I prepare a tonic for the mind?"

Reylin shook his head. "Thank you, Father, but no. I'm merely reflecting."

The mage settled in a flounce of robes beside him and adjusted his glasses. "As am I, my son. This was my first time being so close to such a savage attack. I was proud to see you leading your High Guard through the fray." He beamed, his dark eyes beads inside the indigo band.

It was said the indigo band gave Temple mages the sight of I'ya. Did Kaiadin see him for who he was?

"I thank you for the blessing before the battle," said Reylin, recalling the dusting of magical powder.

Kaiadin ducked his head as though embarrassed. "Oh, it was nothing, my king. Just a bit of low magika for protection and healing. I'm afraid I'm not much use in a fight beyond that."

"I appreciate the sentiment, Father, even if I am learning to heal on my own. Father? Do you . . ." Reylin paused, his tongue tripping over itself. The doubts he had hidden from Gillead and Patreagh came spilling out. "Do you think the fyr deserved—"

"Peace, my son," said Father Kaiadin. "Be at peace. You fought in defense of Mirat's innocent today. The miners are not knights, and they would have been greatly endangered without your support. You suggested that you wish to be a king who does not shy away from risk, for the sake of protecting others. You must adhere to those principles, son. Allow no one to sway you. I see something special in you, my lord beneshel, my young mage-king, and I must believe it is for a great purpose. I believe you when you say who you want to be."

Kaiadin gave him a respectful gesture, one a Temple mage would typically give another.

"I believe you, my son, and I believe *in* you."

ONON M. SAAD.

31

Check the babe from head to toe,
Examine every part.
Inspect the babe, and if you find the blemish,
Take its heart.

The Midwife's Training

"YOU'RE A FOOL IF you believe he loves you," the baroness spat, her tea forgotten in the moment.

Syrana listened with a tightly set jaw and a prim, frozen smile. Undoubtedly, her mother had more to say.

"Until you mother an heir, you're just a plaything," Ana continued. "I thought you were wiser, that you would try harder, and instead you allowed that useless Priscilla to get the first opportunity."

"Ma, she was already pregnant when Reylin and I married."

The baroness glared, her expression pure poison, and Syrana dropped her eyes.

"You should have taken care of it sooner." Her voice was icy, merciless. Then she sipped her tea with the utmost elegance, the picture of a noble and respectable woman.

"I tried," Syrana stammered. "I used cha, like you said, and I prayed daily. I even—" She paused. Even her mother might balk at the use of red magika.

The baroness demanded her answer, though, and Syrana admitted her more recent witchcraft attempts. She didn't mention the minor assistance she had received thus far from Father Kaiadin. Ana didn't seem surprised or taken aback by the nefarious applications of burned feathers and blood. "Well, you really *are* trying," she said, subsiding somewhat. Then she added, "Why aren't you pregnant yet?"

Syrana shook her head in frustration. Perhaps she truly was barren, a more than adequate reason for Reylin to discard her. She confided how she had stolen several spell sheets from the temple, but fertility hadn't been included on most of them.

Her mother examined her with pity. "Stupid girl. Fertility spells wouldn't be questionable to request from the temple. Father Kaiadin or that graybeard Ma'thell would have gladly given you assistance."

Syrana felt herself blush. She was a fool. Months of guilt and shame, alternating with modest hope and optimism, had passed. But she was trying. She *had* reached out to Kaiadin, but the mage was treading carefully and methodically through the most viable options. He hadn't yet surpassed her own witchcraft when it came to red magika.

Her mother was going on about how she had begotten Syrana's brother, Abonn, within two quick moons of marriage. "Do whatever it takes to bind your future to the king, you useless thing," she said in conclusion, "and pray Priscilla has a girl."

Ana left the parlor where they had privately had their tea. Syrana pondered her mother's words while sipping the last of her drink. The calming scent of lavender and citrus filled her nostrils, and she began to feel better. Having collected herself once again, she left the parlor as well, seeking out Reylin's company.

He had returned from the East Face Mine just the evening before, accompanied only by his High Guard and a very small contingent of cavalrymen. He had seemed in a fine mood, having accomplished his mission to deliver men to the mines and learned a small bit of Water magika under Father Kaiadin's tutelage, and he had welcomed her into his arms like a victorious warrior.

He was, in fact, victorious, for he had arrived just in time to deflect a savage Halmani attack. Syrana shuddered to think of such foul creatures, such danger to the miners of East Face.

"He's gone to the quarry, m'lady," said Sir Bonnehad, "along with your father and brother."

Syrana pursed her lips. Abonn, as the heir, was trained in the mining craft and spent his days at the quarry or checking other mines farther up the mountain. They shared little affection, as he had been at the guild hall when she was younger, and had returned for journeyman tenure at about the time she was sent to wait on Lady Shildra. They were likely sharing a dull conversation over ores and lodes, one she would have to feign interest in with a bright smile and occasional intelligent remarks.

She had hoped to leave most of that behind when she went to court, but she couldn't seem to escape Camdry or her mother, no matter what she did.

She dismounted gracefully near Reylin, who did indeed seem deep in conversation with Abonn regarding gallite demand and pricing. He barely acknowledged her kiss before shifting into questions on gemstones, quality versus quantity, and appropriate pricing for the rare orange gems they might find at East Face and beyond.

Just then, they heard the clopping tempo of a galloping horse. A figure in flowing indigo robes rode up to them and dismounted breathlessly.

"My king"—Kaiadin addressed Reylin with a quick bow—"a Whisper from Ironhold. The Princess Priscilla has gone into labor early."

Internally, Syrana groaned. She had barely managed to edge a single word into the men's business conversation.

Reylin had hardly looked at her. Her mother's words seared through her heart, along with a deep-seated fear that he didn't love her. He cared about Priscilla and the babe struggling to emerge from her womb.

Reinforcing that thought, Reylin's eyes widened with excitement, and a wide, toothy grin spread across his handsome face. He took a step toward his tethered horse, then paused and turned back to the group apologetically. "I should go to her."

Bonneser harrumphed and waved his hand. "May your son be strong as alisite, Your Highness."

Abonn echoed the same, flashing a subtle look at Syrana. So he felt the same as Ana. Wonderful.

Syrana stewed where she stood, swaying, torn between demanding Reylin's attention and exuding an image of joy for the occasion. The latter was more appropriate.

Reylin thanked them and moved to his horse.

"Hold, m'lord," interjected Abonn. "No need to end this discussion prematurely or exhaust your horses. Give me a moment." He ducked his head and called for one of the elderly servant women, leaning down to speak in her ear.

Her wrinkled eyes lit up as he whispered, and she bobbed her head. "I'm happy to try, m'lord. He'll be proud to serve the king in such a manner."

"Take my horse then," said Abonn.

The woman nearly ran to Abonn's mare, leapt onto her back with surprising agility, then disappeared up the mountain road.

The baron furrowed his brow momentarily, then seemed to understand. He grunted.

The group continued their discussion of mining logistics, price balances and tariffs, until Syrana wanted to scream. She had hardly been acknowledged and found herself peeking repeatedly at her husband, but he was invariably distracted.

Then a shadow passed over them, and several of the working miners cried out in surprise. They all looked up.

A fearsome dragon with a wingspan greater than Cordan's house blocked out the Eye for a moment, circling overhead. Two riders waved at them, one in black and one in a servant's skirts. Kaiadin grabbed his horse's reins to keep it from panicking and bolting, and Syrana was thankful someone had tied hers with the others. The frightening dragon landed in the meadow below, a respectable distance away, and its riders beckoned at them.

Reylin cast a doubtful look toward Abonn, but Abonn shrugged. "Keeper Davon lives up the mountain, Your Highness. Keeps to himself most of the time, but it seems he can help you get home a little faster."

"You trust him completely, Sir Abonn, Baron Bonneser?" said Sir Gillead, his hand on his sword pommel. "And the beast?"

Abonn reassured them all, as did her father. "He's a good, loyal man, merely a loner. The old woman is the only one he interacts with, but he'll do anything you ask in the name of duty."

Gillead and Patreagh still looked dubious.

Syrana accompanied Reylin and his High Guard down to the meadow, tripping on her gown to keep up. The beast was overwhelmingly large. Its scales shone the color of rust, and its eyes were rubies. It watched them impassively as they approached, and Syrana reached for Reylin's comforting hand.

Davon greeted them with enthusiasm. "Highnesses, I was informed you might have need of Ar'we's and my services. We came as quickly as we could." He helped the elderly woman down from her position in front of him with a ginger hold on her elbow. Her gray-streaked hair was wild with wind, her cheeks flushed with windburn.

Syrana noticed how tenderly Keeper Davon treated her, how his black-gloved hand slipped along her arm first for security and then lingered. They smiled at each other for a long stretch, and something seemed to pass between them.

The elderly woman's smile seemed to widen further, and she clamped her thin lips together to suppress anything else. She began to pull away, but Keeper Davon leaned all the way down and brushed his lips across her fingers in farewell.

Her ruddy cheeks flared with color as she curtsied low to Reylin and Syrana. "Your Royal Highnesses," she intoned. "Keeper Davon." She curtsied again, awkward as a teenager, then scurried away.

Davon watched her go, then hopped down from the saddle strapped around his dragon's neck. He bowed respectfully, but Syrana could tell his attention was on the receding figure. How bizarre.

Reylin offered a handshake, as was due a dragonkeeper, but glanced nervously at the dragon's hovering head. Syrana herself was locked in place, squeezing Reylin's other hand hard. She gulped and struggled through a polite expression, then tried to lessen her desperate grip so Reylin didn't get annoyed.

Davon apologized. "This is Ar'we, Prince Reylin. Ar'we, my heart, not everyone is used to you." His tone toward his beast mimicked what a normal man would use toward his lover, and a shudder passed through Syrana at such impropriety.

I'ya's blessings, said a pleasant voice in Syrana's head. Ar'we pushed her long snout toward them to better focus both spinning eyes on them. Syrana felt like prey.

Her discomfiture must have been obvious, for Davon flushed and conferred with the dragon silently.

Why? said Ar'we petulantly, nonetheless pulling her head back from them.

Syrana sighed with relief, but then she realized Reylin was pulling her forward. "Keeper Davon," he was saying, "thank you for the kind offer. Could you get us home to Ironhold?"

Davon straightened his shoulders and asserted that he could, but then he hesitated. "Your Highness, my saddle is only designed for two, but I will gladly come back later for the princess and your knights, if needed."

He turned to Syrana and squeezed her hand lovingly. "Is that all right, Syrana?"

Her heart fell. He was choosing Priscilla.

"Go, my love," she assured him with a false smile. "By the time Keeper Davon returns for me, the babe will already be born. Just send a message when you have news, and return as soon as you can. My parents planned a banquet for us tonight, but they can postpone till tomorrow." She leaned in for a long kiss, hoping to leave him with an impression, but he merely pecked her on the cheek in hurried thanks.

Davon gave him a thick black jacket and goggles, then helped him into the leather saddle strapped around Ar'we's powerful neck. The dragon leapt into the air. With a rush of air that blasted dust into Syrana's eyes, Ar'we gave a

mighty downsweep of her webbed wings and pushed upward, catching a draft and soaring southward.

By the time Syrana blinked the grit out of her eyes, they
were gone. The High Guard knights all looked as disconcerted as she was.

Kaiadin appeared on his mare, leading her horse with
one hand. He handed the reins to her and offered encouragement. The purple band across his face was darker along
his smile lines, and nearly black spiderwebs sprouted at the
corner of each eye. "Don't fret, my lady. Priscilla will be fine,
and the babe healthy," he said. "High Holy Mage Ma'thell
will send a Whisper as soon as he has news, and Whispers fly
nearly as quickly as a dragon."

The message arrived early in the morning as the second
moon rose, and Kaiadin woke her from her lonely sleep. He
handed her a written note, transcribed as received on the
wind:

> *The babe is female and is without Mark or
> blemish. She has been named Amber. Priscil-
> la is unwell, Reylin remains.*

32

SHOCKINGLY, MOTHER DIDN'T DENY Taiuki's new role as a trainer, although she sneered at the idea of her lecturing on strategy. Perhaps she realized that, in matters of war, Sashiro truly was in charge. His role as arch commodore had been inherited properly, for he had once been Second to Taiuki's own father, Rentai, and he was an ultimate authority in such things.

Taiuki thanked the current for her uncle's intervention, without which she might have been shunted into some sort of castle duty, away from her men and women—and away from Tan.

Sashiro had approved her somewhat irregular petition for a split schedule: five days of intense battle and riding lessons, two days in the castle learning her new duties as a Kritali queen, and rest day. (Her blatant lie to Sashiro made her queasy with its unfamiliar disrespect.)

She had likewise lied to Steward Wehan, arranging courtly lessons in the evenings five days per week, followed by two days she claimed to be at the barracks and a rest day. If all went well, neither party would know, for Sashiro was distracted with the Jijiton-jin war, and Mother and her entourage rarely left the Air-filled passageways of the castle except to visit the Upper Market in the open city.

Four days later, she packed a slim shoulderbag for her trip back to the remote Mountains of Mourning, where the Order was hidden.

The castle was eerily calm in the early pre-dawn, with the heavy silence that accompanied an underwater cave settling like a fog in the lower levels. A dull whisper of light streamed into the lower gates and windows, creeping into her bedroom, which had been private since she was seven years of age. Taiuki moved quickly but quietly, hoping not to awaken Kei next door. She dressed as she would for weapons training, not only to assure her ruse in the event someone saw her departing, but also because travel to the island could be dangerous. Armor was wise, although a bit heavy. She considered forgoing her gauntlets and helmet, but then she recalled the lacer in the kelp grove. No, it would be foolish not to be prepared. Still, certain items might be more useful than others.

Taiuki left the plate-metal pauldrons, gorget, and cape, instead choosing a chinespine and wicked, urchin-like pauldrons. The chinespine, braced to her back and cinched to her breechbelt and chest, was a strip of outward-facing spikes much like a fish's dorsal fin, a good deterrent for most predators. As she strapped the device to her belt, she sadly noted her choice to change rank decorations; this breechbelt was simpler. It had a longer, tougher skirt of chain mail to guard her thighs, and no rankstones beyond that of a cavalier. Tan would appreciate that, she thought with resignation. Better for him, and better not to draw more scrutiny than necessary. She armed herself with blades, one long and one short, and a small speargun. The bolts went into a snug quiver strapped alongside her chinespine. Then she adjusted her hydrodynamic helmet and strapped it securely at her chin. She was ready.

Bag strapped to her back much like the quiver, Taiuki snuck out. She packed lightly, as she could hunt and forage easily now that she carried the tools. She had stashed a small metal bowl and fork, as well as firestarting rocks, and a few other minor tools that would come in handy on the island. Sandals would be helpful too, and an extra shirt. She needed little from the castle, and her heart yearned for It'tholl.

She easily avoided the busyness of the upper gates, heading down from her room to the underwater gates. Best to avoid the Lower Market and the Garrison Gate; too many soldiers would be awake by now. Instead, she stepped through a smaller side gate near the garrison and slipped away.

Passage to the island was uneventful, and before long, she could see the land sloping up to meet the shore. Her heart leapt in joy as she approached the cove. She could see several shadows above, floating on the surface and soaking up the sunshine. Taiuki popped up among them with a grin. Uth'hal trumpeted. It'ma rolled over and snorted a salty spray toward her.

I'ya's blessings, Taiuki. Are you well?

"Bright day, It'ma," she replied, bowing. "I'm well. How's It'tholl?"

At that moment, a piercing keen echoed through the cove, bouncing off the high rock face and over the water. It'ma snorted again. *She has missed you. Go to her quickly.*

From the wavering cries, Taiuki could tell It'tholl was in the cave, and she proceeded to shore, stepping out onto sand with fresh legs and nearly running to the cave mouth. She threw aside her chinespine, shoulder bag, and speargun, then stopped short in the abrupt darkness, letting her eyes adjust just as she was bowled over by It'tholl. Joy and enthusiasm emoted from the little dragon, and Taiuki could only laugh as they nuzzled each other in renewed love.

Where were you? You were gone! It'tholl was sad. Sad. Sad!

A rending sadness did indeed course through their conversation, and Taiuki knew exactly how It'tholl had felt. Lost, like a sailor tossed from his vessel and clinging to flotsam in the unending waves. A sympathetic tear ran down her cheek.

"Me, too, It'tholl," she reassured the creature with a scratch on her forehead. It'tholl leaned hard into it, and Taiuki realized the tender skin was nearly raw from growing so quickly. "Oh, It'tholl!" She looked around for her bag. "Come with me."

They exited the cavern, and Taiuki retrieved skin salve from her bag. There wasn't enough for many applications, but she had brought what she needed to make more. She used what she had, rubbing it into It'tholl's itchiest spots.

The dragling crooned with relief. *It'tholl is happy.*

Yes, me too. Taiuki responded, keeping the thought in her head quiet so it was just for them. They lay on the beach for a while, relaxing in the sun, which baked the sand almost to the point of discomfort. Taiuki embraced it; her muscles were tired from the morning journey. Before long, she slept, a deep and dreamless sleep of exhaustion that had chased her all the days without It'tholl. It'tholl did the same.

Taiuki was industrious that afternoon, and It'tholl teetered behind her everywhere she went. After a quick meal of fruits from the trees and fire-baked fish, they went about making more salve. The easiest recipe Taiuki knew was fish oil, but that would take a few weeks to prepare. Instead, she intended to make a combination of rendered palm nut oil, purple groundmint, and beeswax, all items she hoped to find nearby. She assigned It'tholl to collecting fallen nuts into a large pile while she gathered groundmint, which grew in loose mats among the shrubs along shore. Its tiny purple flowers made it relatively easy to find, and she had collected an armful in little time. Then she set to work splitting open the nuts, pouring the milk inside into a skein for herself.

It'tholl helps!

Taiuki smiled and showed It'tholl how to slice the innards of the nut out, something the dragling could attempt with her razored pinions if Taiuki placed the opened nut just so between several rocks. It was difficult, and Taiuki switched to having It'tholl simply score the insides, allowing Taiuki to pop the chunks out onto a skin blanket. She would need a much larger bowl for this process, she thought, as she squeezed each chunk's juices into the small bowl she had brought. It would only hold the contents of seven, maybe eight, nuts. Perhaps Uth'hal could capture a large turtle for her.

Certainly, replied Uth'hal, who had been watching.

Taiuki glanced up in surprise. She often forgot how loudly she must think. Uth'hal equated it to shouting, she remembered sheepishly.

"Thank you," she called after the dragon as he lumbered into the water and disappeared.

They didn't wait long before Uth'hal returned with an adult redking turtle, which flailed uselessly in his gentle mouth. Taiuki hesitated for a moment as Uth'hal set the large turtle down in the sand and restrained it with the single thumb pinion of his wing. Although her people ate turtle regularly, redkings were considered somewhat unique and majestic. This one didn't look so now, flapping its fins against the sand repeatedly, but Taiuki felt a little bad nonetheless.

"The coral towers, I'd guess?" she asked Uth'hal, stalling somewhat. Redkings were the rare inhabitants of places like that, lounging among the coral formations, eating crabs and lobsters. They would emerge and cater to ships as well, plucking barnacles from the hull.

Yes, Uth'hal replied matter-of-factly.

Taiuki nodded, then stepped forward with her spear gun. A bolt solidly placed into the brain cavity would be most merciful, although even then, it would take a bit for the powerful old animal to die. Then she could strip the creature down, harvesting the carapace for a bowl and the plastron for a platter.

Uth'hal snorted in disdain and promptly bit the turtle's head, ripping it off. He swallowed the bits, then looked at her. *It is done.* He stepped back, leaving the still carcass for her to clean.

Taiuki swallowed back bile at the bloody mess, entrails half-pulled from the shell, and began cleaning it. It'tholl happily scarfed the chunks of skin, muscle, and organ as Taiuki removed them, first slicing the edges of the shell and then prying out large pieces from the middle. The turtle was gigantic, a fine specimen and certainly generations old. Taiuki found herself regretting her strident refusal to bring anything large and obvious from the castle; it would have been easier and more merciful.

She finished the rough cleaning job and thought how best to split the fused shell. A cleaver would have facilitated this process as well as the nut splitting; she mentally noted the need for more knives. That was a subtle enough thing she could pack. In the meantime, she found a thin, sharp-edged rock and a striking rock to serve her purpose, and she shortly produced the two shell halves, one deep and concave and the other broad and flat. She placed them in the shallow pools along the cliff wall, affixed with heavy rocks, so that the marine life could clean them thoroughly. The rest of this work would have to be completed tomorrow.

Taiuki returned to the large pile of palm nuts and pondered the small batch she had started. It would have to wait, as she hadn't yet searched out a beehive, and wax was a key ingredient for stabilizing the salve. She could use the few hours remaining in the day to figure out a way to make fish oil, something she could manufacture in the volume needed for the growing dragling. Unfortunately, she likely needed several more large bowls, she thought to herself—quietly this time, as she couldn't stomach the idea of Uth'hal ripping another redking apart that day. Perhaps she could make the fish keep of leather, dripping down into a bowl catchment. That would allow her to make the keep larger, and she could sew additional pieces on as she snuck them out of the castle. She nodded to herself. Yes, that was a smart solution. But she had brought only one leather skin this time, thinking to use it as a blanket, and no sewing tools. Again, she mentally noted the items she would need next time.

She fed the small fire, then leaned back against It'tholl, who was snoozing with a full belly in the low afternoon sun. Taiuki popped the spent pieces of sweet palm nut meat into her mouth; they reminded her of a candy she had eaten as a child. She wrapped the unsqueezed pieces up in the skin, twisting it shut against flies and bothersome crustaceans, then set the bag aside. Closing her eyes, she soaked up the last of the sun.

A good day, she thought. This was everything she needed.

The second day of Taiuki's sabbatical was equally industrious, as she immediately sought out a beehive. It'tholl followed her as she worked her way inland. Broadly reaching apita trees, with their aggressive, knobby roots, eventually gave way to taller trees interspersed with splayed ferns. The undergrowth was sparse enough to walk through, and the canopy overhead eventually thickened enough to provide regular shade. The atmosphere was quiet, as if the foliage dampened all sound, save for the buzzing of insects and the occasional flitting of birds from branch to branch. Underwater, sound traveled so easily—the world was humming with taps and scrapes and whooshing. Even the castle, half submerged as it was, was a world of echoes and softly muffled sound. The island was silent by comparison, and Taiuki had a disconcerting sense of being watched by the forest. It'tholl felt it too, but didn't seem to mind.

Forest sees, she remarked casually, jumping awkwardly at a small bird in the greenery. The bird easily evaded her and peeped angrily, then swept away to a more distant branch to watch them.

Taiuki looked about her. "Yes, it's odd, isn't it?"

It'tholl looked at her quizzically.

"It just feels like there's someone here besides us, but there isn't."

Forest sees, reaffirmed It'tholl, as if that fully explained Taiuki's feeling.

They continued wending through the foliage, inspecting trees and fallen logs. The way was somewhat steep, and Taiuki's calves were getting tired when she realized she could hear a stronger buzzing from one direction. They turned and followed it, coming upon a fallen giant pillar tree. Its root wad, wider across than the height of a man, was a latticework of honeycomb. Taiuki smiled with relief at the find.

Honeybees were relatively calm, but she warned It'tholl to stay well back as she approached the hive with knife in hand. Taking it slow, she reached out and grasped a piece of honeycomb, slicing a large chunk cleanly off and placing it into her shoulderbag. The bees didn't seem too troubled by her presence, but they were thick on the hive, industrious as ever, and her arms were becoming a regular resting spot. She stepped back, shaking a little with nerves, and remembered to take a breath. The bees stayed with the hive, departing from her skin and returning to work.

Successful in their endeavor of the morning, the pair turned and made their way back home, which took another hour. It'tholl went to hunt small game in the shallow pools, awaiting a larger meal brought by the adults of the Order. Meanwhile, Taiuki ate a noon meal of spent nut meats, honey, and fish, then resumed the salve-making process. The shell bowls had been flawlessly cleaned overnight by tiny crabs and minnows and could now be used. She stripped all of the palm nut chunks into the larger bowl, yielding a vat of creamy liquid, which she heated slowly in the embers of her fire. She then cooled it and skimmed the emergent oil from the liquid's surface. She placed all of the oil into her small bowl and rendered it, then added the stripped flowers. It would be several hours before she was ready to strain the mixture and finish the process, so she relaxed and languidly topped off her skein with clear milk from the plastron bowl. The excess was poured into empty nut hulls for drinking that day. She'd have to remember to bring more skeins, Taiuki realized as she precariously balanced the other half of a hull on each one. They weren't sealed and could easily tip over, wasting the nutritious liquid into the sand. She sipped on one as she relaxed, watching It'tholl leap from pool to pool, attempting to capture fish or crabs.

The dragling was developing so quickly, already a hand taller at the shoulder than when she had emerged from the shell, and she was always hungry. Her motor skills had certainly improved since then too, but she was still an infant, bobbling around and leaping without ceremony at her quarry. She hadn't managed to catch anything yet, save for a voluptuous sea cucumber, which was toxic enough to make one sick. Taiuki made her spit it out.

She was more graceful in the water, as were all the Water dragons, but still unpracticed and easily worn out. Even now, she squealed a tiny yawn and came over to curl up near

Taiuki, where she promptly fell asleep. Taiuki stroked her muzzle gently, regretting only that she had to depart again so soon.

The remainder of Taiuki's time with It'tholl was less eventful, and she absorbed the precious moments with her partner swimming, playing, hunting, and relaxing. Taiuki's remaining ambition was applied to finishing the salve and storing it in nut hulls where it solidified, and to building a nest for herself and It'tholl in one of the cavern's side rooms. She constructed a small table of rocks with It'ma's assistance, upon which she placed her cooking tools, flint, and small bowl. Her bed was layer upon layer of palm fronds, which also served as her blankets for the moment. It would have to do, as she didn't know how to tan hide and could only sneak so many out at a time each visit.

On the third day, Taiuki ate her noon meal slowly, staring wistfully at the populated cove. She belonged here in her heart, but also with her people. With Tan. It was time to return, but it was impossible to make It'tholl understand.

Taiuki leaves It'tholl again, the dragling whined, recently awakened by Taiuki's troubled thoughts.

"I must, It'tholl."

It'tholl hates being alone.

"It'ma and Uth'hal will look after you. There's nothing to worry about."

It'tholl is still alone!

Half-alive, interjected Uth'hal knowingly from his favorite spot in the wavebreak.

Taiuki started at the realization that her pain at being apart from It'tholl, her incompleteness, was once her reality and was still Uth'hal's. All of the Order except It'tholl had lived entire lives without bonding. They would not bond at this juncture, as it was something that only happened at the hatch or shortly thereafter, and instead relied on each other in close fellowship. But from what she gathered, it was a shadow of what she and It'tholl had.

Small wonder she sometimes detected a yearning sadness in their speech, although they didn't show it otherwise.

"Yes, but half-alive is better than dead of a myrman's spear," Taiuki chided. "It's the only choice we have, It'tholl. Behave, beloved." She embraced the dragling tightly, stroking her freshly oiled scales and scratching around It'tholl's eyes.

Then, resigned to her duties, Taiuki dressed for the journey back, affixing the chinespine to her back and slinging her emptied shoulderbag over one side. She needed only her weapons and light armor, and each visit would bring more supplies to the cove. Skins, various knives and tools, resin—she ticked off the items in her head, hoping she wouldn't forget anything next time. With one last scratch, she bade farewell to It'tholl and waded into the water. As she shifted and dipped underwater, she heard It'tholl initiate a piercing scream from the beach.

33

TAIUKI'S RUSE WAS EFFECTIVE, and she achieved a regular schedule of deception between Steward Wehan and Master Sashiro, facilitated by Sashiro's imminent return to the front. When one believed she was at court, the other believed she was at the barracks. She still managed to get quality time training with Tan, who had improved greatly over the past few weeks. She had to admit, as well, that tutoring him had forced her to develop herself. Seeing his errors in form or oversights in planning made her far more self-aware, and she was the better for it.

Since that awkward first day together, she and Tan had become an inseparable pair. Thanks to Master Sashiro's requirements, Taiuki led them in morning stretches and forms, stepping thoughtfully through each perfect movement in preparation for sparring. Master Sashiro would frequently pair them in battle, or would call upon another to spar with Taiuki as he took Tan for himself. After that exercise, Sashiro would lecture. Tan and Taiuki sat together, ate together, and rode together in the afternoons.

Tan was improving on his black-headed whale, Nimoka. Moka was a gentle animal, biddable to a fault and somewhat languid. Tan loved her fiercely, mucking her stable daily and rubbing her with salve twice as frequently as she needed.

Now they rode in battle formation, completing a jaunt around the southern edge of the castle, through the kelp farms and back to the garrison, switching pace and formation a number of times depending on their surroundings. She and Hachi communicated seamlessly, and the time raced.

As she rode, body low to Hachi's back in front of the dorsal fin, she considered his halter design. With a strong bit and snug noseband, the halter overlaid the creature's head just in front of the eyes, with attachment points to cover them in battle. At the top of the girth was a flare, which helped the rider hydrodynamically, and a saddle attachment further secured at the back by a rear girth. The assembly was effective for the cetacean mounts, but adjustments were needed for alternative creatures.

These bits and straps would never work on It'tholl.

The thought intruded on her otherwise sure focus, and Taiuki inadvertently allowed a soft smile to play across her lips. It'tholl's razored teeth and powerful jaw would slice immediately through the bit used on Hachi. It would have to be similar to what Sashiro used with Benn. Benn didn't have a bit, but rather a heavy metal cheekhook on each side, which communicated more of a request for turning than a command. Further, it allowed Benn to join the battle too, thrashing his victims and tearing them with his ferocious, tooth-filled maw. Taiuki shuddered at the thought.

On the other hand, perhaps she didn't need reins at all, for It'tholl could communicate directly with her.

With that sinuous, spiny neck, It'tholl would require an entirely separate girth, and a unique saddle design. If Taiuki could sit between the wings, just behind the neck spines, she could ride with relative ease, even grasping the rearmost spine as a pommel.

She shook herself to the present. Hachi was slightly deviating from formation, likely because of Taiuki's careless control of the reins. She patted his side in apology.

As the afternoon ended, she and Tan stabled their whales.

"You should introduce her to Hachi," said Tan. "She would love it."

Taiuki ignored him, instead caressing Hachi's muzzle and offering him a fish from her satchel.

"Yuki-sho, you know she'd love it. She could pet him through the gate."

Anella. That little girl was like a parasite, latched on to Kei day and night and trodding in Taiuki's footsteps constantly. She answered Tan, "She's afraid of the lower levels. She won't even venture to the shallowest gate."

Taiuki never called it the Whale Gate anymore; it made her remember too much.

"Maybe we could get her to come down just one level," said Tan. "I'm sure she would like it, once she saw it. And the Lower Market is fun, and the villages and the garrison. I bet she's never seen anything like it!"

"She's a landwalker, Tan. She won't see its worth, no matter what you do." Taiuki felt bitterness welling up inside, and she was thankful her tears dissolved into the sea without making a show on her face.

"You might be surprised," Tan insisted. His jaw was set, but his child-chubby cheeks ruined his attempt at being stern. "I've been escorting her horseback riding— Don't give me that look. She wants an escort. Anyway, she's fun and nice, not what I expected after having met Godrig."

The duo reentered the castle's Garrison Gate, shifting smoothly to human form, one after the other. Taiuki loosened her grip on Tan's hand when he was all the way through, and he grinned appreciatively. They walked down the open corridor, a wide public walkway paved with decorative stone and painted with murals, passing several noble homes with large, strong doors and high walls, the second-story windows open to the corridor. A woman passed, shadowed by a snuffling waterdog with a leather collar. She saluted them politely. The evening was settling on Shiggo City, and they would be expected for supper. They made their way up the several levels of the outer shell, past the Lower Market and the shallowest gate. At the lower-level entrance to the castle proper, they walked through a massive tunnel with multiple heavy doors, guarded by Shiggon-jin soldiers. They all touched their foreheads formally as the two passed.

Tan leaned over and whispered, "They never used to salute me like that."

Taiuki was torn between snorting with laughter and sighing with frustration. "You're arch-commodore-in-training now, little brother. You're the Second."

Tan looked down at his breechbelt, as if newly surprised by the embedded andesite rankstone. "Oh, right." He threw his shoulders back. *Tall like Tai, and like Father.*

She didn't bother looking down at her own belt with its vacant rankstone. Whether the world pitted them against each other or not, she would love him forever.

Supper was tedious, with Anella sitting between her and Tan. The little girl was impeccably polite at meals, and Taiuki noticed she had already picked up on *myr* table manners. The girl copied Tan as he shucked a shellfish, placing the undesirable remnants in a waste bowl.

"I've never had to peel them myself," she whispered to Tan with a self-deprecating giggle.

Taiuki tightened her expression, popping a shellfish in her mouth and making a point to eat it. "Children peel the shell, but you really should eat the entire thing," she said.

Tan reluctantly admitted she was right, but then added, "You can taste more flavors that way, at least."

Anella pursed her lips primly, but she tried an unpeeled shrimp nonetheless. Politely, she chewed and swallowed, nodding agreeably. With Taiuki's eyes on her, Anella ate the rest of her shrimp without peeling them. She looked at Taiuki for approval. "How was your whale riding today?" she asked after receiving no reaction.

"It was wonderful. We practiced a new echelon formation with me at the lead," Tan said with a happy grin. "You know, you should meet them."

Fear flashed across Anella's face, but she controlled it. "I'd love to, really, but . . . but . . ."

"There's nothing to worry about, Nelly," said Tan. By the current, he could be naive.

"She's afraid to go to the lower levels. She knows about Tai." Kei's voice was pure ice. Taiuki didn't look at her;

she couldn't. "Godrig probably told her. Now stop talking about it before Mother hears you."

Anella blushed, looking miserable and apologetic. "She's right. I am afraid."

Tan patted her hand and helped her off the bench. "You don't need to be afraid now. That happened a long time ago. You should come with us, and we'll introduce you to Hachi and Nimoka."

Anella hesitated, and Taiuki prayed she would decline.

"You'll be safe with us," Tan assured her. He put a comforting hand on hers, and she relented.

"Okay, I'll do it. As long as I'm with all of you."

"I'll be right there the entire time." Tan gave Taiuki a foolish grin at their victory.

She scowled.

Taiuki took a deep breath, pulling deliciously salty water through her gills and expelling it through her mouth. Hachi echoed her calm, always studious of her emotions and emulating them when they rode. This jaunt brought them only to the castle's outer shell, to the Kelp Gate, which opened to the great fields tended by Shiggon-jin farmers. As it was not yet harvesttime for another few months, the traffic through the gate was low, and Taiuki pulled her whale mount up the vertical face of the large portal. Nimoka followed behind on a lead.

Tan and Anella stood eagerly on the other side.

Anella clenched Tan's hand in a combination of wonder and fear as she stared at the magical portal. Then she saw Taiuki on the other side, and her jaw dropped in the most discourteous manner. The little girl shook herself and blinked before lighting up with the most genuine smile Taiuki had seen since her arrival. "Princess Taiuki!" she called in a high voice, waving with her free hand.

Taiuki patted Hachi on the muzzle and commanded him to stay and be friendly. Then she crossed the threshold with the long reins in her hand. Her tail split and morphed into delicate feet, and slender legs ran up to a skirt of leather ribbons hanging from her breechbelt.

Anella's mouth was open again, and Taiuki realized the girl had never seen a transformation. Until this day, she had only been in the upper levels of the castle or outside, riding that silly landwalking horse. She had resisted Tan's invitation for weeks, admitting that she heard frightening stories when she was younger. At least she was honest. Finally, Tan had maneuvered her down to the Kelp Gate, which was only the second level underwater.

Anella's gaze traveled down to Taiuki's bare legs and feet. Kritali girls, even ones as young as Anella, didn't reveal above the ankle, and they certainly didn't go barefoot. Those long, bulky dresses Anella flounced around in were impractical. And shoes! Taiuki squeezed the soft sand with her toes and cleared her throat.

Anella apologized and redirected her attention to Hachi and Nimoka. Her pale cheeks were marred with scarlet.

"I'ya's blessings, Hachi, Nimoka," said Anella formally. She released Tan's hand so she could curtsy properly, billowing her skirts out in a flutter of soft pink and periwinkle.

Nimoka squealed a nicker from the other side of the gate. Hachi eyed her a bit longer, then overcame his reluctance. They both pushed their noses close to the interface between water and air and clicked at her.

"You can pet them, Nelly," said Tan.

Anella glanced at him doubtfully, then at the portal. "Is it safe? Out there?"

Tan got a mischievous look, then offered his hand again. "I'll show you." He guided her hand through the shimmering vertical face of water and onto Nimoka's muzzle.

"Oh, she's so smooth . . . oh, she's beautiful." Anella was ecstatic.

As her brother helped Anella overcome her temerity, Taiuki stood in a daze.

Is it safe? It's not so scary. What's to be afraid of? Screams. Eternal screams. *Why did you leave me, Tai?*

She blinked the memories away, violently.

"What's wrong with you?" Kei's haughty voice invaded her thoughts. She had come up to them in a rush and now proudly revealed a sealed letter from the folds of her dress. "Nelly got a letter from home."

Anella gave Kenji one more pat on the nose and pulled her hand from the water. "Oh, dear me," she murmured, looking around for a dry towel. Kei gestured to her lady-in-waiting to proffer a cloth, and Anella opened her letter and read it aloud.

> *Dear sister, the plague is spreading amongst the lower born in Krita Port and outlying towns. Signs of sickness include blackened eyes and violent, erratic behavior. The king has assigned me to investigate the extent of disease in neighboring kingdoms, as it is rumored to have spread to Mirat and Marlemet. Beware of those ill-bred. I am coming to Shiggo first to ensure your safety and that of the Tatami family. Branig sends his greetings; please convey his regards to all.*
>
> Godrig

Kei leaned in to catch the details. She loved bad news, especially if it gave her something to gossip about. "Is that *all* he said about the plague?" She was wheedling, as if that would draw freshly inked letters out of the paper.

"Godrig is coming here?" Taiuki did not welcome that prospect. "He should go to Mirat and Marlemet first, where there are reports. This disease may not even affect Shiggon-jin."

"What makes you think so?" asked Anella.

"Our people have the form of the true god, the essence of Water," Taiuki replied, sounding far more sure than she was. She didn't believe in I'ya, but she did believe in that. "All myr do."

Kei scoffed but didn't say anything.

"It is the Way of the Current," Taiuki insisted, irate at her sister's continual denial of everything she said.

"You're one to talk," Kei muttered.

Thankfully, Anella didn't seem to notice the looks exchanged between sisters, for she tucked the letter away and returned her attention to the fascinating creatures on the other side of the Kelp Gate.

Godrig, Crown Prince of Krita, eldest son of King Rigaran and Queen Déllani of House Crayer, was coming.

34

THE NEXT DAYS PASSED quickly, and Konan bemoaned the growing sense of running out of time. Every time he mined, he felt as though someone was following him: the soft shuffle of boots or sandals echoing through the dark tunnels, the slight slip of cobble beneath the feet. Yet every time he turned, there was no one. His awareness was taut, his observation sharp, and still he never caught a glimpse. Nonetheless, the sense of being monitored remained.

Meanwhile, Lyra spent her waking hours practicing her magika with Thordrin, using Air to enhance her precision and speed in knife throwing. Those skills were identical to what she needed in the larger plan, but her practice was limited to the afternoons, when a light breeze was natural. She could hardly practice at the scale needed, and in truth, none of them knew whether a sandstorm was within her abilities.

Given the flatness of the landscape, the distance to deliverance—the distance at which their group of three could no longer be spotted—was long, and Konan had never seen her maintain a spell for that amount of time. Such a thing was a massive manipulation of Air, larger than anything he had ever seen.

Then again, he had been in Tahayi Mines for a very long time, and people with magika didn't usually end up there. Commoners, to begin with, rarely carried elemental power in their blood, making most of the mine's residents fairly harmless.

Lyra was an enigma.

Although her ribs still gave her sharp pains when she moved wrong, and she complained of nausea each morning, her deep, angry bruises had receded to faded hues and then, finally, disappeared. Her swollen eye, so bloodshot and welted, had opened up, and the sclera had cleared, leaving behind only that diamond color on white. The split in her lip had closed, revealing plump pink lips that occasionally curved into a brilliant smile—when they did, Konan couldn't look away. She moved more freely, as if the stiffness of her pelvis and ribs and damaged muscles had at last relented.

He knew the deeper hurts weren't healed.

Neither were his.

"Hey, you, what do you need all them rations for?"

He stopped as two men approached him, both wearing gray tatters that may have once been blue. One had a long, greasy beard that hadn't been trimmed in years. Parts of it were twisted into braids with beads, but other portions were wildly frayed and filthy. The other looked like he could barely grow hair on his chin, but his age was revealed by the scattered white hairs pushing at odd angles from his eyebrows.

He snuck a glance at the guard tower; it was a little far, although it cast its shadow back toward them as he headed west from the well.

One man pointed an accusing finger at the food sack. "We don't trust what's been goin' on lately, so you need to tell us."

Konan scowled and signed, despite knowing they wouldn't understand. "Leave me alone." He set his small canvas bag on the ground and adjusted his skein behind him, freeing both hands.

The two ex-mariners looked at each other doubtfully. "He ain't gonna tell us nothin'," said the one with the beard. "He can't talk right."

"Maybe he is an idiot, like we was sayin' to Cap," said the other. Then he thrust a thumb toward his chest. "Thordrin promised me somethin'. You understand a deal, right? Thordrin made a deal with me."

Konan could feel his body shivering with energy, ready for a fight, and he knew, if they started it, he would kill them. Perhaps the guard tower would sling an arrow down to stop him, or possibly to help him, or simply wait and watch so they could see if his wall score changed. At a minimum, they would be entertained.

The bearded one winced, and his whinging voice shifted to entreaty. "Come on, we ain't got no problems with you. Go easy. We just wanna know what's goin' on with Thordrin."

Konan's scowl deepened as they advanced a step.

Then the bearded one paused. "I seen him fight."

"Yeah, he's a devil, but I want me knife," replied the gray-browed one.

"He don't know nothin', look at him. Fuckin' idiot."

Konan held their gazes, his shoulders high and his stance ready. He flexed his fingers and tightened them into fists.

The gray-browed one ground his jaw and sneered. "Fine. Maybe he don't know nothin'."

The bearded man looked almost relieved as they both relented, backing away at first and then melting into the camp as swiftly as they'd come.

Konan watched where they had gone: the shadows of shacks on the edge of west camp, farther back from the wall toward the waste pits. Heart pounding, he hastened to the shack where Thordrin and Lyra waited. They would eat the largest meal they'd had since Lyra's arrival, a triple ration, to get them steady on their way.

"You ready, Lyr?" asked Thordrin, tearing into a larger hunk of bread than usual. He winced at it and licked his gums, then dipped it in a small bowl of water to soften the stale corners.

Lyra nodded. "I won't be any more ready tomorrow. I rested all day. I didn't even send a Whisper to my mam."

"It is well we are leaving," said Konan as he settled down. "Two of your men followed me to the well, inquiring of your knife." He nodded at the white-handled blade at Thordrin's side. "They mentioned someone they called 'Cap,' and I don't think they were talking about you."

Thordrin looked sharply at him. "Yeah, it's about time then. Coulda done with more rations, but we'll run out of water long before we run out of food. Drink up now, and we'll refill before tonight."

Evening fell, and Konan watched the sun set with Thordrin from a vantage point on the rooftop. The sun was yellower today than usual, a reflection of the dryness of the air. It winked at him one more time as it dipped below the westward dunes. Was it a sign of good luck, or an omen?

"I'm coming for you," Thordrin muttered as the sun disappeared, as if making an oath to the Eye.

Both men entered the shack, where Lyra was finishing the arrangement of rations. She had fashioned longer cloaks for all of them from the spare garments, as well as three large sacks that could sling over their shoulders with rope. She hung the small skein from her corset on her own waist for the first time. They hadn't allowed her to wear it before, as it was too valuable and could have drawn more attention. She twisted it around her waist to hide it beneath her cloak, then offered Konan his new cloak.

She attempted to fling it around him, but she was too short, catching the edge on his shoulder. Lyra blanched as he knelt, and she finished tying it in the front.

"Thank you."

Blushing, she handed him a longer pair of pants; she didn't wait for him to put them on.

He was suddenly aware that his current pair was so tattered, they went up to his scarred knees. Unlike Thordrin, he had never killed solely to get new ones—he simply hadn't prioritized it, instead using spare cloth to add to his cloak.

Lyra continued to Thordrin, offering him a better cloak as well. He complimented her work, for once sounding almost genuine.

Lyra had useful skills as a wayfarer—sewing surely enough, as Thordrin pointed out—but her true strengths were creativity and tenacity. The shoulder bags were ingenious, the fixes to their boots and addition of socks beyond smart for a long trek. And all of it with materials poached from corpses, a concept with which he knew she was deeply uncomfortable.

Lyra fomented a light, almost pleasant breeze as the sun went down, just enough that the guards might believe a sandstorm was coming but not enough to drain herself. The wind tousled the hair of those who remained outside, including the guards. It dried their eyes and slowly became grittier and grittier.

They waited for night to settle over the camp. Raucous shouts from Thordrin's gang quieted as most shrank into their corners to sleep; only the gang's watch stayed alert across the rooftops.

The breeze had grown to a solid wind, which not only irritated the eyes but also provided a whispering cover of sounds. The trio stole out from the shack together, evading Thordrin's own watchmen as well as the tower guards by sliding along walls and between shanties. They stole from shadow to shadow, edging their way deeper into west camp toward the waste pits, then turning eastward toward the salt flats.

They were over halfway, fully immersed in the claustrophobic sea of dilapidated wooden huts, when a silhouette stepped into the dim moonlight.

It was one of Thordrin's men, Yantry, former captain of a pirate vessel. Moony's former commanding officer. Thordrin sucked in a sharp breath through his teeth. Not a good sign.

Yantry, a stout man with a surprising pooch of a belly, smiled maliciously. The cap on his front tooth glinted. "Say, Thordrin, you're out awful late." He eyed them, pausing on the bulge of a full water skein on Konan's hip.

Konan nudged Lyra behind him. She looked both frightened and incensed, but she couldn't fight effectively while also summoning the sandstorm.

"Focus," he signed without taking his eyes from Yantry. Two others emerged behind the pirate captain; Konan recognized one as a miner from his daily work trips and the other as the gray-browed man from the well. He groaned internally. He had hoped that, former pirate or not, the man wasn't still subservient to Yantry. Certainly not enough to tell him about Thordrin's order for extra rations.

"Let us pass, Yantry," Thordrin said coolly. His stance remained confident and dominant, without a shade of self-doubt.

"You're in my part of camp now," growled Yantry. "Call me Captain. Better yet, call for mercy, for I'm thinking all of west end should be mine."

The gray-browed man nodded emphatically. "I want me knife, as promised." He thrust out a demanding hand.

Yantry smiled even wider. "You promised my man a knife."

Thordrin spat at him. "I didn't promise you anything, saltfucker. It ain't your concern, so let us pass."

Yantry snarled with disgust, and two more silhouettes slunk from the shadows behind him.

Lyra whimpered, and Konan took her shoulder and spun her toward the towers. "Cover us now," he signed urgently.

She nodded and elevated her spell to a blustering wind, nearly knocking everyone off their feet. Sand flew, whipping in violent, short-lived whirls and then flailing off into a straight-line westerly wind.

Yantry's men muttered with dismay as they regained their balance, but their leader urged them forward. "Now, you dogs! I want the knife. Extra rations for whichever scum brings me the knife!"

The four men rushed forward, forming a semicircle around them. Thordrin and Konan backed Lyra against the wall of a building.

"Keep going," Thordrin shouted at her. He drew two long knives, one of them the white-handled blade in question.

Despite her terror, Lyra blasted a powerful wind around the nearest guard towers. Her arms extended, and her focus intensified, and sand flew high into the sky, blocking the stars above the towers.

One of Yantry's men attacked, and Konan was suddenly drowning in the chaos of battle. He flipped the man over his shoulders, snapping his as he did so, then kicked him away. Another flew at him, a chipped stone knife in hand, but Konan dodged to the side and elbowed the man's chest; the man stumbled back, coughing, and Thordrin swiped across his neck in a gleeful dance.

The two men entered a deadly rhythm, each using his own strengths to dispatch or imbalance their attackers, sending disoriented men to each other for finishing blows. Several of the men Konan had tossed or flipped found themselves not only staggering with broken bones, but also losing blood from holes in their backs. However, for every man that crumpled before them, another seemed to crawl out of nowhere. One actually dodged Thordrin's lunge and flung sand in the assassin's eyes. Thordrin instantly dove into a roll to one side, and the attacker instead found Konan's fists. They were hard pressed, but the number of attackers was dwindling. Men limped or crawled away, if they moved at all.

Lyra yelped, and the windstorm collapsed. Konan risked a glance behind.

A muscular arm was strangling her through a large crack in the shanty wall. Yantry.

Anger clouded Konan's consciousness, much like the sandstorm Lyra had summoned. It overwhelmed his vision and narrowed his focus. That was dangerous. He reined it in, but his hold on his own fury was temporary. He grunted at Thordrin, who spun and sliced the arm open wide in a single, fluid movement; he continued, spinning into a lunge at another man, dancing away with a wild, blood-hungry grin.

Yantry's arm, split wide with bunched muscle and tendon, disappeared inside the shack, and he howled.

Lyra shook violently, a hand to her reddening throat. She edged away from the crack, but she was otherwise frozen.

"Cover us!" Konan signed as he continued to fight, dispatching two more men.

"Cover us, damn it!" cried Thordrin.

The gray-browed miner was still there, but he looked unsure whether to move forward. Urged on by Yantry's screaming curses and his own desire for the knife, he looked as though he might lunge with his tiny chipped stone blade. Two more men rejoined the fray, and he grew more confident.

The pounding of horse hooves sounded from the iron gate. The guards had seen them. Torches bounced up and down in the distance, coming closer and closer until Konan could see the outline of mounted idraka galloping toward them.

He grabbed Lyra's hand and yanked her behind him. He and Thordrin broke past the gray-browed man, with Thordrin feinting beneath a weak attempt at a clever move. Thordrin sank his white-handled knife into the man's stomach and twisted it.

"You wanted it. You can have it," he hissed.

They ran. Northward past shanty after shanty. The hoofbeats got louder, and Konan turned back to see soldiers surrounding Yantry and his men. One soldier, a knight with a tall helmet plume of yellow feathers, pointed toward them with his sword, and several of the soldiers took off at a gallop.

"Shit," muttered Thordrin.

They nearly reached the edge of camp when the idraka encircled them, reining in their escape. The plume-feathered one began barking orders.

Lyra sucked a breath in.

It was the warden.

Thordrin sent his white-handled knife sailing, knocking the man's torch from his grip and sending a finger flying. The flame tumbled through the air, landing on the wooden roof of a shack beyond; it alighted like parched tinder.

The flames crackled over the shack in a moment, growing to a sudden conflagration that consumed its neighbor. Thordrin hooted with triumph.

The idraka whinnied in terror, bucking two soldiers off. Another galloped out of control, its rider disappearing between burning buildings, his fingers entangled in the reins.

The warden fell to the sand, clutching his bleeding hand.

Konan fought the two coherent soldiers, tossing one into the fire. The man's screams were drowned by the sound of cracking wood and shifting timbers as the building collapsed on itself. As he snapped the last soldier's neck, he watched the flames leap from building to building; the camp was destined to burn. The fire had spread to every nearby structure, and residents stuck inside were crying for help. Some burst out of doors and windows in panic, fleeing the growing inferno. As the prisoners made for the fort wall, more horsemen advanced, abandoning Yantry's group and pursuing the source of the fire.

Thordrin leapt back as the warden sliced at him with a sword, narrowly missing his abdomen. His belt snapped, releasing his pouch of rations, and his skein wasted into the sand. Thordrin snarled and disarmed the man, but at that moment, three small black shadows cut through the air, accompanied by a sudden breeze.

A trio of chipped stone blades embedded in the warden's belly, and he grunted and sank to his knees. He looked down in surprise, then up . . . at Lyra.

Her eyes were cold, nearly white in the flickering fire. Her lips twitched, and she shook. Then she blinked, and she seemed to realize what she had done.

"Time to go," said Thordrin, glancing at Konan with a brief expression that was difficult to interpret. "Cover us, Lyr. Bring up the wind now." He took the warden's sword and opened the man's belly, spilling his organs out, then jabbed the end into the man's crotch with a bitter smile. "Burn in the lowest Gate, you piece of shit."

He yanked Lyra's knives out and turned back to them. The fire played reds and oranges across his face; his eyes were mad with bloodlust, probably much like Konan's.

Lyra seemed to be in a daze, staring at the warden, and no more wind arrived. Konan peered into her vacuous face. Her eyes were unfocused, playing out terrors he couldn't see. Her breath came in hitches.

Thordrin raised a hand. "Lyra, wind!" he barked as he let his open palm fly. Konan caught him and growled. The two men strained against each other for moments, but Lyra did flinch with the arrested motion in front of her face. Her tears sparkled in the firelight, and she launched a new spell. Thordrin smirked and tore his arm from Konan's grip.

A stiff wind rushed into the camp and twisted around them, whipping the sands into a frenzied storm. The fire roared like a furnace behind them, and they could hear idraka and horses spooking and soldiers yelling through the chaos. They ran, encircled by her most powerful conjuration yet, until Lyra stumbled in the salt flats. She didn't catch herself, so focused was she on the storm, and Konan scooped her into his arms and kept running. She remained enthralled in her own summoning, barely blinking as she spun a web with twitching fingers.

He and Thordrin looked back, and a triumphant, malicious smile twitched the corner of Thordrin's mouth.

Tahayi Mines burned.

LYRA POURED HER MIND into controlling the massive firestorm.

It required dedicated thought and a continuous outflow of power, like a pitcher eternally streaming ale. Bouncing in Konan's arms, she lay with her limbs somewhat loose and her eyes half-closed in concentration.

The air from the west was scathingly dry and hot, even in the night. It coated Lyra's tongue with a dull dustiness. As it met the sea of shanties, its flavor altered to choking ash. Even from this distance, she could sense the change made by fire.

Konan slowed after a long stumbling run in the night, doggedly loped along for a while and finally halted, his chest heaving as he set her on unsteady feet.

"Cover our tracks, Lyr," said Thordrin, his lighter panting a contrast to Konan's.

She tried to obey, pulling the windstorm closer and rushing it over the flats they had crossed. There would be no sign of their escape or intended direction. As she allowed it to fade, relinquishing her hold of the element like sand pouring between her fingers, the wind died, and an eerie calm replaced its screaming.

The night sky cleared, revealing the gray sliver of a waning quick moon. It shed little light on the sands below. There wasn't much to see ahead; the sand flats stretched endlessly before them into darkness, far beyond the edge of sight and imagination. Behind, a bright orange glow flickered like a candle. Tahayi Mines.

"Bitch lit up like a funeral pyre," Thordrin snickered.

Lyra heaved a long, quavering sigh as she prepared to walk. The storm summoning had drained her frail, barely healed body of all energy, and the thought of trudging onward exhausted her. But she had to.

She thanked Konan, and he merely nodded, the glisten of sweat apparent on his brow.

Lyra looked back at the tiny light in the distance and blanched. "A lot more people probably got hurt, besides the soldiers."

"Who gives a shit?" Thordrin replied. "No one in there was innocent. Scum of the world, the worst of this Gate." Lyra's expression must have given her away, because he tittered again. "I've dreamt for a while about burning that place to the ground. Good work, Lyr."

She clenched her jaw, biting her tongue against telling him what was really bothering her. The burning of Tahayi Mines was an accident, a byproduct of their fight to escape. The wooden shanties were naught but tinder, waiting for prime conditions and a spark.

The death of the warden was not an accident.

She turned away so they wouldn't see the tears that suddenly stung her eyes, and she began to march northward in a weary walk across unending flats. Each foot sank into the soft, wind-blown sand, and each step burned in her calves and thighs. The paltry meal of bread and cheese they had eaten earlier (ages ago?) had done little to abate the clenching hunger in her stomach. The summoning seemed to sap all of her energy far more quickly than any physical exercise.

Early in the morning, sometime after the slow moon had risen and arced low across the horizon and the Eye threatened to show itself within a bell's time, she fell. She landed with a grunt despite the softness of the sand, and although she was unhurt, she remained sitting with her legs splayed out.

Thordrin and Konan had been walking ahead. Konan had taken the lead, insisting that something lay in the direction he was heading, and Thordrin had followed at the pace he preferred. Konan glanced back at her regularly, and she once spied Thordrin doing the same. They both returned, one on each side, and she expected them to usher her into limping onward.

She stared dully at her awkwardly placed legs. Like the men, she wore pants, and her ankles showed up to her lower calf. She was too tired to care for propriety at this point, especially in front of them.

Konan knelt. One side of his brow went up in entreaty, the other taut with scar tissue. "Have you any energy left?"

She sobbed and began to rise, but Konan placed a gentle hand on her shoulder and eased her back down.

"Please hide us," he requested, gesturing around them in a circle.

Lyra nodded, then whispered out to her element. The wind answered her, moving in a sluggish whirlwind around them. She raised a slow mound of sand with them in the center, visible only as one low dune among thousands of others. The whirlwind subsided, and motes of finer sand drifted down and settled back in place amidst a deep silence. The wind died entirely.

"Well done, girl," said Thordrin, but Lyra was already asleep.

The next days were much the same. They slept when the heat was unbearable, then trudged onward through the evenings and nights and mornings. They had little bearing beyond the sun and moons' rising and setting. There were no landmarks, no mountains shimmering in the distance, not a bush or a bird to be seen.

It was lonely.

Lyra had gotten used to laying her head upon Konan's knee, to his presence emanating like a hearth fire, his fingers sometimes touching hers in comfort, but the wastes were far too hot for any of that. Their cloaks were their only protection from the sun, and during the height of the day, they would huddle individually with their faces covered, trying to stay cool as they rested. At least she was too exhausted to have nightmares.

Every thought eventually meandered its way back to the warden. Sometimes he was alive, and sometimes he was dead. Sometimes his deeply lined cheeks would twist into an evil, ugly smile. Most frequently, her mind flashed back to that moment when she had allowed her hatred to guide her movements, when the livid voice inside shrieked for satisfaction. She pulled her knives from her bracer, smooth and easy, and with a violent flick of the wrist and push with the Air, the three blades had sailed to their destination.

She had felt them enter his slightly pudgy body. Immersed in her Air spell, she had pushed the knives where they needed to go and felt the resistance when they stopped. And she had rejoiced.

"Are you all right?" Konan's signs waved in front of her face, and she realized they had paused. The Eye seared down from just past its zenith, and the sand seemed to shimmer, it was so hot.

She looked at her feet. They were pink with sunburn in every spot her skin showed. She had wrapped her feet with a semblance of stockings, cinched in place beneath her sandal straps, but the fabric was worn and weak, and far from stretchy enough for such a use. The stockings hadn't lasted more than two days' trek, and now they hung from the straps with split seams along the heel and ball of her foot.

Konan encouraged her to sit and handed her the skein from his belt. "Only a sip," he warned with a heavy sigh.

"Is that all of it?" Thordrin asked, taking a single swig as well, then scowling at the ruined skein on his own belt. "Damn that warden to the nethers."

"I think so," Lyra said, prodding the smaller one on her own belt. "Mine is empty."

They shared a small meal, bread and cheese. As Thordrin had forewarned, they would run out of water long before they ran out of food, a truth that now chased them through the wastes like a feral dog, nipping and catching.

Lyra lay down to rest, but Konan beckoned her closer and stared at her. "Are you all right?" he repeated.

Her breath hitched and she looked away, her eyes sting-ing. No, she was not. The tears didn't fully form, however, as though the spare moisture were immediately sucked into her dry eyes. Likewise, the stuffiness that would normally fill her sinuses did not appear. Her mouth was parched, and her nose was stiff and sore with dry blood.

He watched and listened, and she moved to lay her head on his knee. In that familiar place, perhaps she could manage to say it aloud.

His larger hand dwarfed hers such that she clutched only three fingers, and his other lightly brushed her stray hairs from her forehead.

She curled into a tight ball and adjusted her cloak to cover her skin, then twisted enough to see him.

He waited expectantly.

"I—I killed the warden," she mumbled. Each word tasted like a road-filthy penny.

Konan's hand didn't stop its rhythm, and if not for their time together, she could almost believe he didn't hear her or understand. But she could see it: the slight flutter of his right eyelid, the tic in his cheek, and the glow of the copper flecks in his right eye as he processed her meaning.

"I *chose* to kill him," she added.

He looked as though he might respond, but Thordrin interrupted.

"You may have intended to, girl, but *I* killed the warden." Lying nearby, the Phantom turned away from them with his face covered.

"I threw my knives," Lyra argued, the guilt that wracked her conscience traveling into the pit of her stomach.

"Fucking rabbit-stickers," he answered dismissively. "*I* sliced his belly open, with his own sword. Did you see his guts spill out? Fucker was trying to push 'em back in." He sniggered.

Konan's expression gave little away as to whether he thought Lyra was responsible for the warden's death, and in truth, she didn't know what she wanted.

One part of her lamented her choice—she had fallen from a higher moral standing and was drowning in a morass of guilt. She had scorned the beautiful gift of Air magika from the Five-Faced God. She had used it to hurt someone instead of help them. She deserved nothing, not forgiveness and certainly not salvation.

The other part of her danced with bitter triumph, shrieking vindictive adulation for her retaliation. *Finally*, it cried. *Justice!* That thought sent a rush of blood roaring through her ears.

She thought she might be sick, but she swallowed it back. She failed, and she turned away from Konan barely in time to retch on the sand. Her entire body convulsed, rejecting what she had done, and the small meal of bread and cheese came right back up.

"Damn it, girl, you have any idea how dehydrated you already are?" Thordrin complained as he scooted farther away. He released a dry, raspy cough. "Don't rinse your mouth out. Fucking swallow it."

Lyra panted and looked to Konan. He wouldn't meet her eye as he offered the skein. He agreed with Thordrin. She apologized as they moved to a different spot, and she swallowed the acidic gulp of water after swishing it between her teeth.

Konan offered his lap, and she gratefully arranged herself on his leg. The panicked roaring in her ears was replaced by the steady thrum of his heartbeat, a powerful pulse in his thigh. He hunched over, fluttering his cloak out to provide more shade for them; it looked uncomfortable. He seemed to fall into his own light slumber, and Lyra tried to do the same.

She dreamt of Mam and Elden, interspersed with Adrian making her laugh or smile, or memories of the caravan passing through the grassy plains of south Marlemet. Then she dreamt of the warden. He plagued the darker corners and depths, and she would emerge terrified that she was again covered in fresh welts, that her ribs had been kicked and shattered, that she was bleeding and blind. The horror was suffocating, like drowning, and she would strain for the surface. In that nebulous dream state, where the warden was both alive and dead, she would find Konan's touch, his warmth and presence and heartbeat. It thrummed through her dreams. Distracted from the looming nightmare, she returned to her caravan, joyfully reuniting with Mam and dancing to a new rhythm of barrel drums.

They ran out of water shortly after that.

Thordrin alternated cursing the warden with cursing Lyra for her seeming waste of water through puking or crying. It didn't matter—she hadn't done either for days.

However, she was exhausted, much more so than the men. They were physically far stronger than she to begin with, but she had also pushed her still-healing body to its limit with the sandstorm, with no opportunity to recover. As evening approached, bringing with it a slight reprieve in temperature, Lyra became more and more aware of her parched lips, the tender boils of sunburn on her skin, the dryness of her throat.

They paused for bread, a dissatisfying meal that crumbled to dust in their mouths. Thordrin rummaged through the rations bag and grimaced.

"Not much left, love. Now would be a good time to bring some rain." He hacked a cough.

Lyra nodded. Her show of power in the mines had given them all hope, but she feared it was nowhere near great enough. She was tired, thirsty, and hungry, more than she had ever been in her life. Whether she could summon anything at all was the question. "I can try to bring clouds, but whether they hold rain . . ." She shrugged helplessly and hung her head, dejected. "I don't have power over Water."

"By the Light, try," Thordrin answered, flopping to the ground with less grace than she was used to seeing.

And she did try. As the Eye glared orange and then red, its last vestige of grandeur in purple dissipating over the horizon, Lyra sought in all directions. She reached as far as she could, testing the Air, feeling its weight and power, tasting its dryness.

There was hope far to the west. She grasped on to it in her mind, willing it toward her with all of her might. A sudden breeze lifted, a constant westerly wind that seemed to spout from an eternal source. Sand grit flew into their eyes as the breeze continued, on and on, until the sun had gone entirely. The new quick moon was all that shone, a mere sliver of light.

A shadow briefly covered the crescent, an incomplete haze. Lyra reached toward it, urging it near. A cloud, carried on the wind, scurried toward them, but it was thin, as wispy as an old woman's hair.

Thordrin masked the glimmer of hope lighting his eyes, whereas Konan remained stony as ever.

The trailing fingers of the cloud passed by the moon, then hung over them in the dark sky. No rain. No water.

For a long time, no one spoke. The stars began to wheel across the sky, and the pale moon shivered wan light. It seemed colder than before, as though I'ya had truly abandoned them.

Finally, Thordrin spoke. "I thought you said there was something out here. You fucking idiot. There's nothing here."

Lyra flinched, although he directed his glittering green anger at Konan.

"There is," Konan answered, heaving a sigh. "There must be."

Thordrin cursed at his hand gestures with a snarl and dismissive wave.

Lyra began to sob without tears. She had failed them. That summoning was the last she could muster without some kind of relief or rest.

"Let's go," Thordrin commanded. He got up and headed north without looking back.

Lyra didn't budge. Exhaustion pervaded her bones, her muscles, her will. Exhaustion and something else. Despair? It ate into her ability to move.

"Damn it all, walk!" Thordrin shouted over his shoulder. He stomped away, his lean, muscular figure becoming a dark silhouette in the dim moonlight.

Konan took her arm and pulled her along, unwilling and defeated. He looked as forlorn as she felt. They trudged through the rest of the night with their feet dragging more and more.

Lyra was truly thirsty. Her throat burned; each breath came ragged and sore. The dryness of Tahayi Desert seemed to pull the moisture from her tongue and airway, leaving behind cracks like a canyon incised in the earth. Instead of a trickle of water at the bottom of each crack, it was blood. She could taste it in the back of her throat.

She began to imagine what it would be like, happening upon a verdant green space, a spring bubbling from the center and surrounded by flowers: a patch of life in the waste. How she would fall upon the ground with her face over the spring, splashing the cool droplets into her mouth and over her face, rinsing the salty varnish off her skin. How delicious it would be, what relief to fill the cracks in her throat with a torrent of water.

Stumbling over her own feet, she fell.

Someone pulled her back up, and she kept going in a daze, doggedly following behind the other two dark shapes in the night.

After what seemed an eternity, the east turned gray, then a pale yellow. The sun peered over the sands without a single cloud to defray its brightness. It became a furnace emanating heat; its power was merciless and its movement slow as it crept across the sky. The Eye of I'ya.

She cursed him, cursed how he watched their torment and suffering, *her* torment and suffering, and did nothing.

They had not stopped for hours.

The air was still and stale when Lyra realized she was no longer sweating. It was difficult to tell in the first place, as any perspiration quickly evaporated from her forehead and neck and armpits. It did, however, leave behind a thin white crust that nearly sparkled on her skin like a sheen of jewels.

Now she felt truly dry, as though all the moisture in her had been wrenched out. She was dizzy, her limbs ached, and her vision blurred. *Think of the oasis,* she told herself. *Think of the water. There must be something out here, like Konan said.* But her mind wandered instead to her mother, to Elden, to the blue-eyed King Hemil of Shayal and whether he liked his gemstone-studded belt. Even to the Shayalese baron. He hadn't been so bad, but she had never gotten the chance to know him better. Had he been disappointed when he failed to find her again? Did his steward like the horse saddle? Would the baron have liked her enough to bind himself to her?

A wretched thought screamed through her meandering mind: *You're not unblemished by another man. He would never accept you. No noble man would.* And then, as clear as the sky, the warden was in her mind, bearing down upon her and grinning madly.

"Little bitch, you're mine now," he cackled as he reached for her neck with thick, grasping fingers. The lines on his cheeks deepened, and his face contorted into that of a demon.

"Mam!" she shrieked, and fell backward, manifesting a final weak Whisper with her last breath. It cocked its head at her as if surprised she had nothing more to say, then careened southeastward on half-formed wings.

36

KONAN HAD BEEN WRAPPED in his own muddled memories when he heard Lyra fall.

She toppled over herself, uttering a high-pitched yelp and flailing her arms as she rolled down the dune. Her movements didn't seem directed at catching herself, but rather were blindly reaching and struggling. She ripped part of her tunic, her nails catching on the cheap, thin fabric as she stared at some unseen spirit. Her chest heaved, and then she screamed in terror.

Konan rushed back to where she lay. He shook her, but her scream only faded as she ran out of breath, then it weakened to a moan.

Eventually, she came back to him. Her glossy gaze refocused, and she trembled violently and crawled into his arms, nestling her head in his chest. She sobbed, and all Konan could think was how much water wasted away down her cheeks and into the hot sand. Worry gnawed at him.

They were dying.

"We don't have time for this," complained Thordrin, turning back. Konan held out a hand for food, and Thordrin begrudgingly gave him a small hunk of bread.

Lyra ate it without thought, gulping it down and coughing on the dry crumbs. She panted, a rapid, shallow huff that seemed at odds with her fitness. Injured though she had been, she had a good physique from dancing, and she shouldn't have been that tired from the pace they walked.

Konan brushed her hair back and examined her more closely. Her skin was dry as parchment scrolls, and nearly as pale beneath the pink of sunburn. Her forehead burned hot and red, and her lips were cracked raw with scabs. Her blue eyes seemed hazy and dull, and even now, she barely seemed aware of his presence.

"She needs water," he signed to Thordrin, who merely stared and then jutted his bearded chin out.

"I'm fine," Lyra said in a strange voice. She brightened and staggered up, then continued walking northward. Brushing at her sand-covered knees, she stumbled up the next dune.

Konan and Thordrin followed.

Lyra muttered words he couldn't understand, intermixed with "Elden" and "Litis" and occasionally "Ada." Then she laughed; it was like a bell toll, a joyful sound that rang across the empty sand. She tripped through a sudden twirl, humming a song that was vaguely familiar. Her voice, normally a high, lilting soprano, broke erratically, but she didn't seem to notice. She swayed from side to side, arms fluttering in a drunken routine.

Then her foot sank into a soft bed of sand. It sucked her down, but she continued forward. "Blasted cattle," she mumbled.

Konan shouted, but his voice came out as a hoarse cough.

Both of Lyra's feet were disappearing into the sinking sands, but she kept moving forward, shaking her head in disgust. One ankle was already submerged, then her calves.

Konan sprinted forward, using a last burst of energy to dive. He grabbed her flailing right arm as she danced, staying its wild movements.

Sunk to her knees, Lyra muttered and stopped trying to walk, then sat abruptly on the sinking sand. Her hips went under as she muttered curses to herself.

Thordrin appeared, grabbing her limp left arm, and they pulled desperately, digging into the soft sand and shoving backward toward solid ground.

Lyra's body had gone listless, although her eyes were still open. She still wore a faint smile.

Finally, they managed to pull her free of the sinking sand and drag her a short distance before laying her down. Both of them heaved for their own breath, but she looked far worse. She was only partially conscious. Her skin burned hot, dry, and red. Her eyes rolled back into her head, and her blistered lips mouthed inaudible words. She no longer sang.

Konan knelt over her, trying to shade her from the sun. "She's going to die if we don't find water soon," he signed.

Thordrin heaved a defeated sigh. "We need water. Girl's too soft for this place."

They sat in silence for several minutes. The sun beat upon their shoulders, and heat shimmered off the burning sand.

"Do we leave her?" Thordrin's voice was flat, devoid of emotion. His jaw was set.

Konan scowled and signed. "You have no honor."

"Her family can find her in the next Gate, Konan," Thordrin insisted. "This world is not made for people like her. She's better off dead."

With one more heaving sigh, one he hoped would imbue him with energy, Konan shook his head and wearily scooped Lyra into his arms. He stood with an effort. Even he felt the exhaustion, and he had acclimated to Tahayi years ago. He trudged forward, around the sinking sands, and heard Thordrin follow after a few seconds.

"You're wasting your energy, Konan," came the man's deep bass from behind. "She's going to die of the heat, and you'll end up dying for your efforts. Is she worth it? Is she really worth giving up your own life? Your own chance at vengeance?"

Konan didn't answer, focusing all of his energy on continuing onward with a corpse-like weight slumped in his arms. As light as she was in normal circumstances, Lyra was still an extra burden, throwing him off balance and dragging at his weary muscles. She had stopped muttering and now hung entirely limp; he slung her over his shoulder when his biceps could no longer bear cradling her. In truth, he wasn't really sure she wasn't already dead, or at least inevitably destined for the next Gate, and he couldn't bear to check.

Was she worth it? He was certain she was. He had languished an eternity in the mines and for much of it with such paltry hope that escape was laughable. Yet with her help, truly with her initiative, they had escaped. It was the first light that had shone in his heart in an interminable amount of time.

If they managed to pass through this trial, if he could carry her far enough, they could achieve not only a reunion with her family, but also freedom for all three. Liberation. Konan had not dared dream of it in so long. He would be free to pursue a life, any life—perhaps one with her, if she would have him.

He shook himself, a motion that made him dizzier than it should have. Lyra didn't need *that*. She needed her family, the comfort of familiarity and security. Home.

And what did he need? Home? He wasn't sure what that meant, but there was only one place he knew to look for it.

He and Thordrin walked onward, their footsteps creating a double trail of loosely defined indentations. The sun reached its apex, then lazily descended while sending forth its most deadly heat in the midst of the afternoon stillness.

Thordrin tripped as they descended a long, rolling dune.

Konan watched as the Phantom haphazardly tumbled to the bottom, bereft of any grace or athletic form; Konan stumbled down after him. As Thordrin tried to push himself back up, he muttered about a bed and a whore, then collapsed with one last word. "Rigaran."

Konan lay Lyra gently down beside him, rolling them both to their sides so their burnt faces were shaded. He pulled up their hoods and covered their feet with their cloaks. Both were unconscious. They were also overheated and getting worse, and he knew he was not far behind.

They had been going all day, for endless days. He wasn't sure how many times the Eye had passed over them since they stole away from the burning mines, but it seemed like a repeating nightmare. Despite his years of endurance in the hellish desert, Konan could feel his own strength waning.

Even if he could carry Lyra a short distance further, he could not carry them both.

He repressed a sob of frustration. He had been so sure there was something out here. Even now, he could feel it. He could nearly taste it. Water. Life. Hope.

As he lay down next to Lyra, the gritty sand beneath his cheek was like fire, and for a moment, he thought of the past, the terrors that had altered his course and sent him to hell. But then the sand cooled, or his skin burned to numbness; either way, it felt a little better after a few seconds. The fire had burned away everything he loved, and he had been sent to the mines, but he had also found *her* there. And she was a brilliant light, brighter and more intense than the Eye had ever been. She was a tempest, a whirlwind that utterly changed the landscape of his world. Her zeal, her passion, her love for her life and her family—it all infected him. It coursed through him irresistibly, flushing into exhausted limbs and eating at the carefully constructed layers around his heart.

He wanted to live.

It was a strange feeling. At first, it seemed good; it filled him with a foreign-tasting sense of hope, which had been absent for long years. Then panic and dismay crept in. They were dying.

Konan closed his eyes briefly. It would be good to rest, and after they rested, they would keep going. To freedom. To put things right and return Lyra to her family. To avenge Thordrin, and perhaps even to claim his own birthright.

He gulped one last breath of dry desert air, reaching for the water he thought he could taste just beyond him, and wished desperately for salvation.

Konan awoke suddenly, noticing that his face was shaded in the late-afternoon sun. The Eye strained to touch them through a layer of palms, tall frond-covered trees with lanky trunks.

An oasis!

Konan shook Lyra and Thordrin, one at a time. Thordrin groaned but managed to inch his way up. He rubbed his eyes and squinted in confusion at the shade and the cooler feel to the ground. Ungainly, he scrambled between the trees, and Konan heard a splash as he found water.

Lyra didn't respond, so he desperately dragged her by the arms.

The oasis supported palm trees and wispy grass, and from the center, a small spring seeped. Thordrin lay prone, sucking it greedily from the ground. Konan splashed the tepid water into his mouth and onto Lyra's red face, then her neck and legs. She was on fire; every part of her he touched was hot. He parted her mouth and dripped some water in from his cupped hand. Then he continued splashing her body, trying to cool it down. The meager splashes seemed to dry instantly.

Panic rose from his belly.

Konan pulled her tunic off. Her chest was splotchy with an angry red that disappeared under her bindings. He could feel the heat emanating from her. She barely seemed to breathe.

Thordrin cursed at him as he pulled her closer to the spring. "You'll muddy the water," he complained, snatching Konan's skein from his belt and refilling it before Konan managed to drag Lyra all the way.

Konan soaked everything: her underclothes, her skin, her face and head. By the time he was done, he was panting with exertion.

After a long while, Lyra coughed and sputtered, then retched weakly. Nothing came out.

Konan trickled water down her throat, one handful at a time, until she had to lie back down. She immediately fell asleep again, this time into what seemed a fitful rest instead of full unconsciousness, and Konan rearranged her away from the spring. He poured water over her again, dampening her curls and soaking her tunic before putting it back on. Then he soaked his own cloak and laid that over her as well, confident that she was finally cooling, protected from the Eye's merciless rays.

He slumped against a palm trunk and let out an audible sigh. Thordrin threw him a look, relief mixed with absolute understanding of Konan's feelings.

"I don't know which god saved us, but I don't think it was I'ya," Thordrin muttered with a weak, sarcastic smile that cracked his burned lips.

Konan grunted, and both men closed their eyes.

They were alive.

PART TWO

37

REYLIN FOUND HIMSELF GRINNING foolishly as he tucked the soft-woven swaddling into his arm and clutched the bundle closer.

If he turned her just so, he could block any overt breeze from the balcony and simultaneously marvel at the tiny pink cheeks that glowed between the layers of silk-lined velvet. Amber slept soundly. Her thin, wispy hair was a shade of brown, but it was impossible to tell how dark it might become over time. Her tiny nose was slightly upturned, like her mother's, and her ears mirrored his own. There was a shocking blue to her eyes, but Father Ma'thell had suggested that would change.

Looking over the long valley and braided river, Reylin sent a brief prayer to the Eye. *Thank you for not cursing her with the Mark.* He squinted at the pinkish tone of the dawn, which was hindered by a light fog. The mist rising from the Sikrat veiled the brightness of the sunrise, and although he knew it would burn off within a few hours, the day until then would be somewhat bleak.

He had inspected Amber himself, keen for undue marks and blemishes that could curse the child, despite the assurances of the Temple mages and lady attendants. Her chubby folds and tiny toes and fingers bore his fearful examination, but her skin was blessedly clear of any evil affliction. Bolstered, Reylin held her close, finally allowing his relieved adoration to flood out. *My daughter. My perfect little one.*

He tried not to allow his mind to return to the problems inside, but he couldn't help it.

Priscilla had nearly passed the Gates during the birth, and she had bled excessively, fainting with a euphoric smile as they presented Amber to her. She had not yet woken, and Reylin feared interrupting her exhausted rest in any way.

High Holy Mage Ma'thell had given most of his energy to saving her, first by imbuing several potions and then by staunching the blood as best he could. His frail old body had finally wavered after three bells, and in the dark hours before dawn he had been carried away by magusi to recover in the High Temple.

Although Priscilla seemed out of immediate danger, Reylin had sent Keeper Davon back to Camdry Quarry immediately with orders to retrieve Father Kaiadin. While Reylin could wait for the rest of the party to return on foot, at a leisurely pace for the sake of Syrana and her handmaiden, he needed Kaiadin now.

Perhaps Kaiadin knew more potions that could bolster Priscilla's strength—perhaps he could help Reylin apply some sort of healing to his first wife. In addition to Reylin's concern over Priscilla's delicate state, he also no longer trusted the other Temple mages.

Someone had placed that ward upon him, and he didn't know who. There was only one mage he was certain was *not* involved—Kaiadin.

The morning brought more servants and magusi into the room, checking on both Priscilla and Amber. With great reluctance, Reylin surrendered his tiny bundle to Priscilla's matron-in-waiting and broke his fast on the balcony.

His wife continued to sleep, and Reylin noted how the servants traded bloodied sheets for fresh white linens. She was still seeping blood, and her skin had lost its typical rosiness. A sickly pallor had spread, but the magusi assured him that Ma'thell would return soon, within another bell. Meanwhile, the lesser temple workers applied healing salves, dripped liquids down Priscilla's throat, and prayed over her. Their chanting droned into a buzzing monotony, and Reylin finally left to finish his meal in peace.

He settled in the west-facing Crimson Drawing Room, where the large windows afforded him a broad view of the main courtyard. The Crimson Room featured portraits of the Harkin lineage back to the days of the Empire's fall, but the most important was in the center. Hung high on the wall and framed in gilt gold, his family stared down upon him.

King Rolis stood with a sweeping orange fur cape around his shoulders, affixed to enameled rondels indicative of his military status. Gillead may have been lord commander, but Rolis was the kingdom's authority over all, and a vicious fighting king he was. He glared from the portrait with such a glint in his eye, one could have sworn he was real. His heavy brow was lightly furrowed with the worries of governance, and his tight lips and strong jaw hid a soul that had made too many difficult decisions. Over his dark, wavy hair—identical to Reylin's—perched the royal crown, an intricate working of fine-spun gold that wrapped orange gems and rubies in an ivy-like latticework. It was the crown Reylin should have been wearing now, but instead it was stored on a cushioned pillow, awaiting his Ascension.

Queen Leyalin sat in front of Rolis on a chaise. Her gown flowed down her figure and hung off the cushions in folds, hiding her legs and feet in a sea of rose and auburn. Its fashion was elegant to the degree of impracticality, littered with the tiny chains of diamonds used in Mirat to show status. Her golden crown matched Rolis's, and her warmth exuded from the painting; her maternal smile was blissful and proud. In her arms was a babe, swaddled in bright orange silk edged with more diamond frills.

Reylin stared bitterly at the portrait as he finished a pastry, chasing it down with hot pitlan cider. House Harkin, or all that it *was*.

He really should commission a new one with his own family to replace it. Priscilla, Syrana, precious Amber. Perhaps he would wait until Syrana bore him a son, although he didn't want to wait too long. He hated staring at the existing portrait. Its overbearing size alone dominated the Crimson Room.

Davon arrived in a flash of crimson through the window, and Reylin rushed out to escort Father Kaiadin. The junior mage bobbed a polite and awkward bow to Davon and then to his dragon Ar'we, his own overwhelm apparent.

Reylin understood.

I am simply me, said Ar'we, almost petulant, but Davon smacked her lightly.

"My heart, please try to be civil," he uttered in a strangled voice. "He is to be king."

Like the Order Elder? Ar'we continued, cocking her head. *Then who is king now?*

Davon paled significantly and dropped to his knees in a show of remorse. He bowed to Reylin. "Please forgive her, Your Highness. She really doesn't know anything about politics."

Reylin smiled tightly at the pair, torn between fury at the disrespectful tone from Ar'we and pleasure at the countering veneration from Davon. He didn't bow or even nod to the keeper. Instead, he waved Ar'we toward the high towers and the mountains beyond. "Thank you for retrieving Father Kaiadin. Stay, Keeper Davon, in case we have more need for expedient travel."

"Of course, anything you ask, sire," said Davon fervently. He shared an exchange with his dragon, and the large creature dipped her head until her jaw scraped the flagstones.

Yes, sire, she repeated obediently. *I did not mean to be rude.*

Reylin spun on his heel, beckoning Kaiadin to follow, and rushed to Priscilla's bed. He had no time for this ill-fated exchange. He had heard dragonkeepers were somewhat separate from the hierarchy, but he didn't know why. Perhaps it derived from their connection to the creatures who clearly didn't respect position as much as they should. Nevertheless, Davon had performed well, bringing Kaiadin to him more quickly than he could have hoped.

Priscilla was breathing so shallowly that the mage first placed his ear against her chest to verify she still lived. Satisfied, he proceeded to examine her vacant eyes, her cold skin, and her abdomen. He turned to Reylin with a pensive sigh.

"I can do nothing for her, my young king." His solemnity cut through Reylin's chest, right into his heart, and Reylin reeled into the nearest chair. But Kaiadin continued in a methodical, assured tone, placing a comforting hand on Reylin's knee. "I cannot, but you can."

Reylin looked up, panting with overwhelming terror for Priscilla.

The man looked sincere. His gaze was steady, and Reylin latched on to the knowledge that such indigo-painted eyes would know the truth of the matter.

"Your wife is torn, inside," Kaiadin explained. "She will bleed to death unless someone can bind her together again. Even High Holy Mage Ma'thell does not have that much power, if he has already failed to do so, but you do. If you can control it, you can save her, my son."

"How?" Reylin demanded, panic still looming.

Kaiadin shook his knee again, gaining his full attention. "I can teach you, as best I know, from the Temple's scrolls. Trust in me, son. You've already done it once, binding your own injury back together, but we must hurry before she runs out of time."

At that moment, Ma'thell shuffled in, his feet dragging and scraping as he failed to lift each one. He was escorted on each elbow by young magusi, apprentices by the looks of their raised hoods and covered hair. He sank into the chair Reylin had vacated and began invoking healing, reaching his trembling hands over Priscilla's abdomen. He bowed his head in silent prayer and ignored the rest of the room.

Father Kaiadin pointed his chin toward the door, and they slipped out without a word. At this point, Reylin didn't believe Ma'thell could save her.

They headed to the archives, a musty, stack-filled room in the basement of the High Temple. The ceiling was low and the lamplight dim. Reylin marveled at the contrast between the room and the rainbow-filled gallery above. Kaiadin rummaged through a number of scrolls sorted along the wall, each tucked into its own cubby hole with esoteric and faded labels.

Kaiadin pulled a few out, but after peering over their titles put most of them back. He finally tapped one with his index finger. "Yes, this to start," he murmured. He traced his finger along the words, all scribbled in the Old Language. Then he looked up with some surprise. "This reads much like a physician's instruction. 'Healing requires examination of the injury, a probing . . . identification of injured parts . . . stitching back together . . .' Perhaps it would help to have a drawing of the female anatomy as well."

He gathered an armful of scrolls and beckoned awkwardly to Reylin, nearly dropping one of them in the process.

Reylin caught it and took some of the mage's burden.

"Son, let us go to Priscilla before it is too late."

They rushed back to the castle, where Ma'thell still prayed over Priscilla. She lay as still and pale as before, the bed seeming to yawn open and consume her. Her skin was ghostly white as the linen, making the contrast of blood below seem all the more garish. Reylin was thankful it was covered up by a fur, for he could hardly bear to face it.

A lady-in-waiting sat nearby, wringing her hands and mumbling prayers, while a wet nurse fed little Amber in the corner. Neither woman could bear to leave her sickly mistress.

Ma'thell looked up when the men entered. "She is barely holding onto life," he said sadly. "I've kept her stable only by intervention, and I am at the end of my gift." The old man tried to sit up straight and swooned. His assistant swept in and caught him by the elbow, righting him in his chair. Ma'thell gave the magus an appreciative look; nonetheless, tears filled his graying eyes.

"Please, High Holy Father, rest," Kaiadin said politely. "We may have a solution."

Reylin gave him a sharp look. Was it wise to reveal the truth to Ma'thell?

With a subtle nod, Kaiadin continued. "Father, Prince Reylin discovered an incredible gift from I'ya while traveling."

Ma'thell scrunched his wild eyebrows together and turned slowly, his pale, half-blind eyes searching for Reylin.

Kaiadin rushed through the story, focusing on the miraculous magika rather than the tragic deaths of Sir Cordan and his wife. He conveniently excluded the breaking of the ward.

Ma'thell listened, all the while assessing Reylin. Again, Reylin wondered how much the man did see, and how much he really knew. When Kaiadin finished explaining where they had been that morning, the elderly mage turned his gaze to the wet nurse and her tiny charge. "Amber Sallis Harkin," he murmured to himself. Then he addressed Reylin. "Exchange places with me, son." Ma'thell had his magus help him to another chair to the side. "Your love has saved someone once already. Let it be so again."

Reylin obediently took the seat by Priscilla's side, although he suspected Ma'thell did know something about his past. All these years, Reylin had trusted the old mage implicitly, believed in his unwavering support and care; he had once thought Ma'thell to be one of his champions on the Elder Council. Now he wasn't so sure.

He reached his hands over his first wife, caressing her cheek. It was clammy. He tried to focus on her body condition instead, tearing his thoughts away from hopeless dread. Probing with his fingers an inch off her skin, Reylin moved down her form, feeling the pale shiver of breath in her neck. Her breasts were full of a Water that was heavy, warm, and nurturing to his senses. Then he moved to her belly, then her pelvis. There, something felt wrong. Humors and thin blood were where they should not be, and the tissues felt disarranged and torn inside. He didn't know how he knew, but his senses told him it was true. His wife, the lovely and kind Priscilla, was bleeding out from the inside, just as Father Kaiadin had said.

"You know how to fix it, my young king," said Kaiadin in a low voice. "You've already done it once on a smaller scale. You can do it again." He unrolled one of the scrolls, far more detailed than Reylin was comfortable with, indicating the precise anatomy of a woman on the inside. "Perhaps this can help your understanding of what you are sensing," Kaiadin suggested, pushing his glasses up the bridge of his nose. He looked equally uneasy.

"It hurt when I did it," Reylin murmured, thinking back to the sting of healing on his own arm. Would he hurt

Priscilla too? But it was necessary. He examined the chart, then Priscilla, back and forth as he gained his bearings.

The damage was in her womb, as he had already thought, but it did help somewhat to see a reference.

The junior mage's encouragement bolstered Reylin, and he poured himself into his outward touch. He was with Priscilla, in her, connected to her.

Like the strange sensation as he probed his own arm, sensing the jagged edges and the seeping of blood, Reylin could feel the wrongness of tissues out of place. He could sense where Ma'thell had attempted to pull some of them back, half-healed but inadequate to stop her fading. He began taking the broken tissues and binding them back together, Water to Water, edge to edge. The metallic taste of blood overwhelmed his mouth.

The massive wound in her uterus slowly closed, sealing shut with nary a scar from what he could tell. Reylin probed it again with a sigh of relief, then continued on, healing smaller tears and tissue damage farther down. The blood felt wrong, overly thin and weak, and it didn't stop flowing until each injury was fully sealed by his intervention. When he felt no other tissues out of place, he was satisfied. He relinquished his intent focus and looked up.

Priscilla lay unconscious as before. The high holy mage slept on a chaise in the corner, propped up by a large pillow and watched over by his magusi. The sun in the window had shifted position, casting its rays over the elderly man as he rested. Kaiadin had taken a seat next to Reylin and gave him an encouraging smile.

"You've done all you can?" asked Kaiadin. "Son, I'm so proud of you."

"How long was I—" Reylin began, realizing the sun had burst through the morning fog.

"It's been two and a half bells, son," Kaiadin said gently.

Reylin looked down at his wife. She was still so pale, her skin nearly translucent. She lay in a pile of stained sheets. "Why isn't she awake?"

Seeming to understand his apprehension, Kaiadin examined her more closely, feeling her pulse and listening to her shallow breathing. His own expression changed to one of concern as well. "She's lost too much blood, I suspect."

The lady-in-waiting began to wail, awakening the others in the room, "Too much blood. Yea, m'lady bled so much. We couldn't stop it, it's too much. I knew it . . ." Baby Amber began to scream.

Reylin looked to Kaiadin for guidance in the chaos.

The mage took him by the shoulders. "We don't have time for a transfusion. Only you can give her blood, blood from water. You must change it, make it what she needs."

They moved the princess's limp body into the bath, filling the tub with warm water. Reylin followed in a daze, unsure of what he was meant to do.

"Take the water, as much as you need, and join it to her," said Kaiadin. "Make it part of her own blood." He shuffled through the pile of scrolls, searching for some sort of guidance that could help them. He cast them aside one at a time, finding only a paltry description of the value of the humors.

Ma'thell hobbled over, apologizing for his inability to do more, but Reylin brushed past him and knelt by the tub. He placed his hands over Priscilla's limp body and extended his reach once again. The warm water felt comforting but different than what was inside her. Her blood felt richer and full of life, but it coursed through her so weakly, with a diminishing pressure. The rhythm of her pulse was hardly detectable, even with him entirely immersed in her presence. The water, on the other hand, was clear and pure, but empty.

How to make one into the other?

"Will it to be," Kaiadin commanded from somewhere beyond.

Reylin searched for a way, trying to imagine the water shifting into blood, each droplet morphing and joining into a life-giving fluid. But nothing worked. He didn't know how to do this. He didn't even know if he *could* do this. A sob escaped as desperation and terror overcame him.

"Will it to be, son," repeated Kaiadin.

Will it to be.

Reylin pulled away from his intense focus for a moment to give his beloved first wife a long last look. He leaned over and gave her a gentle kiss on her cold lips, then pulled out his dagger and sliced his forearm open. He slumped over the edge of the bath, pumping his own blood into the tub. With his last minutes of consciousness, he joined the swirling redness with Priscilla's body, shoving all of the life force he could back into her. Then a peaceful darkness seeped in, and he knew no more.

*A message for the princess Syrana: Reylin
unwell. Return to Ironhold.*

THE WHISPER ARRIVED TO the Camdry mage's ear late
in the day, and he relayed it promptly to Baron Bonneser's
home. Lady Ana thanked him profusely and sent him back
to the town, then turned to Syrana with an icy look of contempt.

Syrana's shoulders slumped as she realized Reylin was not
coming back for her.

"And he didn't even send that Ar'we creature to fetch
you?" the baroness scoffed. "He expects you to travel the
road alone? It's hardly fitting a lady. Imagine, you and your
savage handmaiden, with ten men, none of whom are your
husband."

Syrana couldn't tell if her mother was gloating or glowering. Either way, she was clearly ashamed.

She searched for an answer that would please the woman. "If he's unwell, maybe he didn't dictate the message," she suggested. "But why would he be unwell?"

"Perhaps that awful blood-colored monster did something to him," said Ana. "It may be better not to go adragonback. I've never thought the animals seemed trustworthy, and their keepers are odd people. In any case, you must return quickly and get back into his good graces. Care for him in his illness. Make yourself indispensable. Clearly, you've failed to do so thus far."

The baron entered the room where they sat and stood in front of the open window, which allowed a summer breeze to freshen the stale indoor air. He noticed the two women. "Was that the priest?" he asked.

Ana affirmed that it was. "He relayed a message from Ironhold. The prince is unwell and cannot return for banquet."

Her father grumbled deep in his chest. It was a sound so familiar to Syrana that she understood it as a complete sentence indicating his unhappiness with the situation. Half of the animals had already been slaughtered and put to roast by the time Reylin had launched onto a dragon's back and disappeared. Half the pies were baked, crusts browned and flaking, fillings tender and spiced to perfection. Reylin's absence had delayed quite a feast, one meant to demonstrate the baronage's capabilities.

Her mother crept up behind him and smoothed the knots from the thick muscle where his neck grew into his shoulder. "I was suggesting that perhaps I could accompany our daughter to Ironhold with a larger contingent, to ensure she gets there safely," she suggested, words honeyed and pleading. *Please, my love, give me what I want*, they said.

The baron grumbled again. *That's a fine idea.*

"And I could handle some of the logistics of assuring supplies are delivered for colonization of East Face," Ana continued. "It sounds like they'll be establishing a fortification to guard against the Halmani monsters. Certainly the prince will wish to continue his collaboration with the guild when he is well again."

That was pleasing to Syrana's father, and he grunted his approval. "All supply runs will come through Camdry." Good business for the town, and taxes in the coffers.

"I'll make sure they do," said Ana, beaming. "Syrana and I will depart in the morning."

The baron turned and exited the room, his heavy boots thudding on the carpet.

"Bright afternoon, my love," she called after him.

He grunted back.

Ana turned to her daughter with a knowing smirk. "See? Indispensable."

The journey back to Ironhold Castle was unpleasant, with Syrana crammed into her carriage with her mother, plus both their personal handmaidens. Ana had perceived immediately that the handmaid was involved in Syrana's private affairs, and therefore spoke openly about Syrana's barren womb and general uselessness.

The only highlight was the occasional visit from Reylin's High Guard knights, who would intermittently trot up to her carriage window to check on her. Sir Gillead, as usual, was dour and serious, but Sir Ronidann usually told her a joke or a story of which the landscape had reminded him. Sir Dorian, the newly promoted High Guard, would regale them with his exploits in the jousting arena, not an entirely appropriate subject for a noble lady but well-meant. Plus, he was handsome. Like most Miratians, he had dark, wavy hair, which he cropped in a military style, shorter than Reylin's. His hard brow and jaw were softened by a refined nose and heavily lashed eyes, which were brighter and more hazel than Reylin's. A woman would kill for lashes like that.

They passed through Lupine without stopping, instead finding a cottager along the road who, overwhelmed as they were for space, appreciated the coins provided to support the contingent's brief stay. After all, the two noblewomen were truly the only ones in need of a proper bed. Everyone else could tolerate a soldier's tent.

Gillead and Patreagh pushed them onward quickly, desiring nothing more than to reclaim their charge. Both men had watched over Reylin since he was a boy, becoming his High Guard upon the death of King Rolis.

Syrana breathed a sigh of relief as they pulled up in front of the stairs in Ironhold Castle's inner courtyard. Her mother was overbearing, suffocating her with disapproval and scolding lectures on being a proper wife. The carriage rumbled jarringly on the brick to a final stop, and a servant pulled open the carriage door. Syrana found herself helped out by none other than Lord Galltry, Duke of the East Valley.

"My princess, we're glad you're home," he said sincerely. There was an odd hollowness to his words and a gauntness in his polite smile, and it seemed the crow's feet around his eyes truly were wrinkles of age.

"Reylin?" she asked, with no patience for formalities in the moment. Worry bubbled up.

Lady Shildra took her arm as Galltry helped Ana descend. "Do not fret, my lady. He is healing, and in no danger of passing the Gates. Now who is this with you? Your mother! Why, Baroness Ana, how lovely to see you." Shildra took the baroness on her other arm and walked them in, chattering about the state of things, the darling baby Amber, the bravado and foolishness of the prince. "As near a tragedy as it could have been," said Shildra, "but I'ya was watching over Mirat that day."

"And Priscilla?"

Shildra's face fell. "Ma'thell didn't tell you in his message?" She looked everywhere but at them, quickening her pace. "He was exhausted. Perhaps he didn't have enough breath."

They hurried on with the High Guard on their heels. Entering the royal suite, Syrana broke away from Shildra to rush to the bed. Reylin was pale, so pale. Covered by more blankets than should have been necessary in the summer, he lay still, with only his face showing. He had been leaned against a mass of pillows so that he was only half-reclined, and his head was nestled comfortably among the cushions. He stirred when Syrana sat on the edge of the bed, and his tired eyes fluttered open.

Syrana gazed lovingly into those richly colored irises, flecked with amber, and began to cry.

"Syrana, you're here," said Reylin. His baritone was muted to a dim, wheezy whisper.

He struggled to get his right arm out of the blankets and dragged it to her own hand, wrapping his somewhat clammy fingers around hers. "It's all right. I'm all right." He closed his eyes again with an exhausted smile, appearing to fall back asleep.

"It was a near thing," came Father Kaiadin's suave voice. The mage stood by the door to the balcony and folded his hands into his indigo robes. "He gave most of himself to save Priscilla."

A cold rage and hatred for the first wife filled Syrana, and she buried her expression in Reylin's chest to hide it.

"Is the princess Priscilla quite well now?" asked the baroness, smoothly covering for her daughter.

The room fell silent, and a glint of hope sparked inside Syrana. She dared not unbury her face from Reylin's chest, for fear of revealing herself.

Shildra sniffled and waved a silk kerchief in the air, as if warding off further poor luck. "She passed the Gates, I'ya bless her soul."

Elation. Syrana prayed it didn't show. She felt her mother place a steadying hand on her shoulder and squeeze; the baroness's dug into Syrana's skin through the fine fabric of her dress.

"What a tragedy." Ana's voice was as smooth as poison. "All hail the crown princess."

Syrana could have sworn her nails would draw blood.

Shildra agreed, then sniffled again. "She left us with a blessing, though—little Amber. Would you like to see the tiny thing? She's quite the dear, unmarked by even a freckle, and with the finest hair." Shildra rambled on, arm in arm with the baroness, who wore a gleeful, maternal expression. Syrana refused; she couldn't leave Reylin. The older women departed to the chamber down the hall.

Lord Galltry excused himself as well. "I'll leave you in Father Kaiadin's sure care, my lady. Pardon me, Crown Princess," he corrected himself with bleak formality. "Father Kaiadin has watched over Reylin these last few days, especially with Ma'thell's exhaustion."

"Thank you, Lord Galltry," said Kaiadin as the man left. The mage went around the other side of the bed, brushing

Gillead aside with more forcefulness than Syrana would have expected.

Gillead grumbled at him, then stationed himself at Reylin's feet next to Patreagh. Sirs Ronidann and Dorian remained on either side of the door, as was expected of them, but Ronidann kept turning his head and peering into the room with a worrisome frown.

Syrana dabbed her eyes with a silken kerchief, then directed her gaze at Kaiadin. "Tell me exactly what happened, Father," she begged. "How did this come to be?"

Kaiadin furrowed his brow, as if he was unsure himself. "Your husband has a great and powerful gift, as you know," he began.

"External trans . . . something?" asked Syrana, remembering Sir Cordan's knife dissolving. Its blade had flashed in the moonlight as it descended upon her, and then . . .nothing.

"Yes, external transmutation," said Kaiadin, bobbing his chin up and down, "but he hasn't learned how to fully use it. We had hardly begun practicing his manipulation abilities, let alone a healing process such as was needed. He did what he could to bind Priscilla back together—more of a manipulation than a transmutation." He paused to ensure Syrana was following his explanation—she wasn't, but he didn't need to know that—then continued. "Manipulation is typically easier to perform, certainly easier to teach and more familiar to the Temple. Most mages have *some* manipulative power, although it is rarely this strong." He nodded to himself, as if affirming his own words. "I taught him what I could in the brief time we had, but when he healed her tissue injuries, she was still fading. She had lost too much blood, so he tried to give her his own."

Kaiadin pulled down the blanket covering Reylin's left arm. The forearm was tightly bandaged.

Gillead groaned, shoving Kaiadin aside to examine the injury more closely. "I should never have let him leave without one of us," he lamented. The other High Guard crowded in, somber as they realized how close they had come to losing their royal charge.

"Damn the boy, praise the man," murmured Ronidann, shaking his head in futile frustration.

Syrana stared at the wrapping, concealing and binding what must have been a long, slicing cut along the artery. If he had died, what would she be?

"He did this for her?" Her voice sounded strange and cold.

"For love, my lady, one would do almost anything," said Kaiadin, tugging the blanket back up and tucking it around Reylin. "Would they not?"

Syrana donned a light, gauzy gown with orange sequins covering the bodice, an appropriate vesture of the proud House of Harkin that ruled Mirat. Her handmaiden assembled her hair in soft coils, twisted round each other so the mass was off her neck, then affixed her large orange gem necklace. Was it too gaudy for such a day? No, but the priests might glower at the head and hair. Syrana wrapped an airy, matching shawl around her shoulders and pulled the see-through material over her head. Her hairstyle was still visible, but she wouldn't be judged for impropriety.

Under almost any other circumstance, she wouldn't have needed to cover her head at all as the queen-to-be of Mirat. Crown princess—now that tasted fine on her tongue, sweet as effervescent wine.

No matter, she thought as she adjusted the veil. Her hair still looked elegant. She nodded confidently into the mirror and drew her shoulders back. Regal, she thought, more so than Priscilla would have looked.

"Did you remember to ochre your lips?" asked her mother.

Syrana pouted her curved lips out as her handmaiden applied the makeup.

"That's good. Any more, and you'll appear to be a woman from the street corner."

Syrana tried to control the twitch in her nose and the irritation in her heart. "And are you ready, Mother?"

"Of course I am," Ana snapped, "but all eyes should be on you today, not me. Crown Princess." She stood and offered her arm to her daughter so they could walk together. Perhaps she could be impressed.

"All eyes will be on the baby," Syrana said bitterly as she slipped her arm into her mother's.

"Don't talk back to me, Syrana. Learn to own whatever room you enter. Shine so brightly that others are blinded, and walk proudly as would any Camdry. You are Syrana, daughter of Bonneser and Ana Camdry, chosen wife of Reylin Harkin of Ironhold, and future queen of Mirat. Act like it!"

"But only second wife," Syrana protested. Always, she was second.

"That's fixed now." Her mother dismissed that concern with a wave of her hand.

The conversation paused as the pair entered a busier corridor and headed toward the Great Hall, where they would meet the rest of the baptismal party. They were only meeting there, then walking in formal procession to the High Temple. As the steward, Gordrew, opened the door and announced them, Ana leaned over to whisper in Syrana's ear. "Own the room."

Syrana swept in, gracefully moving through the open hall toward Reylin, who rested on his throne. Syrana's bodice shimmered in the early-morning light that streamed through the windows, and the gauzy gown flowed behind without weight. Reylin glanced up and seemed to be riveted; a tired smile appeared on his face. Syrana returned a coy look, curving her lips just so.

As she reached the dais, smoothly ascending the few steps without revealing her feet, Reylin looked down. He cradled an orange-swaddled bundle. A tiny arm flailed out of the folds, reaching awkwardly for his face. Reylin smiled again, this time with such warmth that Syrana felt cold by comparison. She forced herself to beam down at the baby and then touched Reylin's shoulder gently.

"My love, you look tired. Let me take her," she said.

Reylin handed the bundle to her, gently supporting the head with special care, and she stood tall, swinging the baby to the side farther from him. She tucked the flailing arm back into the swaddling and pulled it up to hide Amber's face from Reylin's view. Unpleasant, distracting little thing. The baby babbled at her.

"Thank you," said Reylin. "I didn't feel tired when I awoke, but dressing and walking over here was enough to make me weary again."

"You are too hard on yourself, my love. Are you sure you want to proceed with the christening today?" It had been nearly a week, longer than one would normally wait, but they had mourned Priscilla first and waited for Reylin to recover.

Reylin assured her that he did. "Father Ma'thell does not approve," he added with a grimace. "He says I need more days of bedrest, but I've had enough lingering."

Syrana saw an opportunity and took it. Something to make him smile, something to make him linger on her. She was leaning in to whisper about other things that could be done while confined to the bedroom when little Amber cooed. The tender moment was gone.

Damned little demon. She adjusted the babe again, bouncing it a little to help it fall asleep.

The guests, including Ana and guards in front and behind, formed a parade through the short streets between castle and temple, wending their way through the common folk and followed behind with loud cheering. Syrana straightened her shoulders and preened until she realized how few of the rabble eyed her gauzy splendor. All gazes were affixed on the wretched swath of orange in her arms.

The baby Amber Sallis Harkin, first daughter of the son of Rolis and Leyalin of the Miratian kingdom, was to be christened in the name of I'ya in the temple of glass and light. What a day for merriment and gratitude. She struggled to keep a sneer of discontent from marring her features.

Syrana spent the remainder of the day hovering over Reylin, simultaneously cursing his stubbornness and generous love. He had collapsed midway through the christening, faint with poor health, and would have knocked his head on the smooth temple pavers if not for Dragonkeeper Davon's reflexive diving catch.

Now, Reylin slept as if all the vigor had been drained from him. So little exertion had wearied him so much.

Damn that Priscilla to the Nethergate. Syrana wanted to scream.

The lords and ladies present had murmured in dismay, leaning toward each other with exaggerated concern and quietly loud words. *Reylin is weak. Reylin should be more careful. Reylin brought bad luck upon us from the north. Poor Lady Priscilla.*

Syrana shook her head. It was all farce, all doubt sown for the benefit of the dukes and duchesses in power. She had noted that Shildra was the most vocal regarding Priscilla's tragic demise; the woman continually lamented the sadness of a child growing up without her mother. Lío spoke bitterly of the fortuitousness (or was it?) of fyr attacks and Priscilla's decline occurring when Reylin was nearby. And there was this: If Reylin hadn't gone to the mines, perhaps he could have succeeded in his healing efforts. By the Light, *that* rumor had shot through the nobility and Temple mages like lightning.

If Reylin hadn't insisted on bringing troops to East Face himself, perhaps . . . perhaps . . . perhaps. It was all meaningless, and yet it wasn't, for there was far more power in the vicious gossip of the nobility than in the truth.

Syrana realized that Father Kaiadin, who continued his duty as primary herbsman for her husband, had retired to the balcony while Reylin slept. She followed him out.

The mage stood tall and thin, almost gangly, overlooking the valley of Mirat with his arms raised and his palms up to the sky. He seemed to be praying as his eyes were closed, leaving naught but a solid purple band across his face.

He spoke in his strangely solid bass, a sound at odds with his ungainly nature. "What troubles you, my daughter?"

She crossed her arms and didn't answer.

He slowly dropped his hands and turned to her. "A great many things, then? Speak what is in your heart." Kaiadin patted the cushioned bench.

In truth, Syrana had no idea what to tell him or request of him, and she was beginning to have trouble tracking which things she should know. "I'm afraid, Father. Afraid of departing this world without leaving a legacy with Reylin, a child, and of seeing him depart this world without leaving a legacy with me. I'm afraid of death." It was true, in a way.

Kaiadin nodded. "I thought that might be. But death is no more than a passing through another Gate, to go onward and forward to something else."

"I don't care about what's in the next Gate, Father. I care about this one."

"Have a care, my daughter. Your choices affect which Gate opens, in the end."

Syrana began to tremble. He had no idea what choices she had made, but none of them were wrong. They were all for her love of Reylin. "I merely want to be a mother, Father Kaiadin, to give Reylin a son as would fill his heart. Please, help me. Use red magika if you must, as long as it works."

Kaiadin evaluated her for a long while, and she regretted speaking so openly. "Is it worth dying for, my lady? Red magika is very dangerous, viewed less favorably for its terrifying efficacy. I've been reticent to try it until we exhaust our other options."

Syrana's chest tightened. She wouldn't cry, for it would ruin the face of rouge and paint her handmaiden had so meticulously applied, and she'd never hear the end of that from her mother. Instead, she clamped down her emotions and clenched her fists until she felt her nails digging into her palm.

"Reylin's condition has given me a sense of urgency, Father," she managed. "Nothing we've tried yet has seemed to work. What if I had lost him?"

Kaiadin gave her a sympathetic look and shook his head. "Daughter, it's hardly been weeks since you came to me. You must give your body a chance to react to the medicine."

"Please, Father . . ."

He patted her shoulder. "I understand your desperation. Losing Princess Priscilla was hard enough—a tragedy, truly, which will be felt throughout the kingdom—but praise the Light you have Reylin and little Amber. She is such a treasure, isn't she? Reylin *will* rebuild a family from the ashes of the Great Fire, and nothing can stop him."

Despite his friendly smile and his warm encouragement, his words sliced into Syrana's heart like an arrowhead. Reylin *would* rebuild his family, and if she was unable to provide him an heir, he would undoubtedly find someone who could.

"Are they really saying all that?" Reylin's voice was so muted, he felt as though he were speaking to himself.

"Yes, sire," said Keeper Davon. "I'm so sorry to have to tell you."

Reylin sighed. "Give me my daughter."

Father Kaiadin placed several more pillows behind Reylin's back, and the nurse obediently placed the swaddled bundle into the crook of Reylin's arm.

He nuzzled Amber to him. Her button nose demanded a tender kiss, which he gave, and her thin-drawn lips twitched as she slept. Father Ma'thell had said she couldn't smile at him yet, but he thought the twitch was something.

"By the Light, she's perfect," he murmured.

"Ar'we says Amber is beautiful," said Davon in response. Reylin was surprised he'd been able to hear. "She calls her a 'bright light.'" The dragonkeeper's lips curled up possessively, and his tone shifted. "That's very kind, my heart."

Clearly, those last words were not for Reylin.

"Thank you, Keeper Davon."

Davon swayed uncertainly from foot to foot, seemingly unsure whether he was dismissed. Arrayed in all black, a combination of wool-lined riding gear and darkly dyed cotton and leather, Davon had the bearing of an independent man. Despite his position as an honored guest of the castle, he refused to change his attire, as he might at any moment decide he needed to be with Ar'we, soaring through the sky. He was polite, but he carried little formal decorum. Reylin supposed it was his common background and lack of education. A herdsman, was it?

Nevertheless, he seemed a decent and honest man.

Reylin nodded toward a chair. "Remain, Keeper Davon. I appreciate your report, but even more so your timely assistance in getting me and Father Kaiadin back to Ironhold. Your service is not only welcome, but essential."

Davon sat, and Reylin mulled the cruel rumors over in his mind.

On the lips of every wayfarer and spilling from every street corner: He was in poor health, unfit for hard leadership. He was delicate. He had foolishly left his wife to seek glory on the battlefield, and he had missed the birth altogether.

And then, veiled by the whisper of shuffling skirts and laced fringe, the words of the nobility: He had been infected with the madness in Lupine. He had killed Sir Cordan in cold blood, a fit of juvenile rage. He had started a war he could hardly finish. How could he protect an entire nation when he couldn't even protect his wife?

And the words spread like wildlife, feeding into the churning mill of Ironhold's gossip, hot on the lips of every washwoman and stall vendor.

He couldn't pinpoint who was spreading such insidious rumors, but each one seemed to imply his inability and lack of wisdom. Yet, he could never have foreseen half the events that had gone so terribly wrong. The Elder Council couldn't either.

Davon apologized profusely. "It doesn't matter what they say, Your Highness. It doesn't change who you are. Ar'we didn't think I should even tell you some of those things."

The dragonkeeper spoke like a familiar friend, a fact that both grated and pleased, and again Reylin was reminded of the fact that Davon had not the first clue of appropriate courtly behavior. Then again, was Reylin not drowning in courtly politeness already? He'd had quite enough of the false smiles from Galltry, the overbearing pleasantries of Shildra and her entourage, and the haltingly careful encouragement of Father Ma'thell. He believed none of it to be genuine.

He decided something. "Keeper Davon, why are you here?"

Davon started, then gnawed on his lip. "I can leave, Your Highness, if you please."

"No, no, that's not what I meant. When Lord Abonn sent for you, he suggested that you rarely leave the mountains you call home. Why did you come?"

Davon's eyes seemed to unfocus and then refocus. "I would not have refused the call of the king, Your Highness, but I must add that Ar'we also wished to help."

I am helpful, the dragon declared loudly in Reylin's mind, making both men grin, but then Davon frowned.

"I am only sorry, we still were not quick enough. I'm so sorry for the loss of your wife, Your Highness. I'm sorry that I could not do more." He seemed to diminish, his shoulders slumping, his bearing heavy with shame.

Reylin acknowledged him, again marveling at the man's straightforward manner. Nobles didn't speak so bluntly, and no one else had yet talked about Priscilla's death so brazenly. Instead, they spoke of legacy and fond memories, lovely gilded words that failed entirely in reducing the ache in him for Priscilla's death.

"How exactly did Ar'we hear all these things?" he wondered, hoping to reinvigorate the dragonkeeper. Amber stirred and babbled in her sleep, and Reylin inadvertently smiled.

"She spends most of her time on the cliff above the castle," Davon answered, "but during the busier times, she likes to perch on the main tower so she can watch the people and the animals. She can hear a good deal from that vantage point."

Dragons must have phenomenal hearing, thought Reylin. "I appreciate the information. Keeper Davon, you've proven yourself true to your king, and I cannot thank you enough for it. I'd like you and Ar'we to continue listening and reporting what you hear, and to stay with me in Ironhold for the time being."

Davon nodded quickly. "As you please, Your Highness. I'm happy to serve in any way you desire."

"Father Ma'thell can send a Whisper, or perhaps a bird given his current weakness, to inform those at home that you will not return for a while."

Davon flushed the slightest bit, and he shook his head. "No need, Your Highness. Ar'we and I live alone."

Reylin pondered the man in front of him. He had perhaps ten years on Reylin, and yet . . . "Keeper Davon, may I ask you something personal? Have you ever loved anyone?"

"Yes, Your Highness." Davon returned to chewing on his lip.

"And you lost them?"

Davon gave a slow, single nod, then furrowed his brow. "It was necessary for us to be apart. I could not give her the happiness she deserved."

Reylin thought he understood. He often wondered if he himself was capable of loving his wives as thoroughly as he ought, or whether the darkness of the past, the pain of loss and rejection and loneliness, would compose a permanent shadowy wall between himself and others. He wasn't certain Priscilla had known of his true affection or his appreciation of her. He needed to be loved, and yet he felt alone.

As a dragonkeeper, Davon was set apart too, and Reylin had heard additional points about dragonkeeping that would further hinder a normal relationship.

"Was it the servant woman? Did you love her?"

Davon didn't stop biting his lip, but the corners of his mouth turned up, and a softness entered his eyes that Reylin had only seen once before.

"I've loved her all my life," he said, looking down. "And I'll love her until my death, Your Highness." He swallowed and blinked rapidly. "May I be excused? I think Ar'we would like to taste the sunshine."

Davon departed in a hurry, leaving Reylin with all that remained of Princess Priscilla. Amber had woken and was now wriggling inside the swaddling. She managed to pop an arm out and flung it wildly, catching her own cheek in the process. Although she seemed unaware of the fine red line that appeared, Reylin sucked a breath in.

He shushed her and traced the scratch with dismay, then with hope. Yes, the damage was minor, and so similar in nature to the cut Kaiadin had given him on his arm. He trailed a finger along it, pulling the edges back together. The red mark disappeared, and he tucked her arm back into the blanket.

"Well done, my king," said Father Kaiadin. "Such care, such tenderness, healing with your power. She hadn't even realized she hurt herself yet. As you are father to Amber, so can you be father to your kingdom. May I?" He took Amber and sent the nursemaid out. "I think the revelations from Keeper Davon and Ar'we demand discussion. Whom do you trust?"

"Bring in the High Guard," Reylin said in agreement. "And Syrana."

"The problem is two-fold: misinformation on one hand, and untimely revelation of information on the other," said Father Kaiadin. "We haven't had a chance to test anyone regarding their knowledge of your ward, and now the entire city seems to know you have some power. Worse yet, the world was not ready to know of the madness. That information must be controlled somehow, now that it's out."

"A problem for the Temple," Gillead snarled with a dismissive wave.

"A problem for our king, for his enemies may be in the Temple," Kaiadin answered.

The two men glowered at each other, although Gillead's deep-lined scowl was far more practiced.

Reylin bid both of them sit back down. "Father Kaiadin is right, Sir Gillead. The lords think I'm a fool for many reasons. The best I can do is prepare the lords for a disease that spreads unpredictably, while continuing to learn Water healing. If I give them aid, they may find greater value in my leadership."

The men agreed, and Syrana nodded emphatically. Kaiadin had numerous suggestions for how to word a formal warning to each duke, and Reylin could hear the man scratching rapid notes on a parchment at the far end of the room.

He leaned back, exhausted. His arm still ached, for he had spared none of his healing energy for himself.

Kaiadin set his quill down. "That's one item resolved, and one which will require more attention as it worsens. However, we must publicly address the misinformation regarding your health and your role in attempting to save Priscilla."

"The people of Mirat would not be surprised to learn Prince Reylin is gifted," said Sir Patreagh. "His mother was gifted, and his great-grandsire and granddam, one on each side."

"It's the timing that's strange, and we don't wish to alert his enemies to our understanding of the ward breaking," said Father Kaiadin. "We must exclude that information entirely, revealing only that Reylin has powerful healing magika, a gift of Water, and that he sacrificed himself to save the princess."

"He nearly died," Syrana snapped.

"Yes, yes, and that's the point, my dear," Kaiadin replied. "The people will love you all the more for your willingness to give everything to save your wife and child." He beamed at Reylin. "At some point, the will of the people will turn the will of the Elder Council."

Reylin still scowled, thinking back to the cataclysmic baptism ceremony. "How many people saw me collapse, Sir Gillead?"

The lord commander hesitated long enough to irritate Reylin but finally acquiesced. "Two hundred and eighty-seven people were in the High Temple, my prince."

Reylin groaned with embarrassment.

"But they saw a man who gave his lifeblood for his wife, a father doing right by his offspring, a king facing his future instead of lingering on the tragic past. For once, I agree with Father Kaiadin, Your Highness."

Reylin shook his head violently; it made him dizzier than it should have. "They saw no king. They saw a weak boy, the scarred and broken boy who survived the Great Fire. By the Light, Gillead, I couldn't even save her."

"You did more than anyone else," said Kaiadin. "Let us prepare a public declaration in honor of Princess Priscilla, focusing on your sacrifice and the miracle of little Amber."

"I'll spread similar information amongst the ladies at court," added Syrana. The sweetness of her smile melted the angst away. If anyone was in tune with gossip, it was the constantly hovering women of the court. It was a smart strategy, and Reylin told her so.

The group moved on to the confusion in the north. Lady Ana had ensured an initial order of supplies was commissioned for East Face, and had even pushed Steward Gordrew into announcing the colonization effort and calling for volunteer tenants. Despite the chaos surrounding Priscilla's death and Reylin's incapacitation, the first large train destined for East Face was nearly ready to depart Ironhold.

In the meantime, the troops deployed had cleared a swath of land around the mine, and Knight Captain Theodar reported by bird that the keep foundation had been laid out and prepped. No more fyr had yet attacked, but they would remain vigilant and proud.

Reylin finally began to relax, and a torpor crept over him. He sent the High Guard out, and Syrana went off to fulfill her mission with the ladies of Ironhold.

Father Kaiadin remained.

"I'd like to continue our magika lessons," Reylin said, pushing himself up in the nest of pillows with an effort.

"My king, you're hardly well yet," Kaiadin protested. The indigo paint wrinkled into black worry lines around his eyes.

"I'm only physically drained, low of blood, but I can learn and am mentally fit. And furthermore, if all you say is true, I can heal myself with a bit more education and practice."

Kaiadin pursed his thin lips. "Son, you must not overextend yourself. You are important. Your life is important. You've seen how Ma'thell stretched himself too thin; he's still as exhausted as he was a week ago."

"I am not he, Father."

"So very true, son."

Reylin steeled his jaw, despite the kind sentiment. "Father, Priscilla should have survived by my blood. If I had the knowledge and training to transmute, as you wanted and encouraged me to do, I wouldn't have been forced to do what I did, and I could have saved her easily. Now, that same knowledge could help me recover more quickly. I must learn this transmutation skill, this 'destruction' and 'construction' that you speak of, if I am to fulfill my potential."

Kaiadin's worry did not seem to diminish, but he considered Reylin's words with a tired nod. "Very well. Greater knowledge is less risk, for you and those you love." He stood. "I shall hasten to the temple and return with some more teaching scrolls, but until then you must rest, son."

At the door, Kaiadin stumbled directly into Lord Galltry, who was typically measured and refined. Yet now, the older man was breathing hard, and despite recovering his balance, his eyes remained red and his face troubled.

"My prince, I apologize for the interruption," he said, stammering. He took a seat on the edge of the bed and gathered himself. "I know you are convalescing, but . . ."

"Tell me, Lord Galltry."

The High Guard knights crowded in, and Kaiadin lingered in the doorway.

"My prince, I have terrible news. This morning, there was an attack near East Face Mine, an attack on one of *my* outlying villages on the edge of the Loi al'Halmana." His voice shook. "They came during the day, sweeping out from the grasses by air and bird. Few survived."

Reylin's mouth dropped open. "An open ground attack? Mounted cavalry?"

"If you can call those running birds a cavalry," spat Ronidann. "Damned savages."

Sir Gillead called the other knight to task. "Lord Galltry, our troops are prepared to deploy in defense of Mirat." He looked pointedly at Reylin for the command.

Reylin agreed, his head spinning. Not only were the miners at risk, but also Miratian citizens, just as he had warned Galltry of weeks before.

But Galltry waved his hand. "The Elder Council is meeting now to discuss it. I came only to inform you—"

"But I should be in that meeting," Reylin exclaimed, pushing himself up in the bed.

Galltry took his shoulder and forced him back down. "Son, you must rest. The Council shall handle this, and with a strong hand as your father would have done. I expect we shall need Gillead to select at least three more platoons—"

"A company," Gillead interrupted gruffly. "I'll decide the final battle strategy."

"A company then," agreed Galltry, "along with my own district's local knights to bolster the northeast border villages."

"And another platoon for East Face Mine," added Reylin.

"We shall consider it, my prince."

Reylin fumed at Galltry's nonchalant answer, at everything that had been revealed. He had been right, and Miratians were dead because of their lack of aggressiveness with the fyr. And yet, even now, Reylin was excluded from making the decision to destroy the fyr, to even be in the room where the decision was made.

Galltry patted the bed. "Rest now, prince. I've called an emergency meeting of the Elder Council to address our next move. Lío and Ennedrew have already turned around from their journey home. Sir Gillead, we would like your input as well." They left together, and Kaiadin melted away, leaving only Reylin's three remaining High Guard. None of them spoke.

His forehead burned with more heat than he had felt in days. Galltry hadn't cared about the fyr threat until his own citizens bled. The savages were becoming more bold, if they had ventured close enough in the open grasslands to attack Galltry's towns.

"Reminds me of the days we fought under Rolis," muttered Patreagh. "The fyr had noticed Galltry's weakness, and they battered the eastern border like wasps."

"We annihilated them," Ronidann added with a vicious smile. "Let us do it again. I'll skewer a few birds whenever I can."

"I may need to get a handle on this madness instead, Sir Ronidann," Reylin warned before the knight got too excited. "Knight Captain Theodar will command the men in our stead."

He must push for a war on the fyr, a final destruction of their savage kind. Claim the Loi al'Halmana for Mirat, and take its fertile soil under hoe and plow. Mine its shining riches. The fyr, hateful monsters that they were, could be reduced to a nightmarish memory, brought up by candlelight to frighten children to bed and never otherwise. If only the Elder Council would get out of the way.

All of Mirat would see his work, his leadership, his readiness. And concurrently, as the fyr death knells tolled out from the Temple and his soldiers basked in victory, Reylin would learn to use his magika. Such power was another sign of nobility, handed down from ancient times, and his newfound strength echoed his right to the throne. If he could control it, demonstrate it, and use it when needed to protect those he loved, no one could protest his demand for Ascension.

Command, not demand. He would *will* this to be.

KONAN'S NERVES TINGLED WITH anticipation before he ever opened his eyes. His burnt skin crawled, and he tensed for a quick offensive in the dark. His muscles responded sluggishly, demanding rest and hydration, and his eyelids scratched instead of soothed as he peeked into the night.

Someone was watching them, and their gaze was intense. He could feel it creeping over his face and noting his position: one hand on Lyra's shoulder and one splayed out to the side rather than on a weapon of any sort. He hadn't heard them coming either.

He could feel Lyra's shallow breathing, her cheek nestled on his thigh. She was probably still asleep.

Only moments until whoever watched them attacked.

Konan slitted his eyelids as a dark-cloaked man slid from the darkness, emerging from between two palms as though strolling through a garden. The stars gleamed over him in the clear desert night, allowing Konan to make out his figure. The man wore a loosely layered, ankle-length robe, one made of a single piece of cloth wrapped expertly around his body and then covered by a draping outer cloak. He wore a turban with a dangling end that covered the back of his neck; it was also a dark shade but inlaid with silvery beads.

His wrinkle-wrapped, violet eyes bore into Konan, seeming to pulse as Konan struggled to move.

His muscles didn't respond. He couldn't stand, lift his arm, or warn Lyra beyond a faltering grunt in the back of his throat.

The elderly man snaked forward, peering at them and stepping with a staff, and then knelt over Thordrin and leaned into his face. Nose to nose, eye to eye. The man chuckled with somewhat cruel-sounding mirth.

Thordrin glared back, obviously wide awake and seething, but he didn't move either. Even with his quick reactions, his fingers had merely twitched toward his dagger. His cheeks reddened with the exertion, and he groaned like Konan had.

Was this an immobility enchantment? Konan had never experienced one before, but the impotence of it infuriated him. His anger poured out, not white and hot like usual. Instead, it was black like charred skin. He writhed against it, resisting with both body and mind, and felt it give slightly. Perhaps he could break through it with his own will.

The elderly man of the desert merely grunted, waving a careless hand toward him like Thordrin would, and Konan felt his muscles stiffen toward painful contraction.

He uttered a low moan. Every muscle seemed to cramp simultaneously, each fighting the other. His fingers curled into trembling fists, and even the arches of his feet screamed.

The old man straightened and declared, *"Hale mwa'hoa, mikkat'taslam!"*

Torches alighted all around them, and he felt Lyra jolt violently at the startling noise and light, and she pulled her legs in and cringed into Konan. She didn't crawl up to his chest, and he suspected she was under the same enchantment. She uttered a weak whimper.

A knot of horse and idraka-mounted men encircled them, each one adorned in more soldierly garb than the original man, but all with long outer cloaks and turbans. Half of them held their bows drawn, and the other half bore torches in one hand and curved swords in the other.

The elderly man chuckled again in a high, mad-sounding voice. He repeated himself. "*Mikkat'taslam, waruhui'la'a.*" He stood and stepped back, leaning casually on his staff.

At that moment, Thordrin seemed to wrench himself into motion, flipping his dagger from his belt in a smooth motion and growling.

The elderly man swiftly raised a palm, and Thordrin's swift motion halted. The dagger fell from his shaking grip, and the elderly man laughed merrily, stepping from one foot to the other in an absurd dance. "*Waruhui'la'a, hale, hale!*"

The desert men began to chuckle as well, their expressions no longer hostile but rather strikingly amused.

Konan seethed inside, wishing he could at least pull Lyra to him, behind him. She shook like a leaf by his side, and he suspected she was on the verge of lashing out, given a moment's chance. The diamonds in her eyes glittered hard and clear, and power seemed to emanate from her in shimmering waves.

Don't do anything, he thought. *We don't know how dangerous these people might be.*

One of the horsemen, a husky-built man with a thick chest and stout arms, dismounted and approached, lowering his face covering. He glanced from Konan to Thordrin, then leaned down to retrieve Thordrin's dagger. He flipped it casually and handed it to a man behind him. Then he took the warden's sword from the other side of Thordrin's belt and measured it with his eye, toying with its balance. He likewise handed it to a man behind him, then smiled. He sported a well-manicured black mustache and goatee, as well as good teeth.

"Our Godspeaker believes you are harmless, and he has shown us the same." He spoke in a thick Tahayi accent, one which Konan had heard in a few of the lower servants of the mines. The big man chuckled heartily as Konan shook with fury. Then he sobered and gestured at the elderly man— the Godspeaker? "However, I believe it is rude to hold guests under enchantments while they stay with us, so I will ask him to let you go. *Magika'hale.*"

The Godspeaker bowed deeply. "*Ja, alis.*"

Thordrin's outstretched hand was released and fell to his side, and he sat up stiffly, still red in the face from humiliation. He sneered at the surrounding riders and cursed under his breath.

Konan could finally clutch Lyra to himself, and he pulled them both up so they could face the desert men together. His own body ached of exhaustion and soreness, and he could feel her lethargy as she staggered up alongside him. As they surveyed their captors, he felt her shoulders tense, and she backed into him.

Her desperation and fear flowed out, and the oasis seemed to vibrate with a sudden accumulation of power. The fronds above whispered against each other, and the wispy grass fluttered outward in pulses.

Don't, he wanted to say. They were far outnumbered and possibly outmatched in their exhaustion, and they didn't truly know whether these people were enemies.

The Godspeaker pointed at her, and the clan leader addressed her directly. "Do not, daughter. We have no ill intentions for you or your companions."

Lyra's eye twitched, and her chest began to heave harder and faster.

"*Barna'arathi, thral ol'I'ya,*" said the Godspeaker with utter calm. He placed a hand over his heart and bowed low to her, almost as low as he had bowed to his clan leader.

The Air stilled, and Lyra gaped at the elderly man. The wind passing amongst the palms dissipated, once again revealing a peaceful night. She glanced up at Konan in confusion. The white fire faded to a pale blue, reminding Konan of glacial pools in summer.

The Godspeaker then directed words in a different language toward the clan leader, and the big man laughed a deep, bellowing laugh. "You are more than you appear, daughter. Much more." His thick belly bounced in time with his mirth, and Konan wondered whether the man was genuine. Although obviously in charge, the man's robes were nearly identical to the others save for a small brooch on his chest. It was gold, beat into the shape of a bird eating a viper. The bird's eye glinted in the starlight, much like Lyra's did.

The Godspeaker approached in shuffling steps and reached a shaky, wrinkled hand out toward Lyra.

She cringed into Konan, and they stepped backward in unison until his back hit a palm tree. Unable to escape, Lyra turned away and hid her face in Konan's chest. He wrapped her into his embrace, holding her wild curls against his heart with one hand, glaring at the oncoming Godspeaker.

The Godspeaker creaked up to Konan with a merry grin, unbothered by their reaction and seemingly harmless. He tugged lightly at Lyra's shoulder and spun her around, then peered into her face.

"*Barna'arathi, thral ol'I'ya,*" he repeated slowly, then beamed at her with a mouth of missing teeth.

"*Barna'arathi, thral ol'I'ya,*" she repeated. Her small, high voice cracked through the air, seeming to shake the air around it. She looked near to passing out, and Konan maintained an arm around her in case she went limp.

The Godspeaker gave her a small, satisfied nod, then retreated to stand by the clan leader.

The leader pushed his chest out. "I am Shirkaa, Alis ol'Manalal. Who are your companions, thral ol'I'ya?"

Lyra worked her jaw, but no words came out, and she broke into a hoarse cough. The stiffness in her shoulders from earlier softened, and she sagged into Konan as the body-wracking effort drained her.

Konan helped her to the ground to recover, then offered the water skein. Too late, he realized it had been emptied, and the idraka had muddied the tiny spring of their salvation. He sighed and squeezed her hand in encouragement, but Lyra seemed almost oblivious to his assistance. She was fading fast, now that the initial shock of being found had diminished.

Although Alis Shirkaa and the Godspeaker waited expectantly, Thordrin interjected, introducing himself. His tone was confident and friendly, as though he hadn't been fuming moments earlier. Konan grimaced internally. Was anything about their colleague genuine? Then again, was anything about Alis Shirkaa genuine either?

Thordrin indicated him. "And this one is known as Konan; he's mute."

Konan acknowledged that fact with a solemn nod, and Alis Shirkaa seemed to turn toward Thordrin as the group leader.

"You are a warrior, Master Thordrin."

"I was, m'lord." He hacked a dry cough and spat.

Shirkaa chuckled again. "That title is not one that can be stripped away. Well met. And her, the thral? Lyra? Welcome to my desert, friends. Ah, but I have forgotten my manners. The Desert Mother has not welcomed you as easily and kindly as I. She is sometimes a cruel hostess; she refines by fire. Perhaps you are thirsty and hungry?"

Lyra tried to get up so quickly she swooned, and Konan barely caught her as she fell into another bout of coughing. Someone pushed a full waterskein to her parched lips, and she drank greedily, taking deep breaths between long swallows.

Konan watched as water dribbled down her chin, every part of him shouting to conserve it. He accepted the skein next, tipping it back on his own and giving the Manalali soldier a grateful nod.

Never had water tasted so sweet. He swallowed quickly, feeling the liquid course down his dry throat and settle into his shriveled stomach. He could almost imagine it filling the yawning cracks in his insides the way a flash flood crashes through fissured desert pavement.

When he realized the skein was being pulled away, he clutched for it. He found himself staring into the brown face of a desert man, who shook his head solemnly and held the skein out of reach.

"That must be all for now," said Shirkaa from beyond the man, "or you will get the water-sickness. Our Desert Mother punishes greed harshly."

Lyra began to cry, her arms outstretched toward the skein, and Shirkaa seemed to give her a real expression of empathy.

"More later, thral," he assured her.

She sighed loudly, but Konan squeezed her hand to draw her attention. "Thank you, Lord Shirkaa," he signed. "We owe you a life debt."

Lyra's eyes widened, and she repeated his words timidly.

Shirkaa responded with a wide grin. "A life debt? Ah yes, that remains to be seen. I did not kill you at the advice of the Godspeaker; he believed he detected something special in this miraculous oasis. Now I myself have no liking for debts, but I do have a liking for trade. Perhaps you will trade with us?"

Konan noticed Thordrin's face twitch, but the assassin covered most of his reaction. No doubt the man was familiar with the kind of trade the Manalali clan leader wanted. Konan had heard similar rumors about the northern desert tribes. They liked to trade favors and goods, but tended to be lucrative and tricky in their deals. The Shayalese didn't trade with them at all, although the Manalali trade practices were far from the only reason for that interdiction.

"What would you like to trade, m'lord?" asked Thordrin casually, as though he were hardly concerned.

Shirkaa gestured at the three of them. "Your lives for a single service." He continued to smile, although the mirth had gone from his eyes. "In this, I think it is trade in your favor."

Konan steeled his jaw. He wasn't surprised, but he was irked. Shirkaa and his clan undoubtedly believed they could demand anything they wanted, in exchange for not killing them on the spot. He waited to hear what service they might demand.

Shirkaa continued. "My people the Manalal, they are a happy people. They live in the arms of the Desert Mother, closer to the Eye than any others in this Gate. We feel the heat of her bosom, the cold of her absence in winter. We follow her gifts as she walks through her desert, touching each oasis with the gift of her Water. We have lived thus for generations upon generations, and I, Shirkaa, Alis ol'Manalal, have guided them as the Mother's Favored."

His men muttered agreement, and the idraka and horses snorted. Some of them looked as though they pined for something, while others looked at each other nervously. Shirkaa's tone shifted to a bitter, low growl, and his gesticulations became short and violent.

"But our happiness has been overshadowed. Another tribe, the Haralal—no more than depraved, uncivilized beasts—has stolen our most precious desert flower."

The muttering of Shirkaa's men rose, and anger flashed amongst them. The Godspeaker stamped his staff for order, and Shirkaa leaned forward to emphasize his next words.

"The Haralal have taken my daughter, my beautiful Shirasa."

Lyra gasped, a high and heart-wrenching sound. She looked to him, eyes wide with fear. Konan could almost see the nightmares playing out inside her head.

Shirkaa smiled sadly. "You understand, do you not? She must be retrieved, and the aggressors punished in the name of the good Desert Mother. If you three help us destroy the Haralal, I will give you passage through my lands."

Konan considered the clan chief, who stood with his arms spread like a benevolent Temple mage. Little could be derived from his expression, which reflected pure fatherly compassion and muted hope as he looked to the three ragged prisoners. The man had lost a daughter. How old, Konan didn't know, but it was likely she was in danger regardless. Yet, something in Konan doubted the man's sincerity or honesty.

He noticed Thordrin's eyes narrow. If Thordrin truly had been a Phantom assassin for King Rigaran of Krita, then he had worked for money and power, not clemency. The concept alone was offensive, equivalent to slavery. And that was what Shirkaa offered, whether he admitted it or not. This "trade" was being executed precisely as a life debt would be.

Konan looked at Lyra. "We don't have a choice," he signed, "but if we accept, we will be able to help the girl. Then we can leave with their blessing."

Lyra blinked back tears and nodded slowly.

"Tell him we accept." He took both her hands and squeezed them.

She interpreted in a soft, frightened mumble, but she didn't take her eyes from him, as though she were afraid to look anywhere else. "The trade is acceptable. Our lives are yours, Alis Shirkaa."

Thordrin muttered a curse.

41

THE MANALAL WERE RIGHT about water-sickness.

Lyra swallowed down a seedy, unleavened bread and a mouthful of dried meat, and battled the immediate urge to retch it back up despite the growling of her gut. Her insides twisted and clenched; she imagined her stomach shrunk in upon itself like a raisin. The gulp of water had started a new process of wrenching and gurgling, and her thirst battled with her nausea.

The Godspeaker pointed at her. "*Iyasan anthe'brin,*" he murmured in the Old Language. Water-sickness.

The Manalal swiftly cleared the camp after she and the others had eaten. They gave Thordrin and Konan horses of their own.

Thordrin hopped onto his bareback gelding easily and gestured to Lyra to take his hand, but she recoiled. He cursed at her and gestured toward Konan. "You think he's a better option, girl? You're a fool. Boy hasn't ridden anything in years." He paused, then smirked at his own joke. He looked at her for validation, and she made a face at him.

Konan did seem to stare wistfully at his own mount, an elegant black mare with particularly toned muscle and long legs. Lyra approached her cautiously. The mare snorted at her proffered hand and swished her tail.

Lyra's thoughts drifted to her caravan, to Ada, to Mam, and she sighed. Exhaustion pervaded her bones to the marrow, but they could make it farther astride a horse than on foot, even if it did take energy to ride. She glanced at Konan, hoping he didn't mind her riding with him. The thought of riding with Thordrin twisted her insides too much, even though she knew he was safe.

His gaze traveled the length of the large mare, halfway been appreciation and trepidation. He pressed his twitching lips together, and his throat bobbed up and down. He lifted his scarred hand toward her and hesitated, a scowl furrowing his uneven brow.

"Konan?" She took his tentative hand and guided it toward the mare's nose, offering it for evaluation.

The horse snorted again and eyed them.

Lyra guided his hand over her muzzle, and Konan released a nervous breath as he stroked the velvet. He blinked rapidly, again reminding her of a person in the depths of dreams. Then he brushed the mare's cheek and trailed a light hand down her slender, powerful neck. She nickered. What did he recall? If he was noble, as she believed, he had surely had a pony once.

A young man reminiscent of Lord Shirkaa trotted up on an idraka draped in colorful beads and an ornate light saddle. "You ride, yes?"

Konan gave the briefest shake of his head, neither affirming nor denying.

The young man snapped his fingers at another horseman and spoke in Manalali, and the horseman dismounted and began to remove his own saddle. Then the young man urged his idraka forward and leaned down, offering a handshake to Konan. "I am Jikaa, son of Shirkaa. You need a saddle, I think, but this mare is the best option for two riders, especially inexperienced riders."

"I ride," said Lyra softly, but she was looking at her toes. Jikaa likely couldn't hear her.

"The Desert Mother provides," replied Jikaa, giving her a respectful nod followed by a smile. "You make sure he does not fall." He said something in Manalali, and the men around him chuckled.

Konan's right cheek darkened as he watched the saddle get strapped onto the mare, attentive to every adjustment. He pursed his lips again. Then he pulled himself awkwardly up, swinging his leg high and around, and proffered a hand to Lyra.

He lifted her effortlessly, and she abruptly found herself in his arms. She could feel the heat of his chest against her back, and undeniable panic rose like bile. She battled it down, but she felt she was losing as the world closed in around her.

Konan's hands appeared in front of her. Even backward, the signs were familiar.

"Forgive me."

She grasped onto those repeating signs, willing her body to stop, and her breathing finally slowed. She was astride a horse, in front of Konan. The mare's powerful back shifted as the horse perceived her panic, and Lyra stroked her black mane to soothe her. The coarse texture grounded her, and the sense of power and sensibility and sturdiness in the mare's body beneath her. And then Konan's hands, the hardness of the calluses of his palms and the thickness of the skin on his fingertips.

She heaved a sigh and leaned back into him, completely enveloped by his shoulders and his smell.

"No, forgive *me*," she whispered. "I don't know why that just happened."

Konan adjusted farther back in the saddle and then signed in front of her. "Is this okay?"

"Don't squeeze your legs too tightly," she answered, arranging his arms around her, his hands gripping the pommel. She herself took the reins. "Try to move in rhythm with her," she rambled, adjusting his sitting position slightly and trying to get comfortable, but she could feel his look.

Lyra spun and found him, the copper flecks glowing like gold in his right eye. The discolored iris drowned her in its milky depths. She chewed her lip. "I really am okay, I think. I am."

"Nethers, if you ride as slow as you mount, we'll never get to somewhere civilized." Thordrin's impatience was echoed by his gelding's prancing. "Let's go. The whole clan can't all be men."

Shirkaa and his son exchanged dubious looks, but then Shirkaa turned and led them eastward at a trot. Lyra guided their mare forward, and they were suddenly out of the tiny oasis and into the open night sky once again.

They rode for many dark miles through the vast, empty desert. The quick moon was but a sliver, and its pale light barely illuminated their tracks in the sand.

Huddled into Konan, Lyra followed almost mindlessly, for she could see nothing to guide the Manalal but the stars. They were a sure general guide, but certainly could not be helpful for finding specific landmarks in the endless expanse. She saw nothing to the south or north, and the only thing behind them was the miniscule oasis. Nevertheless, the Manalal rode with assurance of their route.

At one point, they took a short detour to the left, circling around an open sandy area with no unique features she could see.

"Sinking sand," Thordrin muttered from alongside them. He rose easily, his gait comfortable and his legs perfectly placed. He coughed and spat. "Good thing they can see it. I don't see a fuckin' thing."

Lyra shuddered, and she felt Konan's arm tighten against her. She barely recalled the sinking sand, but she did have a vivid memory of the *feeling* of suction and suffocation. That moment, like the time after, was a blur intermixed with visions of her family crossing the Loreni grasslands. She had stepped into waste from the caravan's haulbeasts, and she had cursed in front of Elden, to Mam's dismay.

She shook her head. Her hallucinations had felt so real—the soft muck on her toes, the unique grassy scent in her nostrils, the chagrin on Mam's face—all so much more real than this reality of discovering an oasis. Of rescue by people who seemed to respect her magika and not something else.

After an hour and a half riding, the near-full second moon rose. Wisps of dry grass appeared, punctuated by an occasional cactus or burnbush. The cacti were flowering, and although their color was dimmed by night, their luxurious scent drifted into the riders' paths. Lyra took in the intoxicating perfume of desert flowers. It reminded her of the plaza in Shayal City.

She glanced back at Konan. He was looking all around as well, taking in the growing life surrounding them. His right eye glistened.

"I knew it was here," he signed, then quickly grabbed the pommel again. His balance was poor, but he adjusted continually based on her muted comments.

The party slowed, and they passed several makeshift fences before entering a village and coming to a stop in a wide yard surrounded by large tents and a long, open stable. The desert men dispersed quickly, dismounting and unsaddling horses and idraka with minimal conversation and disappearing into their homes.

Thordrin leapt from his bareback gelding and handed it off to a Manalali, then came over to Lyra and Konan. He crossed his arms and smirked up at her.

"Watching you two ride was like watching a new who—"

"Please don't, Thor," she managed with an exasperated sigh.

"You don't want my help, girl?"

His offer to assist her down was likely as generous as he would get, and she was weary beyond comprehension, but she narrowed her eyes and glowered.

Thordrin snorted and raised his hands, backing away a few steps. "Fine."

Stabilizing herself on Konan's forearm, Lyra tried to dismount on her own from the tall mare.

Her fragile ribs tweaked and sent searing pain through her side, followed by a wave of nausea. As her feet touched the ground, the world suddenly spun, and she crashed to her knees.

The heavy scent of cactus blooms flooded her nose, and she couldn't seem to regain her composure. Swooning, she vomited onto the sand, then dry heaved several times before the Godspeaker appeared by her side with a waterskein.

He gave her some, and she rinsed her mouth out, but then he took it away with a sorrowful expression.

"*Iyasan anthe'brin,*" he repeated, slinging the skein back around his shoulder.

Lyra whimpered. "No, please . . ."

He backed away.

The Manalal seemed to believe giving one too much water right away would make them sick. The water-sickness, as it translated. She couldn't imagine needing anything more than she needed water now. She crawled away from the vomit and sat on the sand.

She heard Konan groan. Thordrin chuckled as he helped the bigger man dismount, then slipped Konan's arm over his shoulder to help him walk. They'd staggered a few steps toward her when a number of women appeared. Thordrin's eyes lit up with his own hunger.

One of the women helped Lyra stand, and she did so with an effort. She managed to catch up to Konan, who limped almost comically. *You ride, yes?* If he ever had, it had been long ago, and riding required muscles he likely hadn't used in years. She pressed her lips together. He would be terribly sore for a while.

They were all ushered toward two adjacent tents, but as they got closer, the woman guiding Lyra yanked her to one doorway. The men were pushed toward the other. Lyra protested, fear bubbling up once again, but the woman at her arm hoisted a small waterskein and said something in Manalali.

Lyra followed the woman all the way to the bed inside, a lush pile of cushion and furs elevated on a dais. The woman gave her a small drink, and Lyra sucked it down greedily before the skein was once again pulled from her lips. She fell back onto the bed, overwhelmed with weariness, relief, and exhaustion from the fear of death.

The woman servant pulled a light fur over Lyra, and before its tanned edge touched her chin, she was falling into a dark, deep chasm of sleep.

Even after the sun's first pale rays shone across the village, revealing a cactus-strewn land of life and color and people, Lyra rested.

It was the first time she hadn't had nightmares in weeks.

42

KONAN'S INNER THIGHS WERE so sore he could hardly move.

He spent the first minutes awake tentatively stretching and suppressing more groans.

"Sounds like you're fucking a maiden over there," joked Thordrin, earning a glare from him. Thordrin grinned in response. "Or at least giving yourself a good time." He chortled and arched his back until it cracked, then fell into a fit of raspy coughing. "You ride," he laughed between coughs. "Yeah, you do. Like a novice."

Konan ignored him and tried to rub the stiffness from his legs. It had been over a decade since he had last sat astride a horse, and knowledge and practice were two different things. He wondered briefly if his pony was still alive (a dappled brown and white named Jester, imported from the far south), then berated himself for such a trivial concern. He had lost everything back then, and trying to rebuild any kind of life from scattered pieces was more difficult than starting over. Even returning to Mirat and claiming his inheritance was a questionable plan.

Would it not be easier and more fulfilling to start anew with Lyra? Perhaps her family would allow him to join the Maskalan caravan. He could easily refine his tailoring skills, and he had always loved horses. The mere flash of Jester's splotched chin and streaked mane made his breath catch in his throat.

He pushed against his inner thigh with a knuckle and grunted at the pain. It was as tight as when the Godspeaker's immobility spell had forced everything to contract.

Shirkaa burst into the men's tent, adorned in fresh blue robes lined with silver thread and layered with colorful textiles and beads. "Bright morning, my friends," he exclaimed. "You slept well, yes?"

Both of them nodded and Shirkaa clapped Thordrin on the back.

"Excellent! Then please avail yourselves of our hospitality. Your long journey is done, and you must ready yourselves for what is next. You will see that we, the Manalal, are generous hosts, and you shall not want for anything in my service." He puffed out his stout chest at that, then beckoned some women in from outside.

The stream of young women ushered them into a larger tent with a sleeping alcove and a bathing room to one side. They had prepared two long tubs with clean water.

Konan hesitated as one woman tugged him toward the bath, gesturing at his rags and murmuring in Manalali. Another did the same to Thordrin.

Thordrin immediately discarded his clothing, flinging his tunic without a thought and dropping his pants before the women even had a chance to look away. He stepped into the water with an exaggerated sigh and sank under.

"By the Darkness and the Light, this is what I've been looking for," he said, leaning back in the tub after going all the way under and wetting his sandy-blond hair. He slicked it back with one hand and chuckled. "A good bath, and then you-know-what. Availing myself of Shirkaa's 'hospitality.'" He raised an eyebrow at Konan. "What are you waiting for?"

With a deep, steadying breath, Konan dismantled his coverings: first his hood and face mask, which had been wrapped securely to cover most of his face, ears, and hair. The woman assisting him squeaked with dismay and covered her mouth, then focused on taking his clothing. She could have counted the threads in the cloth, she stared so hard. Konan untied his long, draping cloak and let it fall, then removed the threadbare tunic he had worn for years, revealing his scarred chest and shoulder in full.

Thordrin's eyes widened. "Fuck me, brother . . ." For once, those were the only words he had.

Konan silently placed his pants in the woman's arms and stepped into the tub with an effort. Raising each leg seemed like a bigger challenge than trudging through the desert. He sank into the warm water, and the woman stepped forward.

She cringed as her violet eyes, much like the Godspeaker's, scanned his scars, but she proceeded to wash him with a scrubbing cloth.

He closed his eyes and soaked the experience in: the warm, mineral-rich water laden with floral scents from floating petals and oils, the slickness of the soap. How many years had it been? *Too many*, he thought. *Far too many*. He had become so immune to the stench of Tahayi, he didn't even know what he might smell or look like. In fact, he hadn't really wondered about it until Lyra had appeared, frightened beyond capacity and overwhelmed just as he had once been.

Did he reek of sweat? Did his hands smell of sulfur, with fine yellow dust dried under the nails? What did he look like? Isellan had always encouraged cleanliness, rinsing their faces and arms at the well after working, but there was nothing like a bath with soap.

"Do you think they're maidens?" Thordrin's plaintive voice interrupted his peaceful rumination.

Konan looked over. Thordrin's woman was pretty, with a polite smile and a light laugh. She was murmuring continually in Manalali, chattering meaningless phrases while washing Thordrin's shoulders and gently pushing him to where she wanted him.

Thordrin caught her hand. "Your name, love?" He gave her a suave smile, one which would surely have won over most ladies if not for his ragged hair and unkempt beard. She giggled nervously back at him. He pointed at his own muscled chest, which sported a pectoral tattoo. "Thordrin."

He winked, then pointed at her and raised his brows in query.

"Mirra," she said softly. She pulled her hand away and continued washing him, moving past his shoulders to his chest and abs, but then murmured something with another nervous giggle. She held the cloth out and averted her eyes while pointing below the water.

"Damn it all to the nethers, you *are* a maiden," muttered Thordrin with genuine disappointment. He took the scrubbing rag from her while she prepared a shaving soap.

Konan snorted lightly, and Thordrin scowled at him.

"You laugh, brother, but you don't know what you're missing," said Thordrin. He dunked himself underwater once more, then stretched out and leaned his head back. Mirra began to rub frothy soap into his blond beard. He simpered winningly up at her, the image of trust and trustworthiness, and Mirra smiled back.

Konan's helper began to do the same, and he straightened as she brought out a sharp straight blade. He shook his head, all of his nerves firing with trepidation. She pursed her lips—with disgust?—and advanced, extending the blade toward his neck. He grunted his rejection, a visceral reaction derived from years of defensiveness, and knocked her hand away.

She scowled openly, and he scowled back. Then she railed at Mirra in what sounded like Manalali, although it seemed a bit stilted, and Mirra replied with calm, friendly words. She slammed the shaving soap and blade down on a side table and crossed her arms, revealing a viper-shaped brand on her wrist.

"You pissed her off, you idiot."

"I've never shaved," Konan replied, despite knowing Thordrin wouldn't understand his signs. He gestured at his scruffy mess of a face and shook his head.

"That's what the girl is for, by the *nethers*," Thordrin scoffed.

"I don't trust her," Konan signed, still scowling. His nerves hadn't stopped shivering, and he willed his reaction to calm. It wasn't that easy to overcome over a decade of training in the belief that most people were not trustworthy or safe. No, not a belief. Knowledge. Absolute certainty. Most people were not trustworthy or safe.

Thordrin leaned over the edge of his tub and stared at Konan, serious for the moment. "We made an agreement with Lord Shirkaa, Konan, and desert men are men of their word. You should fear him more than that pretty wench, if you break his trust. Let her do her job." Then he resumed his relaxed position. "Better yet, send her over here. She doesn't seem to like you very much." He winked at Mirra and beckoned her to swap places with the other woman.

After a moment of confusion, Mirra set her blade down and chattered at the other woman. Konan's helper willingly switched positions, eyeing Thordrin with open admiration when he drew her hand toward him.

"Praise the Desert Mother if she exists, this one's a flower that's already opened," he said with a lascivious grin. He reintroduced himself and begged for a more thorough round of washing, and Konan looked away as the woman complied. Her attitude toward Thordrin was vastly different, a fact apparently noted by Mirra as well, for she grimaced slightly and shook her head.

Mirra politely offered the shaving soap and blade once again, and Konan agreed. As she smeared a fresh lather on his cheeks and chin, he closed his eyes to better ignore Thordrin's exploits in the next tub. Mirra stroked his skin with the sharp edge, slowly and carefully, first on his good cheek and then working her way across. His adrenaline still coursed through his veins, and he struggled to be still when she nicked his scars. She murmured apologetically but kept going.

Then she washed and trimmed his long, ratty hair to shoulder length, muttering with dismay as she worked over his scarred temple. He could see the questions in her wide, kind face. Her dark complexion and violet eyes showed empathy, not revulsion, a look reminiscent of Lyra. For a moment, Konan was thankful Thordrin had insisted on switching. Mirra rubbed a conditioning oil into his hair and brushed it smooth.

Meanwhile, the other woman gave Thordrin all the attention he wanted, and Konan could hear him whispering compliments and entreaties to her as she worked. The man's thick beard disappeared, and he had his hair trimmed short as well. He displayed his gratitude with a mischievous kiss, which she didn't seem to mind. She shifted to massaging his shoulders and body, admiring a large tattoo on his shoulder by delicately tracing it with her fingers.

Konan sighed and tried to shut out the sounds coming from that side of the room. With permission, Mirra kindly massaged his legs, which had loosened somewhat in the warm water. She moved to his ankles and feet, sending waves of relief through him.

Afterward, both men were rubbed with fresh, richly scented flowers and dressed. Konan's tunic was light colored and hip length, with split sides for mobility; it hung over colorful pants made of varied textiles. His draping, hooded robe sparkled with thousands of tiny beads in swooping and square patterns. He was further adorned with a golden necklace, and his pants were held in place with an ornate leather belt. Signs of favor?

But the most welcome amenity was the pair of well-made leather sandals Mirra tied on. Konan's large feet had been cramped into undersized boots for years, but that had been preferable to going barefoot on the burning sand. He wriggled his toes, then splayed them out. Mirra smiled.

Thordrin looked the same. "See, brother? Shirkaa will take care of us well, as he agreed. Told you desert men were men of their word. He'll be nice till he gets what he wants, and he'll follow through on getting us out of Tahayi." He rubbed his smooth jaw, seemingly satisfied, then slid a hand over his short hair. "By the Light, it's good to be clean-shaven. Even you don't look like shit—almost civilized if I look at you from an angle."

Konan scowled and subconsciously ran his hand through his hair, then startled at its new feel. He hadn't hacked any off for years. In fact . . . He swallowed. Isellan had cut his hair last, and since then, Konan had been a man in mourning. He tugged thoughtfully at the oil-smoothed length.

"That look doesn't help." Thordrin laughed. "Maybe just keep the one cheek turned toward Lyr."

Another woman entered and spoke to Mirra, who tugged at Konan's cloak. She spoke rapidly, entreating them to follow. They exited the tent, and she pointed at the neighboring one. The tent flap opened, and two maidens led Lyra out.

43

CROWN PRINCE GODRIG ARRIVED on the largest of three Kritali naval vessels.

Like a victorious knight captain, he stood at the bow, one hand cocked on his sword hilt and one casually rested upon the gunwale railing. His bright blue cape snapped behind him, fastened on both shoulders by matching rondels in the traditional landwalker style, a stark contrast to his short-trimmed military hair, which bore only a thin gold lattice crown. He glowered when he saw the party awaiting him at the docks of Shiggo City.

Anella ran up the gangplank, skirts lifted just enough to keep her from catching her own voluminous godets, which forced body into her mostly Kritali dress. She had gotten it adjusted on the bodice after Taiuki suggested its cut was inappropriate.

The princess met Godrig at the top and flung her arms around him. Taiuki and Kei awaited at the foot of the gangplank.

He scowled at them all and pushed his little sister back. "I told you to beware, Nelly," he said in a low voice that carried. "Why are you out of the castle? And what are you wearing?"

He locked eyes with Taiuki and bowed stiffly, then escorted Anella back down the gangplank.

She had to admit, Godrig appeared to be of refined blood despite his inferior breeding. His square jaw and hard cheekbones, while undesirable on Anella, were somewhat attractive in an exotic way, belying his personality. His chin bore a thick, dark stubble, and his build implied a trained fighting man.

Godrig skimmed the port with a look of distaste. "I did not expect a welcoming party, Princesses," he said as he stepped onto the dock. His hard gaze took in the entire wakeway, the myriad docks and jetties, then moved on to the city with a suspicious, creeping flicker.

He had gotten taller and bulkier since last she had seen him. She could almost believe him to be kingly if not for the unpleasant, far-from-diplomatic turn of his lips.

Kei slipped her arm into his and implied that Taiuki should do the same. She didn't. Anella took Godrig's other arm with enthusiasm instead, and they proceeded along the dock together, shadowed by both Shiggon-jin and Kritali guards, who examined each other with distrust.

"There's no need for concern, Prince Godrig," said Taiuki, walking slightly ahead of them. "Not here."

"One cannot be too careful," Godrig replied. He leaned forward. "You fools have no idea what's happening in Krita."

"And you have no idea what's happening here."

Godrig's grimace deepened at her retort, and he blinked as he tried to cover sideways glances at his men.

Kei glared Taiuki into silence. Then, with an entirely different tone, she said, "We've so enjoyed having Anella here, Prince Godrig. She's natural with a brush and needle, and lovely in conversation. Such a well-bred girl." She beamed at Anella, who smiled brightly back.

"She's quite accomplished for her age," he said without feeling, as if stating a fact.

"Will you be staying with us long? A few weeks perhaps?" Kei continued pleasantly.

Godrig shook his head as he helped each of them into the waiting carriage.

The step was high, but Taiuki made an effort not to lean on Godrig as she got in. Her leather cuisse skirt, slit high in several places, revealed her knees as she ascended, and she felt Godrig's unseeming glance upon her skin. She looked sharply at the Kritali prince, but he was already dissembling, his jaw set and his eyes focused on something distant. She had intentionally retained military dress, having just come from drills with Tan, as a dual message. First, she had more important things to do than greet him, and second, she did not receive him as a friend. Furthermore, her uniform both adequately covered the chest and revealed enough of her legs to thoroughly offend his tastes.

She had failed to consider his perverted desire to see the slim muscle of her upper thighs.

Kei smirked from her seat as Taiuki settled across from her. The only open seat was next to Taiuki. Of course. Godrig's breadth invaded her corner, and the carriage rolled through town, escorted by Kritali cavaliers.

"How long will you be staying?" Taiuki asked him, adjusting her shoulders. Her voice sounded harsh even to her own ears.

"Only until I've determined the extent of any danger, my lady," Godrig replied. He could speak more freely now that they had some privacy. "Then I must cross the Crack in the Earth to Marlemet."

"Well, then your stay will be brief," said Taiuki. "There is no disease here." He must have been referring to the Lai'akala Trench. A fearful landwalker *would* so absurdly name the furrow in Father Mana Loi's brow.

Kei tapped her with a foot hidden by the length of her Kritali-style dress. She had been wearing more and more of them with Anella around, a fact that irritated Taiuki even more than most things about her sister.

Then Kei gave Godrig a magnanimous smile. "Yes, but we'll enjoy your company while we can, right Taiuki? Now tell us, what news from Krita?"

As the carriage trundled to the castle of House ol'Kada ol'Tatami, Godrig told them. The madness was trickling outward from every location where it had been found, and new cases were manifesting in the capital. Unusual deaths were occurring, with farmers skewering themselves on pitchforks and seamstresses flinging themselves to the street from second-story windows. A blacksmith had thrown himself into his own forge and was found, half-burnt, by his son, who shortly after went rabid and was being held by Temple mages for closer examination. More cases of mindless murder and cannibalism, with bodies found tucked into the darkest alley corners, their faces shredded and their soft innards pulled out. The perpetrators weren't always found either, and panic was spreading in the slums.

Even stranger were the deaths by animal. The madness frightened pigs, dogs, and horses alike, and several people had been attacked by their own domesticants. It was predictable enough that truffle-trained pigs were now being used to scour the streets of Krita Port, and sick people were being captured and restrained.

"If there is any disease here, it must be snuffed out immediately," said Godrig, pounding a fist into his palm with a smack. "You must take heed."

Taiuki was surprised at the sincere urgency in his voice. He was taking his new responsibility seriously. "As I said before, Shiggo hasn't been infected," she insisted.

"I'll see for myself, Princess," Godrig answered dismissively. "Now I must speak with the queen regent."

The carriage stopped outside the upper keep, and they disembarked. Godrig gave them due civilities and then hurried inside to find their mother. Kei at first curtsied, then realized she should accompany him and rushed behind with an indignant cry. Anella followed, curious to hear more gossip from home.

Taiuki found herself standing in the courtyard, surrounded by a platoon of Kritali horsemen and a platoon of Shiggon-jin warriors.

Her soldiers saluted her before dispersing. The Kritali cavaliers all ignored her, dismounting and giving their horses to the stablekeepers under Marshal Kinota's watch. The courtyard emptied, and Taiuki heard the warning bell for the noon meal. Morning courtesies were done, and she had no intention of spending the meal gagging on a pretentious, empty conversation.

No, she would find Tan at the barracks. His drills had continued without her, and he'd likely be ready for a break accompanied by a lecture. With one last resentful glance at the upper keep, she turned to the lower castle entrance and went on her way.

Godrig's presence rankled Taiuki far more than Anella's ever could.

Within a bell of his arrival, Anella had changed dresses back to one she had brought from Krita, a cut far too low for a girl her age (and too low in general), with heavy trusses of tulle and soft blue cloth, and her conversation had dimmed to a very polite set of responses only. She didn't initiate a single question at supper, despite the curiosity Taiuki knew was exploding out of her. In that way, she was very much like Tan—when Godrig was absent, at least.

The younger girl snuck into her room late in the evening, startling her and Tan as they worked slowly through a series of movements. She peeked surreptitiously into the hallway, then slipped the door shut without a click.

This was only the second time she had ventured into the level with royal bedrooms, the first time being when Taiuki had returned from seeming death.

"Forms? That's what this is, right?" Anella had changed back to the dress she had worn at the docks.

Taiuki evaluated the girl anew. Interesting.

"I mean, 'Forms, Your Highness?'" She curtsied, then scowled at herself and saluted in the myr fashion.

Taiuki waved her over. "You don't have to do it our way. Do it your own way."

Anella nodded, then did an odd but respectful half curtsy and one-handed touch to her forehead. "May I participate, please?"

"Glad you're here, Nelly!" Tan's teeth shone in the lamp light, but then his smile faded. "What's wrong?"

Anella broke into a sad smile of her own. "You're the first people to talk to me in hours, you know? And you want me here." She blushed.

"Of course we do," Tan answered, furrowing his brow. He pulled her over to the open area and gestured where she should stand. "You can stay. You can learn forms with us. We practice almost every night. Yuki, help."

Taiuki did, arranging them both into proper stances for an upper body-oriented set of motions, then demonstrated for them. She explained the purpose of their exercises to the girl, emphasizing the precision and specificity of each movement.

Repetition was the way to perfection, she thought, a flawless routine that seared into one's muscle memory for use in dire moments. It was also the way to discipline and inner peace, although she struggled to find that last aspect even in the endless choreography of forms.

Meanwhile, Tan chattered about his day with "Old Sash" and Marshal Kinota.

"Kinota wants me to ride my landwalk—er, my horse more frequently in the afternoons," he said, rolling his eyes. "I suppose I could, but Moka won't like it."

Taiuki shook her head as she guided Anella's posture, then she waved at Tan to focus on his own. "Do not allow yourself to be so easily distracted, Tan-sho, or I'll insist you not speak."

"May I ride with you on drills?" Anella asked. "I got better clothing for it like you suggested."

"It requires knowledge of the formations and weapon use, but is also a matter of discipline," said Taiuki. "This builds the foundation for everything else. You'll have to ride together during Tan's free time."

"Is it because I'm a girl and not a soldier?"

"No, merely that you don't know the advanced cavalry formations, nor is your horse trained for battle. Now take a break. You need appropriate clothing to practice other forms."

Without complaint, Anella watched them eagerly, and it struck Taiuki again how innocent the princess was in the mess of relations with Krita. It was no more her fault that Godrig was her brother than it was Taiuki's fault she was thirdborn. They were both thirdborn daughters, conceived in different kingdoms of different mothers, yet equally devalued, serving no purpose beyond strategic marriage. For the first time, Anella seemed to see the iniquity of that arrangement. Perhaps she wasn't a landwalker clone of Kei or a female version of Godrig.

Taiuki continued until both Nelly and Tan stifled yawns. She sent Anella to bed, and the girl repeated her half curtsy, half salute at the door. "Thank you, Princess Taiuki, for being so gracious to me."

"It's just Taiuki," Taiuki conceded. "Before tomorrow, ask your Shiggon-jin maidservant to fit you with our style of clothing, at least to the degree you are comfortable. You can't practice effectively wearing a dress."

Anella beamed. "I'd be honored to dress like you, if that's okay. Oh, thank you, Taiuki. I'll make you proud, I promise!" She bounced away with a skip, heading toward the main stairs to her distant room on the first level above ground, in the new wing.

Tan delayed for moments. "Admit it. She's nice."

Taiuki shooed her brother out. "She'd appreciate an escort to her room, not for safety but for company. Go on. I'll wake you at dawn."

How can they possibly be related? she thought as she forced herself to maintain a polite look of vague interest.

Godrig was escorting Taiuki through the royal beach gardens, an expansive greenspace along one of the castle walls. He paused briefly when he realized they had already walked halfway down the path.

"I had hoped to find a slightly more solitary place to speak, Princess," he muttered. He swept his eyes across her, lingering on her slim, olive legs and bare feet. He jutted his chin out slightly. "The gardens of Castle Crayer are endless, rank upon rank of greenery and flowers, the finest hedge maze in Midgate, the most elegant rose garden with certain varieties which are found nowhere else—"

"The gardens here continue onward for those capable of visiting them," she interrupted, her voice cold. She met his sharp glance and was satisfied when he noted how the garden sloped seamlessly into the ocean.

He swallowed.

"This is as much seclusion as you'll get with me, Prince Godrig, so I suggest you speak."

He seemed to chew on his next words, then stumbled through them. "Our houses have worked for years to join meaningfully. When news of your disappearance reached Krita, the king and queen were quite distraught."

"And you?"

"What?"

"Were you distraught, Prince?" She gave him a coy look as his forearm tensed beneath her fingers.

He looked away. "Certainly. A man would certainly be distraught at losing his betrothed."

"Don't lie to me, Godrig."

Scorn flashed across his face. "You have a sharp tongue for a woman. Such behavior won't be accepted in the Kritali court."

Taiuki pulled her arm away and faced him. He was much taller than her, being of Kritali blood. Northern landwalkers tended toward height, and myr did not. Nevertheless, she scowled at him as if he were a misbehaving waterdog. "I take that to mean the marriage contract proceeds, despite word otherwise."

Godrig ground his teeth and nodded. So he wasn't the ardent suitor, despite the lascivious examinations he tended to give her bare skin. More than likely, he was under as much duress from Rigaran as she was from her mother.

"Marriage is a mistake, Godrig. I want nothing from you. I suspect you feel the same."

"Do you think nothing of duty, Princess? Or are you as selfish as they say?" His harsh words drew a wild rage up from within, and she burst.

She shoved him backward. "My duty is to my people," she snarled. "I carry no duty to you or your kind."

His hard features darkened, and he raised a hand to strike her. She blocked him with one arm and brought the other up to his handsome chin. Godrig stumbled back with the blow, and his face reddened with fury. He winced as he rubbed his stubble.

Taiuki planted her bare feet into a balanced fighting stance. She had no armor or weapons, for she had worn a traditional myr dress of trailing silk and ruche sleeves. That wouldn't stop her from fighting him, nor from breaking his prideful jaw. She had been thirsty for this for years.

She leveled her gaze at him. "If you believe in beating your betrothed, Godrig ol'Crayer of Krita, know that your betrothed will joyfully take blood for blood. And if you bring that violence into the marriage bed, know that I will kill you without a hint of regret or reservation. I'd rather see Krita collapse than tolerate your undesired attentions."

Godrig sneered at her but didn't advance, and he finally looked away. "It doesn't have to be this way, Princess." As he turned, Taiuki couldn't help but send one more barb at him.

"You may wish to grow that beard out, Prince."

His look was acid, and he stalked away, kicking at the smooth, sand-worn rocks scattered through the garden as he went. He drew his sword and whacked at several bushes as he passed.

Unbelievable disrespect, Taiuki thought as he ruined the carefully manicured garden path. She watched until she was sure he was gone. With any luck, he would go for a ride through the city on one of his absurd patrols. With even more luck, perhaps her people would decide they'd had enough of his unwelcome insertion into their world, his rudeness and arrogance, and they would turn on him as one. The man could use more than a small bruise on his chin to put him in his place.

Satisfied, she wandered deeper into the garden, stepping into the gentle lapping water of the protected cove and entering the submersed haven of tankos and coral and carved statues. From there, she could exit the other gate and seek out her blue shark cavalier, if he wasn't still too leery of her like he had been.

44

TAIUKI VENTED HER FRUSTRATIONS upon numerous trainees in sparring, but none could match her, not even Tan.

If only I could be with It'tholl. The litany tapped at her constantly, lending her an extra measure of speed. Her jiansword slashed through both water and air with a fury fed by bitter loneliness and rage.

When caged in Shiggo City, adherent to her assigned duties, she haunted the garrison, Lower Market, and lower levels of the castle, all places avoided by Prince Godrig. The man had insisted on staying longer under the pretense of checking for disease, and his presence overflowed from the newly constructed wing of landwalker-friendly guest rooms. She could sense him polluting the upper levels, his musk lingering outside Anella's room and trailing behind him as he stalked the halls. He had even dared to propose entering their Water temple, which she had staunchly rejected. The entrance was below the surface, and he had capitulated after a vicious verbal assault on her forethought and sensibility.

Focus, Taiuki. Teach well, as a Second should.

She demonstrated the move by which she had disarmed her sparring partner once more, slowly and methodically, for all the trainees to see. They alternated repeating the move in pairs, filling the training hall.

Taiuki dismissed the soldier and called Tan up. "Demonstrate the proper counter, first to avoid disarmament and then to recover with a counterstrike."

Tan did so, a grin splitting his face as they whirled into a familiar dance and paused for the trainees to absorb the lesson. They repeated it several times, with each repetition accelerating until their exchange rang out through the hall in a clash of steel. They ended each time with Taiuki in a defensive position, ready to spring forward into a new attack.

"How would one proceed from here?" she asked the group. She received a variety of answers, some calling for another step backward to avoid an aggressive move from Tan and others calling for immediate forward motion. She could see Tan's eyes sparkle as he considered each possibility.

"Full speed, proceed as you think is best," she instructed her brother.

As she expected, his impulse was to charge forward, raising his jiansword high with the intent of crashing down upon her shoulder as she feinted away. Taiuki spun forward and shouldered him off balance, twisting as she went and leaving a score upon his unguarded side. He grunted in surprise.

Dulled blades or not, their weapons struck true and without much restraint. Tan would bruise.

He chuckled as his sword arm fell to cover his sore ribcage, then sobered. "I should have predicted you wouldn't retreat."

She agreed. "To know an opponent's nature is to know their strength, their strategy, and their soul. Should you fail to identify their nature, you will know their steel. I shall react as I normally would again, but you should reconsider your move. Again."

The pace slowed once more, and this time, Tan combined a nimble hop kick with his own spin to halt Taiuki's advance and regain distance between them, after which he could use his jiansword once more.

The lesson continued, with each pair of trainees waltzing through the parry and lunge, the sweeping turns and arcs, until the hall shivered with near-perfect coordination.

Taiuki released them for the noon meal, noticing that Vice Commodore Reihotto was lounging at one of the entrances, her stance easy and her arms crossed. She wore a faint smile as Taiuki and Tan approached.

"Second." She saluted Tan first but accorded equal regard to Taiuki with her second salute. "Your Highness."

"Have you just returned from the front, Vice Commodore?" asked Tan, his eyebrows raising with eagerness.

Reihotto appraised him. "I have, and I would consult with you both if you have time?"

Tan looked to Taiuki, who nodded her assent. "The latest cohort will be occupied in the mess till the next bell, and the captain can resume their training with Kinota this afternoon."

They left the garrison together, shifting from air to water and back as they entered the Garrison Gate.

The arch commodore's office on the second underwater level of the castle was a long, low room cluttered with sheaves of maps stored in water-filled cisterns, but the greatest feature was the massive, three-dimensional map built into the floor of the adjacent war room. Reflecting the distinct bathymetry of the Mana Loi, the model showed the water line even with the floor, as well as the coastline and mountains exceeding the surface. The myrkingdom boundaries were clearly marked: Shiggo, Nagawa, Fumaya, Merchan to the far north, Jijito to the southwest, Riyogo and Tedami to the south, and Hakkan to the southeast, beyond the Holy Mountain. The landwalker kingdoms were shown as far inland as was relevant, with particular detail on the island nations of Krita and Towun.

Reihotto gestured at the map, which showed troop locations and movements indicated with figurines. Estimated locations and numbers of Jijiton-jin were shown in a different color. "You can see our current status here, but Arch Commodore Sashiro and I differ regarding the next move. I'd like your thoughts."

Taiuki studied it before answering. She had been expressly forbidden from lingering in the war room without invitation. Mother had been adamant about that, implying that Taiuki's role in the war with Jijito was nonexistent. Tan, however, had fed her several updates before Sashiro had returned to the front, and she wasn't surprised by the changes since then.

"We reclaimed this atoll?" She pointed. "And this ridge? Well done."

Reihotto nodded. "But we lost ground here, and here. My princess, the Jijiton-jin have not backed down despite the routing in both of these towns. In fact, they have pushed forward over the Lai'akala Trench to the far south, here, where it shallows on the steppe. The number of slain are beyond counting." She looked up, her face marred by tragedy. "Arch Commodore Sashiro equates the Jijiton-jin behavior to that of a blueback: vicious, wild, and without restraint or ethic. I've never seen such violent destruction as I have at these border towns."

Tan made a sound, a groan of sorts. His black eyes were wide, overwhelmed. "That's not like any of the battle strategies you or Sash have taught me about," he muttered.

"That's because it's not the Way," Taiuki answered, guiding him to a chair and giving his shoulder an encouraging squeeze. "Their tactics are risky, shooting small contingents out in erratic spurts of violence and then pulling them back just as quickly." She pulled up a chair beside Tan and sat, staring at the map. "Are these locations all up-to-date, Vice Commodore? Sashiro's main fleet sits here?"

Reihotto nodded.

"And he shored up this atoll, and this one?"

"Yes, he divided the force here and here, so no group was too small. My fleet is down here, to the south."

Taiuki sighed. They had too many holes in their defense, exacerbated by the wide spread of Jijiton-jin attacks and the natural myr unwillingness to divide schools into smaller factions. She was shocked Jijito would do so, but as Sashiro said, they were acting like wild beasts, lone predators without schools. It was barbaric.

Tan listened as she and Reihotto strategized over troop movements. Taiuki suggested shifts in their defense groups, moving the stronger defense closer together and pushing the northerly forts toward the smallest groupings acceptable, strengthened by two squadrons from Taiuki's trainees. Rei-hotto cringed at the numbers, urging her to push them back up; they compromised. Taiuki then suggested an aggressive counterattack, pushing directly toward the Jijito capitol, which might force the enemy soldiers to coalesce.

She didn't state her most desired solution: an assassination party, a very small contingent to go in and slaughter the Jijiton-jin arch commodore at his command post. By the current, if one was willing to go alone, a single skilled soldier could complete the mission. But that wasn't the Way of the Current, and she knew it.

"How long will you remain in Shiggo City, Vice Commodore?" Taiuki knew the woman was stretched thin, no doubt leaving command of her companies to her most capable commodores.

"I was told to remain here until Master Sashiro relieved me, providing oversight to the Second's training." Reihotto flushed slightly at the potential offense to Taiuki, and she bowed her head to indicate her shame.

Taiuki clasped her shoulder. "It is well, Vice Commodore. I am unable to spend as much time with him as I'd like, for Wehan demands a portion of my own days at the castle." The half-truth slipped across her lips so easily, she felt gutted. But Reihotto could not know anymore of her altered schedule than could Master Sashiro. "In fact, I report to Wehan and Hannaka for castle duties tomorrow, and do not return until after rest day. I planned to cede leadership to Captain Kutachi during the intervening days, but with you here, I'll cede it to you."

"I shall conform, Your Highness." Reihotto saluted. "Thank you for your time." She acknowledged Tan as well, then led them out of the office with a respectful farewell.

Tan watched her disappear down the walkway, heading back to the Garrison Gate. He crossed his arms and scrunched up his face. "You're busy again, for *three* days?"

"That's what Sashiro and Wehan agreed to," Taiuki answered quickly. "A balance between garrison and castle time. Remember, I must dedicate significant effort to learning the expectations of a Kritali queen." Her rancor must have leaked out, for Tan gave her a look.

"And you're okay with that?" Doubt colored his voice.

"I'm doing what is needful," she answered carefully. Above all, she regretted any false words from her lips to Tan-sho. Even dishonesty by omission pained her.

"You must be with Wehan a lot," he muttered. "Half the time, I can't even find you at night."

"I've been spending more evenings at the barracks, to get away." A blatant lie, but Tan smirked as if he understood completely.

"Your cavalier again? *Your* bed is probably more comfortable." He subsided, suddenly glum. "I just feel like we're farther apart, even though we spend more time together in some ways."

She controlled her dismay and slung her arm around his shoulder, a motion that was getting more and more difficult as he grew. "I'm here, Tan-sho. We can go for a ride this afternoon and practice forms tonight, at least."

As usual, Anella joined them for forms. She wore a bizarre outfit that had made Tan laugh at first, one at which she giggled herself but which allowed her to participate—a man's tunic with a high neckline, supported and bound by a colorful corset to support her growing body. The tunic flared out at her waist, reaching below her hips, and although it was slit on both sides, none of her leg was revealed, for she wore a long, somewhat loose pair of pants underneath, another piece of Kritali men's apparel. She abandoned her shoes at the door.

Dual forms were a beautiful interchange from one warrior to the other and back. Elevated beyond the slow, intermittent starts and stops of new students, dual forms were almost sexual, and as predictable an act in most cases. They were a balanced dance of blade and body, an essential basis for rapid response in hand-to-hand combat. Not that Anella would likely experience that anytime soon, or ever, but she could practice with them if she really wanted to.

"Princess Taiuki? May I ask you a question? Will you teach me how to actually fight?"

Anella's question caused her to pause as she was adjusting her position.

"Please, I want to be more like you . . . You're strong, and people are intimidated by you. People respect you even though you're a girl."

Tan grinned, and Taiuki really saw the young Kritali princess for the first time.

Anella was slightly chubby with the fat of childhood, but had already grown a finger taller since her arrival. She was likely to end up tall, like her brothers. The contours of her face were square and could be regal once she grew a little more, but what made her beautiful where Godrig was repulsive was that shine of pure-hearted friendliness in her eye. She was kind, despite how many times Taiuki had turned her away for being Kritali, for being the enemy.

Then Taiuki recalled her courtly lessons with Wehan and Hannaka, and aggravation devoured her. "You don't need to know how to fight in Krita."

But the girl caught her hand, breaking form to beg. "I'm not in Krita," Anella said. "I'm in Shiggo. You know, I was terrified to come here because—because of stories I had heard about myrpeople. Please don't be offended. I'm telling you because I'm not terrified anymore. Your people are different than mine, yes, but not in a bad way. Your queens are strong, and your women fight alongside the men. You tame wild sea animals and speak about politics and war. I want to be like you." She brushed her hands nervously down her ill-fitting tunic and straightened her shoulders. "Besides, did my father and mother not send me here to learn more about Shiggo's ways? That's the whole purpose of a foster, isn't it? Perhaps they wanted me to learn these things."

Taiuki couldn't help but snort in amusement. There was more ambition in the girl than she had realized. When Anella arrived, Taiuki had assumed she was a classic product of the landwalkers: a biddable, weak, delicate creature accustomed to jewels and regular tea times. And in many ways, Anella appeared to be so. She was talented in the so-called feminine arts, she was well-mannered and overly soft-spoken, and she dressed in clothing that was entirely impractical. Or, she used to.

"That would be fun," Tan interjected. "Better than forms."

Taiuki resisted an open smile to match his. "I suppose I could teach you something."

The expression that stretched across Anella's face gave her dimples, and her eyes sparkled. "Oh, thank you, Princess Taiuki, thank you! If it helps at all, I'd be happy to work with you on Kritali culture too, if you please. I know it's not your favorite subject, but it is something I know."

She decided to teach Anella a different form of martial art than what she and Tan had been practicing. The girl would benefit most from a defensive art that utilized leverage over brute strength, especially when she returned home to Krita. If she paid attention, Anella might have to worry less about rough treatment from dangerous people who didn't value her pretty covewater-colored eyes and white teeth, her charisma and passionate interests, her audacious nature.

Taiuki still doubted whether Kritali people in general were like her or more like Godrig, but if it was the latter, the girl could use all the help she could get.

⁂

No matter how many times she left and returned, her return to the Mountains of Mourning was heralded by the piercing cries of It'tholl, a desperate dirge which seemed to neither begin nor end until she was safely wrapped around her dragling.

It'tholl does not want Taiuki to leave, wailed It'tholl, curling her glistening tail around Taiuki as the surf crashed around them. She redoubled her feelings with a sad croon that vibrated through Taiuki's entire being.

"I know, beloved." Taiuki did know, for she and It'tholl exchanged their emotions as surely as two ocean currents mixing, an unstoppable swirl and interchange until it was unclear who had expressed first. "I must return to Tan."

It'tholl itches.

Taiuki stifled a laugh and attempted to cover her reaction. It'tholl had already figured out that Taiuki would linger given a good enough reason, and her rapidly growing body continually ached and itched. Her scaly shimmer flaked in places, especially along her stretching limbs and torso, and her teeth hurt.

"One more application on the bad spots," Taiuki relented with a quick look at the setting sun.

It'tholl nearly howled with delight, then scampered up the beach to the tarp dripping fish oil. Numerous nut hulls brimming with thick salve lay in careful stacks nearby, the result of patient weeks of oil collection and rendering.

Taiuki rubbed the flaking skin and grimaced. "Uth'hal, is this normal? She's growing so quickly, her skin can hardly keep up."

The Bond affects growth, Uth'hal responded from his position in the breakwater. He preferred lounging in the crashing waves, his head resting upon his own shoulder, casually watching the sea.

She will grow faster with you near, added It'ma. *But it is well. The slow life without the Bond is very long.*

Again, Taiuki wondered whether she imagined the sorrow in the elder dragons' voices. None of the al'Laiakala Order had bonded save It'tholl, and none of them would. It was too late.

She couldn't help but grieve for their loneliness, one that she had shared until the moment she spied those sapphire eyes in the hatching cavern. Within that black slit of a pupil, within those whirling pools of Water-infused life and color, was the world.

Do not lament, child of I'ya, said Uth'hal. *We rejoice for our offspring, and that is enough for this lifetime.*

"Is it?"

It'ma leapt down from her spot at the top of the cliffs, half gliding on wings not designed for flight. The ground shook at her landing, and she tramped up to them using her forewings as stilts. She touched noses with It'tholl, then brushed Taiuki's forehead with her massive muzzle. *It is enough. The Order has returned to the Land of Light, something for which we had prayed for many years. I'ya has already blessed the Order beyond what we dared hope.*

The Land of Light, echoed several others.

Tears threatened Taiuki's vision, and she blinked them away as she rubbed more salve into It'tholl's skin. She needed to go. Even with It'ma's or Uth'hal's accompaniment, she would arrive at the edge of Shiggo's settlements late in the day.

"I do have one more question for you, Elder Uth'hal, Elder It'ma, but I have had trouble putting it into words." Even as she spoke, her stomach turned over, and It'tholl whimpered with matching discomfort. Why did the subject bother her so, as though her entire being rejected the nebulous idea that clamored for freedom from the cage in her mind?

Ask, child.

Taiuki shuddered a deep breath, attempting to steady herself even as waves of fear came over her. She leaned against It'tholl. "When we first came to the Mountains of Mourning, in the coral towers . . ." She swallowed convulsively. "What happened with the lacer?"

It attacked, and we killed it, It'ma answered, cocking her head to one side.

"But after?" She forced the question out, even as her mind clouded with an intense fear. It darkened her comprehension, closing her from clear recall of the moment. Perhaps she had only imagined the clear orb around her and It'tholl as they had shrieked in terror together.

It'tholl whimpered again and huddled against her.

You defended yourself, It'ma said, as though nothing strange had happened. *But without control.*

For reasons she couldn't explain, Taiuki fell into a heaving panic. *No blood in the water.* Her lungs spasmed, and her heart thudded as though it might explode from her ribcage. The cloudiness in her mind consumed everything else, a dark thunderstorm billowing over her ability to perceive or understand, and she fell to her knees and retched.

It'ma and Uth'hal spoke to her, but their voices were nonsense. Uth'warran spoke as well, and again his deep confidence broke apart into drivel.

She felt as though she were drowning, if that was a sensation she could even imagine. *But myr don't drown . . .*

Taiuki, It'tholl is here. It'tholl loves you.

The terrifying void lessened at the dragling's desperate plea.

Taiuki had a grasp on reality again, a tangible clutch upon It'tholl's forewing. She struggled back to her feet, realizing she had vomited onto the sand. What was this darkness in her memory, tied to her recall of the lacer attack, of the spear? Of the ale glass beading sweat and then shattering into nothing? She couldn't bear to think of it fully, so she shied away from it as she usually did.

Unable to stomach more, she bid farewell to It'tholl and hurried back to Shiggo City. It'ma escorted her to the edge of the farms, allowing her to move far more quickly than she could have alone. The elder dragon spoke little until they parted.

You will find greater power in the Bond, child of I'ya. Do not fear it. Return soon, for It'tholl cannot live without you. It'ma turned away and melted into the endless blue of the Mana Loi.

Taiuki swallowed back the senseless overwhelm and made her way to the barracks, seeking out Reihotto.

She found the vice commodore lounging in the training hall, enjoying an ale in one of the alcoves. Reihotto stood quickly and double-saluted before offering Taiuki a seat.

Taiuki settled quietly opposite Reihotto, her mind still reeling from the joint pleasure and terror of her secret holiday.

"My princess?" Reihotto cocked her head and furrowed her brow, then pushed the ale across the table.

Taiuki stared at it, her thoughts warring with each other. The ale glass. She tapped her fingers on the cool glass, then took a gulp with an appreciative nod at Reihotto.

"Hotto?"

Reihotto straightened. Rarely did Taiuki use her nickname, but she was coming to the woman as a friend rather than a soldier. She needed to ask someone she trusted the questions she was terrified to voice, and yet she couldn't find the strength to do so.

She took another swig of the ale, hoping to fortify herself. "You have known me longer than most."

Reihotto listened, merely nodding.

"Is there something wrong with me, Hotto?"

Reihotto's eyebrows rose up, and she leaned forward slowly, speaking in a low voice that would not carry beyond their alcove. "My princess, I don't pretend to understand your doubt. You are *my* Second, and I have never known one more suited to the position than you."

Taiuki looked sharply at her. "I am not Second, Hotto. At best I was always Third, and now I am nothing."

"Do I speak as vice commodore, or as your friend?" Caution had suddenly darkened Reihotto's eyes; the yellow flecks had dulled to a pale straw color as she diminished.

Taiuki regretted her response, and she shook her head as if to dispel the unchecked anger. She tried to smile. "As a friend, please."

Reihotto clasped Taiuki's wrists from across the table and squeezed affectionately. "As a friend, Princess, I say that you are exceptional and worthy of the title denied you."

Exceptional. Taiuki considered that. Myr were not meant to be exceptional. Being different reduced the potency of the school. Being different was dangerous.

Reihotto seemed to read her thoughts, and she knitted her brow. "The school follows the strongest. Every school has a master, every fleet a figurehead at the bow. Without it, the school plunges into chaos. This *is* the Way of the Current."

"Your words would be encouraging were I to be the Arch Commodore, but I am no longer." Taiuki pulled her hands away and finished the ale with a heavy sigh. "I wish I were not exceptional, Hotto. It gives me an unease I can't explain, as though the world is crashing down around me, by my hand." The thought sickened her. Even a friend recognized the fault within her.

"It is no doubt lonely," Reihotto answered with a grim smile. "Yet, I do not wish normalcy upon you. You are the blood ol'Kada ol'Tatami, and you were not bred to blend into the rest of the school."

Taiuki pondered her words for a while, then managed a weak half-smile in response. "And what would you have said, as a soldier?"

"As vice commodore of the fleets of Shiggo, I would have said that I cannot recognize you as my Second, as I have been commanded otherwise."

"And you shall conform, as you must."
"I shall, my princess."

45

"You requested my presence before I departed, Prince Reylin?" Lío's gruff voice would have soured Reylin's mood, if not for the confidence he had in shaking Lío from his superior attitude.

Reylin forced himself to remain relaxed. He leaned back against the smoothness of the silk pillows, the soft billow of the down inside. Despite his convalescence, he had regained a healthy pallor and adequate strength to sit alert, and he had ordered his crown to be placed upon his head for the audience.

Lío paced at the foot of the bed, snarling at the summons. Reylin enjoyed it for a moment or two longer before beckoning the man's attention.

"I called you here for a private discussion, Lord Lío, something the Elder Council may not be ready to hear. It affects your district, and I believe you'd prefer to handle it privately if possible."

That had the effect Reylin had hoped, for Lío was a prideful and independent man. He would resent interference by other lords as much as Reylin resented it. Reylin smiled to himself as the man paused his pacing and looked sharply at him.

Reylin continued. "Much has happened in the past few weeks, including revelation of a new danger to Mirat, a sickness."

"What sickness?" Lío growled.

"Have you not wondered *why* Sir Cordan would attack me in Lupine? He was no traitor."

"I assumed it was dementia," Lío grumbled, but he looked far from sure.

"Of a sort, Lord Lío, but not brought on by old age." Reylin reveled in the moment. "In Lupine, we found a sickness of the mind, the first detection in Mirat. However, as isolated as the incident was, we suspect your district is most at risk of future infections."

Lío glowered, although Reylin suspected the nasty sneer wasn't directed at him. The man resumed pacing suddenly. "I would have heard about it by now."

"The Temple has been keeping information tightly bound, my lord." Father Kaiadin stepped in with quiet authority. "As a sickness of the mind, the madness would typically be dealt with by the mages, but this disease has evaded our healing. However, I do believe healing is possible."

Lío ground his teeth, then gave Reylin a begrudgingly grateful look. "I'm listening, Prince Reylin."

"The disease has infected Krita," Reylin said with all the assurance he could muster. "They have kept this information from the world, trusting they could resolve it, but Father Kaiadin tells me they have failed to do so thus far. There is great danger of infection in our seaports, particularly a busy one like North Mara. You must initiate a close watch on incoming ships, perhaps a quarantine, and engage the local temple."

Lío grumbled again but didn't argue. He crossed his arms. "I must say, communication with Krita has been poor of late. Fewer birds, almost no Whispers." His eyes widened. "By the Light . . . Mother Morsey suggested something strange not two weeks ago, that some violent criminal had been apprehended. She suggested I come in person to make judgment."

For the first time, Reylin saw a glint of fear in the sturdy man's eye.

"So it has already begun," murmured Father Kaiadin. He adjusted his glasses and looked at Reylin.

Reylin straightened. The weight of his crown was heavy on his exhausted neck, and he took a deep breath to ensure the words that came out next were strong. "Return to your district, Lord Lío, and investigate North Mara Port. Report your status to Father Kaiadin via Mother Morsey, and inform me of anything you need. We do not wish to cause a public panic, but this disease is dangerous."

Seemingly speechless, Lord Lío nodded.

Father Kaiadin stepped into the silence that followed. "His Highness has omitted one fact in his humility. He himself has the ability to heal, and where the Temple has failed, it is possible he will succeed."

Attuned to any reaction from Lío, Reylin noted the slight goggling of the duke's eyes, the tempered shock, and then the vague hopefulness masked by a gruff frown. Lord Lío inclined his head with more respect than Reylin had ever seen before.

"A miracle," he muttered. "I shall return to the west and report back immediately, Your Highness. I thank you for your discretion; I shall control this disease within my district if possible."

"Ensure Mother Morsey communicates any messages directly to Father Kaiadin." Reylin excused him, and Lío hurried out, leaving only Father Kaiadin with him.

"He couldn't have known of the ward," Reylin suggested. "He was genuinely surprised and relieved to have some hope of healing."

"Perhaps, my son."

Reylin winced. "But what if I can't heal them, Father? What if I try and fail, yet again?"

Kaiadin eased Reylin back down into the bed and set his crown on the side table. "The Temple has already failed, but I saw what you did in Lupine. You are specially gifted, and may succeed where they have failed. It is a matter of training and learning now. You, my lord, may be the best defense Mirat has against the madness."

"Can I truly stop it?"

Kaiadin shrugged helplessly. "We know so little about it, and we know even less about the extent of your power. Perhaps you can feel what is broken in them, and heal them as you did your wife."

"I failed at that, Father." His last word cracked in his throat.

"You healed her physical wounds, son. You cannot blame yourself for how much she bled before you arrived, due to the inabilities of others. All you can do is push yourself to learn more, to grow."

"Then let us train and learn." Reylin yawned. "If it is true, then I should be able to heal myself." He lifted his aching left arm, which still bore the long line of blood-letting. "I'm confident I can heal this, as I healed Priscilla's tissue injuries, but that's not where I failed her."

Kaiadin agreed, pulling out a scroll on anatomy from the desk. "It was in fortification of the humors, a more difficult challenge as it required true transmutation. Your concept of binding your own blood was not a poor idea, however. Son, you did all you could in the time you had been given, with the knowledge you had available."

Reylin swallowed hard, recalling Priscilla's snow-white skin, the faded glaze of her dark, pretty eyes, the limpness of her hand where it flopped over the side of the tub. She was gone, interred in his family's mausoleum in the cliffside. He had placed her crown on her head himself, deciding to make a new one for Syrana in any case, and he had been the first to place a delicate mountain flower in her coffin. It had been a friendly yellow, bright like her and one of her favorites. All he had left of her now was little Amber.

Kaiadin waded through descriptions of humors and skin layers, arteries and veins, particularly those in the arm, and Reylin listened. Reaching into himself with his power, he could sense much of what the mage described, making sense of the thick sinew and cord-like tendons, exploring the variety of tissues. Each humor tasted different. Even the blood seemed unique depending on which direction it flowed, toward his fingertips or back toward his shoulder.

After a thorough foundation had been laid, he worked to seal the self-inflicted injury entirely shut, bypassing at least a week of healing if not more. It burned all the way through, as freshly tender as a new cut. He was forced to stop several times, his body resisting the slow and intentional hurt. It took most of his reduced energy, and he had to wait until the next day to continue on.

Father Kaiadin was patient as ever. His lessons were a combination of academic study of what was known by Mirat's High Temple and practical application. However, it seemed the High Temple knew less than he would have liked.

"Manipulation seems more straightforward," Reylin lamented, staring at the bowl of water by his side.

"That it does, son," the mage agreed, removing his glasses to rub his eyes. He grimaced as some of the indigo paint smeared his thumb and forefinger, then clucked his tongue. "However, it would be a valuable skill to attain for many reasons, not just your recovery now. You could rejuvenate your humors without magika, given a little more time, but what of those situations in which we do not have time? No, we must figure this out."

Reylin nodded slowly. He knew mages with transmutative magika existed, scattered across the continent, serving a variety of purposes. Kaiadin had mentioned one who served a hemophiliac lord, and another who served an elderly lady with weak blood, and yet another who helped provide fresh drinking water on a trio of miniscule islands in the Mana Loi.

"Do you think Priscilla scarred?" Reylin murmured, staring at the thin line on his forearm. "Do you think she would have been able to have more children?"

"I don't know, son. We do not typically cut open the dead."

"No, of course not," he mused. If he had more practice, he might have healed the wounds without any lingering hints of the injury. He hadn't considered the possibility before, but how heartbroken Priscilla would have been if the scarring had inhibited her from carrying another child. She had always spoken of having three.

As for himself, he needed at least one son to assure a legitimate heir. Amber was perfect in every way but that. Whether Reylin liked it or not, a proper heir would further legitimize his claim to the throne, defraying one more concern of the Elder Council.

"Do you think . . . Syrana can?" He finally voiced a worry that had nagged at him lately. She should have been with child by now, given their nightly (and daily) activities. She had made good on her threat to ensure he wasn't bored while bedridden.

Kaiadin's expression tightened. Was that pity Reylin spied in the stiffness of his brow, in the squint of his eyes? "I do not rightly know, son. She may have ten children in time. Until then, rejoice in little Amber and your beautiful Chosen."

They returned to their exercise using the bowl of water. Kaiadin had pulled out a small number of lessons derived from myr Waterpriests, but he cursed the Temple for not retaining more.

"The Waterpriests are not an official division of the Temple as they reject the holistic perfection of I'ya," he explained to Reylin. "They believe the Water aspect is the true form of God, and that the other aspects are lesser subsidiary powers. However, they have a thorough understanding of Water magika. If only we had closer ties to Nagawa, or even Fumaya were Lord Yarris willing to facilitate . . ." He trailed off in thought as he parsed the ancient script. The myr scrolls bore a combination of Old Language and myr, and they could only read half of it as a result, plus the messy, scribbled notes along the margins where someone had translated.

"We already trade with Nagawa and Shiggo, albeit through the intermediary of Krita Port," said Reylin, unsure what the mage was considering.

Kaiadin perked up. "Shiggo has a number of talented Waterpriests. I wonder if they would be willing to send an emissary to you, in exchange for shipments of stone and lumber. I believe I heard something about a building project there, and Shiggo doesn't produce its own construction materials."

Reylin nodded. "An expansion of the royal castle at Shiggo City. I heard the myr queen is building a new wing aboveground to host guests from human kingdoms."

Kaiadin rubbed his clean-shaven chin thoughtfully, then adjusted his glasses. "Queen Regent Furuhaki, yes. She seems much friendlier to trade relations than before her husband passed. Hmm . . . I'd be happy to assist in contacting their Water temple. Until then, I will continue to teach you all I can from our stored texts and my own experience tutoring the magusi."

"Thank you, Father." Reylin was sincere, despite his shared frustration regarding the paucity of information on construction of materials using transmutation. A place like Shiggo, where the people themselves carried transmutative magika, should have far more information and training. He had found himself relying more and more upon Kaiadin, given Father Ma'thell's questionable allegiance and poor health.

Compared to Reylin, the high holy mage had been slower to recover from his overexertion of healing. The elderly man rarely left the rainbow-filled temple, overseeing daily prayers and occasionally sending abbreviated Whispers across the kingdom, but he had begun delegating sermons and events to Kaiadin and other junior mages. More birds had been flying from the dovecote, for Ma'thell could no longer bear Whispering every message. Reylin worried, despite himself, that the old man had extended himself too far.

Reylin asserted his mind onto the bowl of water, pulling away from his sadness for Ma'thell. It was nearly certain that Ma'thell had played a part in warding Reylin's magic. Who else could have done so? And Reylin enjoyed these lessons, repetitive as they were, for each time, he felt the elemental connection a moment sooner, succeeded in rippling the surface a little deeper, and felt less drained by the minute movements. He hovered a palm over the bowl, tapping his fingers over the surface and feeling it echo back with splashing laughter.

"Can we return to manipulation, Father? I have little energy for much more today," he suggested.

Father Kaiadin looked up from his esoteric myr scrolls and sighed. "Yes, son. I'm sure we can draw an emissary soon enough. Now, I'd like you to try splitting the water, half on each side of the bowl, without getting your hand wet. This requires more than dabbling and stirring."

Reylin twisted his wrist so his palm looked like it was making a chopping motion. The exercise was more difficult, as he would have to push half the water in one direction and half in another. He lowered his palm into the bowl, pushing out and away with his mind.

The water leapt in all directions, soaking both Reylin and Kaiadin and nearly ruining the open scroll laying nearby.

The holy mage flinched as indigo tears washed off his purple eyeband. "Oh, by the Light, son!" he stuttered.

Reylin laughed. His bedsheets were soaked. Thankfully, he wasn't leaking indigo dye on anything like Father Kaiadin was.

Kaiadin dabbed his face, disregarding the stain on his dark robes. "Well, perhaps less mental effort in the push next time. A delicate touch..." He looked at the empty bowl, then realized the scroll was wet on the edges. "Grace and mercy upon me," he muttered, quickly pulling the scroll from the damp bed and fluttering it in the air.

"Wait," said Reylin. He raised his hands toward the scroll.

"With utmost care, my son," pleaded the mage.

Reylin closed his eyes and, probing with only his mind, felt the outline of the map with its water-sodden edge. He could see the shape of it. Echoing his mental image with his fingers, he gently grasped the wetness and nothing else, and pulled it into his palm. Holding an accumulation in one hand and picking with the other, he worked until the scroll was dry. When he opened his eyes with a triumphant grin, he relinquished his careful hold.

A quivering orb of water in his left hand collapsed and poured onto the edge of the bed, splashing Kaiadin's boots, but the scroll held by a relieved Kaiadin was entirely dry.

"Shadows find me," Reylin cursed.

"Nay, it was well done, my young king," said Kaiadin warmly. "Thank you. That scroll is a rarity."

"Perhaps I should call in a keepmaid," said Reylin with another laugh. The power gave him a sense of calm and confidence in himself, despite his exhaustion.

Kaiadin beamed at him, streaky cheeks looking absurd. "You should continue practicing by returning the water to the bowl. I, on the other hand, must return to the temple, first for a change in robes but also to send a message to Shiggo." He excused himself with as much dignity as he could muster, leaving Reylin in good humor as he collected the spilled water covering the bed and floor.

46

DESPITE REYLIN'S BEST EFFORTS, he could not transform the water presented to him into anything else, and he was forced to wait for his body to recover on its own.

Syrana kept him company.

She was a vigorous companion, as luscious as the day he first saw her peek through the gossamer curtains of her carriage and catch his eye. As he had marched down the castle steps, shoulders thrown back so the wind fluttered his orange cape, he had first noted the depth of her dark eyes, a stark contrast against the white.

He fell into them like a chasm, tumbling endlessly, and he had never emerged.

She had worn a creamy beige and green dress, and her black trusses had been pulled back into an elegant mass hardly done justice by her requisite hair covering.

He stroked the locks back from her face now, glad she no longer had to cover her hair as a maiden would. She sighed and kissed his chest, then snuggled closer.

"I love our moments alone," she murmured, her wandering fingers revealing that she was in fact awake.

"You haven't had enough of them yet?" Reylin allowed a smug look to cross his face, despite his realization that he hadn't been able to endure her salacious touch as long as he normally could. He truly had approached the Gates with his sacrifice, and it had been a slow recovery. He felt almost normal now, but it was frustrating.

Syrana teased him with a coy look. "Never enough, my love."

He inadvertently looked toward the door. There was so much to be done, once he gathered the resolve to get up. The war, the mines, the Council . . .

"Leave your worries outside the door to this room," Syrana whispered, moving on top of him once again. "In this room, it can be just us."

He groaned and acquiesced.

By the Light, what had he done to deserve her? She loved him so thoroughly, he could almost believe he was worth something.

Priscilla, wonderful as she was, had been obligated to him through arrangements made by her own father and his regents. The lords regent, Father Ma'thell, all had cared for him because they had to do so, for his lack of parents. The women he had before marrying, the desperate and clinging pretty faces of court (as well as a number of serving girls), had all desired him for his crown and status, not for himself.

But Syrana was different. She had stepped down from that carriage with a shy smile, despite believing him to be the castle steward. Her remote home at Camdry had given her a practical understanding of economy, of the function and role of mines in Mirat, as well as proper noble mannerisms instilled by the baroness. Reylin could not say the same of many of the other ladies at court; they were beyond useless in terms of conversation. Furthermore, she didn't carry that haughtiness that the women from the larger cities did.

Well, not in public. She was not humble when he celebrated her perfect naked form. He could tell she relished his verbal and unspoken compliments, both delivered with an eager tongue.

Their lovemaking was interrupted by a knock at the outer door, renewing all of Reylin's worries for the world outside. He winced.

"Don't leave me, my love," Syrana purred, pulling him back to her.

"I must," he answered upon hearing Father Kaiadin's voice outside. It had to be an important message. He wrenched himself away, leaving Syrana with an arm outstretched and the sheets hanging halfway off her hips.

She pouted, and he lingered on the shape of her lips as he pulled the door to their inner bedchamber shut.

With a huff to fortify both his mind and body, he yanked a pair of trousers on and bid Father Kaiadin enter.

The mage strode in. "Praise be, you're up and walking, my king," he said, but his ebullient expression faded almost immediately. "A bird from Lord Lío, conveyed via Mother Morsey. I thought it urgent." He bowed his head and offered a letter bearing his own seal.

Reylin took it and collapsed on the couch. After breaking the seal, he read it silently. He called in his High Guard, who crowded in from their stations on either side of the outer door.

A message from Lord Lío to Prince Reylin: The madness is here. King Rigaran has admitted a spreading of the disease at Krita Port to our source, and the sailors coming from Krita are being checked at anchorage for signs.

Sickness has been stamped out once, when an infected ship arrived with three maddened sailors. They murdered two crewmates during the voyage before being restrained in the brig. They are now held in my dungeon at North Mara, and the Temple of I'ya is working to heal them. The first report from Morsey also appears to be the same disease.

> *Please advise any new findings regarding healing.*
>
> Respectfully, Lord Lío

Reylin leaned back against the soft cushions and groaned.

"Lupine was only the beginning," muttered Kaiadin.

Gillead grumbled low in his throat.

"It's obviously traveled inland with someone once before," muttered Patreagh, scratching his head.

"Which means Lío missed it in North Mara Port once before," added Ronidann with a grimace. "How long do you think a man could carry the disease before going mad?"

They all grew quiet.

Dorian glanced from one man to the other, unsure how to react.

Reylin shuddered with horror. Was it days? Weeks? Was it possible his own consort was infected in Lupine and didn't realize it?

"Worry not, my young king," said Kaiadin quickly. "The word in the Temple is that it doesn't spread like a normal plague, and when it infects a new victim, the effect is immediate."

Reylin could hear the collective sigh whisper through the room, and some of the tension left his own shoulders. He handed the note to Father Kaiadin to burn. The frightening words flaked away to ash. "Lord Commander?"

Gillead straightened. The corners of his mouth were turned down, deepening his ruddy scowl lines. "Highness?"

"Send at least two platoons to North Mara Port to support him in this outbreak."

"My prince, I can and shall do as you command, but any man you send west cannot fight in the east."

"I thought we had whole companies in reserve."

"We do, but Lord Galltry requested I keep the barracks here as full as I could in case the fyr attacks escalate." Gillead looked apologetic, his brow knotted and his gaze cast toward his boots. "He's nervous with the latest attack on his eastern border, although not nervous enough to actually deploy the force needed."

Reylin fumed at Galltry's subtle selfishness. Lord Lío had just as much right to kingdom soldiers as he. Troops were commanded by the lord commander in any case, who technically answered only to the king. Gillead was being yanked between two conflicting sources of authority. "Lord Commander, they are your men, and my men. Send two platoons immediately to North Mara Port. I nearly lost my wife to this madness, and I refuse to allow my people to suffer just because Galltry wants a reserve for his own use. Wait—better yet, Gillead, let us deliver the men to North Mara ourselves. Let us bring a whole company."

Sir Gillead stared at him. "My prince, that seems unwise."

"I didn't ask if it was wise, Gillead. The lords believe the road to be safe enough not to deliver troops, don't they? Then why should I not travel on it to deliver a needed boon to my subject?"

Gillead stuttered and looked to Patreagh for support, but a proud grin twitched at the other knight's lips.

"Just like your father, Prince Reylin," said Patreagh.

"The Elder Council doesn't meet again till the next moon, and I don't believe it appropriate to wait that long for decisions. I shall lead them myself, so we can study the disease in person. I may be the only one who can heal it, and I cannot give Lío guidance without learning more." If Lío was the one blocking his Ascension to kingship, such a move would surely convince him that Reylin's leadership was a good thing.

"North Mara is infected—" Gillead began.

"It was caught early and contained," said Kaiadin in a low, steady voice. Reylin glanced at him with gratitude.

"I do not wish to hear your opinion on this, Gillead," said Reylin. "Ready the troops for departure, and select a knight captain you trust."

Sir Gillead gave Reylin a long look, then nodded. "As you please, Your Highness. May I ask, how do you wish to respond to the situation in the east?"

Reylin leaned into the comfort of the couch and closed his eyes, willing the fury simmering inside not to boil over. "Galltry's made it very clear that I'm not welcome in that discussion." Priscilla would have said something kind, something that bolstered him, in this moment. *It's your pro-*

ject, Reylin. Your initiative. A small idea hatched in his mind, but he clenched his jaw under Gillead's watchful evaluation.

Gillead was so careful compared to him, so conservative, but Reylin wanted to be in the fight.

"Must we go west, Your Highness? Taking more troops east to the grassland would be a lark," said Ronidann, nudging Dorian playfully.

Gillead cleared his throat, a guttural sound that was almost a growl. "In truth, I'm more comfortable with the devil I know. If you wish to fight alongside your men, Your Highness, I'd much rather it be a fight with the fyr than against some devilry. I can guard your back on the battlefield. I don't know how to protect you from this madness." He shook his head.

"The madness doesn't seem to infect noble blood," Reylin argued, although he was equally torn between the two directions.

The colonist train had departed several days before, trundling and trudging its way to East Face with a gaggle of hopeful homesteaders and a mass of supplies and tools. A bird from Master Daiunek indicated that he and Wethers had found another potential mine farther downslope; it tasted sharp with rubies. Daiunek had named it "Halmani Mine," for it overlooked a long expanse of grassy meadow that eventually opened up to the broader Loi al'Halmana.

But the west was where Reylin could truly prove he was special. If Father Kaiadin was right, he might be able to heal the sick, and to heal such a terrible disease would prove his mettle and worthiness, his pure nobility and holy gifting. What more could one possibly want in a king? The Elder Council would be practically forced to abdicate.

"We're heading west," he said with all the authority he could muster, then dismissed Gillead to make arrangements. It would likely take several days to gather an entire company, especially with other troops likely headed elsewhere.

With one more regretful glance at the inner bedchamber, he heaved himself off the couch and dressed fully.

"Remain with my wife," he ordered Dorian, who obediently stationed himself outside the door to the inner chamber.

He left with Kaiadin, trailed by Patreagh and Ronidann as always. He found Galltry in the Council Room alone. Did the man never go to his own castle? Galltry and Shildra's district technically encompassed Ironhold, but their home, a massive fortification of stone and painted plaster and gold gilding, was a day's ride to the southeast along the foothills.

Galltry pored over a massive map of northeast Mirat and the wilds beyond. His scruffy brows rose briefly at Reylin's entrance.

"How good to see you walking about, Prince Reylin," he said somewhat stiffly. "Are you feeling quite recovered from your collapse?"

"I wish to speak of the war, Galltry," said Reylin, raising his chin and gazing down his nose at the shorter man.

Galltry cleared his throat and straightened to face Reylin. He waved across the map at his grassland border. "We've endured a significant loss of life as a result of this aggressive push for the sake of the Miners Guild, Your Highness."

Reylin caught a slight emphasis on the last word, as though Galltry were spitting it out like poison. The anger from earlier boiled over. "Enough, Lord Galltry. The Council knew what we were getting into by supporting the East Face Mine, and it agreed with me. It's a viable direction for Mirat to grow; it just needs military support. Did you send a company like I asked?"

Galltry crossed his thin arms. "The Council did not deem it wise to respond with such a hostile display to the fyr. As you know, they're very reactive and territorial. Their ground attack was a direct rejoinder for the recent establishment of Halmani Mine. If we stop now, then the attacks should halt."

"That's beyond foolish," cried Reylin, slamming his fist on the table. The map edges fluttered outward. "It is time to eliminate the fyr, not bow to them. Where is your pride?"

Galltry didn't answer; he merely turned to the map and brushed it flat where Reylin had creased it. He pointed solemnly. "This border village is gone, Prince Reylin, because of Mirat's heedless expansion. Almost a thousand dead, injured, or homeless. Are you proud of that, son?"

His ribs seemed to crush inward as his chest tightened; his breath caught in his throat. A wave of hot rage burned through him—he could feel it flushing on his chest and neck and ears. He glowered at Galltry with all of his frustration and resentment. "The fyr did that, Lord Galltry. The fyr have pushed your border before, and never been met with a decisive answer to their savagery. It is time to end it and take the Loi al'Halmana for civilized people."

Galltry kept a level eye with him, despite Reylin's attempt to tower over him. He was calm, and he spoke in that reasonable, quiet tone, as a parent would to a child. "The Council decided to pull back from Halmani Mine, Prince Reylin. It presents a careless and needless risk. Consider the loss we've endured of innocent Miratians." He brightened with an almost fatherly smile. "Perhaps you should prepare a few words for the Summer Solstice Festival, to commemorate them."

A tingling warmth built in the corners of Reylin's eyes, but he blinked the irritating feeling back. "A speech, Galltry? That's what you want me to do?"

"The people would appreciate hearing you address such an unnecessary tragedy, and hear your revised plan. Something more reasonable for East Face's future."

Neither of them broke away from each other's gaze. Reylin's was fierce, as he wished he could burn a hole right through the man, and Galltry's was piteous. *Errant child, back down and remember you're not in charge.*

The idea in the back of Reylin's mind burst from its shadowy corner and into the light, and he relented with a gracious smile. "A speech you will have, Lord Galltry. I'll look forward to the Summer Solstice Festival."

Whether Galltry was aware of the relief flooding his lined face, Reylin did not know, but the tension between them dissolved, and the older man returned to examining the map.

Reylin watched the older lord and silently ground his teeth, then spun on his heel and marched out, ignoring Ronidann and Patreagh entirely. Kaiadin followed, his gliding movement sedate compared to Reylin's measured stalking. Both men exited the wing of the castle in which the Council Room sat and descended a flight of stairs. They had nearly reached the foyer before Kaiadin put a staying hand on Reylin's arm.

He leaned over to whisper in his ear. "West is wisest, my son, where you can demonstrate and develop your exceptional gift, but a foray to the east would not be a poor idea, if you could move quickly enough."

Reylin peered down each hall for listening ears, but there was no one besides a short Halmani slave dusting the decorative vases. The long arcade stretched beyond, filled with statues and carvings and more vases, and yet it seemed so empty. The entire castle, all of its grandeur and history, was meaningless to Reylin; his heritage was a joke and a lie. He broke into a bitter smile. "Precisely my thoughts, Father."

Father Kaiadin bobbed his head in understanding, and they hurried down the corridor to the gardens. Patreagh grumbled a little, confused at the next move, but Ronidann said nothing.

Reylin found Davon in the garden, playing with a strange creature in one of the large fountains, which was surrounded by a massive brick plaza. Reylin nearly tripped over his own toes as he stared at the scene. Davon's black attire dripped, and his dark hair clung to his skull. A crimson animal that looked somewhat familiar romped through the shallow water, circling the central pillar featuring several figurines of naked women. Every prancing movement splashed more water upon Davon, who laughed uncontrollably from where he perched, his arm slung around one of the figurines for support. The naked woman bore a string of tiny violets upon her bronze hair.

Both paused and looked up like adolescents caught in a mischievous act, and then Davon grinned.

"Your Highness, umm, Ar'we and I were just..." He cleared his throat and leapt from the pillar, then climbed out of the fountain and bowed properly. His breathless smile still stretched across his common visage.

But Reylin couldn't look away from Ar'we, who looked beyond disappointed at the abrupt end to her game. She observed him while languishing and rolling in the fountain, twisting her head every so often as a dancer would.

Bright day, Prince Reylin, she finally greeted him. He could hear the pique in her tone.

Davon reddened.

Reylin would have been slightly annoyed, but he was still processing Ar'we's appearance. "Keeper Davon, where are her wings?"

Davon straightened. "Oh, perhaps you haven't seen her do this before. Ar'we, come out of there and reassure His Highness that you can fly."

Of course I can fly, she answered curtly. *I was made to fly.*

"You were also made to dig, my heart." Davon waved her out of the fountain.

Reylin took an involuntary step backward as the massive creature padded toward them on all fours. Her sturdy forepaws were stout and muscled, with thick, elongated claws at the end of stubby knuckles. As he stared, her claws shrank to nothing, leaving only a single pinion, while the knuckles stretched and elongated with webbing in between each finger. She rocked back onto her hindlegs and stretched wide, revealing her rapidly growing wingspan in the bright sunshine. The thin skin stretched between each finger was nearly translucent, giving Reylin the impression that she glowed in the light.

He murmured his admiration, then realized his jaw was hanging slack. He snapped his mouth shut before Davon could notice. "I had no idea they could do that," he managed. His High Guard knights echoed his sentiment.

Davon turned back to them. "I didn't either until I met her." His possessive smile was so intimate, Reylin wanted to squirm. Dragonkeepers were strange people. Whatever this "Bond" was, it was not something he was comfortable with. Davon continued, unaware of the prince's apprehension. "How may we assist you, Your Highness?"

Reylin cleared his throat. "I'd like to visit the Halmani battlefront and bolster the troops deployed there, with your assistance."

Patreagh choked behind him, which Reylin ignored.

Davon's eyes widened slightly, then glazed as he conferred with Ar'we. It irritated Reylin; the dragonkeeper didn't simply obey like a subject should. Nonetheless, Davon agreed, and even Ar'we dipped her gigantic head toward him.

"We would be glad to help, Your Highness." Davon flipped his hair, though his bangs stuck to his forehead. "I'm afraid I must dry my riding leathers first though, or we'll risk sickening from the cold."

"His Highness can help you with that," said Kaiadin with a nod of encouragement.

Reylin raised both hands toward the dragonkeeper. He had never demonstrated this ability in front of anyone else, but the challenge was no different than his exercises with Kaiadin. He squinted to better focus, but he could see the shape of the lanky man in front of him in his mind's eye. Keeper Davon was soaked from head to toe. The algae-laden fountain water thoroughly infiltrated his clothing and sopping hair.

It tasted . . . green. Vegetal like a salad, but also a bit dirty. He should have someone clean this fountain.

He pulled the water away. It slicked down Davon's body and pooled at his feet until he stood in a shallow puddle. The water rolled its way into the crevices between the bricks and settled as Reylin dropped his hands.

Davon stared in shock as he watched the process, then plucked at his sleeve with a vague smile of understanding. "Thank you, Your Highness." Davon fluttered his black tunic loose from his skin, then scruffed his own hair.

Ar'we rumbled, a sound that could have been laughter, and Davon gave her a sharp look. "Well, how was I supposed to know? I couldn't do special things till I bonded with you . . ." He gnawed on his lip and gave Reylin a sheepish grin. "I suppose we're ready to depart whenever you are, sire. I merely need to place Ar'we's riding saddle."

Reylin acknowledged that. "I must retrieve my armor, but meet me as quickly as possible in the inner courtyard. I do not wish anything to hinder my departure."

"My prince?" Patreagh looked apologetic, but he scowled at the puddle like Gillead would. "I beg you not to do this. We cannot follow."

Ronidann's grin fell, and he looked at his comrade. In Gillead's absence, Patreagh had seniority.

"It's not your decision, and I won't be long," said Reylin with a dismissive wave. "Tell Sir Gillead where I've gone afterward."

Patreagh looked like he wanted to argue, but instead, he addressed Davon. "Keeper Davon, Ar'we? We are entrusting you with the care of our prince. Do you accept this responsibility?"

Davon glanced at the dragon, then nodded quickly.

"Swear it."

The dragonkeeper knelt. "I swear, I will serve and protect His Highness to the best of my ability." His words, unrefined and without the embellishments of the Temple or the court, rang true in Reylin's ears. Ar'we echoed them in his head.

Patreagh accepted the oaths solemnly and sighed, seeming suddenly older than he already was.

Ronidann's grin returned as they returned to the castle. "My prince? When the fyr attacked Miratian soil, they *fouled* up." He snorted at his own wordplay, then sobered at Gillead's rebuke. "Be careful, Your Highness, and bring us back a few feathers."

TERROR ATE AT LYRA. Despite a dreamless sleep, praise the Light, her fear had returned upon waking without Konan, in a strange tent with a strange girl watching over her.

The girl had left immediately and returned with the Godspeaker, who finally gave her a much longer draught of water. He spoke in the Old Language to her, explaining again that she had the water-sickness but would improve soon with rest and careful recuperation. Cupping her face with his ancient hands, he examined her eyes.

Lyra struggled to find all of the words to reply. As a people of deep faith and as practitioners of both low and high magika, the Maskalan had spoken some of the Old Language, but it wasn't exactly a conversational tongue. She was fundamentally aware of how limited her vocabulary was.

Suggesting they would meet again later, the Godspeaker left her to the girl, Korahel, with a wrinkled smile and respectful bow. Lyra had never been bowed to by anyone but a suitor, and those bows had been more nods of the head accompanied by formal kisses on the hand. No one bowed to her. She looked after the Godspeaker with some confusion, but then remembered how awed they had been to realize she was a thral ol'I'ya.

She flinched when Korahel took her hand but followed the girl to a larger tent with a bed and bath, where several others about her age were waiting. Lyra spied the long tub with fresh, clear water. Delicate pink and orange blossoms floated on the surface, and Korahel added a bowlful of pink salts that gave off an energizing scent as they dissolved. Beside the bath was a tray of soaps, oils, and scented cleansing sand.

Apprehension twisted inside of Lyra as Korahel led her to the middle of the room and began to chatter at the other helpers.

They all seemed friendly, but she couldn't help trembling as one unclasped her cloak and swept it from her shoulders. They pulled at her piecemeal clothing, tugging at the tunic and muttering at the dingy cloth. Once that had been pulled from her head, the breast binding was unknotted. Lyra crossed her arms and covered herself, battling tears of fear and anger. The girls exclaimed at her beautiful form with what sounded like words of encouragement, and one plucked at her forearm with a bright smile.

She lashed out in a fluster, flicking off the girl's hold of her arm. Air accompanied the motion, knocking the girl back into the gaggle and shocking the crowd into silence. Lyra hadn't meant for it to happen, but the irate voice inside refused to apologize. She crossed her arms once again and hugged herself. She felt utterly exposed.

Korahel approached carefully, her lilac-colored eyes wide with concern. She looked over Lyra's form, her half-undone bindings, then knotted her brow and said something sharp to the other girls. They quieted and turned away as one.

Korahel gestured at her pants and then to the discard pile, then waited to see if Lyra understood. Lyra nodded. Quietly, the girl stepped around to her back and finished unknotting the breast bindings, then stepped away with her eyes averted.

Lyra darted into the water and immersed herself, torn between resentment and guilt. She sobbed, but then gulped it back. The women were trying to help, and none of them wanted to hurt her, but the idea of anyone staring at her made her want to rage like a windstorm. It made her want to destroy things, to suffocate the offenders.

She caught herself. Only part of her wanted that. The other part thanked Korahel as the maiden handed her a scrubbing cloth.

Korahel released the other girls to assist, and they fluttered about, offering her soaps and fresh cloths, adding flowers and salts to the water and chattering amiably amongst themselves. It made Lyra sick with nerves. Korahel watched patiently, restraining the others' eager hands, although helping was precisely the function of all the girls.

Lyra didn't want help, or more accurately, she didn't want to *need* help. She focused on scrubbing her skin clean of the countless weeks of grime—sweat, blood, urine, dirt. She rubbed the areas that had been purple or yellow a month before, as if she could scour the warden's touch away. That thought made her scrub harder, turning her skin an angry pink in several spots. She wept, locked in her memories. It couldn't be cleaned. No matter how hard she scrubbed, bringing tiny red spots out in fresh bruising, it couldn't be cleaned.

When her skin smarted too much for any more, she held the cloth out to Korahel with a trembling hand.

Korahel took it away, then showed her a new bowl of pale green salts. Although she explained in Manalali, Lyra thought she understood. The bowl smelled of grassy herbs and calcium, ingredients of spiritual cleansing. Lyra would have mixed something similar for purification and sold it as green magika. Korahel dumped the entire bowl in; it hissed and bubbled, and its volatile scents grew stronger. She gestured for Lyra to wet her hair.

Lyra knew Korahel merely wished to help, and she swallowed back her hesitation as she dunked her curls. Seeming to perceive her discomfiture, Korahel began to sing a lilting melody as she rubbed soap into Lyra's long mat of tangles. The other girls joined in. The song sounded like a lullaby based on its rhythm and notes, but Lyra didn't understand the words. Korahel worked her scalp to a lather, massaging as gently as she could through the knotted mess. Lyra almost sighed despite herself.

Mam used to wash her hair, long ago when Lyra had developed her bouncing ringlets.

"Cut it once, and it's never straight again," Mam had declared, shaking her head with dismay despite the fact that Lyra's curls were nearly identical to her own.

The slight tug and massage reminded Lyra so much of her mother's touch that she began to cry again. Korahel paused, and Lyra apologized. "I just miss my mam," Lyra whispered, allowing her to continue.

Korahel had the string of helpers bring in fresh buckets of warm water, and she dumped them a pitcher at a time over Lyra's hair, rinsing it cleaner than it had been in ages. The girl seemed almost contrite when she gestured for Lyra to get out of the tub, offering a large, supple drying hide and commanding the others to look away. Korahel rebound her breasts with a proper underbody corset, cinching the garment securely and quickly, and Lyra scrambled into a light, short shift.

When the other girls were allowed to turn around, they made no comments on Lyra's body, nor did they flutter about touching her. Korahel had her sit, and they worked a conditioning oil into her hair, starting at the bottom of Lyra's kinky lengths and sliding the knots out one stubborn tangle at a time. Eventually, Korahel was able to comb it through until it flowed, and Lyra had to admit there was something mesmerizing and calming about that. As her hair dried, it got frizzier and lighter, but the oil helped. Korahel secured it with several ornaments and bands, drawing it back from Lyra's face.

Then they insisted on dressing her. First, they pulled a thicker dress over her head, this one decorated with gleaming silver beads and sequins on the chest and wrists. Although their touches were delicate and unassuming, Lyra's stomach still twisted and churned with nausea and nerves. One girl's fingers brushed her belly, and Lyra recalled the warden kicking her in the gut—the pain after, the ugly black mark that had spread across her abdomen.

She convulsed, falling to the ground and shaking for minutes.

Korahel knelt beside her and murmured words of comfort until she recovered. The other women waited in silence until Korahel ordered them to resume their work, dressing Lyra layer by layer.

Over the sparkling shift, they wrapped a bright red patch-work skirt, a gorgeous creation with patterned textiles embroidered and set with more sequins on alternating patches. It didn't have flaring layers like the skirts Lyra used to wear, but it was beautiful. Korahel cinched a looser-fitting fashion bodice with beadwork patterning on the front; this style reached high over Lyra's chest instead of emphasizing it. She sighed with relief. Manalali clothing was conservative, but also airy and well-adapted to the constant summer sun.

They slipped a sleek black open-fronted robe over her shoulders, and she pushed her arms into the long silken sleeves. A gauzy black shawl edged in crimson thread and silver coins floated over top of the robe, and a heavy sil-ver-chained necklace with dangling garnets was fastened around her neck. Jeweled handflowers were placed on her wrists, connected with delicate silver chains to rings on her fingers. Each handflower was embedded with tiny rubies and garnets that matched her necklace.

Finally, a woman placed a silver circlet studded with a ruby and minute orange gems on her head. The circlet had a skirting of silver coins covering her ears and back of her head, and they attached a matching gauzy black veil across her face. The servant murmured to another, and the second one's eyes widened; she stared at Lyra with renewed awe. "Thral ol'I'ya . . ." she murmured in a soft voice, then lowered her gaze and bowed. They both stepped back, and Lyra got a reprieve.

As one, their tone changed from friendliness to awe, and she began to understand that she was dressed as an honored guest. The circlet alone was an indicator; orange gems were never worn by anyone without high station. It had to be the work of the Godspeaker, who had already called her a thral once before.

She touched the veil fastened across her cheeks and sighed with relief at the anonymity. Her handflowers sparkled in front of her eyes, and she realized she had never worn anything so stunning in her life. She had seen plenty of small decorative rubies and garnets inset into their products, but the Maskalan didn't specialize in jewelry.

Korahel took the bejeweled hand and guided her toward the door, where Lyra paused to draw in a slow breath. Despite the draping, loose layers and Korahel's care, she felt vulnerable in this strange new place.

Then she stepped into the bright sunlight of late morning.

She blinked as blindness shimmered into an extraordinary blue sky, sandy pavement, sage-green grasses and bright green cacti, and brown hide tents. And two familiar silhouettes, which resolved into men.

Thordrin and Konan stood in front of her, both of them clean-shaven and with their hair trimmed, both adorned in practical Manalali clothing, plainer than her own but still striking. Thordrin crossed his arms and gave her a smug look, holding his chin high. His closely cropped hair reminded her that he really was a knight. He was no prisoner, and he was finally being treated more appropriately for his station.

"Looking good, Lyr," said Thordrin, breaking the silence with a smirk. He nudged Konan hard enough that the man twitched.

Konan's trimmed hair flowed in dark chestnut locks to his shoulders and had been carefully divided to partially cover the patchy spot on his temple and his malformed ear. His sparse and erratically grown beard was gone, with nothing to hide his pocked cheek. His scars, as wickedly shocking as they already were, bled in a few spots, and they looked redder and angrier in the bright light.

Konan looked down at the ground, then back up at Lyra. "You look beautiful," he signed. His one cheek turned scarlet.

A strange, nasty-tasting sense of self-loathing filled Lyra, and she rejected his compliment, squeezing her eyes shut against the dark thoughts that battered her.

Then she felt his roughly callused finger and thumb on her chin, and she pulled herself from the mire. She was face-to-face with his intense gaze. Any hint of a smile—if there had been one—was gone, and he looked terribly sad again. One eyebrow knotted, while the other stayed stiffly in place. He reprimanded her kindly. "No one can take that away from you, Lyra. Do you understand?"

She nodded.

"Don't be ashamed of your scars," he signed. His powerful gaze slid to her wild curls, and he brushed them back with a tentative touch, seeming to appreciate the smoothness imbued by the fragrant oils.

She tore herself from his mismatched eyes, which now explored her mane of hair along with his fingers. How could she not be ashamed? But he wasn't.

His beige tunic was cut down the center and loose-fitting, and she found herself reaching up to brush across the fine dark hair and push the collar aside. She heard him suck in a breath, and his chest rose and fell a little faster. She traced the lines of scar damage, so much more visible in the sunlight and without his old layers of coverings; they ran up his neck and throat like lightning. His chin and cheek looked sore—he had been nicked several times. Lyra grimaced for him, for his pain old and new, then realized his gaze had returned to her as she touched the wavy hair by his ear.

She blushed.

His hair was unexpectedly soft, properly trimmed and treated. He had probably not felt that himself in years. She dropped her hand.

"You do look beautiful, Lyra," he repeated. Then he contorted his face. "Although you were beautiful before."

He stumbled through a few other signs, then stopped with a frustrated exhale and clenched his fists, as if to stop himself from speaking further.

"The fuck are you two saying?" Thordrin complained. "I hope more than the clan leader and his son can speak the common language. I'm sick of you both."

Her words caught in her throat, so she signed at Konan. "Thank you." She did mean it, she realized soberly. She was barely maintaining composure, bathed by a gaggle of curious women and dressed in foreign clothing and forced into a new environment that was somehow even farther from home. Konan was a pillar.

An elderly woman approached them and pulled Lyra from his hold, drawing her away while bantering in Manalali. Her hand trailed back toward Konan, who wore a look of dismay as her fingers slipped from his. Korahel muttered warnings, and Lyra whimpered, but then Shirkaa's confident accented voice boomed out behind her.

"Do not worry, my friends," he announced to Konan and Thordrin. "Old mother will introduce her to the other women of the village, and then to the Godspeaker. Come now, and I'll show you the village."

Korahel squeezed Lyra's other hand, as if searching her for signs of panic, but the old mother would not relent, and they were dragged along regardless.

The women of the village fussed over Lyra, giving her water and feeding her a scathingly spicy meat dish over porridge. She attacked it voraciously, but then the women hovered over her, commenting on her hair and plucking at her clothes. Korahel, who was apparently assigned to her as a handmaiden, seemed to understand her apprehension and increasing unease, and swept her away as soon as was socially acceptable.

Korahel guided her to a large, well-appointed tent with scarlet-dyed canvas walls. The tent opened into a foyer with a bench and chairs, and they removed their shoes. The floor beyond was carpeted, and the next room exuded a wild combination of scents.

The old man beamed at Lyra's entrance into the work room, which was stacked with baskets and pots. Everything exuded powerful herbal and floral scents; the Air contained so much of everything that Lyra thought back to the vineyards of Marlemet. She had to stop to take it all in.

It was clear the Godspeaker was the tribe's most powerful mage, and perhaps its religious leader. He was likely their herbsman as well, a medicine man. His supplies reminded her of the caravan's herbal storage wagons, where her aunties would go to produce the many spells and potions for sale. Only somehow, his collection was even more vast and diverse, and riddled with strange-looking jars containing items with which she was unfamiliar.

Korahel bowed respectfully to both of them and placed herself in the foyer, out of their way.

The Godspeaker, unassuming as ever, shambled up to Lyra and gave her a wizened grin. His glittering violet eyes peered out from the folds of wrinkles. "Thral ol'I'ya," he stated in stilted Old Language. "Thral, you know how Manalal find?" His command of the Old Language was better than most, but still halting and piecemeal, and it was the only tongue they shared.

Lyra shook her head. So much from that night and the time before was a dream interspersed with a nightmare, the edges blurred and the words muffled. Sinking sands. Cattle droppings. Ada grunting a warning and Elden laughing. Waking from a dehydrated stupor, she had seen the desert warriors and tried to call upon the Air, but the old man had stopped her with an immobility spell. She had never experienced *that* before, but it had felt as though the power drained away from her, as though she were an empty shell. She had been so weak, so dizzy, and seeing things that she now knew weren't there. She hadn't even been sure it was a spell until later.

Now, she was actually quite sure it hadn't been that powerful of a spell. If she hadn't been so weak . . .

The old man shook his head solemnly. "We follow Water."

"You knew the oasis?" Lyra's practice of Old Language was mediocre but serviceable. She was surprised she remembered the word. Or was that the word for "green"?

"Tahayi Mother is dry, her children few. Sands hold little, even for great Manalal. No, thral, we know no Water until we feel it. Like sandstorm, we follow."

"Thralais, I don't understand," Lyra replied, recalling the honorific for a mentor mage.

"You called the Water, thral?"

Lyra was confused at his line of questions. She had summoned the wind, certainly, but the oasis had been a miracle of the Five-Faced God. She recalled the disappointment on Thordrin's face when she pulled the pathetically wispy cloud from the west. She recalled Konan's stoic acceptance, his lack of anger at her failure. In fact, she was fairly certain he had turned that anger on himself for insisting they go north.

The oasis was their salvation. Perhaps she wasn't abandoned.

She finally answered the Godspeaker, but he peered intently at her, seemingly into her. "Thral, Mother did not send this Water. You bring Water." He stamped his staff, completely assured of his words.

Lyra thought to answer, but a sharp pain coursed through her body, and she staggered. The spicy breakfast lurched up the back of her throat, and weakness loosened her muscles. Fear blasted out of her bones, and she lashed out with a wave of wind.

The Godspeaker fell backward, tumbling ungraciously in a pile of bones on the rug-covered floor, then uttered a shielding spell and came to her aid.

The lancing pain frightened and confused her, and she lashed out several more times before diminishing in a trembling heap. Her blood pounded in her ears, and she curled into a tight ball and sobbed.

The Godspeaker squatted beside her, clutching to his staff for balance. "Do not fear, thral. Mother gives you power, much much power, but Mother punishes greed. Iyasan anthe'brin."

She shuddered, and they sat together a while longer. Korahel lingered a few steps back, looking unsure, but then the Godspeaker ordered her about. In a moment, they presented Lyra with a tonic for water-sickness.

Lyra recovered shortly but continued to mull over the Godspeaker's words. Had she called the Water, as she called the Air? Had she somehow created the oasis? She had never heard of anyone with that kind of magika.

Even the wayfarers, blessed as they were, did not have such power in their ranks. The legends they told, the ballads they sang, and the stories they danced implied that the magika had once burned inside the great warriors. It alighted King Shastid like a torch barreling down the battlefield and fueled the fire on Gattlin's battle-axe, but such things had faded over time. The blood had thinned and finally been staunched during the dark days of the Empire's fall, when the Luminaries did their bloody work. The Maskalan, like many wayfaring caravans, had endured that age by running, fast and far, with their families to the ends of roads, to the edges, to the difficult terrain where the Empire's priests did not follow.

Powerful, transformative, world-changing magika had nearly died out in the more sedentary peoples of Midgate as the Great Cleansing washed over the land.

Lyra had power, but not over Water.

Neither did Elden, nor her aunties or uncles. Mam could Whisper a little, and she could control a breeze to cool the horses, and she could sing like a bird in spring, but that was all. The Maskalan were Air-blessed, as well as talented in green magic.

Yet they had brought the Water?

"Thralais?" Her whisper was soft and entreating, and the Godspeaker attended her with a gentle arm, moving her to a low sedan in the foyer. She swallowed nervously and stumbled through the Old Language. "Thralais, can you teach me?"

The Godspeaker's cheeks wrinkled into a gleeful smile. "Mother gives this gift. If is Mother's will, I teach you all," he replied. He drew a soft blanket around her with shaky hands. "Rest now. *I'ya'hakkat* tests you. Harsh dry Mother." He made another potion and set it beside her for later, then left.

Korahel brought several other female servants to attend Lyra, but she felt more and more alone as the day waned. Being alone and awake gave her far too much time to ponder the Godspeaker's words (*I'm different*), recall their escape from Tahayi (*I killed the warden*), and recall the desperate moment in which she gave up (*I will never escape him*).

Relief washed over her when Konan strode into the tent. He flicked servants aside as they pulled at his sleeves to leave, and he finally growled at them before kneeling by her sedan. Korahel slipped out in a huff, discontent riddling her brow.

"I heard you cry out," he signed. "I'm sorry I didn't come sooner."

Lyra looked down. "It's just water-sickness from dehydration. The Godspeaker said it would go away after a few days." She sighed and made space for him beside her. "I've had enough of all of this. I'm neither hungry nor satiated. I'm exhausted but can't sleep for the nightmares. There's so much I need to talk about, to talk through, but we've hardly had a moment to breathe."

Konan settled at her side, and she leaned her head on his shoulder. He automatically shifted to stroke her hair, this time pulling his fingers through the ends of the bouncy curls that hung below the shimmering skirted circlet on her head. The sensation sent a tickle of both pleasure and calm across her scalp, and she buried her cheek against him. He was warm, and despite the veneer of palmnut oil and cactus flowers rubbed into his skin, he still had his familiar musk.

"We're alive," he signed. He hesitated. Then, "I'm glad we are alive."

"So you can get me home, I know." She almost rolled her eyes. "You need to live for more than that, Konan."

"I am."

She twisted her chin up to look at him, and they sat in awkward silence until Korahel pushed her way into the tent, leading the Godspeaker. Her cheeks flushed when she saw how they sat together, and she gibbered irately to the elderly man. The Godspeaker dismissed her, and she stood back and glared.

The Godspeaker chuckled as he evaluated them. "Forgive, friends," he said in Old Language. Lyra translated as he ducked out of the tent and returned with Jikaa.

Jikaa stopped short, then cocked an eyebrow at Konan and spoke in the common language. "A man must not enter a woman's tent unless he is her husband or brother. This is the way of the Desert Mother."

Lyra felt Konan tense beneath her cheek, and his arm around her shoulder tightened in defiance.

Then Jikaa softened. "But you are not of the desert, and you did not know."

Lyra sat up straighter and pointed toward the Godspeaker. "But my lord Thralais attended me himself."

Jikaa chuckled, and Konan stopped bristling. "True, but he is a servant of I'ya'hakkat and has no affinity for man or woman. He is pure like the desert winds." Jikaa offered a hand up to Konan. "However, *you* really must leave. I cannot allow it." He pulled Konan toward the entrance.

Korahel followed, battering at Konan's back and half pushing him as he reluctantly departed. She said something rude-sounding in Manalali and dusted her hands, then remained in the doorway like a guard.

The Godspeaker stooped carefully down to look directly into Lyra's face. He leaned on his staff. "You have Desert Mother's gift, thral. *Benned ol'I'ya'hakkat.* I feel Water gift. You call the Water and more."

She gulped and nodded, her mind still dancing around Konan's words. *I am.* What did that mean?

The Godspeaker stamped his staff. "Thral teaches Manalal; Manalal teach thral." He handed her the tonic, and she drank it in one swig.

48

WHEN THE GODSPEAKER WAS content with her physical condition, he released her from her rest. He warned her again of eating or drinking greedily.

Her stomach grumbled nevertheless, and Korahel revealed that she had prepared a pot of stew over a small fire outside Lyra's quarters. The handmaiden crumbled spices into the stew along with chunks of meat and vegetables. Lyra protested weakly, recalling the heat of breakfast, but Korahel gave her a look. *Trust me. I know what you thought of breakfast,* it said. Lyra subsided and watched the maid grind some round grains into a powder, then add it as a thickener.

Lyra managed to communicate that she wished to eat outside as well, thereby allowing Konan and Thordrin to join her, and again Korahel gave her a look.

The men attended them shortly.

"Are you well?" Konan asked. The corner of his mouth twisted into a lopsided expression when she acknowledged him; the left side, taut with scar tissue, didn't change as much. "Good."

"Hey love," Thordrin greeted her in higher spirits than she had seen him in a long while. "Who's your lady companion?" He winked at Korahel, who merely raised a dark eyebrow as she ladled stew into bowls for each of them. She didn't even look at him.

They scarfed the food down. After malnourishment, a full belly felt strange, as though she were stretching unused muscles. Lyra hoped this serving would stay down, partially because she needed the energy and partially because it was truly delicious. She should have trusted Korahel more.

Konan offered a second helping, and Lyra was about to say yes when Korahel stopped her.

"Iyasan anthe'brin," the girl warned.

To Korahel's dismay, the men eagerly finished their bowls, eventually consuming every drop of liquid in the pot. She flared her nostrils in dismay.

Lyra's stomach churned, and her body ached.

"They really dressed you up, Lyr," Thordrin commented. He gestured at her hair and veil, then the sparkling hand-flowers. "I thought we had it good till I saw you." If he was feigning jealousy, he was doing a poor job; instead, it sounded like a compliment.

"They recognized your power, like a Temple mage," suggested Konan.

"But I'm not a Temple mage," Lyra said quietly, looking down. Her cheeks felt warm. She examined the complex textiles of her skirt, then noticed the garnet-studded leather straps on her sandals. She gasped. Gemstone-studded sandals weren't that common. *The noblewoman of Shayal*, her mind screamed.

"You didn't notice your sandals when they put 'em on?" Thordrin laughed.

"I was . . . It was a lot to take in." She crossed her arms and was pleased to see that the beadwork bodice and undertunic covered her cleavage.

Thordrin chuckled. "It was, but damn it, it was all nice." He scrubbed his smooth chin. "I even found the second step to my escape plan. Remember, Konan?"

"What second step?" Lyra asked.

"Take a hot bath, and then—"

Konan growled at him to be quiet, signing the same despite Thordrin's lack of understanding. Konan shot an embarrassed glance at Lyra, then changed the subject.

"You may not be a Temple mage, but you are as powerful as one. Everyone can see it, friend or enemy."

She lifted her jeweled hands in frustration. "I don't want this special treatment, although I do like the face veil. I like all of their clothing, actually, but I don't like the attention. I just want to go home. I miss my mam."

Konan's mouth twitched again, and his cheek ticced. "Soon."

"We can get out of here as soon as we help Lord Shirkaa," Thordrin declared with confidence. "I don't want to be here any longer than necessary either, but at least he's asking for something easy."

Lyra looked at him with disbelief. "To help him fight a war?"

Konan's expression echoed her own.

The other man shrugged. "Sure, could be fun. Come now, Lyr, you should enjoy it. He said it had to do with his own daughter being taken. Think about that. These Haralal people deserve to die, and you get to be part of it." He grinned.

"I . . . I may think they're in the wrong, but killing is still a sin," she said with weak conviction. Her insides twisted, and the shrill inner voice of anger rejected her answer.

"By whose law?" Thordrin challenged, oblivious to how much he echoed the inner voice. "That of the one who allowed you to be put in the mine? That of the warden? The only law is what you *can* do, and what you *can't* do. What you can make others do, or what you can't make others do."

Lyra thought about that. She was angry. If I'ya was real, how could he be so unfaithful to someone like her? She had worshiped him all her life. Still, where did her gift come from if not from him? What was the Eye, if not his physical form watching over her daily?

"Murder *is* wrong," affirmed Konan.

She agreed, and Thordrin rolled his eyes.

"However, retribution for the girl is not murder," Konan added, catching Lyra's eye meaningfully.

Thordrin had already pulled himself from the conversation, turning his attention to Korahel. She seemed vaguely amused, but not particularly interested in his games, and she eventually escaped to clean up the meal.

Konan touched her hand to get her attention. "Lyra, we will have to do some things we don't want to do, to be free. Think about your family. Do whatever it takes to get back to them."

"And what will you do?"

"I'll do whatever I have to, to make a new life."

She narrowed her eyes. That was more esoteric than usual, but he didn't elaborate.

The Godspeaker and Jikaa approached then and bid them follow. Together, they walked to the edge of the village by a stone well and looked out to an expanse of rocky desert interspersed with cacti and jutting stones.

Konan's stiff gait reminded Lyra that he was likely sore, and she marveled that he was walking at all. She felt bad for not asking sooner.

The Godspeaker began to lecture in Manalali, and Jikaa translated. "This land, the land of I'ya'hakkat, is created of Fire and Earth, not of Water. The Manalal, like many tribes, survive by moving across the Desert Mother's breast from well to well, staying until her milk runs dry. Power of wind and water"—the Godspeaker nodded at Lyra—"is power over this land. Power enough to defeat the Haralal. You will help the Manalal, good children of Tahayi, with this power, yes?"

Lyra hesitated. "I only want to defend myself, Thralais. I don't want to hurt anyone."

"The viper that does not bite will be crushed underfoot," said the Godspeaker decisively. He stamped his staff on the ground.

Lyra stammered.

"And our Lord Shirkaa has crushed many vipers who did not use their teeth," Jikaa added.

The Godspeaker stared at Lyra severely, leaning forward on his staff. His former friendliness had disappeared, and it was obvious he expected her agreement.

Thordrin nudged her and muttered, "You don't have a choice, Lyr. He ain't asking."

Konan agreed.

She nodded fearfully, and so they began. The Godspeaker asked Lyra to demonstrate her power, and she summoned small bouts of wind, which swirled chaotically around the group, pushing them about until they staggered. Next, she summoned a gale, which blew across the expanse, tumbling blossoms off the cacti and stirring up gritty sand and dust. She would begin by bringing her hands low, summoning the power from deep and low, then bringing it forth in a crescendo with her hands raised high before swinging them in the intended direction. Her vision would often blur as she focused on something abstract, something complex that was felt and not seen, and would stay intent upon the target of her magic until the spell was done. She slumped after the gale, and her chest heaved with effort. This magic was not paltry, but powerful. It sapped the energy from her bones.

Konan gently pushed her into a sitting position on the edge of the well, supporting her by the small of her back to ensure she didn't fall.

The Godspeaker absorbed it all quietly, allowing Lyra to demonstrate her strength with only a small shielding spell to keep the winds at bay from his precarious stance.

When she sat, he pondered a moment, then addressed her through Jikaa. "You have created a tempest of Air. Your gift with the wind is impressive, unlike any I have seen. I believe you can do the same with Water, drawing it from one place and sending it to another." He turned to the well, which had been dug deep and had a glint of murk at the bottom. "Do the same, to this water."

With a heavy sigh, she glanced doubtfully down the well, a movement echoed by Konan and Thor. The water was far below. "Thralais, I do not know Water magic," she mumbled in a small voice.

"Relax your arms, your body, your mind, young one." The Godspeaker seemed quite confident. "Close your eyes, guard your thoughts, and focus only on yourself. Feel that strength deep within you, that warmth in your loins, that heat in your belly, the source of all your will to be and sur-vive. That strength made you cross the desert, that faith told you we were here, beyond the terrible mines."

The thought of the mines made her tense, and the Godspeaker nodded approval.

"Yes, *that* source, the center of you that cringes when you're hurt, that tenses when you are afraid, that sickens with your heart. This is where you must begin. Draw from this source, will the magika from this source, and guide it with your mind." The Godspeaker lifted his staff slightly and made a twirling motion with the bottom. The water at the bottom of the well rippled slightly, then began to spin in a weak whirlpool.

Lyra watched it with fascination, leaning forward too far. Konan caught her with a quick arm around her waist and righted her. His grip was sure and warm. They stared down together.

The Godspeaker stopped and again pounded his staff in the sand. The water became still. Then he took Lyra's hand and hung it palm-down over the well. "You can move the water, as I did, if you command it. Again, close your eyes and focus on that strength. Now, extend that focus to your hand. Let it creep out, from your shoulder to your arm, to your fingers, and hold it there." The Godspeaker's voice trembled with excitement, as did Jikaa's translating echo. A strange pulse emanated through the air, a heartbeat, subtle but present, of magic. "Hold that focus, hold that energy, young one. Now, extend it down from your fingertips, reach out to the water at the bottom of the well. Touch it."

Lyra tried. Knowing Konan had her by the waist, she poured all her focus into the exercise, reaching, feeling, although she didn't think she felt anything beyond the dry air in which her hand hovered. His grip on her tightened as she leaned over the well with her eyelids scrunched tight. She chewed on her lower lip, trying to do as the Godspeaker said.

She didn't really feel like she was connecting with the water below, but she did sense an accumulation of power around her. It flowed and ebbed and twitched.

Thordrin cursed under his breath, making Lyra open her eyes. The water below suddenly rippled outward in concentric circles, lapping the wall and reverberating back. She gasped and clutched at Konan's arm with excitement. He stared down into the well, one eyebrow quirked up higher than the other in surprise.

The Godspeaker beamed at her and banged his staff again in excitement. "By the sands, young one, it *was* you. I'ya'hakkat has given your gift for the glory of the Manalal. Praise to the good Mother!" cried the old man.

The Godspeaker gleefully led Lyra through more motions, guiding her focus until the water spun around in a circle, sloshing back and forth against the well walls in a messy, overlapping pattern. He used her hand to guide the motion, although the smoothness of his guiding motions was not reflected in the erratic upsurges below. Konan and Thordrin watched intently, both rapt in their attention.

"You are such a gift from the Desert Mother." The Godspeaker's wide, wrinkly smile cracked from ear to ear. "Rest now, rest well. We will need more of your energy soon." He turned and hobbled into camp on Jikaa's arm, disappearing into Shirkaa's tent.

All three watched until the two Manalali disappeared, and they were alone at the well. The water below had stilled entirely, as though Lyra had never touched it.

"Our service to them will be over soon," said Thordrin, staring after them suspiciously. "Shirkaa told us he called his people in for battle. Some are already here, and the last will arrive over the next week or so."

Konan squinted after the Godspeaker, his face contorted into a scowl. "I don't trust them," he signed.

"What do they need my magic for?" asked Lyra. "I don't want to hurt anyone if I don't have to."

"Nor I," Konan agreed, "but your magika is your strongest weapon. I assume they will want our arms and your power during the battle with the Haralal."

Lyra translated for Thordrin, and he sneered. "Is it really so bad? Who cares who we have to kill to get home? And the Manalal are good hosts; they treat us well." He pulled at his finery, rubbing the soft fabric between his fingers.

It fit him well, emphasizing his athletic build and narrow waist, and the golden necklace contrasted with his emerald eyes. Even without armor, he looked like a respectable, highborn man. If not for how nervous she felt, Lyra would have laughed at that irony.

"They want something from us, that's all," said Konan.

"Everyone wants something, and I'm fine doing it as long as I'm well paid. I hate to fight for Shirkaa's clemency, but if it's a war, there will be spoils." Thordrin spat with disgust, likely directed at the clan leader.

Lyra pondered that for a while. It was true the Manalal had saved them from wretched starvation and thirst, aided them with medical care and comforts beyond anything she had experienced before—she had certainly never had her own pavilion or servants. Thordrin's cough had already eased, and they were clean and perfumed. They each wore clothing generously gifted and of high rank. She glanced down at the crimson-and-black apparel that hung from her frame; the garnets sparkled in the sunshine. Crimson seemed to be the color of the Manalali god, this I'ya'hakkat or Desert Mother. Lyra wasn't sure if it was heresy to wear it instead of I'ya's indigo, but she hadn't been given a choice.

Lyra had her own private tent with Korahel at hand and an unending train of female helpers, and the two men shared a large tent with two dedicated servants. One, Mirra, seemed shy, but the other . . . Lyra blushed thinking about Thordrin's obvious inclination toward that one. Lyra had noticed she had a brand on her wrist, something Korahel and Mirra did not have, but she didn't know what to make of it. The woman was pretty, and no maiden.

Lyra's heart skipped a few beats. Neither was she. Perhaps she shouldn't judge the woman so harshly.

Thordrin was an attractive man, reasonably tall, taut with muscle, with short, dusky hair bleached by the sun. His broad cheekbones supported somewhat shallow-set eyes that twinkled green under a heavy brow and flat, wide forehead. His dark blond beard grew thick, giving him a shadow within a day. Even now, she could see the slight stubble. His jaw was square and his smile easy, creating a dimple on either cheek whether he showed his teeth or not. When he grinned, his narrow eyes would squint with merriment and his cheeks would rise, highlighting his lower lids. His mirth always seemed authentic, even when it was cruel.

She envied his entire outlook on life, carefree and confident. Of *course* he would be successful in seducing his handservant, as Lyra had once been successful in seducing her audience with Miridi's dance. How innocent and carefree she had been once. She sighed sadly, and Konan glanced over at her.

"We must do what is necessary," he said. "I don't like it either, but at least it's for Shirkaa's daughter. Endure this trial, and we can go home. We may even do something good."

"It doesn't feel right."

"You two and your 'sanctity of life' bullshit," muttered Thordrin. "By the Light, I can almost believe you're a noble, with that kind of high-and-mighty ethic, totally disconnected from reality. The world is shit, and there is no right or wrong."

"Better to be a king of hell?" Lyra said, irritated.

"When there is no heaven, love? Sure."

Konan and Thordrin led her through the parts of the village that the old mother had skipped over: the stables and pens, the training yard, and the extensive encampment of residents, men who seemed to be both warrior and herdsman. Many of them appeared to have families with them, and there was no dedicated barracks. Children scampered past, fighting with sticks and screaming laughter, and women scurried about on various tasks. Many of the men practiced in the open yard, including Jikaa.

Jikaa later invited them to a pleasant supper, then informed them of their invitation to Shirkaa's war meeting the next day. Stumbling with exhaustion by the meal's end, Lyra leaned on Konan as they walked back to their tents. He reluctantly stopped at the entrance and peered in.

"Will you be all right, alone?" he asked.

Korahel was the only one inside, and she frowned at him.

Lyra nodded, although she wasn't sure. She offered an apprehensive smile.

He helped her onto Korahel's supporting shoulder, and Lyra entered the tent. A plush bed had been arranged for her, with layers of colorful quilted blankets over a stuffed mattress. Its pillows were softer than those of the previous night, its blankets finer. She sank into the heavenly bed and was already fading as Korahel made herself comfortable in a simpler bed on the other wall.

She slept.

As she so often did, she woke with a shudder and whimpered from the eternal, repeating nightmare. The warden was there, alive in her dreams, chasing her, hitting her, knocking her down and kicking her like a dog. Laughing mercilessly. She burned with hatred, then froze with fear, until she emerged from the subconscious waters in a cold sweat. And then Konan was there, rushing in and catching her as she rolled violently off the bed. Her sheets fluttered outward in a burst of Air.

She landed in his extended arms and nestled into him, still trying to evade the warden in her dreams, and he clutched her close for minutes. Then he laid her back in the blankets and tucked them more securely around her.

Ignoring Korahel's whispered chastisement, he hummed. It was an odd sound coming from him, but one meant to comfort her in lieu of a shush. It reminded her of Ada. Ada was the reason she had learned to sign, she thought sleepily as she gazed up at Konan. Konan brushed her hair from her sweaty forehead, then placed his hand on her cheek and looked at her. His humming turned to a real melody, one she had heard in her childhood as a song of the east.

"Is that a song of Mirat?" she wanted to ask, but instead she listened, letting his baritone vanquish the wretched cries of her mind. Her heartbeat stopped pounding in her ears and faded to a dull drumbeat deeper inside. Her eyelids drooped, and she sighed.

"Is this okay?" he signed.

Lyra nodded and nestled into the down pillow.

His hand tickled across her cheek to her ear, and then he gently pushed through the springy mass and dragged his fingers through her hair from scalp to ends. She felt the slight tug as he untangled the minor knots of the day, the shiver of elation at his touch.

A moan escaped her lips as Konan played with the shorter wisps on the back of her neck, and an odd sensation traveled her entire body. Calm pervaded her mind as he continued humming to a vaguely familiar tune, and she finally fell into a dreamless stupor.

49

KONAN LEFT AT KORAHEL'S insistence. She shoved him outside, muttering in Manalali, and he was almost certain she was cursing. She dropped the tent flap with a final glare, and he could hear her fastening it from the inside.

He slept with his back leaned against the pavilion doorpost, a blanket from his own tent draped over his sore legs.

Konan didn't mind, especially because it seemed the Manalali rule only applied in one direction, and Thordrin had found a willing partner in the pretty handmaiden who had bathed him. Both she and Mirra had small beds along the wall in the men's tent, but Konan was quite certain one of those beds was empty.

He slept lightly, as Isellan had trained him to do, oftentimes in a position much like this one: his back against something solid, his attention alert to anything out of place. He held his hand close, savoring the lingering sensation of Lyra. He had longed to touch those loose curls weeks ago but had been afraid of hurting her. Based on her reaction, she enjoyed the feeling too.

He watched the sun rise, alert to the waking of the camp and the sleep of the nocturnal desert. Earlier, he had caught the swooping whisper of a nighttime bird on the hunt, the scurrying of tiny rodents, and the squeak and flutter of bats, all signs of life that had been nearly absent in the mines. The floral scent peaked at dawn as a minor breeze alighted, blowing smells from the cactus-strewn flat to the west. Manalali villagers began to stir, and the sounds shifted to the nickering of horses and lowing of idraka, the clatter of cookware, and the soft murmur of voices.

He had known this was here. He had been so sure.

And when they had collapsed in the sands, he had doubted and regretted his bull-headedness. He had thought that he brought them to their deaths in the endless wastes, and he had prayed for salvation one last time.

His prayers were answered through a true miracle, which meant I'ya supported his cause. His mission to save Lyra at the very least, for she was a faithful woman of a faithful family, even if she had doubts at the moment.

He leered at the rising Eye. *Was it you?* he wondered. *Or was it her?* He pondered that for a while. The Eye didn't see him, he was sure, but perhaps it saw a woman like Lyra, pure and devoted and innocent.

Korahel emerged to stir up the fire. She glared at him half-heartedly, then proceeded to make a meal large enough for them to share. Thordrin emerged when the meal was ready, his handmaiden hanging at his side. He wore a smug look and winked at Korahel as he sat down.

By the Light, the man was red-blooded. Was the one not enough?

Korahel ignored Thordrin and went inside, then came out pulling Lyra by the hand. Again adorned in Manalali fashion, Lyra was now honored with a brightly beaded face covering more elaborate than the last, a gem-studded circlet, and an intricate, beaded shawl hugging her shoulders. Her colorful gown layers and brocaded bodice still featured crimson, their apparent holy color, but it was even finer than her previous dress. Her hair was plaited thickly with beads and ribbons. Her display the day before must have elevated her status, because they had added yet another boon, a small necklace carved of malagate tokens and strung together with silver and gold. Shirkaa was a most hospitable, if not entirely transparent, host. Whatever he wanted from them, he was paying in overt generosity and homage.

Thordrin whistled. "They like you, Lyr." He nudged Konan, and Konan agreed.

Lyra blushed and adjusted her face covering, then crossed her arms over her chest and hugged herself. She sat beside Konan, their arms touching, but she looked uncomfortable.

"I didn't want *more* attention," she murmured.

"And here I am, dressed as a common prick," Thordrin continued. His own tunic reached only to his hips and was covered by a less colorful belt-length surcoat. Loose trousers billowed underneath.

Konan was likewise dressed, but he felt it was quite appropriate. The outfit allowed far greater freedom of movement than Lyra's robes, and they would likely need the flexibility in battle. It was ornately beaded and featured artful textiles unlike any he had ever seen. It was also unbelievably comfortable, protective of his skin but light and airy. He hadn't been this comfortable in years.

Konan nudged Lyra gently, and she gave him a small smile and sighed. She ate the food offered by Korahel methodically, grimacing when the maiden warned her of iyasan anthe'brin. Korahel limited her food and water but said nothing to Konan.

They ate their meal in near silence, sensing a growing tension in the air. Jikaa had implied they might learn more in this meeting, but he had refused to give them details—that was his father's role.

"Lord Shirkaa is waiting," he finally signed, seeing Jikaa wave at them from afar.

Thordrin snorted but resumed a neutral expression and began walking to the large pavilion of the clan leader.

When Lyra hesitated, glancing fearfully at the large and mysterious tent, Konan proffered an arm. With an effort, she reached out and grasped it, overly tight; her fingernails dug into his bicep, and the gems on her handflowers pressed into his skin.

"Be brave," he signed. "You are strong enough."

She leaned into him for a minute, then looked up at him. "I don't know what's right." Hesitating, she buried her head in his chest, then looked up at him again. "Are you feeling better too? I noticed you limping."

"It's been a long time since I rode a horse."

"I know what that feels like," she answered. "But Mirra helps?"

The question hung in the air for a moment as he thought of the bath, and he nodded.

She looked away quickly, pursing her lips. "That's good. You need to ride more to build strength in your legs. I know it can be rough at the beginning."

Surely she wasn't jealous of the sweet handmaiden. Mirra was harmless, and he was confident Lyra wasn't actually interested in touching him like that. Moreso, he was certain *he* couldn't let her do so without frightening her. The mere thought of her massaging his thighs caused a stirring.

She doesn't need a lover, he reminded himself, berating himself as a fool. He had to stick with Mirra's ministrations; that was wiser.

Konan escorted her to the pavilion, where the canvas door was pulled back by an unseen servant. They entered side by side.

Shirkaa's pavilion was a series of tents fastened to a more permanent structure in the center. It was the shrine of the Desert Mother, a massive stone pillar with an outer ring of stone rooms. Shirkaa's tents were spacious, with the tanned hide walls stretched between permanent timber footings to handle the weight. They were covered in pelts and tapestries, while the floor was laid in furs and carpets. The furniture was as elaborate as any lord's, as homey and full of belongings and decorations as a permanent residence.

A young girl appeared, and she tugged Konan into a carved chair before kneeling to remove his sandals. She wiped his feet clean of dust and set the sandals aside. With a little wheedling, she did the same to Lyra before melting away with both pairs of sandals.

Thordrin waited for them at the threshold to the next room, and they wandered deeper into the pavilion together.

Lord Shirkaa reclined in a large throne at the back of the largest tent, at ease and drinking from a goblet. His honor guard sat on the colorful carpet in front of him at a low table, two on each side. On Shirkaa's right sat a stout, bearded man introduced as Rahar, the chieftain's advisor, and on his left sat his son Jikaa. Beside Jikaa was another man about his age named Hafka. Next to Rahar was Dashann. All four men ranged in age and build but all fit and carrying the confidence of trained knights.

Shirkaa extended a hand and invited his guests to sit at the far end of the low table. Scantily clad servants, male and female, placed small cups of a red tea in front of each of them, then withdrew behind colorful silk curtains. Konan noted that they shared the same serpent brand as Thordrin's handmaid.

Lyra jumped when one reached over her shoulder to place a cup, and the air around them shimmered for a moment.

"Welcome to my home, my friends." He smiled benevolently. "I hope you have recovered somewhat from your ordeal."

Thordrin spoke for them. "We thank you for the gracious hospitality of your people, Alis Shirkaa."

Konan caught Lyra's surprised glance, which she hid behind her tea. Thordrin was capable of speaking without disrespectful words, as Konan had suspected given the man's necessary infiltration of noble and yeoman houses for his work. It wasn't a skill the Phantom utilized often, but he did have it. He dressed well, given the opportunity, and carried himself as Shirkaa's honor guard did: chin high, back straight and shoulders back, hand cocked over the hilt of whatever blade he carried.

Thordrin continued after taking a casual sip of his tea. "How can we be of service, my lord?"

Konan appreciated his initiative. Thordrin seemed comfortable with making deals and politicking, despite his disgust with Shirkaa's "trade," and his experience doing so vastly outmatched Konan's own. He couldn't communicate with anyone but Lyra, and right now she looked so intimidated she couldn't seem to speak. She blinked frequently and had already emptied her teacup.

He reached under the cloth for her knee, and she jumped, exuding another pulse of air that startled the honor guard. She reddened, then gave him a sheepish smile and covered his hand with her cool fingers. Beneath the cloth, she turned his hand over and played with his calluses, but her heaving chest and vacant stare down the table revealed her nerves.

Shirkaa ignored the outburst and beamed. "It is nearly time for you to fulfill your end of the trade, my friends, by serving me in battle." His gaze swept across all three of them, landing last on Lyra and lingering.

Thordrin nodded knowingly. Lyra fidgeted and hitched a breath, then chewed on her lower lip.

"Your arrival is a benned ol'I'ya'hakkat, a sign that we the Manalal are blessed, a sign that we are right in Her eyes," Shirkaa continued. "She called us to you, clearer in our Godspeaker's mind than any sign he had before heard. She beckoned us from our beautiful village into the wastes, blind to what we sought, and She revealed you to us. We are Her Favored, as are you.

"The same cannot be said of our enemies. They are a cursed people, a half-people who abandoned their humanity years ago. They use impure magika to turn into beasts and are no more than animals at heart."

The honor guard around the table murmured in agreement. "Gyr," muttered Hafka with disgust. He made a strange sign, which was echoed by all the Manalal.

Shirkaa straightened in his lavish throne and leaned toward them, balancing his goblet in one hand and using it to gesture peremptorily. "Make no mistake, my friends. The Haralal are *not* the Mother's children. They are bastard offspring of a lesser corrupted god, one which came from a nethergate. They may appear to be men, but they are not. It is an illusion and a lie."

Lyra's fingernails dug so hard into Konan's hand, it almost hurt. Her skin lost its color, and the few dark freckles on her neck and forearm stood out.

Shirkaa's face turned tragic. "The Haralal have committed a sin against Her, and they have sinned against the chosen Manalal, by seizing my daughter and taking her to their squalid war camp."

Lyra gasped and somehow paled even further. She looked near to fainting when a male servant leaned over her to pour more tea in her empty cup. She startled at his sudden proximity, and she flung a hand at him to push him away.

The Air nearly screamed as it rushed outward from her, and the servant flew backward. He tumbled violently against a carved wooden sedan, and they heard a crack as his skull connected with the arm. The sedan legs snapped, and he lay still for moments before whining like an abused dog and crawling away.

"I'm sorry," Lyra cried, yanking her hand back. She shook as she stared at the servant, who disappeared behind the silk curtains. Whispers erupted from there, and Rahar immediately disappeared. They heard a snarl in Manalali, and it quieted.

Shirkaa laughed, holding his paunchy belly and downing the rest of his goblet's contents. "You did no harm." He spoke to his honor guard in Manalali, and they fell to chuckling. "As I was saying, the Haralal are monsters, and now they have committed an atrocity which is unforgivable. Do you remember my daughter's name?"

"Shirasa," whispered Lyra, facing the clan leader.

Shirkaa smiled wide. "My only daughter, Jikaa's baby sister. She is more beautiful than her mother and I could have dreamed. She is the first blossom of the summer cactus, faintly pink and softer than silk and more precious than any other."

Lyra shifted, and Konan saw the glitter of tears in her eyes.

"Shirasa is beloved by all in the tribe, but outside her family"—he placed a solemn palm on his heart—"treasured most by her betrothed, my honor guard and great warrior Dashann."

Dashann turned a tragic face to them, affirming Shirkaa's words.

Lyra whimpered, finally breaking into tears as she looked at the man. He seemed a bit old for a girl younger than she, but then, arranged marriages frequently disregarded age differences. Dashann was a great warrior and therefore a smart match.

After a pause, Shirkaa slammed his palm on the arm of his throne. "She must be retrieved, and her honor restored. Such depravity, such greed, is not the Mother's way. Our Mother punishes greed, and we the Manalal must do whatever the Desert Mother demands to right this wrong. The Godspeaker has conferred for many days, and She had told us to destroy the Haralal. She has told us to remove them from this Gate so their evil cannot spread any further."

"She lives?" asked Thordrin. The question seemed crass, yet neither Shirkaa nor Jikaa seemed offended. It was a practical question, grounded in reality.

Jikaa began to speak, but Shirkaa held up his hand abruptly to command silence in the room. "The Godspeaker knows, as he knows the will of the Mother. Yes, my desert flower lives, but we know not whether they have sullied her body with their wicked gyr touch." He paused significantly.

Lyra sobbed, horrified, shuddering with tears. Her hold on Konan's hand bit with the sharpness of her nails.

Shirkaa began to extoll his daughter's virtues and beauty, her preciousness.

The air in the tent seemed to stale, and Konan knew it was Lyra. She shook and yet seemed not to breathe, locked in a trance of terror and tragedy. Her eyes reminded him of the night they met, fury mixed with fear. As was her nature, Lyra projected it just as fervently to Shirasa as she would feel for herself. Konan admired her for that, despite how dangerous empathy could be.

His own reaction was similar, though internalized and less passionate, as he imagined this man's daughter, probably younger than Lyra, being tossed around a circle of horsemen. It was intolerable. Thordrin looked equally disgusted and was watching Lyra sharply.

Shirkaa finished his speech with an entreaty, his tone more genuine than any Konan had previously heard. "Please, each of you, help us defeat the Haralal—"

He would have said more, but Lyra interrupted. "We will." She raised her red eyes up to the man; their color was emphasized by the crimson of her veil. The air seemed to tremble with energy, a mirage so close one could reach out and touch it. "*I* will do whatever it takes to save Shirasa." She had stopped shaking, and the cold conviction in her gaze reminded Konan once again of *that* night.

There was such strength in her, Konan decided, despite all she had been through. Beyond her Air magika too. Was it vengeance? Anger? Or some other source of strength he knew nothing about?

"Where exactly is she?" asked Thordrin.

"In the main Haralali war camp," Shirkaa replied. "As soon as my people arrive in full number, we will attack and search for my beloved flower. You will fight with us, each with your own skills. You will be Manalal."

It wasn't a question, but Konan nodded agreement nonetheless. Thordrin spoke for both of them.

"You have our word and our swords. We will fight for the Manalal and for Shirasa, and when it is done, we will leave you in peace with your daughter safely recovered."

Shirkaa waved at Rahar to roll out a large hide map on the low table. He pointed at a spot on the map with a dark pillar symbol. "Our village is here, at the shrine to Desert Mother. Our home spans from this oasis here to the black cliffs here, to the eastern coast. We make home wherever we need, following the Mother's tears with our animals and children. We move so we do not exhaust one place; we are not greedy. My tribes span far to the north and east, and my herds are great, for the Manalal are the favorite children of Desert Mother." He spoke as if stating a known fact.

He swept a hand over the land to the west, which had few landmarks. "This cursed land is that of the Haralal. Their only boon is a large palm oasis, but they have built a strong war camp around it with many warriors. This is where they hold my flower. We have called our people here, bringing them home from their wanderings with their cattle, so that we may make war upon the Haralal in their own territory. My warriors are strong, but they are relatively few against the powerful Haralali war camp. That is why I'ya'hakkat brought us to you. You shall tip the battle in our favor."

They all leaned forward to study the map. The Haralal land was mostly empty, with no mark for the oasis of which Shirkaa spoke.

"My lord, how far is the Haralal camp? Will we surprise them in the night, or arrive by day?" Thordrin sounded eager.

Shirkaa beamed. "My friend, they are not far, and we will arrive long before two days' end. You—" He pointed at Lyra, who returned to fidgeting with Konan's hand. Her nerves had frayed again. *Don't relent, Lyra,* he thought, giving her fingers a light squeeze. *You can do this.* She straightened, and her brow furrowed. Shirkaa continued. "You will guide us at the vanguard. Hide us in a sandstorm."

Konan gave Lyra an apologetic look and pulled his hand away. "Are there to be negotiations?" he asked.

Lyra interpreted, her voice cold and stiff. The reason for their war had gotten to her, and her gentleness had disappeared—along with any reticence.

Shirkaa's single-word answer seemed to echo in the tent. "No."

When their meeting was over, Thordrin stood and clasped arms in agreement with Shirkaa, reiterating his word. Konan did the same.

"Until you destroy my enemies, remember that your life belongs to me," Shirkaa stated as he let go of Konan's arm. His grip was tight, but then he gave Konan a broad, friendly smile.

Shirkaa did not seem to expect the same physical agreement from Lyra, and they bowed to each other instead. Lyra was visibly relieved, immediately adhering to Konan's arm and receding into her own thoughts as the trio was ejected from Shirkaa's tent.

50

Lyra had nightmares earlier that night than usual, and Konan brushed past a fretting Korahel to attend her. She panted and shuddered, muttering half-words that seemed to be a mixture of the common language and the Old Language. Konan couldn't understand much of it, but then she bolted up, fully awake.

"That poor girl," she murmured, her eyes wide and frightened. Konan sat on the edge of the bed, much to Korahel's dismay.

Lyra crawled to him, her legs tangled in the sheets, which followed as she tucked her knees up. She leaned her face into Konan's chest and wept.

He adjusted himself on the bed, pulling her tight and close and wrapping the shamble of blankets around her like a cocoon. She smelled of an intoxicating perfume; it reminded him of the early spring mornings just before the sun came up.

She sniffled, and Korahel appeared with a kerchief. Resigned, she handed it to Konan and stood back. He dabbed at Lyra's cheeks, and her fingers crept out from their place on his chest to take the kerchief.

"Tell me about Mirat," Lyra whispered. She shifted, turning within his arms so she could see his hand gestures, and pulled the furs up to her chin.

What could he tell her? Many of his memories were so dim, so dreamlike, he wondered how much he really knew of his home. Was it even home, or was he to make a new one? He tugged at the furs and tucked them around her better, then shook his head. "Tell me about your family."

"Only if you tell me about Mirat," she replied.

He didn't answer, instead pulling her close with one arm and caressing her hair with the other hand. Hopefully his rough hands wouldn't catch too badly.

She sighed as he pulled a knot out, seeming to forget she had demanded an answer. "My family is one of the oldest caravans from Litis, with a well-established trade route to the south and north. We have hundreds of people, a herd of horses and cattle, and fine wagons that hold everything we need. My aunties make potions and spells and incredible gemstone inlays, and my uncles tan the best-quality leather you've ever seen. My mam plays every stringed instrument I know of, and she sings like a professional orator from the guild. We live on the leather, but we live for the music and the beauty of the shifting cultures and peoples we meet. I've lived on the road all my life, chasing the summer."

Her full, pink lips curved into a real smile, and her pale blue eyes shone in the low light of the candle Korahel had lit. Lyra stared into the shadows of the tent as she happily relayed her stories. She told him of the ponies who got lost in a storm and were found by Adrian, who nursed them back to health. She told him of passing by the city of Corronei, the shining capital of Marlemet, and of camping for extended periods along the beaches of the Red Bay. Corronei was where she had seen the spinning lamps that told stories on the wall; it was beautiful, with grand architecture and yellow brick. She told him of Elden's antics, his irrepressible mischief and naughty grin. "I've never seen anyone lift so much from people's pockets. Scamp." She giggled, and Konan froze as he took the musical sound in.

She glanced up at him with a questioning look.

His cheek felt hot, and he looked away. "It is good to hear you laugh."

Konan could see the conflict in her eyes. Her joy at the memories battled with guilt for feeling light under their circumstances. He returned to stroking her hair, and she sighed and pressed against him, her eyes shining. Then she grimaced and pulled away.

"No, you have to tell me about Mirat." She pouted at him, then rearranged herself in the bed, dragging the furs with her. Merciless. The glare she gave him seemed like the most vicious she could manage, which wasn't much.

He did. He told her how the valley looked in autumn, verdant with crops of grain and the braided fingers of the river, the foothills burnished with orange and crimson leaves. He described the eternal snow on the caps of the Sikrat, the thunderous sounds of its collapse in the spring and the rushing of fresh glacial water from its heights. It was all he had: flashes and sensations.

There were real memories somewhere deep within, buried under years of calcified stubbornness and fear. The layers were meant to guard him, and they were difficult to remove. Konan had never wanted to remove them before, and even now he didn't know how. If he did remember something real, could he even articulate it?

In the low candlelight, Lyra peered at his hand signals. Her eyelids fluttered and she yawned, then stilled.

He carefully withdrew, Korahel once more battering him in the back, and he prayed Lyra would dream of home. Before his prayer was even finished, Korahel blew out the candle.

Konan felt a shift in the village's energy—they anticipated war. They whetted swords, made arrows, and outfitted their fighting men. The next days were full as the Manalal tested and trained them.

The Godspeaker seemed eager to see Lyra's powers manifest and took every bit of time and energy she had to work with her. He walked her slowly through drills to be more specific with her actions, using Jikaa as an intermediary. The old man focused primarily on Air magika, assigning her a drill or task and then leaving her to practice endlessly. Controlled squalls, tiny whirlwinds to keep a single flower alighted, microgusts to push a single tumbleweed without affecting others. It seemed to require finesse in pulling the energy from inside and extending it in a thin stream to reach out to her target. Lyra said she could almost see it, a quavering jet of air shimmering like a trick of the eye, a false oasis just beyond the horizon. But more so, she said she could feel it. The focused power was not dispersed in an emotional tidal wave, but rather pulsed with her heart, emanated from her being. Konan noticed that when she tired, it became duller, weaker, quieter, and her winds died down. And when she was immersed in it, she danced.

He, meanwhile, joined Thordrin in getting to know their horses and fellow warriors, often working where Konan could keep an eye on the Godspeaker's lessons. They frequently took breaks, for Konan's sake, to watch Lyra's progress.

Hafka, the honor guard warrior who had sat next to Jikaa, reintroduced Konan and Thordrin to their horses. With Hafka's help identifying a proper saddle, Thordrin got astride his mount and began practicing archery. For once, the man seemed to struggle, and Konan realized that despite the Phantom's extensive experience, he had never loosed an arrow from horseback.

Hafka brought Konan's horse over. The big animal had a good temperament and nickered as she recognized him. Nevertheless, Konan groaned to think of more riding and the saddle-soreness that would come with it, though it was necessary. He requested more assistance through a series of frustrated gesticulations, and Hafka recruited a boy from the tribe. The two walked Konan through proper mounting and riding. The day waned quickly, and Hafka was obviously appalled at the ignorance of a grown man. He spoke quickly in Manalali to the boy, who agreed emphatically and then turned to Konan.

"Manalal teach, day." He struggled with the unfamiliar words in the common language, pointing at the setting sun and then turning a cycle with his hands. "Good?"

Konan thanked Hafka graciously and agreed. His thighs protested, as did his calves and ankles and lower back, but he would have to learn to ride again. If that consumed part of his days until they paid their debt to Shirkaa, at least he could spend the remainder of his time practicing with the sword, knife, and bow. Oh, the things he had forgotten in Tahayi!

When not riding, Konan integrated with the other warriors, practicing swordplay with a wooden saber on the ground. He would be useless on horseback; his thighs still ached from his first ride, and the additional practice on the mare only made him more sore. But he was effective on the ground, combining a rough sword form with the jabs, kicks, and throws of close-quarter combat. For once, he was glad for the years of brawling in the mines—if it could be called that.

The honor guard had talent supplemented with a healthy dose of Manalali pride, and they shifted from practicing in pairs to alternately attacking Konan in a loose circle. Hafka soon joined the fray, smacking his waster hard into Konan's, who rejoined with equal force.

The pair squared off, probing each other's weak spots. Hafka tested Konan's right side with a jab. Konan dodged and closed the distance between them, grabbing the Manalali's sword arm and flipping the man over his back. Hafka rolled himself back to his feet, looking surprised. He pressed another attack, slicing low at Konan's gut and keeping his distance, then swinging high. Konan was less prepared for this, taking a hard thump in the shoulder with a groan. Adversaries in the mines had knives, not swords, and he wasn't accustomed to fighting someone without closing. Hafka seemed to perceive this and switched to a distanced swordplay where he had a definite advantage. When he had reestablished a foundation of pride for the Manalali soldiers, hitting Konan several more times, he called for the others to disperse and worked with him on sword forms.

Exhausted but appreciative, Konan listened to and emulated the warrior. Hafka was a good teacher, and Konan was able to recall more and more of proper form, the fluid motions and arrangements that fit with the longer weapon and its greater reach. The curved edge of the Manalali sabers was a little strange, meant for fighting on horseback, and he wondered if he might find an alternative weapon that suited him better.

Hafka couldn't understand his signs but gathered enough from Konan's gesticulation to guide him to a tent with a variety of battle gear. Konan identified a blade with less curve and a somewhat shorter length, almost a hybrid of Hafka's sword and a knife. Hafka raised a doubtful eyebrow but encouraged him to swap weapons nonetheless. Content, Konan returned to their practice area, fighting Hafka and the other honor guard intermittently. Again, he wondered at the things he had forgotten in the long years.

Thordrin's dagger was returned to him, and he immediately set to sharpening and oiling it. He also exchanged the warden's heavier sword for a saber to supplement his bow and arrows. He enjoyed sparring in any scenario and attached himself to Jikaa whenever he was available, so he had someone to talk to. Konan hoped Jikaa didn't understand all of the depraved speech coming from Thordrin's mouth, but he suspected the man was as bilingual as his father. Such a skill was beneficial to someone looking to be clan leader someday. At least Jikaa didn't seem to take it personally.

Unlike Jikaa, Shirkaa didn't spend much time with the common men of the village, instead staying in his massive tent complex. However, the chieftain did gift them (through Jikaa) with thick hide armor to supplement the weapons they had already been using. The Manalali handmaidens had stopped giving them cloaks during sword practice, since they often took them off anyway. Konan and Thordrin were clearly meant to fight as soldiers, and the Manalal withheld nothing that might enable them to fight more effectively.

Konan spent his evenings recovering, rubbing the soreness from his thighs as Lyra and Thordrin chatted. Between Mirra and Korahel, they were always well fed and provided for, eating outside to avoid any condemnation from the

Manalal. Mirra also offered massage, and he accepted for his calves, feet, and shoulders.

Thordrin's handmaiden, the one with a viper brand on her wrist, kneaded his shoulders and chest. He groaned with pleasure.

"Thor, what is her name?"

"Huh?"

Lyra looked pointedly at the handmaiden.

Thordrin smirked. "Why does it matter?"

Lyra shook her head. "You don't know, do you?" She repeated the question to Korahel and Mirra.

They winced at each other, an odd reaction to such a simple question, and then they ignored it. Lyra looked at Konan, confused, then seemed to eye Mirra's working hands.

She put her empty bowl down with a grimace and clutched her stomach.

"Still feeling unwell?" Konan asked.

She nodded. "I thought the water-sickness would go away by now." She sighed. "Thor, your cough is better."

Thordrin hacked and spit. "Yeah, the old man gave me something for it."

"Actually, I made that," Lyra said in a small voice. She smiled shyly and stared at the flames, then slumped into Konan's side with a yawn. Taking one of his hands with both of hers, she wrapped their fingers into a knot.

They were pushing her too hard, he thought. They wanted to use her magika somehow, but she had barely had time to recover from the mines and long trek. He suspected Shirkaa didn't care if they exhausted her, only that she could do what they wanted. Their war meeting with Shirkaa and his honor guard had stirred a discomfort in him, although he couldn't pinpoint why. Perhaps it was the overt enthusiasm and generous smiles of Shirkaa, his elaboration of how much he loved and missed his daughter. It could be false as easily as it could be genuine.

Konan extracted his arm from where Lyra leaned against him. Her pinkish-blond hair lay like a halo on her head, tickling his chin and neck. He gulped nervously and brushed the strays back down, but her hair was springy and fine. He smoothed it again and again, until he realized he could hear her humming.

In a soft, high voice, Lyra sang an old folk song, one that echoed from his memory in the voices of orators from the past. It was about going home. Lyra's voice was both beautiful and tragic, subdued by shyness and the impending evening as Manalali went to bed. She stared into the fire as she sang, seemingly entranced, and when she was done, she closed her eyes.

They soaked in the pleasant warmth of the fire for a bit longer. Thordrin made an appreciative sound, then resumed his attentions on his handmaid. Even Korahel, who would normally have rushed to clean up the meal's dirtied dishes and cookpot, seemed to appreciate Lyra's song.

Konan carried Lyra inside after and laid her in her blankets. Korahel ushered him out but didn't curse at him, and he returned to his tent, where Mirra massaged his sore thighs for a while. He left before Thordrin's massage escalated into something else, again settling outside of Lyra's tent. With a friendly expression, Mirra brought him a blanket.

51

"Do they not have stewards in Krita?"

Taiuki held a ledger, annotating and cross-checking items as she and Steward Wehan reviewed the contents of an incoming pallet of goods.

"They do, Princess," Wehan replied. "However, the queen oversees more of the process, acting as high steward." Wehan's lessons on castle management, including finances and inventory, primarily consisted of active duty, documenting orders and receipts to the royal grounds.

"Should I not be busy doing other things? Holding court or handling diplomatic negotiations?"

Wehan inspected the small label marking the flat of grain and ran a hand across his bald scalp. "Princess, in Krita, you will not be needed at court at all."

Taiuki glowered at the stack of cheese wheels, counting and categorizing them. "You mean to say I'm not even expected to be present at the hearings?"

"If you are, you will not be expected to speak."

Wehan wouldn't meet her eye, instead making a show of counting the boxes of hops that had arrived from Kyoshu Mountain.

"Wehan?"

"Yes, Princess?"

"How do you know so much about Krita's ways?"

"I studied at their High Temple in Krita Port, Princess."

"You were a Temple mage?" Taiuki snorted. Wehan seemed too practical to believe in that Five Faces nonsense.

"A journeyman," Wehan replied, seeming embarrassed. "I never attained a mastery, but they did develop my mathematic skills after noting my intuition with numbers."

"Why would they send you there in the first place?" Taiuki asked, curious. "Water magika is well taught by the Waterpriests."

Wehan cleared his throat. "Indeed it is. I returned after several years at Krita Port because, well, it felt unnatural to live above the waves." He cleared his throat again, realizing what he had said. "I'm sorry, Princess."

"You're not the one who should be sorry," Taiuki murmured.

"I am—" Wehan paused. "Princess, please know that I have always done what I thought best for Shiggo. I served your father faithfully, and I serve your mother to this day. I will serve your sister Keiki as well. I am myr, and I would die for myrkind, to preserve our kingdom and our way of life. No place should be like Krita, godless and disconnected. Chaotic in its heterogeneous parts, all pushing and pulling to different corners of the Mana Loi."

Taiuki pondered the steward's words while they worked. Wehan had never been kind to her, but he had never been unkind either. He had simply been cold and distant, the regulatory arm of her mother. His role as disciplinarian had increased when her father, King Rentai, had died, and Wehan's place in Shiggo had been elevated to a step behind and to the side of Queen Regent Furuhaki. Wehan was always present during Taiuki's most painful moments.

"And what of Tan? Would you serve him so faithfully?" she asked quietly.

"I would, Princess."

They worked in silence the rest of the afternoon, until Wehan released her to supper. The meal was tolerable until Tan-sho pointed out their recent training successes to Mother, who sneered with distaste over her stewed mussels.

"No, Mother, it's been really good," he repeated. "I got faster. I won a spar against Vice Commodore Reihotto today."

"I'm proud of you, Second," Mother replied stiffly, her narrowed eyes on Taiuki.

Taiuki forced herself not to react, clenching her jaw against the unbidden words that burned on her tongue.

One of Tan's hands snuck to hers beneath the table, and he squeezed. His face was almost as neutral as hers, for once.

"It sounds like the vice commodore's presence has been most advantageous," Mother continued, as though discounting Taiuki's influence. "Thank the current she's returned to prepare you in Master Sashiro's stead." She visibly turned her attention to the steaming bowl of mussels and shucked them open with delicate fingers and a miniature fork. The conversation was apparently over.

Anella leaned closer to Tan. "How do I break this one open if it didn't crack?" she whispered.

Tan gave Taiuki's hand one last squeeze and a silent look of encouragement, then turned to help Anella.

Taiuki bore the rest of the shared meal without a word, for Godrig filled the chair to her other side, and he had long ago given up on polite discourse with her. His shoulders were turned slightly away as he listened to Kei explain what the lower gardens looked like, the diversity of plants and creatures who lived in the tiered intertidal.

Even afterward, Taiuki could not escape the pressures suffocating her, for Mother suggested they entertain Godrig by inviting him to an evening singing lesson with Lady Hannaka. Taiuki groaned internally, but she couldn't deny the request without drawing attention to irregularities in her schedule. At least Mother didn't have interest in attending, instead withdrawing to her own evening rituals without another word. Tan followed on her heels, abandoning the others.

"Oh, what a pleasure to have an audience," Hannaka tittered, guiding their group to one of the upper rooms with a great piano and harp. "Sing well, dearies, sing well."

Despite Taiuki's displeasure, Godrig insisted on escorting her by the arm. His boots pounded and echoed along the hallways, a dull thud to announce his coming everywhere he went. Anella danced on his other arm.

"Oh, Godrig, Kei and Yuki taught me a new song. Do you want to hear it?" She smiled brightly and didn't wait for an answer. "Actually, two songs. I can sing them both without help, except for the parts with clicking."

"Walk like a lady," Godrig growled.

Anella stopped bouncing from foot to foot and returned to a sedate, courtly walk. "Slow down then," she mumbled, trying to keep up with his long strides.

He abruptly altered his pace but glared at his sister, and when they reached the room, he sat in a chair with his arms crossed.

Hannaka didn't seem to notice any of this, busy initiating lessons as she usually did.

Kei sang in a high alto harmonized by Anella's young soprano. Taiuki could never get so high, mumbling in a low alto instead.

"Put some effort in, Taiuki," Kei scowled. "You're not even singing."

"Do fill those lungs, child," Hannaka encouraged as she strummed a harp. "You can't get the range without deeper breaths than that."

"Can we sing one of the songs I just learned?" Anella begged. "Godrig, listen. Are you listening?" She led them in a traditional Shiggon-jin song, one which utilized the sadder notes of the harp in what was almost a dirge. Her soprano could break hearts with its tearful agony.

I once loved a noble man.
He came across the sea Merchan
and courted me with gifts of gold,
of bronze and crystal diamonds cold.

He said he loved my pureness of heart,

> *he suffered every moment apart.*
> *He offered me a Merchan home,*
> *I gave him all my flesh and bone.*
>
> *And when he had what he had,*
> *he left me for my cousin glad.*
> *He showered her with gifts of gold,*
> *of bronze and crystal diamonds cold.*
>
> *He said he loved her purest heart,*
> *he suffered every day apart.*
> *And I was forced from father's home,*
> *broken, ruined, and alone.*
>
> *I wandered till I lost my way,*
> *and stumbled to a lonesome place,*
> *where my broken heart could heal*
> *as bark can scar and wood can seal.*
>
> *Halleluia, mourn the death*
> *of innocence and youth,*
> *Halleluia, mourn the loss*
> *of happiness uncouth,*
> *Halleluia, damn the man who*
> *fooled my naive mind,*
> *Halleluia, praise the pow'r*
> *embracing me all time.*

All three women joined in the chorus, their voices rising high in a final lament and fading away as the harp rose behind them, repeating the last tragic notes.

Godrig seemed to take it all in, his glance continually flickering between his sister and Taiuki. Was that a reluctant admiration and appreciation for the performance of all, or another subtle savoring of her skin and voice? More likely the former, for her voice wasn't all that good.

At the end, his jaw clenched several times before he spoke. "Stunningly rendered, ladies," he managed before giving Anella a look, "but perhaps inappropriate for a young lady such as my sister to be repeating."

Kei gasped. "Oh, Prince Godrig, I didn't even think of that. She heard us sing it, and she liked the melody so we taught it to her."

"Don't apologize, Kei," Taiuki snapped, allowing her scowl to linger on her sister before sliding to Godrig and settling. She raised an eyebrow in challenge. "It is one of our most beautiful traditional songs, Prince, one of false desires, lies, and heartbreak. A young woman would be better served to learn of such things through song rather than experience."

Godrig stood and glowered, his arms still crossed over his chest. "A young lady need not speak of such things, nor think of such things."

"A woman knows such things are true." She could feel the animosity emanating from Godrig in waves, and they remained at an uncomfortable impasse. Despite the nattering of Kei behind them, suggesting perhaps they should have Anella teach them a song of Krita, the air between Godrig and Taiuki was muted, silent without serenity, dead without stillness. A violent hush as each exerted their own will.

It was broken by Tan's entrance. His cheeks were flushed with patchy red, and he seemed not to notice the room's tension as he moped over to a seat beside Godrig. It was Anella who finally broke through the enmity by hurrying to him and touching his arm.

"Are you all right, Tan? Where were you?"

He scrubbed his face, then looked up and caught Taiuki's eye. She abandoned her altercation with Godrig to listen.

"I thought, maybe with all the good progress I've made, that maybe Mother would see how good of a teacher you are," he began, screwing up his face. "So I asked if she would make you Second again. After all, I don't even want it."

"Tan-sho . . ." *How I love you, but you're a fool.*

"She's never spoken to me like that before," he said miserably. "At least the only one who saw was Wehan."

"*Steward* Wehan," Kei corrected mindfully.

"I'm sorry, Yuki," Tan mumbled. "I probably just made things worse."

Anella patted his arm one more time and tried to pull him from his chair, a move that made Godrig's expression twist even more. "It will be okay, Tan. Come on, let's sing the fun one, the victory song about taking down the pirate captain."

Tan broke into a grin and followed, and Hannaka will-ingly moved to the piano for accompaniment.

Taiuki watched as Godrig's dark disapproval shifted to surprise, then condemnation. "These are not appropriate for a young lady to sing, Anella. Call upon me when you wish to demonstrate your talents as a well-bred lady of Krita. A song of home would be pleasant to the ears." He turned and stalked out.

Kei looked confused for a moment, then rushed after him with apologies falling from her lips. Taiuki allowed herself a small smirk.

Although Tan's blunder did result in a one-sided conver-sation in which Mother reemphasized the need for Taiuki's menial lessons with Wehan and Hannaka, the queen regent did not rescind Taiuki's training duties.

I suppose I should be thankful for that, Taiuki thought as she trotted behind Tan on their landwalker mounts. With Marshal Kinota's guidance, Tan led several hunting parties on both land and sea to practice cavalry command.

The earliest migratory seaducks passed by Shiggo City in droves, heading northward toward the Merchan Sea ahead of other species. Led by Tan, the hunting expedition went north along Shiggo Mountain's eastern coastline. Successful ambushing required attack from both land and water, but Kinota insisted both Tan and Taiuki ride their horses and allow her to lead the underwater school.

They harvested a slew of ducks from north of the city, snapping those resting from beneath and shooting those that lifted in panic with a volley of slingshot. Tan missed his mark several times.

"I'm not used to these shot throwers." He shrugged and placed the speargun-like contraption, designed to throw balls of dropshot or stones, on his horse's side.

"Exactly why you must practice with them more often," Taiuki replied with a smile. "Your horse obeys you well, but your weapon handling on horseback leaves something to be desired. Remember, you don't need to lead them so far in the air. A few times, you nearly blasted their bills off, which is why they reared back midflight."

"I'll do better next time."

"I believe you will. Let's try again in the next cove."

The hunting party moved north along the coast all day until each bag and stringer was full. They met with the waterborne party as evening fell.

Marshal Kinota nearly beached her whale in order to speak with them. The stringently trained animal didn't question the order, merely waiting for the next command. "Shall we return at a swift pace, or camp for the night?" Kinota asked, glancing at Tan for the response. "It is your decision, Second. You are in command."

"Oh!" Tan looked to Taiuki, and she shrugged. All she wanted was to be done so she could slip into the night and head east. Tan looked lost at her vague response. "I suppose we could camp. Spend the evening preserving the meat and resting? The party has more than earned a good hot meal."

"Why else might that be a wise strategy, Second?" Kinota asked.

Tan's eyes widened, and he looked around the island and sea. "Well, it's also prime feeding hours for predators like lacers and wild blues, and we passed at least three bear caves along the coast."

"Very observant," Kinota said with approval. "This part of the coast has especially large sea makran colonies as well," she added. Then she raised her eyebrow in a polite query. "Your orders, then, Second?"

"Make camp, Master Marshal," Tan said formally. "Bring the seamounts close and post a guard through the night." Kinota saluted and left to obey. Tan turned to one of the officers nearby. "Likewise, Captain, bring in the horses to that open area with the overhanging cliff, and we will make camp in that shallow cave. Post a guard on both sides to watch for bears." The captain saluted as well, placing one palm to his forehead, then left to organize the men. Tan gave Taiuki a sheepish grin. "They obey like I'm in charge of everything."

"You *are*, brother," Taiuki replied, rejecting the bitterness that threatened to envelop her. "You are Second now, remember? You need to be prepared to take command of any situation, especially with Keiki as queen. She has no military experience at all and will delegate all of those duties to you. *You* will win battles and lead the fleets, not her."

"It still seems like I should defer to you."

Taiuki patted his shoulder. The gesture was ironic, for he was now taller than she, and yet she couldn't help but see him as her little brother. "That's out of our control for now, Tan-sho. Besides, if I was still Second, I would still want to see you cross-trained in the event of my death."

Tan scrunched his eyebrows together, troubled by that thought. "I don't like it. I mean, I like the training, especially with you, and it's funny when they salute me so seriously, but I don't like being Second without good reason. It's not right."

Kinota cleared her throat, startling them both. She saluted them. "Your orders are being carried out. Supper should be ready soon."

They were quiet until Taiuki nudged Tan.

"Oh, right, thank you, Master Marshal," he rushed to say. "You are dismissed." Kinota left them alone again, and he let out a long sigh. "I'm not ready for this, Taiuki. I'm not meant to be Second." His voice cracked, and he looked even more miserable.

Taiuki embraced him with one arm. He was still just a boy, barely past puberty. She didn't know what to say, so she said nothing. They watched the hunting party shift into a camp, popping up tents and lean-tos, rousing a fire, and relieving the mounts of their saddles and sweat. Tan leaned forward, thinking to assist, but Marshal Kinota shooed him away.

"See, what's that about?" Tan whispered. "I've always cared for my own horse."

"You're Second, Tan-sho, in a party large enough to have a stablekeeper."

Tan thought about that and grimaced. "I like handling my own mount. After Moka, that horse may be one of my favorite animals: intuitive, emotional, communicative, a little easily distracted—but that's probably my influence as the rider . . . What are you smiling at?"

"Nothing, Tan-sho. You've always taken exceptional care of your mounts, whether they live in air or water, and I must say I've noticed your horsemanship improve with all those late afternoon rides with Nelly."

Tan grinned. "It's nice to ride for fun once in a while. So you approve of her now?" Mischief sparkled in his eyes.

"She's better than Godrig."

He snorted. "That's an understatement."

"You did well today, brother." She moved to scruff his hair, and he battered back at her with a defensive block, then a counter. They both laughed, for a moment forgetting their circumstances and worries.

The moment was fleeting, and Taiuki sobered quickly. "Decorum, brother. I suggest roving both camps above and below to bolster the soldiers, praise them for a hunt well done."

The next morning did not see them back as soon as expected—one of the hunter's horses came up lame. Marshal Kinota railed at the hunter for failing to check his mount's feet. Taiuki wanted to do the same, for every moment of delay caused her heart to break a little more, pining for It'tholl. Nevertheless, they moved as a school, nursing the limping horse down the coastline, past dark caves and long crevasses leading to the island interior. A massive brown bear lay in one cave mouth, basking in the morning light. It groaned lazily at the passing party, rolling over to watch them and causing a cascade of scree to tumble from the edge of the cave mouth. Tan commanded the party to be on guard, especially with the injured horse in the center, but the bear made no other moves.

Although they could have left the injured horse and rider at the first village, Tan chose not to. "We're a school," he said with some conviction, looking to Taiuki for support and realizing she likely would have left the man behind. He looked confused, then resolved himself. "We *are* a school. We will move together to Shiggo City."

Taiuki resented his decision, seeing only that they could have traded the horse for a fresh one in the village or left the rider. The horse's foot abscess was opened and draining, but it would easily have made it home the next day. Her resentment, however, stemmed more from the fact that she knew Tan had made the right decision for a myr: the preservation of the school in lieu of individual gain.

Why couldn't Taiuki fully appreciate that decision? Was she broken, deviant as Mother said? Was she really myr, or was she some corrupted offspring that should have been abandoned to the current at birth? Taiuki tried to shake off the stray thoughts, but even Reihotto had acknowledged her difference from the rest.

It's all right now, Yuki-sho . . . whispered a kindly woman's voice.

A godly form . . . one with the Most High . . . It was a strange, deep tone in her mind. What was that?

I am ashamed of you, Taiuki. If only it had been you, and not him . . . Her mother's harsh words echoed in her ears.

Taiuki pulled her shoulders back and rode, pouring her energy into proper form and patience. Tan straightened as well, glancing at her posture and emulating the way she held her reins.

By the time they returned to Shiggo City, the sun was only a few fingers from the western horizon. Taiuki excused herself from the party as quickly as possible, intending to disappear to the Mountains of Mourning, but had only gone a few steps when Kinota called to her.

"Hold, Princess. The vice commodore has summoned you for an expeditionary report." Kinota included Tan in her statement.

Taiuki took a measured inhale, trying to appear carefree in front of the master marshal. "Very well. Second, are you ready?"

Tan reluctantly handed his reins to a stableboy, again forced to relinquish care of his own mount in the name of duty. They found Reihotto in the arch commodore's office. She looked up from a dispatch and gave them a grim smile.

"Excellent, you've returned safely. Second Tan, please report regarding the hunt."

Tan stumbled through a description of their hunt, elaborating on what he had improved on and how much game their efforts yielded. When Reihotto inquired whether anything had gone poorly, Tan paused.

Taiuki expected him to explain that they had returned late due to an irresponsible rider who had failed to check his horse's feet, but Tan did not do so. Instead, after a thoughtful pause, Tan explained that their return home had been slowed to ensure the school remained together, and that he claimed responsibility for not overseeing the horse care more closely. Taiuki held back an incredulous huff. That was hardly Tan's fault. The rider should have cared for his own mount.

Reihotto caught her subtle sound and briefly made eye contact with her. "It is well," she said in a measured voice and looking back to Tan, "that you protect the school and the erroneous rider with your words, Second. Your actions are meritorious, and it seems you learned a good deal. Did you address the individual and assign penance?"

"Yes, Vice Commodore," said Tan.

"Excellent. Such is the myr way, the Way of the Current." Reihotto smiled warmly. She sounded much like Sashiro in that moment.

Tan had done well. In fact, he naturally followed the Way better than Taiuki would have. Despite her own military prowess, she lacked the camaraderie required to build cohesion in the school.

Without a doubt, she would have left the injured horse and rider behind in the first town.

Reihotto waved the dispatch in her hand. "An update from Arch Commodore Sashiro. I must bring the most advanced platoons to the front soon. I shall leave Princess Taiuki in charge of your continued training, Second, with Marshal Kinota assisting on these mentored hunts, I think they've been highly beneficial thus far. Master Sashiro implied he may return for a brief time later to evaluate your progress, at which time he may call you to the front for real battle experience, most likely with the princess as your second-in-command—or perhaps myself."

Tan lit up. "I haven't been to the front since last time I was with Yuki, and I didn't even get to fight that time."

"This is not a circumstance to be taken lightly, Second," Taiuki said sternly. "This is real war, real risk. You must train hard to prepare for deployment."

"But you'll be with me. It's not like I'll be in danger."

Taiuki gave him a hard look, and his shoulders slumped a little.

"I shall train as hard as I can," he mumbled. "I shall conform."

Reihotto nodded. "Now, before I depart, I'd like your thoughts on the latest troop movements."

Although her words were directed at Tan, her meaning was for Taiuki, and they moved together to the bathymetric map in the War Room, its figurines scattered farther and farther apart as they attempted to block the insurgent Jiji-ton-jin movements. Everything about it made Taiuki uneasy, perhaps most of all because she could understand the Jiji-ton-jin strategy and, while she believed it to violate the Way in its barbarism and recklessness, she could see why it was effective against traditional myr battle tactics. Had she been their commander, she might have done the same in certain places.

No matter how much she resented it, how much she denied it, she was like Jijito; she was deviant. And she would prove it to herself once again when she snuck off that night, intent upon only one thing: seeing It'tholl.

52

Ar'we soared high through the fluffy clouds, seemingly heading into the Eye.

Reylin had always wondered what it might feel like, and now he knew. Like a fog, clouds were thick and heavy, and at the speed Ar'we flew, dense enough they almost stung as the dragon pushed her way through the air.

Ar'we was in her element, ascending with powerful sweeps of her outstretched wings and then gliding across the mountainous landscape.

Reylin had only seen this miraculous view of his kingdom once before, and he had been so preoccupied with worry over Priscilla's delivery that he had failed to appreciate it.

Mirat was breathtaking.

Far below his boots, the virescent greens of the meadows and deep sage of the underbrush and dark evergreens melded together, the shining white of frothy rapids and waterfalls streaked into the clear water, and the beige and brown of stone interspersed every patch of color. Light glinted off the occasional milky azure lake, pocked with white glaciers. The mountain peaks glittered with remnants of snow clinging to the rock, somehow enduring the summer sun.

The cities and villages stamped their pattern into the valleys and mountainsides, unmistakable even from this height. Their streets stood out in straight lines that cut through the trees, and their rectangular buildings fashioned a weak grid of concentrated civilization, or at least semiorderly lines. In the larger towns, a single pentagonal tower stood out: the Temple of I'ya. Most of them did not have the extent of prismatic windows like the grandiose High Temple in Ironhold, but they were marvelous nonetheless. Their architectural perfection was visible from above, all five sides equivalent and faultlessly straight, with a flat mansard roof for ceremonies and prayers.

The wind roared by, and Reylin thought how appreciative he was for the flight gear Davon had provided. The eye covers were finely crafted Litisian clear glass, and the furred skull cap guarded his ears as well as keeping his head warm. He had packed his battlehelm along with a few other items in the saddlebags, but overall he packed lightly. He wore most of his armor, and his sword hung from its scabbard on his left side. Davon had insisted he wear a warm riding fur over top, to avoid any chill.

I am pleased you are comfortable. Ar'we startled him with her intrusion. Then, *I do not* mean *to be intrusive. You were stating your thoughts very loudly.* Again, she sounded somewhat piqued.

Reylin had never realized dragons were so . . . whatever Ar'we was. She was not merely a mount, like a horse.

Of course I am not a horse.

Reylin made an effort to close his mind. By the Light, no wonder Ar'we had heard the gossip of Ironhold! His realization was overwhelming, for he had never considered the possibility that anyone could hear his personal thoughts. He had to be more careful.

I apologize, Ar'we, he thought intentionally at her. *I have never thought you to be a horse, but I have never met a dragon until you.*

Many hamanool do not remember anymore, she answered with an odd inflection. Was that sadness he detected? *We are daragool, and we are meant to be your equals.*

Reylin considered that for a while. His education included the old legends, and he knew mankind had been more closely bonded to dragons thousands of years ago. But what that really meant, he didn't understand. He had never experienced a relationship with a creature like Ar'we. He imagined it could be a friendship even, for she was intelligent enough, but he still couldn't accept the degree of connection involved in bonding. He would leave that to a man like Davon.

Ar'we, would you mind asking Davon a question for me?

If it is necessary.

Again, her response was so practical and neutral, careless of the respect he was due.

Your Highness, she added.

Reylin closed his mind again, a habit he needed to build if she was that attuned to his mental and emotional state. He debated asking Davon more about the elderly servant woman at Camdry, then decided against it. Such a query was blatantly obtrusive, no matter how curious the exchange between Davon and the elderly woman had been.

He had left his entire High Guard to watch over his Chosen and his babe, and yet his insides twisted at abandoning them. Simultaneously, he worried on another front. He loved Syrana, and she loved him, but if she couldn't get pregnant, he would have to marry again simply to produce an heir. He didn't relish the thought of finding yet another bride, although he liked women. Three wives, for the sake of one son.

Yet here was Davon, a man of indeterminate age, dedicated to a single woman for the long years of his life, a woman who could not warm his bed or tend the fire at his hearth. Reylin had thought commoners could marry for love. What had kept them apart?

They rode in silence for hours, until the landscape ahead suddenly changed.

The fingers of the Sikrat dropped down suddenly, as though some great god had flattened the earth with a giant palm, and beyond was the vast Loi al'Halmana, the Sea of Grass.

Reylin had never seen it before.

Where Mirat was craggy with character, the plains were pristine in their simplicity. The ground seemed to undulate with the breeze, endless tall grasses and grains waving and flickering as a single monstrous beast. Reylin shuddered. Those grasses hid a wildness that could only be tamed by a plow and sword.

He pointed at the distant town surrounded by a small military camp and requested for Ar'we to land. She banked and descended lazily, giving him and Davon a wide view of the ground. They surpassed a smaller village, which lay in ruin. Every building appeared to be scorched, although the fires had burnt out, and a few industrious bodies moved about, dragging carcasses into a mass grave. The workers glanced up at the dragon and pointed.

Reylin straightened in the saddle. They were already in awe of Ar'we's presence, but how much more gratified would they be when they learned *he* was astride her? Their king was here and prepared to exact a painful vengeance upon the fyr.

Ar'we landed with an earthshaking thud, and Reylin took his battle helm from Davon and tucked it under his arm. He strode forward and waited a moment as the military camp mustered itself. Two platoons. That was all Galltry had sent.

He resisted shaking his head in disappointment and anger, for their knight captain approached with his second-in-command. The man peered behind Reylin at Davon and Ar'we, then broke into a relieved smile and bowed deep.

"Your Highness, I was not expecting you, but praise the Light you're here!" he cried. "Welcome to the Halmani front, sire."

Reylin indicated that the man could rise, and he introduced himself and his second-in-command.

"I was concerned, Sir Forin, that you had not been adequately supplied with men and arms. It appears my concern was valid."

Sir Forin failed to control a wince. "Lord Galltry was quite clear—two platoons of cavalry, sire. We're to maintain a protective line out of this town, Edgegrass."

"An apt name," muttered Reylin, "if we never advance. Tell me, Sir Forin, do you believe this is the edge?"

The man stuttered a little. He was a knight from Galltry's barracks, but Gillead had chosen him for command, which meant he should be loyal to the crown. Forin cleared his throat. "It is only the edge for now, sire."

Reylin approved of that answer. "Protect for now, Sir Forin, but I promise you I will seek more troops for your command, that you may push forward for Mirat's integrity and glory."

"Thank you, sire."

Content with the favorable impression he had made, Reylin settled into the military camp, introducing himself to many of the fighting men and encouraging them. The ones deployed to grave duty returned and greeted him with enthusiasm, and he realized Davon had gone to assist them. There was far less fear surrounding Ar'we's presence than he would have expected, and she romped through the camp on all fours like a dog, still shaking dirt from her crimson mane. The rancor for the loss of the other village was raw, and the men were nearly drooling with their eagerness to punish any fyr who approached.

Around the campfire that evening, Reylin considered his next moves. Two platoons seemed so inadequate, although they were powerful cavalrymen. Their chargers were healthy, and their weapons well-oiled and ready. They even had an herbsman with them, for which Reylin was grateful. He suspected that was Gillead's choice, not Galltry's. In any case, the endless grass just beyond the town edge could hide an unspeakable number of enemies.

Sir Forin placed a platter at his side, stacked with a hearty stew, sliced bread with butter and jam, and a variety of roasted spring tubers. "Do you know much of makran, sire? Predators of the grassland, nasty felines."

Reylin nodded appreciatively and took a bite of the food. Forin must have had the local inn prepare a finer meal for Reylin than for himself, for Forin had a simpler platter in front of himself. "Are they presenting a problem?" He glanced nervously out at the mysterious grass; its constant whisper was audible even from where he sat.

"No, Your Highness. I was merely thinking about them because of what you said about living on the edge. Predators like the edge—it's good hunting. The wealth and refinement of Mirat is denser farther in"—he waved toward the rising mountain foothills behind them—"but so too is the security. A fyr warrior would never succeed attacking an interior village, for it would be shot down. Here, though, the brave Miratians of the edge territory face the potential of frequent incursions."

"And you equate these fyr to makran?"

"Any lone predator, Your Highness. Perhaps a falcon is a more appropriate comparison."

"All the more reason to move the edge, so towns like this one are no longer at risk."

The men around the fire muttered agreement, and Sir Forin gave Reylin a look of sincere respect.

I hunt the edge, came Ar'we's matter-of-fact voice. *Does that make me dangerous?*

Reylin's glance around the fire verified that she had projected to everyone. Davon turned beet red. "I'm sorry, Your Highness. She doesn't understand the politics of this."

People need to be protected from people sometimes, Ar'we declared stoutly. *I know this, but do not understand why it is so.* She cocked her head, then disappeared into the camp again, seeking chin scratches from the grave diggers.

Davon released a quavering sigh and gave Reylin a sheepish look. He opened his mouth, then bit his lip and sat quietly, watching the flames.

"Will she fight, if it comes to it?" Reylin asked in a low voice. He closed his mind to Ar'we, assuring she wouldn't hear as she gallivanted between tents on the other side of the camp.

Davon nodded. "We will, Your Highness. We will do anything you ask in the name of Mirat."

It was Ar'we who alerted them the next day.

They are coming, she said simply. *They are very loud.*

Reylin and Davon alerted the camp immediately, and over half of the men managed to mount before a group of Halmani poured from the tall grass and into the camp. They were scattered in threes, charging through the tents on colorful running birds.

The fyr rode their holy birds, tall creatures with swanlike necks and vicious raptor beaks. Raiya. Their powerful legs pumped at pace that could likely exceed that of a horse, and they occasionally fluttered back to deliver violent, clawed kicks. Their chests and necks were guarded by leather armor, and they wore armored helmets that formed a bitless bridle behind their snapping beaks.

The fyr themselves were arrayed to match. Their feathered headdresses and skirts varied in length and color, a stark contrast against their white hair and tanned skin. Smaller-bodied than typical Miratians, the fyr rode comfortably on their two-legged mounts, swinging small, bardiche-like weapons in each hand. The long crescent blades swept by their potential victims as the fyr galloped, and then Reylin saw one dismount. The fyr warrior snapped the two ends together, creating a double-bladed staff that extended his reach substantially. The warrior tumbled gracefully into an acrobatic dance, jabbing at the soldiers around him.

Reylin, who had slept in his armor in case this very thing happened, grabbed his scabbard and rushed toward the melee. His blood rose and thundered through his body; it was invigorating. To be in it, part of it. He wanted this.

He dove between a fyr warrior and a man who was struggling to drag his sword from the scabbard, having only just cinched his belt. Reylin sliced at the fyr's arm, opening a wound large enough that the creature dropped half his bardiche with a squawk. The fyr stumbled away and twisted the staff apart, then turned to Reylin with one good arm swinging. He was fast, unbelievably fast, and Reylin parried, sucking in a breath of surprise. The warrior fought well, slowing only as the unstaunched wound bled out on his other arm. As Reylin prepared for a killing blow, the warrior keened, an odd, high trill that cut across the camp. A raiya appeared, and the warrior wrapped his arm around the bird's neck as it ran by. He disappeared into the grass.

Reylin snarled. Coward.

The camp was in chaos. Sir Forin had not been ready to meet this attack, as unregimented as it was. The fyr had no battle formation, no strategy, but they were fierce. Was this what Galltry meant when he suggested the fyr were reactive?

A sick feeling ran through him. Was this a reaction to *his* arrival? A bonded Earth Dragon could be interpreted as a threat.

He sensed Ar'we gliding overhead. Davon was nowhere to be seen, and Reylin realized the dragonkeeper was with Ar'we. The two dove upon the mounted fyr, with Ar'we dragging her fearsome rear talons across the enemy's backs. She grabbed one and flung it through the air. The flightless bird flapped its undersized wings uselessly, and it rolled into a heap with its rider. A soldier dispatched the fyr quickly as the creature tried to climb out from underneath the plume of feathers.

Ar'we roared, a terrifying growl that shook the ground beneath Reylin's feet.

No, it was more than that. She projected power like he had never felt before, and it reverberated through the earth. Many of the mounted fyr fell from their staggering raiya, as did some of the cavalrymen. Horses bucked, men screamed, and birds scattered in panic without their riders.

Reylin made quick work of two or three disoriented fyr, then realized the camp had quieted somewhat.

The surviving fyr melted into the grass, leaving their dead behind.

Reylin immersed himself in the Water of war. The heavy iron-richness of blood, both man and fyr. The pollution of the air with piss and sweat. The sharp tang of body paint from the corpse at his feet.

He knelt, aware of the hurried movement around him as Sir Forin pulled the camp back together.

Up close, this creature looked like a man, just like the one he had inspected at East Face Mine so long ago. The nose was a bit long and hooked, the eyes hazel with tawny edges. Unlike the one at East Face, this one had never revealed its fyrform, instead riding a tamed flightless bird. Perhaps their cavalry couldn't transform, Reylin considered. Not all of the potential slaves they procured from the Loi al'Halmana could shift; that was why Mirat's royal household retained only the nonshifting ones, like Syrana's handmaiden.

That gave a distinct advantage, if Ar'we and Davon were to remain at the front. Despite their lack of training, they had saved the unprepared soldiers from greater damage, and it was clear Sir Forin needed help. Reylin tucked that thought away for later.

Then he plucked a single feather from the front of the warrior's headdress. It was an iridescent pink. He did the same to the others felled by his hand and tucked the feathers away for Sir Ronidann.

He stood and caught Forin's eye, then exerted all of his authority. With his chest puffed out and his chin high, he had a solid hand and a half over the knight captain, as well as a substantial amount of youthful brawn.

The man awaited orders.

"Burn the grassland, Sir Forin."

Forin licked his lips and looked toward where the last fyr had disappeared. "It is holy to them, Your Highness."

Rather than repeat himself, Reylin merely stared at the man.

Forin cast a doubtful glance at Ar'we, who had landed nearby.

"She's an Earth Dragon, Sir Forin. Torch the grass to a minimum five-hundred-pace perimeter around the camp and town, so this doesn't happen again." He leaned over Forin. "The grass is not holy to me, and I am your king."

The man bowed low, apologizing profusely for the attack, for his lack of preparation, for everything he hadn't done that he could do, but Reylin waved him away. *Don't tell me you're going to do it. Just do it.*

Reylin oversaw the changes in the encampment for a while longer, reassuring the soldiers through his presence. They had endured eight deaths and fourteen injuries, numbers Reylin believed to be inexcusable. Was Forin truly the best person to command this group? What was Gillead thinking?

Then the prince realized—he walked a precarious line between talent and loyalty. Perhaps Galltry's barracks did not contain a more strategic knight who was loyal to Reylin. He resumed a forced smile as he helped the men reassemble the camp. All he could do was build more loyalty in the ranks, bypassing errant leadership from Galltry and his closest men.

He was somewhat satisfied by the time he and Davon lifted off the next morning, heading a shorter distance to East Face Mine. From above, the camp's canvas tents were stark white inside a blackened semicircle of charred earth that extended a good distance into the plains. Nothing could surprise them now, and there was plenty of room to charge. The soldiers bid them farewell with formal salutes as they rose in the sky.

Their flight to East Face was peaceful, and Reylin used the time to manage the warring emotions inside. It was clear that the front needed more military support, although he still wondered if the attack was a response to his presence. The gall of it irked him enough to respond with greater vigor, regardless. Somehow, he would have to force Galltry's hand. Perhaps he could use Davon and Ar'we; they had more than proven their loyalty.

They settled down in the clearing below East Face Mine. The space had been dug out and flattened, stumps burned and removed, and foundations laid in several places for the large fort. The clearing, however, was eerily silent, as Ar'we commented on.

Then he noted the sound of wailing. There was movement as the doors of several of the log cabins opened, and one servant ran into the mine and reappeared with a tired-looking Daiunek.

The normally garrulous guildmaster greeted Reylin with a modicum of formality, then gestured toward a table. He beckoned for drinks, and the servant brought out the heavy tar beer Reylin hated.

"It's a bit early for such a heavy drink, Guildmaster," Reylin said in a low voice. "What's happened here?"

Wethers settled beside them; his swaying cup reeked of putrid liquor. "The Earth gives and takes as she will," he slurred, "but that doesn't mean we have to be happy about it."

Daiunek tore his gaze from his own mug and dragged it up to Reylin. Tears glistened, and it was evident he had already wept, for muddy trails streaked down his broad cheeks.

"Master Oyerton is dead," he said in a gruff, tortured voice. "And many others."

Reylin stared, then forced himself to look about the clearing again. Half of the colonists' wagon train sat unloaded, and entire families peeked out the doors of the small cabins. The children were filthy, their hair mussed; the women were haggard; the men were exhausted and bloodied. "No," he whispered, almost to himself.

"The fyr must be watching us like hawks," Daiunek said with a loud sniffle. He wiped his nose, smearing more mucky stain across his face. "They attacked the morning after the train arrived. They targeted the families. What kind of monster does that?"

Reylin's heart pounded in his ears. "Did my soldiers help at all?"

"They did all they could. They gave warning, and they fought well. There were simply too many fyr, coming from every direction in the sky and targeting those who couldn't fight back. The colonists were hit hardest." Daiunek beckoned for refills.

Despite himself, Reylin gratefully drained his mug, hoping the stout alcohol would ease the tightness in his chest. Was it a mistake to have encouraged colonization?

"What of Halmani Mine?"

Daiunek scrubbed his dirty beard. "Abandoned for now."

"Rich with rubies," Wethers mumbled. "Light's end, she tasted sweet."

"Doesn't matter now," snapped Daiunek.

The other man grumbled into his cup.

Daiunek looked expectantly at Reylin. "What can we do, Prince? The guild wants security, but if we establish East Face as a town, then it goes beyond the guild's means to guard it. How quickly can we raise this fort, and how many men will be stationed here when it's done? We simply need more resources, both men and materials."

Reylin swallowed back his sharp retort. He already knew all these things.

He just hadn't expected the situation to go so wrong, so quickly. He thought they had a little more time to build the walls, solid stone against which a feathered monster could batter itself all day and night and not leave a scratch.

"I'll get you both, Guildmaster," he promised, clenching his jaw. "Would it help to have aerial support?" He glanced at Davon, who hadn't touched his mug.

The dragonkeeper gave him a sober look and a slight nod.

Reylin controlled his ire at the implied permission, but he was certain Ar'we had picked it up, for she came over immediately and inserted herself. The colonists hiding in the houses yelped in fright, and some of them shut their doors.

Wethers goggled at the intimidating creature he found blocking his view, but Daiunek recovered quickly. "Such a boon would change our fate, Prince Reylin, Keeper Davon. My thanks are but one small voice in a hundred." That seemed to change his attitude, and he finally looked across the clearing with hope. "East Face could be a glorious place to live, rich in the metals of Earth and blessed by her hand, a gorgeous view and the clearest night skies I've seen in years. I've half a mind not to return to the Masterhall at all."

"Then so it will be, Guildmaster." Reylin gave the brawny man a firm handshake. "Grace us with a little time, for Keeper Davon must return me to Ironhold before he begins his duties here. He'll provide regular oversight at Edgegrass as well."

"Frighten the birds away," Wethers mumbled into his mug. He tipped it upside down; it was empty. Without so much as a farewell, he staggered away, undoubtedly to find more of that magical liquid that chased off bad memories.

The worst had happened. Oyerton and a vast portion of the first group of homesteaders, brave-faced and bold as they marched toward a bright future, were dead.

53

SYRANA HAD PRACTICED THE fawning look for Reylin in the mirror a hundred times, and yet when he returned, she felt entirely unprepared.

How could he leave her without warning?

She hurried down the steps with as much elegance as she could afford. Her heeled shoes sparkled with diamonds and, despite their extremely ill fit, drew the eye as she hitched her heavy skirts above her ankles.

The High Guard were right behind her. They hovered like fretting mothers, having nothing else to concern themselves over while Reylin was gone—especially Sir Gillead, who wore a sour grimace constantly. It was irritating, although she liked the occasional attentive conversation from Sirs Ronidann and Dorian.

Father Kaiadin remained at the top of the steps, reserved and patient. He folded his hands inside his draping indigo robes and merely watched.

Reylin leapt down from the Ar'we creature's back with a hard look she couldn't read, and he strode over to her and stopped. He held his head high and yet kept his gaze toward the clean-scrubbed flagstones, working his jaw.

After a beat, Syrana flung her arms around his broad shoulders. It required an ungainly hop, and she prayed her mother wasn't watching from a window somewhere, but she quickly found herself clutched in his desperate grip. It almost hurt, for he still wore hard plate armor. She controlled her reaction to the cold metal and reached up to kiss his bristly neck. It was sharp with the growth of several days.

She felt his chest heave, and then his hands curved down her buttocks and pulled her up. Her ready lips met his in a rough kiss. It was followed by a long, wandering one as he explored her lips, her chin, her cheeks. Her feet hung without touching the ground, and she adjusted her hold around his neck.

"I missed you, my love," she whispered.

He didn't answer beyond a low grunt as he buried his face in her loose black hair. It reminded her of her father, a man who often communicated with grunts. What was he feeling? She had expected a smirk, almost mischievous at his demonstration of independence. Galltry had been livid, but couldn't do anything about it, and she was certain that was precisely the intended effect.

He held her like that long enough that she began to feel embarrassed. At least they were in the inner courtyard. Who was watching that hadn't seen more? The High Guard had seen plenty of displays; even Father Kaiadin had seen them in more intimate situations due to his tendency to interrupt with important news. She embraced his need and began to play with his somewhat long hair.

He never cut it short like a knight, instead keeping it somewhat loose and thick to the nape of his neck. She stroked it lightly, regretting wearing the number of rings she had, for they would catch and yank if she wasn't careful. Reylin grumbled into her hair again; she could feel the heat of his breath behind her ear.

"Tell me," she commanded. "Give it all to me."

He unburied his face and seemed to see the others for the first time. "Is Galltry here?"

"No, he returned home when he heard you had gone."

Reylin almost smiled. "Probably feeling insecure about his eastern front. Good." He released her, placing her gently back on her feet. The pain of her shoes immediately shot through her arches and ankles.

Sir Gillead bowed. "Welcome back, Your Highness." His tone was measured and stiff, then eased with what seemed to be genuine concern. "We received a bird from Sir Forin at the eastern front, but I'd like to hear your perspective and experience."

Reylin's hand on her shoulder tightened. "No birds from East Face?" He glanced at the towers, the countless windows overlooking the courtyard, then suggested they go inside. "Council room," he stated simply, then turned behind him. "You too, Keeper Davon. Father Kaiadin, retrieve the baroness as well by the next bell."

In the privacy of his council room, after a bath and a change of clothes, Reylin gave a shocking report. Syrana had little role for commentary, but she listened.

No wonder he had been in a dour mood.

Her mother had numerous questions regarding the condition of the colonists' train, the state of their supplies, and the number of lives lost of each age. She produced convincing tears, but Syrana knew she was merely tallying the gaps created by the fyr attack. Reylin tasked her with compiling a new train and coordinating extensive lumber and stone supplies from Camdry.

"Your Highness, are you certain—" Sir Gillead began.

"I didn't ask you, Gillead." Reylin's words were harsh, infused with the aggravation of responsibility for the former train. He would need comforting later. "Master Daiunek and I already agreed to pull back from Halmani Mine. I refuse to give more ground than that."

Sir Gillead acknowledged him and leaned back in his chair, while Sir Patreagh scrubbed at his bearded chin, but said nothing.

Reylin surveyed the other High Guard, then pursed his lips in a tight smile. "I value your advice and leadership as lord commander, Gillead, and we can strategize later on precisely whom we should deploy both eastward and northward. But I will not retreat. For now, I have a gift for *you*, Ronidann." He pulled several feathers from inside his jacket. His cocksure smirk finally appeared, matched by Sir Ronidann's open grin. "One for each fyr," he said, placing the handful on the table and sliding them toward his knight.

Sir Ronidann chuckled. "Well-fought, Your Highness." He selected a single one in sunburst yellow with white edges, then pushed them back. "Thank you for the gift, but you should keep the others as mementos."

Sirs Gillead and Patreagh both grumbled in their throats.

Syrana expressed an appropriately ladylike mixture of appalled horror and admiration, her gaze lingering on Reylin's face.

He looked pleased. He had fought at East Face Mine, but this Edgegrass battle sounded far more violent, more dangerous, and more unexpected. He had saved the day with Davon and Ar'we.

Reylin ended their meeting quickly, leaving Davon, Gillead, and her mother to finalize defense and supply plans for East Face. Gillead insisted the men he had already mustered for their westward move were best redirected to meet the needs at East Face and Edgegrass, necessitating a delay. Reylin acquiesced with surprisingly little fight.

"I must be present at the Summer Solstice Festival in any case," Reylin said, gesturing for Gillead to go. "Deploy the men you've readied to East Face, and Davon shall accompany them."

He even dismissed Father Kaiadin in his eagerness, and they headed toward the gardens.

Before long, Syrana had him to herself. His hand enveloped hers as they meandered through the hedge maze, a twisting fountain- and statue-filled labyrinth of greenery that made her feel as though they were alone, despite the shadowing steps of the High Guard.

She gasped with delight when they entered one of the hidden clearings. A picnic was laid out, along with a pile of plush blankets and down pillows. Halmani slaves stood at attention in the grove entrances, ready to serve. The central statue was one of two lovers in the throes of passion.

"How did you manage this?" she wondered as he pulled her into the grove.

The gold in his eyes gleamed with desire, and the darkness that had lingered over him as they walked retreated. "My Chosen . . ." he said, his voice rough. "I'm sorry I left without warning."

She debated a response. Ire and pouting? Or abject amnesty? She leaned up to kiss him. The latter was what he needed.

They dined, made love, and talked over enough glasses of Marlemetian red wine that she lost count, until the near-summer sun dipped behind the mountains. The slaves lit their candles, and the grove flickered with the soft glow of a hundred firebugs. And still they remained, tumbling among the soft blankets in a passionate frenzy, each desperate for the other's affirmation.

Syrana plucked a slice of citrus, a rarity imported from Tamorín, from the platter and savored its uniquely sour flavor. It paired better with the effervescent from Loreni, and she beckoned her handmaiden to pour her a fresh glass. She leaned back in a mound of pillows, naked under the stars and utterly content.

Reylin watched her, his eyes dark and possessive as they traveled down her figure.

She gave him her most seductive smile. "My love? Don't leave me behind again."

His dark lashes fluttered away in self-deprecation for a moment, then back. He crawled to her, trailing a finger up from her navel to her chin, then kissed her softly. "It wasn't practical or safe, Syrana. My High Guard didn't come either."

Now she pouted. "Then promise me this: anywhere you go with your High Guard, you shall bring me. I want to be with you always, no matter how dangerous." She bit his lip on the next kiss, preventing him from pulling away, and lingered close.

"I must keep you safe," he murmured, his expression softening. His breath had quickened, and she knew he thought of Lupine. How close she had been to losing him, and he to losing her.

"I am safest by your side, my king."

He nodded, then pressed against her urgently. "As you please, my queen."

The solstice arrived too quickly.

Syrana had ordered several dresses from the master tailor for the event, one for the daytime and one for the evening, and three more for the market that followed on subsequent days. Her mother laid each one out, evaluating their cut and quality.

"You should wear this one last. It will be most forgiving of bloating should you overeat." Ana pointed at one.

Syrana sighed. "I'm not Priscilla, Ma."

The woman twitched her finely plucked eyebrows up just enough to express her displeasure. "Don't talk back to me, you useless girl." She handed the selected gown to Syrana's handmaiden, who hung it carefully along a rack of chosen dresses. Ana picked another. "This one should be first. It will highlight your physical traits during the feast. Nice bust line, corset well cut to accommodate sitting as long as you keep your back straight like a proper lady." She didn't wait for Syrana's approval this time, instead snapping her fingers at the handmaiden to take care of it. Then she stalked back and forth from the remaining line of dresses, no doubt to choose the best ball gown for dancing.

"Have you chosen your *own* dresses already?"

"Days ago," her mother replied. "How can one be adequately prepared for such an event without thought and time? Or perhaps you hadn't considered that." She leered at Syrana then, daring her to speak.

Syrana's throat felt dry, and she inspected her toes, which showed beneath her thin shift. Her mother had insisted she try each dress on again, to ensure it fit well and that Syrana had not gained undue weight.

"Straighten your shoulders and raise your chin," Ana snapped. "You cannot command a room slumping like a farm-worn peasant woman. Now, tell me, why am I disappointed with every one of these dresses' cuts?" She waved an imperious hand across the beautiful gowns, each unique and brightly colored to match the season.

Syrana, chin high and neck straightened, stared hard at the wall and blinked back tears. "Because they're not cut for a woman with a showing belly."

"You've had months, Syrana. *Months*. Are you trying anything novel? Are you trying at all? Stop crying, you'll ruin your rouge. Did you have *fun* during your little garden party? Because fun is not the reason you're here. You have the opportunity to be Heir-Mother and Queen Consort. Don't ruin it."

Syrana nodded continually, wishing only that the conversation was over. Why had her mother insisted on leaving Camdry?

When Syrana had gone to court to serve as the duchess Shildra's lady-in-waiting, she truly believed she had escaped. She had thought she could define her own place and persona, and yet here she was. The pale and deficient imitation of the commanding Baroness Ana ol'Camdry, who'd single-handedly organized the colonization of East Face. The barren and unwanted daughter, a poor substitute for the second son Ana had desired. Her mother had once told her that she had been named "Seran" in the womb, but she had emerged without the correct anatomy.

The baroness finally relented, leaving one more insult to Syrana's Halmani handmaiden lingering in the air as she swept out.

Syrana could hear Sir Dorian bid Ana farewell from beyond the door. Reylin never left her alone entirely, although Dorian and the others didn't post inside the rooms she was in. For that, she was glad, for her own conversations were primarily secretive and shameful.

She slumped onto the chaise, and her handmaiden approached cautiously with an herbal tea that reeked of green magika. Syrana cursed at her and covered her eyes for a moment, then sat back up.

"Dress me. We must do more. Father Kaiadin will understand, surely. Let us seek him out."

Her handmaiden bowed and dressed her, then fixed her makeup without commentary.

The deep, grounding breath Syrana wished to take was hindered by the tightness of her corset. Her toes were pinched in stunning shoes, her handflowers so elaborate with hanging stones that glittered and clinked in dangling stringers, they made her hands useless. All she could do was touch the tips of her fingers together in prayer, which was precisely what she was going to pretend to do.

They headed to the High Temple, trailed by Sir Dorian.

The temple floor shone with jewels of light, broken occasionally by worshipers crossing the gallery to each shrine. The central mirrored room hosted not only Syrana and her handmaiden, but also a secret. She followed Father Kaiadin through a hidden door that led down a tightly curled stairwell to the basement. Her handmaiden stayed in the mirrored chamber to ensure their privacy, and Sir Dorian, clueless as he was, remained outside the chamber with his right hand comfortably cocked over his scabbard. To all those outside, it would appear Syrana had entered the shrine for private prayers, a ritual she completed daily as a woman of great and unadulterated faith.

Kaiadin guided her with a dim lamp to a small storage room with crammed shelves. The air was thick with herbal scents, overwhelming the more subtle smells of feathers, sheaves of stretched and dried leather, and powdered metals. Vials of blood, scent secretions, and tears were arranged carefully along one wall, but in no order Syrana could identify.

"Are we trying something new today?" Syrana asked. "I don't believe the tea is working, nor anything else we've tried. Father, I'm desperate for your help. Reylin could have died or been grievously injured at Edgegrass, or even at East Face."

Kaiadin nodded as he searched the shelves for a particular ingredient.

"Ah, yes, here it is. Rabbit blood," he muttered, squinting at the dusty vials and blowing on one of the labels. He sneezed and adjusted his falling spectacles.

Syrana wrinkled her nose. "Pardon, Father?"

Kaiadin turned to her with an unstudied look. "Rabbit blood, very good for fertility. We can prepare this treatment now, but have you given the tea a full month?"

"Nearly, Father, but I feel no different," said Syrana, "and I am certain I'm not with child." She gulped back her tears. The week had been a dismay as her body resisted her efforts; her mother acted unsurprised and made her feel no better about it. *"Damned useless girl, even with Priscilla gone you cannot stake your claim."* Syrana wished with all her heart that her mother would go home, but she realized how integral the baroness was to handling logistics for Reylin, assuring marks and supplies made their way to Camdry and onward to East Face. Why, even a contingent of cavalry! *"See, Syrana? Indispensable."*

"Do not worry, my dear lady," urged Father Kaiadin. "I can see that you fear losing the prince's love, but he does not love you for your womb alone."

Kaiadin guided Syrana through a new preparation, mixing the rabbit blood with her own along with a variety of powdered herbs. The mage then prayed over the bowl, invoking the Old Language in a rhythmic chant that Syrana didn't understand. When Kaiadin was finished, he poured the mixture into a glass bottle with a dropper and handed it to her.

"Twelve drops per day, Princess, with your tea or meal."

Syrana recoiled in disgust. "I have to drink it?" She had assumed the blood was to be injected directly, or applied as a wash. She'd rather bathe in blood than drink it.

"The enchantment is far more powerful if the potion is ingested," Kaiadin insisted. "Such is most red magika."

Syrana reluctantly took the vial and hid it in her dress.

"Take the potion daily for sixteen days before doubting, Crown Princess," Kaiadin continued. "It is a more powerful intercession than most require, and I am confident it will improve your womb's receptivity."

Syrana thanked him and headed for the stairwell. "I shall trust in I'ya, good Father."

Kaiadin saw her out, bidding a polite farewell to her handmaiden as well. "Show it to no one, daughter. Go with my blessings, and trust in the guidance given."

Her hopes renewed, Syrana considered how pleasing her finery was, and after taking a draught of the potion mixed with juice from a street vendor, she figured she should seek Reylin.

She stepped along carefully, trying to move with elegance despite the pain of her heels, and cursed herself for not calling upon a litter.

When she was nearly back to the castle, Kaiadin hurried up beside her, matching her stride and, after a moment, offering her a gangly arm.

"Father," she greeted him with surprise.

"Crown Princess," he said as though he hadn't just spent time with her in the Temple's darker recesses. "An urgent message has arrived for Prince Reylin. Might you know where he is?"

Syrana quickened her pace. "I'll take you to him, Father." Excellent, she thought. Reylin often spent this time of day doting on Amber in the ivy-and-rose-canopied pavilion of the south garden. This was a fine reason to pull him from attending the distracting babe, who wouldn't remember his time and attention in any case.

It was exactly where they found him. He lay on the brick plaza beneath the green-spackled shade of intermingling vines above, Amber swaddled and held to his bare chest. He stared up at the pink roses with a faint, foolish smile which faded quickly with the shuffle of their approaching steps.

Father Kaiadin half-bobbed while also trying to pull a sealed note from his robes. "My young king, another bird from Lord Lío," he stuttered. "It could not wait."

Syrana leaned down and took the babe. Amber began to wail as she was yanked from the cozy spot, and Syrana made a show of remorse before handing the bundle off to a waiting nurse.

Reylin sat up and took the note, snapping the wax apart and reading intently. He glowered at the message.

> *My prince, I fear the effects of this disease. According to our source in Krita Port, it has not yet affected any noble lineages, but the sick are aggressive and unpredictable. If the disease infiltrates the common population, we may be endangered without additional mil-*

itary support. Therefore, I request immediate dispatch of several platoons to North Mara Port to quell any violence.

Respectfully, Lord Lío

He handed it back to the mage.

"We'll depart immediately following the festival. Lord Commander, is that enough time to muster a company?"

Sir Gillead inclined his head solemnly. "Yes, Your Highness. Just enough."

"We shall lead them west, rather than lingering for the market days." A strange glint in the amber flecks made Syrana wonder at his words. He seemed to look forward to the festival, a strange attitude given Galltry's audacious request for a silly speech about "loss of lives" and the "East Face tragedy." Surely, Reylin wasn't anticipating *that* embarrassment.

"Lord Lío will appreciate your responsiveness, my young king," said Kaiadin. "And then we shall have an opportunity to study this disease firsthand. Truly, a wise move."

Syrana shooed the nurses away with a subtle look and gestured for Ronidann to assist Reylin in standing. She couldn't do so herself with the dangling jewels wrapping her fingers and wrists, nor could she sit down on the filthy pavilion to join him.

Reylin kissed the diamonds on her middle finger after dusting himself off. "My lady, are you ready for the adventure you so fervently demanded?"

She allowed her hand to fall delicately, and she gave him a sweet smile. "I would have it no other way."

"Then how can I refuse?" he answered. "Will you forgive me for disallowing the public display of your new gowns?"

She tossed her hair coquettishly. "I shall wear them when and how I please. Why not North Mara? However, you, my love, have likely not selected your finery for the first day." She left the last word on a high note, half implying a question as she recalled Reylin's thoughtful commission of matching clothes for the Festival of Remembrance. He likely cared less for the solstice, but . . .

He kissed her cheek and began to escort her back inside. "In truth, I have."

She wasn't sure whether her surprise or pleasure showed more, but he wore a self-satisfied half smirk that told her enough.

Ana's gown choice could be tossed aside.

Syrana felt her lips curl into a genuine smile.

54

LYRA'S INEXPERIENCE WITH WATER magika frustrated her mentor—and his translator, Jikaa. Between wind exercises, the Godspeaker would have her sit on the edge of the well, reaching down to the water and attempting to "touch" it, slosh it about with smoother and smoother motions. Sometimes those exercises worked, and sometimes the water would be completely still. Lyra had no idea why.

The fourth morning burned away, and the camp began preparations for the noon meal. A woman shuffled up to the well with an empty pot and gestured at Lyra. Lyra immediately stepped back, apologizing and allowing the woman to retrieve water using the long rope. Several other women followed, each using the well in turn and averting their gaze from the strange, scarred man nearby.

Konan had been riding his mare, but Lyra could tell he needed a break. His development reminded her of the younger children in the caravan, who eventually all learned to ride expertly. She had seen many boys and girls learn, but it had never occurred to hear that a grown man might not know how.

It struck her yet again that Konan had been in Tahayi Mines for a very long time—he still hadn't told her exactly how long. She knew he had once hailed from Mirat, for his descriptions of its beauty were raw and dreamlike. The copper flecks in his right eye gleamed when he spoke of the mountains, and sometimes he didn't end his ruminations with that familiar sadness. There were good memories to recall, she wanted to remind him, but she was afraid of pointing that out in case it grated too much. If he loved Mirat as much as he seemed to, then he knew what he had lost.

The last woman in line carefully drew the bucket up, grasping its edge to tip it into her pot. She whimpered. A thin stream of muddy water poured out, barely enough for a bowl of stew.

The well was exhausted.

The woman dropped to her knees and crawled to the Godspeaker, gibbering Manalali and plucking at his crimson-and-black robes. Her wails drew Konan's attention, and he half cantered over at an awkward pace. Thordrin appeared shortly after, still sweating from his drills with Hafka and Rahar.

The Godspeaker spoke soothingly to the woman, placing his wrinkled palm on her head, then turned to Lyra.

"It has not rained enough for nearly two seasons," he said somberly. Jikaa translated, his face stricken as the woman's. The Godspeaker continued, tapping the well's edge with his staff. "This was our deepest well, the well of life and the fruit of the Mother's shrine. It has sustained us these last months, but it has dropped as the Haralal gained power. We believe it is their curse."

Hafka and Rahar muttered to each other, and Lyra heard the word "gyr" once again.

The Godspeaker stamped his staff in the sand. "In our time of need, we the Favored children followed the signs of water, and Desert Mother brought us to you. That is no coincidence. You must be the well of life for our people. You must bring us water."

Lyra quailed at the thought.

Konan winced as he dismounted and came beside her, then peered down the well. He seemed dubious.

The Godspeaker pointed down the well. "You can, and only you can. I *feel* your strength. Reach into this well and pull the water up."

Lyra shrank from the old man, overwhelmed by the thought, and found herself backed against Konan's broad chest. He squeezed her shoulder in encouragement, but his dubious look remained. Embarrassed, Lyra gathered enough strength to stare down at the muddy bottom of the well. Far below, only a small puddle remained in the moist sand, too small to scoop with the bucket. Konan and Thordrin did the same.

"Lyr, do you have any idea how to do that?" Thordrin said, raising his eyebrows.

"No."

"Focus your energy," came the Godspeaker's voice, confident as ever and echoed by Jikaa. "Collect it inside. Extend it through your arm, through your fingers, and reach out to that pool as you did several days ago. Touch it and feel it, just as you do the wind."

Knowing Konan had her secure, Lyra sat on the edge of the well and leaned. She extended her hand, a physical reflection of her mental reach, and splayed her fingers. As usual, she was fully aware of the element around her. The day was clear and dry, and the air was fresh and clean, with the mineral flavor of dust. The air inside the well shaft was slightly different in character: barely damp and slightly heavier, still where the well wall blocked the desert breeze but not stagnant.

She didn't believe she could feel the water below in the same way, but she tried nonetheless. Fingers outstretched, she reached. Konan's grip around her waist tightened as he leaned with her, and she felt power pulse and quaver down the well.

A delicate touch shimmered the surface, but this time the extension of self stayed there, like keeping a palm to a warm fire to absorb its temperature and essence. Lyra leaned into the feeling, imagining the water to be slick and cool, fresh and pure.

"Good," the Godspeaker said in a guttural whisper. "You feel the water on the surface. Now, extend your reach deeper and feel the water below."

Lyra took a deep, slow breath and closed her eyes, trying to focus. Konan's grip was sure and warm, and she could feel his essence enveloping hers. She was completely off-balance, extended over the distant puddle, and Konan reached his own arm out to support hers. He wouldn't let her fall, and she poured herself into the exercise.

The empty well shimmered in her mind as though a bright rope extended from each fingertip. Probing, she was certain there had to be more beneath the surface, more coolness and wet in the earth below.

"Close your hand and grasp it." The Godspeaker's voice vibrated with excitement. "Grasp it and pull it toward you."

Immersed in the power she felt around her, Lyra closed her open palm into a fist and pulled back into herself from the bottom of the well.

Thordrin swore, and Lyra opened her eyes. The trio stared down the well together, and Lyra gasped in amazement. The bottom was no longer wet sand, but a pool several hands deep. Konan pulled her back when she leaned too far, curling her own arm around her in an innocuous embrace. His left eyebrow was stretched taut, and his mouth was half-open as he stared at her and the well.

"Holy fuck, Lyr," muttered Thordrin. "You did it."

The Godspeaker pounded the ground repeatedly with his staff and danced with glee. Tears welled in his squinting eyes as he gestured at Lyra. "Again, thral. Again, draw the water up!" he cried. He cackled wildly, speaking so quickly that Jikaa didn't even bother to translate.

Jikaa, for his part, reevaluated her with new respect, a look that made her cringe. The woman who had begged the Godspeaker to do something fell to her knees and crawled to Lyra, placing her forehead against the sand as she thanked Lyra. She gibbered and tugged at Lyra's skirt, and Lyra struggled not to kick her away.

Konan tightened his secure hold as she pulled her legs away. The woman continued to beseech her, clutching and grasping and wailing, and the wind suddenly rose. The world spun for a moment, and then Jikaa yanked the woman back.

The Godspeaker stamped his staff. Lyra locked on to the sound, trying to steady herself, and the breeze calmed to a shiver.

"Again, thral," repeated the Godspeaker. "Do it again."

Lyra went through the motions once more, surrounded by Konan and Thordrin only a step away. The water slowly drew upward with repeated summoning, until finally the well was full.

The woman's wailing turned to an elated cry, and she immersed her pot into the well by hand. The rope was no longer needed, lying coiled to one side. Clutching her filled pot, she dipped into a half bow and rushed away.

The village became an uproar as men and women left their noon meal preparations to see the well, and Konan pulled Lyra back from the busy noise. The Godspeaker danced from foot to foot.

"I'ya'hakkat provides," he cried and pointed at Lyra, "through Her servant Barna'halais."

"Barna'halais," the crowd echoed. Some of them approached, falling to their knees and crawling to touch the hem of her skirt.

She flinched violently, and the wind whipped up around her, and she finally turned and hid in Konan's cloak. Lyra heard them passing near and felt the slight tug at her clothes, and she heard the slosh and splash of people dipping their basins into the well. Jubilant laughter mixed with excited chattering.

I've done something good, she repeated to herself over and over. *I've done good with my power.* She clung to the thought and fought her panic.

Konan held her close and rocked, occasionally snarling at the villagers. He pressed his hand against her shoulder; it felt odd. She peeked out to look at his fingers.

"Okay?" he signed. He tapped the sign against her skin.

She shook her head and buried her face again, and he stroked her hair while pulling her farther away.

"Barna'halais," she heard over and over amid the Manalali speech.

Shirkaa's voice boomed out and extolled her achievement loudly, repeating the term several times. He must have come down from his pavilion.

When it quieted, Lyra peeked out. The crowd had finally dispersed, leaving only the clan lord, his son, and the God-speaker. Thordrin stood back with his arms crossed and a bemused smile, watching the well like it was a show.

Konan got her attention. "What is Barna'halais?"

She shook her head and asked Jikaa, who repeated the question to the Godspeaker.

The wizened man smiled winningly, making his face a maze of wrinkles, and replied. "Giver of Life."

"Nethers, you made an impression," murmured Thordrin low enough that Shirkaa and Jikaa couldn't hear. "They're damn near worshiping you."

Shirkaa rubbed his black goatee thoughtfully. "The Desert Mother provides. I wonder, do you have enough energy left to do another boon?"

Lyra gulped. The exercise hadn't drained her as much as she expected, though, and she was afraid to tell the clan leader "no" in any case. She inclined her head respectfully.

Shirkaa beamed. "The water you brought up will help this well of life stay full, and our people and cattle sustained. Praise the Desert Mother for your gift! But, if you were to draw in the water from the surrounding lands to this camp, draw it from far off where it is dispersed and thin, and bring it here, an oasis could flourish. Our people, the Manalal, would need wander less. We would have security in this home for a greater part of the year, and we could build more permanent dwellings. I'ya'hakkat brought you to us, and I believe it is for this purpose above all. Barna'halais, will do you this great thing?"

Lyra swallowed. Her throat felt suddenly dry, and the intermittent nausea rose. It was a more difficult task, a much larger task, and she was no more certain she could do it than she had been drawing water into the well. But Shirkaa had asked, and he didn't seem to be a man familiar with disappointment. He hovered expectantly, so she nodded another affirmation.

Shirkaa broke into an even larger grin than the one he usually wore for them, and he slapped both Thordrin and Konan on the backs heartily.

Lyra could tell by Konan's stony expression that he didn't like it.

Shirkaa then pointed to the north and west. "Blessings of the Desert Mother, Barna'halais. May rains fall upon your lips. Now draw the water from that direction, from as far as you can reach."

Jikaa stepped forward and muttered in Manalali to his father, but Shirkaa brushed him off. Then he put on an almost pathetic expression of supplication, perhaps even more dramatic than the one he had worn for his daughter, and he leaned forward to beg. "Bring life to my people."

Something about his intensity made Lyra deeply uncomfortable. *You are doing something good with your magika,* she reminded herself.

She turned to the northwest and stared out, seeing nothing but desert pavement sprinkled with cacti. It seemed empty, like so much of Tahayi. It *felt* empty.

She straightened and raised a trembling hand toward the expanse. Konan stood immediately behind her, steadying her balance as he did by the well. She squeezed her eyes shut and projected outward.

There was power, raw and wild, and it channeled out through probing mental fingers. It touched the earth at their feet, then tiptoed outward, passing beyond the village edge, then farther. It pulsed and emanated from them as a palpable, tangible force. It tumbled through the cacti and across the wispy grass, over the low dunes at the horizon.

Lyra's fingers stretched wide, and she shook until Konan supported her arm once again, sliding his touch from her elbow to her wrist with a tickle that shivered through her. She imagined the faintness of the water beyond the edge of her sight, the cool and sustaining essence. She imagined it was at her fingertips like a blanket at the foot of the bed, drawn toward her with a curl of the fingertips. She dragged it inward by the ends of her fingernails, clawing at it several times and then slowly pulling her reach back in.

She heard Konan heave a breath. Lyra was leaning into him hard, and he staggered back a step to keep them balanced.

The desert seemed to shudder, as though a mass of something had shifted through the earth from far off. It came to them as the epicenter and stopped, and Lyra knew it was done.

She opened her eyes. The surface of the well water trembled and drew upward slightly, then reverberated against its walls like a dance. The magika transpired, and the feel of power slipped away, seeming to trickle back into the sand. She dropped her hand and turned to Konan.

His expression was identical to earlier. He stared out to the expanse, his jaw slack and his gaze searching the view in wonder. Then he looked down at her.

"Incredible," he signed.

Lyra couldn't help but smile. If the ground around them was filled, it could feed plants on the surface and allow the Manalal to flourish on its goodness. The village's foundation was now sustained, not only for the season but forever. This unfathomable power of Water was hers to yield, and she could bring life with it. Barna'halais. She had never had control over anything like this.

The entire group was breathless as they realized what had been done. Lyra felt like fainting, and she collapsed into Konan. He caught her with a grunt before himself falling into Thordrin. The man steadied them both with a half-hearted curse.

They settled on the edge of the well once again. Konan seemed as overwhelmed as she was and kept staring at the well water that was now within arm's reach.

Shirkaa beamed triumphantly. "A job well done, Barna'halais. Truly."

Jikaa agreed, although he furrowed his brow a little. Maybe he didn't know much about elemental magika and how draining it could be.

After they caught their breath, the trio was escorted to a noontime repast outside of Jikaa's home. They ate well, for numerous grateful families appeared with gifts of stew and meat and bread, glasses of milk and chunks of soft cheeses.

The train of offerings continued until Jikaa finally instructed them to go rest.

"The Manalal know a blessing when they see one," he warned. "They will not stop giving you gifts until they are certain you understand what a boon you have given the Mother's Favored."

55

INSTEAD OF RETURNING TO their tents or to additional lessons with the Godspeaker, they headed to the training yard, and Lyra watched Konan and Thordrin as they sparred. Thordrin was unbelievably fast with blades, especially dual-wielding knives, which seemed to be his favorite. Then again, he was talented with a longsword and bow, and proficient on a horse. If not for his lack of chivalry, she would have thought him to be a knight from a long-established preeminent lineage. Konan, on the other hand, seemed fond of brawling, most effective at disarming others and using their own momentum against them. He used a shorter sword and dagger effectively, but most often integrated his moves with throws and bodily twists. He was fast despite his larger bulk.

"Get your knives, girl," called Thordrin after a while. "Your magic may be spent, but you need to work on that too."

She wrinkled her nose at him, but Konan agreed. "This is a safe place and a good time to practice." He looked exhausted himself but kept going, so Lyra obeyed. She had them on her, having insisted on strapping a new leather bracer to each forearm beneath her robe sleeves, which Korahel hated. Thordrin twisted one side of his mouth up when he saw her pull them out. Was that pride?

They were all exhausted by the time they returned to their tents that evening. Konan leaned on Thordrin, complaining of his thighs being sore. Thordrin snapped that his own shoulder was sore from Konan's toss but carried him nonetheless.

They ate voraciously, even Lyra, and for once, Korahel didn't stop her.

Thordrin leaned back afterward. "That was quite a show today," he said. He beckoned his handmaiden. She slunk over and massaged his neck while he groaned.

Lyra blushed. "I still don't know how it worked. It's completely different than manipulating Air." She slumped onto Konan's lap, and he looked down at her.

"It was incredible," he signed, "both at the well and then later. The way you reached down, deep into the coolness of the earth. The groundwater is near the surface now, not deep and unattainable."

She smiled up at him.

"What did it feel like, Lyr?" asked Thordrin between groans of pleasure. He pulled his handmaiden onto his lap and ordered her to keep kneading his shoulders and chest. She obeyed.

Lyra stared at the sky. "I don't know. I guess it seemed clean and pure?"

"Gritty," signed Konan. "Pure, but with fine grains of sand dancing through it. Right?"

She stared up at him.

"And cold," he added, raising an eyebrow in query.

Lyra pulled herself up slowly and stared at him. "Did you feel it? Did you taste it?"

He blinked, then looked at Thordrin in confusion. "Through you," he answered.

She scrambled on top of him to look in his face. She studied his scars, his milky iris, the lost look on his face. "*I* couldn't taste it, Konan."

He breathed hard and glanced down at her knees splayed out on his lap, then up at her. "It felt slick, like worn flagstones in early spring, when the moss grows. It tasted of dust in a sandstorm, but the pollution was heavy enough to be separate from the water itself."

Lyra couldn't help but stare at him, awestruck. "By I'ya, it was you."

"What?" Thordrin emerged from his attentions on his handmaiden. "What was Konan?"

Lyra ignored him and leaned closer, edging further onto Konan's lap. "What did it feel like underground?"

Konan grasped her hips and pushed her a little ways back, then cleared his throat and signed. "It was cold, reminiscent of the ice that forms on the eaves in winter. I was immersed in it like swimming in a lake, and its purity was mixed with an earthy, rough flavor."

"What the fuck is he saying?" Thordrin demanded.

Lyra translated, utterly shocked as she repeated the words. "Konan, I felt none of those things. I could sense the power, but now I realize it wasn't coming from me. It was you, Barna'halais." She was nearly bouncing in excitement and clasped both of his hands.

They were all silent for a minute, and Konan fell to stroking the tops of her hands. He looked almost embarrassed, his smooth cheek a patchy pink. Then Lyra gasped.

"It *was* you."

"You already said that," complained Thordrin.

"No, I mean, the oasis." Lyra pulled her hands away and touched Konan's ruined face, forcing him to look at her. "The Godspeaker said we brought the water with us. Somehow, you did that, and that's how they found us."

His right cheek warmed under her hand, and he scowled with his confusion.

"You gotta tell us who you are, Konan," said Thordrin. "Few have the power we saw today. Lyr has it because she's a wayfarer, but most people with gifts are noble."

"He's noble," Lyra whispered, biting her lip at his flushed cheek.

"But not all nobles have gifts," Thordrin continued. "Not even all royals have gifts. That prick Rigaran is as useless as a fucking bull's teat. You're highborn, Konan. Tell us."

Konan stiffened, and his scowl darkened.

"Come on," Thordrin jibed. "You have to tell us anyway. I made a knight's agreement with you to kill your enemies, and I am a man of my word. How can I have my fun if I don't even know my targets?" He laughed and buried his face in his handmaiden's chest, kissing his way up her neck without a hint of shame.

Konan hadn't taken his eyes from Lyra, and the right one glistened. She realized his left one never made tears, maybe an aftereffect of the burn that had discolored his iris. Smiling, she brushed at the lone tear with her thumb.

"Tell me please."

He pulled her hands from his face and placed them gently on her lap. "I was a prince," he signed at last.

Lyra stared.

"The fuck did he say?" Thordrin interjected when he noticed her expression. He could be attentive to two things at a time, apparently. She answered, and he leered. "The *fuck* you were. Princes don't end up in Tahayi Mines. Prince of what? One of those petty kingdoms on the Miratian-Lorenian border? A no-name province with a single fort and a twelve-man army?" He laughed.

Konan glowered.

Thordrin's taunting grin faded, and he rolled his eyes.

Konan retreated into himself, steeling his jaw and gazing into nothing. His eyelids twitched with waking nightmares, and the sadness in his lost expression grew. He was once again the nameless prisoner of Tahayi Mines.

Lyra adjusted herself, realizing how inappropriate her position was. She swung her legs around to sit in his lap with her knees together and wrapped her arms around his neck, placing her head in the curve where it came together with his shoulder. The spot was rich with his scent, and his scars tickled her cheek. She could hear his heart thumping more rapidly than normal.

"Please talk to me," she whispered. "Which kingdom?"

"Mirat," he answered.

"You were a prince of the *Kingdom* of Mirat?" she repeated, dumbfounded.

Thordrin snorted. "Mirat's not missing a prince, brother."

She could hear Konan grinding his teeth, a disconcerting grate that echoed through her skull. His entire body stiffened, and he clutched her like a man drowning.

"I think those high and mighty assholes running Mirat would know if they were missing their charge," Thordrin insisted, looking fully at the younger man before returning his attention to his handmaiden. Lyra could hear him inhaling, his face buried in her hair.

She cringed and focused on Konan's response.

"That's impossible," he said. His scowl deepened, and his eyes glittered, reflecting not only aggravation but also—was it dismay? The milky spot seemed to swirl and churn, a storm of anger and frustration encapsulated in a tiny but expressive part of him.

"I've been there, Konan," Thordrin assured them without looking. "Mirat's belonged to the same royal family for generations. They were nearly wiped out in a massive fire. Killed the king and queen, but the son lived. Prince Reylin's been at the Miratian council's mercy ever since."

"I am Prince Reylin of House Harkin," Konan signed with an infuriated grunt. He threw his shoulders back and sat tall, forcing Lyra to straighten and look at him anew.

From the right side, at an angle, she could hardly see his deformities, and for a brief moment, she saw a noble face: the strong forehead with a darkly drawn, commanding brow, high and prominent cheekbone, and a narrower, diamond-shaped jawline. His lips were thinner, like most northerners', and his soft hair loosely wavy, another northerner trait. His nose was straight and not overprominent, nor pointed like hers. His eye was beautiful, like topaz and obsidian. His right eyebrow arched naturally, giving him a constant appearance of skepticism.

Then he turned to her as if beseeching her support, and the moment was gone. His ugly left-side visage was twisted in dismay, and he glowered, as angry as she'd ever seen him. "I *am* the rightful heir to the Miratian throne," he insisted.

She tightened her hold of him, feeling the tension in his neck. "I believe you," she said softly. "I believe you are who you say you are."

"I don't," said Thordrin.

Lyra spun toward him. "Then why did you ask? If you weren't going to believe him?"

"Calm down, girl. I'm telling you Mirat has a prince. He's called Reylin." Thordrin licked his lips and lifted the handmaiden up in the air. Her legs were wrapped around his waist, and she giggled. He carried her off to the men's tent without a backward glance.

Mirra and Korahel muttered to each other with seeming revulsion, then went about cleaning up the meal.

Lyra turned back to Konan, and they stared at each other for a while. Then she drew her fingers through his fine hair, a deeply burnished brown that hung in dark locks that could have provoked envy in anyone. She played with the ends at the back of his neck, then trailed her fingers down his neck and returned to the rough scar tissue on his collar bone. She traced it up and down and whimpered in sympathy for his hurts.

If Konan really was who he said he was, then he had lost everything all those years ago. His family, his freedom, his identity. Thordrin had said there was a fire, something Konan had mentioned once before (although he had skipped the part where it was the royal castle). She felt horrible for ever having judged his appearance, for being almost afraid of looking at his terrible face because she couldn't control where her gaze went.

He glared after Thordrin, then looked upon her; the softness and the sadness returned. "How can it be that they don't know I'm missing?"

Lyra didn't know. "You told me once that you knew how it felt to be abandoned in Tahayi, to lose a part of yourself. I didn't think anyone could really understand how lost I felt, but you did. You've lost so much. I'm so sorry." She traced the pockmarks on his cheek, then placed her palm over it. "Maybe Thordrin really can help you reclaim your home. He's being . . . himself right now, but he gave you his word. Whoever this council is, whoever this Prince Reylin is that says he's you, they are in the wrong. You can tell them the truth, and fight for it if you have to, and then maybe you can live in peace in the beautiful mountains you told me about."

He was still. Then his mouth twitched. "'Endure it'?"

She smiled, recalling their discussion of Isellan's days in the mines. "Overcome it."

"Will you sing a song, Lyra? Please."

He enveloped her hands in his and bowed his head, and she realized he needed her comfort, not the other way around.

She kept her voice quiet as she sang, embarrassed about drawing attention beyond their small fire. Mirra and Korahel paused and sat to listen. It was another folk song about the caravan life, about treading the paths from north to south, trudging through the muckier wetlands of the south Aklimian-Marlemetian border and embracing the endless sky of open Litis, of tasting the dusty track to Shayal. It was one they usually sang on the road; Ada loved to hum along to it. Then she sang of the night sky in the Marlemetian plains, and then of the mariner's voyage east across the Mana Loi.

Konan was deep in thought through most of it, not even massaging her knuckles like he normally did, and she finally declared it time for bed. He obeyed, escorting her from the fire to her tent.

Before she entered, she turned back to him. "You also told me once that I'ya may have given me my gift to do good in this Gate, to defend the innocent and fight for justice. Maybe it's the same for you."

He looked at her strangely, and she crossed her arms.

"You know I'm right."

He searched her face, then brushed her wild curls back. The line his thumb traced left a trail of fire, and she shivered. Then he signed. "Perhaps. Thank you for singing. Bright night."

When she got to the privacy of her tent, Lyra sent another Whisper to her mother. She had already spoken of their rescue, of her protectors and her own safety on previous nights. Mam needed to know of her development of magical skill and of Konan's amazing discovery of his own magika. Lyra also prayed that the caravan was well and told Mam she would be coming soon, as soon as she gained passage through the Manalali lands. She told her of Shirkaa's official plans and offer, and of Lyra's decision to do whatever it took to save Shirasa.

"Maybe I can help someone else, maybe keep them from going through what I went through," she whispered, clasping her fingers so tightly they whitened. "Maybe it's not too late for Shirasa."

She nestled her precious message in her hands and stroked its ethereal feathers, then pushed it through the folds of the fabric at the rear of the tent.

"To Elaisa," she breathed.

It whisked away to the south and east, leaving her with the smallest hope that one would eventually return with a reply. She stared out at the bright stars for a while, then resigned herself to the fact that no one else could Whisper as well as she. Temple mages supposedly could, but she had never actually met one.

Korahel watched, although it was unlikely she could see the birdlike Whisper herself.

Lyra lay in the bed, wriggling under the furs and nestling into the down pillow. As Korahel tucked her in, Lyra caught her hand.

"Don't be afraid of the Whispers," she said to the handmaiden. She nodded toward the spot where she had released this most recent one.

Korahel looked away and struggled through a few thickly accented words. "Is good magika, Thralais." She glanced toward the entrance, where they heard Konan settling himself and thanking Mirra for a blanket.

Lyra sighed and released Korahel. She was such a wonderful help and a thoughtful companion, intelligent and perceptive despite their lack of shared language. Mirra was too.

The thought of Konan's handmaiden sent a troubling surge of feelings through her, and she imagined Mirra kneading Konan's sore shoulders and legs. What a strange thing to think of. She buried her face into the pillow. Mirra was incredibly kind and polite, with an easy, friendly smile. Lyra quenched any other thoughts and went to sleep.

She didn't really understand her own feelings until she woke up later, wracked by a terrible nightmare of strange Haralali warriors mutated into monsters with demonic, glowing eyes. A gorgeous girl with Jikaa's eyes and skin screamed, and then they were fleeing together through the mucky bogs of southeast Aklim. Their feet dragged.

She woke to Konan, who held her until the turbulence of the air stilled. Korahel scurried about in the background, rearranging overturned furniture and replacing the rugs that had shifted and flapped against the tent walls.

Konan drew his fingers through her hair, and when he touched the spot behind her ear, a shiver of pleasure ran through Lyra. It traveled down her spine and into her loins, and then out like flames along her inner thighs. Before she could restrain herself, she moaned, and then she understood.

She must have flushed red, for Konan paused and stared at her. Then she recalled how he'd pushed her away when she crawled onto him so inappropriately, and she blushed even harder. The guilt overwhelmed her like a wave crashing down upon the beach. She began to cry, and Konan pulled her into their usual position and merely held her, rocking back and forth and humming a variation of her earlier song. She wept again for Shirasa, and for herself, and for the feelings inside her that both terrified and excited her.

The shrill voice within declared its opinion, but the soft, ashamed voice argued back in certain terms. She was unworthy, filthy, and inferior to a prince of Mirat, no matter what she did. She was nothing, and she was broken.

She didn't know when Konan left, but when she awoke again in the morning, he was gone.

56

LYRA TRIED NOT TO think about him, an impossible task given their constant proximity. Once they told Jikaa that Konan had been the one who moved the water, the Godspeaker insisted Konan spend a little time with him as well, although they now seemed more interested in Lyra's Air magika.

Under the Godspeaker's tutelage, Lyra quickly became more proficient in subtle wind manipulations, realizing that the delicate touch was similar to the push she used to guide her throwing knives. It was almost a nudge, keeping a cactus blossom alighted. Nudge with the left, then with the right, back and forth from hand to hand. If she pushed too hard, she would send the blossom awry. If she missed, it would float gently down and she would have to start over. It became easier with each trial as she honed her focus.

In truth, she had never been formally taught the use of magika. Wayfarers accepted it and allowed it to grow organically within the caravan family, but they knew far more green magika than they did about the higher powers of I'ya, the powerful magika that formed the world. Green magika was primarily herbal, and black magika was telluric; red magika was corporeal. The Godspeaker's guidance was extremely useful to her avidly listening ear.

Having bored of the blossom, Lyra examined the broad desert before her, scanning it for anything of interest.

"Thral." The Godspeaker interrupted her trailing thoughts, with Jikaa echoing. "Can you now rouse the winds from east to west? Can you make a sandstorm?" His eyes glinted with curiosity.

Lyra nodded. She had once before, and it had helped save them from the mines. But it drained the energy from her bones, and it had likely been the reason she weakened so much sooner as the trio desperately wandered toward their death in the sands.

"Please." The Godspeaker waved his arm over the expanse.

Lyra complied. She stared to the east horizon, summoning from inside, feeling the strength pour out of her, down her arms, and beyond. Both hands reached to the darkening horizon and pulled at the sky in a broad swath. Dust appeared, leading a front line of wind that blasted across the land in front of them. It was not especially wide, only enough to prove to herself and the Godspeaker what she could do. It spanned the expanse as it rolled westward, crossing their view in a roar. Lyra swept her hands westward, pushing the sandstorm away to the setting sun and finally allowing the storm to die down.

She gasped at the effort and sat heavily on the edge of the well.

Konan looked up at her from the sand, where he sat resting from his morning horse antics, his eyebrows raised in surprise. "You've improved so much already." He turned back to the expanse, which was now eerily calm. "That was somehow more directed than the first time."

She looked away, her cheeks warm, and he struggled up with a grunt, approaching her.

He wore the garb of a Manalali warrior, but in all black and crimson like her. Mirra had refrained from giving him a veil or handflowers, but the other signs of his status as a thral were there. His hide armor had been upgraded to thin silver plates, and his billowing pants were of much finer material than Thordrin's. The villagers had switched to calling him "Barna'halais" instead of Lyra.

He reached for her arm but hesitated when she jumped. "Are you okay?"

She didn't know how to answer and instead clamped her mouth shut. Her eyes traveled from his feet to his ornate belt to his beaded decorative chestplate, then to his face. "I . . . no."

His face fell. "Is it about the war? We escaped Tahayi Mines, Lyra. We'll find our way home."

She shook her head and couldn't help but smile.

"Konan, get over here," Thordrin called. "Knives, and I'm bored of Hafka."

Konan grimaced and held out a hand for hers. She relented, and he drew it to his forehead and then kissed it in a formal manner. With that, he pressed a folded paper into her fingers.

"Later then," he signed.

Lyra followed his departure, her curiosity mixing with apprehension, then unfolded the paper. It had writing scribbled on it in a sloping cursive, sprinkled with ink splatters. She quickly folded it back up and tucked it into a pocket. She couldn't read.

The wait till that evening was hardly bearable. Despite her fear and nerves, enough to make her sick to her stomach, Lyra also needed to talk to someone, and that someone was Konan. He surprised her by arriving with two saddled horses, his big mare and a sleek black gelding, a half bell before the sun set.

"You want to ride more?" she said, incredulous as she admired the gelding. He was a handsome animal, and friendly.

Konan snorted. They rode a distance away from the village, into the cactus-filled pavement, where there were more flowers and overwhelmingly sweet smells. He dismounted stiffly and offered her a hand down, although she didn't need it, and then laid out a colorful blanket for them to sit on.

They didn't speak at first, and Lyra took in the freshness of the air. She had never welcomed it so much in Tahayi Mines, although it wasn't all that different in character.

"Lyra, what's wrong?"

She felt the heat on her cheeks as she thought about how to answer. "Last night . . . I—I'm afraid."

"Of me." It wasn't a question. His expression darkened. "Forgive me."

She reached for him, drowning in her own shame. "It's not your fault. I'm . . . I'm so confused. You shouldn't even be around someone like me."

He gave her a completely flustered look, and her vision began to blur with frustrated tears. In her confusion, she sought safety, and she found herself leaning against him, nestled into the crook of his shoulder. He swept his cloak around her like a blanket and held her close with one arm.

The sun sank below the horizon in a flurry of pinks and oranges on the thin clouds.

"Lyra, I don't want you to be afraid of me."

She sniffled. "I wasn't."

His chest heaved, and the airy, hollow sound of his lungs filled her ear.

"I realized that I don't like Mirra taking care of you, even though I know she does a good job. It's a horrible, selfish, silly feeling, and I hate it." Her hand trembled as she tentatively reached toward his leg. She had no idea why she was doing it or what she wanted to accomplish, and part of her shrieked in terror. Her fingers slid across his muscles and squeezed, but then he grabbed her hand and pulled it away.

He sucked air through his teeth and winced, placing her hand back on his chest. "I can't, Lyra. It's not safe." She saw him swallow.

A part of her was relieved, and she sighed. That seemed to verify something for him, and he pulled her closer and placed his chin on her hair.

"Not yet," he signed. "When you're not afraid, I'll be here waiting."

His words sent the same kind of shiver through her that his touch did.

"But you're the prince of Mirat."

"I'm a man first, and the son of Isellan second. I don't know who I was meant to be, but I haven't been that boy for a long time."

"But when we leave here, you'll go to Mirat?"

"Only if I'm not wanted elsewhere."

She peered up at him in the dim evening light, then nuzzled closer. Was *that* what he had meant by his cryptic statement a few days earlier? His face was unreadable, and he had receded into himself somewhat.

She didn't understand at all. She didn't understand how he could want to be with her, or anywhere near her, when she was so inferior to him and unable to return his affection. Her lesser blood combined with her corruption may have been tolerated by a man like Thordrin, who had been common-born himself and elevated to knighthood. Even then, she was now most appropriate for emmisarying to another caravan. That's all she was: a maunderer. Besides, it would be absurd for Konan to not return to Mirat when he had such bright possibilities awaiting him.

Yet he held her close without reservation, and the only thing keeping them apart was her own reticence. He held her with no expectations and no demands, only tender care.

"Konan? What if I'm never ready?"

He squeezed her shoulder.

"That's okay."

He indicated he was done talking by wrapping his other arm around her and plunging his fingers through her hair, and they sat until full dark. The nighttime plants opened, sending a new fragrance through the desert, and Lyra regretted taking two horses, for she wanted nothing more than to stay in his arms.

In exchange for the Godspeaker's training in elemental magika, Lyra worked to prepare small potions and medicines in his tent, an essential part of the Manalali war preparation. However, she also taught him what she could, creating a constant learning process for both of them.

The Godspeaker pointed her to needed ingredients one at a time which she fetched, scanning the foreign marks on each label when there was one. They meant nothing to her, but some seemed almost like glyphs at which she could guess.

"Bluetail bat wings, thral." She could hear the amusement in the Godspeaker's tone as he spoke in broken Old Language. "Quicken the horses." He pointed at the vial in her hand. "Makran saliva, gives Manalal lust for blood."

Lyra gulped, gladly ridding herself of the clear vial and its liquid contents. The Godspeaker had a frightening array of red magika experience, which wayfarers rarely touched. The blood and bodily fluids could be dangerous and were only to be used in minute amounts if at all. Yet the Godspeaker confidently dumped a volume of horse and idraka blood into a large basin, then nicked his own fingertip with a small blade. His blood dribbled into the mixture.

"To join man and animal," he explained. He stirred it smooth with a ladle, murmuring an incantation in a hybrid of Old Language and Manalali, and seemed satisfied. He called a servant to take the bowl, and when the servant had gone, the Godspeaker turned to Lyra. "Now we prepare medicine. You know medicine. Yes?"

She nodded.

"You teach, I teach." The Godspeaker nodded to emphasize each point.

Lyra obliged. Although she couldn't read any of the labels on the vials, she recognized many of the herbs the Godspeaker kept stored in dried bundles, which overflowed from a basket. Wetspice, good for hacking coughs; alliun, to strengthen a weak body; brownbed's root, best ground into a tea to reduce fever. His collection was admirable considering their distance from main trade routes, but some things she needed were missing.

"Do you have cow's tongue?" she asked. The large-leaved plant would be necessary for helping the wounded.

The Godspeaker shook his head. "What is for?"

"It is good for staunching blood from a wound."

"Aah, yes, we have desert plant." The Godspeaker nodded knowingly and pulled a bundle of thick succulent leaves from the basket. "Pound into paste, this stops blood."

Lyra took the leaves and examined them. They were far different from cow's tongue, but perhaps she could use them in a similar manner. She added them in a mortar with several other herbs: ginger, alliun, and yewflower to fight infection, milktree sap to bind and thicken, and a small amount of blood-purifying nansbane.

The Godspeaker watched curiously, noting each item she added and helping her find ingredients. When she was done, having mashed the leaves into a thick paste, he took the mortar from her and placed the medicine into a large, lidded pot. He bid her make more, and he likewise did so until the pot was full. Then he taught her a different mixture, one for deep arrow wounds, to be used on both man and mount, which contained a combination of herbs, lizard gland, and horse urine. Again, they made enough to fill a large pot, which was sealed and set aside. The days flew by, and pot after pot stacked up, piled with other supplies needed for battle.

More families arrived each day, leading their cattle and idraka into the joint herd and setting up more tents on the edge of the growing village. The days were hot and sunny, and the landscape seemed to parch in the breeze that rose every morning and evening. The full well was a much-used blessing, and newcomers constantly appealed to Konan and Lyra with their gratitude, calling him Barna'halais and bowing deferentially to her as a thral.

Each afternoon, when the sun had dipped close to the far horizon and the wind naturally picked up, the Godspeaker would have Lyra summon a large sandstorm in practice. It was a welcome reprieve after the burning heat of each day, which contributed to a stagnant heaviness in the Godspeaker's tent that was difficult to work through. Lyra reveled in the power of the cooling wind, an emanation from her own fingertips. She felt free when she embraced it, released from her troubled memories and concern for her family.

Sometimes, she even spun in a dance, surrounded by swirling air that rushed and moved with her.

No other member of Maskalan had this power, she was sure. Even Elden, who had typically replied to her Whispers, had never shown this measure of aptitude. He was spritely and wildly energetic, followed by a tumultuous breeze wherever he went. His presence spurred the cattle forward almost like a whip, and his high voice could always be heard singing at the nightly fire. He had watched her craft her messages as a child, and shortly after began mimicking her. It seemed so natural to the young, Lyra recalled, and soon they were able to send notes back and forth between wagons.

Their abilities came in handy for the long train, as Lyra would sit toward the front and Elden toward the back. Although they sent many official messages from one wagon-master to another, they also shared a multitude of hidden codes and side notes. Of course, onlookers without any magika couldn't see the Whispers bouncing back and forth, zipping through the caravan between horse's ears, so they sometimes saw Lyra and Elden fall into fits of laughter for no reason. Even among the wayfarers, their gifts were exceptional, their connection to I'ya strong; these were a source of pride among the caravan. Lyra, Elden, and the other gifted children were the most likely to be strategically emissaried to another clan to strengthen the blood of all wayfarers.

She caught herself smiling.

Only if I'm not wanted elsewhere...

She bit her lower lip, then remembered how silly the dream of being with Konan was, and all the reasons why she was a poor match for him. Her sandstorm faltered at the intrusive memories, and her sadness returned full force. The sand fell into an uncontrolled drift, lazily dispersing to nothing.

Lyra dropped her hands. Tears shone in the corners of her glistening eyes, but she blinked them away. She felt sick, alone with terrible thoughts that clawed at her.

"You good, love?"

She spun at Thordrin's voice. Both of the men were astride horses. Thordrin looked eminently comfortable with a bow slung around a shoulder, but Konan's mare kept prancing from side to side, reflecting and feeding off his nervousness.

Lyra guarded her tears as best she could and put a positive tone into her voice. "Yes, just distracted." She forced a smile.

Thordrin nodded slowly, then abruptly turned his horse and rode toward his tent.

Konan glowered as his horse turned to follow, and he attempted a countermand. The mare resisted, spying a patch of grass in front of her, and Lyra quickly ran up to grab the reins. In a well-practiced exercise, she calmed the big animal while controlling the head, gently exerting authority over the horse. The mare responded to Lyra's caress and calm, becoming still and straight with a snuffle.

"Thank you," Konan signed. His right cheek flared red.

Lyra tore her eyes reluctantly from the horse and met his gaze. Now he gave her a penetrating stare, searching her for prevarication. She tried to give no indication of her troubled thoughts, changing the subject. "You've improved so much in a few days. Hafka and that boy have been helpful."

He gave her nothing back, finally breaking their tableau with neither a smile nor a frown. He pulled another paper from his tunic and handed it to her, his right cheek flaring red. The paper had scrawls and messy ink splatters on it once again, and she wondered what it said. He never brought the notes up in conversation, just slipped them to her when Thordrin wasn't looking, and surely he suspected she wasn't literate. Most wayfarers and other commoners weren't.

Evidently he was, which made sense if he had learned when he was young. He could write, and as rusty as he had been when they joined the Manalal, he certainly knew aspects of swordplay and horsemanship.

As he turned his horse to trot away, leaving Lyra to walk at her own pace in her own thoughts, she held the note up. His embarrassment couldn't be worse than her own. "What are these?" she managed.

He tensed and wouldn't meet her gaze. "Memories," he signed, "but I'm not sure which ones are real." His expression turned tragic, and he yanked the horse's reins, spurring her away.

She folded the note with care and tucked it with the others, secure inside her breast binding where they couldn't fall out.

57

THE DAY ARRIVED WITH a bleeding sunrise, an unexpected wisp of clouds that marked the horizon red when the sun tried to burst through.

The Manalal took it as a sign, and as the sun rose higher and shimmered across the camp with a growing heat, Shirkaa bid Konan and his companions to the large pavilion once more.

The camp bustled with renewed activity as men mounted saddles upon their mounts, adjusted leather jerkins, padded the chests of their idraka for protection, and packed supplies onto the backs of larger but slower hauling cattle. Women scurried about, packing up the village itself by taking most of the smaller tents down and loading wagons pulled by idraka and haulbeasts. As quickly as the village had expanded, it contracted toward the Desert Mother's shrine.

Konan escorted Lyra on his arm. She had been different since their conversation. Not aloof—she wasn't capable of that if she tried. Perhaps still afraid, though, as if being nearer to him was overstepping an invisible boundary. He regretted who he was.

You can be someone else. Why not be the son of Isellan and nothing more?

Only one tent remained of Shirkaa's pavilion complex, the one with his table and throne. Its carpets and curtains had already been removed, so they didn't need to remove their sandals. Without the heavy dividing curtain on one side, they could see into the tabernacle of the Mother's shrine, where the Godspeaker and numerous boys and girls prayed. The shrine exuded an overwhelming smell of incense.

Shirkaa stood upon their arrival and welcomed them to the low table with his honor guard. "Break your fast, my friends. Today is a blessed day."

He offered them food and drink, which they gladly took. Shirkaa's meal was no less elaborate than usual, and his servants brought an array of heavily spiced meats, unleavened bread with smooth, creamed butter, and fresh, berry-like fruits. A cold, fruity tea was poured to counterbalance the meat.

Shirkaa continued to speak as they ate. "This day we march on the Haralal and continue into the night. We rest briefly, then attack their main war camp at dawn tomorrow. All of my people have come in, and I'ya'hakkat has declared it time. See how she makes the sky bleed? We will fertilize this land with the blood of the Haralal, a right and proper sacrifice to Mother." His strong voice, normally hearty in nature, shook with bitterness. "My scouts have verified that my desert flower lives, but the Haralal beasts have sullied her."

Lyra gasped, then began to weep.

Shirkaa went on to describe their roles in the upcoming battle, and they departed the tent to find the camp nearly packed.

"Shit, they're fast," Thordrin commented.

Lyra was quiet, and Konan could tell she was thinking of home as she scanned the wagons of rolled tents and furniture and cookware. He touched her fingers, and she looked up at him with a weak smile.

"Focus on Shirkaa's daughter," Konan signed.

"Tighten that lower lip, girl," Thordrin said at the same time. "You know what the girl may be going through, and for once, the right thing to do about it is also fun."

Konan shook his head and tried to reassure Lyra more. "They only want you to cover their attack. You won't fight."

"And then I'll be in the herbsman tent, healing." She looked relieved, then hardened. "I almost wish I *could* fight, for Shirasa's sake."

Thordrin scoffed. "Lyr, they put you in a position of honor next to the Godspeaker. Nethers, they've put both of you in positions of honor. Meanwhile I'm still dressed as a common fuckin' nobody." He plucked at his soldier's clothing with a tragic expression, then gestured at them. "Thral ol'I'ya and fucking Noble-Heart Barna'halais."

Konan looked down at himself. His tunic, incredibly soft with tightly woven material, hugged his form with custom fitting, and his jeweled swordbelt hung with proper clasps and sheaths for his daggers and sword. The crimson of his cloak was as bright as fresh blood, and the garment sparkled with silver thread and coins along the edges. His plated armor shimmered in the morning sun, but it was still armor.

"They only want me to fight in this battle, like you," Konan replied.

Lyra translated, then added, "They respect both of you as warriors. You should be honored by that from such a territorial people."

Thordrin dismissed her compliment. "I don't need to be respected. I want to be feared. The Haralal will tell stories of the Phantom after this, if there are any left when we're done." He showed his teeth in a nasty grin, having recovered his confidence.

Lyra balked, and again Konan tried to bolster her. "Use your power for justice, for Shirasa."

She nodded, knotting her delicate eyebrows.

The Manalal fighting men adorned their battle garb and assembled in the large area where the training yard had been. Each man wore red and yellow war paint. Most carried bows or scimitars, but a few had spears as well. Piecemeal layered hides served as armor for many, although family clan leaders stood out with metal plates similar to Konan's. Hundreds upon hundreds had come, accompanied by their families and livestock, bringing the village's population to many thousands.

Konan didn't believe in the Desert Mother, but the Man-alal did seem to be unusually blessed. A small measure of satisfaction flickered in Konan's chest, knowing he had been responsible for drawing more precious water to their home. The small children running about, the young trainees of the Godspeaker who prayed in the shrine, all of them would have a better home with greater security. Permanent structures, as Lord Shirkaa had suggested. It would be possible eventually, once more plants grew, and they would likely need to bring some materials in from the edges of their territory.

Shirkaa emerged from his pavilion, a grim look of pride painting his face as he surveyed his warriors. Only he was adorned from head to toe in elaborate battle armor. It gleamed in the sunshine, revealing nary a scratch or imperfection. It was thin but heavy-looking, with each plate cinched to the next with leather strips. The chest plate was embedded with small, glinting jewels in a rainbow of colors. An impressive feline creature, perhaps a form of makran, served as a headpiece with its teeth bared. Its mottled fur flowed back as a cloak with frays of colored beads around each edge.

The Godspeaker chanted a protective mantra over the chieftain, smearing red paint over his cheeks in a final blessing. The old man repeated the process for each clan leader and for the honor guard, then approached Konan and Thordrin.

Konan could feel Lyra backing away to hide behind him. She had already been arrayed in an elaborate dress of crimson and yellow, and she glowed like the Eye. Her handflowers were topaz and polished sunstone, and he suddenly appreciated the value of the mining he had done for all those years. Properly shaped and polished, sunstones were striking, and even more so on her. Korahel had matched the necklace and veil to the handflowers, and Konan could see through the sheer yellow silk of the veil. Lyra was blanching as the Godspeaker chanted over Thordrin.

Konan recalled her distaste for red magika, as well as her desire for less attention. He stepped in front of her and offered himself to the Godspeaker, then remained as he was.

The Godspeaker merely chuckled and said something that Lyra seemed to understand, and he moved on to the Manalali ranks. Lyra sighed as the old man had each warrior drink from a bowl of red liquid.

Konan glanced questioningly at Lyra, and she wrinkled her nose.

"It's mostly blood, but also bull semen, powdered malagate, water, and a few other things," she said. "Red magika mixed with black, to give you strength, courage, and bond you with your mount."

Thordrin cursed and spat. "I just drank it."

"It's not bad for you, and it may even work. The Godspeaker is very talented, and I helped him make it." Lyra paled a little as Thordrin glowered at her, and she clutched her stomach as though she felt sick.

Thordrin mounted his horse without another word. He jutted his chin toward Konan, whose mare was prancing in the little boy's care. Taking the reins with a sign of thanks, Konan dismissed the boy, who chattered in Manalali. It sounded like encouragement.

Konan guided his horse and Lyra toward the Godspeaker's wagon. He settled Lyra on the plush seat next to the old man, who had been wrapped in layers upon layers of shawls. The Godspeaker smiled toothlessly at them.

Lyra clutched his arm. "Where will you be?"

Konan nodded toward Thordrin, who had taken his place behind the honor guard. He was gesticulating at Jikaa, likely telling some story of his own prowess on the battlefield.

"Can you ride with me?"

"You should rest now, while you can," he replied, denying the warm feeling that spread through him. He swung onto his mare so he could match her height; the horse danced. "When we're closer, you'll be with me."

Lyra chewed on her lip, and Konan couldn't tell whether that thought made her more nervous or content. He forced his mare closer and reached for her, bidding farewell by placing his forehead to her hand and then brushing his lips across her knuckles. Then he pulled another note from his tunic and curled it into her fingers.

She clutched the note to her bodice with a bashful smile and sat back on the wagon with her silky layers shrouding her. Her curls were tamed by pins and a hemmed circlet, but he still thought of a halo, as light and fluttering in the wind as her shawl.

Then he trotted to his place behind Hafka and Dashann. The war train departed. The pace was quick enough to cover leagues but not exhaust the animals or outpace the idraka- and cattle-drawn wagons. The heat bore down on them, and the landscape became drier and drier. The cacti and bushes that characterized the area around the Desert Mother's shrine waned to nothing, and Konan was back in a featureless desert of windblown pavement.

He understood now why the Manalal had packed so much water, normally an excessively heavy item but apparently necessary if there were no wells.

They paused for a noon meal and rested for several hours, guarded from the burning sun by small, temporary awnings that folded out from the wagons. As the sun began its descent, they continued north and westward at the same brisk pace. For a breath of a moment, a terrible thought crossed his mind, but it was too nebulous for him to comprehend. Evening fell, and a breeze graced them for a few hours before night settled.

Onward they rode into the night, using the moonlight to guide them through the open landscape. Both the first and second moons were full—yet another sign from the Desert Mother. Hopefully, Lyra was sleeping.

He had spied her tucking the note away somewhere inappropriate, and it made his blood quicken. He knew she probably couldn't read them. Not only was his script nearly illegible from lack of practice, but she also likely didn't know her letters. It was almost a relief for him. He merely wanted to write his thoughts down, and with the Manalal had finally procured the proper supplies for doing so. The quill felt strange in his hand, the ink unpredictable, the paper thin and prone to wrinkles and tears. Regardless, he could articulate better in writing than he could any other way.

By I'ya, if only I could speak to you, he thought. *Then again, I'd probably stutter.*

The quick moon set, and the second slow moon hung low in the dark sky. It was the Nether hour, the darkest part of night, and dawn would be upon them in a few hours. The air held no heat, and the night could almost be chilly.

The war party stopped to eat a quick repast and rest. Konan immediately broke rank and rode back to the Godspeaker's wagon, where Lyra huddled.

With another toothless, almost mischievous smile, the Godspeaker prodded her awake with his staff, then beckoned for food.

Lyra shivered, but upon seeing Konan, she smiled. They ate quickly, and she settled with her head in his lap as he leaned against the wagon wheel.

"Are you ready?" he asked.

"No, but I have to be. I hope my magika is helpful."

"It will be, and then your healing skills afterward."

"I'm still wondering about your gift," she mumbled with a yawn. "I understand that you pulled the water, but where did the oasis come from? The Manalal didn't seem to know about it, and they know every part of this desert."

She rolled over, nestling her face into his abdomen and pulling the furs closer around her, then grumbled sleepily. He tugged the covers over her shoulder and stroked the soft skin on her neck. Sighing, she fell into a deeper sleep before he could respond.

The entire war party quieted, tired after the long ride. They closed their eyes for what seemed to be only a moment, and then the Godspeaker was prodding Konan again. Shirkaa stood over them.

"Time to use your gift, thral ol'I'ya," he said. "We are nearly there. Summon a sandstorm and push it ahead of us until we reach the war camp. After, you will remain with the Godspeaker and help the wounded."

Lyra sat up, her eyes wide, but Shirkaa stooped down and spoke with genuine urgency. "Remember my daughter, my flower." His words overflowed with entreaty, the desperation of a forlorn father, and Konan felt conviction fill him.

As he had seen before, the limpid pools of Lyra's eyes froze to a perfectly clear ice, like a glacier. She tensed, raising her chin. Tears threatened and then flowed freely. The fury inside of her pulsed out in waves, and Shirkaa stepped back with a grim satisfaction.

"You are the first assault, honored thral, and must ride at the front until we arrive."

The chieftain bowed as he would to the Godspeaker, then mounted his armored idraka and rode away.

Konan helped her up and wiped her cheeks. "For Shirasa."

Lyra shuddered. "She doesn't deserve whatever is happening to her. It would have been more merciful for her to be dead than to be . . ." Her breath hitched, and Konan held her until she recovered.

"She's alive," he signed, trying to steady her. "So let's save her."

She nodded. "And punish those who hurt her." The coldness that exuded from her was as chilly as any winter night in Tahayi Mines. She was ready.

He mounted his mare and pulled her up after. Lyra adjusted her billowing skirts on both sides of the horse and nestled her hips into him, then declared herself ready. Her knobby shoulders fit perfectly inside his, and her hair tickled his neck like the touch of a feather. Her back and pelvis felt cool against his burning body, her slender fingers outright cold as they wrapped around his forearms. He closed his eyes and took her presence in, then turned the mare toward Shirkaa and Thordrin at the vanguard.

The Manalal moved surely into the night. Dawn was approaching.

Still gripping his armored forearm for stability, Lyra reached one palm out and trailed it behind her. Her eyes darted behind her lids like those of one dreaming. Her fingertips quivered as though reaching, and then she spoke.

"I couldn't feel the water, Konan," she whispered, "but I can feel the air. It flows around us, light and sinuous. It's forming a wake behind the wagons and curves around each mounted warrior like a river." He felt her open her chest and inhale deeply, and then she began to push her trailing arm forward.

The breeze shifted direction, giving them a tailwind, and Konan's pulse quickened with it.

The bulk of the wind moved in front of them, roaring forward until it picked up sand and swirled into a behemoth wall. Some of the war party shouted, a combination of surprise and excitement, but they were hushed by their neighbors. The wall widened as Lyra intensified her spell. Her clasp on Konan's forearm was uncomfortably tight as she used him for grounding and support.

The sandstorm churned ahead of them, blocking their view, but Shirkaa led the party confidently forward. They increased their pace, shifting from a quick walk to a trot. As they rode, the landscape began to change.

A gray light appeared on the horizon behind them, forewarning of the dawn, and they entered an area with jutting rocks and shallow canyons. Such a place would have threatened ambush, but no Haralal would see them coming. Konan noted several warriors splitting off to the sides to ensure no scouts of the rival tribe survived, if there were any.

Lyra continued to hold her palm forward, but the arch of her back lessened, and she took a panting yawn of a breath.

"Okay?" he signed, tapping the symbol against her thigh so she could see and feel it.

At first she merely nodded, not opening her eyes beyond glancing at the sign. Then she spoke, but her voice wavered with exhaustion. "I feel nearly empty."

Shirkaa began shouting commands, and the pace quickened again. He called back to Lyra. "One more push, thral."

Thordrin checked his horse slightly to ride beside them. He wore the wild, mischievous grin of a madman, and a sharp lustiness for death sparked in his eye.

"Almost there, girl," he rumbled in his deep, smooth bass. "And then it's my turn. Konan, I'm pairing with Jikaa in the archery vanguard. Follow behind with Hafka?"

Konan nodded, and the Phantom spurred his horse onward.

Lyra released his forearm, her eyes still squeezed shut, and he felt the power gathering near her core. He held her steady with a hand around her belly, where a bright heart of light and power seemed to emanate. She shoved both her palms forward with what was likely the last of her energy. The storm pushed just ahead of the mounted Manalali, many of whom were now hooting and brandishing their weapons as they formed multiple cavalry lines in the center. Jikaa led the archery line on the fore left, and Rahar led the one on the fore right.

A town far advanced in comparison to the migratory camp of the Manalal emerged on the near side of her windstorm, just as dawn broke. The archers immediately launched several volleys toward it. The eager arrows fell in waves, landing upon the silhouettes of people and cattle in the encampment. Shirkaa roared, and the cavalry smashed into the war camp.

Lyra slumped with a hefty huff, and the winds dispersed. The sands fell to the ground instantly, giving a clear view in the early morning light.

Konan grasped her tightly and wheeled around, looking for the Godspeaker's wagon, but they had left it a bit farther behind in the final advance. He set Lyra down gently. Her feet were unsteady, and he clamped one of her arms until she gained her bearings. She panted and tried to straighten.

"I have to go," he signed. "Will you be okay?"

They both glanced back at the oncoming wagons in the distance, and she nodded, just barely. Then her gaze hardened, and emotion filled her eyes. *Diamonds*, he thought. *Unbreakable.*

"Save her, Konan," she said, almost at a whisper. "And punish them for what they've done."

He obediently kissed her hand, then spurred his horse onward, hoping to catch up to the vanguard.

Guided by her last words, he homed in on the enemies ahead. His mare galloped into the second wave of cavalry led by Dashann, and they burst past the town's outer walls, sweeping through wide streets and narrow alleys without mercy. He trampled several Haralali men underfoot of his big mare and finally leapt off, knowing he was more effective on the ground.

The warriors he met sneered at him, cursed at him, and he was thrust into memories of Tahayi Mines. Of being forced to defend himself and constantly be on guard. Of killing his first man at the age of thirteen over a meaningless rations dispute. Of Lyra the night she arrived, beaten and bloody.

Rage flooded through him. His muscles burned like fire, and his vision clarified as in a dream, where things immediately in front of him shimmered with liquid clarity and everything else blurred. It was dangerous; he wasn't fully aware of his surroundings.

But he dove into it anyway, slicing and cutting and striking.

Punish them for what they've done.

He eventually met Hafka, and they slid into a paired stance, guarding each other's backs and cutting men down with broad, confident sweeps of their swords. They danced through the streets of the Haralali town, utterly destroying the resistance they encountered. Konan wasn't sure how long he fought, nor how many fell at his feet, but his rage blinded him to everything beyond the next fight.

Numerous times he heard Thordrin hooting, and once he saw the man shooting fire-tipped arrows into roofs and people as he galloped by on his horse. Jikaa did the same, although he wore a grim and determined expression without a hint of mirth. The town was ablaze.

The Haralal fought poorly but bravely, falling under them as they cut a bloody path toward the center of the town. The time passed quickly, and the battle was suddenly done.

When they finally reached the center, the heart of the Haralali oasis, they found the last holdout. A small group of Haralal held one of three towers oriented about the oasis garden. Engravings covered the mud bricks from top to bottom, each glyph painted in different colors. One tower adorned in primarily red glyphs featured a large engraving of a lizard, another with blue glyphs featured a bird, and the last in yellow glyphs featured a palmnut tree.

The Haralal hid in the red tower, blocking the single door from the inside, and Shirkaa commanded a battering ram be brought.

The shrine didn't hold long, and the first two warriors to burst out with sword arms raised fell to arrows.

Thordrin cackled in the background as Manalal shoved into the shrine. Konan entered behind Hafka, and they cut down several more warriors until they found their quarry in the last room of the upper level.

The girl had the gorgeous olive skin and dark eyes of Jikaa, the short stature and wide shoulders of Shirkaa. She held them back proudly as she faced them, and she said something in Manalali to her father.

Shirkaa didn't reply, merely dropped his weapons and opened his arms as he approached her.

She raised her chin, and her nostrils flared. She looked as though she were fighting a breakdown.

Shirkaa embraced her, crying praises in Manalali, and rocked back and forth. Jikaa and Dashann joined them, and the foreign cries began to turn into a sort of song. The honor guard of Hafka and Rahar sheathed their swords as one and joined in the sound, then ushered the group out. Rahar turned back and examined the room, his expression twisted with hatred and disgust.

There were no signs of struggle, nor bindings to hold the girl, but perhaps the Haralal had not been keeping her there until the battle.

Rahar took a lamp from the wall and poured its oil out on the wooden furniture and sedans, and Hafka did the same to the plush, yellow-patterned carpet. Then Rahar struck a light, and the room lit up.

He gestured to Konan to do the same to the next level down, and they burned everything. The floor level contained far more wood, decorative wall paneling and sconces and tables, and far more cloth. Wall tapestries and curtains and rugs flared up with lamp oil, and the men rushed to exit the burning pillar. Black smoke billowed from the few windows of the shrine, dirtying the red-painted mudbrick.

Thordrin patted Konan's back when he exited and backed away. "Nice work, Noble-Heart. Let's burn the other two."

Jikaa stopped him. "Other shrines are not corrupted. Other shrines belong to I'ya'hakkat."

Thordrin's grin faded, and he narrowed his glittering eyes as Jikaa mounted and turned away. "Fucking Desert Mother," he muttered at Jikaa's back.

The desert men trotted away as one, with Shirasa held in front of Dashann. The Manalal troops eagerly began stripping the unburnt buildings and corpses of spoils, gathering the livestock, and taking anything of value they saw. Konan scowled at the ugliness of the war around him, but he hardened his heart as best he could.

They had won.

58

THE EYE SMILED UPON Mirat the day of summer solstice, piercing through a few lingering trails of clouds hanging from the peaks and promising a gorgeous day of revelry.

Reylin looked down from his bedchamber's high balcony, which gave him a view of the massive plaza beyond the castle walls. It was milling with activity, a swarm of movement and color, even this early in the morning. Those plying goods had entered the fortified section of the city the day before and claimed their places on the streets, packed end to end along the busier ways with their carts and wagons and open-fronted tents. At least eight wayfaring caravans of substantial size had come for the festival, and all of them provided some form of value, be it in goods or entertainment. He saw a group of Faraldin making final arrangements on their temporary stage, while another group wearing different family colors decorated the permanent platform in the center of the plaza. Faraldin children skipped about the working adults, screaming with laughter that reached his ears even from his height.

Despite their poor breeding, the young wayfarers brought a foolish smile to his face as he thought of Amber. He imagined her hair would stay dark and wavy. *May it never be cut.* Her eyes would surely darken, like his, although he had enjoyed the slightly green tinge to Priscilla's hazel. They wouldn't stay blue—that simply wasn't in his Harkin blood.

He straightened. He *was* a Harkin, and he was prepared to declare it so.

Reylin turned back inside to check on Syrana.

"Are you ready, my Chosen?" he called, knowing full well how long it took to prepare her hair and jewels. Nevertheless, it gave him the pretense to watch her dress.

She gave him a level look as he settled in a plush armchair. Her handmaiden was cinching her underlayer corset, drawing the silken strings tight with a slick, whispering sound. Every crossing of the strings further emphasized her tiny waist, lifting her breasts and forming a balance with her impeccably shaped hips.

Maybe he couldn't watch—if he wanted her to finish dressing.

Her soft, pouty lips curved into a seductive smile. "Thank you for the gown, my love," she managed, although her breath puffed out of her on the last word as her handmaiden finished tying the final corset knot. The gown lay splayed out on the bed, ready to adorn her. It matched his own.

Reylin stood, unable to hide his desire, and told the maid to move the dress and leave. She nodded and disappeared.

He towered over his wife and tipped her chin up. "I need you," he whispered, leaning down for a kiss.

She returned it but then pulled away. "My corset could rip, my love."

"Do you love me?" He sought her lips again, and she answered as he wanted her to. "Then I'll do everything."

And he did. The edge of the bed, raised upon a dais, was just the right height, and he managed to satisfy her without mussing her perfumed hair or ripping her tight corset. He did tear the edge of her underskirt, but no one would see that in any case, and it was worth it. By the Light, he felt powerful.

She made him feel capable and worthy with every gasp and fingernail. She made him feel like a king.

Smiling, he pulled her in for one more kiss, this one soft instead of desperate. He brushed his thumb across her lower lip, her chin, and then trailed down to her taut stomach. Perhaps it was *this* day. Wouldn't that be fortuitous, a re-markable story to tell later?

He called for the handmaiden as he readjusted his own clothes. She mumbled something as she touched the fray in Syrana's skirting, but then she went about her duties silently, a tightly controlled look of irritation on her savage features. She was an extremely fair-haired woman of small stature and unusual features. Her hazel eyes gleamed green with tawny brown edges, far more multi-colored than a human Mirat-ian, and her nose projected out and downward in a slightly hawkish hook.

Reylin returned to his armchair, entirely at ease for the moment as he watched Syrana adorn the gown he had or-dered especially for this occasion.

From a distance, it flowed with gorgeous sheer layers of orange, so light and thin they fluttered from movement alone. Even without a breeze, the dress rippled with the color of House Harkin. And yet, it was not made of orange mater-ial. Instead, the airy layers were crimson, the color of strength and potency, and yellow, the color of joy and celebration, so thin and intermingled they melded and flowed like wa-ter. The ribbed bodice was more crimson, embroidered in a sunny yellow and white—the color of truth. Every glittering jewel sparkled in clear perfection.

It matched his own. The fine cloth of his pants appeared orange but in fact was stitched with alternating thread col-ors, and the silky layers of Syrana's skirt were echoed in the ruffles on his neck and sleeves. His vest paired with her bodice, the embroidery forming a complex collage of elk bulls and jaybirds and mountain florals.

It was a message, directed above all at the Elder Council members, all of whom had arrived except Lord Lío.

Reylin was unsurprised, given Lío's recent message. In lieu of himself, the duke had sent his son, a young man of far better temperament and great naivete. The boy could hardly think to stand against Reylin in the Council, but he likewise would not serve as a strong ally. That was all right; Reylin didn't need it today.

He also knew the underlying motive: Lío wanted his son at Ironhold's court while North Mara experienced such duress. The man feared for his heir. A reasonable fear, given the ease with which a heritage could be stolen away.

Syrana's preparations took another hour, and as the alabaster perfection of her skin was covered, he grew bored and went back out to the balcony.

The city was waking, and Reylin found more and more of the crowd turning to point and wave at him from afar. He deigned to wave back.

The plaza shimmered with a rainbow of color as glorious as the High Temple as festivalgoers milled about, seeking a small breakfast before the banquet—or a full noon meal if their status did not allow them to enter the castle. The noblemen wore elaborate tunics and light summer vests, prancing like proud stallions with pretty gowned women on their arms. The Temple mages, some local and some visiting for the festival, dragged long robes of indigo with white half-sleeve overtunics, their wrists dressed in jingling golden bracelets and their long hair hung with purple beaded headdresses. Those with higher status, the holy mages who had mastered various Temple subjects, had indigo stripes painted across their eyes, that they might see with the eyes of I'ya. They rustled through the crowd sedately, blessing guests with a smile and children with a pat on the head. Reylin looked for Father Kaiadin, then for old Ma'thell. The elderly high holy mage had not been well since his healing attempt on Priscilla, and Reylin wondered if he could handle the crowded plaza. The five-sided white tower shone on its other side, farther down the main road. Reylin wasn't aware of any times of late in which the old man had emerged from its arching doorway.

A large number of orators milled around in deep blues and yellows, not only revealing their specialty by their dress but also by the instruments each held in their hand, at their belt, or slung over their back. Several masters were present, and so they wore their hair braided with blue and yellow ribbons, while the apprentices scurried after with navy cloth hoods covering their heads. They would not have the honor of showing their braids until they were at least reputable journeymen. In addition to the entertainers and holy men and women, various other guildspeople sifted through the crowd: a trio of turquoise-robed artsmen; individual jewelers showing their wares upon their ears, noses, and clothing; and proud, hulking miners in their earthy brown and evergreen fineries. Reylin gulped and looked away from the group, although they doubtless couldn't feel his gaze from this distance. They huddled around a tar beer vendor's tent.

The Eye had not yet reached its zenith, and they were many mugs into their own revelry, if it could be called that.

Last but not least, a small number of men in black, most of them still wearing their riding leathers—dragonkeepers. Some feared them, some respected them, and others ridiculed them as the last of their rare race, spread across the world as thinly as their dragons. (Their dedication to protecting the creation of I'ya, by ensuring peace or leading in battle, was absurd in this modern age. A war of that scale had not been waged since the days of Mirgawn the Brawn, from whom Reylin derived his noble Harkin blood.) Their calling was pure, however—no one could dispute that. Dragons chose their keepers, and dragons knew the will of I'ya. Three massive beasts lounged upon the cliffs above Ironhold. One was a burnished red, one a deeper brick color, and one a bright azure.

None were Ar'we, for he had sent Davon north with the homesteader caravan and another contingent of soldiers. He vaguely regretted it, as Davon's presence would have eased him about the presence of the other dragonkeepers. He knew none of them personally.

"I'm ready, my love," called Syrana, her voice somewhat strained by the restriction of her ribs.

Reylin shook his darker thoughts off and examined the yellow silk of his neck ruffle. Today was a day of celebration, whether the Council truly knew that yet. Solstice meant the shift in the year's balance, a change in the weight of darkness and light, and an eternal indicator of new beginnings.

He marveled at Syrana for minutes, admiring the elegance of her pinned hair, fully exposed as was proper for the queen-to-be and set with the new golden crown he had made for her. She wore multiple gems of I'ya, the indicator of royalty and chosen blood, and she looked at him now with a slight question in her eyes. She had noticed the symbolism, then.

Reylin chuckled and raised her fire-opal-decorated hand to his lips. She wouldn't want him to smear the fresh ochre on her lips. "You'll understand, my queen," he said softly. "Let us enjoy the festivities a little, before the meal."

He escorted her to the busy plaza at a sedate, authoritative pace. Sirs Gillead and Patreagh made way ahead of them, declaring the crown prince in gruff but proud voices. All stood aside for the royal couple, and then for the train behind them, for beyond Ronidann and Dorian were the nurses with little Amber and a gaggle of handservants to ensure that he and Syrana had whatever they needed.

They entered a mass of colorful, garrulous celebrants. The courtyard was all motion and chatter, fried food and fresh soap and a hint of sweat as the Eye poured down its warmth. They progressed through the crowd slowly, beaming at old friends and advisors, welcoming unfamiliar faces, and nodding respectfully to those of greater standing.

Father Ma'thell approached them as they enjoyed their first sips of a new fruity effervescent from Loreni. He tottered, leaning heavily on the arm of a young magus, but his wizened smile was as genuine looking as it had ever been. Reylin couldn't help but smile back and incline his head respectfully at the high holy mage, the master of Mirat's entire temple community, even as bitter and suspicious thoughts muttered in the back of his mind.

"High Holy Mage Ma'thell, may I'ya smile upon you this day," he said in formal greeting.

"And upon you, Your Highness," croaked the old man.

Formalities done, Reylin continued. "It is well to see you out of the temple, Father, but are you wise to walk with only a magus's assistance? Might I call a litter for you, that you may visit more revelers?"

Ma'thell's eyes disappeared in indigo-painted creases. "A kind sentiment, my son, but I fear I am not wise." He chortled, a raspy sound that devolved into a cough. "The years have blessed me with enough trials, yet I have not heard the lessons for my deafness. Perhaps you can enlighten an old man with the wisdom of youth. I had it once, but I seem to have misplaced it."

Again, Reylin couldn't help but smile. This old man had given him nothing but love and care since he remembered. Surely, Ma'thell could not be the one who had placed the magical ward upon him, binding his strength and limiting his potential. "Which youthful wisdom do you see in me, Father?"

The mage clicked his tongue and nodded to himself. "Ah, that is the right question. I see love. I see the potential for great love, and I beg you not to forget it like so many youthful wisdoms are forgotten." He beamed at them, then patted Syrana's hand, which lay on Reylin's arm. Ma'thell's graying eyes were nearly blind, although the painted band supposedly helped him see other things. His rough, timeworn voice was almost melancholy. "The pure and uninhibited love that comes in youth is a kind of wisdom I no longer know, unembittered by jealousy or grudge, unpoisoned by the darkness of the world. You must hold on to that love, my son, or all will be lost. You must lead and triumph, but you cannot do that without love." He leaned into Reylin, nearly staggering, and Reylin desperately wanted to back away from the man's intensity and unsettling words.

His doubts returned. Did Ma'thell know more than he pretended?

Reylin steadied the elderly mage with his free hand, straightening his shoulders and hoping that all around them could see that he was a pillar of strength and leadership to the religious man. "I know what it will take to lead Mirat, Father, and to triumph against the evil in the world. I know what it is to face adversity, even from unexpected places." He raised his bearded chin and caught Ma'thell's eye.

The man paused, giving him a long and trembling stare. He creaked back onto his magus's support. "My son, I fear you do not understand the evils of this world, not yet. I fear your anger clouds your vision to see how much you are loved."

Reylin felt his temper rising. High holy mage though he may be, Ma'thell had no right to speak to him this way. He towered over the man, pulling Syrana up as well. He patted her hand. "I am loved, High Holy Mage."

"Your parents loved you too," Ma'thell said very quietly. "They loved you more than you can imagine. And Shildra, she has loved you like a mother, in your time of greatest need." His near-blind eyes glistened, but Reylin heard no more of his words.

The plaza echoed with tumultuous laughter and spatters of conversation, shouts from vendors, and chords of music from orators scattered about the crowd. Father Ma'thell bowed his head and turned away, still appearing distraught, and disappeared into the crowd.

Syrana squeezed his forearm, her handflower jewels biting into his skin. "What in the name of I'ya was that about?" she whispered, clearly upset.

Reylin forced a light smile, painfully aware that some in the crowd might have heard part of the awkward exchange. He placed a fresh glass of wine in her hand. "Fret not, my Chosen. I am merely learning who my enemies are. They will not stop me from becoming everything I was meant to be."

Reylin wasn't prepared for the next conversation either, but he couldn't wait until after the banquet to reassure the miners who attended the festival. He needed their support.

The tight, hulking circle of russet and evergreen was stationed near the tar beer vendor, as they had been since the last bell. They turned to him as one, and his heart pounded. It was Guildmaster Daiunek, Journeyman Wethers, and a number of local guildsmen and women.

Daiunek wore his shaved head uncovered, and for the first time in months, he was also clear of dust—and blood. His finery was immaculate, the smock dyed manifold shades of green reminiscent of the mountain pines, embroidered with white paisley designs and embedded with small topaz and sapphire. His leggings were a lighter green, as was his cape, which hung over his massive shoulders by two identical brooches emblazoned with the miner's seal.

Reylin noted the big man's careful intake of their outfits, then his grave acknowledgment. "Well timed, Your Highness," he said in a low voice. "We were about to toast Master Oyerton."

Reylin gestured for the High Guard to grab a round of tar beer for everyone, even Syrana, although he knew she didn't prefer it. He raised his mug to all. "In memory of your

pioneering miners, the fearless first to advance Mirat. I am
indebted to all of you, including Master Oyerton, for your
bravery in the face of blind hatred, and I am proud to know
you." His words were paltry compared to the guild's loss. If
the Elder Council had only listened to him, taken his desires
and concerns seriously. If they had sent all the men he had
requested without delay or question, this tragedy would not
have occurred.

Wethers attempted to stand, but he swayed hard onto
Daiunek with a dark, mumbled curse, and Daiunek helped
him sit back down on his bench.

Daiunek raised his mug high. "The Earth listens and gives
as she will, and takes as she will."

Most of the group repeated the miner's mantra obediently, but Wethers growled into his mug. "To the nethers with
the fyr savages. They're not *of* the Earth."

"The Earth listens and gives as she will, and takes as she
will," Daiunek repeated, his deep voice so intense it made
Reylin's chest constrict. "May she take Oyerton into her
womb. May she guide him to the next Gate, a Gate of fertile
soil and boundless riches. May he never need again."

Their mugs clinked together, a somber sound in the midst
of the revelry, and Reylin washed the prayer down with
thick, over-rich stout. It clung to his throat, as bitter as
the loss of the master miner and the first homesteaders. It
was a wretched drink in the heat of summer, but no more
wretched than his guilt and frustration.

"I've deployed more troops to you under Keeper Davon,"
he said quietly to Daiunek. "They should never have been
delayed in the first place."

"I know, Prince Reylin. Davon is the reason we were able
to attend. No, the new caravan hasn't reached East Face,
but he and Ar'we flew ahead to inform us of its imminent
arrival and to ensure the skies remained clear. He recruited
another dragonkeeper to transport us here as a kindness."
Daiunek examined him for moments, then called for a refill.
"We've drunk to the past. Now that's done, let us drink to
the future."

"The past is the future, the future is the past," muttered
Wethers from his seat. Whatever he was drinking wasn't tar

beer; it reeked of sharp, unrefined liquor. "Dust only exists because of rock, and rock only exists because of dust."

Daiunek shushed him and bid good day to Reylin. "The guild will speak to the necessity of the military presence you've provided, Prince Reylin, should the Elder Council challenge that during their upcoming meeting."

This wasn't a poor outcome, Reylin thought as he raised his mug a second time. "Then let us drink, Guildmaster, to the East Face Mine and all it will yield, to the hidden precious minerals of the next valley, and to Miratian pride."

59

REYLIN ESCORTED HIS BEAUTIFUL wife through the crowd for a while longer, but the time was imminent.

He couldn't afford to miss anything, for he himself would initiate the banquet. Galltry had verified several times that Reylin would provide the first speech of welcome, but the lord had deceived him before. As the afternoon belltime approached, he guided her back into the castle courtyard and to the keep doors. They turned together at the top of the steps, and Reylin waited for the crowd's attention.

"I invite you now to share a great supper in our banquet hall," he announced, straining to overcome the constant hum of conversation. He was pleased with how authoritative his baritone actually sounded, level and demanding of attentiveness. "Please enter and enjoy the feast!"

The crowd cheered, and honored guests immediately began weaving through the melee to reach the stairway. Lords and their ladies, guildmasters, the black-adorned dragonkeepers, and high magusi of the temple entered the doors behind them, chatting amiably amongst themselves. Behind them flowed in the sons and daughters of high houses, the journeymen of various guilds, and the other confirmed magusi. After that, the gateway to the feast became a free-for-all of apprentices, yeomen, and traders, bustling and jostling each other to get through the doors and obtain a seat in the massive but swiftly filling banquet hall. Long tables had been set out with shallow wooden bowls, shining gallite forks and knives, and beautiful floral centerpieces featuring the summer lilac blooms.

The upper tables were raised upon a dais, reserved for those of status, and were festooned with delicate flower petals in every color, but especially the soft rosy hue of wild kiltberry. Elegant glass vases flickered with colored oils, priceless lamps from the southern kingdom of Litis. The plates were pounded of silvery fusianate which shimmered in the licking lamplight, and the knives and forks were accompanied by cloth napkins embroidered with unique scenes of dragons, warriors, and maidens.

The king's table was set higher still, upon a second dais, and was draped with a deep orange cloth that ruffled around the edges as its richly embellished lengths folded up at the base of the dais. The outer edge was shaped in a crescent, and only eleven people could sit on its straight edge, facing the expansive hall.

Reylin helped Syrana into the chair to his right, the place of the first consort. A brilliant smile lit her beautiful face, and he leaned down to kiss her despite the ochre—she would ruin it sipping on her wine glass in any case. After a moment, he beckoned the nursemaid carrying Amber to the chair on his left. The woman blanched, but no one would notice her. They would notice his baby, swathed in a bright yellow and dangling with topaz bangles. Dukes and duchesses filled the rest of his high table, with the notable exception of Lío's position being taken by his son, who looked a bit overwhelmed at the admirable placement.

Galltry had proposed moving the young man to the secondary table and elevating Lord Porin, but Reylin had staunchly refused. After Galltry, Lío was by far the most influential duke, and his son was acting as his proxy.

No mages sat at the king's table, as they claimed to be immune to the temptation of great stature, frequently choosing instead to sit amongst the yeoman and apprentices at the low tables. Kaiadin acknowledged him from the second table with a more-than-adequate nod. Ma'thell, on the other hand, had humbled himself to the point of situating at a low table of youngsters between his magus and a garrulous apprentice orator. Ma'thell's graying eyes squinted merrily as the apprentice rendered a rough performance of "The Forgetful Mage of Mundi" with his sitar, plucking the strings and beating the wood during the bridge, in which the forgetful mage taps his head in thought. The other children at the table were yowling the words in time to the music, clapping and squirming in their seats. Other mages were scattered about the lower and upper tables, many of them in slightly more dignified company. Reylin controlled a subtle shake of his head. The man was talented at appearing harmless.

The great, heavy doors to the banquet hall swung shut, and the last of the guests settled on benches at the lower tables. Reylin rose to his feet, exerting his presence as best he could. Strands of music hushed, and voices stilled. He adjusted his tunic importantly and threw his shoulders back. Syrana looked up at him with such adoration that he licked his lips. Then he cleared his throat.

"My honored guests," he began, "welcome to the Summer Solstice Festival, a time of change and new beginnings."

The hall shook with cheerful applause and hoots of agreeable merriment.

"This day marks the change in our world, when the Eye blinks down with its highest potential and smiles upon those who dance below its gaze. A day of celebration!"

Again, a buzz of agreement echoed through the room. How desperately he wanted to look at Galltry, who had demanded words from him but had failed to specify which words. Well, he wasn't going to get a eulogy to the dead miners of East Face, nor a guilt-laden lament of the ashen village near Edgegrass.

Reylin raised a hand to the crowd, testing and feeling their energy. They were ready, and if they weren't, he was. "I cherish your presence at this festive moment, not only to celebrate the solstice, but to join with me in celebrating my new beginnings. Behold, my firstborn, my daughter Amber Sallis of House Harkin."

He took Amber and held her high for all to see, a sure impression to replace that of his fainting in the Temple, if anyone in the banquet hall had been present at that disaster. Plus, there were hundreds more with a fresh impression, crowded and rabid for a view from the lower tables. Then he pulled Syrana up.

"And behold, my Chosen wife Syrana has entered her new role as first princess consort, a woman bound to be your queen." He grinned at the wild fervor shown by the audience, and he finally spared a glance at Galltry. The older man had paled, and Lady Shildra's mouth hung slightly open in shock.

He continued, commanding the hall to silence with the strength of his next words. "My faithful people, proud Miratians and dear guests, today I ask you to bear witness to a new beginning."

Every eye, sober or glazed over with inebriation, was glued to the prince. "My beloved people, my honorable lords and dedicated servants, this year brings the fruition of my own apprenticeship. The Elder Council who has guided me so wisely since my youth has given me honest guidance, true wisdom, and devout love, invaluable service which I can never repay. I have taken that wisdom and used it to guide Mirat into a new era, one of fearless partnership as we expand in the name of civilization and glory. Elder Council members, please rise and be recognized, that our guests may thank you as I do. Thank you for your service."

Syrana sucked in a quick breath through her teeth, and he knew she now understood. Reylin was announcing his own Ascension.

There was a short, breathless stillness. Then Ma'thell creaked to his feet, leaning upon his apprentice for assistance. The mage's pale eyes were no wider than usual, and he had a bright, hopeful smile upon his wizened face. Lord Porin, however, appeared to be quite shocked, his jaw slightly awry as he gawked. His wife nudged him, and he shot to his feet abruptly. She nudged him again as she rose gracefully, and he shut his mouth. Lord Lío's son grinned openly and stood with enthusiasm, banging his mug on the table before raising it high. Suddenly, Guildmaster Daiunek staggered to his feet, a drunken bear of a man. All miners in the hall followed suit as he sloshed tar beer from his mug in a toast.

"To Reylin of House Harkin," he bellowed. "Once our boy who survived the fire, and now our grown lord and king. May I'ya shine upon your rule!"

A great clatter went up as the hall clinked mugs.

"King! King Reylin!"

Reylin drained his mug of ale, then sat with his chin held high as he looked over the hall. The clamor continued to rise as his declaration of independence hit home. He had been an apprentice lordling since that fateful fire so many springs ago, leading his kingdom under the watchful shepherding of the Elder Council. Or rather, the self-serving and conservative control of the Elder Council. And now, they were publicly denied that control, to the violently loud adulation of the masses.

Praise the Light for the Miners Guild. Their support would convert half the city by word alone. And Lío's son—the lad had demonstrated that the councilmembers could safely defect from Galltry's miserly control.

He dove into the meal, drowning in a combination of ale and his own satisfaction.

The air rolled with the pervasive aroma of freshly baked bread, crispy-skinned meats, and sweet mountain flowers. A cacophony of innumerable conversations rolled like the rumble of an avalanche in the mountains. The room echoed with raucous laughter, authentic stories and absurd tales, greetings and good tidings, screams and giggles from the children, shameless jokes and haughty rebukes. The journeyman orator beside Ma'thell was particularly loud-voiced, making the children around him giggle.

As the day wore on, drink replaced food as the primary object of consumption. Tankards were brought out and placed on each table, chilled and tapped. Now, the feast became more riotous. Beers had been imported from kingdoms throughout the east and west, including the heavy and malty black tar beer of Fumaya's outposts, the pale and fruity wheatbeer from Loreni, the deep golden amber with an aftertaste of magasberry and thindelfruit of the Miratian highlands, and the hoppy bitterroot beer of the southern Tamorini subtropics.

Many of the orators took out their instruments and began to play, sometimes solo and often in groups, their well-trained voices lilting above the noise as they sang of glorious battles and valiant dragonkeepers, strange riddles and terrible deaths, beautiful sunrises and heartbreaking passion. Capers milled from table to table, performing jests and sleights of hand, breathing fire and smoke like a dragon, and dancing with each other foolishly. Miniscule tumblers came out, slaves from the fyr tribes of the Loi al'Halmana; they were dressed in bright feather skirts made from their precious birds, and absurd feathered caps covered their shaved heads. Their smiles were strained, and they seemed uncomfortable in their costumes. Reylin smiled, recalling the audacity of their bird-riding cavalry. If he recalled correctly, only warriors wore feathers, and those they took only from the birds of men they had triumphed over in battle, just as he had done. They deserved every bit of this humiliation for their people's affront to Mirat.

The tumblers tussled and wrestled each other, then performed wild acrobatics throughout the hall, throwing each other through the air and flying across tables on ropes of silk. One incredibly drunken man picked one of them up and tossed him carelessly, hollering, "Fly, little man, fly!" and then guffawing as the fyr hurtled onto a table, knocking off plates and platters of food. The barbarian scuttled back to his feet to the sound of laughter, his lips tight and white as his cheeks burned a furious red. He clenched and unclenched his fists tremulously but then diminished with a curt bow to the drunken audience. As he pranced away with a feathery rustle, even the royalty at the king's table clapped.

The feast continued, and a dessert course was laid out, featuring a massive thindelfruit pie spiced with cinnamon and platters full of pastries, wafers, and fresh fruits dipped in chocolate. Everyone's cups were refilled, this time with sweetwines and beers. Reylin preferred the harsher ales, but a delicate winter wheatbeer would mix well with the pie.

Galltry had said almost nothing to him. The man still hadn't managed to look like he wasn't choking, a fact that gave Reylin almost more fulfillment than his own declaration.

His beloved Syrana remained beside him, sipping a goblet of ale. Reylin shook his head; she had to be reeling inside, but she held her liquor well. It was a matter of Miratian pride to keep up through the meal, even if she retired from drinking for the rest of the day (as she very well should).

He peered over at her. She was engaged in a very polite conversation with Lord Shiften and his wife. Unsurprisingly, as he was Shildra's brother, he was overly tense and struggling through light conversation. Reylin could have laughed, had he not wished to maintain a kingly air through the entire meal.

Stuffed almost beyond comfort and somewhat woozy from the volume of ale consumed, he signaled for the end of the meal. The hall doors were flung open, letting the brisk spring air in and the people out. Many of the lesser guests departed the hall to continue libations outside, where they might find more diversions. The gambling would begin in earnest, and bets would become increasingly risky as the night wore on. The capering jesters, jugglers, and fire-breathers would run their shows out of doors on the various stages that had been assembled throughout the large outer courtyard, as would the bards and orators. Furthermore, at least two wayfarer caravans had arrived for the festival, one specializing in dance and entertainment and one specializing in sculpture and art.

His noble guests thanked them for the fine meal as they got up, most of them expressing adulation and admiration to the royal couple. Reylin helped Syrana out of her seat, and they all moved outside in the company of Lord Galltry. Lady Shildra clung to his arm.

Father Kaiadin appeared nearby, a bolstering source of strength as Reylin considered what Galltry might have spent the last few hours planning to say.

They emerged into the orange light of the afternoon; the Eye sank toward the horizon in a riot of rainbow colors, again emphasizing the presence of I'ya on this day.

Kaiadin pointed it out. "The Five-Faced God blesses this day," he declared.

The dancing wayfarers had set up on one of the central stages, adorned in varied costumes and preparing for a major performance. Their caravan, the Faraldins, were well known for their presentations of history, and their offspring were frequently apprenticed to the Hall of Orators in Krita Port. Some were even elevated to masters on occasion, a high rank for ones so lowborn. Of course, the guilds were quite dedicated to ignoring the social status of their novices. Their detachment from the nobility elevated the importance of dedication to the guild, from which alone guildsmen derived their status. It was whispered that Master Daiunek had come orphan from a mining camp, although Reylin hardly believed that absurd claim. More believable was the rumor that the Master Farmer was no more than a lowborn bastard born in a hovel in Litis.

Lord Galltry led him to the stage, finally stationing himself on Reylin's left as Reylin refused to release Syrana from his right side. *Know* your *place, old man,* he thought. Galltry chewed on his cheek a few times, seeming to struggle with producing words, and then he stroked his white beard and scowled a little.

"Your Highness . . ."

"Duke."

The use of Galltry's formal title gave him pause, but then he seemed to shake it off. "Your Highness, summer solstice is such a time, isn't it? Truly, a time of change. But as you know, the light exceeds the darkness up until this day. It consumes more and more of the night, threatening even the nether-hour with an early dawn, until, upon this day, it begins to diminish to winter."

Reylin hardened, but he bit back an immediate reply and waited.

Galltry raised his grayed eyebrows in supplication. "Son, such is not the right day to declare your kingship. It is riddled with bad luck as much as good, with such a change in the season. Your Ascension cannot be this day."

Reylin took a deep breath in, swelling his brawny chest. A miner he was not, for Galltry had denied his apprenticeship and eager learning, but he had gained the stature. He glared down his nose at the man, hoping his eyes flashed with as much fury as he felt coursing through his blood.

"Don't call me son. I am not your son, Duke. You will address me as is proper to my station."

Galltry's brow knotted, and his jaw trembled, and again he was rendered speechless.

Reylin spared a brief look at Lady Shildra. She looked so beseechingly at him, with such care and concern, that he inadvertently recalled Ma'thell's words. *She has been like a mother to you.*

"Crown Prince—"

"King." He said it with finality, his glare darkening even further until Shildra took a step back.

Galltry recovered. "Your Highness, the Council *must* convene to discuss this with you."

Perhaps it was the thrill of his earlier declaration still rushing through his veins. Perhaps it was the ale lending him the confidence he needed, further swelled by the ire and frustration of years of being reined back. Perhaps it was Father Kaiadin's presence directly behind his shoulder. He leaned into Galltry's face.

"No," he said simply.

The lord subsided, and they stood uncomfortably watching a new troupe of Faraldin performers array themselves on stage. Several musicians nestled on stools to one side: a sitari, a lutist, two drummers, and a reedsinger. A lithe young man stood in the center, and his clear tenor voice rang out over the crowd.

> *The tales to be told*
> *of greatest deeds old*
> *kindle in hearts all afire,*
> *but embers alone*
> *are no more than stone*
> *when tales do fail to inspire.*
>
> *So lend us an ear,*
> *some laughs and some tears,*
> *and let your heart light into flame.*
> *Dear ladies fair,*
> *your wishes declare,*
> *and gentlemen call out the same.*

The singer paused, listening to the cacophony of shouts.
"The Last Battle!"

"No, the Juggler of Normance!"

"Miratian March! Miratian March!"

"No, no, the Battle of the Kings!"

The singer signaled for quiet and announced, "The tale to be told shall be the Last Battle of the Five Kings."

The crowd cheered as torches were lit, encompassing the stage like a wreath. The performers arrayed themselves throughout the hall, their faces solemn as they prepared the storytelling art which they had mastered. The lead singer leapt upon a barrel, flourishing his hand at the audience, and began.

Reylin leaned close to Galltry. "Duke, I will give you one concession. Information."

Galltry and Shildra leaned in, striving to hear over the raucous pounding of feet in the crowd and the crowing battle-screams from the stage.

"I am not only king of Mirat, responsible for the glorious advancement of our border and a new and binding agreement with the Miners Guild. I am also a mage, a wielder of Water magika, and my power will not be fettered by someone weaker than myself."

Lady Shildra gasped, her eyes wide, but she covered her mouth quickly.

Galltry remained stubborn, the lines of his face drawn tight.

"There is a new threat to us of which you know nothing," Reylin continued, feeling even more pleased with himself. Lío would forgive him later for revealing the debacle touching his district. "There is a sickness, a deadly and insidious one that has thus far resisted Temple mages and lower magika practitioners alike. I am one of few with even a mote of the potential needed to cure it."

Kaiadin placed a supportive hand on his shoulder and acknowledged his words for the truth they carried. Galltry and Shildra, meanwhile, exchanged frightened looks.

"I ride for North Mara tomorrow, Duke. Nothing will hinder me. I go to heal this madness, before it destroys Mirat."

The Faraldin finished their battle dance, and Galltry's response, if there was one, was stifled by wild applause.

60

THE ARCH COMMODORE RETURNED from the front a number of weeks later, full of praise for the vigor and discipline of the new platoons. In his formal way, he elucidated the strengths of each: one was an exceptional blue shark cavalry group, moving in great concert that could only be the result of extensive drills; another was a highly effective archery group, talented in both bolt and sling.

"I shall accompany you on the next hunt," he announced, stroking his white mustache thoughtfully. "I'd like to see Tan's leadership on a more difficult mission."

Taiuki nodded. "A large colony of spotted sea makran have been attacking the fish farms near the Green Hills, sir."

Sashiro hummed his approval of the idea, then raised a finger. "Princess, one more thing. Have a seat."

She moved from her stance at attention in front of his desk to the chair.

Sashiro continued plucking at the long thin braid on his chin. "The vice commodore provided an extensive report of your work with the Second, all highly positive. Well done."

She acknowledged the compliment.

"She also brought a few novel ideas for troop adjustments when she relieved me at the front," he continued. "More aggressive than usual for her, but well considered. We implemented some of them." He raised a white, scruffy eyebrow.

Taiuki accepted the information, feigning ignorance, although she knew full well he suspected the ideas were hers.

"We could never take so many troops from the several villages along the northwest plains, leaving so few together." He gestured at the bathymetric map beyond the door.

"Of course not, sir."

"That is not the Way of the Current," he warned.

"No, sir."

Seemingly satisfied, he moved on. "Nevertheless, I understand the temptation. The Jijiton-jin aggression has spurred our southerly neighbors, and I worry for the Riyogon-jin border."

Taiuki took the information in. Jijito was a true threat; to the south was likely the typical border dispute, which rarely led to such violence. Then again, if one myrkingdom abandoned the traditional ways (was she ruminating on Jijito, or on Shiggo?), why would another myrkingdom not do the same?

"Sir, why are you telling me this?" The question was straightforward, which Sashiro would appreciate. She was unranked, after all, and her role in training Tan was temporary at best.

Sashiro tugged at his length of braided beard. "Because I need you to prepare the Second. With Jijito a constant harassment, Reihotto and I are pulled in every direction, stretched like tanning leather with too much sun. Princess, we *need* your leadership, even if it is only to train your replacement."

She swallowed back her feelings with difficulty. "I will gladly do more. But precisely what, sir?"

"You must not only train him to fight, but also to strategize, and eventually to kill. Reihotto and I do the same, but our words pass through his ears as a fleeting breeze. Yours settle on him, in him, become a part of him like the river meeting the sea. He has grown so much since this all began, primarily under your tutelage. He needs you, Princess."

Taiuki saluted deeply and with both hands, giving the arch commodore all of the respect and fealty he deserved. He dismissed her.

She paused at the door to his office. "Sir?"

"Yes, Princess?"

"If the Jijiton-jin abandoned the Way, can we not respond in kind?"

"No, dear niece. No."

Tan was ecstatic with the next hunting assignment: the destruction of a sea makran colony that had grown too bold.

They followed him now, riding in a wide-scouring hunting formation far to the east of the outer villages. Moka forged the way forward with Hachi and Benn to either side and behind. The rest of the formation fanned out in a broad chevron. Sea makran traveled in packs and had a reasonable level of intelligence, so it would take some coordination to eliminate the threat. This was Tan's test.

Benn was attuned to some scent, and with Tan's approval, Master Sashiro gave him rein to lead the hunting party where he would. Eager for blood, the blue shark turned slightly and led them into a thicker patch of the kelp forest, a wilder area that hadn't been harvested for some years. The kelp grew tall and thick, forcing the wedge pattern to break down. The water smelled mustier, older in this part of the forest. Each soldier slowed, moving into the growth in an uneven zigzag, working only to keep his neighbor within sight. Ahead, a clearing appeared, an open spot around a large rock formation that formed an island.

"They're close," clicked Sashiro in warning when Tan didn't seem to slow.

Tan paused, then signaled. "Circle around and assume attack formations, moon echelons. Initiate together with a single volley."

The soldiers folded around the large glade on either side. Taiuki held Hachi back on the edge of the clearing; he trembled with adrenaline. She could see Tan a distance away on

Sashiro's other side. Nimoka appeared to be very calm, but Tan was grinning under his helm. This was his first hunt with Sashiro.

"Attack!" Tan commanded, his click shattering through the water to reach every ear. A single round of bolts flew from top-level archers above the surface and pounded into the island's residents. Then he spurred Nimoka forward, and they all tore into the glade.

Taiuki and Master Sashiro followed closely behind Tan, urging their mounts across the opening and to the incline of the island. Near shore, they shifted and drew their jianswords, bursting from the water onto a colony of sea makran. The predatory creatures began trumpeting alerts and scattering from their lounges on the warm rock, but it was too late. Taiuki sliced into a smaller cow, then spun around a large bull. She slashed into his fat back, opening a massive cut into which she could jab the blade. The bull roared but then collapsed as its lungs filled with blood. Another bull, younger and faster, charged at her. She rolled out of the way, and the animal splashed into the water, where Benn and Hachi were waiting.

Taiuki recovered her feet and looked around. The rocky island was covered in corpses, the shoreline pink with fresh blood. She saw Master Sashiro dispatch another cow, who had been fiercely guarding two younger pups. Tan and another soldier swept in from either side and killed the pups shortly after. Her brother's smile was gone. She killed another juvenile that burst back from the water in a panic, then wiped her jiansword clean on its chubby body, leaving a film of grease. No soldiers appeared to be hurt on the island, and they turned their attention to the underwater battle.

Benn was ripping into a bull, and Sashiro slipped back into the water to regain control of his mount. Taiuki followed with a deep sigh.

The water reeked of blood and oil from the sea makran. Taiuki breathed it in, controlling her heart rate with long, deep inhalations until her lungs disappeared. With her gills reformed, she tasted everything. A halo of death surrounded the island, dissipating into clear water beyond the glade. Makran corpses littered the glade underwater as well, floating just under the surface.

And there, Hachi.

Taiuki rushed to him. The whale lay contorted on one side, unable to swim upright. His pain was evident, but he also communicated it with her in a storm of clicks and emotion. His panicking eyes were glassy, and his trill was one of pain and fear. Taiuki pulled out her injury salve to treat his wounds. He had been bitten farther back on the left side of his belly, and a large chunk of flesh had been ripped out. Blood poured profusely from the open wound. Taiuki could see organs protruding from the hole. Worse yet, his tail looked as if it had been crushed and was already bruising. A broken spine. Hachi could die.

Taiuki staunched a sob as she tried to calm him, assuring him he was safe. Hachi resisted, and she forced him to be still with a firm hand on the reins. She spread salve on the edges of the open wound and looked around for something to wrap him with.

"You should leave him, Princess," said Master Sashiro. "He is dead already."

Taiuki looked up and realized the arch commodore was watching from his position on Benn's back. Benn looked extremely satisfied, attuned to the scents in the water, turning his head back and forth with bloodlusting jubilation.

"I can't," she replied. "He can heal."

"No." Sashiro's clicking conveyed no admonition, only finality.

Tan rode up on Nimoka, his face pensive. "Hachi?"

Taiuki shook her head sadly. Her whale mount trembled under her fingers, as if he knew they were discussing his fate. He whined at her. She didn't have the strength to leave him behind for the crabs. She turned to Sashiro. "He can heal. Let me try, sir," she pleaded.

Sashiro gave a slight grimace. "Second, at your command."

Tan's eyes widened, and he was at first speechless. He winced as Nimoka joined Hachi's wailing cry with a moan of sympathy. She nuzzled her fellow blackheaded whale, but Hachi was oblivious in his pain.

Tan stuttered. "I—I cannot leave any of the school behind, right, sir?"

"If they can bolster the school later," Sashiro said slowly. "But one which is at the Gates?"

"A single one must not put the entire school at risk," Tan admitted. He shook his head. "If Yuki—er, the princess—if Princess Taiuki believes he can heal, then we should not leave him behind."

"He will not survive." Sashiro's voice was harsher now. "Knowing this, what is the right call?"

"To leave him to the current," said Tan, bowing his head. Then he raised his chin. "I do not wish the soldiers to return in the dark. Please escort the main party back to Shiggo City, Arch Commodore. We shall catch up."

Sashiro gave Tan a long, measuring look. "Have a care for the Way of the Current, nephew." He turned Benn and led the hunting party out of the glade.

Tan handed a roll of binding cloth to Taiuki from his pouch. "I'll stay with you," he clicked quietly.

Taiuki placed a few fat kelp fronds over the open wound and bound it tightly. Then she led Hachi by the reins, praying he could make it back to the stable. They fell behind the hunting party after mere minutes, but at least Tan and Moka were with her. Once they got out of the older kelp forest, the landscape was fairly well colonized by farms and didn't likely host any serious threats. Nonetheless, she suspected Master Sashiro was intentionally forcing her and Tan to see the danger of falling behind for the weakened whale. It was better to leave Hachi to the current, to sacrifice him for the good of the company, but she couldn't.

They arrived at the stable late in the day, and Taiuki re-dressed Hachi's open wound with proper medical supplies. She treated the gouged edges with gloryflower-steeped milk-tree jelly, then stretched the thin skin from a feeder fish over the open area. The whale moaned in pain, but his protesting had grown subdued. He had lost so much blood and fluids, and Taiuki could tell he was fading. She attempted to splint the tail, but the bones inside were likely shattered. She made him as comfortable as she could, allowing him to slip into a woozy slumber. Hachi drifted to a vertical position and became very still.

"Do you think he'll live?" Tan asked from behind her. He had watched all of it in silence, gnawing on his cheek the entire time.

She couldn't be too optimistic. Broken tails were a death knell for whales.

They swam to the training hall and entered. It was mostly empty, as the soldiers had already eaten supper and returned to the barracks. A few sat in the alcoves, throwing dice or cards in small groups.

Master Sashiro appeared, still wearing the same grimace from earlier. "You abandoned formation today," he said stiffly, "for a dying mount." He looked at both of them, his disappointment tugging new lines on his battle-worn cheeks.

Taiuki tried to meet his eye but couldn't. "I couldn't give up on him, sir. He could live, and he's a good mount, well trained and intelligent."

"But he is only one," replied Sashiro, his voice hard. "And I was speaking to the Second. What if we had met a lacer on the route home? What if you had? Did you consider that?"

Tan stuttered, failing to answer.

Taiuki blushed with shame and spoke in his stead. "I didn't think it was likely, sir, and I had Tan and Nimoka with me."

"And they had you." Sashiro's voice was contemptuous, and Taiuki looked up in surprise. He rarely spoke with such a tone. He must have caught himself too, as his face softened. Gripping her arm, he forced her to look him in the eye. "Princess," he said urgently, "it is not enough to consider yourself. You must consider the company, the troops, the kingdom as a whole. The myr that lives alone, dies alone."

Tears welled in the corners of Taiuki's eyes, and she saluted deeply to the arch commodore to hide them. She stayed that way, staring hard at her palms, until he released her. Then he turned to Tan.

"You are the Second now, Prince Tan. You must consider the effects of your decisions on the school. You abandoned your post as leader of the expedition to stay behind, thereby dividing the school."

As Sashiro turned to walk away, he said, "His tail is broken. I expect his stable to be cleaned out within a few days.

I suggest you consider a blue or a sawtooth for your next mount, Princess; you're ready for it."

His steps echoed in the open hall, and the door to the barracks made an audible thud.

Taiuki shuddered out a breath. Tan remained beside her, then awkwardly patted her hand.

"It's okay, Yuki. I'll help you take care of him," he suggested, his irrepressible hope lighting his expression. "He could get better."

"He'll never hunt again, even if he does survive. Master Sashiro is right," she whispered, grasping at the harsh reality in front of her, then changed the subject. "I need to return to the castle. I'm late."

"For what?" he asked. "They already ate supper without us."

Taiuki caught herself. "Nothing important. Wehan was expecting me after the evening meal, that's all."

Her brother nodded despite his lack of understanding, then brightened. "I can stay with Hachi if you want."

Taiuki squeezed his hand. Such a trusting and impulsive soul, he would pour all of his energy into Hachi's care without questioning why she couldn't for the next few hours. He still believed she completed courtly lessons on the full days before rest day, not in the evenings between supper and forms practice.

Even knowing she had to put the whale down, Tan would nurse Hachi until his end. Taiuki resigned herself to her evening lesson, sure to be dull and unsatisfying, and made her way to the castle.

Hachi was stable the following day, although he slept a great deal and moaned when he was awake. His skin color had deepened from its grayish pallor of the previous evening, a good sign that the bleeding had been staunched. He couldn't move much without ripping the tender wound open on the edges. The fish-skin patch was frayed on the edges and leaked sour, clear fluids.

Taiuki smeared the edges closed with more sap-based salve, which would not dissolve in water. Hachi communicated his pain and relief to her in a combination of clicks, whines, and body movements. She could tell he understood that she and Tan were helping him, despite the tenderness when they touched his bandaging or splint. Hachi was such a clever beast. Raised from a weaned calf, Hachi had been hers for nine years, and they had been riding together for seven. Taiuki sighed. No more. Hachi could not likely swim effectively again.

She had probed his tail more carefully after he had survived the night. As she suspected, his tail had been crushed by a vicious bite. The dorsal ridge had sustained a series of pinhole injuries, top and bottom, from a large makran mouth, probably the dominant bull. The delicate bones at the end of the spine, on the narrow peduncle, were shattered, inhibiting future tail movement and coordination. If the vessels inside were overly destroyed, the tail could lose blood flow altogether, leaving the flesh to senesce and rot away. Taiuki caressed Hachi, scratching around his eye. He didn't respond, as he was in a stupor of shock and gloryflower numbing.

Taiuki completed her morning training, but her forms were careless and imperfect. Sashiro knocked her to the ground several times in sparring, jabbing or slicing her with a wooden jiansword at each opportunity. After the humiliating match, the arch commodore dismissed her to check on Hachi, recognizing where Taiuki's mind was, but he bid her return later.

Master Sashiro placed Marshal Kinota in charge of the cavalry that afternoon, sending Tan and the other trainees off to work with landwalker mounts. He then led Taiuki down to the blues' territory on the far edge of the village. Benn swam up eagerly in greeting, swaying his head back and forth, and Sashiro gave him a freshly dispatched feeder fish. The shark swallowed it whole.

"Blues are fierce, but loyal," said Master Sashiro. "They are natural guardians, being both territorial and partner-specific. However, they are also very independent and can be stubborn."

Taiuki nodded as she watched the pair interact. Benn circled slowly around them in a protective loop, brushing his head under Sashiro's outstretched hand on each pass. Some of the other blues nearby adopted his protective looping, easing around them in loose, languid motion. Blues were naturally pack animals, like the myr. It was no surprise the arch commodore preferred them, but he also had his own strength of character to partner with a stubborn mount. Taiuki wasn't sure she was ready to choose a beast that required such overt command, especially when there was blood in the water. She told Master Sashiro as much.

"Are you certain? That blue with the white crescent mark is an excellent young animal." Sashiro clicked at the juvenile shark, and it approached somewhat cautiously. He gifted it another fish from his pouch. "She is one of Benn's off-spring," he added proudly. "You may find that you and she are very much alike."

Taiuki thanked him for his recommendation but requested they move to the sawtooth stables before she decided. Sashiro looked disappointed. Nonetheless, he brought her to the large pens where the sawtoothed whales were kept. They stayed in family groups, away from the other whales, but they were friendly to humans. Taiuki swam into the enclosure and was immediately surrounded by curious animals. Several swam up and down, clicking at her in their excitement.

"They're so intelligent, like Hachi," she said.

Master Sashiro begrudgingly agreed, then pointed to several of the juvenile calves. "That one is bred from Vice Commodore Reihotto's male Tsuya, and that one from Marshal Kinota's new female. Both matings chosen by the master herdsman."

Taiuki examined the calves. One had a uniquely shaped eye patch, and the other had especially mottled coloring. They were beautiful creatures, well-bred and well-conditioned. The master herdsman should be proud. Both animals regarded her, curiosity counterbalanced with timidity—sawtoothed whales tended to be shy at that age. She clicked to them, calling them to her and assuring them that she was safe. The mottled one tentatively swam forward, then paused to glance at its mother. Emboldened by the exchange, the calf came closer, nudging Taiuki's hand with its muzzle.

"A quality animal, well formed," said Sashiro. "He will serve you well in battle, better than any blackheaded whale." He had never preferred the more demure whales, but they were the easiest to break and ride.

"I have to start over with training," Taiuki replied, smiling as she stroked the mottled creature. His nose was beyond smooth, perfectly slick as only a juvenile could be.

"A good exercise regardless," answered Sashiro.

Taiuki agreed. This calf would have to replace Hachi, as she had no interest in a blood-loving blue shark, no matter how noble its lineage. Sashiro was obviously disappointed in her final choice, but he didn't push her harder.

"I've given Marshal Kinota additional instruction to assist you in breaking your new mount." *And to verify that you've emptied Hachi's stall*, were his unspoken words. Then his face became more serious, and he leaned in to click at a lower volume. "The Way of the Current is the only way, Princess Taiuki, the only true myr way. Give Hachi to the current, let him return to I'ya, and focus on being here with your people." Again, his true words remained unspoken, conveyed only in the hardness of his yellow-flecked black eyes. *Your defiance to the school's conformity for the sake of your whale confuses Tan.*

He left then, allowing her more time to bond with the mottled calf she had chosen.

That evening entailed the last of her courtly lessons for the week. Before she could sleep, she checked on Hachi one more time. The blackheaded whale rested, but his color looked far better than it had. His wound had sealed and appeared to be clean of infection. However, his peduncle was purple with bruising, with a sickly yellow on the edges, and his tail was limp and gray. He whined as she left, but she promised him she would return soon.

Taiuki slept lightly, tossing in her blankets until the early hours, when she lifted her tired body from the bed. It didn't matter—she would sleep when she got to the island, to It'tholl. She smiled tenderly at the thought of her dragling. It'tholl would be surprised by her arrival this time.

Taiuki dressed in silence, armoring herself with the light scalemail and chinespine as she had done for weeks now. She worried she might need it this time, and she added several more bolts to the quiver on her back. Her slim Nagawan knife slid into its sheath on her right, and a jiansword on her left—an extra protective measure.

She was ready.

Taiuki slipped out of the castle via her usual route, using the side portal near the garrison to sneak into the stables. She lifted a chariot harness off the rack and examined it. The device would have to do. Hachi greeted her with a weak but excited whine, and she shushed him. She arranged the chariot harness on him, flipping the lead straps backward so they ran toward his head instead of his tail. Then she adjusted each girdle's tightness, ensuring the harness would not fall off.

She stopped. Had she heard something? The stable was still, the water heavy with the reduced oxygen of night. The other blackheaded whales slept soundly, and only Hachi shifted in his harness, creating a delicate sound of stretching leather that seemed loud in the darkness. Taiuki waited a few more seconds. She had to go, or someone would catch her.

She urged Hachi out of the stable and closed the gate. Then she pulled the long leads forward and tied them to either side of her breechbelt. Hachi was the chariot today, and she the draught. With one more look toward the dark barracks, where the young trainees and Master Sashiro slept, Taiuki led her beloved mount out. Both moons were nearly full, and there was enough dim light to navigate, even this early. By the time the sun rose in the world above, she would be an adequate distance from Shiggo to escape notice. She arranged her speargun comfortably on her chest harness, then commanded Hachi to swim.

The exhausted whale followed her command, although he was sluggish, and her lead guided him and kept him properly oriented. His tail appeared to be nearly useless, and he used his pectoral fins to flutter forward.

Taiuki steeled herself for a long, strenuous trip. When nighttime waned and the sun peeked through, she would have to be especially guarded against feeding lacers. With a deep breath of resolve, Taiuki swam eastward, Hachi in tow.

61

TAIUKI DRAGGED HERSELF OUT of the coral reef late in the afternoon. Hachi could do little but maintain buoyancy, despite their long rest hidden in the towers and foliage. Finally, they had only to ascend the incline to shore, and they would be home.

The whale moaned in pain.

"Advance," Taiuki commanded. At this point, only their training, years of discipline and practice, was maintaining their progress. It was possible the exertion alone would kill Hachi, but she had to try to get him to a safe place. The island was the only such place she knew.

Hachi moaned again.

"Please, Hachi, we're almost there. Advance!" she clicked, desperately pulling him forward. Her body was sore and chafed from the harness.

Child of I'ya? Bright day. Uth'hal's deep voice entered her head in a friendly greeting. A large shape emerged from the murky distance, morphing into a familiar shape as it swept its magnificent wings sedately.

Hachi saw the shape and began to struggle in the harness, trilling an alert.

"Calm!" cried Taiuki as she was yanked backward. "Uth'hal, stay back!"

The massive dragon paused a long distance away, but his size and predatory shape remained obvious.

Hachi screamed an alarm and tried to swim away, but his fluttering was feeble. Taiuki unclipped the chariot leads from her breechbelt and regained control of her mount with a tighter grip. She grabbed the loose reins hanging from his mouth.

"Calm, Hachi!" she commanded, asserting her authority.

The whale held position but rolled his eyes in panic.

Is it food? asked Uth'hal. He edged closer, snaking his long neck toward the whale and sweeping his wings once more.

Taiuki rejected that thought vehemently.

It looks like food, said It'ma, likewise appearing from the direction of shore and pausing a ways away. *What else would it be for?*

It'tholl is hungry! Taiuki brings It'tholl food! The dragling's voice was more distant but clearly petulant. Taiuki couldn't even see her yet, but she was approaching fast.

"He's not food!" Taiuki shouted. "He's my mount, Hachi. He's very sick, and I need you to protect him."

She could feel the scorn exuding from the adult dragons.

Why is he important? He is neither hamanool nor daragool, said Uth'hal.

"He's mine. I raised him from a calf, trained him, hunted with him." Terror grew in Taiuki's stomach. This was not the welcome she had expected, and she realized that she had brought her whale into a den of predators. Hachi shifted uncomfortably from side to side, desiring to bolt but held in place by discipline and Taiuki's firm grip. "Please," Taiuki continued, addressing all the dragons within hearing range, "he is precious to me."

It is only a whale. We do not understand, said It'ma. Nonetheless, Taiuki could feel the hungry nature of their interest wane, replaced by confusion.

It'tholl's smaller figure appeared and came closer, but Taiuki warned her to slow.

It'tholl wants Taiuki! The dragling pressed forward eagerly, sweeping her wings like a ray and speeding toward Taiuki.

Hachi squealed in fright, ripping the reins from Taiuki's clutch, and pumped his broken tail with all his might. The whale labored westward to the reef, crying with each ineffectual sweep of his tail.

A figure burst from behind a rock and grabbed his reins, yanking him back under control. The figure turned to face Taiuki, and they stared at each other in a shocked tableau.

Tan.

Taiuki was barely conscious of It'tholl wrapping herself around her, entwining her neck covetously around Taiuki's torso and her tail around Taiuki's leg. They both squealed when It'tholl squeezed too hard on a chinespine, which broke her skin. Then It'tholl exuded pure, unrestrained bliss that infected Taiuki until she unwittingly smiled.

Tan mirrored her smile for a brief moment, then reverted to disconcerted awe. His jaw hung loosely open, and his eyebrows kept knitting and unknitting, his expression morphing from a troubled scowl to utter confusion. He stared primarily at Taiuki and It'tholl, then seemed to realize the import of the large shapes beyond her. He pulled Hachi forward a short distance, torn between terror and curiosity.

Uth'hal and It'ma examined him calmly in return.

Tan gulped visibly and placed his right hand on his jiansword as if to reassure himself.

I'ya's blessings, child, said It'ma.

Tan swiftly looked around, unsure of where the voice had come from. Taiuki chirped a nervous laugh. Her brother grinned sheepishly at her but dared not come any closer.

"Sis?" he clicked.

Taiuki shook herself out of the initial trepidation that had immobilized her.

Tan had followed her. Of all the foolish things she could have allowed to happen, this was the worst. If Tan got hurt . . . He wasn't even properly outfitted, wearing light leather and carrying only a jiansword. No helmet, no chine-spine, not even a Nagawan blade.

"Oh, Tan-sho, why did you follow me?" she clicked.

Tan's grin came more easily this time. "I knew you had a plan for Hachi." He swam a little closer, allowing his awe to shine as he peered at It'tholl.

It'tholl was entirely possessed with Taiuki and paid him no mind. She kept repeating Taiuki's name in a childish, happy rhythm.

"Is that her, singing?" asked Tan with amazement.

Taiuki nodded.

"I can hear her," he clicked. "Is she . . . What is she? What are they?" This time, he looked beyond them, where Uth'hal and It'ma still floated, watching. "Are they dangerous?"

Not to you, child of I'ya, said Uth'hal. *You have nothing to fear.*

Tan looked around wildly, realizing where the voice was coming from. He pulled Hachi forward. The whale had given up resisting, thoroughly exhausted and stressed beyond his capacity, and had gone vertical in a half-conscious stupor. Tan pushed his chest out and lifted his chin, then passed his hand respectfully in front of his face. "I am Prince Tan ol'Kada ol'Tatami of Shiggo," he said proudly.

I am Uth'hal, second elder of the order al'Laiakala, replied Uth'hal with some amusement.

And I am It'ma, first elder of the al'Laiakala, added It'ma.

It'tholl is It'tholl, the dragling said happily. Satisfied with her display of affection for Taiuki, It'tholl loosened herself and made loops around Tan and Hachi. *Food is Hachi is not-food*, she declared, looking at Hachi.

"That's right, beloved," said Taiuki. "Hachi is not food."

Taiuki was torn between a fiercely burning ecstasy to have Tan with her, and terror that he now knew her precious secret. Nonetheless, she allowed him to close the distance between them. He was flushed with excitement, and he looked up at her with complete confidence. She broke into a relieved smile and wrapped him in a tight embrace. She found herself weeping uncontrollably.

"What's wrong?" her little brother asked.

Taiuki couldn't answer, but she felt like a weight had been lifted from her.

Taiuki is happy, It'tholl is happy, declared It'tholl.

"I'm sorry I followed you, but I didn't think you'd let me come with you," said Tan.

"I wouldn't have," Taiuki said, half laughing and half sobbing. She released him. "But you're here now. Come with me."

She led him to shore, and they tied Hachi's reins to a shallow rock formation so he could rest. In his utter exhaustion, he remained as they left him.

She shifted her fin into legs thoughtlessly as she reached shore, pulling Tan behind and supporting his balance as he shifted too. Stepping out of the waves, they breathed in the fresh coastal air, delicious with purity edged in salt. Dragons lounged all over the beach, in the shade of the cliff and on top. It'tholl had emerged and was trouncing through the shallow pools, snapping at crabs and darting fish. Tan stopped and took the scene in.

"By I'ya, they're beautiful," he whispered, his mouth once again hanging open.

Taiuki agreed. "They're incredible creatures, Tan. And It'tholl, she's perfect."

"You found them?"

"They found me. They saved me, Tan, and brought me to her."

All of the dragons were watching them now, their interest piqued at the new visitor. Taiuki introduced Tan as her little brother, and the dragons echoed a welcome filled with a myriad of names that was impossible to pick apart. Tan took it all in with a bewildered, wondrous smile. He already seemed so comfortable with this reality, this world where sea monsters existed that could cover a section of the Lower Market with the span of their wings. He didn't balk at their terrifying size or razor teeth, only basked in the beauty of their iridescent verdigris scales, their lithe and powerful tail fins, and their magnificent, hypnotic eyes.

The sun was low when a terrible thought passed through Taiuki's mind.

"They'll be missing you at the castle," she said. Fear twisted her gut worse than the butt of a spear.

Tan grimaced. "I'll lie. No one expects much of me anyway. I'll just say I wanted to relax after how hard the hunt was, and went to the Shrine ol'Tatami."

"We have to get you back. No one can know about this, Tan." Taiuki pleaded for him to understand.

"I know."

"*No one.*"

"I know!"

"If Mother found us out . . ." Taiuki's voice trembled. "She would—"

"I won't tell anyone, Taiuki." Tan sat up. "Especially not Mother."

"Or Kei," she said in rejoinder.

"No, not Kei," he agreed. "I'll go home tonight and pretend it was nothing. Although, you need to be more careful yourself."

"What do you mean?" Taiuki thought she had been exceedingly clever.

"You're not at court sometimes. When old Sash or Reihotto send me on errands, sometimes I look in to see where you are, and you're not there. And you disappear after supper, and you go to bed late most nights, even when you're not with that cavalier. Someone is going to catch you."

Taiuki swallowed some of her errant pride. She had been too confident. And how to get Tan back safely and without causing more suspicion?

I can take him, said Uth'hal. *I can leave him at the edge of the farms, away from the villages.*

She nodded. "Tan," she said, "please keep this a secret, and we'll make a plan together when I get back."

"I'd die before telling," her brother declared. He grinned, then walked into the water with Uth'hal, giving her a casual wave before going under. "See you in a few days, Yuki-sho."

Taiuki gulped back nervous bile; it burned in her throat. "See you in a few days," she whispered at the orange-streaked water.

Hachi's injuries remained Taiuki's primary focus, but there was little she knew to do for the exhausted whale. Despite her field medical training and the pouch of supplies derived from Shiggo's garrison, she still could only staunch the leaking of fluids and give him rest. His cries echoed through the cove from his pasture, a shrill but intermittent wailing that threatened to break her in half. It'tholl didn't seem to care, driven to visit him more by curiosity than by a desire to help.

Hachi-food-not-food suffers, she stated plainly.

"Bring him small fish, please," Taiuki instructed before returning to Shiggo City. "Keep the others away and minimize his stress."

We have no interest in the whale, child of I'ya, said It'ma somewhat haughtily. *Not if it is claimed as yours.*

If it were possible for a dragon to be snippy, that was it. Taiuki apologized and begged the Order to protect Hachi while she was away, then returned with Uth'hal to Shiggo.

I need a new whale to speed this trip, she thought as she paused at the sawtoothed whale pens. She spied her selected calf and pulled a small fish from her sealed pouch. He responded shyly to her clicking, easing toward her once his mother agreed.

Tan appeared. "You're back."

"Hush, Tan." Taiuki scanned their surroundings thoroughly to ensure no one could hear them. Sound carried so well underwater; it would be foolish to speak of this now.

His smile faltered, but then he nodded in understanding. "How's this little one? Not too scared of the dark, is he?"

Taiuki glanced up at the graying water above, a sign of impending night. "He knows he's safe here."

She beckoned the mottled calf with the small fish, then pulled another out for his mother and sister. The calf eagerly grabbed at the food, his juvenile teeth razor sharp. Taiuki chastened him calmly, then offered again with a clicking command. The calf rolled his eye at her, trying to understand, and hesitantly plucked the fish from her hand. Taiuki praised him with an encouraging click and scratched him under the jaw.

"I think I'll name him . . . Kenji."

Tan stroked the calf's side. "That's a good name."

"What do you think, Kenji-sho? You like your name?" She showered him with affection. As much as she hadn't sought a new mount, this beautifully colored creature was an excellent-quality product of the Shiggo herd. The master herdsman thought Kenji was the best of the breed thus far, derived from a long-celebrated lineage owned by Reihotto's family. Reihotto had been ecstatic about Taiuki's choice.

"I like Kenji," Tan agreed. "He's really cute."

Taiuki agreed. The sawtoothed whale had an exceptionally vermiculated back with dark patches over tawny brown, fading to a light tan on the sides, then to a bright white belly. His face had asymmetrical mottling, with a dark patch on one eye and not the other. At this young age, he was already twice as long as she was tall, and would continue to grow rapidly. Kenji was only partially weaned, a boon for trading his whale mother for a human caretaker without much struggle for dominance. Despite his size relative to Taiuki, he was timid and unsure of himself, much like a human toddler.

"We have so much to learn together." Taiuki smiled despite herself. Kenji really was an incredible creature, capable of learning a broad vocabulary and the perfect age to do so. They would swim together for another month or two, building trust through constant handling and generous salve rubs, halter and saddle training, and integration of human vocabulary into the whale's communication method. Taiuki barely remembered this process with Hachi, as she had been Anella's age at the time and had received a good deal of assistance from Marshal Kinota.

She offered her last fish to Kenji, who took it delicately and swallowed it whole. She praised him, and he squealed an effusive high pitch, moving up and down in the water to proclaim his contentment. Taiuki encouraged him to return to his family group for the night, and she and Tan headed toward the Garrison Gate.

"How are we going to get out of here?" asked Tan.

"Later, Tan," she said. Even in clicks, her words sounded short and snappy.

Tan screwed his face up but stopped. He was bursting, likely had been since the moment they parted. How could they adjust their training schedules? When could he go with her? How was Hachi? How was It'tholl?

"Well . . ." Tan was searching for an alternative subject. "Anella would really like Kenji, if she would come down to meet him. She could pet him through the gate like she did with Hachi."

They arranged it that week, encouraging Anella down to the Kelp Gate once more. Her apprehension had faded, but she didn't explore the lower levels alone.

Godrig and Kei came with her, trailed by two Kritali soldiers.

Godrig leered through the gate, his arm securely linked with his little sister's as though he needed to guard her from danger. His square chin jutted out, stubbornly insistent upon ensuring that their interaction was miserable, and he wore a permanent glower as he gazed out of the vertical portal.

Anella bounced from foot to foot in her excitement as Taiuki and Tan guided the sawtooth family closer to the portal. Taiuki guided the mother by a harness. Both Kenji and his sister adhered to the mother's side, as sawtooths always did at younger ages. The princess's exclamations pinged through the portal with full clarity, and Tan grinned.

"Told you she'd love him," he clicked.

"Tell Godrig to back up," Taiuki called to Kei. "The calf is young enough to be shy."

Kei complied, and Godrig pulled Anella backward with him.

Taiuki sighed. "Tan-sho, would you hold the reins please?" She handed control of the mother to him and stepped through the portal, splitting her tail in one smooth motion. Her toes reformed just as her foot met the ground, and she emerged from the water into the air-filled side of the Kelp Gate.

Anella's cherubic face, as always, was filled with wonder, and she half curtsied, half saluted. "Bright morning, Princess. May I pet him?"

Godrig's face twisted into a distrustful snarl, and he clutched her arm more tightly. "Stay back, Nelly. You can look at it from here. It may bite."

Taiuki checked her temper and gazed coolly at the man. "*It* is a *he*, and he is more intelligent than your horse, I guarantee it." She advanced, pulling Anella from Godrig's tight hold with an assertive glare that matched his. The repeated clenching of his jaw gave her a rush of pleasure—likely the only pleasure to be had from him—and she smiled sweetly like Kei would do.

Nelly willingly approached the portal, withholding her wild enthusiasm with careful steps and a tentative hand. "What's his name?"

"Kenji."

She glanced at Taiuki in utter awe. "Like the great king you told me about? Your ancestor? That's a really good name then."

Godrig held a neutral expression, but it was obvious he didn't know who Kenji was. Did they not teach any history of other cultures in Krita? She checked herself. Admittedly, she didn't know what they taught in Krita either, at least not beyond what Wehan had been drilling into her.

"Kenji was the warrior king who ruled with Queen Noriko during the Great Massacre," Kei explained, flipping her hair back and sidling forward despite herself. She wore heavy-laden skirts that disallowed her shifting, but at least she wasn't afraid of getting her laced arm wet.

"They flooded the entire city," Anella added as she offered her hand to Kenji on the other side of the gate. "To keep it safe from the Luminaries." She giggled as Kenji nuzzled her fingers, then turned to peer at her with one eye.

"You mean the Great Cleansing," said Godrig.

"We call it what it was, Prince," Taiuki replied, her voice bitter enough that the gate's guards glanced over.

Godrig sneered. "All of the histories I've read call it the Cleansing."

"Perhaps you should read more diverse texts." Taiuki's honeyed smile was not lost on him, and he shook his head as if to himself.

Anella jumped in, her child-chubby cheeks pink with embarrassment as she attempted to bridge the gap between them. "They have a whole history we never learned about, Godrig. Everything that happened underwater while Krita faced the Cleansing with the other land kingdoms."

Godrig feigned indifference. "In any case, that's ancient history. And besides, the Luminaries mostly targeted *lower*-class citizens who were disrupting society with their use of magika."

"And how do you think they treated people with magika in their blood?" Taiuki snapped, her voice a harsh echo in the cavern.

The gate guards looked up, now openly scowling at Prince Godrig and leering at their Kritali counterparts, who had stiffened, hands on hilts, at the tone of conversation. Tan's mouth hung open as the mother sawtooth strained against her harness; she was picking up on his agitation. Even Kei huffed, finally giving Godrig a disdainful look.

Godrig ground his teeth, and his hands curled into fists at his side, but he didn't apologize. Instead, he offered a hand to his sister. "Come on, Nelly. Let's go for a ride in the fresh air."

Anella backed away from him, nearly bumping into Taiuki and wetting the edge of her skirts on the portal interface. She crossed her arms. "I want to stay here."

"Now, Nelly."

"No."

"I must depart for Marlemet soon. This may be your last opportunity before I'm gone for a while."

"Then stay here with us." Anella raised her chin much like Kei had, but her young face was so much softer, lacking the squareness of Godrig's or the elegance of a grown woman's.

Godrig's now-familiar glower deepened, and he growled a rude curse before turning and stalking away with his soldiers on his heel. Anella watched him go, her face twitching as if she were about to get into trouble, and she swallowed several times.

Taiuki gently turned her shoulder back toward the gate and encouraged her to pet Kenji. "It's his choice not to be excited about Kenji or any of the things you've learned while being here, Nelly."

Tan clicked an agreement through the water, and although Anella didn't seem to fully understand, she did comprehend his friendly smile.

Brightening, she turned her attention to the whales. She scratched Kenji's chin and patted his smooth muzzle, then gave him small fish from Taiuki's belt pouch, completely disregarding the slick fish oil sticking to her fingers. When all the fish were gone, she stepped back with a soft, melancholic smile.

"I'm really sorry for what happened to Hachi," she said quietly. Her pretty green eyes struck Taiuki. Were those tears, for a myr whale? By the current, she was a sweet girl.

"It's all right," Taiuki said, her voice rough. She cleared her throat. "War mounts rarely live a full life."

"I know you loved him, though," Anella insisted. "He was a really good whale. I liked him."

Taiuki nodded, then gestured to Kei to take the girl back up to higher levels. "Tan and I will return Kenji and his family to their pasture," she said, managing to control her expression and the sting in her eyes until she could pass through the gate. "We'll join you at supper."

Once again, Anella shone with hopeful excitement, for after the evening meal was training, and she had proven to be a faithful if inexperienced student.

Taiuki had to admit, she liked her.

As if reading her thoughts, Tan glanced over at her as they swam and winked.

THE HARALAL WERE NOT ready.

The Manalal swept into the expansive settlement that appeared as the dust of her sandstorm settled. It was a large town. From her vantage point, she could see a deep green in the center surrounded by three towers. They shone with bright colors in the morning light. The green spread outward, with palms and grasses and cacti flourishing in every street and between every building. The homes were mostly mudbrick with thatch roofing.

A terrible realization hit her, and she fell to her wobbling knees.

The Manalal cut the unwary Haralal down like scythes upon grain. Lyra shuddered and watched with dull eyes as people emerged from buildings for their breakfast preparations; they dropped their cooking pots in shock as arrows pounded into their chests. The cavalry trampled people down, and from where Lyra sat, the people on the ground looked like children. Those who dismounted took wood from the cookfires and tossed them onto the flammable thatch, and the nearest side of the town began to burn. Pillars of smoke appeared, making the scene hazier and hazier.

Cries of terror emanated from the town, followed by wailing and the bleating of panicking herdbeasts. Cattle and idraka burst from between buildings and scattered into the desert.

It was like a bad dream. This place was no war camp.

Some Haralali managed to arm themselves, shooting horses with bows and halting the cavalry charge with long spears, breaking the initial charge and forcing the first company of Manalal to the ground. Konan and Hafka swept a bloody path down one of the main roads together, fighting back-to-back. Shirkaa and Rahar fought together as well, pushing from house to house with thirsty blades. They spared no one. Thordrin galloped through the houses recklessly, sending arrows from ever-changing vantage points at the Haralali defenders. She saw him toss several burning pieces into new buildings with a gleeful whoop, then gallop down a street, killing three people with the sweep of his blade. The entire Manalal contingent, well over a thousand warriors strong, had entered the town now, and before the sun had risen, the place was ablaze. The streets wept with blood, and corpses were strewn everywhere.

The last vestiges of resistance were smoked out of their defenses, abandoning two of the towers in the center of the village as they burned, and most of them were cut down. Lyra watched a single group of idraka-mounted riders escape to the north, but the rest were destroyed.

Lyra's stomach clinched with nausea and pain.

This was not a war camp.

"Haralal are not ol'I'ya'hakkat, thral," said the Godspeaker gently. He had appeared suddenly, leaning on his staff, and Lyra realized the wagon train had caught up. Women were raising a medical tent as they spoke.

The horrors playing out were the result of her own helping hand, but the Godspeaker patted her hand with a reassuring smile. His squinting, violet gaze was cool as ephemeral spring blossoms.

"Haralal are gyr," he added, as if that comforted her at all.

Lyra didn't know the difference between the Manalal and these gyr, but she knew it had been wrong. She had imagined a war camp bristling with aggressive and wicked warriors who had Shirkaa's daughter bound in the center. After learning the latest reports of Shirkaa's scouts, her imagination had further darkened, and her wagon ride had been far from restful. Her dreams were flashes of Shirasa mixed with the terrible physical sensations of her own memory, torrents of biting midges crawling under her skin. She hadn't truly slept until she was with Konan.

From her vantage point, she had seen the surprise and fear as Haralali villagers fell under bow and blade. The Manalal had killed women and elderly too, not only the fighting men. The Haralal had been cut down as they prepared their morning meals, as their children played with their dolls and their livestock munched on fresh piles of grass.

And something else had seemed wrong. Most of the people had not put up much of a fight. The elderly swayed and swooned, and the women staggered to their knees like they were already dying. The men who fought on the Haralal side fought weakly and moved sluggishly, as if they were exhausted before the battle had even begun.

Lyra didn't understand any of it, but her conviction was that she had made a mistake helping Shirkaa. She felt like puking. Her gut cramped, and the nausea overflowed into her limbs and closed her lungs.

I wanted to do good with my magika.

The world pulsed in and out, and she battled the panic attack.

I wanted to do good.

Lyra tore her eyes from the scene and focused on helping the Godspeaker. They quickly began ministrations to man and mount as the injured arrived. She bent to her work sorting out salves and supplies, bringing items to the Godspeaker as he needed, and working her own green magika on the wounds presented to her.

This was more familiar, more comfortable, and she hid from her shame with great focus and industry for hours, barely noticing how morning had matured into day, and that the Manalal had erected a temporary camp all around her herbsman tent as the Haralali town burned to ashes and dust.

The medical tent was an open pavilion overflowing with injured men and horses. Most injuries were small enough: lacerations and dislocations. A simple poultice would serve to heal cuts without infection and fever, and dislocations were straightforward, although painful. Her wayfaring knowledge provided her ways to alleviate the pain, and her education with the Godspeaker expanded upon that foundation. However, some men were deeply wounded with arrows, spear tips, and swords; some had lost digits or even limbs. There was less Lyra could do for these men despite her medical repertoire. Blood could be slowed efficiently with earth and potherb, imbued with light magika and wrapped with cow's tongue, but a lost limb had to be cauterized with hot metal. Sometimes those men would fall asleep and never wake up.

Lyra had never seen death so close, and she kept thinking she saw their souls leave from the side of her vision. She always looked away, soldiering on, working side by side with the Godspeaker, continuously learning from him and teaching him as new subjects came in.

I can still do something good, she repeated to herself, trying not to drown in the death. Colors and smells kept assaulting her senses: flashes of lightning and a sulfur smell like the mines, waves of fresh growth combined with blood that must have come from the Haralali oasis.

She was midway through treating an idraka arrow wound when a pang seared across her body. She inhaled roughly, clutching her stomach, and there it was again. Clenching pain exuded from her abdomen in rays, and Lyra found herself kneeling on one knee next to a toppled bowl of medicine. The idraka brayed as she leaned against it, trying to stand. The cramping wouldn't leave; her pelvis ached, and her body radiated heat.

She felt a wet seeping under her skirt. The discomfort made its way down her leg and meandered to the sand.

With a shaky hand, Lyra lifted the edge of her crimson-and-yellow skirts, revealing a pool of blood. She screamed.

Everything bright faded and blurred. The desert became a white, distant vacuum, the sky a pale expanse. The tent evaporated, as did its tenants, and Lyra was alone again in an empty space. The space began filling with bright red, crimson like her skirts. She grasped wildly at her abdomen, trying to keep the mass inside as it shifted.

So much had already been lost to the sand and was percolating its way down to poison the wells of the desert. So much lost already. *So much lost*, her mind screamed. She didn't know if it was the shrill, angry voice or the frightened one; their words were intermingled in a shrieking wail.

She cried out again as a tangible shape passed from her body, as small as a cactus flower, and lay still between her legs.

Lyra trembled as she scooped it up. The thing fit in the palm of her hand. It had miniature digits and a smooth, rounded face. Incomprehensibly tiny ears and a shadow of eyes.

No.

A bright portal seared open in front of Lyra, revealing a figure silhouetted in light. A Gate? Sunshine brighter than that of the desert poured out, washing Lyra's face with warmth and a sense of life. She could smell the verdant fields, ripe pome fruits on the trees, and rich, musky earth. Bees hummed along their wavering paths, and birds sang a chorus of mismatched but beautiful songs to each other. The figure took measured steps through the Gate.

"Mam?" Lyra whimpered. "Mam."

Elaisa wore simple garments of fine cloth. She had no shoes, but her feet were clean. She knelt beside Lyra and gave her a proud, sad smile, brushing Lyra's hair behind her ear.

Her hands were ever so delicate as she took the baby from Lyra. It wriggled in her palm, dancing with all four tiny limbs. Lyra's mother's smile broadened, emphasizing the slight wrinkles around her eyes, and she cradled it against her breast and sang softly.

There was no blood.

Lyra reached out, seeking the minute life, and her heart swelled when she touched it. It was warm, soft. She thought she could feel its pulse.

And then it was gone.

Mam removed Lyra's hand from the baby and clasped it tightly against herself. Then, wordlessly, she turned and passed through the Gate with her precious cargo. When the Gate closed upon the otherworld, so green and rich, darkness crashed in from every direction, consuming Lyra where she sat.

63

Konan felt helpless.

He had arrived at the herbsman pavilion, although he didn't need much aid, having gained only a few cuts and bruises. Instead of receiving ministrations, he found Korahel fretting over Lyra's reposed figure. Her skirts were a ruin of blood, and she lay in a nonresponsive stupor. Her pinkish skin was pale as a dead woman, and he scanned her for injuries.

Korahel hissed at him when he realized the blood's origin and touched the hem of her skirt.

Thordrin appeared. "What in the lowest Gate . . ." he muttered. Then he glared at Konan and snapped, "Where the fuck did you leave her?"

Konan scowled, bristling with fury, but Shirkaa swept up to them and interrupted. He tapped his temple. "Your mage is physically well, my friends, but she is halfway to the sands inside. The Godspeaker does not know if her soul still lives."

He gestured at Lyra's ruined dress and bloodied hands.

"It was *not* iyasan anthe'brin."

He turned and left.

The two men stared at each other, and Thordrin glowered as he perceived the chieftain's meaning. His gaze traveled up and down Lyra's body just as Konan's had, and he leaned over her.

"Maunderer, come on, love . . ."

Lyra didn't move beyond the slightest fluttering of her eyelashes. She stared unfocused toward the canvas of the tent wall.

Without hesitation, Thordrin raised his hand and slapped her cheek.

Konan returned the blow so quickly that Thordrin staggered backward.

He rubbed his jaw with an irritated growl. "Damn it all to the nethers, you tongueless bastard," he began, advancing with a hand on his dagger hilt.

Lyra stirred, and both men stopped. Tears streamed down her cheeks, and her mouth hung open in shock.

Thordrin eased, then smirked at Konan. "See, she fucking needed it. She's awake."

"Don't ever lay your hands upon her—" Konan began.

"Go fuck yourself with those fingers," Thordrin said, walking away.

Konan seethed, but Lyra was weeping softly now, and he turned his attention to her instead.

Korahel shoved him aside, fretting over Lyra even more now that she was half-responsive. The handmaiden railed at Konan, forcing him back with the assistance of Mirra and several other women, and when the circle opened, the stained red and yellow silks had been removed. Lyra was covered by a fur, and the other women dispersed. Korahel remained, dabbing Lyra's hands with a fresh damp cloth. She wiped everything clean, even the sunstone-and-topaz handflowers, murmuring in Manalali the entire time.

The Godspeaker appeared and peered into Lyra's face while chanting in what sounded like Manalali and the Old Language. Konan didn't know if the old man was speaking to her or over her, but she didn't respond in any meaningful way. The Godspeaker made a blessing gesture, then turned to Konan and said something. It sounded encouraging, but his wizened face was tragic, and he waddled away to continue his ministrations of others.

Konan stumbled forward finally, and Korahel made room for him. He touched Lyra's pale, limp arm. She wasn't looking at him, but he signed anyway.

"The battle is over, Lyra. Shirasa is safe."

He thought he understood now. The ruined yellow silks of her skirts made his gut churn with the horror of it. Not water-sickness, not a slow recovery from her battering and bruises, not nerves. A seed of life, forced into her by the warden and now lost in yet another tragedy in Lyra's life.

He tipped her round chin toward himself, his callused fingers catching on the silk of her veil, and tried again.

"Shirasa is safe," he repeated. "You helped save her."

Damn it all, Lyra, overcome it, he wanted to shout.

She startled him when she sat up, nearly bumping foreheads. "We made a mistake, Konan," she breathed. "We hurt people . . . There was something wrong." She was wild-eyed, almost panicking. The air shivered, but Konan didn't understand what she was so anxious about. Did she even understand what had happened to her? She continued so softly he could hardly hear. "We hurt so many people."

Overcome this, Lyra, he prayed in entreaty. *It is the only way. Harden your heart.*

He stopped. Was that truly what he believed? Isellan had taught him to be strong, hard and unyielding as forged steel, and as cold with your enemies. It was the only way to survive.

But Lyra was nothing like that. She was gentlehearted, sweet, as soft on the inside as her skin was on the outside. By the Light, how he wanted to caress her smooth cheeks and take in the perfume on her neck. Her large, expressive eyes said so much more than his own, which were permanently locked in a taut squint on the left side. Hers were simultaneously sky and ice, the fragile light of the slow moon and the lucid depths of a glacial lake. Her tears flowed as easily for Shirasa and others as they did for herself. Her heart, a flickering gem, pattered tenuously, where his marched loudly in time.

And there was a different kind of strength in that, one with which he had previously been entirely unfamiliar.

Telling her to harden her heart was like covering a crystal with a veneer of filth and calling it protected.

She seemed nearly mad, her words still nonsensical, and she slumped back, repeating words to herself more and more quietly until she trailed off. The desert breeze stopped, and the putrid scent of blood and bodily fluids filled the medical pavilion.

Korahel murmured with dismay and gesticulated to Konan. Mirra likewise chattered and prodded him forward toward the bed.

He resisted, unsure whether he would hurt Lyra by moving her, but they shoved him onto the bedding. Korahel carefully lifted Lyra's limp body and nestled her head in Konan's lap, and Mirra adjusted the furs to ensure Lyra was covered. Both women spoke to him urgently, although they knew he couldn't understand.

Her cheek bore a red mark behind the gauzy yellow, and he removed the veil to look at it more closely. *Damn you, Thor,* he thought, feeling anger rise up again. He tamped it down and stroked the tender skin with a thumb. He trailed his fingers along her high, wide cheekbone and back to her ear, then tugged off her mage's circlet. Korahel took it without a word.

Konan leaned over Lyra, one hand slung protectively over her belly and one in her hair. The feeling of light and power he had sensed earlier was gone; she was a shell.

I feel nearly empty, she had said earlier. If she had known her own words were a premonition, would she have been more prepared for such loss?

He sat for a long while, unsure what to do beyond the minimal comfort of stroking her hair and sitting with her. He groaned in frustration at his inability to comfort her or change anything about their circumstances.

The sound seemed to awaken her from whatever stupefying thoughts overwhelmed her, and she blinked up at him.

"Where is Mam?" she asked, furrowing her brow. "Mam was here."

Konan sought the Godspeaker, but the old man was busy, and he didn't have a translator to help.

He signed in front of her dull eyes. "The battle is over, Lyra. You were hurt, but I'm here."

"She took it from me," Lyra continued. "She was here, and she took it from me. I saw the other side of the Gate—Litis maybe, or southeast Marlemet. I could smell the grass, and she touched me and took it." With a faint shudder, she began mumbling words so softly he couldn't hear them all. He caught "Mam" again, and "Elden" and "Gate." Instinctively, he pulled her up into his full embrace.

Korahel and Mirra scrambled to cover Lyra, but he didn't hear or understand them as they railed at his impropriety and roughness. He cradled her close, praying she would find comfort.

She flung her arms around him, weeping, and the salt of her tears mixed with the salt of his sweat as she buried her head into his neck. The blood still seeping through her wrappings dampened his leg and mixed with the blood of dead Haralal in which he was covered.

He didn't understand anything she was saying, but she didn't explain further. She shook and breathed more and more harshly, and the fetid, sickly air of the pavilion began to move again. She did seem almost mad in her anguish, and there was nothing he could do about it.

Eventually, she quieted, having said nothing more of her body's wracking pains or mental agony, and then she nuzzled deeper into his long hair. Slowly, she raised her face to him, her nose nearly touching his cheek. She looked frightened.

"There *was* something wrong, Konan." The tremulousness of her whisper seemed to shiver outward in rhythm with her words, shimmering through the air of the pavilion. "This wasn't a war camp. The Haralal weren't monsters. They were people, women and children and elderly."

Konan's heart, which had previously leapt to his throat, sank like a stone to his bowels.

She searched him. She had seen everything—seen him cutting everything in front of him down, wild with glory and bloodlust and rage. *But they took Shirasa,* he reasoned to himself. *It had to be done.*

As if she could read his mind, she blanched. "And when the honor guard returned with the girl, she was screaming. I heard it."

She leaned her forehead against his scarred cheek and cried.

He left the tent feeling ill at ease. Korahel and Mirra would care for Lyra, but he had to investigate her strange, confused ranting. Something troubled him too, something nebulous and unclear that rankled the edges of his mind.

As he absorbed the late afternoon sun on his wrecked face, Konan pondered the battle. Certainly, the fight had been easy, perhaps too easy. He had not met a single warrior who could match him that morning. He had been fighting since his earliest memories, true, but still . . .

He decided to reenter the Haralali town—not a war camp?—following a similar path as that morning. The main road was cobbled with large, flat sandstone pieces and edged with a variety of palms. The houses on either side were mud-brick, formerly roofed with thatch. Many had collapsed as the fire weakened their structural integrity, and others still smoldered. Still others had been sacked, emptied of belongings and people.

Desiccating bodies lay where they had fallen, their lips pulled back in permanent grimaces.

Konan tore his gaze from a smaller corpse; its face and outstretched hands blackened in the cookfire that burned in a side yard. To the other side, a lithe body lay face up next to a tumbled-over basket of grain, a red line sliced across the chest. Had he done that?

He whipped his gaze away from that scene. Surely he would not have done so, even in a blood-fueled rage. Would he?

Doubt filled him.

Punish them for what they've done.

Hafka had, as had the swarms of Manalal who followed behind in wave upon wave of foot soldiers. The cavalry had trampled everyone they encountered until they met a line of spears; it was easy to accomplish when the bodies being trampled were so small.

Konan shuddered. For all their bluster and posturing, the Manalal were as heathen as their victims. Whatever "gyr" meant, he was increasingly certain that he was with the monstrous ones, that he was one of them.

He passed three women with arrows jutting from their bodies. A wicker basket of shriveled fruit lay on the ground beside them, scattered into the bloody dust. He hadn't done that, but Thordrin might have. Several times, the Phantom had galloped by with a mad, bloodthirsty expression painting his face darker than any war colors. Each time, Konan watched him cut down more people, regardless of what they looked like. Half the fires seemed to be his handiwork.

He wandered toward the central towers, the three shrines of the Haralal. The red tower still blazed, and the heat of its flames had caused a weakness in the outer wall. A portion of its heights had collapsed, leaving a gash of an opening into the upper room where they'd found Shirasa.

She was screaming.

The well in the center tugged at him, and he felt his feet float toward its colorful painted stone wall. It was six times larger than the well of the Manalal's desert shrine, featuring six dipping buckets, an elaborate multipaneled cover, and a colorful awning providing shade over top.

He leaned over the low wall and peered into the well's depths. It was deep, yawning, and empty.

He shaded his eyes from the bright sun, praying his gut was wrong, but his certainty grew as they adjusted. The shadowy bottom was dry sand. Not mucky with low puddles, not damp. Completely parched, like the dusty ground near the mines.

His throat tightened. That strange thought that had nagged at him since their ride northward hit him in full force.

The Haralal had been without water. The numerous residents of the large town had likely tried to scavenge the last drops of life from the bottom of this well, but nothing remained to scavenge.

Konan examined the oasis with new insight.

He noted the shabby state of the central garden's shrubs, the slump in the leaves of the stout palms. The grass withered, and the earth underfoot was dusty dry. The flowers had dropped from the cacti and fluttered away to cover the corpses littering the streets.

Konan groaned and leaned against the well, then staggered to a knee.

Unease surged through him with each gasp. The battle had begun long before they left the Manalali village.

At Shirkaa's disingenuous request, they—he—had called the Water from the empty (not empty) lands to the north and west. He had reached out, clutched at the distant sensation of thirst-quenching goodness and dragged it to the shrine of the Desert Mother. He had clawed at it until it was fully in his grasp, then pulled it in its entirety.

Shirkaa had known what he asked. Jikaa had known. Konan and Lyra simply hadn't realized the truth.

Barna'halais.

The honorific tasted bitter on his scarred tongue. What life had really been given, when other life was sacrificed in its place?

Konan took one more long look down the empty well, and the scars on his eyebrow and cheek ticced uncontrollably. He clenched his jaw, then turned away.

64

THE HARALALI TOWN'S SMOKE wafted upward, black with the miasma of dead men and women, thatch and hide, and a thousand flammable household items. The Manalal settled their new camp around the medical pavilion, allowing their injured warriors to convalesce with their families nearby. As long as the prevailing wind held, it was far enough from the town to avoid the stench.

They moved Lyra to a private tent once again, but this time, they couldn't keep Konan away. Despite Korahel and Mirra's constant fretting, paired with frequent visits from the Godspeaker, Lyra lingered most of the time in a depressed daze. Unlike her worst days in the mines, no winds shook the Manalali camp or screamed erratically by the entrance. She was utterly still, a barely breathing corpse. A shell of a woman.

It worried Konan more than violent outbursts, but he understood at least some of her distress. His own guilt gnawed at him, compounded further by his refusal to tell her the truth.

Barna'halais. The Godspeaker's wriggling, ecstatic dance taunted him.

Telling her would only serve to place another weight upon her shoulders, while failing to lessen the weight upon his. Telling her would be for himself and for himself alone. He clenched his fists and lay back against the base of her raised bed.

As far as he knew, she slept as she had done for several days.

Konan crept out to find Thordrin.

Lord Shirkaa approached them later that afternoon, his arms held wide and welcoming and his smile broad. "The Haralal are defeated, my friends, and my daughter, my precious desert flower, is safe," he stated. He paused significantly. "Your services are acknowledged, and the trade is done. You may pass through my lands freely." He pounded his fist upon his chest and took his leave, sauntering off to his newly erected set of tents.

Thordrin's mouth dropped open and turned a genuinely stunned look upon Konan. "That ungrateful goatfuck."

"A faithless man," signed Konan in agreement.

"We served our purpose, and now he's done with us." Thordrin huffed his disbelief. "I swore a death oath on the last man who did that to me. Worse than a Kritali trader . . ." He trailed off in a string of increasingly violent insults.

Konan hadn't been able to tell him about the well either, not without telling Lyra, but the Phantom was perceptive. He had suggested several times that Shirkaa wasn't trustworthy, and that the honor guard had treated him differently since their victory. Konan could only nod in agreement.

They had routed the Haralal, and Konan knew now that both he and Thordrin had played a significant role in the massacre based on their share of the spoils.

Jikaa and Rahar had allocated to them a total of four horses, two idraka cows, and six sheep, which Thordrin immediately traded for clothing and weapons. They gained two tents, numerous hides and leather, colored textiles and rugs, skeins and baskets, jewelry of carved bone and rock, rough-spun linens and clothing, some finer clothing and shoes, handflowers and circlets, fringes of beads and coins, stone tools for cooking and sewing, cookpots and serving bowls . . . all the miscellany of a people now dead, which seemed so mundane in ordinary circumstances.

But Konan saw them as treasures. He had lacked for so long things as simple as shoes and blankets. Gorgeously colored thread for embellishment, not seams. Paring knives meant for cooking, not killing. Leather for pretty corsets for Lyra, not waterskeins.

He and Thordrin chose new weapons from an array of long and short knives, swords both curved and straight, and bows with wooden-shafted arrows and black malagate tips. At Jikaa's behest, they took everything they wanted, garnering choice immediately after the honor guard.

"Let's not tell Lyr about the armor." Thordrin chuckled somewhat weakly as they picked through a pile that had been stripped from the dead.

Konan tried to choose items for Lyra too, but he had no idea what would fit her. Then they went to the horses, where again the Manalal gave them first choice.

Thordrin chose a sleek, massive creature, radiant in coat and vicious. It snapped at him as he exerted control. "By the nethers, I'm going to break this beauty," he murmured with admiration.

He helped Konan choose the rest. For Konan, an older gelding with less bite but certain experience in battle. He was a mediocre rider at best right now, and he didn't need a horse vying for dominance. He had somewhat hoped he might keep his mare, but Hafka had made it clear she belonged to the Manalal as breeding stock.

For Lyra, they chose a younger but steady Haralali mare, and as the fourth, a young Haralali stallion: beautiful, trainable, but also worth coin if they needed it. This colt would have a rider with experience, their largest gift of war: a Haralali woman.

After the battle, the surviving women and children of the Haralal had been collected and sifted through. Some of the elderly and young were slaughtered and others allowed to leave, but the able were kept as chattel. Each of them received a wicked snake brand on their wrist. Wrists inflamed with the recent, untreated wound, they stood in a line for inspection.

Rahar stalked down the line first, pulling some of the women out and spinning them about, then shoving them back in line. He took a middle-aged woman and two younger boys who looked alike. Hafka took three pretty women, as did Dashann. Jikaa, having noticed a little girl who cried when the boys were taken away, took her along with two middle-aged women. As he guided them toward his tent, he told Konan and Thordrin to each take a slave.

Konan balked at the choice, leaving Thordrin to select a lovely young woman with dark, tear-filled eyes and copper skin. She trembled when they collected her but followed dutifully to their tent, where she remained, sullen and afraid, until she realized neither of them would use her.

Thordrin's handmaiden spoke kindly to her, and Konan realized she shared the same snake brand on her wrist. Confused but less frightened than before, the new slave quietly prepared their baths and meals, and eventually touched Thordrin's arm to get his attention. She placed her hand on her breast.

"Mikaa," she murmured in introduction.

Thordrin nodded his understanding and replied, patting his own chest. "Thordrin."

"Tho'jinn," Mikaa repeated quietly. "Mikaa, Tho'jinn." She patted his chest, and he caught her hand and winked at her. Then she looked at Konan.

"That's Konan."

"Datch Ko'ninn," she repeated.

Konan shook his head.

"Just Konan," said Thordrin with a chuckle.

"Ko'ninn. Tho'jinn, Ko'ninn." She bowed slightly and returned to her work repairing their torn clothes from battle. She happened to be working on his crimson cloak, and she held it up. "Thral?"

He nodded.

"I hope she's like the other," said Thordrin, licking his lips. "She's the only one we're allowed to take with us." He gave her a winning smile, suave as ever.

Over the next two days, Mikaa revealed a surprising resourcefulness. In the disarray of Haralali goods packed into the men's tent, somehow women's clothing appropriate to her stature had appeared, tucked discreetly into baskets. The collection grew substantially after she observed Konan staying in Lyra's tent so much of the time, and Konan noted the clothing was fitted to Lyra's shape and status. Silks and gauzy layers and veils were wrapped around bejeweled handflowers and ornamental circlets and hairpins. Undergarments, breast bindings, and women's wrappings appeared, carefully organized and folded in specific piles.

He berated himself. He had procured light armor for her, a variety of high-quality slim blades in various sizes, ankle and thigh straps, forearm bracers, even a bodice with sheath pockets for small knives, but he hadn't thought of all the things Mikaa did.

Mikaa had not yet met Lyra, but that night, they would all wisely depart together. Shirkaa had ignored them recently, and Jikaa implied that they should take advantage of their freedom.

Thordrin called the girls into their tent and instructed them to pack. A stilted exchange of Manalali and Haralali followed amongst Mirra, Mikaa, Korahel, and Thordrin's handmaiden, which they all seemed to understand. They sized up the pile of goods and the livestock outside, then began rearranging items into baskets and sacks.

Satisfied, Thordrin stood. "Come on, brother. Let's get rations for the road."

They gathered a collection of dried fruits and grains, salted dry meat, and a dense, seedy bread, as well as full skeins of water. The old mothers were reticent to give them too many, but Konan was less concerned given his newly discovered ability. They should be in far less danger traveling at a horse's pace at night, fully supplied and properly clothed.

Jikaa told them that the landscape changed to the east within several days' ride, shifting from loose-packed sand to cactus-covered pavement and tufts of grasses, and later on to a rocky, crack-filled land. Some ravines had streams in them, surrounded by yellow grass and even trees, and the uplands had fruit-laden cactus as well. The Manalal would typically travel to that side of their territory soon, once their most severely wounded warriors could be moved.

As the sun sank down, Thordrin saddled and arranged his own horse, forcing it into compliance with an iron will. Konan watched and then did the same to his horse and Lyra's.

They were more accommodating than Thordrin's stallion, but they still seemed dubious of him. It would require the building of trust and respect, Konan recalled from his childhood lessons. Mikaa prepared her own horse, again revealing her aptitude.

"Useful," said Thordrin approvingly. "Good prize, whether she fucks or not."

Konan ignored his rude comment. More important than what lay between her legs was her mind. She knew the desert, and her company would be more than welcome as they traversed Tahayi one last time, headed eastward to the Mana Loi coast.

"She can't understand me, Noble-Heart." Thordrin rolled his eyes.

Near ready, they entered Lyra's tent and found her much as she had been, reposed on her cushioned bed and staring vacantly at the ceiling. The Godspeaker finished a blessing before giving them a disapproving grandfatherly look.

Korahel pulled Jikaa in and glared at Thordrin, then proceeded with packing items from Lyra's pile.

"When can she be moved?" Thordrin asked.

The Godspeaker shook his head sadly, and Jikaa answered, "According to Desert Mother's will."

Thordrin snorted. "I'm afraid we can't wait for the Mother's will, old man."

"She is broken here." The Godspeaker tapped his own chest. "Mother has lost children too. Mother will guide her."

Jikaa translated, then grimaced. "You're leaving now?"

"At your father's request," spat Thordrin.

Jikaa nodded slowly, looking ashamed. "I'm sorry for all of it, my friends. I wish you understood," he beseeched Konan, who scowled back at him.

"Dashann has his betrothed. Shirkaa has his daughter. You have your sister." Thordrin was snarling. "And she has *you.*"

Jikaa's throat bobbed up and down. He backed out of the tent with arms wide and waist bent in a bow. "May rains fall upon your lips, Warrior Thordrin, Barna'halais."

The Godspeaker followed, but he turned to give Lyra one long last look and stamp his staff.

"Yeah, go with the Light." Thordrin waved a dismissive hand with blatant disgust, then glared at Konan. "Wake her the fuck up, or I will. We're done with this place."

Konan grabbed his arm. Thordrin's look was acidic, and Konan released him immediately. The man stalked out, and Korahel hissed something in Manalali at his back.

Konan tried to gather Lyra up, but she slumped against him like a dead body. Frustrated, he shook her by the shoulders, hoping he could somehow force her to respond, but to no avail. That wasn't the way, not for her, and it never would be.

He recalled something else about diamonds. They *didn't* break, until they did—until they shattered under intense pressure.

Shaking her was as ineffective as telling her to ignore her pain and soldier on, and it might even worsen her state. With a deep breath, he pulled her gently into his arms and held her closer than ever before. She was so slight compared to him, so delicate, as light as the air she manipulated. She sagged into him, and the intoxicating floral oils of her hair flooded his nose. Konan gripped at her slipping hips and adjusted his position on the bed until she was stable. *Wake up, Lyra,* he wanted to whisper. Instead, a soft groan came out.

Her pain was such a salient reminder of his own, pain that he had pushed down as deep as he could and ignored for years. She didn't do that. She was vulnerable and open, and she had endured things he couldn't imagine. He leaned his forehead against hers and stroked her curls back. His fingertips brushed her supple cheek in the process, and she shuddered. "Wake up, Lyra," he signed in front of her eyes. "I'm with you."

"Why?" she whispered. "All of it. Why? I was right, wasn't I?"

Her soft sobs filled the room.

With an effort, he relinquished his hold to help her stand, and they departed the nearly empty tent with an awkward, shuffling step. Korahel followed them to the door and tugged Konan's sleeve.

She curtsied deeply to each of them. Her tragic expression echoed that of the Godspeaker. "Is good magika, Barna'halais. Thral, good magika."

TAIUKI AND TAN DEVISED a new plan: five days of intense training followed by a two-day joint hunt focused entirely on riding, tracking, and mounted fighting, followed by a rest day. At least, that was the story.

If Master Sashiro could accept Taiuki as Tan's overseer during the hunts, they could go to the island weekly without interference or questioning. On regular days, Taiuki attended morning sessions with either Hannaka—oftentimes practicing the various arts she would be expected to excel in—or with Wehan, completing the duties of a high steward. She no longer had to lie about when her various courtly lessons were occurring, but she also couldn't train Tan and the rest of the garrison in the mornings. They didn't have time for short afternoon rides anymore, but that could be exchanged for the longer hunt, which was better practice in any case. She was still obligated to attend to cultural lessons from Wehan after supper, but he seemed satisfied if she kept up with his uninspired reading assignments. Tan, in turn, would continue spending his mornings at the training hall, apprenticing with Sashiro or Reihotto, depending on who was around.

When they brought their proposal to Arch Commodore Sashiro, his gray eyebrows arched quizzically, and he gave them both a dubious look as if he knew they were up to something. Taiuki and Tan stood side by side, both wearing masks of innocence. Sashiro frowned at one, then the other, then relented somewhat.

"I don't see why not, although your schedules are highly irregular," he said. He tapped his index finger on the table at which he sat, then added, "I am concerned, however, about an extended hunt without a chaperone. I realize you, Taiuki, have extensive riding experience, but your new mount is young and unbroken. And you, Tan, with Nimoka, you've only been riding two years." He darkened.

"But sir, we'll bring Kenji's mother and sister along, so we'll be part of a pod," Taiuki said.

Sashiro's frown deepened at Taiuki's impropriety, and she examined her feet in shame. Speaking back to him was never acceptable—it hadn't been even when she was Second.

She prayed he would give in. A sawtoothed whale pod would easily protect them, instinctively maintaining their family group with coordinated attacks and razor teeth. And with adequate oversight, they would allow Nimoka to re-main nearby, although they wouldn't embrace her as their own.

She and Tan would be safer than she had been these last weeks, sneaking off alone like she did.

In her peripheral vision, she saw Sashiro ease and return to tugging at his beard. "I should assign Marshal Kinota to hunt with you, but she is needed here to train the other troops. Perhaps when Vice Commodore Reihotto returns from the front . . ." He sighed. "We are all stretched thin. She needs to be here as much as you do." He gave Taiuki a stern look.

"Pardon me, sir?" Tan interjected politely. "If Reihot-to—sorry, Vice Commodore Reihotto—attends us the first time and feels comfortable with our skill level, perhaps we can proceed together, just the two of us? That way, she is not removed from her duties training the troops."

"Two is hardly a school," murmured Sashiro. His voice was full of worry. "Highly irregular . . . but you two are a powerful pair." He straightened and cleared his throat, realizing he was oversharing his thoughts. "I know you are both capable, but you also have so much to learn. I must insist the vice commodore accompany you, at least this time, and provide a report of your hunt before a further decision is made. What is your quarry?"

"Diving birds, sir," said Taiuki. Again, she was prepared for his question. With enough detail, he would be assured of her planning, another safety measure.

"Ah, yes, the young redfish are moving this time of summer, aren't they?" Sashiro stopped rubbing his chin and nodded. "Very well. Tan, learn well from your sister in this. I can only justify her involvement if her tutelage clearly benefits you. Do you understand?"

Tan saluted formally, although he couldn't control the enthusiasm in his face.

Taiuki saluted as well, but with a different expression. She knew Master Sashiro was sincere. The extended hunts had to contribute to Tan's training, as did all of Taiuki's time spent with him, or she would be ushered to the castle for redirection. Sashiro didn't seem to want that any more than she did, but he would fulfill his duty to the arch-commodore-in-training with impartiality. She thanked him, and they headed to their afternoon training session, both with unspoken enthusiasm.

Sparring one-on-one, both underwater and in air, Taiuki and Tan battled. Taiuki was faster and better, but Tan was learning so quickly. His slim practice blade swept through the water like hers, fluid and without resistance, as if the water parted before him. Their jianswords clashed violently, and their staffs resounded together with a rapid clatter that echoed in the training hall. Their styles were so similar, they could often match each other for an extended fight, with neither gaining substantial points over the other. Eventually, Taiuki would win, but she was impressed by Tan's fervor and rapid advancement.

Sashiro left for the front shortly after, taking two more platoons with him.

"When Vice Commodore Reihotto returns with the injured, she will continue to utilize you in training, and she will oversee your first hunt," he said in departure. He saluted Tan with both hands, then Taiuki with only one.

"We shall conform, sir," Tan replied.

"Go with the current, Arch Commodore." Taiuki covered her face and bowed, unable to bring herself to lie to a man she respected as much as Sashiro. She would not conform, but she would do everything in her power to keep Tan safe.

By the end of the week, they were both exhausted.

Although he didn't need to, Tan awoke when she did to help with Kenji's morning routine scratches and feed, seeing her off regretfully when she was expected by Hannaka or Wehan. They spoiled their mounts before supper with feed and salve rubs, and then he stayed with her in the evenings, following her perfect motions through each precise drill and sparring lightly with Anella. Sometimes it was so late, it seemed the entire castle had gone to bed.

Taiuki missed It'tholl, and she was wrenched between impotent fury at Sashiro for assigning a chaperone to them and frustration at Tan for suggesting it, exasperated by angst that she wouldn't be able to visit It'tholl under Reihotto's watchful eye. This hunt would have to be legitimate to defray suspicion, but Uth'hal and It'ma were expecting her back at the island. All she could do was rest until morning, and pray they didn't worry so much that they sought her out.

The hunting party left early the next morning. Tan rode Nimoka, while Taiuki led Kenji by a long rein. Kenji's mother accompanied them with glee, swimming in circles around her mate, Reihotto's mount Tsuya. Kenji's sister, who was a few years older, joined them without hesitation, but adhered to her mother. She was saddle-broken as well, making their trip preparations easy. They packed saddle bags with overnight supplies on each whale, allowing Nimoka and Tsuya to carry only their riders with light armor and weaponry.

They headed eastward to the open plain between Shiggo and the Mountains of Mourning. The redfish were schooling, and they successfully routed not only a number of redfish, but also three massive migratory birds with elongated wings and long, sharply curved bills. They fed most of the redfish to the whale pod but dressed the remainder and sealed it in a packbag. They camped that evening on the edge of the kelp forest, eating some of the redfish raw with tanko fruits and savenberries. The summer had grown late, and the ocean bore more and more rich fruits with salty sweetness.

Taiuki barely slept, yearning for It'tholl. She felt like her mind was wailing, calling into the night. They were so close to the island where her heart was held, but she couldn't even look that direction for fear Reihotto would notice.

The vice commodore had already commented several times on the strangeness of their new training schedule, but she also seemed to like the idea of intense hunting.

"I suspect the arch commodore will reassign you both to the front soon," she mused, "so you can hunt the Jijiton-jin instead of wild animals."

They hunted more the next day, riding through the wide plain for hours in pursuit of the high-flying predacious birds that occasionally lanced their way into the ocean like a bolt from a speargun. Between opportunities, Tan perfected his riding stance, and Taiuki worked on harness guidance with Kenji. Reihotto reminded Taiuki of some of the early training conventions, pointing out certain behavioral differences between sawtooths and blackheads. Despite herself, Taiuki had to admit Reihotto's presence was helpful.

As the day closed, they headed west to Shiggo City. When they got close, Taiuki suggested that she wanted to go for one more short jaunt with Kenji. They had already reached the farmland edge, so Reihotto saluted them both and went on her way with Tsuya and their harvest satchels.

"Well done, Second, my princess," she said as she left. "I shall report to Sashiro, but I expect he will favor independent hunts and assign me to the garrison."

Tan and Taiuki watched her disappear in the distance. She looked back once, a furtive, hurried glance, and Taiuki wondered if she was suspicious.

Then Tan looked at her. "Liar." His face was full of mischief.

"I *have* to go back, Tan-sho. They were expecting me yesterday. It'tholl is probably frantic." Taiuki began pulling Kenji eastward, followed by his mother and sister.

"I'm coming, right?" Tan turned Nimoka as well, but Taiuki held her hand up.

"I'm afraid they're watching us too closely right now. Can you do this for me this time? Stay, and pretend you've been with me during rest day."

Tan's face fell.

"Please, Tan."

"I will." Her brother slumped his shoulders with disappointment as he turned Nimoka back toward Shiggo City. He swam low to her back, his head dipped a bit lower than was proper.

Taiuki watched him until he was a distant mote passing among the fields.

I could have returned him promptly before morning. Uth'hal's voice was deep and brimming with a dry humor.

Taiuki spun. By the current, they were here?

It'tholl is being restrained by her mother, Uth'hal replied. *They are at the cove, waiting for us. Will the meat creatures follow?* His silhouette appeared in the distance and grew. How in the netherworld had he gotten this close to Shiggo without them noticing?

Kenji's mother peeled out a warning and moved between Uth'hal and her babies. Taiuki called her to task, grabbing her rein along with Kenji's. The mother whale was well-trained but seemed furious at the instruction. She hovered back and forth, drawing a line across which she would not allow Uth'hal to pass. The dragon paused his advance, aware of the whale's anger.

Can you leave them? Uth'hal asked.

"No, the young one is in training as my new mount," Taiuki replied. "He needs to get acclimated to you."

And the others?

"They will attend him for a few more weeks at least; they are a family unit, and he is a babe yet."

Very well. Uth'hal's disdain for the whales was obvious. He turned east and led the way at a quick pace, one Taiuki would have preferred for all the former months but could not risk swimming alone. Following far behind Uth'hal's dark mass, Taiuki tugged a reluctant Kenji and matron along, tailed by a nervously twitching sibling. The creatures would have to learn to coexist, just as they did with the blues.

Finally, she was going to It'tholl. She was going home.

Back in Shiggo City again, Taiuki watched Godrig's fleet loose their lines from the quay with a pleased smirk. She stared unblinking at the tall figure on the raised deck, who glared back at her while proffering a stiff, unfriendly wave. Finally, one less stressor haunting her in Shiggo City, one less set of eyes tracking her every move.

Godrig had insisted Anella stay at the castle, where it was "safer." In fact, he had insisted on all of them staying, rather than riding with his party to the city docks, and Taiuki had staunchly refused.

"What kind of hosts would we be if we didn't provide you a sendoff?" she had said in a voice sugared as sweetkelp. It sounded like Kei. In truth, she wanted the pleasure and assurance of seeing him disappear over the horizon.

Godrig had glowered at her. Maybe he wasn't as foolish as she had thought, because he seemed to note the caustic sweetness in her tone. "This disease emerges in the thin blood of the lower dregs, exactly the sort who live near the docks. I may not have found disease here yet, Princess, but I'm sure it will be here soon. You have to be careful." He had attempted to touch her arm like someone familiar, someone with whom she would share her life, and she had expended a great deal of energy to not lashing out.

"I am careful, Prince, and I can defend myself," she had flashed back, fuming at his presumption to tell her how to behave in her own city. Breaking his arm would have brought her a great deal of pleasure. "My kingdom is clean. The myr are clean. This disease does not exist for Shiggon-jin. You have wasted enough time here."

Godrig had snorted rudely, then insisted she have a guard of at least six men attend her, if she was going to be so foolish as to leave the castle.

And that was why she was here, sitting proudly on her landwalker mount with her back arched and her head high, without accompaniment. Her myr clothing, split high at the legs to allow both riding and shifting, revealed her bare legs above the knees. Her hair was done up with a distinctively myr style, traditional and elegant and draping with pearls, topped with a royal crown. Her fitted shirt of soft, stretched leather, dyed in a myriad of colors, covered her upper body respectably, as was proper, and was topped by a light, gauzy shawl. Her decorative breechbelt bore the royal emblem as well as an elaborate edging sparkling with gemstones. Her high status and feminine stature were both unmistakable, even without a busty figure like Kei had. Her feet were bare in the modified stirrups, and her copper-skinned calves were all taut muscle.

Remember me like this, Godrig, she thought as she raised a single arm in an informal wave. *I am not yours to command or own, and I never will be.*

The distant figure dropped his arm and stomped out of sight.

Taiuki allowed her sweet, prim smile to twist with mischief. She turned her horse from the edge of the docks, nearly swinging into a bulky mariner who stood within arm's length. His face was gruff and hairy, his shoulders broad. Even on her sleek horse, Taiuki felt his daunting presence.

Is he sick? The thought flashed through her mind, and for the briefest of moments she worried that she might have too carelessly dismissed the danger of a virulent disease. If it was all over Krita, how could it not be here? But Shiggon-jin were myrpeople, she reasoned, bred superior, with powerful blood from the purest form of nature.

The mariner hefted a box net to the side and bowed quickly. He touched his palm to his forehead in apology. "Beg pardon, Highness," he said sincerely. Then he moved around the stack of nets and continued working.

The vibrant sounds of the wharf returned to her ears: wood creaking, ropes stretching, banners flapping, wake splashing. All was well in Shiggo. She breathed a sigh of relief, mixed with a weak, self-deprecating chuckle. Surely, they were safe from the madness here. Flicking the reins, Taiuki trotted through the city streets toward the castle. Mariners, dock workers, scampering children, all made way for her with deferential salutes and bowed heads. They knew she was Taiuki, thirdborn of the royal family, former arch-commodore-in-training and dangerous in her own right.

Beyond that, she had the distinct feeling that something about her made them timid and overly apologetic as they shifted their eyes from their tasks to the ground. She didn't know what it was, but she could feel it. Before her betrothal to Prince Godrig, she had always assumed it was simply recognition of her high status as Second, but now Tan was Second. Now with her bonding to It'tholl, she suspected her deviation from normalcy was even more exaggerated, but could people see that? She wasn't Second, and she didn't identify as a dragonkeeper.

She was . . . nothing. Myr didn't alter the birth order; such practices were the landwalker way. In any case, such deference as she saw in the splayed fingers of the saluting masses was not due to a woman being bartered to Krita like chattel.

A horsed rider blocked her way, jolting her out of her scattered thoughts. A familiar roguish grin met her.

"You followed me?" she asked, irked at the thought that Godrig may have perceived Tan as a guardian for her.

Tan shook his head at her unspoken concern. "No one saw me. I know you wanted to bid farewell to your Kritali prince on your own." He smiled even wider at her discomfiture. "You two need your alone time, right?" He chortled, finding his own joke far more hilarious than she did.

With a grimace, Taiuki commanded her horse around him in the busy street. He turned and followed, pulling up next to her so they could ride side by side.

"Now that Godrig's gone, we can go?" he asked eagerly.

"It is almost time for a hunt," she said with as much dignity as she could muster.

Tan laughed.

66

THE PAIR TROTTED BACK to the castle together, handing their landwalker mounts to the stablekeepers, then rushed down to their beloved Nimoka and Kenji. Both whales were prepared for a long excursion, strapped appropriately with travel bags and weapons. Taiuki was cautiously grateful for their recent pattern.

After only a few weeks, Vice Commodore Reihotto had verified their allowance to hunt without oversight, as long as they maintained the five-member pod at a minimum. Thus, Taiuki and Tan were able to openly supply themselves and depart the stables, waving as they passed the barracks and training yard, and head east without question. The speed at which they arrived at the island was a reprieve for Taiuki after months of traveling by fin, eloping from Shiggo City in the early hours and moving slowly to avoid predators or attention.

They arrived at the island by early afternoon with appetites churning in their bellies.

It'tholl keened at them from the beach, an eerie sound that echoed strangely through the water. Nonetheless, the dragling resisted bailing into the sea to tackle her bonded mate. Taiuki and Tan settled the riding whales with Hachi, who was tethered in what had become known as the Pasture, a large area with kelp copses and sporadic coral formations where Hachi knew he was safe. Like the other whales, he was still dubious of the nearby dragons, recognizing a predator when he saw one, but both sawtoothed and blackheaded mounts were also intelligent enough to understand that the dragons had not attacked them yet. It was no different than having the blues swimming the edge of the city, in sight of the stables.

Uth'hal had grumbled a disdainful laugh when Taiuki asked for verification that they would not bother Hachi in his convalescence.

We will not eat the food, Uth'hal had promised. *He is half-rotten with bad meat.*

Hachi's tail had indeed become a flapping fleshrot, hanging limp and discolored by patchy lesions. Taiuki knew she would have to remove it, but she lacked the confidence to do so. She stroked Hachi's jaw, and he nuzzled into her with a low, moaning cry. He was in pain. Taiuki hugged his giant face to hers and apologized to him for his misery. It would hurt less if she cut off the infection, but he might easily bleed out.

"He doesn't look too good," Tan clicked, inspecting the broken tail with a glum expression. "What do we do?"

Taiuki shook her head. "I'm no herbsman, Tan-sho. I don't know what to do."

"I wish we could bring help," Tan clicked quietly, then flushed at her sharp look. "It's just . . . he needs medicine we don't have."

"Sashiro told me to put him down," Taiuki replied, her clicks sharp and concussive in the water. "He should be with the current, had I conformed."

Taiuki leaves Hachi-not-food, called It'tholl. *It'tholl waits!*

Tan chirped a nervous laugh, cutting the tension. "She won't hold back forever, sis. I think she's about to break."

Taiuki resisted rolling her eyes. The dragling was dramatic sometimes, although she herself understood the desire completely. The desire to be with It'tholl, to touch that sleek, scaled body, fix her hurts and itches with oil and good scratches, to gaze into the eyes and soul of that wonderful creature who understood her and loved her—nothing matched the experience.

Somewhat reluctantly, she patted Hachi's muzzle once more and told him to rest.

Brother and sister emerged from the Pasture and onto the beach, both shifting smoothly and enjoying the squelch of sand between their toes as they walked together.

It'tholl scampered down the beach and pranced in ungainly circles around them. She was getting too large to safely tackle Taiuki on land. Already, her front shoulder was nearly as high as Taiuki's head. She trilled a happy croon out loud while repeating *Taiuki Taiuki Taiuki* in a childish singsong.

Also, It'tholl itches, she added between refrains.

"Of course you do, beloved," laughed Taiuki, letting her rancor for Hachi's state fade in the presence of her bonded dragling. She quickened her step to the makeshift tarps of fish oil. Her early attempt at a solution to It'tholl's rapid growth had worked well, yielding large amounts of rich, slick oil for treating the dragling's tender skin. Tan had helped her strengthen and enlarge the contraption, stabilizing the large tarp holding a heavy load of decaying fish which dripped down into their collection bowl, a broad redking shell. The oil was wonderful directly applied, but they also rendered it into a concentrated salve whenever they had time.

"We should make some more today," said Tan, thinking along the same lines. He leaned against a driftwood log and stared out at the water, then added, "or maybe tomorrow." Uth'hal snoozed in the breakwater, and Tan looked like he wanted to do the same.

"Bright day, It'ma," Taiuki called to the matron dragon, who lay on a high vantage point at the top of the cliff.

I'ya's blessings, children, It'ma replied, stretching her sinuous neck out to bob a greeting. *We are pleased to see you. We have news to share with you both.*

Tan perked up from his sedate position on the beach, and Taiuki exuded her curiosity openly to It'ma. She had slowly been learning to withhold or share her thoughts and feelings intentionally, as the dragons did.

The order al'Laiakala has a new first and second elder, It'ma announced. *Ind'arra is now first, and her mate Kar'nak is now second.*

Taiuki could read no emotion from It'ma's voice, so she was unsure whether the dragon was displeased with loss of her status. She had not worked out how the dragons governed themselves either, but they rarely seemed to conflict with each other. "I didn't realize the Order rotated its leadership," she said carefully, again allowing her curiosity to project.

Uth'hal chuckled dryly, a mental laugh coinciding with a low rumble in his throat, then opened his glossy eye to peek at them from his comfortable lounge. He *had* been listening, thought Taiuki.

The first and second elders earn their right to lead the Order, he said matter-of-factly, then rolled over to sun his other side.

It'ma leapt from the cliff and landed on the beach with her hindlegs, shaking the ground slightly. *Come, children of I'ya, and I will show you why.* She walked on all fours, using her wing pinions as forelegs, and worked her way inland on one of the enlarged paths the dragons had developed with their frequent passage. Even so, she moved quickly, her massive strides easily outpacing the myr.

Taiuki looked at Tan with an eyebrow raised, and he shrugged back. They waited for It'ma's long, sweeping tail fin to pass by, then followed.

It'tholl danced around them, humming a song to herself, before exclaiming, *Forest sees!* She scampered into the brush. Birds twittered at her as they flitted out of her path.

"What does that mean?" asked Tan as the dragling disappeared.

The trees around them stifled their conversation with a strange closeness, and they only heard the scuffle of their own footsteps and the thud and scrape of It'ma as she moved up the path.

"I'm not certain," said Taiuki. "She's said that before. When I ask, she explains that 'forest sees' means that 'the forest sees.'" She flashed a helpless smile at Tan. "Sometimes she's so literal."

Tan grinned. "It does feel like something is watching us. I've always thought so when I come here. No wonder people think it's haunted."

"All the more reason I chose it for our home," said Taiuki. "No one comes near here."

"Kei read me a story once," her brother went on, "about this island."

Taiuki smiled pensively. Kei used to read her stories too, but that seemed like a very distant memory, one so nebulous and gray she wasn't sure if it was real.

"Kei said it was haunted by the spirits of broken-hearted women, who came here to kill themselves."

A light breeze whispered through the forest suddenly, almost like a gasp of indignation.

Despite the summer heat, Taiuki's skin shivered into gooseflesh. She peered into the trees, then noticed that Tan had done the same. His hand was on his belt knife, as was hers on her own.

They both broke into strained chuckles, but neither of them took their hands off their hilts.

"Haunted, you say?" she said.

Tan shrugged. "I can't imagine what could break your heart badly enough to want to die," he said.

Taiuki choked, suddenly sober. "I can."

Tan looked at her, then nodded and bit his lip. His mirth was gone too. "In any case," he said, trying to recover, "Kei said the island was guarded by forest gods, so the troubled spirits of the dead could rest."

"As long as people believe that, we'll be safe here," said Taiuki. "I'll tout the existence of any god . . ."

I'ya cries out for you, child, said It'ma from ahead. The sinuous dragon had led them out of the forest, where the path disappeared, up the mountain to a rockier area at the base of the volcanic peaks. Steam exuded from fissures in the ground, and the area was hot and muggy.

Ind'arra lay curled around an object near the fissures. Her gleaming scales shone an unusually irradiant turquoise. Kar'nak lay a distance away, enjoying the sunshine that gleamed on the rocky opening; he trumpeted a greeting.

Blessings, hamanool, he said.

"Good day, Kar'nak, Ind'arra," said Taiuki with a bow and a formal salute. "Congratulations on becoming the head elders of the Order."

Thank you, Ind'arra replied, *but we suspect you do not know the reason why.* Her voice held neither scorn nor humor, only a straightforward factuality.

Taiuki admitted Ind'arra's correct assumption with an embarrassed nod.

The dragon lifted her large wing.

A clean, white orb lay in her protective embrace.

Tan gasped. "By the current . . ." he murmured. He rushed forward, rocked back on his heels as he checked for Ind'arra's approval, then approached the egg with glee. "It's amazing, Ind'arra! Kar'nak! Taiuki, come see it."

She looked to It'ma, then back to the new parents, a slow smile curling her lips. An egg—a new life, a new dragon.

You may approach, said Ind'arra. *We welcome hamanool presence. In fact, we would not have expected a dragling so soon without you here.* Her voice was warm and motherly.

Taiuki neared the egg. It sat in the midst of steam vents, absorbing heat, and the air was heavy with Water. The rock at her feet burned, but it mattered little compared to this miracle of an egg.

"How often do dragons . . ." she began, but she bit her tongue, worried her question might be offensive. "I mean, I know the daragool are longer-lived than humans." She felt foolish stumbling over her words.

"I was wondering that too," interjected Tan without looking up from the egg. He had his palm placed gently on it, and his face was filled with wonder. "How often do you have babies?"

By the current, thought Taiuki. *Please don't be offended, Ind'arra/Kar'nak/It'ma.*

We are not, the trio replied jointly.

Taiuki reprimanded herself for thinking so loudly yet again, but she sighed in relief at the dragons' serene reply. They really were unbothered by social blunders.

Ind'arra snaked her head around to nudge the egg, then examined Tan face-to-face. *The al'Laiakala Order has not had the joy of two births in such a short time for many years,* she said, *but proximity with hamanool causes a quickening of the blood. We are grateful for Taiuki returning the al'La-iakala to the Land of Light.*

The Land of Light, whispered It'ma and Kar'nak in conjunction. It was a prayer of praise, sent to the heavens. All three briefly pointed their muzzles up to the sky, where the Eye burned.

"So it's because we're here?" Tan asked, brightening. He looked Ind'arra in the eye without flinching, despite her gigantic visage, which had to consume his view.

Yes, Ind'arra replied.

"And that makes you the leader?" Tan continued, piecing things together.

Taiuki cringed again. Tan really would ask anything. Still, the dragons did not seem offended at all.

Yes, the Order is led by the most recent parents, said It'ma, *a fair and regularly exchanged honor.* She did not seem at all distressed to have lost her First Elder position.

Taiuki wondered at the dragons' political system. No nobility, no birth order, no seniority beyond the simple measure that the first and second elders were sexually mature. What a beautifully simple, equitable system, she thought.

It'tholl bounded from the forest. *Taiuki sees baby. Baby egg is beautiful, isn't it?* she called happily. Scree flew beneath her scrambling pinions and back legs, and she came to a wild halt immediately in front of them. *Baby egg is dragon.* She said the last statement very seriously, as if informing them of a new fact.

Taiuki laughed and caressed her dragling. It'tholl leaned into it, begging for a scratch, and Taiuki obliged. "You were inside an egg once too, It'tholl."

It'tholl's eyes spun into a brighter whorl of colors. *It'tholl was?*

"Yes, you were inside an egg for a while, and then you hatched right when I arrived, as if you were waiting for me," said Taiuki, radiating gratitude to It'tholl.

The dragling basked in the emotions, returning them in full. *It'tholl remembers. Taiuki was Light in darkness.*

It was such a mature statement from her childlike mind, Taiuki was astonished for a moment.

She grows quickly, reminded It'ma. *A quickening of the blood, because she is with you.*

And a slowing of yours, added Kar'nak, so dismissively that the import of his statement was lost on Taiuki for a minute.

"Pardon me, Kar'nak?" she said.

Tan managed to peel his eyes from the egg and looked at the male dragon as well, although his palm still caressed its smooth, finely pored surface.

Both your lifespans are affected by bonding, said Kar'nak. *It'tholl will not have to spend the ages alone; she will* truly *live*.

This time, Taiuki was certain she could hear the subtle grief in Kar'nak's voice as he spoke of an experience he could never have.

As will you.

Taiuki and Tan returned to the beach after gawking overly long at the new egg. Ind'arra and Kar'nak remained with their nest.

"I can't believe it," said Tan as they enjoyed the last minutes of sunshine. "A baby Water Dragon. I wonder how long before it hatches."

"I don't know," said Taiuki. "Last time, I arrived just before It'tholl was ready to hatch."

They rested against the bone-white driftwood log and watched the sun descend below the horizon in a final flash of color. As the last bright sliver disappeared, the dragons hummed a farewell to the sun that made the air tremble. Then Uth'hal and the others tramped into the cave for the night, curling themselves into worn-in nooks that had become home, and the cove stilled. Taiuki absorbed the gentle splash of tumbling waves as they broke on the shore, the light sea breeze that kissed her cheeks, and the coolness of the damp sand just under the crusty surface broken by her toes.

"Thank you for this," murmured Tan. He was looking at her, then back at the sunset, abashed. "This life, I mean. This island. There is nothing I would trade for this." He squinted out at the water. Far beyond, over the curve of the horizon, lay Shiggo City. "Are you sure Kei . . ." He trailed off.

"She wouldn't, Tan," Taiuki said firmly.

"What about Nelly?"

"No. She's too young to keep this secret, and she's a Kritali. We couldn't get her here in the first place, and I wouldn't want to."

"I thought you liked her now."

"It's too dangerous to tell her this." Her reply came out too harsh, making It'tholl glance at them from where she lay watching the sunset.

Tan shook his head. "I just don't understand how someone could see them and not appreciate how amazing they are. Uth'hal—he's massive, powerful, the size of our largest trade ship. Ind'arra is flushed with this amazing color that gleams rainbow in the sun, even brighter than It'ma."

"People fear what they don't understand, Tan-sho," said Taiuki. A sadness weighed on her that she couldn't fully explain, but she knew that she was right. "And they kill what they fear," she added.

"But they're not wild animals," Tan declared, indignant. He sat up straighter and leaned a hand on her arm, his face full of hope. "They're intelligent, smarter than Moka and Kenji put together. Smarter than Benn or any of the blues I've met. They have their own culture and government, and they seem to share our religion."

"Yours, maybe," said Taiuki with a jaundiced look.

"I'ya is real, Taiuki."

She didn't want to argue with him, so she just sighed deeply and pursed her lips.

"The dragons know things," insisted Tan. "You saw how they all watch the sun, how they obsess over being in the 'Land of Light.' They know he's there."

"Just don't tell anyone, Tan," Taiuki said, changing the subject. "Kei would tell Mother in an instant. Nelly would tell Kei. You know how they like to gossip. She's just too young."

Still, Tan didn't relent. "Would it be so terrible to have dragons in Shiggo City? To live with them side by side? Isn't that how it used to be, like in the stories?" His eyes shone in the receding red light of the evening.

By the wind and waves, only Tan could be so naive. Taiuki shook her head once again.

Tan's face fell, and he leaned back, allowing his hand to fall from her arm, utterly dejected. "You really have no faith," he said sadly. "People are better than you think, Taiuki. They would appreciate the dragons."

"They would see monsters," she reaffirmed. "Nothing more."

They speared fish the following day, dining on black par-rotfish with honey at noon and then topping the broad canvas trap with surplus fish. The vat of oil beneath was exchanged with another empty redking shell, a gift from Uth'hal. Taiuki focused on rendering the oil to make more salve, mixing it with beeswax and herbs, while Tan sought out more honeycomb in the forest. He returned with a sack full of sticky comb and a puzzled expression.

"Did you call me?" he said, sloughing the bag from his shoulder and taking a seat by the fire.

Taiuki gave her mixture a final stir and began filling empty nut hulls with the salve. "No, why?"

Tan shook himself, then held the hulls in place for her as she poured. "I thought I heard you. There really is something odd about this island, a presence. You know what I mean?"

A light breeze whispered through the cove in response, and they both looked around apprehensively.

It'tholl paid them no mind, splashing in the shallows in leaps and calamitous, flopping dives. She seemed to be focused on splashing It'ma, who floated contentedly in the middle of the bay with several others.

Taiuki thought she might ask again about the odd feeling, in case It'tholl had more insight.

Forest talks, came the reply. It'tholl didn't pause in her sprightly efforts, instead diving under It'ma and buzzing beneath her companions to the other side, then popping up. *It'tholl likes the sun!* she declared.

Tan snorted. "She's no help."

Taiuki agreed with a chastened smile. Despite It'tholl's unconstructive response, Taiuki knew the dragling was not being uncooperative. Her explanation was simple, and her attitude implied that they should understand without further elaboration. It'ma had answered in a similar way earlier.

"It'tholl, beloved," she called, "*how* does the forest talk?"

Trees talk. Leaves talk.

"Like the wind?" suggested Taiuki.

Leaves make *wind talk.*

Taiuki and Tan exchanged glances, then burst out laughing.

Hachi-not-food smells bad bad bad, said It'tholl, careening around her mother.

"What?" Taiuki set her work down and focused on It'tholl's words.

Hachi food-not-food, sang It'tholl. *Bad food, Hachi is bad food!*

His flesh rots, child, said It'ma. *He is dying.* As usual, the dragon conveyed little emotion, only a dismaying pragmatism.

Taiuki knew It'ma was right. Hachi had looked pale when they arrived; his breaths were labored as he whimpered. His tail, once so powerful, was a limp and swollen mass of infection. But what could she do?

Return him to the sea, said Uth'warran from beyond It'ma, his voice laden with cold practicality. Taiuki knew she failed to filter her burst of rejection and distress, because Uth'warran lifted his massive head and looked at her. *It is the wisest choice, child of I'ya.*

"What are they saying?" asked Tan, aware of the exchange but unable to hear it.

"They think I should euthanize him," she replied, "and end his suffering, just like Sashiro said."

Tan's face fell. "No, there has to be another way," he exclaimed. "Hachi is a good animal; surely he can heal if we give him a chance."

We can smell the death upon him, said It'ma. *Even if he was acceptable to eat, we would not eat him.* She said it for both humans to hear.

Tan's eyes widened in horror at the statement.

"I'd better check on him," Taiuki murmured, setting her bowl down and heading toward the Pasture.

"You're not going to do it, are you?" asked Tan, staggering to his feet.

Taiuki shook her head emphatically. "I couldn't possibly give up on him, not after he made it this far. He and I have been together for so long . . ." Her eyes welled up, and she found herself choking on her words. "So many years, Tan. He was my first adult mount, and he's so fierce and so smart . . ." She turned away so he wouldn't see her cry.

"I wish we could bring an herbsman here," Tan muttered. She could hear him kick the sand in his frustration.

It'tholl appeared, looping around Taiuki and digesting her concern, which seemed to depress the dragling's nonchalant perception of the situation. It'tholl understood the extremity of Taiuki's distress, just as Taiuki could sense the practicality and mercy of ending Hachi's life. The pair entered the water, shifting simultaneously to their water-breathing forms, and headed to the Pasture down the shoreline.

Poor Hachi, Taiuki thought to herself. *If only there was something more I could do.*

But there wasn't. Hachi was dying.

67

THEY DEPARTED AS THE sun kissed the horizon and the heat of day dissipated into a pleasant evening with a natural light breeze from the north. Lord Shirkaa bowed magnanimously as they passed his tent pavilion; Thordrin barely nodded an acknowledgment.

Lyra found herself astride a handsome mare with powerful muscles and a healthy sheen. She made the motions of an accustomed rider, but her mind was fastened on Mam and that small bundle. It all seemed a dream.

Both had smelled of life, an overwhelmingly rich and pure scent that had swirled out of the Gate and enveloped the baby. And then they were gone, and the green light streaming through the Gate, much like that of an open meadow, had winked out, and Lyra was left alone again in a cruel realm ruled by pain and grief.

She didn't recall much afterward except a sharp jolt across her cheek. The Godspeaker peering at her with concern. Konan burning with rage, a scowl skewing his twisted features, as Mirra shoved him back. Korahel fretting.

The damp cloth on Lyra's cheek was refreshing, the tonic from the Godspeaker bitter.

His normally kind features seemed ragged and his gentle smile forced, and he had chanted over her quietly using the Old Language mixed with Manalali. She caught "I'ya'hakkat," their word for the desert goddess, and "hale," requesting release, but she didn't understand the full invocation. It was not one of the healing prayers sung by the wayfarers, or perhaps she wasn't listening well enough in her daze.

Korahel and a blur of other faces tugged at her and pulled at her. Her hips and thighs ached and pulsed, and then Konan was there.

She had felt words bubble out of her in a torrent of anxiety, but she didn't even know what she said, and then she faded away.

There had been a brief waking when her abdomen clenched again. Groaning to consciousness, she'd looked up to see a different ceiling and darker surroundings; she was in her own tent. The Godspeaker immediately began grinding new herbs in a bowl, intentionally showing her each step as he prepared a numbing salve. She wept as he applied it, but her muscles relaxed somewhat, and she realized he was newly arranging the various herbs, powders, and skeins, seemingly dividing them. She queried him.

"*Thralais'haralali* now with I'ya'hakkat," the Godspeaker replied sadly. "This . . ." He gestured to the array of medicinal goods. "This belong now to Favored Manalal." Now he gestured to her. "To warriors of Manalal."

Spoils of war. The Godspeaker had received the items of the defeated Godspeaker, a powerful boon to a people gifted in magika and medicine, but there was no delight in it for the old man, and Lyra thought she understood. Following the old ways, servants of I'ya were linked together. It was what had connected them at the oasis, when the old man had called her a thral, what had caused her to stop her spell and go with the Manalal in peace. And now a brother of theirs was dead, by their hands.

"Manalal teach medicine for pains." The Godspeaker insisted on mixing additional salves and the bitter tonic for her, showing her how to use the foreign ingredients. The remainder were stowed carefully in small jars and baskets and taken away by a dark-skinned woman just older than her. The woman slipped in and out quietly, and Lyra had not seen her again until now.

She was named Mikaa, and apparently she was their Haralali slave. Lyra didn't know what that meant, but she rued the angry sore on Mikaa's wrist, the twisted brand of a serpent.

Mikaa was a good rider. She sat comfortably on her horse, an energetic creature that had likely only been recently broken. As was tradition for the desert peoples, she used colorful cloths and a light saddle, spurring her steed with a light whip. She towed two idraka cows behind her, each harnessed loosely in a line and meticulously piled with their earnings. Lyra could see the baskets of medicines tied in place in the fading light.

Realizing that she was staring at the Haralali woman, she sheepishly looked away.

Thordrin led the party out of the camp, heading eastward. Mikaa followed with the idraka, then Lyra, and Konan took up the rear. Lyra focused on riding. Despite the Godspeaker's attentions, her pelvis and inner thighs ached, and her stomach churned erratically. She was uncomfortably aware of how much she still bled into a cloth beneath her, a remnant of the event three days before.

How was it so long ago? Where had she been? Besides the briefest flashes of moments and the intense teaching of the Godspeaker, most of that time was a blur except for the sense of being in Konan's arms. His scars had come into focus, but then she had been entranced by the amber flecks in his right eye, the heat of his breath, the certainty of his hold. His rough brow scar tickled her forehead, and his dark locks swung over to frame his face until the world beyond no longer existed. He was with her, and he would take her home.

It seemed only hours since she had touched her mother's hands. Mam's fingertips had brushed her palms as they swept up the tiny mass. But why was she there? How? Her mother was hundreds of miles away, hopefully more if the caravan had heeded Lyra's initial warning whispered on the wind ages ago, as she clattered to Tahayi Mines in a prison wagon. The caravan should have left Shayal City and headed back south on their trade route. It seemed perhaps they had, as the greenery in the gateway behind Mam had reminded Lyra of south Marlemet, where the grassland intermingled with forested glades along the rivers.

She was certain that that was what it was: a gateway. She had vague memories of the lore surrounding Gates to the other realms and other parts of the world, but so few Gatekeepers existed, even the Maskalan family didn't have expertise. How had the Gate opened, and why now?

Lyra gathered her thoughts into a short message. *Mam, caravan okay? Baby?* In her mind, the message was shaped like a bird with translucent wings. It capered from foot to foot, waiting for its destination. *To Elaisa.* The bird leapt to the sky with a whoosh of Air, somersaulting with triumphant freedom and then soaring southward. Lyra's mare nickered, flicking its ears in the sudden breeze, but it continued trudging onward. The bird rapidly faded into the background of the dark sky.

Lyra hoped it would reach its target, as she had prayed for the countless Whispers sent before. Mam couldn't Whisper, but she would recognize the message; several other caravan members might then attempt a reply, if they were strong enough and not too far away. Lyra wasn't really certain that her own strength was great enough to get the message to them if they had gone south, but if she had reached them at Shayal from the road to the mines . . .

Her work with the Manalal had built her confidence. She was strong enough to create a windstorm that blinded men. Surely, her message would arrive at its destination, no matter how far the caravan might be.

Lyra bit back the guilt that accompanied that thought.

Mikaa glanced back at her audible sigh. The slave had to be only a few years older. Her breasts were full, and her face had lost all of its childlike roundness. Her narrow face and long, slightly flattened nose projected an elegance that matched her proud posture. She wasn't tall, but the desert people didn't seem to be blessed with height. Even Shirkaa had barely matched Thordrin's stature, and he was considerably shorter than Konan.

Lyra scanned the south where the slow moon would eventually arc on its low path. The Whisper was long gone, a wisp of wind sailing over the sands and mudflats, careening over the steep malagate cliff and onward past the sprawling city of Shayal. If the Maskalan caravan had gone to Marlemet, the bird would follow the river toward the Red Bay and then southward along the wagon ruts through tall grassland, spotted with occasional copses of trees.

Perhaps it would find them there.

Konan trotted up to match her, and she tried to smile. He didn't smile back.

"Are you well?"

She was being too quiet.

He nudged his gelding closer. The horse pranced a little at the guidance of an unfamiliar hand, but eventually it obeyed. Konan searched her, and she felt herself blush.

"Please don't look at me like that. I'm . . ." *So broken. So ugly. So inadequate and foolish.* "I'm ashamed."

He darkened. "You have nothing to be ashamed of."

She didn't want to talk about her aching pelvis, her broken heart, the glimpse of hope in the Gate. Finally, she composed an answer. "I thought my magika was a tool for good. I thought we were helping to free an innocent girl from men like Selen and the warden." She choked on the last word and winced.

"We did." His expression was hard.

"Everything about it felt wrong," Lyra whispered softly, staring at Mikaa's back. "This is the third time I've used my gift against evil people, and the third time I regretted it in my heart."

They rode for a while, neither speaking, but she knew something bothered him too.

"Konan? If I scorn the gifts from I'ya, do you think I'll be punished? Do you think his Faces will turn away from me?"

"I believe the Haralal had to be punished for taking Shirasa, and your actions were justified." His cheek flickered in the moonlight, the violent tic visible even to her. He avoided looking at her.

"But it wasn't a war camp. It was a town. I saw the children." By I'ya, the weight in her gut when the dust of her storm had settled to reveal the open streets and humble buildings. The horror as she saw the devastation unfold, all facilitated by her power. She bit her lip hard enough that she tasted blood. Konan wouldn't meet her eye until she clutched his arm. "Konan, how could it be right?"

"Justice must be harsh and swift, lest it be ineffective." His discolored eye was murky and expressionless, and his entire face was more guarded than she had seen in a long time. He seemed to notice her sharp look and elaborated. "We know Shirasa was taken by the Haralal, and we know what happened to her while she was with them. We found her ensconced in one of the three towers, in the highest room, and guarded by Haralali soldiers. Regardless of the circumstances, it was right to fight for her."

She could see him swallowing, and she let her hand slip from his arm. He seemed off. Although everything he said was logical, it still felt wrong. Although she believed in defending Shirasa's honor, she reeled with doubt whether that honor had truly been in danger. Shirasa had squealed in Dashann's arms, and her gibbering had sounded like protests to Lyra's ear as she lay in the medical tent, consumed in her own pain.

Konan seemed to have no doubt, and yet she had seen him sweeping through the streets with Hafka, killing every civilian who approached. Was it so easy for him to send others through to the next Gate? She glared at him, and his brows rose in surprise.

"You couldn't possibly understand, if you value life so little," she said bitterly.

Lyra snapped the reins and rode ahead, unable to look at him any longer. It was unfortunate that the view ahead was Mikaa's back. The Haralali slave rode at a comfortable pace, hips swinging with her stallion's gait, shoulders back, head held high.

The blood of Mikaa's family was on Lyra's hands.

The woman heard her crying and looked back, curious.

Lyra examined the ground. Mikaa, beautiful and dark, was now one of only a handful of Haralali survivors. Because of Lyra, she was alone.

Konan left her on her own for the rest of that night, and she seethed at his cold attitude. She had expected it from Thordrin but not from him. She lay down as the noontime heat rolled in.

Mikaa had arranged a shelter, a makeshift tent meant for quick pitching. The thin leather covering was stretched wide over a single rope tied from a spear to the ground, giving a swath of angled protection from the sun.

Lyra lay awkwardly in the low interior side and ignored Konan, who sat beside her. Feeling his gaze, she cringed into a ball with her knees tucked up. Her body hurt, and she was exhausted.

She cursed when she awoke facing the other direction with her hand in Konan's, much like during their early days in the mines. Snatching her hand back woke him, and they went through another long night of silence.

The desert overflowed with rich scents from cactus flowers, carried on the pure breezes that rolled over the land both morning and evening. There was so little sign of man in Tahayi, so few tribes and settlements. No distant fires or lamps burned, no roads or beaten paths wended through, no cities shimmered in the distance. There was only the expanse in front of them and the hoofprints behind.

The moon was a bright but waxing sliver, and Lyra could only see a few hundred paces out. They carried no torches themselves; it was a waste of fuel given the moonlight. The way was flat and even, and the livestock were sturdy and sure-footed.

And so they trudged through the night again, and again. As Hafka had said, the flats became harder, turning into pavement like near the Desert Mother's shrine. The low-lying, wedge-shaped cacti, few and far between, gave way to taller cousins and gnarled bushes. Gnats buzzed from bush to bush, searching for the tiny white blossoms hidden among fingerlike branches. Small lizards dashed from shadow to shadow, hunting the gnats. There was life here, but still so little water. At least, not that Lyra could feel. It was full of powerful wind; the air was thick with it.

But she felt nothing else.

She caught herself wondering if Konan could feel anything, then cursed herself. He had not relented of his view, but neither would she, and she was drowning in her guilt alone for the first time.

Thordrin made a small fire, and Mikaa made a thin stew of dried meat and savory tubers from their supplies. Lyra ate her supper as quickly as she could, avoiding conversation with either man. Thordrin made several comments, but he eased up when both she and Konan glowered.

"Fuck's sake, you two are the worst," he grumbled, and stood to help Mikaa with the shade. She heard him flirting and wasn't surprised.

She began to stand, but Konan caught her hand and gently pulled her back down without forcing her close. She scowled, then realized how much pain was behind his eyes, how much the amber flecks shone when they were wet. His tic was going wild, making his left eyelid twitch.

Now confident she wouldn't leave, he began to sign.

"I do value life."

His cheek reddened.

"I value justice, and I hate the ugliness of what we've done." He looked at her, pleading, and she gasped at the depth of feeling in his face.

"You fought as any warrior was commanded to do," Lyra began, but he rejected her comment with a violent shake.

"I did, but that's not all. You said something seemed off. You were right. I went back into the town afterward, and I was drawn to the well in the center, in the midst of the oasis that fed the Haralali people, women and children and elders. It was empty, drained entirely, and the plants withered." He shuddered. "The water that fed the Haralal had been taken away, a week before, by me. They were already dying by the time we arrived with the army."

With that revelation, he crossed his arms over his knees and bowed his head.

Lyra choked back a sob, suddenly understanding his aloofness. Shirkaa had asked for their help—a "boon" for the Favored—so innocuously, so politely, and yet specifically enough to accomplish his end. The Manalal would be well supplied with the most valuable resource of Tahayi forever, and simultaneously their enemies would starve. Lyra vaguely recalled the momentary hesitation of Jikaa, who had understood the chieftain's intent the moment he made the request. Nonetheless, Jikaa had acquiesced to his father and allowed it to happen, and Konan had drawn all of the water from the farthest reaches of Haralali territory.

He had pulled it inward to himself, shifting the ground-water and the underground rivers to the land of the Manalal.

Shirkaa's people would flourish in the renewal of the land around I'ya'hakkat's shrine, and the few remaining Har-alal would die thirsty as they clawed their way through the parched sands. The terror of death she knew after escaping the mines? That same terror would course through every Haralali vein, and no one would save them.

Konan had Haralali blood on his hands too, far more than she had realized. Even without the edge of a blade, he had cut down the scrawny children and helpless wrinkled mothers of the town.

She crawled to him and touched him. He sulked without raising his head, his shoulders and arms stiff as iron and his own fingers clenching his elbows hard enough to leave red marks.

Empathy bubbled out of her uncontrolled, and she thought how strange it was for their roles to be reversed. Fighting her body's innate resistance to the intimacy, especially when she had been furious with him minutes before, she wrapped her arms around him in an awkward side embrace.

"I'm sorry, Konan," she whispered in his ear. She buried her face in his soft brown locks and cried.

He nuzzled her, and she felt a powerful arm wrap around her as he adjusted his position. They were suddenly face-to-face. A tear leaked out of his good eye, and Lyra traced it with a delicate touch. It was slick on his cheekbone, rough on his stubble.

"Why didn't you tell me?" she asked.

His throat bobbing, he released her. "You didn't need more."

Her ire surged back. "You carried this alone because you didn't think I could handle it."

Konan blinked.

"You're a fool, Noble-Heart," she snapped, even as she sidled next to him and slid her arms beneath his cloak. She hugged him with all of her strength and all of her frustration, and she heard him heave a wavering sigh. She could have crushed his lungs, she was so angry at him. Her voice was muffled as she buried her face in his musky shoulder. "I needed you more than ever the last few days, and you weren't there. We carry the same weight, so why not carry it together?"

His arms instinctively took her in, and his fingers sought her hair, and they comforted each other in a slowly rocking embrace. Lyra could feel his heart thumping in her ear, a drumbeat that made her think of battle, and she squeezed more tightly.

His fingers were rougher than usual, and she could tell he was wrapped in his own thoughts. He couldn't talk while he held her like this, but she wasn't willing to let go yet. All of her angst surged and swelled like a tide on the Mana Loi, and it broke against him. She hadn't realized just how much she needed him, his confidence and his constancy, until it was missing.

And he had withheld it, thinking she was in too much pain to handle more. *By the Light, you fool.*

They lay down in the shade with Lyra tucked in the most sheltered spot on the inside, and for the first time, Konan lay next to her, hip to hip, his breath tickling the back of her neck and his arm tucked protectively around her belly. His presence consumed her like a blanket.

It was the most restful sleep she'd had in months.

68

THEY HAD BROUGHT LITTLE water. The old mothers had been reticent to gift them many skeins due to the dryness of the Manalali war camp, and Thordrin had insisted that Konan could handle any need as they reached better land.

Konan himself was dubious, for he had hardly had time to hone his manipulation skills. In retrospect, the Godspeaker had minimized training time with Konan after the ground-water had been shifted to the Desert Mother's shrine. The Manalal had needed Lyra's magika more once that trick was done.

He could vaguely sense the underground source that fed the land through which they traveled, and the plant and animal life subtly increased. Small rivulets riddled the pavement, dry now but revealing the seasonal rains that must occasionally visit, sloughing off the pavement into ephemeral streams.

His suspicions were confirmed two nights later when a brief but tempestuous rainstorm alighted the sky, releasing precious drops onto them. They collected what they could with tanned hides, stretched at an angle to drip into basins. They topped their skeins and filled the basin enough times to water the horses, and Mikaa offered a Haralali song to the flashing sky.

It was wise they did so, for the next week was dry.

Rock began to dominate the landscape. The empty stream beds deepened and widened. Poking from the hard ground were stubborn trees, mangled from a difficult life but leafing nonetheless. Their roots split cracks in the rock, creating a miniature habitat for an airy, dry moss and tiny, buzzing insects. Konan suggested that the groundwater was becoming shallower, a distant and cool sensation far beneath their feet, but the stream beds remained dry. He resisted Thordrin's proposal of pulling it up for fear of destroying another area that people depended upon, and they argued, both hot with their tempers and without resolution.

Lyra had tried not to interfere, knowing the ache and weight of his guilt, but ultimately she snapped with irritation at Thordrin. He cursed them both.

They continued traveling mostly at night, resting during the height of day to avoid exhausting the animals and to reduce their water consumption, but they ran low once again nonetheless. Thordrin's suggestion sounded more and more reasonable, although he had eased once Lyra explained Konan's stance. Thordrin had shrugged carelessly, though he seemed lost in thought after as well.

Mikaa kept repeating something in Haralali and finally dismounted in a huff. She pulled a serrated knife from her cloak.

Thordrin chuckled. "Figured she found a knife."

Lyra balked, but Konan was no more surprised than Thordrin. Mikaa was more than clever enough to have armed herself the moment she was left without supervision, and she seemed feisty enough to use the blade without hesitation.

Mikaa sawed off a nearby cactus leaf and wrapped it in a cloth. She wrung it tightly, squeezing the water into her skein, and kept glancing at each of them to see if they understood.

"Aye, we get it, girl." Thordrin dismounted and made to slide a large chunk off the nearest cactus.

Mikaa ran to stay his hand, chattering in Haralali and shaking her head. She pointed at the cactus he had chosen, then at her choice. One had orange flowers, one yellow. She plucked a flower and proffered it, chattering and pointing at the petals.

Thordrin and the rest of the party nodded. Guided by Mikaa, Konan harvested other leaves, cutting only a few from each plant. Lyra didn't carry a large knife, so Thordrin assigned her to harvesting the water. She squeezed each chunk into a catch basin until they had enough water to refill their skeins, water the horses, and wet their own throats. The idraka could continue without for a few more days, so they moved on, hoping the streams would fill soon.

Their hopes waned after two more nights' travel. They found themselves following a broadening streambed, a sandy path waving its way across the rocky surface and very subtly deepening, but it was still dry.

Dawn approached, and the horses trudged onward, navigating the loose rock with tentative hooves.

They were near exhaustion, and the idraka lowed with their thirst.

"Do you hear that?" Thordrin's deep bass broke through the empty silence.

The party stopped and listened.

Water.

It was the slightest of sounds, a trickle. Thordrin and Konan spurred their horses and leapt off near a large stone pile in the middle of the streambed. As the sun peeked over the eastward horizon, it shone upon the stone pile. A tiny stream dribbled from underneath, pooling slightly on a flat stone and then dripping off. It trickled downstream for a short distance and then seeped back into the stream bed.

Thordrin whooped with elation, and Konan sent a prayer to the Eye as he knelt to suck the water across his parched lips before beckoning Lyra over. She dismounted with a veiled wince, and Konan scowled internally. She tolerated a lot of pain without complaint. Was she not the one who suggested they carry such weights together?

Water.

"It's here, but we need more than this to replenish," said Thordrin after drinking his fill.

Konan nodded. "It's a shallow spring," he signed.

"Can you pull more up?" Thordrin raised an eyebrow as though doubtful, but he didn't succeed in hiding his hopeful, lopsided grin.

Konan clenched his jaw and looked at Lyra, and warmth spread through him at her reciprocating gaze. She nodded encouragement. "It's already here. You won't hurt anything."

He knelt by the rock pile and dabbled his fingertips in the moist sand, recalling the Godspeaker's instructions and Jikaa's methodical translation. He called out to the damp, picturing its origins beneath the surface, down, down below the surface rocks and percolating through layers of broken stone. Deeper and deeper to the water beneath the earth. He clutched at it and drew it upward.

His hand echoed his mental motions, grasping mucky sand into a raised fist, and the spring burst forth like a fountain upon his cheeks. He stumbled back in surprise.

Both Thordrin and Mikaa laughed and merrily began watering the horses, then the idraka.

The weary party rested at the spring for the day, allowing the horses and idraka to drink to satiation. The horses moved on to munch on the scattered swaths of yellow and green grasses, while the idraka munched on the scraggly bushes and their white flowers. Tiny lizards appeared with the emergent stream. They skittered across rocks and hid in shadows, occasionally popping out in jolting movements to grab a buzzing insect.

Konan chewed on salty meat and wizened fruit, refilling his skein several times to slake his thirst.

Lyra rummaged through the food packs, roughly counting their rations as she pulled out a sweetfruit peel. "We have one bag of sweetfruit left, and another of that orange one. And four days' worth of dried meat," she announced.

Thordrin didn't open his eyes from where he rested on a large flat rock. "Aye, love, we're getting low."

"We've been rationing for days," said Konan. He joined Lyra by the idraka cows, who slept contentedly by the spring.

They'd arranged the packs carefully nearby, giving the cows a needed break.

"Put those knives to good use, girl," said Thordrin. "Fresh lizard meat would be nice."

Lyra slipped her long sleeves up to reveal her bracer of throwing knives, then looked at Konan doubtfully. She wrinkled her nose.

"You should." Konan felt his lips twitch at her expression. "They're food."

She went to stand with a hand on her bracer, but he pulled her back down. "They've disappeared with the heat," he signed. "They'll return later in the afternoon."

She nodded, then smiled and let him pull her close. They leaned against the idraka. Its unique, bestial scent was somewhat goatlike but also foreign, and its high-humped back cast a pleasant amount of shade over them.

Konan tugged their draping cloaks over their feet, and Lyra curled her knees up to be closer to him. He adjusted her hood over her frizzy hair, ensuring that her ears were covered, and trailed his thumb across her chin as he dropped his hand.

She did the same to him, but his heart fluttered as she traced his scars on one side, then brushed his stubble on the other.

"I should help you shave soon," she suggested, inspecting his chin.

Embarrassment flushed through him in response to her soft tone. He would never grow a proper beard, not with the damage on the one side.

Lyra kept playing with the stubble, picking at it with her nails, then paused. She leaned back with a mock scowl. "What, you need Mirra?"

He shook his head.

She attempted to glare at him. "Are you afraid of me hurting you?"

Konan shook his head again.

"Are you afraid of me?"

Her dangerously bright eyes glittered with mischief. That had to be what Elden looked like. Konan resisted a twitch at the corner of his mouth as he answered. "Terrified."

The mischief drained away with her color, and then she blushed so red, it highlighted the pink in her curls.

She buried her face and laughed. By the Light, it was music.

They huddled together despite the heat, resting. The spring lent a coolness to the ground beneath them, granting some relief while they slept. As evening fell, Lyra talked around her aching body, speaking of the windstorm and the Gate and her family, but he could tell by how she moved that her thighs were still sore. Beyond that, she battled the heartbreak of it all, and all he could do was hold her and commiserate in silence.

If only I could speak to you, he lamented. *I might say something foolish, but at least I could say something.*

The lizards reemerged, and Lyra stood with a sigh. She pulled a slim blade from her bracer and held it awkwardly, twisting her wrist in an unpracticed throwing motion.

"Told you to work on it more," said Thordrin with a snide chuckle. He peered at them from under the tent shade where he lay next to Mikaa, but he seemed more interested in the lithe body next to him than Lyra's struggle. Konan could hear him teaching her words.

Lyra huffed, but Konan stood to help. He molded her fingers as they had done so many times before and walked her through the motions, and she nodded.

"I remember. I should have practiced more," she whispered, seeming ashamed. Nonetheless, she turned toward one of the small lizards, which was focused on a jumping insect that clung to the dry grass blades.

Konan felt a swirl of air spinning around them. It funneled along her arm and forward, and the blade spun through the air in a flash of steel.

The lizard toppled across the rocks and lay impaled, and Thordrin jerked up. "Not bad, love."

Mikaa let out an exclamation—she sounded impressed.

Lyra beamed at Konan. He nodded toward another lizard, and she tried again. This time she missed, and the blade skittered across the rocks. The lizard scuttled into a crack at the startling sound, as did the others nearby, and they were left with only the buzzing of insects and the subtle trickle of water.

Lyra's face fell.

"It's okay. Keep trying." Konan stepped over to the first lizard's body and picked it up, pulling out the pointed blade.

Lyra huffed again, frustrated. "But they're gone."

He wiped the bloodied blade on a kerchief and handed it to her, then pulled his own dagger out and gutted the small creature with deft slices. He rinsed the body cavity out in the spring, rubbed it with salt from their baggage, and slid it onto a spit. He handed it to Mikaa, who had casually watched the entire scene. Now she moved to prepare a fire off to the side.

"There's no hurry. Concentrate on your technique."

Eventually a lizard poked its head out and emerged from hiding. Lyra's blade met its target that time, and the next. One throwing knife struck the rock face and dulled the tip, and she got flustered, but Konan took it and began striking it back into shape while she continued hunting.

Lyra didn't stop until seven small lizards filled the spit, roasting in the white smoke of Mikaa's fire. Konan handed her sharpened blade back, and she thanked him as she tucked it into her bracer with the others.

"You're better than you think you are," he commented.

With a meek smile, she joined him under the tent shade, and they enjoyed the respite from their long journey while the meat cooked.

Tahayi Mines seemed like a lifetime ago.

He wouldn't have imagined it could ever be. Tahayi Mines *was* his life, and now its miserable confines, its dank sulfur smell and constant tension, had faded to a horrid memory. Konan had no obligations to his keepers, no debt to pay. He still didn't feel free, for the weight of his guilt was heavy, but he finally shared it with someone who made it feel lighter.

Returning to Mirat didn't matter. He had pined for those frosted mountains and lush valleys for over a decade, but they paled in comparison to her. Besides, what kind of king could he possibly be? He was a monster and a murderer.

If Lyra would tolerate him, then he would beg to join her caravan. He could tailor, and he could keep her and her family safe on the trade routes. Thordrin would demand his services first, but afterward, perhaps Konan could live a peaceful life, one that atoned for the sins he'd committed against the Haralal.

He tightened his hold on Lyra, and she mumbled sleepily. His eyelids sagged, and the last thing he spied before falling asleep himself was Mikaa tending the fire.

She was alone, because of him.

69

WHEN LYRA OPENED HER eyes, the fire was smoldering, and Mikaa was gone.

Konan stirred behind her, and she felt a new sensation pressing against her. The whirlwind of emotions that resulted were panic mixed with arousal, fear mixed with desire, and she managed a squeak of dismay before the wind exploded outward from her. Konan shot awake, then looked down at himself and pulled away.

She forced herself up, a fire burning through her and wakening new tremors she hadn't thought she could feel again. The air shivered around her, flapping the torn tent flap. She had ripped it right off the tree branch with her outburst.

The terror shuddered out of her again, and she squeezed her eyes shut against the wretched memories.

"I'm sorry, Konan," she whispered, but he refused her apology, signing one in return.

"I knew it wasn't safe," he said. He scrubbed his pock-marked face with his own rage.

They sat awkwardly, each unable to look at the other, until they heard Thordrin approaching. Lyra rushed to scoot out and industriously check the smoking carcasses, spinning the spit with great care and attention. Konan remained by the tent, pulling its fastenings down and attempting to mend the tear.

Thordrin fed the flames with tufts of grass and sticks from the small bushes that grew around them. It rolled with aromatic white smoke, and the savory scent of cooked meat filled the air as the cool evening breeze set in.

Dusk approached, and Mikaa appeared with a sack thrown over her shoulder. She chattered in Haralali and laid it open. Tiny fruits spilled out. Proffering one to Thordrin, then to Konan, and finally to Lyra, she spoke. "*Pakla*. Eat good."

"Good girl," mumbled Thordrin as he ate. He caressed her arm appreciatively, and she gave him a sweet smile. He looked at Konan with a smirk. "Told you she was a good prize."

"She's a person," said Lyra irritably.

The fruit was tart, puckering Lyra's cheeks, its sourness unbelievably refreshing after weeks of dried goods.

They spat out the hard seeds, and tiny ants emerged to carry the remnants away. Mikaa gave them each two handfuls and stored the rest in a woven basket, then tucked the sack back in her belt for future foraging. With a look, she obtained permission from Thordrin to take a skewer and ate quietly by the fire.

Lyra marveled at the woman. She was truly surprised Mikaa had come back, when running away seemed more than attainable. In this desiccated place, the woman knew how to find water and food, and she always seemed confident of the way despite the fact they were in the territory of her people's enemies.

Lyra choked a little. Mikaa had no people. The Haralal were dead, whisked away like sand in a desert breeze. No trace of them would be found in the lonely dunes of Tahayi.

Konan settled beside her with a sheepish look. "I didn't think she would return," he signed before retrieving the second skewer and sharing it with her.

Lyra agreed.

Mikaa's loss also made her think of her family.

When she was young, the caravan would pass through Marlemet along the seacoast at high summer, and the children would play on the beach. Castle towers and wagons and horses arose from the damp, white sand, frozen in eternal battles and trades. Every piece of greenglass, worn to smoothness on the edges, was a beautiful myrmaiden. Every stick was a banner, and every stone was a jewel.

Lyra smiled to herself and wondered again where her family was. The Gate had looked like the precise area where the Mana Loi tumbled its waves onto her favorite stretch of beach. There was a crossing where a large river entered the sea, feeding a verdant tidal marsh. The bridges over the swampy areas were threefold, hopping from solid foothold to solid foothold, north to south. Trees and birds abounded, and the air had both the fresh saltiness of the ocean and the greenness of the woods.

"Mam, Elden, where are you?" she Whispered. The bird cocked its head, then burst into the sky and away, to the south and slightly west. Lyra watched it disappear. Perhaps someone would answer this time, though she didn't have much hope. It was likely her fleeting Whispers had died out on their way to the caravan, dissipating into a meaningless breath, and even more likely that any response would have done the same.

Had they even received the first warning? She prayed they had. Anxiety rose in her belly even as she reminded herself that the world behind Mam's Gate had obviously not been Shayal.

"What was that?" asked Konan, knotting his brow. He set his skewer down and cupped her hands in his, sending another shiver through her.

"You could see it?" she replied, too shocked to be afraid.

"See what?" asked Thordrin, munching on another pakla fruit and spitting the seeds in the flames.

Konan glanced at the sky, his face twisted in confusion, then back at her hands as though he had seen a miracle. His scarred cheek ticced, and he dropped her hands in embarrassment. "I saw something, or felt it."

"A Whisper. You can see it?" Her heart swelled with untempered delight, and she grasped his hand as he had hers. "You *can* see it."

"See what?" Thordrin repeated. His petulance revealed his annoyance at her cryptic, distracted answer. "Nethers, there are other people by this fire, you know."

Lyra's enthusiasm faltered, and she gave Thordrin an apologetic look. "It's a message, like sending a pigeon, but with Air," she said.

Konan nodded slowly, and the red flush that hit him illuminated the white scar tissue not only on his cheek, but also on his forehead.

"I didn't see anything," said Thordrin.

"Most people can't see them, unless they're Air-blessed—or at least gifted with higher magika." She beamed at Konan.

He pulled his hand away to answer. "It was formless to me, but it seemed birdlike in a way."

"I can't believe you could see it at all," Lyra said, once again elated in his companionship.

Thordrin looked skeptical, then scoffed. "You two and your magika! By the lowest Gate, I've never met anyone who could do that except for fucking Temple mages."

"I've heard of it," Konan signed. "Very useful, nearly instantaneous communication from one place to another, albeit in one direction."

"You know of others?" Lyra asked. She bit her lower lip as she realized she was smiling, but Konan reached over and traced her lip with his thumb, his own mouth twitching at her happiness.

He stopped and then frantically signed, "Is this okay?"

She broke into a sheepish grin again. "Did you know Temple mages who could Whisper?"

Konan paused, then shook his head. A shadow of that reminiscent sadness flickered back into his face. "I don't remember. I know of it, that's all."

Lyra sighed, berating herself for reminding him of what he'd lost, and then for falling so easily into needing his solidarity. She couldn't hold him back from what awaited him in Mirat; she *wouldn't*. He deserved to rediscover the clarity of home, not this paltry set of half-memories and images that seemed to only drag at him. What would his smile look like?

Thordrin tore loudly into his lizard, staring hard at Konan the entire time. He slitted his already-narrow eyes. "Are you still claiming to be Reylin, Crown Prince of Mirat?"

Konan nodded.

"And you knew Temple mages and scholars and lords? And you can see Lyra's Whispers?" Thordrin sneered, still doubtful.

"Why would he lie to you, Thor?" Lyra asked.

The man scowled, turning his physical attention to Mikaa and offering her more food, which she accepted with an alluring smile. He spoke with assurance. "It's simply not possible, my pretty little maunderer. There's a prince there already, dancing by the strings of an Elder Council. Tell me, brother, how long were you in Tahayi Mines?"

Konan withdrew into himself, his expression darkening.

Lyra turned toward him and forced him to look at her. As he so often did to her, she brushed his long locks over his ruined ear and traced the straight line of his jaw. "Please tell us. I barely know anything about your past."

His scowl twitched, and he stared into the flames as if seeing demons. "I was there for over ten years," he said. "Ever since the fire."

Lyra gasped. Ten years? How old was he? He couldn't have been more than a young boy. She ached for him, and she again touched the scars as though she might erase them.

"The fuck did he say?" complained Thordrin. When she translated, he frowned. "The famous Great Fire of Mirat was *more* than ten years ago. Everyone knows that," he muttered. He abandoned Mikaa and stalked away, but she soon followed.

Lyra stayed where she was, begging Konan to open up more. Ten years in Tahayi Mines? It was amazing he was alive, let alone a decent man.

With an effort to overcome her own body's confused reticence, she pushed his legs down and climbed into his lap. She wrapped her arms around his wide shoulders and pushed his slouching head up enough that she could place her forehead against his, although she had to close her eyes to focus on not allowing her body to panic.

After a moment, Lyra began to sing a lilting lullaby, one of her earliest musical memories and one that she always heard in Mam's alto in her own mind. That alone eased her fluttering heart.

She felt Konan's body shift, and when she opened her eyes, she met his intensity. Her breath hitched, but she continued, rolling into a happier song about the rivers in springtime, then a ballad about a knight and his love.

Konan never looked away, but one hand found its way to her elbow, clutching as though desperate for grounding. The other snaked around her hip and settled on her lower back; his palm burned like a brand.

When she finished, and her high voice faded away in the breeze, he hugged her delicately, as though she were glass. His eyes said everything, but he signed nonetheless.

"Thank you."

He told her what he remembered: stories of stealing pies and playing jacks and stones with boys on the street, reading books with a scholarly mage over his shoulder, sparring with an older man in knight's armor. He spoke of his mother, who sang to him before bed, and his father, who guided his morning prayers in the private chapel. Litisian windows like those she dreamed about, casting rainbows of color across the room.

He also told her about being bucked off his pony, of getting lost in a frightening hedge garden, and of the unending pain of searing burns, including his tongue.

Lyra glanced at his mouth without meaning to, then bowed her head in shame. He never smiled. Behind those chapped lips lay a severed tongue cauterized by fire.

"I'm so sorry for everything that happened to you, Konan," she whispered, nearly weeping from the awfulness of it all. "You deserve happy memories again, to see the snowy Sikrat and your castle at Ironhold, to pull the pieces back together." She ran her fingers across his chest and down, feeling the hard-muscled ridges, which bore more scars beneath the fabric of his tunic.

He shuddered. "That's not safe, songbird."

"You're the safest thing I've ever known." With those shy words, Lyra turned and nestled against him. She leaned back, fully aware of his state. Every part of him was iron. A part of her chattered nervously of her inadequacy, but the stronger voice declared that she was perfectly fine. As long as this was it, she was fine.

"Okay?" he signed on her thigh.

She reassured him, pulling his arms around her, and they sat together and listened to the nocturnal desert awaken. She wanted to ask him a thousand more things, but they were all derivations of the same question. A question she refused to ask, for his sake.

When they reached her family south of Corronei, and she was handed back to Mam, and Elden jumped on her shoulders and clutched her like he would never let go, would he leave her?

70

REYLIN RODE OUT FROM Ironhold at the head of an entire company: two platoons of the best swordsmen in Ironhold, one of pikemen, and one of archers. He imagined any fight against wild-eyed madmen like Sir Cordan would primarily involve hand-to-hand combat, if it could even be called that.

Cordan had been a rabid animal, almost feline with his predatory hunger but less coordinated. His wild blackened eyes had popped madly from his skull, as though they wished to jump right out from their lidded prisons.

The festivalgoers, many of whom had been forced to camp beyond the fortified city wall, stared at the orderly lines of marching soldiers first with jaws dropped, then with enthusiasm and acclamation. The several caravans of wayfarers, sprawled in the fields in countless concentric circles of wagons, broke into song, and the strumming of battle songs hummed in the air.

Reylin held his chin high. His neatly trimmed goatee was likely identifiable from a long distance, but he also wore his crown rather than his battle helm, a difficult choice given the gorgeous flail of dyed horsehair boasted by his helmet. He tried to ignore the presence of the same prince's crown he had worn for years, for Galltry had insisted that his king's crown required a substantive and elaborate ceremony. It was the Miratian way, and Reylin wasn't going to risk making his crowning questionable.

And so he led his men from Ironhold at a working trot. His handsome stallion Farrion seemed to perceive the grandeur required and clopped along in a perfect rhythm, ringing out the cadence for the entire company. The way-farers matched the cadence with their song, and he felt the excitement ripple through the troops.

He glanced back once to spy Syrana peeking out the window of her carriage with a prim, pleased smile. She gave him a lascivious look, one which told him not to stay at the head for too long. There was plenty of cushion and curtain in the carriage, and her Halmani handmaiden could easily walk.

He slowed as the city faded behind them, for the pikemen were on foot and could not keep such a pace for the two weeks it would require to reach North Mara, and eventually he relinquished leadership of the succession of soldiers and horses, carts and wagons to the company knight captain. The man had come highly recommended by Gillead, a better planner than Sir Forin and far more experienced in ground combat. Apparently he had fought at Patreagh's side during Rolis's campaigns. The man saluted as they exchanged places at the head of the company, and Reylin reined Farrion back to await the carriage with thinly disguised relief.

In truth, he wanted the better commander with him, headed toward the unknown threat of madmen, a problem that had grown beyond Krita's ability to control. Gillead must have considered the same.

He rode a while longer, appreciating the stamping rhythm of the small army behind him, the creak of working wooden spindles and iron-clad wheels, the hush of the summer breeze at their backs. I'ya had blessed this day, further feeding into his confidence. He had chosen his timing well, throwing the regent lords into utter disarray and bafflement at their own sudden demotions. And yet they were forced to smile for at least two or three more days in front of the solstice celebrants who packed the streets of Ironhold.

"My king looks well," declared Father Kaiadin from his position on a supply cart. The mage, in his holy humility, had insisted upon not infiltrating their royal carriage with his presence, instead finding a place next to a capable driver with a cushioned seat. The supply wagon was near the front, carrying items the queen consort Syrana—even the thought of the title pleased Reylin's ears—might decide she wanted at any moment.

Reylin paused beside the mage and realized he was grinning again. "It is a fine day to look to the future, my good father."

"Well spoken, son. Mirat is twice blessed to have its king, a proper Harkin bred of strength and adversity *and* a gifted mage."

"You'll continue to work with me each day, Father?"

"Of course, but I suspect you will learn far more once we reach North Mara. We can only imagine the chaos within one of the sickened bodies, or imagine the proper treatment." He adjusted his slipping glasses with a look of exaggerated tragedy.

Reylin agreed heartily. The truth of it was that he hosted a chaotic war of worries in his own mind.

East Face had to remain safe, especially while its fortification was under construction, and Edgegrass had to hold the line. Both were graced by the watchful eye of an Earth Dragon, however, which bestowed him far more peace of mind as he himself withdrew from the eastern front.

Ironhold remained under the official care of Steward Gordrew, Lord Ennedrew's cousin and a man from several proud generations of military men. His own brother had served as a High Guard knight at one time. Amber remained with him and Lady Ana.

Galltry and the other dukes could do nothing to halt the events Reylin had put in motion. Their own barracks were ultimately faithful to Lord Commander Gillead, a fact of which Galltry had been harshly reminded as Gillead deployed more men to Edgegrass. Still, Reylin would have to watch them all carefully.

Kaiadin had intimated that he might have a way to assure their faithfulness, but he had been somewhat vague. Perhaps something to do with birds and Whispers? Some magecraft Reylin had not yet seen?

Reylin had leagues to consider these things, and he'd had quite enough for the moment. He gave Kaiadin a polite farewell and hopped into the carriage. The Halmani woman exchanged places with him immediately, taking his horse to be tied behind and making herself useful.

Syrana awaited him.

"She appears to be healthy," said Reylin, peering into the dark cell at the woman who hung by shackled wrists.

"Physically, perhaps, but she must remain shackled," said Mother Morsey, the lead Temple mage of North Mara Port. The middle-aged woman sighed and shook her silver-streaked head. "She has only paused due to exhaustion. She screamed all night until her throat was hoarse and empty."

"Has she tried to hurt anyone?" asked Kaiadin, stepping forward.

"Only herself," the woman replied in a low voice as she led them to the next cell.

The man inside perked up when they blocked the torchlight in his door's tiny, barred window. He began to shake back and forth, wringing his wrists against the metal shackles till they bled from the abrasion.

"Let me out," he crowed. "Let me out so I can play, all the live long day, all the day long live, all the love I give . . ." He cackled wildly and began howling while plunging his body at them. His blackened eyes glistened like the wet slime on a fresh corpse, bursting outward from his skull. Shackles held him securely in place, but Reylin nonetheless retreated from the tiny window.

"*That's* the madness," said Morsey. She folded her hands together and offered a quick prayer to I'ya, supplicating for the man's soul. Kaiadin joined her as she made her final symbolic gesture, sending the message upward. Somewhere beyond, through thick walls of stone and mortar, sailed the Eye, looking down on them and listening.

Reylin felt a hard lump grow in his throat. The man's erratic movements were certainly reminiscent of Sir Cordan, as if he were trying to climb out of his own skin to reach them. He seemed to want to slough it off like a tunic, revealing a monstrous demon of exposed muscle and yellow fat. The madman's noisy disturbance seemed to stimulate the woman they had just seen, for her voice now emanated from the cell.

It was thin and high, wavering like a reed in a montane marsh. "Save me, by the Light," she wailed. "Save me from this curse."

Reylin stepped back to her cell and peered in. Her head hung low, her body slumped so much of her weight pulled upon her arms, which had grown so pale they seemed translucent at the wrist. Her fingertips tinged toward blue.

"How?" asked Reylin. He said it quietly, speaking to himself and contemplating the woman without much optimism.

The woman lifted her head and met his gaze. Her eyes were wide, frightened. *Save me,* she mouthed. Then a terrible, toothy smile stretched across her face, and her eyes turned black, and Reylin thought he was looking at a devil. "Save me," growled the woman, "by letting me out." She began to yank on her chains, rattling the metal with an echoing clamor that filled the dungeon. "Let me out, and I won't hurt anyone anymore." She launched into a high-pitched, ululating shriek, as if she were being branded or whipped.

The madwoman's rant aroused the entire dungeon, and screams echoed out from every cell. Trailed by his High Guard, Reylin followed Morsey and Kaiadin away, passing the group cells that had been packed with criminals who did not have the sickness. They threw their arms through the bars, grasping and pleading for release. Their terror was infectious, and Reylin quickened his step. They exited the dungeon, and Morsey turned to lock the heavy door despite the presence of guards on either side of the threshold.

"You see, Your Highness, why Lord Lío did not come?" she said, despair thickening her voice. "There is so little hope for these people, so little the Temple has been able to do." Reylin noticed an indigo-stained tear dripping down her eyeband and staining her cheek with a dark trail.

Kaiadin's expression was sober, and he nodded as if he understood. Even the Temple had limitations. Not many, but some.

Reylin stood digesting the experience for moments, then straightened and looked at Morsey. "Thank you for showing us what North Mara has been dealing with, Mother," he said formally. "Clearly this disease is a serious threat. I must speak with Lío now." He bowed to the high mage, not even waiting for a reciprocation before he turned away. He needed to ensure that Syrana was safe, and he praised I'ya he had left Amber at Ironhold. The situation in North Mara was already serious, with the dank lower dungeon cells full of madmen and women bearing an unexplainable and, thus far, incurable disease. And not all of them had arrived from Krita in that state; some had come down with the disease after a member of their household sickened and died. Despite those cases, Morsey still couldn't tell them how long the disease incubated before revealing itself, or how contagious it might be.

All they knew for certain was that it attacked those of lower blood. Sir Cordan was the highest-ranked victim yet, and he had derived his status through service to Reylin's father Rolis, not by birthright. Even he might be considered a man of common blood, no more than a hedge knight.

An inkling of regret tugged at Reylin for disregarding Gillead's caution and warning, for rushing so rashly to the port like he was their only salvation.

"My king?" came Kaiadin's low voice. The mage peered at him with concern, and Reylin realized he was glowering at the holy man.

Reylin apologized. "I was thinking, worrying." He patted the gangly man on the shoulder. "I appreciate you coming, Father."

Kaiadin bobbed awkwardly and gave him a nervous smile. "Of course, my son. I promised that I would remain with you, guide you, and assist in any way. This terrible disease can be resolved, I believe. You must have faith."

"But what more can we do?" Morsey lamented, throwing her hands in the air. "I'm at the extent of my abilities. Even High Holy Mage Ma'thell may not be able to help."

"He is unwell," murmured Kaiadin, confirming the woman's fears, "but there is more some of us can do."

Reylin marveled at the man. He seemed so sure of what he said, but without the heady stench of arrogance. He simply *knew* that Reylin could help. The man's faith made Reylin's that much stronger, despite the proximity of the wretched prisoners mere steps behind them.

Lord Lío stalked up to them as they emerged into the main corridor. "That's seven new cases since I sent you that message," he growled.

Reylin prickled at the man's disrespectful greeting, but Kaiadin intervened.

The mage calmly spoke, with emphasis on Reylin's honorific. "*His Highness* has already begun a new healing effort with the Temple, my good lord duke, and brought a contingent of soldiers to supplement your barracks. He further petitioned the High Temple for more mages to be assigned here, in lieu of Ironhold." The tall man didn't glare, but his steady look and neutral expression made Lío squirm uncomfortably.

The man acquiesced. "Thank you, Your Highness."

Reylin considered him. Lío was deeply prideful, almost arrogant in his insistence on managing his district as he pleased, including trade negotiations with the many kingdoms connected through the Mana Loi ports. Yet, he was reasonable enough to ask for assistance and to be grateful upon receiving it.

The man had hardly flickered an eyelash when Father Kaiadin announced him as "King Reylin, firstborn of Rolis and Leyalin, commander of Water, savior of Edgegrass." He merely jutted his chin out, harrumphed, and muttered "Galltry must be livid" with a dour laugh.

Kaiadin continued while removing his spectacles to clean them. "You, however, have overlooked a serious issue in your dungeon, good lord duke."

Lío bridled at the comment. "What could I have overlooked? Each madman is in their own cell," he snapped.

"We don't know how infectious the disease might be," said Kaiadin forcefully. "Those group cells are an epidemic waiting to happen. If one man falls to the sickness, they all might, or the madman could hurt others in the cell."

Lío sneered. "They're all criminals, and there's nowhere else to put them. This disease has filled my dungeon."

"What crime could they have committed that earned them a slow descent into madness?" he replied. "Lord Lío, such is not justice."

Lío glowered at the mage, then turned to Reylin. "The Temple can concern itself with justice in the eyes of I'ya, but justice in the world is accomplished with steel bars and taut ropes. I'm not releasing them, and I have nowhere else to put them."

Reylin maintained a steady composure, but inside he praised the Light that Lío was calling upon him for aid against Kaiadin's censure. "I must agree that such is not justice, Lord Lío."

Lío growled, his cheeks turning scarlet. "You're but a boy yet, and you have no idea what justice is."

Reylin raised a finger, resisting the ire that naturally welled up to meet the duke's temper. He had control. "I am King of Mirat—"

"And I am your regent," snapped Lío.

"—and I have an idea that may serve Mirat well."

Lío's snarl eased.

His wife tugged at his shirt, desperate to keep the peace. "Please, my lords," came Lady Falicia's velvety voice. "Highness, please forgive him. It has been a stressful few months, and the fear of disease weighs upon us all."

Lío yanked his shirt sleeve from her without breaking eye contact with Reylin, but he capitulated. "I am doing what I can, Your Highness, but the Temple has not cured a sick man yet. My dungeons are getting full. What would you have us do?"

Reylin could see his route to winning this interaction. Lío was a man of reason, after all. "Can we forgive any debts, allow the minor infractions to go home?" he asked hopefully.

"Stay that thought," warned Kaiadin, backed by a stuttering and fearful Morsey. "We don't know the incubation time; they could be infected."

"Perhaps a quarantine?" asked Morsey.

"Where?" Lío asked irritably.

"The Temple, perhaps," suggested Kaiadin.

Morsey was stunned for a moment, staring at her fellow mage, then accepted the logic of it with a reluctant nod. "We can more easily work with diagnosing the disease there," she agreed. "We have a small holding cell, but there is a mad-woman already there under observation. We could retrofit a storage room or two . . ." She drifted off.

"It's only a temporary solution," Lío warned. He wagged his finger at Kaiadin, but Falicia nudged him. "The Temple can only take so many, and like I said, my castle dungeon is already brimming with madmen and women. If we can't control it, we could end up like Krita."

"And what of serious infractions?" asked Falicia. "Not all of those criminals can be set free."

Reylin was ready with an answer. Forgiveness without trial or punishment was no form of justice, not for thieves and violent felons, and certainly not reflective of his desired kingship. Likewise, punishment without trial was no justice either. His eminent authority would be questioned if he instituted executions without trial, although they seemed like a reasonable solution in the current situation.

"After quarantine, they will be conscripted and deployed to the eastern front as ground troops until trial," he suggest-ed. "If they are found innocent, we'll pay them as we pay the other soldiers."

Lío raised his eyebrows with apparent admiration, then cleared his throat. "It's a fine idea, Your Highness."

The two men, a generation apart and formerly separated by a wide gap of disrespect, reached a new understanding. Lío grunted, seemingly pleased.

"Let's see if there's anything we can do for those poor people under your care, Mother Morsey," suggested Ka-iadin.

"What do you believe can be done?" asked Falicia, trailing along behind them.

"Our prince has powerful Water magika," said Kaiadin enthusiastically, "but our Temple's knowledge is somewhat limited compared to that of the Waterpriests."

Morsey looked at Reylin with wonder, then dipped into a bow. "I thought I could feel something, Your Highness, a glimmer of power exuding from you, but I'm not a sensitive. I'm sorry I did not realize sooner."

Lío cleared his throat. "I must remain, Your Highness. There is much to figure with the altered trade coming in and out of the port." He excused himself and his wife.

Reylin debated calling for Syrana but didn't, loath to expose her to the ugliness of the disease. He had left her under the care of Sir Dorian and several other knights.

Shadowed as always by the other High Guard, the three departed Lord Lío's castle and headed for the Temple of I'ya, where a lone madwoman awaited in her solitary confinement.

71

SYRANA HUFFED HER FRUSTRATION.

She had hardly expected the journey to North Mara to be more enjoyable than the destination, but Lío and Falicia's oceanside castle tended toward a gloomy fog both morning and evening. The rotten stench of ocean creatures tainted the freshness of the breeze that eventually cleared the fog, a disappointing and sickening contrast to the purity of the mountain slopes. A horrid teal layer of slime mold clung to the outer walls far below, where the spray of the waves kept the rock continually wet. Syrana considered the fall to the jutting rocks below, a jumble of wickedly jagged boulders, and shuddered.

Reylin had been busy since they arrived, loping between Temple and castle with hardly a spare wink or impassioned kiss.

"Milady?" Her handmaiden stood with head bowed, proffering a blood-infused brandy in lieu of tea.

Syrana couldn't stomach the red magika's harsh metal flavor, steeped with delicate herbs and dried flower petals. She nearly retched now, even with the aggressive liquor to cover it up. Still, she swallowed it quickly and demanded a sweet tonic to chase the medicine.

The handmaiden melted away to the next room.

Halmani could be useful, Syrana thought, and occasionally observant. Her own girl was intelligent enough to maintain idle conversation and prepare most of the magical potions and powders, and wise enough to keep her mouth shut otherwise.

"Milady, your husband comes," the girl murmured in her strange Halmani accent. Despite her years of service in the royal castle, and the constant company of respectable nobility, she still retained that foreign sound. Not that anyone would confuse her for a human, given her diminutive stature and bleached hair.

Reylin, finally.

At least she had enjoyed his attentions during the carriage ride, a pleasant diversion to break up the monotony of the long days of trundling along overworn tracks. She felt like a maundering commoner by the end of it.

Reylin strode in, his orange cloak trailing behind. His royal crest decorated both rondels in a gleaming gold, and his tunic was fine enough that Syrana suspected it was one he had intended for the solstice festival. It clung to his skin, emphasizing his trim, muscled abdomen and the breadth of his powerful chest. He smiled possessively.

"My Chosen." He swept her off her feet and spun her around once, his breath hot in her hair. "I praise and curse the power that brought you here by my side. Why did you want to come?"

"To be with you," she murmured as she sought his lips.

A slightly troubled look flashed across his countenance, but she could tell he was in a fine mood overall. He shook his head. "Is it worth the danger? The dungeon, Syrana . . . it was terrifying. The several we've moved to the Temple for closer observation revive the Lupine incident in my memory like it was yesterday." His kiss was desperate, demanding some verification that she was still there.

She returned it despite the painful scratch of his upper lip.

He pulled away after a minute and set her back on her feet, then looked around the room with wonder. "And yet, despite everything, I feel different here. I feel powerful and empowered, as though the air itself carries magic that bolsters my steps and clears my head." He looked out the window, which boasted only a view of endless dark blue. "Father Kaiadin said it was the water, the source of my gift. I've never been to the Mana Loi before." He grimaced, and she knew he was thinking of Galltry.

Reylin seemed to take the view in with one hefty breath, his hand cocked on his sword pommel and the other thumb tucked in his belt. All of a sudden, he exuded greater confidence. Maybe he truly did absorb some kind of power from the vast waters.

A moment later, he offered her escort to supper, his free hand caressing her delicately placed fingers on his forearm.

They were stopped by a scurrying Father Kaiadin, whose cheeks looked wan beneath his indigo paint. He bobbed at the waist. "My king."

"We're heading to supper, Father. You'll join us, won't you?"

Kaiadin nodded but leaned in to speak in a low voice. "I have unfortunate tidings you must hear."

"Speak."

"Shiggo has denied us an emissary, son. However, they welcomed us to attend their experts in Shiggo City." The lean mage ducked his head in shame.

Reylin's gliding touch paused on her ring-bedecked fingers, and his forearm tensed. Even as he steeled his jaw, he acknowledged the message and then sighed. "Even that is a rare concession from the myr, isn't it? I must admit that I am disappointed."

"As am I, son."

Reylin stood a minute longer, and the flexing of his forearm eased beneath her fingers.

"We need their knowledge," Kaiadin lamented. "So few guides on Water-based transmutation remain here in Mirat."

"It is well, Father. Attend us now." Reylin pulled Syrana forward and resumed his light touch, which sent a shiver of excitement through her. He was strangely calm, reining his temper in better than usual.

Perhaps the nearness of the sea did make a difference, but she certainly couldn't tolerate it for long. Praise the Light she had been sent to Ironhold rather than to one of the dukes' lesser courts. The only handsome one in any case was Lord Ennedrew, and he presided over a sea-oriented district as well, just southward of Lord Lío. Syrana much preferred the majesty of the Sikrat ranges, with their clean, crisp air that didn't make your gown stick to your belly.

Lío and Falicia offered hospitality for all of Reylin's officers, but Reylin suggested they keep the group small for open conversation. The food itself pleased Syrana's palate enough, although she avoided the odd-looking textures of seafood. A heavy bread rolled in seeds and nuts provided a vehicle for sopping up the thin summer vegetable stew, a creation with squash slices, potato chunks, and a lightly spiced lamb sausage. The platter of early fruits and soft cheeses was excellent, with the exception of the smooth liver terrine, which reminded her far too much of her red magika. She picked on the various courses and listened.

Lord Lío complained of the diminished trade with Krita, interspersing his whinging with explanations of Krita's fault in the matter.

Lady Falicia echoed her husband's thoughts. "Meanwhile, we must consider the danger of encouraging further trade with Krita," she added.

Lío turned to her. "Of course, I was going to bring that to His Highness's attention," he snapped. His wife bowed her head demurely, and Lío continued. "It's been five ships now, coming from Krita Port with sick mariners and travelers. Thankfully, the crews kept them under lock and key each time, and the sick ones are now in the dungeon you just left. However, we may not catch the next ship in time, or the passengers may not be showing signs yet. Krita is doing *nothing* to control this plague. King Rigaran won't reply to any birds!"

The older man's frustration emanated in waves, and Lady Falicia grasped his shoulder in comfort. He shook her off and stabbed at a cut of meat on a silver fusianate platter.

"How bad does your source say it is now?" asked Reylin.

Lord Lío shook his head, clamping his jaw to contain his anger. He managed to serve himself, then reddened as he realized he should have served his wife first. He cut her portion from his own and placed it on her plate.

Lady Falicia spoke up. "We know it is percolating through Krita Port, affecting a broad swath of commonfolk in a growing number of sites, but not spreading like a normal plague. The port continues to do business, according to the mariners, but with more soldiers patrolling the streets." She shrugged helplessly. "That's all we know with the reduced number of birds coming from Krita. I venture that the Temple at Krita Port has been overwhelmed with the sick, disallowing much communication via Whispers, and you know the king and queen are dealing with a situation most dire. Look at our own circumstances."

"They're ignoring us," grumbled the duke, shoving red meat into his mouth and chewing loudly.

Lady Falicia gave his shoulder an affectionate, encouraging shake, her expression one of entreaty. "I hope it is only an oversight, my dear lord."

Syrana smiled as Reylin cut her a slender portion of meat as well. He was strangely composed given the recent refusal from Shiggo's Waterpriests. She would have expected him to rage and stew over it, perhaps to stalk the halls and or batter steel with Sir Gillead for a while, and then come to her for comfort.

"It seems a diplomatic mission to Krita Port may be necessary," he said slowly. His almost neutral gaze sharpened as Sir Gillead opened his mouth to dispute the idea, and the lord commander leaned back in his chair. Sir Patreagh merely turned down the corners of his mouth.

Lío's frown darkened, and Syrana wasn't sure whether it was because the man didn't approve of the danger or because Kritali relations were his dominion.

"Such a voyage would allow us to learn more of the madness," suggested Kaiadin. He adjusted his spectacles nervously as Lord Lío turned his scowl upon him, but continued anyway. "His Highness has seen what he can here in North Mara, but based on your report, the situation has escalated in Krita Port. We could examine the victims in a more advanced stage of the disease, perhaps revealing a solution."

"And then on to Shiggo," said Reylin, nonchalant.

Syrana gasped as the long table erupted into arguments.

Sir Patreagh pleaded with Reylin; Gillead jutted his chin out and glared with disapproval. Ronidann wore a faint, excited smile, while Dorian looked clueless. Lady Falicia implored him not to take such a risk in a timid, polite voice, while her husband smacked the table and flatly refused.

"I cannot approve, Prince Reylin, and Galltry would never approve. The Council would never approve. It's too risky to your person."

"I approve," Reylin stated loudly, his smooth voice filling the room and quieting the table with its confidence. "And I am a man grown, *king* of Mirat, commander of Water magika, and a healer. I am going."

Lord Lío's thick, slightly chubby cheeks reddened, and he smacked the tabletop in dismay. "And I am your regent. Your Highness, I beg you not to put yourself in such danger."

"I do not believe we will be in serious danger," Reylin interjected. "My contingent includes noble-born soldiers and servants, Father Kaiadin, and myself. We are all immune, and capable of self-defense in any case."

"Your choice is right, son," said Kaiadin. "Your magika could be the key to resolving this madness, and we *must* hasten to Shiggo for help. Krita is a logical stop; we could learn more through observation of the disease whilst resuming trade relations."

"And me?" The words slipped past Syrana's lips before she realized what she was saying, but as they did, she dedicated herself to the idea. "And me," she repeated with more surety.

Adhered to Reylin's side, Syrana would escape the restrictive bonds that had followed her to Ironhold. She would remain with Kaiadin, applying whatever means necessary to procure success in her womb. Perhaps the healing arts of Shiggo would yield alternative remedies she had not heard of. And above all, she would fill the space on Reylin's right arm, his first and Chosen, his queen consort.

To her chagrin, Reylin appeared uneasy, his authority fading. "I had thought to return you to Ironhold. Krita sounds like no place for a lady at the moment."

"I go where my king and husband goes." She tossed her hair and pretended to be engrossed in eating a berry-and-sour-apple pie.

Reylin yielded. He turned back to Lío.

"I expect your best ship outfitted in two days. Meanwhile, I will continue to assist Mother Morsey and Father Kaiadin in the temple. I believe the criminals we've quarantined may be sent east within a week, and you may rotate another group out of the dungeon."

The ill-tempered duke seemed to chew on the inside of his cheek, contemplating, then inclined his head toward Reylin. It was the first time Syrana had ever seen any of the regent lords fully submit to Reylin's command. "A ship shall be ready, Your Highness."

They discussed the supplies needed for a voyage, and servants scattered to obey their terse lord's commands in the short time demanded.

The remainder of the meal was fairly pleasant, despite the fearful madness creeping toward the castle gate, for they also felt the warm flicker of hope stirring amongst them. Reylin had saved her at Lupine, and he had already demonstrated a magnificent aptitude for Water manipulation and tissue binding. There was likely more ability brimming inside of him, an untapped pool of power that could change the frightful circumstances in which Mirat had found itself.

He exuded certainty of the path forward, further bolstered by the faithful Kaiadin, and as they returned to their room for rest, even his posture and stomping steps rang with conviction.

Reylin didn't relent until he and Syrana fell onto the bed in their private chamber. He pulled her onto him and put his palms on her cheeks.

"I'm sorry if I surprised you," he murmured with a worried grimace. "You don't have to come to Krita or Shiggo, for both may be unpleasant. Would you not rather be with your mother and baby Amber?"

Syrana controlled her reaction, a morass of conflicting emotions. "I'll miss them as much as you will," she said enthusiastically. Removing his crown, she twirled his hair around her finger. "But I cannot stand to be apart from you that long."

He pressed his lips firmly against hers, then pulled her to the window overlooking the sea.

The gray of evening fog reminded Syrana of the stories of ghouls and spirits who haunted places of death. Its monochromatic haze caused the dark waves below to merge with the night sky, making the Mana Loi appear to be an infinite space of crashing noise and cold. Syrana winced internally. Soon, they would board a ship to attend an island kingdom of sickness, strange and wretched foods, freed slaves and street whores, and odd-looking foreigners from the far south, and they were doing this intentionally. Krita had a reputation, one which seemed to her quite unsavory, of trading in everything but slave peoples. Such a place would meet all of the sordid conventions of a typical seaport but on the scale of a capital city.

"It's overwhelming, isn't it?" Reylin mused as they stared out. "Rich with an energy I can hardly describe. It calls to me, Syrana. I *know* that what I need—be it knowledge or simply the power to change things—is out there."

"Then let us seek it out together, my love."

Despite her qualms, her reaction after was genuine, for he finally did what she expected: sought comfort in her. As sure as he acted in front of Lord Lío, as brazenly as he treated Lord Galltry, Reylin was not sure of his path. She could see it in the flicker of his dark eyes and feel it in the hard grip of his hands on her hips as he directed her where he wanted.

He was desperate, a man drowning in his own insecurities as they rushed into the unknown. And in his fear, he needed her. He chose her.

Syrana ol'Harkin, first and Chosen, queen consort of Mirat and, eventually, Heir-Mother.

72

"One herbsman could change his fate," Tan whispered urgently.

"No." Taiuki pushed Tan away, beckoning him to sit straight in Nimoka's saddle. "Focus. Command the soldiers."

Tan lingered on her for a few defiant moments, then looked away.

The top line platoons awaited the next order, although some of them had glanced back after no command shivered through the water to their waiting ears. Taiuki admonished them with a glower and a hand signal. The soldiers whipped their faces back round, facing the target island in unity once more.

"Rank One, ascend, fire, and rotate," Tan pronounced.

They watched each platoon shift in synchrony, the first line rising above the surface with spearguns raised. They loosed simultaneously, and a black line of bolts flew through the air toward the empty spit of sand. Taiuki pointed out the individuals who slipped from the pattern, arcing their bolts at an erroneous angle or failing to maintain the rhythm. Tan clicked corrections. The line of archers sank back and down, allowing the next rank to rotate to front. while they reloaded.

"They are getting better," murmured Tan.

"Repetition leads to perfection," Taiuki replied automatically. She gestured toward the platoons.

"Rank Two," called Tan before turning back to her. "Listen, if I'm really the Second, then my commands cannot be denied, right?"

"Superseded only by the queen and the arch commodore," Taiuki replied, wondering where he was headed with his line of thought.

"Conformity above all, right?"

"Yes, Tan-sho."

"Then why not command an herbsman to silence?"

The tightening of her abdomen, the nervous churning of her stomach, the dulling of the current's song in her ears—all were reactions she tightly controlled. Her expression revealed nothing, but she couldn't control the fury in her voice or the strength of her grip as she reached over to Tan's arm.

"You shall do nothing to reveal them," she choked out. "Nothing." The last word concussed in their ears, seeming to reverberate through the water like an echoing cavern without walls. Instead, she was floating in an eternal space, an endless vacuum of water that flushed and trickled, laughing at her. She shook his arm again. "Nothing, Tan. You must obey in this."

The redness of his eyes revealed his agitation over Hachi's health, over his inability to do anything about the whale's injuries beyond praying. She knew exactly how he felt, but she would not risk everything they had by bringing a stranger to the island.

Tan grimaced at the troops rotating, then clicked a loud corrective to one flagging soldier who had broken rank as his speargun jammed. "Rank Three," he called before patting her own hand, which still curled around his bicep. He wouldn't look directly at her. "How can I let him die when there's something I could do?"

"You don't understand the risk, Tan-sho," she said more gently. "If that person defied your order in any way, even to their spouse in confidence or to their children while telling a bedtime story, the truth would be out. The Mountains of Mourning would no longer be a haven for the Order, a safe place where they can simply live. They would have to abandon their merry life again, perhaps even return to the trench to escape those who don't see them as worthy."

Tan chewed on his lower lip. "I don't understand why they can't live openly with the myr. They were meant to be in the Light, just like us."

"Because people will hurt them."

"Why?"

"Because they reveal our inequities and our weakness," Taiuki replied, finally putting into words what she had struggled to explain to him for weeks. "Because they are everything we're not, our antithesis in some ways. Where we are flighty, they are staunch. Where we are fearful, they are stoic—"

"Where we are curious, they are indifferent," Tan interrupted. "Where we are sensual, they are dispassionate. Isn't it obvious we are meant to be together, to make each other better?" The yellow flecks in his black eyes shone like flames in the dark, his eagerness spilling from him in waves. "Imagine a world where hamanool and daragool are joined again, as it once was and is clearly meant to be."

She stared at him, torn between dreaming the same dream and cringing in terror at the possibility of everything going wrong. He met her eye, pleading. Her fear won out, and she clamped his bicep in warning.

"Bringing the dragons into our society without violence would require utter control of the school's sentiment, on a scale that no one could possibly achieve. Controlling the fear, the reticence of something new or different—it cannot be done. Do you understand, Tan-sho?"

His enthusiasm washed away, diluted by the reality of human failings. He dropped his gaze once again.

"Will you conform, brother?" She needed to hear it, need to gain his undoubted compliance. It was both a command and an appeal.

His face wrinkled into mournful distress, and she knew he wept for Hachi. Finally, he nodded. "I shall conform, sister," he whispered.

Despite Tan's promise, Taiuki felt a growing unease.

Her brother's knowledge of the island was dangerous enough, but his continual desire to join her on her truant egressions was even more problematic. Every "hunt" they conducted was riddled with lies regarding where they went, how they spent their time, what challenges they faced while retrieving whatever meat was desired that week by Wehan or Mother.

In truth, they did hunt, but with a much larger and more menacing school than they claimed. Uth'hal always accompanied them to assure It'tholl's safety, and often his brother Uth'warran followed. Depending on their quarry, others from the Order would join them as well, for they thoroughly enjoyed routing certain species of fish and turtle.

Tan so desperately wanted to share their successes with someone, and he occasionally tripped over his own tongue in his eagerness to describe his hunting prowess to Anella, or even to Kei.

Both woman and girl listened avidly as he explained their latest escapade in morbid detail, his hands flying in wild gesticulations in mimicry of the blueback shark they had tracked and slaughtered.

"Good riddance," Kei said, snippy as usual, when he had finished. "The fewer there are of those monsters in the world, the better."

"What does a blueback look like?" asked Anella. She tore her gaze from the large portal window at the end of the room. They lounged in one of the drawing rooms, a comfortable room on the first lower level with a fine, wide view facing the sweetgrass fields and trade current. Distant caravans pulled by whales moved in the distance.

"Massive," said Tan, throwing his arms high and wide. "Dark like the night sky on top . . ." He reached down and took both her arms, pulling her from her place on the couch and spinning her around. He turned her forearms over, revealing some of the paler of her Kritali skin. "White like your arms on the belly, invisible from both directions in the open sea until . . ." Tan gnashed his teeth with an audible click at her arms, and she squealed with frightened laughter. Grinning, he set her back down beside Kei. "Until they open their maw, revealing blood-red gums with thousands of teeth, and then it's too late."

Anella giggled, her face filled with admiration. "And you chased after one on purpose? That's incredible! Kind of like hunting a frostbear. It sounds terrifying."

"Like I said, good riddance," Kei repeated with pure hatred. She caught Taiuki's eye and held it briefly.

Taiuki swallowed back her feelings, hoping Tan would move on with his story sooner rather than later. Her own memories of bluebacks were too vivid, too raw. Hunting this one had been hard enough, drawing her entire body into a panicked cringe that she hid from Tan. Recalling it now only led to more recall, scents in addition to sounds, flavors in addition to graphic flashes of horror. *Blood in the water.*

She inadvertently shuddered, and Tan paused his heroic retelling with an apologetic look.

Anella caught it; she was getting more observant like that. Her smile faded in the sudden tension of the room. "Do you kill every one that you find?"

"Every single one. Ol Shiggo'lo." Taiuki turned to the window and looked out. The long whale caravans below slipped through the current on the easiest path; the few ships above followed the same path. The arteries of the myr world, both bringing life and flushing the death away.

Anella nodded emphatically, as if she understood, but Taiuki knew she didn't. The girl opened her mouth as if to ask another question, then clamped her pink lips shut again. She did it a second time before folding her hands in her lap and straightening.

Kei patted the girl's knee. "Let's talk about something else, Tan-sho," she suggested. "How are your trainees doing?"

"Good." Tan shrugged. "Yuki is really the one leading most of the time. I'm still training myself."

"You're doing well," Taiuki admitted, forcing a support- ive smile. "You will be able to command the fleet one day, and you are an excellent cavalier and swordsman already."

Tan touched his forehead in thanks, and his cheeks flushed. "I admit I liked it better when the blades were only blunted points and dull-edged wood. I have a lot of bruises and cuts these days." He rubbed his ribcage with a grimace.

"Get better at blocking," suggested Anella. Then she cov- ered her mouth, seemingly shocked by her own words, and broke into a nervous giggle.

Tan mock-glared at her, then chuckled. "Fair enough."

Anella *would* know. Tan had a tendency to charge in dur- ing hand-to-hand combat, forgetting to block in his eager- ness to strike. His habits showed even in the slower-motion drills with Anella each evening. Taiuki had been focusing on breaking him of the poor strategy, and she had been somewhat merciless in her lessons.

"Nelly is right though, Tan. You should never count on your opponent missing an opportunity to strike, nor on a blade to be dull. Assume the worst, and act accordingly."

"Hey, I'm not the only one to have gotten struck in sparring," he exclaimed, his cheeks reddening further into uneven splotches. He gave her a pointed look. "You lost with spears that time."

"One against four."

Tan threw his shoulders back and mimicked Sashiro's gruff, deep voice. "For the warrior, the number of opponents matters no more than the number of fish in the sea. The battle is fought for hope, not for fear." His eyes widened. "You know, we never did figure out what happened with that spear . . ."

Taiuki pursed her lips, hoping her expression would push him to silence, and nausea curdled in her stomach. It had to do with It'tholl; that much she knew. Why the inherent anx- iety? She didn't know, but she didn't want Kei and Anella to know about it.

"What spear?" Kei perked up. *Too late.*

Oblivious, Tan shrugged and bounced onto the couch next to Anella. "I don't really know. She broke it in sparring, but no one could find the pieces. I didn't see it happen."

Taiuki could feel the power of Kei's disapproval burning into her, and she finally slid her gaze from Tan to her elder sister.

Kei had knotted her arms across her chest, and her chin trembled. Was it fear, or rage? Either way, it was intolerance.

That sickening feeling of being irreparably broken, polluted in some way that made her not true to the myr, sank into Taiuki's bones once again, and she ducked her head. Sashiro would be ashamed of her.

"You *know* what happened, don't you?" Her sister's voice was frigid with hate.

In her peripheral vision, Taiuki could see Anella's face swinging from one to the other in confusion, but the girl didn't break into the palpable tension between them. Taiuki swallowed and barely nodded in acknowledgment of Kei's words.

"Why, after all this time, would you . . . I thought they had fixed this."

"Fixed what?" asked Tan.

"Why can't you just conform?" she demanded. "Why do you have to make it so damned difficult for yourself and everyone around you?"

Anella gasped at the language.

But Kei wasn't done. She stood, arms still tightly clutched against themselves, and leaned over Taiuki, exuding the most authority Taiuki had ever seen from her. *Just like Mother.* "Life would be better for you if you would just give in. Everyone else has to. What makes you think you're so damned special?"

Taiuki stiffened. "What is so wrong with being different, Kei? If you know so much, tell me."

Her sister sneered. "It weakens the school, the fleet, and the kingdom. You know this is true. You lash it out of the trainees in the garrison. Mother has tried to lash it out of you. Don't you see that it weakens all of Shiggo, and could tear it apart?"

"Don't you see that your dalliance with Krita does the same thing?" Taiuki was beyond anger, beyond any sensibility of Anella's slack-jawed presence. All she could comprehend was the blatant hypocrisy of Kei's and Mother's actions and perspective.

Her sister winced as though she had been slapped, and by the current, Taiuki wanted to make that a reality. But she wouldn't. She was not their mother.

Kei backed down and flounced to a different chair, a high-legged one next to an elevated round table. She snapped her fingers at Tan. "Get me a drink, Tan-sho."

He rushed to obey, cracking a cabinet in the back of the room and pulling a bottle out. He sloshed its contents into two glasses and handed one to each of his sisters, begging without words for them to resolve their differences.

When neither eased, he sighed and poured a third for himself, then sat heavily next to Anella. "Anyway, I think our latest platoon of archers will be ready to deploy soon," he muttered. "When the arch commodore rotates back with the injured, we'll send them to the front."

Kei looked bored. "Enough of war. Want to hear something funny? A few weeks ago, we received a message from the land kingdom of Mirat, *summoning* a Waterpriest." She snorted and took a sip of her drink. "Some blather about their prince needing their expertise. It came off rather presumptuous and demanding, so Mother and I declined." She gave them a prim, nasty smile as though she had won some game, and directed it mostly at Taiuki. "So if you think we bow to anyone, you're wrong."

"I never said—"

Kei dismissed her protest with the flick of a hand. "We Shiggon-jin are the most powerful people in the sea, the most powerful *anything* in the sea, and so it will remain. I'm willing to treat with kingdoms that bring glory to Shiggo, so I told them they could come here. If they want to learn something about the Way of the Current, the most powerful and important of the five elements, they can do so on our terms." She emptied her glass and set it on the table with a clink, then hopped from the chair and once more crossed her arms, challenging Taiuki with a cold, lingering look. "No matter how much advice I give you, you ignore it. No matter how good of an example I set, you ignore it. *You* are hopeless, and I'm done worrying about it. Swim alone, *all the way to Krita.*" She clicked the last few words, likely to save face in front of Anella. Then she swept away, her elegant Kritali-style train rustling along the floor.

The drawing room was still for a while, the silence broken only by the hushed words of comfort Tan was giving to Anella as he held her hand. She looked stricken, her cheeks wan and her eyes glassy.

Taiuki tipped her glass back and realized it was empty. She needed more, something strong to sear the memories away, to fog the clarity of all her nightmares and worries. As she moved away, Anella caught her wrist.

"Yuki, I'm sorry."

Taiuki raised an eyebrow. "For what?"

"I know you don't want to marry my brother. I know you don't want to live in Krita. I'm sorry you don't get to choose." She sniffled, and Tan handed her a kerchief. The princess blew her nose in a very unladylike fashion, and it began to redden. "Most of all, I'm sorry that I'm one of them. Everything you hate. Everything Keiki hates, although she won't admit it. The only thing she likes about me is my clothes." She had worked herself into a shuddering, hiccupping cry.

Tan looked lost as to what to do, so Taiuki handed the kerchief back to him and pulled Anella to the window. She turned the girl's shoulders toward the vast Mana Loi.

"Look. Do you see the farmers, tending the fields?"

Anella sniffled again and nodded.

"Do you see the trade caravans in the distance? The ships filled with mariners?"

Again, a disheartened acknowledgment.

"The city on the slopes, small homes and shops, townspeople going about their business?" She turned Anella toward herself and gave her shoulder a light squeeze. "We are different, but not as different as I once thought. I don't hate you."

Fresh tears poured down Anella's cheeks, but this time they were joyous. She beamed back, the pretty shades of green—as varied as the mottled depths of a kelp forest—sparkling in her Kritali eyes. Without warning, the girl threw her arms around Taiuki and hugged her.

Taiuki grunted with both surprise and dismay, and pushed her lightly off. "Decorum, Nelly."

Not unexpectedly, Tan laughed.

73

THEY TRAVELED ALONG THE waterway without much conversation, save for Thordrin's one-sided chatter at Mikaa. The nights had darkened with the new first moon, and their progress slowed until the larger second moon, just now waning, emerged low in the sky.

Summer was waning too. Despite the daytime heat, Tahayi didn't hold its temperature in the darkness, and some of the nights could be chilly. Likewise, winter was miserable with a bone-penetrating cold that screamed across the flats from the north. Autumn was coming, and the cooling nights reminded Konan of his last moments with Isellan, a bitter memory he'd rather not have. Konan thanked the sky he wouldn't have to endure another season huddled in the crack-filled shack, his grimy shirt and patchy pants freezing to his skin.

In any case, this night was a bit cool, as though a squall were forming.

He could sense the heaviness of the air, something he formerly would not have put faith into, but now . . .

Melancholy filled him as he reflected on the dead Haralal, and he spied Mikaa, who rode comfortably at the lead beside Thordrin. Twice she had guided them around sinking sand in the flats, and she pointed them down the most practical routes through an increasingly difficult landscape. She foraged more pakla as she spotted it, tossing the fruits into her satchel so thoughtlessly he almost doubted she had properly identified it. Navigating Tahayi was simple for her.

Konan wasn't sure what to call her. A servant? A slave? The Manalal had meant for her to be a slave, but he certainly didn't want her. It wasn't right to own another person's soul. He suspected Lyra felt the same way; he was nearly certain wayfarers didn't have slaves in their caravans. Thordrin was the one most likely to keep Mikaa, although he didn't treat her poorly and hadn't done anything to restrain her yet. His flirting was shameless, his repetition of the common language persistent if not patient. There was little reason for Mikaa to leave with her tribe gone.

The stream trickled down a sandy flume in the rocks, which became more and more of a gully as they moved. Mikaa eventually directed them away from the riverbed and up the sloped bank, where they could see the landscape ahead.

Looking eastward, Konan saw the stream grow to a small but permanent feature, accumulating enough strength to carve deeper into the earth. It smoothed rock walls as it splashed by and cascaded over larger rocks. A canyon developed far off, large enough that they would not likely want to stay by the river despite the flat path, for they may not be able to get out again.

Instead, they began to follow the upland edges and flat areas when available. The going was rougher as the more abundant water fed an increasing number of scraggly bushes, gnarled and lean trees, and wispy grasses. The cacti abounded, not only in random sentinels, but also spiky ground cover and round patches of low-growing bulbs. The variety of vegetation was astounding for what was still temperate desert.

Konan had never imagined Tahayi could be like this.

The sand gave way to colorful shale chips and red, granular soil, overlaid on a red-and-pink-striped sandstone. Among the thickets, more and larger lizards scurred, tiny birds flitted across the canyon diving for minute flies, and small rodents dove for burrows as they passed by. Lone birds of prey occasionally dove upon the skittering flashes of movement, silent and deadly, and Konan even caught a glimpse of a dusky brown fox.

The presence of animals was a boon and a relief, for they could easily hunt for more as well as forage.

As the landscape became more treacherous and variable, they rested for a greater part of the night, from a few bells after dusk till the Nether hour. Konan knew that Lyra was frustrated with the pace, as desperate as she was to return to her family, but they had to be cautious as they neared their destination of the seacoast. An injury through misstep would be incredibly foolish at this point.

You're a fool, Noble-Heart. Her half-furious, half-teasing words echoed in his mind. The sensation of her touch was enough to excite him in the saddle, and he thanked the Light she rode her own mount. She knew the effect she had on him, and although she didn't seem to revel in it, she came to him each time they rested. It confused him, for she consistently encouraged him to return to Mirat, to claim his birthright and dispense justice as he must.

The dawn brought no light, for the sky churned with tumultuous black clouds. They danced down from the north, burgeoning into a threatening storm, something he had never seen in the mines.

They threw their camp together in a protected hollow. Thordrin built a small fire mound, stacking it with sandstone slabs in such a way that it might survive the rain. The fuel was plentiful and dry, and before long, he had a warm bed of coals. Konan pitched the tent, stretching it across as much space as possible, while Mikaa and Lyra prepared a meal of stewed cactus fruits and sliced succulent leaves. It was a sour but refreshing meal, and Mikaa straightened at their compliments.

She crept beside Thordrin, who nestled his back against a large, vertical slab of pink-streaked stone. The stone reflected the fire's subtle heat pleasantly, and he stretched his legs out, alternately extending each one with a groan.

Mikaa extended an inquisitive hand over his thigh and raised her dark eyebrows in query. "Good?" She gently massaged him, working along both inner thighs, then his calves and ankles, rotating his feet expertly.

He sighed with relief. "Told you she was a good prize," he muttered.

Mikaa made the same offer to Konan, but he refused. He could sense Lyra considering, and she even reached over to his knee. Her fingers hesitated above his skin, and he stopped her.

"But you're probably more sore than he is," she murmured, her expression a mixture of confused feelings and guilt.

He pulled her hand to himself and brushed his lips across her knuckles, then proceeded to massage his own legs. She was right. He was stiff and exhausted. She watched him, then proceeded to knead his shoulders.

Konan kept looking up at the sky. Its heaviness was overwhelming, its wetness crackling with energy. He wondered what it felt like to Lyra, for the thunderstorm seemed to combine their elements so thoroughly the two aspects couldn't be separated. She kept glancing up as well, biting her lip nervously.

The wind rose.

They all piled into their shelter right before the rain came, a downpour accompanied by flashes of lightning and pounding thunder. Konan had supplied them with a pile of furs to defray the chill, and he tucked Lyra into the inner corner.

To his delight, she rolled over and tugged him closer. As she lay her head in the crook of his shoulder, and her fingers danced across his tunic to the opening where his chest hair protruded, she laughed. "The Air is electric with power," she said. "I feel like I'm drowning in it. You know what I mean?"

He acknowledged her, reveling in the feeling. The rain was immersive, ripe with energy and refreshing to his body as it splashed a few inches from the top of his head and toes.

Lyra shivered with the sudden chill and cuddled closer.

She doesn't need a lover, he warned himself. *Not yet, and perhaps never.*

Another slim, cold body crept under the blankets, wriggling up between him and Thordrin. Mikaa nuzzled into the Phantom with a coquettish smile. "Is good?"

Thordrin traced her shape from shoulder to hip beneath the furs, then wrangled her close, and she lay her head on his chest much like Lyra had done to Konan. However, her fingers seemed to wander far more than Lyra's did. Her hips shimmied until her legs were over his, and Thordrin's smug, ever-hungry expression appeared as they settled down.

By the Light, if Lyra ever looked at Konan like that . . .

He watched the desert light up intermittently with the storm for a few more minutes, and he inhaled the power around him with a deep, slow sigh. Lyra already breathed the regular, soft rhythm of sleep, and he stroked the ticklish wisps of wild curls from his chin. She smelled of pungent cactus flowers, subtly spicy herbs from her medicines, and the richly perfumed palmnut oil of her hair. He ached for her, for everything about her. Her pain was his, as was her joy. Finally, basking in the storm and everything it wrought, he slept.

Late afternoon revealed a new desert. The greenery was virescent, the blue sky azure. The wind was fresher, and the stream in the canyon below sang with the influx of lightly turbid water flashing downstream.

The sun reappeared and dried everything more quickly than Konan could have imagined, and he got up reluctantly. Lyra moaned resistance, and he tried to tuck the furs back around her as he slipped out. She woke up anyway. With a shy smile, she brandished a knife and departed for a quick hunt, wandering down the rocky escarpments toward the water.

Konan, for his part, foraged near the camp, hoping to find more pakla or the particular succulent that Mikaa recommended for stews. Shortly, he praised the Eye Lyra had gone.

For from the shelter, he could hear rustling and moaning, then Thordrin's low bass as Mikaa gasped in excitement. Their sounds became rhythmic.

He shook his head.

That man.

He couldn't believe Mikaa had already fallen for his antics, just as easily as had the other Haralali handmaiden. He still didn't know that one's name, and he suspected Thordrin didn't either.

Suddenly, Thordrin's exclamations turned to curses, and he shouted in alarm.

Konan drew his dagger and rushed back, where he found Thordrin staggering from the tent with his tunic unlaced. He spun and made a quick grab for his pants, then backed away.

Mikaa emerged, proudly naked, and babbled at him. She stamped her foot, then dressed herself in a huff. She glowered at Thordrin the entire time.

Konan sheathed his knife and looked from one to the other. "What happened? Did she hurt you?" He gesticulated, trying to convey his question to Thordrin.

Thordrin snarled with frustration. "She fucking—I don't even know! She's not fucking human." He yanked his pants over his manhood and snapped his belt through its loops.

Lyra appeared and goggled at the scene, then stepped up beside Konan. He wrapped his cloak around her shoulder as though she needed protection, but Mikaa didn't seem that dangerous. She seemed spurned.

She glowered at each of them in turn, then began gesticulating with a sharply pointed finger (he didn't remember her having long nails before) and shouting in Haralali.

The woman went on for minutes, and tears streamed down her face as she grew more and more incensed. Her cheeks darkened, and her pupils grew until her eyes were entirely black. Her nose shrank somewhat, and her nostrils turned to slits. The finger now pointed at them elongated to a claw, and her skin extending to her shoulder shimmered with brownish-gray scales. She finally stopped, leaving her final furious scowl directed at Thordrin.

Her transformation was followed by a brief silence.

"By I'ya," Lyra finally whispered. "The Godspeaker said the Haralal weren't people."

"Hafka said the same thing to me," said Konan.

Thordrin echoed his words at the same time. "Jikaa called them monsters—didn't give a shit about slaughtering them all, man, woman, and child."

As they watched, Mikaa reverted to fully human form as she calmed, but she still glared.

"She looks human now," said Thordrin. "What the fuck."

"The Godspeaker called them 'gyr,' I think," Lyra suggested in wonder.

This seemed to spur Mikaa into another attempt to communicate, this time with exasperation rather than anger. Her smooth, dark skin repeatedly flushed into scales and back, and her pupils shifted to black slits again. Konan caught "Tho'jinn" and "gyr" in her response.

That roused a vague memory for him, of studying the Five Faces and their unique properties in a dusty, dark room with the walls covered in scrolls. The mage repeated something, tapping the paper with a thick finger. The room smelled of herbs and dry parchment.

"Gyr, the people of Fire," he said.

"Impossible," said Lyra, squinting. "There weren't any people of Fire left."

"Like the myrpeople, they still have magical form in their blood," Konan signed, still staring at Mikaa. "They can change."

Lyra interpreted, and Thordrin sneered. "Into what? Damn it all." He straightened his tunic and tucked it back into his pants, cinching his belt tight.

"The gyr were reptilian," he signed slowly, trying to recall those vague lessons. "They were hated by the Empire. I don't know much more. It was a fragment of history I didn't appreciate at the time."

Lyra interpreted automatically, then let out a horrified gasp. "After the Cleansing," she whispered, "they must have run to the edge of the world to escape, and even now the Manalal hate them." She began to tear up as she stared at the other woman. "Oh, Mikaa."

A dark, beautiful creature, Mikaa stood proudly, as though she knew exactly what they were talking about. She seemed to comprehend their shift to reluctant tolerance, and she lowered her accusatory finger. "Mikaa gyr, Mikaa good," she insisted, raising her chin. "Tho'jinn, Ko'ninn, Lee-ra no gyr."

"Tell her it's okay," signed Konan.

Lyra repeated his suggestion meekly.

Thordrin winced with chagrin, but he put on his best conciliatory voice. "Mikaa, you are good. We may not be gyr, but we're good too. We're friends." He opened his arms, although Konan noticed he didn't step forward. It was the most reluctance Konan had ever seen in the Phantom, especially for a beautiful woman. Was that what she was?

Mikaa examined Thordrin doubtfully, scanning him up and down as though displeased that he was fully clothed. She repeated her heavily accented words. "Mikaa are gyr, Mikaa are good. Yes?"

"Yes," Thordrin affirmed.

"Yes," Lyra echoed passionately, her tears unrestrained.

"'Friends' are fam'lee?" Mikaa cocked her head and waited for their answer.

"Yes, Mikaa." Thordrin finally stepped forward and touched her arm in a conciliatory gesture. "Friends are family."

Konan raised his brows at that, wondering how she knew the word for family, but then again, she was an attentive listener. She probably picked up more than they realized, and Thordrin had been blathering at her since the battle.

Mikaa flickered her slitted gaze down to Thordrin's touch, then his face, and seemed satisfied. She gave him a haughty expression and tossed her black hair. "Mikaa fam'lee are no gyr, fam'lee are yes good."

74

LYRA TORE HERSELF FROM the scene as Thordrin consoled Mikaa with exaggerated affability.

Mikaa encapsulated everything foreign to her: sexuality, effortless beauty and confidence, and this strange, frightening, demihuman character. Gyr? People of Fire?

She had heard of myrpeople, of course. They were a known part of the world, if secluded and supposedly somewhat barbaric. She had never met one, as they tended to stay in their underwater kingdoms and refused to trade.

But gyr? Reptilian people who could shift their skin and senses—that was a lost aspect of humanity wiped out by the Luminaries a thousand years ago. Yet Mikaa seemed to see in the dark and could sniff out water and food in the vast, parched land she called home.

She pulled Konan with her to hunt, and to talk.

"I should have realized, that's why Korahel and Mirra didn't like the other handmaiden," she lamented. She had judged the woman so harshly, especially because her licentious behavior with Thordrin reminded Lyra of her own brokenness. "I thought the snake was simply a slave brand, but it was a specific label to set the Haralal apart."

Konan nodded, somber as ever, and pointed at a lizard that scuttled after the buzzing insects. She threw, but she missed. The lizards were more active at dawn and dusk, and she realized that Mikaa was too, and that when they rested during the daytime the woman, would often bask unprotected in the sunshine. It was a miracle she wasn't burnt, like Lyra would be. Perhaps people with Fire in their blood couldn't burn.

She hit her next mark, and Konan gutted and rinsed it as she continued hunting.

"Mikaa is so alone," she continued. "When I heard Thor shout, I thought he was hurt, and I was terrified, but then I saw something beautiful. She *belongs* here, or she did until we took her away from her home." The tears spilled out uncontrollably. Her chest ached and her stomach churned with the awfulness of Mikaa's solitude.

Konan finished the next carcass and came over to her, placing a staying hand on her knife and motioning for her to sit beside him. Tucking her knife into her wrist bracer, she did, and his knotted bicep burned against hers. *By the Light, if only you would hold me.* Instead, he signed.

"We cannot undo the past, songbird," he said. His signs were ponderous, as though he himself were wading through the mire of confusion and guilt. "We did what we believed to be right to help the Manalal, as we had to do, and in turn hurt Mikaa's people. Guilt is a bleeding wound in the heart, but it will heal if you let it."

"Should it, though?" she wondered.

His throat bobbed up and down, and he nodded. "One of a thousand scars that become a part of you. Don't deny it, for we did a terrible thing to Mikaa and her people. Accept it and let it guide you."

"Claim your scars," she repeated, staggering between resigned acceptance of his words and irate rejection. His own melancholy revealed his shame for their sins.

Lyra pushed under his muscular arm and tucked herself against him, and he wrapped her in his embrace. She buried her head in his chest, where she didn't have to think. The fine, dark hairs above his shirt line tickled her nose, and his musk mixed with sweat and dust in a way that both frightened and entranced her. She breathed it in with an audible sigh, and she heard his heart thump a little harder.

Turning, she compiled her private thoughts into a tiny Whisper, which formed on Konan's knee. The bird cocked its head at her when she told it to find Elaisa or Elden, and it chittered at her before launching into the sky. She raised her head to watch it fly, then settled back against Konan.

He followed its path and released her to sign. "Did that head due south?"

Lyra nodded, somewhat surprised herself. His aptitude for detecting her Air magika was impressive, although he said he couldn't see them clearly. The Whispers' routes had shifted as their party traveled eastward, implying to Lyra that her family may have stopped in a town before reaching Corronei. That was slightly behind the caravan's typical schedule, as it would miss the high summer dances in the capital. Such events represented a substantial piece of income—the winemakers of Marlemet were often generous with their product, and coin flowed as freely as the wine. Why, the Maskalan would make entire marks in a single week. She had thought they'd have passed through weeks before and would now be south of Corronei along the coast.

Lyra peered southward, as if she might see some sign.

"We cannot be that far from the sea," said Konan. "Perhaps we should follow the Whispers and meet up with your family now that we've left the dry territories. I don't think the Bleeding Wall extends this far east." He trailed off, squinting southward like she did.

"I would appreciate that," said Lyra. All she wanted was to hug Elden and ask Mam how she had opened the Gate, crossing Tahayi instantly to take Lyra's undeveloped baby. Bitterness and bile rose up from her belly at the reminder, and Lyra flung a knife out in a huff, impaling and bowling over a large lizard.

Konan quietly redirected his intensity at her. His big hand slid down her arm and pulled her closer, sending a shiver through her, and she felt his thumb begin its usual caress on her skin. She buried her face once again. He always knew her thoughts.

"Nice throw, love," called Thordrin.

Lyra peeked out. The man perched on a large rock nearby, casual as ever, munching on a pakla fruit.

Konan straightened. "Let's head south from here," he signed, pointing in the direction the Whisper had flown.

Lyra translated, beseeching. "My family is that way," she added.

Thordrin rolled his eyes. "By the Darkness and the Light, girl, we're so close to the coast. If we head a little farther east, we might find some fishing villages. I'd like some blackeye and crab after all these days of dry desert fare and stringy meat."

"My caravan can't be far," she insisted.

"Yeah, I heard." Thordrin scooted off the rock. Nonetheless, he moved to retrieve the lizard and gutted it with a practiced hand. "When this is cooked, we'll go."

"South?" Lyra asked.

Thordrin glared at her, but Konan grunted and pointed southward, his jaw set and his gaze hard. The other man made a mock bow. "*Yes*, m'lady," he said, dripping with sarcasm. "Fucking pakla for another week . . . You'd think I was serving a queen again." He stalked away, muttering curses, then called back, "I can't wait to drop your whiny ass at that caravan and move on with my life. Damn it all to the nethers."

"Thank you," she whispered to Konan.

He didn't reply, merely presented her with another mysterious note and held her for a while longer. She held the paper close to her heart. His memories, even if she couldn't decipher them, were precious to him, and thus precious to her. She would keep them safe.

They adjusted their heading to that of the last Whisper, nearly due south, and continued at a steady pace. The horses and idraka were content, having had their fill of cool spring water and fresh grass, and they trudged through the thick scrub in a loose group. The vegetation now included richly green bushes with narrow leaves and yellow florets; sprigs of wildflowers in pure white, bluish violet, and flaming orange; and the occasional apita tree.

Mikaa dropped back to the end of their caravan, apparently out of favor and unneeded as the terrain eased to the south. Again, Lyra wondered why she stayed. *She has nowhere else to go,* said the bitter voice inside her. *She is one of your bleeding scars.*

Thordrin led the way as usual. He spoke little, a rare thing for him, sulking quietly except to mutter curses directed at Lyra.

Konan rode beside her whenever he could, until he suddenly reined back on his gelding. Lyra noted how much his horsemanship had improved since they first met the Manalal. She reined back as well, and both their horses nickered.

Konan sat now with a stiff posture, partially proper but overly rigid, and stared eastward. He wavered as he stood in the stirrups.

"Do you smell that?" he signed. "Salt and minerals . . . perhaps the ocean?"

"You can sense the ocean?" Lyra asked, awed. When she felt the air, it had such character, such strength and purity, and she reveled in it. Was that how he felt as they neared the Mana Loi?

Thordrin groaned. "You're telling me we're *that* close?" He turned an acidic look upon Lyra, and she became flustered.

Konan shook his head. "It's like a weight, drawing me eastward from far away. It feels . . . massive but not heavy, dynamic but permanent." He came to himself and gave Lyra a sheepish look. "It tastes like salt." He spit to the side as if trying to rid his mouth of the flavor.

Lyra laughed, a childish giggle that startled her own ears with its lightness. She understood. When the caravan had stopped in Shayal City, the wakeway had reeked of fish and waste; the scent had polluted the air in such a thorough manner that she had nearly been overwhelmed. "Have you ever seen the ocean?"

She rued asking, for he turned stoic and sad once again.

"Well you would have by now, if we hadn't turned," Thordrin rejoined. He sneered at Lyra. "Damn you, girl. When I get rid of you, I'm gonna do what I want. Kill Rigaran, and then kill Prince Reylin Harkin, first of his name, for *this* fucking madman."

Konan growled, but Thordrin reached over and stayed his reins.

"Don't misunderstand me. I'm going to help you. A king for a king, justice for the wicked." He grinned and let go.

Konan's expression hardened, and he whipped his reins to move away.

For once, Thordrin didn't vie for the front position. Instead he pulled back to ride next to Lyra. He patted his stallion, urging them south as she had demanded. The horse whipped its head with reluctant acceptance of his touch. He had broken its fury through a combination of hard will and tender affection, a strange side of him to see. The man threw one more snide comment at Konan's back. "Nethers, he's touchy for someone who thinks he can be king."

She measured him with a dubious side-eye, and her mare picked up on her nerves with an audible, nostril-flaring blow.

"You do realize he's fuckin' mad, right? Be glad you're not coming with us, girl. That stubborn goatfuck's gonna throw a whole kingdom into chaos."

"And you're not?"

Thordrin shrugged carelessly. "Rigaran's got sons, and he deserves it." He flashed a toothy, cold smile at her. He was like a predator, a ghastwolf or a makran, baring its fangs.

"I don't see how it's any different. You're planning to murder someone."

Thordrin snorted his disdain. "It's hardly murder when they've already tried to kill you. It's retribution. Your 'prince' is the one murdering."

Conflicting arguments raced through Lyra's mind. "Unless his story is true," she struggled to say. "Then it's retribution too. He's not hurting innocent people by reclaiming his crown from a usurper."

"You tell yourself that every time before you fall into his arms?"

She felt the heat of embarrassment tingle across her neck, face, even her chest.

"Anyway, that was twelve years ago," he continued as if trying to convince himself. "Konan said he was in the mines for ten."

More than ten, she thought. "You really don't believe him?" she asked.

Thordrin scoffed. "You do? Look, Lyr, some men are dangerous because they're sane, others because they're not. But sane men are at least predictable. Konan is going to create havoc, whatever he does."

"Then why is he burned?"

Thordrin's expression darkened, and he seemed to seethe at her question. Without another word, he adjusted his pace and moved ahead.

Wispy strokes of cloud painted the horizon as the sun fell lower in the west, yielding a burnished red and orange sky-line. Less than an hour of daylight remained as they climbed a steep, malagate-infused bluff, the trailing end of the Bleeding Wall. Konan paused at the top, waiting for Lyra and the others to catch up. He squinted into the sky to the south.

Lyra followed his gaze. Like a flock of seagulls, Whispers soared in lazy, uncoordinated circles over a copse of apita trees on the next hill, their lost cries piercing Lyra's ears.

"Are those—" Konan began, but Lyra spurred her horse into a gallop.

Her family was close.

She closed the distance, madly waving with one arm and screaming into the trees. The Whispers high above called back at her.

"Mam! Elden!" she cried, urging her mare onward faster with a deft squeeze of her legs. The horse tore into the copse, yielding an opening in the center. Lyra shifted her full weight back, and the horse whinnied as it came to a panting halt.

Raucous, distressed Whispers and the heaving froth of the horse's breath were the only sounds in the expansive glade. The charred remains of numerous wagons lined the edges of the circular opening, piles of snapped and collapsed tinder. Rotten canvas hung in frays from matchstick bows, which arched awkwardly into the air, their original wagon base fixtures now gone. Hundreds of bodies, skin blackened to sheets of stretched leather and bones partially exposed, littered the glade.

Lyra's horse snorted and pranced about, echoing Lyra's own reaction. Everything was clear, lucid like the radiant colors one would see through wet eyes right before the tears flooded out. Brimming. The bone was stark white, bleached where it was exposed on ribcages, and there on the neck and jaw. Eye sockets were shadows. Laughing grins were incomplete as teeth dropped away and buried themselves in the soil. Desiccated skin crumpled itself onto hands and legs like large swaths of coal-black wet paper.

The leaves on the late summer apitas were a rich evergreen—*Was that the verdant world beyond the Gate?*—and the soil a deep fertile brown. The blood pooled under corpses was not red like the setting sun, but rather a polluted blackening of the earth, a lingering stain. Brightly patterned bits of textile burst from the scene, adhered to their corpses in decomposing glory, shouting their magnificent weave and color.

Lyra's eye was drawn to a familiar swatch, which flapped off a skeleton leaning against a half-burnt wagon wheel. Burgundy, finely woven with black and purple stitches forming a floral pattern, edged with tiny bells that had now fallen to the ground. A slight patina of copper told her they were still there. An arrow pierced through the eye socket and was lodged in place, and most of the skin had already peeled away from the face. But the hair remained, a tangle of reddish-blonde curls with gaudy, colored beads woven to the ends. Elaisa laughed at her daughter with gleaming white teeth.

Not taking her eyes off her mother, Lyra slipped off her horse and stumbled to the body, falling to her knees and half crawling to the corpse. Everything around it was a blur, but the body was more resolved in her vision than reality, like a fever dream. She fondled the edge of the burgundy fabric.

"Mam?" she whispered, barely managing to form the word.

A bird alighted on the ground next to them and cocked its head at Lyra. It cheeped at her several times, then looked pointedly at the skeleton, then back at her before taking off again to circle with the other Whispers. Their cries were intolerable, their confusion overwhelming.

Immersed in the chaos of her lost Whispers, Lyra wept.

75

KONAN RUSHED AFTER LYRA, urging his own horse to an uncomfortable pace between a gallop and a trot. He didn't have the stride quite right. Lyra's excited shouts bounced through the trees to his ears, and he eagerly pushed his horse faster. Lyra's exultation was infectious.

But there are no signs of a camp, no smoke and no movement, a small voice said inside, just as he burst into the copse's broad meadow opening. *No sounds.*

The glade was still, save for Lyra's prancing mare, which sidestepped away from them with a fearful wicker. His own gelding adopted the same anxiety and bucked, tossing Konan to the ground. He landed on a rotten haulbeast carcass with a clattering of bone on bone, but he quickly got up and ran to Lyra.

She sat on her knees near the remains of a wagon, her head limply bowed. She had crawled so close to a corpse, her nose almost touched its sternum. Lyra's mouth hung slack, and her eyes were dull and glazed as she panted in shallow, uneven gasps. Then she began to plead with the body in indecipherable mumbles, burying her tears in the frail red cloth that covered half of it.

Konan stood back, watching her as she clung to the corpse. Little but cloth and integument held the body together, but he felt any interruption of Lyra's grief would be an unwelcome infringement, so he resisted pulling her away.

"Unholy fuck," murmured Thordrin from the edge of the opening. His voice traveled far in the deafening silence. The Phantom mastered his stallion, and Mikaa likewise controlled the entire train of livestock. They had entered the copse quietly and at an indolent pace, being in no particular hurry to meet the Maskalan clan. Mikaa tied her horse and train to a tree in the copse, away from the massacre, then captured both stray horses for Konan and Lyra. Thordrin dismounted and looked around, taking the entire scene in as he walked toward Konan. He heaved a depressed sigh. "I guess I'm not getting rid of the girl then, eh, Noble-Heart?"

Konan narrowed his eyes, feeling the tautness on his left brow.

Thordrin shrugged helplessly, then raised his eyebrows, which created a few shallow furrows across his flat forehead. He seemed to take the massacre before them in stride, as if the stench of decay didn't fill his nose or linger on his boots.

"You're an asshole, Thor," Konan signed, flinging the insult with sharp hand movements.

Thordrin scoffed. "Hey, I know that one. That's rude. I expected more refinement from a prince."

"If you have no respect for her, at least give homage to the dead," Konan replied, signing furiously at the man, who promptly ignored him.

Mikaa approached, examining her surroundings with obvious distress and stepping with care to avoid the polluted puddles of blood dried into soil. She stopped short when she saw Lyra stretched over the red-cloaked body.

"Lee-ra fam'lee?"

Konan nodded.

The woman shook with horror, and she slumped with knees quavering.

"By the Darkness and Light," Thordrin cursed as he caught her by the elbow, gently letting her all the way down.

Mikaa didn't seem to notice as she relived her own tragedy for minutes. Then she crawled over to Lyra, muttering platitudes in Haralali and plucking at Lyra's dress.

Lyra didn't acknowledge the other woman, instead clutching tightly to the half-rotten corpse. The tenuous connection between the corpse's skull and body gave way, and the entire skeleton buckled with a horrible sound. The skull hung by its piercing arrow, which had lodged deeply into the wagon's wooden frame. Lyra gasped at the dreadful sight and leaned back, then retched. She made no effort to remove herself from the mire, returning to a despondent slump, and Konan and Mikaa pulled her backward out of the vomit and rot.

What struck Konan was how utterly still the meadow was. No breeze ruffled his hair, and not a leaf twitched on the apitas. The miasma of horse and man sat like a fog. Catatonic, like her. The sun set, and still no hint of breeze touched them. The fog of graying necrosis hung over the copse, weighty and stale.

Lyra lay where they put her as they rinsed her filthy hands and face with water. He found a spot without bloodied soil and pulled her into his arms. She reeked of stomach acid and putrid decay, and she did not return his embrace. Instead, she sat in a stupor.

Lyra. How badly he wanted to talk to her, to comfort her. A sound escaped his lips as he shifted her body, pulling her hips closer to his and her knees to one side. He turned her head toward him, nuzzling her under his chin and stroking her hair. Her skinny arms were limp at her side, and her breath was shallow. For once, she didn't continue weeping. Her glazed eyes had dried, now as nonreactive as the rest of her. He rocked her for a while, fighting his own gathering tear that tickled down his right cheek into his rough beard.

Mikaa frantically chattered and worried over her, plucking constantly at her skirts. "Lee-ra, Lee-ra, we are fam'lee. Mikaa fam'lee. Fam'lee good." Then she digressed in Haralali. She shot a panicked look at Thordrin, but the Phantom merely shrugged.

"I suppose she'll come with us to Krita then," he said to Konan, crossing his arms. He sounded annoyed.

"Her family deserves justice," said Konan, disregarding in his haste that Thordrin wouldn't understand. "We should inquire in Corronei. Do you think it was bandits?" He didn't believe his own words. Everything was wrong. Hundreds of corpses littered the glade; hundreds of Maskalan wayfarers. Women, children, horses, dogs.

Thordrin looked around. "Like I've said before, you can do anything to a maunderer, and no one cares." He stepped toward the skull and yanked the arrow out, making the skull clatter to the ground on top of other bones. A tiny bell tinkled. He inspected the arrowhead. "This was military. Had to be. Fuck's sake, there's over 250 bodies here."

Lyra twitched, and her crystalline gaze finally focused on him. She mouthed a word so softly he couldn't hear it, and he pulled her closer. He sensed her summoning power, forming it and spinning it into a tiny, birdlike shape on his shoulder. The weak thing bobbed to his ear and dispersed.

"Justice," it chirped in Lyra's voice.

She pulled away, staggering to her feet. Her chest heaved, and her mouth opened and closed over and over as she surveyed the massacre.

Konan jumped to his feet to accompany her, to ensure she didn't trip or faint.

She shuffled a few steps forward, back toward the vomit-covered corpse and wagon, then paused. Her half-clenched fingers trembled in front of her face. And then, she let out a soul-wrenching wail, high and torturous and disconsolate.

Konan caught her as her cry diminished, her lithe frame so light in his arms that he believed she really might be a shell, emptied of every ounce of life she had once contained. He swept her up and dipped his forehead to hers.

I'm here, Lyra.

He couldn't stand to look at the devastation any longer. Although it had gone unspoken, the place of death was not where they would rest their bodies or souls.

Lyra had slipped into a coma-like state, dull and dispassionate. Konan resolved to carrying her. The rot of the corpse was on her clothes and skin, paired with vomit. He settled her securely in front of himself, thanking Mikaa as she took the mare and tied it to their line of animals.

They intercepted a major road farther southward and rode through the night to reach the outskirts of Corronei, where they found an inn. The motherly woman who opened the door gasped with horror upon seeing their state, and she nearly snatched Lyra from him.

"Light's end, draw a bath," she commanded her bleary-eyed husband, who disappeared to a backroom immediately.

The woman evaluated Konan with a combination of horror and distrust, her soft chin jiggling and her mouth pulled down at the corners.

Thordrin barged past him and snapped at her. "We're *with* her, woman. Don't look at him like he's responsible. We need a room for the night." It was the least suave Konan had ever seen Thordrin be, and the woman placed her hands on her wide hips and frowned.

She softened when Mikaa entered and tugged on Thordrin's cloak, then pursed her lips and sighed through her nose. "Come, come in. Be welcome and find your rest. You're obviously with her, and you smell like you need a rinse too. Warm your heart by our hearth, *after* your bath." She looked pointedly at Konan.

She showed them to a room, then pointed at a bathing room where a tub was available. "My husband will fill it shortly."

Konan watched her disappear into an adjacent room with Lyra slung over her hefty shoulder. Her husband exited the room and locked it with a key around his neck, then proceeded to fill the available bath with an elaborate faucet mechanism connected to pipes.

"I hope you can pay for this," the man muttered.

Konan nodded and jingled a coin purse on his belt.

The innkeeper harrumphed but brought him into the room. "Not sure we have much to replace your sullied clothing, but we can wash what you're wearing."

Konan indicated that he had clothing in the room; Mikaa had brought a small sack in already.

The man grumbled, taking his filthy Manalali clothing with a disgusted frown. "I'll return these in the morning then." He left a loose outer robe and a drying towel.

Konan washed swiftly, attuned to the sounds in the next room. Through the thin walls, he could hear the innkeeper's wife dismayed exclamations mixed with idle chatter meant to distract Lyra. Lyra said nothing, nor did she whimper or cry.

He thought of the stillness of the glade. The stillness of death.

The halted breath of Isellan, the blood seeping into the sand and coagulating. The black ring of Lyra's knife target.

What once was savory and rich with life was gone.

What remained?

He trudged toward his room and paused outside the door, hearing the telltale sounds within.

Mikaa moaned, and Thordrin spoke in a low voice, words Konan couldn't understand. The Phantom had his own way of processing his aggravation, and apparently Mikaa did too. Loneliness did strange things to men, and any solace seemed like it would be welcome on this dark night. Anything to make it feel less suffocating. The two escalated their attempts to fill the empty void. Thordrin stopped speaking, and Mikaa's moans lengthened and loudened.

He left quickly.

The innkeeper sat on a stool outside Lyra's bathing room, his jaw set and a hand on his belt knife. He grimaced at Konan's approach but then pulled another stool over.

"May as well have a seat."

Konan obeyed, shifting his mass onto the small, creaking chair and leaning against the wall with a sigh. He could feel the man's eyes on him.

"What happened to her?" the innkeeper asked.

Konan signed and pointed to his mouth. "Forgive me."

The innkeeper took a deep breath through his nose, much like his wife had done. "I see. Well, my wife said she didn't look to be physically hurt, but she's quite distraught at the girl's condition."

Konan nodded.

"She's with you?" It wasn't really a question, and the innkeeper eased back to a more conversational tone. "Strange things been happenin' around here. Violence, fear in the streets, rumors like you wouldn't believe."

Konan perked up, giving the man his full attention.

He shied back a little. "You haven't heard? Come from the west, have you? Seems like it hasn't touched there."

Konan grimly nodded again.

"Yessir, the folks traveling from Shayal talk about nothing but the summer drought and the fire at their mine, not sure if they were connected. Folks from Corronei proper, though, they been sharing some pretty odd tales. Seems like some sickness came in through the port, nasty business."

"Tell me more," Konan signed, beseeching with his contorted facial expression as best he could.

"Not much real information to tell. Knights mutter nonsense about security. Mages don't respond at all. What I heard was that the sickness messes with your mind, makes you go feral. I heard tell there were groups of madmen scouring the countryside out here, murdering travelers, but there's no evidence. A whole caravan is said to have disappeared, but the man who told me that was certain that was only a rumor. The sick are mindless—they fight without reason or strategy. An entire caravan would be nigh impossible to take down."

He shook his head and clicked his tongue. "What I do *know* is we've seen a lot of strange deaths, like the baker's son committing suicide. He was a happy young man, prime of his life, set to marry some pretty gal from a vineyard west of here. The baker and his wife committed suicide shortly after. Then their neighbor disappeared, hasn't been heard from since. Then a string of murders, terrible violent, the next hamlet over, no connections among the victims. And just last week, one of the farmers who came in for market came down sick while in town, went to head home, and got trampled by his horse. Creature stomped him to nothing, then ran off."

The dour man sighed again.

"I really don't know more than that, sir, but I can say I'm glad you brought your women to a safe place for the night. Streets are risky right now, whatever's going on."

Konan mulled over the innkeeper's words in silence, unable to respond in any meaningful way. He ground his teeth. Was it madmen? The extent of the destruction of the Maskalan caravan was incomprehensible, the mercilessness unimaginable. Beside Lyra's mother's corpse had been a smaller shape, a child. He assumed it was Elden. What kind of disease would cause that sort of violence, or was it explained by something simpler: the inherent evil and cruelty of man?

It wouldn't fix a damned thing, but perhaps Lyra could find closure in knowing what happened.

They both straightened at new sounds from behind the wooden door. The innkeeper stood and unlocked it with his precious key, revealing Lyra hanging despondent on the older woman's shoulder.

She was clean, hair freshly oiled and combed. The innkeeper's wife had dressed her in an overly revealing traditional nightshift, too low in the neckline and too high on the ankles. Lyra's breast bindings peeked out from the generous cut, and Konan could tell his notes were missing. He scowled and took her gently in his arms, trying to avoid looking at the exposed skin.

The innkeeper's wife put her hands on her hips and frowned. "What, I wasn't going to put her previous clothes on without a wash, not a chance in the lowest Gate."

Her husband agreed, and she raised a finger at Konan and chided him. "If you think I was going to put those filthy rags back on her . . ."

She paused when he mimicked a writing motion, then retreated into the bathing room with a thoughtful look. Returning, she stuffed the notes into his hand with a tentative smile.

"Do you know where she had them?"

He nodded.

"Can you put them back?"

He shook his head quickly, and her smile stretched across both cheeks. He and her husband turned their faces away as the woman tucked the notes back in place.

She put her hands on her hips again. "Stranger, you are welcome to warm your heart at our hearth anytime. Go on to bed now, and we'll see you in the morning. You all look like you could use a good rest. Sleep does wonders, you know. It'll all seem all right in the morning, by the grace of I'ya *and* a bowl of rice porridge with my special seasonings." She ushered him down the hallway and into the dark room, closing the door softly behind him. "Take good care of her, sir."

Konan laid Lyra down on the bed next to Mikaa, then arranged himself at her side, adjusting her pillows and tucking the blankets tightly around her. She stared dully into the dark rafters, and a small sound escaped her when he wiped the dampness from her cold cheek.

"Endure it," he signed, knowing that wouldn't help. "I'm here."

Lyra nodded, just barely, then leaned her head against his knee. Realizing her want, he readjusted so her head was in his lap and stroked the soft hair at the base of her neck. His other hand grasped hers—her fingers were like a dead woman's—and he leaned against the headboard and closed his eyes.

76

THE NEXT DAY, THORDRIN chartered a ship to Krita, promising Konan passage to North Mara from there.

"I've been there, brother," Thordrin assured him, "plenty of times. All ships stop in Krita Port anyway, so we'll take care of Rigaran first."

They sold all of the horses but Thordrin's stallion, and the idraka made enough profit to pay for the passage. Thordrin lamented Lyra's passive condition as he and Konan made deals to sell most of the Haralali war spoils. They kept a few herbs they had seen her use for pain medicines, some of the finer clothing and jewelry, the armor, and the weapons. Thordrin then purchased a chest for them to store everything, along with a rich black-and-gray Marlemetian suit indicative of his rank.

He parceled out coins to each of them in individual purses: two crowns and a pile of marks. Mikaa marveled at the gift.

"Mikaa are fam'lee?" she inquired, almost confused.

"Yes, Mikaa, you're one of us, and a free woman." Thordrin ruined his response by smirking at Konan. "And even freer in bed. You shoulda seen her scurry last night. And she does bite."

Konan ignored him, intent on securing Lyra's purse somewhere safe on her person. He had instructed Mikaa to dress her in full Haralali mage clothes, something he thought might make her more comfortable, and she sat quietly on the bed in a fine set of crimson robes. The black bodice hugged her figure but sat high on the neck, with a heavy brocade stitched with iridescent beads in the pattern of flying insects. Her skirt fluttered with layers of thin dyed linen, topped by a gauzy black with diamond coin studs. Mikaa had reined in her enthusiasm with jewelry, skipping the pricy handflowers. She did, however, hang a large sunstone from Lyra's neck, insisting it was necessary.

He would have worried that their finery would draw too much scrutiny, but he quickly realized that even in this outer village of the Marlemetian capitol, the fashions were far different. Their Haralali clothing wasn't as resplendent as the form-cut silks of Corronei, and the beauty and complexity of their textiles was wasted on Marlemetian tastes. Face veils weren't common, defraying attention rather than drawing it, which Konan suspected was exactly what Lyra would want.

He raised her silver-coined fringe veil now, fastening it to her headpiece. They were nearly ready to leave.

"Songbird, I learned something about what may have happened to your family," he signed. "Do you want to hear it?"

She blinked slowly.

By the Light, the pain that glittered there.

Then she shook her head the slightest bit.

Konan chewed his lip as he considered his next question. He didn't want to ask. He wanted to decide for her, but he couldn't. "Do you want me to stay?"

The pause before she answered was interminable, and then she weakly shook her head again. His heart fell, but her fingers clutched his cloak with more strength than he thought she had, and he thought to ask one more question.

"Do you want to come with me to Mirat?"

Lyra's nod was enough, and he pressed his forehead against hers, nearly shaking with the gladness it gave him, before carrying her outside. If she thought Mirat was a worthy destination, then to Mirat they would go. Together. Perhaps there they would both find freedom from their nightmarish memories, and he could give her the garden she dreamt of.

They had rented a cart for the short ride farther into the city, and Konan couldn't help but marvel at the beauty of Corronei. It was hard to imagine the yellow-bricked streets being dangerous; everything was clean and colorful. Oversized lamps lined the main ways and hung from buildings, and the fresh sea air grew stronger until he felt he was swimming in it.

When they boarded the ship, a large passenger vessel with wine-red flags, they found themselves in the midst of a bustle of confusion. Other passengers joined them on deck, unsure of where they belonged in the chaos. Konan would have settled Lyra somewhere comfortable if she could stand, but she was limp and wobbling at the knee. He propped her against him.

Many of the other passengers wore shades of red and black, a professional smithy emblem on their shoulders. Most covered their heads with black hoods, while a few displayed their enhanced rank through the proud exposure of their hair, which was often tied with red ribbons. Master craftsmen, journeymen, and apprentices. Each seemed to have at least one heavy trunk of possessions to be loaded and stored belowdecks. Where were they all headed?

The mariners shouted to each other as they prepared the ship for sail. They wore practical clothing with relatively little color, but most carried a blue item—a bandana, a vest, or a beaded braid—to denote their vocation. They scrambled to and fro, nudging their way between passengers with irksome salty curses. Konan pulled Lyra back farther, noting which sailors paused for a second to look at the pretty woman under his arm. He found himself edged against the gunwale next to an apprentice smith, who appeared overwhelmed.

"First time sailing?" Thordrin asked the smith in a jaunty tone. After a haircut and a shave from the innkeeper's wife, the Phantom finally looked at ease, his trimmed beard making him strikingly handsome. At last, his physical appearance fully matched his suave attitude, and Konan could believe that the man had served in a king's court. Mikaa hung on his arm, looking beautiful but out of place.

The smith nodded at Thordrin. "First time to the ocean, sir."

Thordrin smiled broadly, exuding confidence. "No worries to be had, friend. The Mana Loi is a gentle sea. It'll be smooth sailing to Krita."

The smith gulped and nodded again, thanking him for the encouragement.

"A good many smiths on board," Thordrin continued. "Where are you all headed?"

"Mirat, sir," said the smith. "Prince Reylin demanded the smithing Masterhall's services for weaponmaking and basic tools, some big project for their northeastern border."

Konan made a derisive growl in his throat, and the smith looked at him nervously, noted his appearance, then quickly looked down to inspect the deck.

"Must be quite the project," Thordrin continued casually, leaning back against the gunwale.

"Yes, sir," said the smith, edging away from Konan and paling. "I must admit I'm afraid."

"As an apprentice, this must be your first major assignment," Thordrin said, half in inquiry.

The smith shook his head. Finally, he whispered, "That's not what I'm afraid of." His voice was barely audible below the scuffling feet and shouts on deck and the calling gulls in the air. "It's Krita."

Thordrin perked up, now genuinely interested. "What about Krita?"

The smith's eyes widened, and he glanced from one man to the other. "The sickness, sir."

Thordrin knitted his brows and demanded to know more, while Konan groaned inside.

The young apprentice complied in a fearful whisper that carried. "I heard there is sickness in Krita, something terrible that makes people go mad. It's here too, in Corronei. I thank all Five Faces we got to the ship without incident."

Konan caught Thordrin's attention and intentionally rolled his eyes toward Lyra, who hung limp under his arm. She didn't seem to be listening, but she'd likely heard everything.

Thordrin nodded slowly, turning his attention back to the apprentice smith. "What do you know of the sickness in Corronei?" he asked, leaning indolently, as if he couldn't care less whether the smith told him anything more.

The young man elaborated. Their party had traveled the long road from the smithing Masterhall in Shayal, and thankfully they had been a large contingent, well equipped with wagons, weapons, and horses. They passed the dry plains as quickly as they could, pausing at small towns along the way, and had heard tales of wild attacks on the roads. "They say hundreds of people have disappeared," he declared, his eyes wide, "and that's not even the worst of it. Krita is worse. The streets of Krita are said to be filled with cannibals now. I don't mean to even disembark at port, if I don't have to," he finished. "This ship is heading all the way to North Mara, thanks to the dispatch from Prince Reylin."

Konan bristled at the last two words. He gave Lyra a light shake. Her head bobbed with the movement, but she didn't react with more than a slow blink. He glowered. He hadn't wanted her to find out this way.

"In any case, I wish you safe travels, whether you're stopping in Krita or heading elsewhere," the apprentice added with a short bow. "Go with the Light." He nearly ran away from Konan's scowl, finding solace in a group of smiths on the other side of the boat.

"Did you hear that, Lyr?" Thordrin muttered. "Some kind of madness . . . Do you think he's right? Madness?" He grimaced, following his own track of thought. "Madmen. Sick or not, it was people fucking did it." He suddenly barked a laugh, though it seemed without feeling. "Rigaran probably brought it on himself, that treacherous son of a bitch. Maybe there is a God, and may all five of his faces be turned away from Krita. Justice is calling."

Lyra stared at the wooden deck. The cries of sea gulls pierced the salty ocean air, and she looked sharply up, alert for several intense seconds. She watched the birds circling the ship's mast, then returned to staring off to sea with erratic, panting breaths. As she slumped, Konan caught her once again, slinging her into his arms.

He carried her belowdecks, followed by a fretting Mikaa. If Lyra had been "halfway to the sands" before, now she might be entirely gone. That blurry reflection of a beautiful young woman had diminished, tarnished by an unending slew of wretched experiences. He yearned to hear her sing again, if only because it reflected her inner joy. Her laughter was like the shake of a tambourine, her voice high and smooth like a bird welcoming the morning Eye.

They entered a tight bunkroom with two sets of cramped bunks, and he laid her on his lap to remove her Haralali headdress and veil. Mikaa set it aside and arranged herself at Lyra's feet, plucking at her robes and murmuring sadly.

"I'm sorry you found out that way," he signed. "That's what the innkeeper said too."

As he drew his fingers through her long, kinky hair, she resumed more normal breathing, still shallow but at least regular. Nonetheless, she remained in a tearful trance.

Who could be to blame for such a mad curse? He didn't know anything about King Rigaran, but someone had brought the ire of I'ya down upon the world. Lyra's family had paid the price, and now she had too. He leaned over her, forehead to forehead, and begged her not to shatter.

The ship departed late that afternoon, exploiting the cool land breeze that plumped the sails and pushed them from the Red Bay's Corronei West Harbor. Konan reluctantly laid Lyra down on the bunk, arranging her as comfortably as he could, and pulled a light sheet over top of her. She wouldn't eat, hadn't since the discovery of the caravan. Mikaa stayed with her at all times, and he rarely left, although the sea called to him.

Her catatonic condition was unchanged the next day, and the next, and the next. The captain, a blue-swathed man with an elaborately layered coat and doubloon shirt in pastel blue, declared that they were over the Crack in the Earth and were less than two weeks away from Krita Port.

"These good winds'll keep us sailin' strong," the captain said. "Blessed by th'Sea God and I'ya, the ship *Nessa* traverses th'Mana Loi." He broke a bottle over the side, and the crew broke out in cheers. Konan noted a release of tension that evening, as if the Crack in the Earth had made them nervous. But as the evening wore on, the wind slackened to a frail whiff, then disappeared entirely. A heavy weight of humidity settled on the ship, and its forward progress stopped. The ocean became a mirror reflecting both perfect slivers of moon; not a wave or swell disturbed the surface.

Konan and Thordrin both rose when they felt the change in the ship's pitch and rhythm, emerging onto a torchlit deck of shaken sailors.

"Is like the doldrums, Cap," said one mariner.

"Aye, but we're nowhere near the warm waters," muttered another.

"The Crack o' the Earth cursed us," said another in a panicky voice.

"Men, men," shouted the captain, waving his hands in appeal. "It's not a curse, just a shift in th'winds."

"Ain't a shift when the winds disappear," said a man from the back. "Is th'doldrums, Cap'n."

The shouting escalated, until several other passengers woke and ascended from below, scrubbing sleep from their eyes. Konan and Thordrin backed into a dark corner. Konan had an uneasy feeling. The ocean was unnaturally still, dead . . . catatonic. The dynamic feel of it, the steady rhythm that had formerly filled his senses, had disappeared.

A wail echoed from somewhere below, and all heads turned to the doorway to the quarter deck.

Lyra appeared in the doorway with her head tilted to one side, as if sleepwalking. She shuffled forward into the pale moonlight, still in a seeming trance. Her dark robes faded into the shadows, and the only bright points Konan could see were her sparkling eyes. She wasn't asleep.

A rough-looking mariner stepped toward her. It was one of those who had given her a second leer at the beginning of the voyage, Konan was sure of it. "Girl, get back below," the sailor demanded in a gruff voice.

Lyra's hand flicked out so quickly, no one could see the slim blade as it spun through the air and embedded in the man's neck. He fell, spewing blood in a spray that splashed the people nearby. He died with a gurgle. Shock rippled through the crew and passengers, and no one moved. Lyra stayed where she was, intent on the mariner's still body, and her eyes went from glittering to opaque orbs for moments. Her round face, so innocently drawn with those wide-set rosy cheeks and soft lips, became tragic as she stared. Then she tripped forward and fell.

"No, no, no," she muttered to herself. "It's not the right Gate. Not the right Gate. That's not the right Gate. No, no, no." She was hyperventilating, entirely consumed with her vision.

Mikaa burst from below deck and nearly tripped on her in a panic. "Lee'ra kill," she wailed. "Lee'ra bad head, bad friends." She backed around Lyra and ran into the crowd, hiding behind a large, broad-shouldered smith.

"The madness! Seize her," cried the captain. As the crew descended upon Lyra, she flashed several more knives out, dropping five men in a matter of seconds. As others restrained her, she only stared intensely at each body, her own light frame in deathly rigor and her eyes again becoming opaque and dead. Then she violently returned to life.

"It's not the right Gate," she cried. "Not the right Gate! None of them lead to the green lands!" She howled like a winter wind, and rage flooded her face. Her irises appeared almost white they were so bright, and she began to summon as she shrieked and struggled. A mighty gale blasted across the deck, knocking people down. The large smith stumbled backward, shoving Mikaa over the edge. She screamed and disappeared overboard. Lyra was freed and began spinning her hands in wild, desperate gestures of fury. Wind smashed into the ship, then waves. Water poured over the sides, hammering man and mast alike. The sails plunged full forward, then backward, then ripped off into the wind.

Konan clung to the gunwale, his feet sliding out from under him as water rolled by, sucking past his legs and splashing his knees. The ship pitched dangerously forward, and when it whipped back, the main mast shivered and split. Stray ropes cracked by his ears, and for a moment, he got one last look at Lyra.

She had her hands raised, and her glinting eyes were cold, empty orbs of diamond. She wasn't looking at him—she wasn't present. No, she was consumed in her own frantic intonations about green lands and Gates, and her apparent frustrations exuded as piercing blades of wind that shot outward and around. The storm escalated, and the last thing Konan saw was a wall of water twice the height of the ship, descending upon him and Thordrin where they clung to the half-broken gunwale railing.

The railing snapped.

77

As they often did, Tan and Taiuki took care of their hunting and riding obligations on the second day of their respite, for the first day was usually full of caring for the sickly Hachi, spoiling It'tholl with attention, and organizing supplies.

This time, Steward Wehan had requested that they bring back a spectre shark, a horrifying monster of a delicacy from the abyssal plains southeast of the Lai'akala Trench. Spectre sharks were somewhat uncommon, living alone in the deep sea and hunting the small-bodied fishes of the trench, but occasionally they made a meal of squid. Taiuki thought their best opportunity was the edge of the abyssal plains, where the juvenile squids patrolled their paltry territories, and Uth'hal had agreed. As long as they stayed far enough away from Shiggo City's settlements, they could travel as a unit and hunt with contentment and ease. The hunting party swam west early in the day to reach the plains on the east side of Lai'akala, far enough south to avoid the Jijiton-jin front.

Taiuki praised Kenji as he bore her westward. He loved galloping in spurts, but she held him in check to ensure he didn't weary himself. Kenji's discipline training was a large component of Taiuki's focus, as she not only trained him to the halter, but also to It'tholl's presence. The dragling, meanwhile, careened in wide circles around them as they gained distance from the Mountains of Mourning. With Uth'hal's accompaniment as well, not even a blueback would be foolish enough to attack them.

Tan rode beside them on Nimoka, his stance proper and comfortable, and Taiuki clicked only small bits of advice to him when she noticed his attentiveness flagging. Tan was a natural rider and devoted friend to his Nimoka, but these long hunts tested his concentration. Taiuki smiled possessively; only her little brother could be simultaneously so enthusiastic about a hunt and so distracted by his surroundings. Despite their squabbles over telling Anella about the dragons, she would never regret having him with her.

They had expected the day to be long, given their excessive travel, but their quarry was also elusive, and they stalked the edge of the plains for several hours before finding one.

The spectre was half-grown, about the length of It'tholl, and oblivious to them as it nosed about a volcanic cairn in the dim underworld light. The squid who likely called this area home was a distance away, eyeing the shark with irritation. Swinging its long, flat nose around the large tower of rock, the spectre sensed for the small fish that called the rock home.

Taiuki held Kenji steady and pushed him forward just a hair, moving to the nearest cairn behind the creature; Tan did the same. They nodded to each other and discharged their spear guns simultaneously, latching on to the unsuspecting shark from both sides.

The spectre shark screamed silently, whipping its proboscis from side to side. Taiuki pulled back on Kenji, keeping the harpoon lines taut between herself and Nimoka. Tan clicked a command to his whale to pull back as well, then leapt from his saddle. Moka drew her line out till it stretched, leaning her body into the effort, and Taiuki reflected on how long it would be until Kenji had that level of discipline and comprehension of commands. How she missed Hachi.

She patted Kenji with encouragement as he tried to counter Nimoka's weight.

The spectre glared death at Tan as the young man approached with his hand spear, but the beast was caught. Tan slammed the spear directly into the shark's chin and into its skull, dispatching it cleanly. The creature lunged once more to the side, yanking Kenji forward as it died. Taiuki detached her spear line from the harness and dismounted.

A clean kill, said Uth'hal with approval. His mass emerged from the variegated rocky bottom without warning.

The shadow of It'tholl peeled off from him and approached until she was nose to nose with the dead creature, which settled in a lazy drift to the seafloor. *Is food?* she asked.

"Yes, beloved," replied Taiuki, "but not for you."

Myr food, huffed It'tholl, losing interest and switching to a game of chase with the resident squid.

"Stay close," called Taiuki as she watched the dragling's murky shadow alternately coalesce and fade in the distance.

Tan removed each spear tip from the carcass, and they cleaned it together. Crabs and tiny fish appeared from cracks and holes in the magma chutes, gathering nearby and grasping detritus as they floated outward. Taiuki packed each muscle group into sealed satchels for carrying, then latched each satchel onto Nimoka and Kenji's backs. The spectre was a good kill, just the right age. Mother would be pleased—Taiuki was certain Steward Wehan's request originated from her—and even Kei might be excited.

When they had finished, the day was waning.

"We should get It'tholl home," said Tan, looking up into the dark blue beyond. Its hazy, perfect gradient of color made the existence of a surface uncertain; it seemed they were in a world separate from the other. This was a world of water, and water alone. This was *their* world.

Taiuki agreed. "I would guess the sun has just set. It'tholl, closer to the school. We're heading home."

It'tholl comes, called the dragling, abandoning the irritated squid, which had immersed itself in a cloud of ink.

The successful hunt energized the group as they headed eastward, exiting the abyssal plain to a slightly friendlier landscape. Kenji was more nervous at night, but Uth'hal's presence helped keep him in check. To travel in a school, as odd a school as it was, was safer and wiser; even the young whale had internalized that.

Suddenly, the ocean changed.

Taiuki couldn't place the unease she felt, but it seeped into her bones, tightened her muscles, and unsettled her stomach.

"Taiuki?" said Tan. His own dismay was obvious, and he kept looking up toward the surface. "There's something wrong."

They halted, and Kenji huddled next to Moka for comfort. Taiuki reached out to touch Tan's shoulder, but he caught her hand and clutched it instead, never taking his eyes off the surface. His mouth was slack. "The ocean feels wrong," he said.

Taiuki closed her eyes and focused, trying to elucidate what troubled her so deeply, what was so disconcerting, but she couldn't place it.

Water stops, said It'tholl, flitting around as if nothing had changed.

"By I'ya," Tan said slowly, "there's no current . . . especially up there." He pointed.

That's impossible, thought Taiuki, but the distorted reality crashed around her and screamed in her terrified ears. The never-ending current, the ebb and flow of life in the water, the rhythm of the world, had stopped. The ocean was eerily silent, vacant of its usual flush and murmur and delicate push against her skin. The stillness originated, as Tan said, from above.

Uth'hal inspected the distant surface as well, untroubled but certainly curious. *I have never felt this before*, he stated. *There is power in it.*

Tan glanced at Taiuki, a hint of mischief lighting up his eyes in the twilight. "We have to go look."

"I don't think it's safe," she cried as Tan relinquished her handhold and whipped his reins, urging Nimoka upward.

"We have Uth'hal," called Tan. "Nothing can harm us. Come on, sis!"

Taiuki struggled to control her fear as she whipped Kenji's reins furiously to stay close to Tan as he ascended. She spared a glance at Uth'hal, whose languid undulation kept him even with her as he tucked his massive wings in and pushed through the water like a monstrous eel.

Worry not, said Uth'hal, knowing her troubled thoughts.

They'd ascended halfway when the ocean changed again. The surface blackened, and tumultuous waves appeared, sending violent vibrations through the water column.

Tan paused his eager approach and waited for Taiuki to catch up. The mischief on his face was replaced with confusion. "I've never seen a storm hit like that," he said, looking at her for confirmation.

She agreed. The blasts of energy were sporadic and uneven, whipping the surface into a chaotic frenzy. Then they seemed to take on a large-scale rotation much like a hurricane, but hurricanes rarely evolved this far north. Taiuki puzzled and muddled over that thought as she stared at the surface storm. The water was swelling and abating in high billows and valleys now, and it felt as if the heart of the ocean was beating in rhythmic pulses. Darkness had descended, making their underworld even darker, but the surface was lit by intermittent flashes of lightning.

She squinted through the twilight, blinking. What was that? Lightning flashed again, and she could see the silhouette.

A ship.

"By the current, they'll never make it," cried Tan.

Taiuki grabbed his arm and stopped him. "They're only landwalkers, Tan."

"But they'll drown," he said, trying to pull away from her as she clutched harder.

"You could get hurt trying to save them," she insisted. "Don't."

Her brother ripped from her hold with a frown. "Let's at least watch," he said.

She nodded.

The storm intensified, and they could see large pieces ripping off and stabbing into the water like oversized arrows. Taiuki found herself urging Kenji closer to the ship, watching the devastation unfold. A large swell passed overhead, and she caught her breath as it smashed into the vessel. The hull splintered into thousands of pieces, and human bodies appeared in the water above. Some struggled, but most did not. Tan kept looking at her, and she ignored him. There was nothing they could do for the ones who didn't struggle, and those who did were finding wreckage to cling to. The surface was still rocking and littered with floating debris. Heavy refuse from the ship—filled crates, anchors, metal plating and rigging—sank past the myr siblings, disappearing into the black depths forever. It'tholl was highly entertained, dodging the sinking fragments and then following them down in a nosedive before looping back up for another round.

An orb of clear water developed near the wreckage. Taiuki squinted hard. Two human bodies, one lashing ineffectually at the water while dragging another. Despite the one's frantic attempts, the pair sank slowly, enveloped by their sphere of calm water.

A mariner who couldn't swim? Taiuki wondered at the possibility.

Tan tapped her shoulder. "Now can I help?" he said impatiently.

It'tholl helps, declared the dragling, abandoning the corpse she had been following and darting toward the ship.

"No!" cried Taiuki. In her mind, it was a desperate scream. "They mustn't see you, It'tholl!"

It'tholl helps because it is right to help, said the dragling without looking back.

"Please, you don't understand, It'tholl," called Taiuki as terror ripped through her veins. These strangers had no right to her secret—they might destroy everything she cared for. "It'tholl, leave them be!" she cried once more.

It'tholl knows it is right to help, the dragling repeated as she approached the orb. The struggling man saw her as she circled the strange still area, then entered it and neared him.

The figure lashed out with a long knife, and It'tholl squealed. Taiuki grabbed at her own arm with a yelp of pain.

Man hurts It'tholl, her dragling exclaimed, *but It'tholl still helps.*

The man stopped and stared at It'tholl in awe. Clearly, she had spoken to him as well. His attentive demeanor was fading, and Taiuki knew he was almost out of time. The one he clutched was already unconscious and likely dead. The man blinked slowly at It'tholl, then passed out as well. The orb of still water protecting them dissolved into the chaos of the surrounding water, and both bodies drifted apart.

It'tholl swooped in and grabbed each one with a foot, pulling them out of the worst currents. Taiuki noticed that the storm itself was shifting westward, and they burst to the surface just behind the whirlwind. Tan grabbed the man who had struggled so valiantly and expunged the water from his lungs using the magika they had learned from Water-priest Araya. The man retched and hacked, and Tan laid him on an extended wing from Uth'hal, who floated comfortably now that the localized storm had calmed.

Taiuki grabbed the other limp body. This man was still alive, but his pulse was weak, and he was covered in blood. She pushed the water from the man's lungs using a physical maneuver combined with the magika, but he didn't react. She knew breathing for him might work, but had never had to do it before. *Myr don't drown*, she thought to herself bitterly as she laid him on Uth'hal's wing and put her mouth to his. She breathed into him, a deep, full breath laden with life, and she felt him spasm.

He gagged water, rolling over with a groan between hacking coughs. He caught his breath for a couple of minutes, then sat up and stared at her. With a start, he looked down at the leathery surface upon which he sat. His eyes followed the wing to the pinions, to the shoulder, to Uth'hal's oversized and fearsome head, a black shadow hovering over them in the night.

Uth'hal rumbled a greeting.

"Fucking nethergates," said the man, raising an eyebrow. "We made it." His chuckle turned into a cough, and he spat, then rubbed the back of his head. Wincing as his hand came away with blood, he looked suddenly woozy, and his already wan skin paled further.

The other man sat up too, examining his surroundings carefully and measuring in turn Tan, Taiuki, It'tholl, and the overwhelming Uth'hal. He wore a stolid and unreadable expression until he stared into the darkness beyond Uth'hal, following the receding storm. His shadowed face seemed almost disfigured as it twisted with tragedy, and his bulk began to shake and convulse. He covered his face, clutching his long, dark hair as if he were going to rip it out. Taiuki couldn't tell whether his strange groan was meant for them to hear, or some sort of statement to himself.

Nevertheless, It'tholl took it up as a new song: *She's gone. She's gone. She's gone, gone, gone.*

78

REYLIN INHALED THE BRISK sea air. A wave crashed into the ship, and he shivered as the damp morning chill was worsened by the salty spray.

"Must've been a storm from the nethers," said the ship's captain, standing alongside him and enjoying the view.

"Pardon?" asked Reylin.

The captain gestured at the lapping waves that occasionally splashed into the ship as it rocked its way to Krita. "Unusual size and direction for this time of year, Highness. Must've been a good'n."

"We're in no danger, are we?" Reylin asked anxiously. "My wife is not fond of sailing." Syrana was in their quarters, bedridden with nausea. She had insisted on coming despite his encouragement for her to remain in Ironhold with the baroness, and she clung to him like he was her air. His heart swelled at the thought, but he resented the effect the sea had upon her. If only she could draw strength from it like he could.

If Shiggo City was where they had to go to learn proper Water magika and Water-based healing, then to the myr city they would go. His impetuous words in North Mara had seemed impulsive at the time, to continue onward after Krita. Now, he knew they had no alternative, for the myr would not send their own far inland, far from their waters, to a foreign kingdom of terrestrial humans.

But first, Krita. An intentional stop was wise given the reduced communication from Rigaran; the kingdom might have need of help and could provide valuable information about the madness. Reylin could reveal his self-proclaimed status to them and perform his rightful duty as diplomat, thereby shedding the influence of the Council like an elk dropping its aging antlers.

"Augh, no, Your Highness," the captain replied to his query of danger. "Storm's far and gone."

"Skies be clear," muttered the skipper from the helm. He seemed uncomfortable with their discussion.

The captain nodded. "Aye, skies be clear."

That ended any mention of rains or wind, and Reylin took in the peaceful view, a seemingly endless expanse of dark blue water. North Mara was behind them, and Krita ahead. Shiggo lay somewhere beyond, on the other side of the Kritali island kingdom. Reylin had never sailed the Mana Loi, and his insides were a jitter of qualms, curiosity, and exhilaration. At the same time, he felt at ease, immersed in this expanse of water. Kaiadin suggested it was because of his connection to the element, his gift.

A dark sliver appeared on the southwest horizon, broadening minutely until its existence was sure.

"Krita?" asked Reylin, peering at the distant shadow.

"Aye, Highness," the captain replied. "Krita."

79

"Ahoy there," called a voice. "We're throwing a rope. Grab it, and we'll pull you up."

A darkened landscape of endless navy depths and gray skies met Lyra as she emerged from a groggy nightmare. She clung to flotsam, a splintered piece of secondary mast. The ocean around her was littered with pieces of the ship *Nessa*—yet she kept imagining bodies adrift in the cracked timber and floating barrels. The sun had risen several fingers in the sky, but its rays only penetrated the hazy clouds as a diffuse brightening that let her know it was daytime.

"Jump in, you idiot," came a sultry, feminine voice. "Can't you see she can't reach it on her own?"

"Yes, m'lady," said the first voice.

Lyra heard a splash nearby, and then a young mariner swam up to her, hauling a line. She was too exhausted to resist as he tied it around her waist and urged her to let go of the wooden float. The mariner held her like a rag doll as they were hefted up and out of the water. Lyra found herself hauled over the side and settled on the floor of a trading vessel, a small ketch. In front of her stood the captain, a buff but short man, and an elegant lady adorned in far southerner clothing. The captain examined Lyra with a dubious eye until the lady spoke.

"Fetch her a blanket, by the Light, or she'll catch her death of chill," the woman commanded. Mariners ran to do her bidding. "Why, the sodden thing must have been floating since that storm yesterday."

"Aye, and what a storm," murmured the captain, still staring at Lyra. She wasn't sure if he thought she was a miracle or a soaked rat. She accepted the blanket draped around her shoulders, though, and she was soon ushered to the captain's quarters by the other woman.

"We're headed to Corronei, lady," said the captain as she shuffled by. "You'll have passage there, by my word." He bowed, making the pledge with his hand on his burly chest.

Lyra managed to nod at him as she went by. She stumbled through the door, which the other woman shut behind her and locked.

"I'm Lady Riven," said the woman. "Let's clean you up, and you can tell me how you came to be a bit of driftwood on the Mana Loi." She curved her full, ochred lips into a beautiful smile, but something in the expression seemed cruel.

Lyra gulped nervously.

Lady Riven laughed, a high-pitched chuckle laden with humor. "Oh, come, girl. You have nothing to fear now. Those sailors won't touch you if you're with me." She threw her shoulders back and raised her long chin, highlighting her straight-line jaw and perky cheeks. The woman was undoubtedly noble-blooded: melanistic skin, semiwide but perfectly straight nose, flat forehead, and dark, delicate eyebrows. Gorgeous. Lyra supposed she was from far south of Tamorín, as her features reflected those from beyond the reach of the empire. Lady Riven was a few years older than her at most, yet had the bearing of someone much beyond that. Someone in charge.

"You're traveling alone?" Lyra asked, shocked.

Lady Riven laughed again. "Indeed I am." The woman looked around the captain's cabin, a comfortable space for a medium-sized ship. She spied a small washbasin and carried it over. "Looks like the captain has limited fresh water, but we can at least wash the crust of salt from your lashes and scalp."

Lyra gratefully splashed the tepid water on her cheeks, scrubbing a fine layer of grit from her skin. Her cheeks and forehead felt raw, and when she looked up into the silver-wrought mirror in Lady Riven's hand, she saw that they were bright red. She doused her head halfway in the large basin, rinsing to dissolve the bits of dryness adhered to her scalp and hair. It was enough to give her some relief.

Lady Riven rummaged through the captain's drawers and dressers, pulling out vials and fineries as she found them. She handed Lyra a fine perfume and a sweet oil—"For that sea wench stench, Lady Driftwood," she said with a laugh—followed by ladies' undergarments. Lyra hid behind a curtain as she rubbed the oil on; her skin tingled with pleasure as it soaked up the oil. She rebound her breasts, tucking the soggy notes from Konan back in by her heart. She was afraid to unfold them, afraid to see if the ink had bled.

"Try this one on," called Lady Riven, tossing a dress over the divider. "Then come out."

Lyra pulled the dress on. It was somewhat rich, perhaps belonging to the trader captain's wife? And it fit her well. Lady Riven had a sharp eye. The bustle was more formal and stiff than Lyra was used to, and the breasts lifted too high for her own comfort. She cursed her body for the thousandth time and pulled the front up as high as the fabric would go, then tightened the corset to hold it in place. She had preferred the clothing of the Manalal: loosely fitting, with high-necked undershirts and billowing sleeved robes, embroidered textiles in a rainbow of colors, headdresses with face coverings and exquisite, complex beadwork. The silver coins they wore reminded her of her own, which edged her waist belt and flashed when she danced. It seemed ages ago.

"Sit." Lady Riven gave a peremptory flick of her finger at a chair. Lyra obeyed, and the woman began rubbing hair oil into Lyra's tangled waves, working the knots out with a silver comb. "Now then, who are you, and what ship were you on?"

Lyra tried to explain, but her memory of the previous few days was oddly blank, with only feelings and shades remaining. She thought back to playing with seaglass on the Marlemet beaches.

"This is the princess," proclaimed Elden, holding a clear chunk of seaglass high in the air. "She lives in the castle." He mounded the wet sand into a high pile, which sloughed off itself to form a cone. Elden was too young to understand which sand to use to build a good castle, Lyra knew, so she went along with it

.

"This is the Fire Dragon, the mighty and evil Car'rok," she said, flying an orange piece through the air with a whoosh.

"Oh no," cried Elden, holding his princess on top of the castle. "Save me!"

An energetic wave pushed its way just a little further up-shore than the previous ones, breaking over the castle and washing most of it away. Only a low slump of sand remained.

"I lost my princess," said Elden sadly.

Her memory of the ship was just as vague and malformed. Had it been as large as this ketch? A man in the door of her cabin, the warden. No. A man on the floor, in a pool of blood. How did she get onto the *Nessa* again? Konan's warmth. By the Light, Konan. Small bunks. Her eyes closing with relief as Konan stroked her hair and massaged her temples. Her heart pattering with horror and grief and gratitude, with a feeling she had never known before as she thought of *him*.

But there was no green land on the other side of the Gate. No matter which Gate opened, it was never the right one.

"Pardon?" Lady Riven interrupted her verbal scatter.

Lyra turned to look at her with haunted eyes. "I couldn't find the right Gate." Her stuttering voice shook.

Lady Riven paused her brushing and stared at her with new respect. "You can see the Gates?"

"I can, but . . . but I couldn't find the right one." Lyra began to weep, and Riven squeezed her shoulder.

"That's a miraculous ability, Lyra. You opened a gateway to another world? Never mind it wasn't the one you were looking for. Did you go through?"

"Only for moments," Lyra stuttered, "only long enough to realize they weren't the right ones . . ."

"You're a Gatekeeper. By I'ya . . ." she murmured, finally achieving long strokes of the comb without catching tangles. "And then the storm hit?"

Lyra thought hard, but all she could process was a panicked litany. *Not the right Gate. Not the green lands. Mam's burgundy cloak. Not the right Gate. Elden's ring, half-buried in the dirt and tarnished. Men grabbing me, touching me, controlling me. Not the right Gate.* The room reverberated with Air, shaking the silver on the table with a clatter.

"Ah, I see," said Lady Riven in a placating voice.

"You were the storm."

MONON M. SAND

INDEX

Refer to this comprehensive guide to people, places, and things in Midgate. People and dragons are organized into their respective kingdoms, families, and orders.

KINGDOM OF KRITA

Large island country in the Mana Loi, major trade hub. Capital at Krita Port.

House Crayer
Rigaran: King
Déllani: Queen
Godrig: Crown Prince, firstborn son
Branig: secondborn son
Anella: firstborn daughter

Others
Sep: Phantom in service to Krita
Thordrin: Phantom in service to Krita

KINGDOM OF LORENI

Major producer of wheat and other grains, as well as wheat beers and effervescents.

Brigg: King
Wenfa: Queen

KINGDOM OF MARLEMET

Rich kingdom on the western continent, major winemaker and agricultural exporter. Capital at Corronei in the Red Bay.

KINGDOM OF MIRAT

Mountainous and high plains kingdom on the eastern continent, specializing in ore and gemstone mining. Capital at Ironhold.

House Harkin
Reylin: Crown Prince
Priscilla: Crown Princess, first wife of Reylin
Syrana: second wife of Reylin, from Camdry
Rolis: King of Mirat, died in the Great Fire
Leyalin: Queen of Mirat, died in the Great Fire

Others
Amber: lady of Lupine
Ana: Baroness of Camdry
Bonnehad: heir of Camdry
Bonneser: Baron of Camdry
Cordan: knight, mayor of Lupine
Daiunek: Master Miner, Guildmaster of the Miner's Guild
Davon: Earth dragonkeeper of Ar'we, lives near Camdry

Dorian: High Guard Knight
Ennedrew: Duke, lord of the southwest coastal district
Falicia: Duchess, lady of the western port district
Farrion: Reylin's warhorse
Forin: knight captain, commanding officer of Edgegrass
Galltry: Duke, lord of the eastern valley district
Gillead: High Guard knight, Lord Commander of Mirat
Gordrew: High Lord Steward of Ironhold Castle
Gordrim: swordmaster of Mirat, deceased
Hominy: steward of Camdry Castle
Jonathan: High Guard knight
Kaiadin: Holy Mage
Lío: Duke, Lord of the western port district
Ma'thell: High Holy Mage of the Temple in Mirat
Morin: Footservant of Reylin, deceased
Morsey: High Mage at North Mara Port
Oyerton: master miner at Mirat
Patreagh: High Guard knight
Porin: Duke, lord of the southeastern plains district
Ronidann: High Guard knight
Shiften: Duke, a lord of Mirat, Shildra's brother
Shildra: Duchess, lady of the eastern valley district
Theodar: knight captain, commanding officer of East Face
Wethers: journeyman miner at Mirat

KINGDOM OF SHAYAL

Kingdom on southern edge of the Tahayi Desert on the western continent, major mining and gemstone exporter. Capital at City of Shayal.

Dawna: worker at Tahayi Mines
Hemil: King of Shayal
Konan: prisoner at Tahayi Mines
Moony: prisoner at Tahayi Mine, west camp
Selen: prisoner at Tahayi Mine, central camp
Tass: worker at Tahayi Mines
Yantry: prisoner at Tahayi Mine, west camp

KINGDOM OF TAMORÍN

A subtropical southern kingdom on the edge of the Empire's reach.

Riven: a noblewoman from the far south

MYRKINGDOM OF FUMAYA

Myrkingdom to the north of the Mana Loi, blockading the Merchan Sea.

MYRKINGDOM OF MERCHAN

Myrkingdom far to the north in the Merchan Sea.

MYRKINGDOM OF NAGAWA

Myrkingdom in the eastern Mana Loi, specializes in knife production.

MYRKINGDOM OF SHIGGO

Myrkingdom to the west of Krita. Capital at Shiggo City.

House ol'Kada ol'Tatami
Furuhaki: Queen Regent
Rentai: King, deceased
Keiki: firstborn daughter, the First
Taifun: firstborn son, deceased

Taiuki: secondborn daughter, the Second
Tan: secondborn son, the Third

Others
Apakun: Master Mariner, Commodore of Ships
Benn: a blue shark, primary mount for Sashiro
Hachi: a blackheaded whale, primary mount for Taiuki
Hannaka: matron-in-waiting, Tan's wetnurse
Kenji: a sawtoothed whale
Kinota: marshal (in charge of all stables)
Merridan: a disgraced Waterpriest
Nimoka: a blackheaded whale, primary mount for Tan
Reihotto: Vice Commodore, the second-highest military command
Tsuya: a sawtoothed whale, primary mount for Reihotto
Sashiro: Arch Commodore, the highest military command
Wehan: High Steward of the royal castle

Manalal Clan

Shirkaa: clan chief
Godspeaker: a priest of the Desert Mother religion
Dashann: honor guard of the chief
Hafka: honor guard of the chief
Jikaa: son of the chief; honor guard of the chief
Korahel: maiden of the clan
Mirra: maiden of the clan
Rahar: clan advisor, leads half of army
Shirasa: daughter of the chief

Haralal Clan

Mikaa: maiden of the clan

Maskalan Caravan

A wayfarer caravan on the western continent that specializes in leatherworking and high-value gemstone work, spells, and minor potions.

Adrian: Lyra's cousin, stablekeeper
Elaisa: Lyra's mother
Elden: Lyra's younger brother
Isellan: family leader of the Maskalan Caravan, deceased
Lyra: a young woman who specializes in dance, singing, and medicine
Terrasa: Lyra's uncle, stablekeeper

Faraldin Caravan

A wayfarer caravan on the eastern continent that specializes in interpretive dance and history telling.

Al'Laiakala Dragon Order

Ind'arra: female water dragon
It'ma: female water dragon, First Elder
It'tholl: female water dragon
Kar'nak: male water dragon
Uth'hal: male water dragon, Second Elder
Uth'warran: male water dragon

LANDMARKS

Bleeding Wall: a cliff of malagate dividing the Kingdom of Shayal from the Tahayi Desert
Holy Mountain: a floating island that is the religious center for the faith of I'ya
Mountains of Mourning: a twin-peaked volcanic island east of Shiggo City, haunted
Lai'akala Trench (LIE-uh-KA-la)/Crack in the World: a deep-sea trench in the western Mana Loi
Loi al'Halmana (LOI-all-ha-MA-na): tallgrass plains east of Mirat, literally the "Sea of Grass"
Mana Loi (MA-nuh-LOI): Central ocean between the eastern and western continents of Midgate

THINGS

alliun: medicinal herb, immune booster
andesite: black volcanic stone, used as rankstone by myr-people
apita: trees that grow along the shoreline in sparse clumps
blueback: an aggressive shark of the open ocean
bluetail bat: a desert bat species, used in medicine
bracken crab: a crab native to kelp forest
brian bush: medicinal plant used for healing skin, antiseptic
brownbed: medicinal plant with a tuberous root, root used dried and ground to reduce fever
cha: medicinal seeds, homeopathic use to encourage bearing a female child
chinespine: a piece of myr armor worn on the back to ward off predators
cow's tongue: medicinal plant with naturally mucilaginous leaves, crushed to bind wounds
eclipse jellyfish: deadly jellyfish characterized by its large round body and bioluminescence
fenweed: medicinal plant used for healing skin, antiseptic
frostbear: large bear native to the northern mountains and

islands
frostmoss: dark green moss that grows through the winter
fusianate: a valuable silver-like metal
gallite: a somewhat common metal used in combination with iron to make a form of steel
Gem of I'ya: orange gem, very rare
ghastwolf: large wolf native to the northern mountains
gloryflower: red medicinal plant, hallucinogenic, used to induce calmness and sleep
greenback ray: a ray native to kelp forest
idraka: a haulbeast of the desert, can survive without water for long periods
kiltberry: a berry-producing shrub
lacer: aggressive striped shark of the kelp forest
lendrel tree: medicinal plant, anesthetic
makran: large carnivorous cat, harvested for its fur
magasberry: a berry-producing shrub
malagate: black stone with red seams (iron)
milktree: medicinal tree used for its sap, to bind and seal wounds
nansbane: medicinal herb, antibiotic
orangebloom kelp: a plant native to the kelp forest
pakla: an edible cactus fruit
pitlan: a fruit tree used to make cider
raiya: large groundbird native to the Loi al'Halmana, domesticated by the fyr
redking turtle: large, rare sea turtle native to kelp forest
savenberry: underwater fruiting body, savory salty flavor
spectre shark: a deep-sea lone shark, mildly aggressive but adapted toward smaller prey
striated kelpfish: a small colorful fish
sweetgrass: marine grass, mild dragon opiate
sunstone: a translucent gemstone filled with colorful specks, typically found with sulfur
tanko apple: purple marine fruits
thindel tree: a tree with fragrant wood and pitted sweet fruits
wetspice: a medicinal herb, used for hacking coughs
wul: a herdbeast, primarily used for meat and milk but also leather products, also occurs in the wild
yewflower: a medicinal herb, used to fight infection

Afterword

LOVED IT?

Don't miss the next book! Sign up for the newsletter for early access to books, sales and giveaways, and other special announcements. Please provide a review on <u>Goodreads</u>, <u>BookBub</u>, or <u>Amazon</u>. The story continues in *Sundering*. Check it out at:

https://rmkrogman.com/books/sundering/

Plus, you can find more books at:

https://rmkrogman.com/

READ MORE BY R. M. KROGMAN

KEEPERS OF MIDGATE

Recommended Reading Order
Marked (Novella)
Liberation
Myrmaiden (Novella)
Sundering
Desert Rose
Schism
The Chronicles of Thordrin (Novella)

Chronological Reading Order
Marked (Novella)
Myrmaiden (Novella)
The Chronicles of Thordrin (Novella)
Liberation
Desert Rose
Sundering
Schism

ABOUT THE AUTHOR

REBECCA M. KROGMAN IS an epic and dark fantasy author from Iowa, USA.

Her debut novel, *Liberation*, is the first volume of a larger story set in Midgate, a medieval-inspired world of magic, mermaids, and wyverns. She has been developing the *Keepers of Midgate* epic since she was in high school. The main storyline has changed little since then, only gaining more clarity and detail as the characters take on a life of their own. The world has grown in its depth of history, culture, and geography, spawning numerous side stories, prequels, and a sequel.

She loves nature, art, and food, which all funnel into her world-building. Her story's settings span two continents and the sea between, encompassing a diversity of peoples, cultures, and creatures. She is working on a collection of recipes from Midgate, and she loves drawing scenes and characters from the books (although those sketches may never see the light of day). She will never apologize for describing a tree, as she finds trees to be fascinating and far more alive than they get credit for.

When she's not writing about Midgate, she's penning fairy tale retellings. She enjoys mixing familiar pieces from many tales together and may one day reveal to you her *Tinderbox Princess* series.

www.ingramcontent.com/pod-product-compliance
Lightning Source LLC
Chambersburg PA
CBHW030904300726
48970CB00001B/3